DAWN OF CHAOS AND FURY

ALSO BY MELISSA K. ROEHRICH

LADY OF DARKNESS SERIES

Lady of Darkness
Lady of Shadows
Lady of Ashes
Lady of Embers
The Reaper (a Lady of Darkness novella)
Lady of Starfire
Unrelenting Winds (a Lady of Darkness novella)
Treasures of Darkness (a Lady of Darkness compilation)

THE LEGACY SERIES

Rain of Shadows and Endings
Storm of Secrets and Sorrow
Tempest of Wrath and Vengeance
Dawn of Chaos and Fury

DAWN OF CHAOS AND FURY

THE LEGACY SERIES
BOOK FOUR

MELISSA K. ROEHRICH

kensingtonbooks.com

Content notice: *Dawn of Chaos and Fury* contains representation of: depression, sexual scenes, threats of sexual assault/rape (not between the FMC/MMCs), death, anxiety, physical abuse (on page and memories), forced medical procedures, murder, torture, claustrophobia, suicidal thoughts, blood, hostages, alcohol abuse, kidnapping, sexually explicit scenes, gaslighting, slut shaming, profanity, needles, graphic violence, branding, drugging, psychological manipulation, addiction, references to past sexual assault, pregnancy (not the FMC), grooming.

KENSINGTON BOOKS are published by:

Kensington Publishing Corp.
900 Third Avenue
New York, NY 10022

kensingtonbooks.com

All Kensington titles, imprints, and distributed lines are available at special quantity discounts for bulk purchases for sales promotions, premiums, fundraising, educational, or institutional use.

Special book excerpts or customized printings can also be created to fit specific needs. For details, write or phone the office of the Kensington sales manager: Kensington Publishing Corp., 900 Third Avenue, New York, NY 10022, attn: Sales Department; phone 1-800-221-2647.

The K with book logo Reg US Pat. & TM Off.

First Kensington Trade Paperback Printing: December 2025

ISBN 978-1-4967-6036-4 (trade paperback)

10 9 8 7 6 5 4 3 2 1

Printed in the United States of America

Electronic edition IBSN 978-1-4967-6040-1 (ebook)

Interior design by Kelsy Thompson
Chapter head designs by the author, with images courtesy of Canva

The authorized representative in the EU for product safety and compliance
is eucomply OU, Parnu mnt 139b-14, Apt 123
Tallinn, Berlin 11317, hello@eucompliancepartner.com

For those whose balance is unconventional, you don't owe anyone an explanation. Let the world wonder.

Anala
Ekayan Island
Fae Estate
Orinthia
Falein Kingdom
Raghnall Mountains
Caelan River
Dolion Woods
North
Terrarun River
Nisha Forest
Fae Estate
Arobell
Lake Moonmist
Celeste Kingdom
Achaz

a m

Arius

Underground Entrance

Ozul Mountains

Estate

Arius House

Idalia

Castle Pines

The Asning Sea

Sinvon's Lake

Rockmoor

om

Dark Haven

Arius Kingdom

hade Plains

Night Waters

Fractured Springs

Raven Harbor

Wynfell River

om

River of Endings

Serafina Kingdom

osebell

Dreamlock Woods

Fae Estate

Sanal

Astown Port

Serafina

The Un
Leisure District
Penthouse Building
Charter District
Apparel District

rground
HOUSE OF FOUR
DISPENSARY DISTRICT
APOTHECARY DISTRICT

LEGACY SERIES REFERENCE GUIDE

I know. There's a lot to remember and keep straight as you dive into Devram. So here's a little reference guide to help you out!

OUR MAIN PLAYERS

Tessalyn Ausra:
Tes-uh-lin Ah-sruh
~~Fae~~. ~~Legacy,~~ Chaos
Source of the Arius Heir...sort of
A little (or a lot) wild and impulsive

Luka Mors:
Loo-kuh Morz
Sargon Legacy, Theon's Guardian and advisor

Theon St. Orcas:
Thee-on Sānt Or-kus
Legacy, Heir to the Arius Kingdom,
A morally grey, walking, talking red flag
Source to...Tessa? Maybe?

Axel St. Orcas:
Ax-ul Sānt Or-kus
Legacy, Second-in-Line for the Arius Kingdom, Theon's brother, married to Katya

OTHERS OF NOTE

Dex: Dex
Wind Fae, Tessa's ex-best friend
Claimed by Achaz Kingdom

Corbin: Kor-bin
Water Fae, Tessa's friend, involved with Lange, claimed by Arius Kingdom, chilling with Eviana

Brecken: Brek-in
Wind Fae, Tessa's friend?
Claimed by Achaz Kingdom

Tristyn Blackheart:
Tris-tin Blak-hārt
~~Mortal,~~ ~~Legacy~~, Deity, owns Lilura Inquest, Cienna's brother

Cressida St. Orcas:
Cres-ee-duh Sānt Or-kus
Legacy, Theon & Axel's mother

Oralia: Or-āl-eeuh
Water Fae, ~~Tessa's Friend~~
Claimed by Achaz Kingdom

Lange: Lāng
Wind Fae, Tessa's friend, involved with Corbin, claimed by Arius Kingdom, chilling with Eviana

Katya: Kat-ya
Fire Fae, Tessa's friend, claimed by Arius Kingdom, married to Axel

~~Penelope:~~ Pen-el-ō-pee
Fae, personal servant of Theon & Axel

Eviana: Eve-ee-on-uh
Earth Fae, Source of the Arius Lord

Legacy Series Reference Guide

Others of Note

Felicity Davers: Fel-i-sit-ee Dav-ers
Gracil Legacy, Theon's prospective Match

~~Auryon~~: O-ry-un
Huntress

~~Pavil~~: Pah-vil
Sleazy Legacy that works for Valter

Julius: Jool-ee-us
Sleazy Legacy Advisor to Valter

Razik: Ra-zick
Legacy, Luka's brother, Eliza's twin flame

Xan: Zan
Legacy, Luka and Razik's father

~~Desiray~~: Dez-i-rā
A Sirana Legacy who oversees Rosebell and the Sirana Villas

Elowyn: El-ō-win
A priestess in Achaz Kingdom

Nylah: Nī-luh
A wolf that guards Tessa

Cienna: Cee-en-uh
Diety, Tristyn's sister

Ford: Fōrd
Fae, Pen's replacement

~~Metias~~: Meh-tī-us
Sleazy Legacy that works for Valter

Mansel: Man-sell
Sleazy Legacy Advisor to Valter

Eliza: Ee-lie-zuh
A Fire Fae, Razik's twin flame

Bree DelaCrux: Bree Del-uh-crū
One of the four coven leaders of the Night Children who lead the Dispensary District in the Underground

Gia: Gee-uh
A Witch in the Underground, Cienna's lover

Roan: Rōn
A wolf that guards Tessa

A Couple Things & Content Information

steps onto soapbox

Beloved Lovers of the Chaos—

Here we are. The last book in the Legacy series. I cannot believe we're here. But as always, before we dive in, I need to say this one final time. Why? Because some of you don't believe me, you go in blind, and then you proceed to yell at me about something that was included in the Content Information. I wish I was joking, but my emails, DMs, and comment section don't lie.

This is a DARK fantasy romance series. While there is probably some salvation along with the destruction coming, all the characters are still morally grey, and in true dark fashion, that's never going to totally go away. There's redemption. There's heartache. There's growth. There's vengeance. But it's still Devram.

Are you Team Theon? Team Luka? I'm going to need you to be Team Content Information, because again, I don't like to be yelled at when I've provided the answer to that on a silver platter from the very beginning.

You can find all the tropes, tags, and triggers on my website at www.melissakroehrich.com. I put it there because I can easily update it if needed. If any of those things are not for you, it's okay! We give you this information so you can set your own boundaries and protect your mental health. I am begging you not to go in blind, and then message me in disappointment or anger when things happen that were outlined in the information that has always been available to you.

Now that we've covered that—for the final time, welcome back to Devram. Thank you for hanging in there and trusting the process. Thank you for cheering on these traumatized and emotionally stunted babies, even when you were beyond frustrated and furious with them. We've made it to the end. There will be emotional whiplash. There will be redemption. There will be long-awaited deaths.

There will be balance.

A quick reminder that I wish I could pin everywhere: *The Legacy Series* takes place in the same universe as the *Lady of Darkness* series, but this is an entirely new world with brand new characters. You do NOT need to read the *Darkness* series to understand *The Legacy Series*. This series can be read separately. This story has its own conclusion by the end. However, you WILL come across spoilers for the *Darkness* series and some dragon eggs along the way, even if you don't recognize them as spoilers at the time. Some of our favs have found their way to Devram, and we get to see them from a different perspective. I promise I won't reveal any of the big details from *Darkness*, but there will be minor spoilers. You might learn how things end up, but none of the twists and turns that got us to that point.

Grab the wine, turn on the playlist, and settle in. This is the longest book I've written to date. We have lots of pages to spend together. See you on the other side—

XO,

Melissa

Tempest of Wrath and Vengeance Quick Recap

AS TOLD BY CYRUS

Hi, Darling! It's hard to believe this is the last rundown I get to give you. It's even harder to believe I still haven't gotten the chance to go to Devram—

Scarlett: I swear to the gods, Cyrus. I'm going to need you to stop.

Cyrus: And I'm going to need *you* to stop sending our family to other realms. We haven't heard from Eliza and Razik in months.

Sorin: We're all worried about them, Cyrus.

Cyrus: Well, maybe if they hadn't been sent there alone—

Cassius: We have discussed this numerous times. We all miss them, and we're all worried. You know as well as I do that Scarlett has spent countless hours holed up with books in the mirror chambers. She's trying. We're all trying.

Cyrus, *glancing at Scarlett:* Yeah, all right. I didn't mean . . .

Scarlett: It's fine, Cyrus. Let's just do this so I can get back to the Wind Court. Ashtine found more texts that might be useful.

Cyrus: We head back to Devram to find Theon not doing well. Tessa had left him on his knees. He'd sent Luka to go after her, and he has no idea where his brother is. Tristyn Blackheart shows up and takes him to the Underground, where he meets Eliza and Razik, who we very graciously sent to help them. And if Eliza gets stuck in a realm where Fae are treated as less than, I pity anyone who crosses her path.

Meanwhile, Tessa is hanging out with the Achaz Lord, and her visions keep changing. She slips out of a Tribunal Hearing when Luka shows up, making her way to the Pantheon. On her way there, she runs into the Keeper, only to realize there is more than one. She finds her way to the mirror gate beneath the Pantheon and summons her grandfather, Achaz, himself. *(Pauses.)* That's a choice, and not a great one.

Axel is locked away somewhere, falling prey to some insane bloodlust that is driving him . . . Well, insane. At some point, he's taken from the locked room only to meet with Bree DelaCrux, one of the leaders of the Night Children in the Underground. She proposes they join forces to take the Underground and eventually all of Devram. She leaves him to the bloodlust to . . . help him decide? What a bitch.

Scarlett, *snorting a laugh*: That's the understatement of the century.

Cyrus: I can see how that would be effective though. I mean, look at Gehenna.

Cassius, *muttering*: Can we please not bring the Sorceress into this?

Cyrus: Anyway, Luka goes on to the Achaz Kingdom because that's what Theon wants and Guardians are notorious for bending over backwards for their Wards.

Cassius, *flatly*: I'll bend you over backwards.

Cyrus, *with a wink*: I know.

So Luka shows up, hoping Tessa will help them find Axel. He ends up making a Bargain with the Achaz Lord, which cannot be good, and Tessa is furious when she finds out he will be staying in Achaz Kingdom for the foreseeable future. She has lots of reasons to not want him around, but one of them is a big secret being kept beneath the Faven Palace. Luka doesn't like being there any more than Tessa likes having him there, but he suddenly has bigger things to worry about when Tessa starts pulling him into her dreams.

Theon and Tessa are finally reunited when she shows up at Arius property, and they have it out with their magic. *(Snickers.)* Nice. Do you think they destroyed a building like we do when we're pissed with each other? Anyway, Luka intervenes, but he also discovers Eliza and Razik, noticing the latter is clearly related.

Tessa leaves Theon to his mess, going to the Wynfell River where she's attacked by Night Children. Auryon and Tessa's wolves come to her aid, and Roan is gravely injured.

She begs Luka for help, and they end up at Arius House, where Theon has a Healer specifically for his hounds and horses. It comes to light that Nylah and Roan are Trackers, creatures created by her father, Temural. Huh. Those are new.

Scarlett, *wistfully*: I know. I wish I'd known when we were there. I have so many questions.

Sorin: They can't speak, Love.

Cyrus: They're probably grateful for that. I can't imagine how quickly they'd get sick of you.

Scarlett, *scowling and flipping him off.*

Cyrus: Speaking of questions, Theon has a lot too, and so does Katya, who's been hanging out with Razik and Eliza. Kat finds a book, and they all learn about the twin flame bond and how the Source Marks are a gross manipulation of them. Finally. Thank the gods they finally put that together. Kat also realizes that—Shit. *(Looks up at Scarlett.)* Is that true?

Scarlett, *softly*: Keep going, Cyrus.

Cyrus, *swallowing thickly*: Kat believes that Axel is her twin flame and asks Eliza to give her the twin flame Mark in the hopes it will help them find Axel.

Tessa takes a field trip to the Sirana Villas where she learns that Fae are being . . . bred for their power. That is fucked up.

Scarlett: And I trust Eliza and Razik to help stop it.

Cyrus, *muttering to himself*: Eliza is going to burn everything when she learns of this.

Brecken helps sneak Tessa away to one of the buildings, where she breaks into some files. She learns things about her friends, but she also learns that Valter's Source has a daughter. Tessa vows to destroy the Villas, and Brecken asks her to wait a few days to give him time to get the innocents out. She does, and a few days later, she returns and demolishes the Villas. Thank. The. Gods.

While all of that is happening, Theon, Kat, and Tristyn go to the Shifter Alpha and Beta to ask for help finding Axel. They agree, but only if Theon finds a missing Shifter Prince first. He also learns that Tristyn has history with the Shifters *and* that he and Cienna are siblings.

Axel suddenly finds himself freed by Bree, and he follows a voice in his head that leads him to Kat. Where he attacks her. *By the gods.* Thankfully, Theon and Tristyn show up to pull him off her, and he learns that Kat is pregnant with his child. Holy Anala. Can this guy not catch a break? Apparently not because a little while later, Cienna shows up and confirms that he has triggered the curse and will turn into a Night Child. The twin flame bond he shares with Kat will die once the transition is complete. Knowing he's a threat to Kat and his child, he leaves and . . . returns to Bree. This is a ruse, right?

Cassius: Cyrus, seriously. We all understand it's fucked. Just keep going.

Cyrus: Yeah, but . . .

I guess Theon has taken on the duties of the Arius Lord since his father is being held captive in the Achaz Kingdom cells. Trying to use that as leverage against Rordan, he attends meetings with the other rulers. They decide to move forward with a Gala, with funds going to the rebuilding of the Villas. For fuck's sake.

Cassius: Cy—

Cyrus: Yeah, yeah, I know. Keep going.

Tessa has been training with Luka as agreed, and he wants her to master Traveling. Auryon shows up, annoyed that she is having to track down the Hunters Tessa keeps summoning. Auryon warns her she needs to stop, but Tessa argues the Hunters answer to her.

Luka goes to see Theon to ask if he knows how Tessa is pulling him into her dreams. While there, he officially meets Razik, where it is confirmed they are full-blooded brothers. Razik doesn't appear to care, and that seriously tracks for that broody bastard.

Tessa is learning more and more as Dex and Rordan continue to pressure her into acting. In an attempt to breathe and get away, she goes to visit Roan, who is still recovering from his injuries. She finds Theon being remarkably human as he plays with his hounds and tries to convince Roan to join in. Desperate to not feel anything, she drinks too much tea that has been prepared for her and is pulled into a vision. Luka is there when she wakes, panicked at how long she was unconscious.

Axel decides to return for Kat after a chat with Bree, where he realizes the Night Child had let him go to kill her. He seeks out Tessa for help, only for Tessa to reveal that she intends to end his bloodline. Not trusting anyone, he waits until dark and goes to Kat. They exchange words, and ultimately, she returns with him to the Underground.

Tessa accompanies Luka to go talk to Razik about his theories as to how Luka is entering her dreams. They believe it is a manifestation of gifts from her various bloodlines. When they return, Luka is upset about how little his brother cares. Tessa offers to take his mind off it, but he resists . . . until Theon agrees down the bond. Honestly, good for them. Tessa never agreed to a relationship with Theon, and Luka is noble enough to make sure his friend is fine with it before acting. That's something you don't see in Devram.

In a wild turn of events, Tessa has been sneaking down to the room where Eviana, Valter's Source, is being held. Despite the female's clear apathy, Tessa returns time after time, leaving various things for the female including boots, clothes, and weapons.

The Sirana Gala happens, and Theon is forced to go with Felicity Davers since she is his Match. During the event, Rordan surprises everyone and announces a Match for Tessa as well. Forced to keep herself under control, she dances with the male. Then she finds herself dancing with Theon. They both slip into the hall to the same alcove where this all started.

Furious with Tessa's actions at the Sirana Gala, Rordan once again berates her for not acting. Trying to figure out a way out of her mess, she is attacked again. This time by the Augury, and we learn Theon's mother has been working with them. Tessa summons her Hunters, but they go rogue because they were summoned within Arius Kingdom. Auryon had warned her of this, and the Huntress ends up being killed in the battle, leaving her bow to Tessa.

Luka takes Tessa back to his . . . Really? He has one too?

He takes her back to his cave where Theon is waiting for them. Theon immediately has to leave to go defend his Kingdom, once again leaving Luka with Tessa. The two of them finally give in to the feelings and tension they've been harboring for months. Things seem to be going great until Tessa lets it slip that she's known this entire time that Luka's father is in the Faven Palace cells. They have an argument, and Luka sends her away. Tessa finally Travels.

(Long pause.)

All of that just . . . sucks.

Cassius: Just wrap this up, Cyrus. Please. We have other things to do today.

Cyrus: We're almost done. Relax or you'll shift.

Cassius, *grumbling*: I swear to Sargon, some days . . .

Cyrus: Unbeknownst to Eviana, Tessa has entrusted two of her friends to free Eviana. Lange and Corbin show up and convince the female to go with her. She learns of a Mark to block her bond with Valter, and in the end, she blackmails Lange and Corbin into helping her. Helping her do what? No one knows, but we can assume it has to do with her daughter.

Axel and Kat have a run-in with Bree. They end up getting married, only to also discover that Bree has confiscated all the blood rations in the Underground, leaving Axel in a bind.

Tessa returns to Faven, where she hands herself over to everything going on after discovering text messages from Theon. She's taken to the cells beneath the Pantheon until her fate can be decided. But Theon has never stopped fighting for her. He shows up with Tristyn, and they break her out. In the process, they are unexpectedly aided by the Achaz Heir.

Luka tricks his brother into helping him free their father, who Razik very clearly has no desire to ever talk to or see. They then race to help Theon. Theon explains he's figured everything out, and the Fates will come for Tessa and destroy Devram in the process. He tells them all to leave, giving Luka a final order to protect her. Then he . . . walks away. Giving her the freedom she's always wanted and sacrificing the realm for her. Well, fuck me. Talk about a shocking turn of events. Where do you think they're going to go?

Scarlett: I don't know. I've been trying to figure something out, but she'll just continue to be hunted across the stars.

Cyrus: Here? Can't they just come here with Eliza and Razik?

Scarlett, *glancing up at Sorin*: We've discussed it, but I cannot allow that. Not yet. Not when we are still recovering from our own battles with Achaz, but I'll figure something out. I'll . . . The Oracle says they need to fight their own battles. That we've interfered enough already.

Cyrus, *slinging an arm around her shoulders*: Let's go to the Citadel, Darling. I'll bring the mugweed to help.

Scarlett, *scoffing*: How will mugweed help?

Cyrus, *drawling*: I suppose we won't know until we try it. But if anything, you'll relax some. One would think Sorin would be helping with that . . .

Sorin: I heard that, you prick.

DAWN
OF
CHAOS
AND
FURY

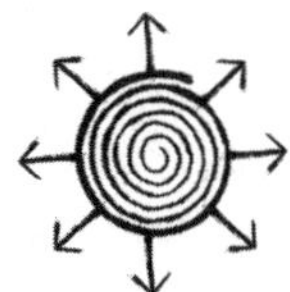

Who Will Be Left Standing?

There was nothing but rocks and dirt and rubble under her bare feet. The sky that had been clear and blue when she'd first stepped here was quickly turning grey the longer she stood among the ruin of a world that had once been grand. Wicked and cruel and broken, yes, but the shell of it had been grand. The beauty of the outside had hidden the poison that spread among the realm, killing and taking and breaking—

Lightning crackled at her fingertips, flecks of silver and gold, white and black, flickering among her power. She took a deep breath, calming the fury that was building in her belly. She'd told no one she was coming here. Only one knew. The one who'd helped her get here. But perhaps she should have brought Roan or Nylah just to help keep her grounded. It'd been decades since she'd been in this world. She hadn't thought it would still make her . . . feel.

But she should have known.

It would forever make her feel.

Because it was the last place she'd seen him.

Because it had always been more than a bond.

Tessa looked back over her shoulder. The mirror gate she'd stepped through stood several paces away, but the Pantheon that had once housed it was in ruins. It was nothing more than cracked pillars and crumbled stone. She could see straight to the courtyard where the fountain had stood once, large and regal. Without having to navigate the passages of the Pantheon, she reached the disintegrating structure quickly. Half of the fountain was gone and water had long ceased flowing, but the other half still stood, albeit fractured in several places.

She ran her hand along the lip, finding a crack that had been there before this world had died. A crack she'd put there with her power, summoning a Hunter to her side. Peering over the side, a gasp of surprise fell from her lips. Somehow the mosaics of the six First gods and goddesses were still pristine and perfect. Not one scratch or chip on the tiles. Tilting her head as she studied them, she couldn't help but think they'd gotten some of it wrong, particularly Celeste. Just minor details here and there, but not Arius. That mosaic was perfect with the dark hair and emerald eyes. The arrogant tilt of lips. It even managed to capture the aura of his darkness and power. Looking so much like him.

Odd really, when he was hundreds and hundreds of generations removed from Arius. How had he looked so incredibly similar? Genetics or no, it seemed implausible.

Straightening, she intended to make her way to a townhouse that had once almost felt like home, but as she turned, she stilled. This world was dead, the Fates having destroyed it in their search for her, and yet . . .

"Hello, clever tempest."

She said nothing.

Only stared back at him.

*The inky black hair that always found a way to fall across his brow. The emerald irises drifting with darkness and sin. The suit sans jacket. The rings on his fingers. The Mark of Achaz—*her *Mark—forever on the back of his left hand.*

When she didn't speak, he slipped his hands into his pockets, rocking back on his heels slightly. He slowly took her in, eyes going from her head to her bare toes and back up again. As though he was trying to take in as much detail as he could.

"Are you a phantom?" she finally blurted, unable to help herself because how was he here? Nearly a century after Devram and everyone in it had been destroyed? How had he survived?

He smiled, and her stomach dipped as a dimple appeared. Only then did he take a single step toward her, his head canting to the side a little with the movement.

"You look beautiful," he said, going still once more.

Tessa looked down at the black dress with deep slits up the sides. Her bow was looped across her chest while her golden hair was loose and flowing around her as the wind picked up.

Meeting his gaze once more, she said, "You didn't answer my question. How are you still here?"

He appeared to debate his answer before he said, "I'm not entirely sure. Do you wish I wasn't?"

"I . . ." Her fingers curled at her sides, power and more flaring, because she

didn't know what she wished. She didn't know why today, of all days, she'd finally found her way back here.

He reached her in a few long strides. Gently taking her chin, he tipped her face up to his, and she shuddered. It may have been decades since she'd seen him, but a part of her soul remembered him. Always would. Her power calmed. Her fury banked. The Chaos that was always trying to consume her rushed to his touch, seeking him out. A small sigh escaped her when he brushed his thumb across her bottom lip.

"Better?" he asked, his voice gruff and low as he searched her eyes, concern lining his features.

She nodded, swallowing thickly. "How did you know?"

That small smile tilted again. "I always know what you need, little storm." They stood like that for a long moment, staring at each other, before he lightly cleared his throat. "Where is Luka?"

Tessa shrugged, looking back at the mirror gate. She wished she hadn't. His hand slipped from her face, and the thing inside her immediately thrashed, reaching for him again so violently, she stumbled back a step. Her hands curled, fingers already reaching for her hair, but wisps of dark wrapped around her, soothing and calming.

She shouldn't have come back here, and yet . . .

He'd been able to touch her. A phantom couldn't do that, could it? Then again, the Hunters had been able to touch her when they'd wanted to.

"You're thinking too hard, Tessa," he said gently, watching her.

"Is this the After?" she asked instead.

He huffed a laugh. "By the gods, I hope not. Then again, if it brings you to me, I'll take it."

"It's been decades."

His brow furrowed for a few seconds before quickly smoothing back out. "I'll take whatever you'll give me."

She nodded, still unsure of . . . everything that was happening. The last time she'd seen him . . .

Lifting her chin, she glared at him, fresh fury coursing through her. Fury she'd shoved down for years and years. Fury she'd told everyone she'd dealt with, when in reality, she'd simply learned how to hide it, master it, use it when needed. Fury and chaos. Chaos and fury. Wild and untamed. Untamed and wild.

There'd never been any such thing as balance when it came to her. She'd only given them the illusion she'd found such a thing. Found a balance. Found a semblance of peace and belonging. Found a sense of purpose. The truth was, she'd simply found a way to survive, letting the chaos and the fury consume her. She knew Luka sensed it. He'd tried, she supposed, but in the end . . .

"Luka tells me . . ." She trailed off, letting her fingers flit through the darkness drifting around her and hovering close. "Well, everyone tells me, I guess, that I was never the same after we left here."

"Who's everyone?"

She shrugged, too many emotions trying to claw their way out of the dark places where she'd shoved them. "Luka. Tristyn. They're the only ones who really knew me from my time here."

He nodded slowly, his eyes never leaving her.

"You broke me," she stated.

"I know, Tessa. I know I did, but I had hoped that if I got you out, it would . . ." He shoved a hand through his hair, a frustrated growl escaping him. "I was hoping it would atone for some of it. Keep you safe. Save you from a fate you never deserved. That's all I ever wanted for you. To be safe and happy and—"

She shot forward before she fully knew what she was doing. Impulsive. Wild. Her hands slammed into his chest, and he caught her wrists, keeping her there.

"You broke me when you walked away from me!" she cried, finally letting that fury win.

To fury they both lose.

"You promised. You were the one person—the one *person—who never balked when I showed you my worst. You promised I would always . . . You were my only constant in the end, and you walked away from me," she finished.*

He said nothing, pulling her fully into his chest. Her head rested against him, and she could hear his heart beating, rapid and erratic.

"It was all to save you, Tessalyn," he murmured, his chest rumbling with the words. "Always to save you because I love you. Please tell me you understand that. It's the only way I know how to . . . I love you."

"And I hate you," she replied.

He was silent for a few of those too-fast heartbeats before he said, "Yeah, little storm? How much do you hate me?"

"So godsdamn much," she answered, pressing into him more, because like this, her soul was almost calm. The fury almost banked. It did this with Luka too, but it was never enough. Peace and contentment just out of reach. The world almost silenced for once in her immortal existence.

His hand drifted along her hair, tangling in the strands as she clutched at his shirt. She breathed him in, letting his scent fill her lungs. Memorizing his touch. Some part of her wished she could stay with him. A bigger part of her knew she'd left a piece of herself here, and it was why she'd come back.

How bizarre to want to stay with a phantom.

As if he could still hear her thoughts, he whispered, "You can't stay here."

She stiffened, his fingers trailing down her spine.

"It's too dark for you here, little storm," he continued. "You hate the dark."

"As much as I hate you," she retorted.

His fingers paused on her lower back before a low huff of laughter escaped him. "Always a battle with you, right?"

Despite herself, a small smile tilted on her lips. "Always."

"Tessa, I—" But he broke off, his entire body tensing, and she pulled back to look up into his face once more.

His gaze was fixed on something beyond her, and she turned to see a figure off in the distance. This far away, she couldn't make out much, even with enhanced senses. She could only see the long black hair blowing in the increasing winds around a distinctly feminine form.

"Is that . . . Auryon? Is she a phantom here too?" Tessa asked, moving to take a step closer, but his hold on her tightened, keeping her close.

"You need to go," he said. "It's not safe for you here right now."

"When was it ever?" she countered, her voice hardening.

He cupped her cheek, regret and longing staring down at her. "I'll always find you. I'm forever yours."

Tessa pursed her lips, lingering a second longer before stepping from his hold. She wouldn't argue with him. It hadn't worked before; she wasn't under any illusion that it would do any good now.

Adjusting the bow across her chest, she didn't say another word as she made her way back to the mirror gate. The figure across the vast expanse watched, not moving.

"You broke me too," he called after her, making her pause. "In ways I never could have imagined. So hate me, Tessa. Hate me and break me and make me feel it all, but would you save me? If you could?"

Her fingers traced along the symbols etched around the mirror, searching for the one she needed. She pulled a dagger from where it was sheathed at her thigh, slicing her palm and pressing it to the marking before she looked over her shoulder one last time.

"Maybe," she answered, before she stepped through the mirror.

PART ONE

ENDINGS

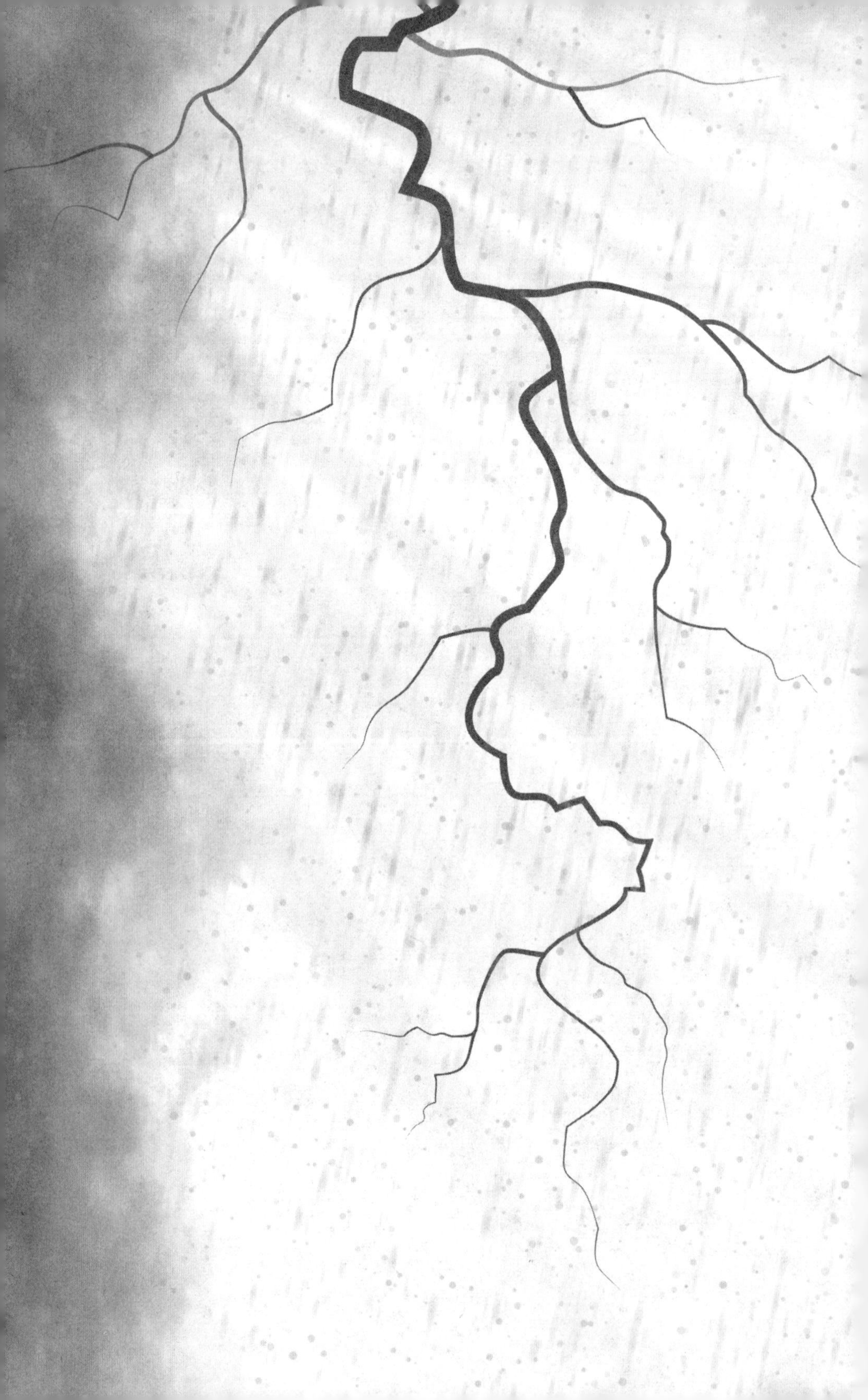

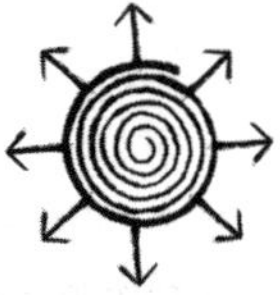

1
TESSA

The chair was empty.

It was always empty when she woke. But she knew he sat in it while she slept. His scent lingered in the room, so strong and fresh he must have just left. She wondered if he could still feel her stirring down the bond despite how broken and fractured it was now. He would hate that. Hate that he was bound to her in any way. He valued loyalty above all else, and she'd betrayed that. Betrayed him.

But for the first time since Theon had left them in that chamber, she wished Luka was sitting in that chair when she blinked her eyes open. For the first time, she wished he was there, just to calm the turmoil in her soul.

Truth be told, she wasn't sure how long they'd been here. Days for sure. Weeks? Possibly. They tried to talk to her, but she couldn't hear them. Sounds were muffled. She was too lost to herself, her thoughts, her fury. Trying to make sense of something, anything. But she couldn't get her thoughts in order, and even if she did, she had choices to make.

So many choices.

It was what she'd always wanted, and now there were so many, it felt crippling.

Sliding from the bed, Tessa made her way to the floor-to-ceiling windows, pressing her palms to the cool glass. Every room of this three-story penthouse had them. On the top floors of the towering building, she could see over the vast expanse of the Acropolis below. The Pantheon in the center, grand and regal on the hill it occupied in the center of the city. The Tribunal building a few blocks away. The shopping centers to the south, while the building she was in sat in the heart of the corporate district to the west.

And while she could see everything outside, she knew there were more spells and wards on the glass than there were floors in this building. No one could see in. She would expect nothing less from a male who changed his identity on a regular basis. Tristyn Blackheart had been here for centuries, and only in the last few months had he dropped all his glamours.

Had he felt guilt, living in this luxury while his sister had been banished and hiding in the Underground, being hunted by the Arius Lord? Had any part of him felt an ounce of regret? She doubted it. He had his own purposes and motives, and he didn't seem to care who he used to obtain them. His sister could suffer. Injustice could reign. And her? He could keep any secrets and plans from her until it benefitted him the most. She'd thought he was different from the rest of this godsforsaken realm.

I can have motives and still care. It does not have to be one or the other.

Power flared at her fingertips. Bright light refracted back into the room, but there was more. Sparks of energy. Embers of black and white. Faint flecks of silver and gold.

She inhaled deeply, trying to calm her soul. Not that it worked. It never worked.

Tristyn's words rattled around in her head.

It does not have to be one or the other.

But she had a purpose too. A purpose that could be fulfilled if she simply left this world. Let the Fates come and do what they do best.

Fuck over everyone and everything.

But that would mean—

"We agreed you weren't going to do that anymore," came a growl that had her pausing.

She hadn't realized she'd stepped back from the windows. Had started pacing. Had her hands in her hair, tugging at the strands.

Slowly, she turned, lifting her gaze to his as Luka tossed something onto a nearby table before striding across the room. Hands still in her hair, she backed up with every step until her back pressed to the window. She said nothing, unsure of what he was referring to. She didn't recall agreeing to anything.

Reaching for her hands, he methodically untangled her hair from her fingers. There was no tenderness in his touch. No soft glance or reassuring look. Just . . . duty.

That was what she'd become to him. A duty given to him by his Ward.

Not that she could blame him.

And maybe it was better this way. It was easier to do what needed to be done when you were alone.

"So we're going to continue with the silence, then?" Luka asked as he finished, taking a step back from her, his stare hard.

She slowly lowered her hands to her sides, fingers curling into the fabric of the shirt she wore. It wasn't his. She actually had no idea where the clothing had come from or when she'd changed into it. She didn't even remember coming here.

Folding his arms across his chest, he added, "You should shower and get dressed. Everyone is meeting in an hour to discuss our next moves."

She watched his irritation grow when she only stared back, gritting her teeth as everything in her soul strained for him. Her power wanted his, and again she wondered if he could feel her struggle.

With each day that passed though, she was sure he couldn't. Neither could Theon because she couldn't feel them either. The silence down the bond was deafening, telling her just how broken it was. The quiet was so loud, it made her want to scream and rage. Leave and stay. Save and destroy.

At some point he had moved. She didn't know when, but he'd stepped closer. She felt the barest of touches as his fingertips trailed down her arm, as if this was the last thing he wanted to be doing, but again, she was his duty. But that touch . . . Gods, that touch calmed everything just enough to give her some reprieve from the madness, and her eyes fluttered closed.

There was an audible sigh before he murmured, "What am I going to do with you, Tessa?"

Her eyes snapped open, and she lurched away from his touch.

What was he going to do with her?

The wild, untamed, chaotic thing that could never do as she was told or be what she was supposed to be.

What was he going to do with her?

The one who could never clean up her own messes and who always needed saving.

What was he going to do with her?

The Source that couldn't submit, and the one expected to understand everything, yet be told nothing.

A dark bark of laughter fell from her lips, a sound tinged with the madness that had laid claim to her soul.

He should be asking what *she* was going to do with all of *them*.

"Fuck," Luka muttered. "That's not—"

But she was already walking away from him, striding for the bathroom. The cold tile of the bathroom floor helped her feel grounded as she spun and looked back into the bedroom. Luka hadn't moved, but his eyes narrowed as she held his gaze.

Then she slammed the door shut.

Moving to the vanity, she found her reflection. Her violet eyes were glowing, and she didn't know how to make them stop. She didn't know if she wanted to anymore. For so long, she'd been told she needed to learn to control it. For so long, she'd feared it. For so long, she'd thought herself weak for failing to conquer it. But maybe . . .

She lifted a hand, light pooling as gold and silver flecks appeared and swirled among it all. Flickers of lightning. A storm in her palm.

Maybe in the end they'd all been wrong.

Her eyes still on her reflection, she smiled. For the first time in all her years, she let herself embrace what she was at her core. She would not change herself to suit others. Would not shove down her light or deny her longing for the dark. Would not cower and let others save her.

Pulling her shirt over her head, she slipped off the loose pants she was wearing, discarding it all in a pile on the floor. Then she stepped into the shower, turning the water on and letting the hot water wash over her.

What am I going to do with you?

Dex had said it.

Theon had said it.

Luka had said it.

They would do nothing with her. Not a godsdamn thing.

But her?

She was ready to fulfill her purpose her way.

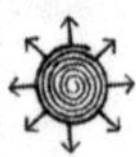

"Nice to see you up and about, wild fury," Tristyn said, his tone light and playful when she entered the large sitting room.

Tessa met his gaze, but she didn't say anything. There was no tilt of her lips or arched brow, and she watched his small smile falter.

Luka had been waiting for her when she'd emerged from the bathroom, hair still dripping and skin bare. Neither of them had spoken. He'd only pointed to the bundle he'd tossed on the table, which turned out to be a pair of leggings, a sweater, and undergarments. No socks or shoes; not that she'd have worn them anyway. Then she'd followed him down a flight of stairs to where everyone else had gathered—Razik and Eliza, Cienna and Gia, Tristyn and Xan.

The eldest male's soulful sapphire eyes watched her carefully, just as they'd always done from behind a pane of enchanted glass. He still had the white stone collar around his neck. Apparently no one had figured out how to remove it yet.

At the extended silence, Tristyn looked at Luka. "Has she said anything at all?"

"Not a word," Luka clipped, brushing past her.

Tristyn visibly hesitated for a moment before he hedged, "And down the bond?"

"Nothing from either of them," he answered. Broody and stoic. Identical to two of the other males in this room.

"There's food, Tessa," Tristyn said, returning his attention to her. The teasing note to his voice was gone, replaced with something softer. Kinder.

Cautious.

"But if there's something else you'd like, I can make that happen," he added.

She drifted over to the spread of food that had been laid out along a wall. Fruit and breads. Doughnuts and crackers. Various jams and cold meats and cheeses.

Tristyn appeared at her side, holding out a steaming cup of coffee, and she glanced up at him again. His voice was low and only for her when he said, "Come on, wild fury. It's a peace offering."

As if a cup of coffee could fix her. Fix this. Fix anything.

But she took it anyway, the hot cup warming her hand as she reached for a cracker and took a bite.

"Let her be," Luka said from across the room, where he'd commandeered an armchair. An ankle propped on his knee, he steepled a finger along his temple. "She doesn't need to be coddled. If she wants to act like a child and give everyone the cold shoulder, let her."

He was probably expecting her to bristle. React in some shape or form. But she didn't even bother glancing at him, instead setting her cup down and filling a small plate with a bit of food. If he wanted to go back to how they were before, she could do that. Him a broody prick, and her . . . Well, she wasn't going back to how she was before, but if he wanted to pretend they'd never been anything, she could do that.

Swiping up the cup of coffee, she moved to stand near the windows, setting her dishes on a side table as she stared out, biting into a doughnut she'd picked up. The grey sky swirled with snow, a storm of flurries and ice that drifted to the ground. The snow should be lessening as they moved towards the spring equinox, but the weather had been cold and dreary.

She didn't notice the weighted silence that had settled over the room until Tris lightly cleared his throat. "It's been two weeks since we . . ."

"Stole her from the Pantheon cells?" Cienna supplied.

"I guess we can call it that," Tristyn muttered.

"I don't know what else you'd call it."

"Freeing her?"

"Tempting fate?" Cienna countered.

"We're tempting fate every day we stay here," he retorted.

Cienna hummed in agreement. "And now it is time to step away and let them dictate their own steps, Tristyn. We've interfered enough here."

Interfered?

It was an interesting choice of word since neither of them offered any guidance until their hands were forced, and even then their guidance was vague.

"That's simple enough," Luka interjected. "We need to leave. That decision has already been made."

"And go where exactly?" Tristyn said. "Isn't that what's been holding us back? Well, besides . . ."

He trailed off, and Tessa watched in the glass reflection as he gestured in her direction.

"If she doesn't want to speak and contribute to anything, then she can't complain about not having a say and not having choices," Luka said.

Still she said nothing, only taking another bite of her doughnut. As if she'd let anyone take her choices from her again.

"You are sure Scarlett won't let us go to Halaya? Just until we figure everything out?" Luka finally said.

"We've discussed this several times already. My answer isn't going to change," Razik said, his tone sounding as irritated as his brother's.

"And if we simply show up?" Luka asked. "An 'ask forgiveness later' type of thing?"

Tessa huffed a laugh to herself at his response, picking up her coffee and taking a sip. It tried to warm her bones where a permanent chill had seemed to settle. She didn't know if it'd ever thaw again.

"That's a terrible idea. You should always have a plan," Razik replied.

"That is the plan," Luka shot back.

"And if she denies forgiveness?"

"Stop it. Both of you," Eliza cut in. "Perhaps the best course of action is to summon her in the mirror and ask her. Even if she says no, she'll likely have an idea of where we could go."

"Or," Razik drawled, "the male who clearly prefers to travel the realms and doesn't want to be tied down could give us some ideas."

That was the comment that had Tessa peeking over her shoulder to see how Xan would react to his elder son's clear vitriol. Luka looked like he was holding back a retort, and Razik was glaring at his father, refusing to be the first to break the stare. And Xan?

He sighed, crossing his arms. "I've tried multiple times to explain myself. You refuse to listen."

"Because I don't care. All I care about is getting back to my actual father. The one who raised me as his own. If that is the plan here, to leave, then let's get the fuck on with it," Razik retorted.

Tessa watched Xan debate what to say, and she found herself wondering if she'd let her own parents explain their actions. Or would she simply not care like Razik didn't care? It wouldn't change anything, and she didn't owe them her forgiveness for choosing to abandon her in a realm where she'd been forgotten. She didn't think that was how love worked.

And yet that was what everyone who claimed to love her seemed to do.

Leave her.

Abandon her.

All in the name of trying to protect her and keep her safe.

If she loved someone, she'd fight for them. Do whatever it took to stay with them, even if it meant every day was spent in danger. If she loved someone, they'd fucking know it because she'd destroy a world for them to keep them safe. Not fucking abandon them. Not walk away from them. Not leave them behind.

"Tessa."

Her name was a sharp command that broke through her thoughts, her gaze sliding to Luka, who still sat in that godsdamn chair as if he didn't have a care in the world.

His eyes dipped down her body as he said, "Control it."

She looked down, her palms glowing with embers crackling at her fingertips. But instead of reining it in, she let it grow. Let it loosely wind around her legs, her waist. Let it call to the rest of the power in the room, and she watched as every single person who stood before her stiffened. Knew they were keeping their own straining magic from reaching for her. Knew her power was calling to theirs.

Knew it was affecting Luka the most.

And even when she felt a calmness brush against her, Tristyn or Cienna trying to use their Pax gifts to pacify her, she remained impassive. Turning back to the window, she picked up her coffee and stared at the Pantheon. The Tribunal building. The Acropolis. The center of a poisoned realm. Only then did she let her power wane except for the bands of light at her wrists.

"Has she expended any of that power since she was brought here?" Xan asked, everyone collectively releasing a breath of relief.

"Not that I'm aware of," Luka answered.

"And you think that is a good idea?"

"I think she's stubborn and is trying to prove a point, and per usual, it's going to bite her in the ass," Luka answered.

Tessa ignored him, setting her coffee aside and picking up an orange, starting to peel it.

"Can we get back to the topic at hand?" Razik cut it. "Because my answer remains the same. Scarlett will not allow that kind of power into Halaya, where we are still recovering from a war we nearly lost. Not when Tessa will continue to be hunted throughout the realms."

"So then we are left with summoning Scarlett to the mirror?" Tristyn cut in. "Unless you do have other ideas, Xan?"

"I have ideas on where we could go, but we will still need the World Walker High Queen to allow passage," he answered.

"Then it's settled. We go to the Pantheon, summon Scarlett to the mirror, and go from there," Tristyn said.

"When do we go?" Eliza asked.

"Honestly, we're lucky Tessa hasn't been tracked here yet. The enchantment that prevents her from Traveling is still active. She's been too . . . We haven't had time to work on removing it," Tristyn finished.

"We've been sitting around doing nothing for days," Razik cut in.

"We should go sooner rather than later. We're all prepared anyway. We have been in case we needed to escape," Tristyn said.

"Then we go tonight. Under the cover of darkness. It's our best chance," Luka said, and from the reflection in the window, Tessa watched him rise from the chair.

"Agreed," Razik said.

"Cienna?" Tristyn asked, and Tessa tilted her head to the side.

She could see her in the window reflection too, her gaze catching Tessa's and holding. Tessa popped an orange slice into her mouth, waiting for the witch's reply.

"I think we cannot interfere here anymore," she finally said.

And Tessa smiled.

Wise choice.

She turned on her heel, crossing the room without ever uttering a sound. She didn't acknowledge any of them as she left and found her way back to the stairs. Taking another bite of her orange, she climbed to the room she'd been staying in.

They had made plans, but she had her own.

And now she could finalize them to fulfill her purpose.

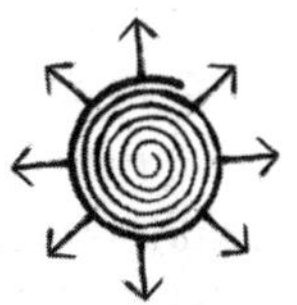

2

LUKA

At least Tristyn waited until they all heard the door to her room click shut on the floor above before he rounded on Luka.

"That's it? What the fuck, Luka? We need to do something," Blackheart spat, hurling his cup of coffee across the room.

The ceramic mug shattered where it hit the wall, and Luka couldn't help but smirk. He'd been handling the tantrums of the St. Orcas brothers and the Arius Lord for over two decades. Males who were used to commanding a room and being obeyed without question. He should maybe be concerned that Tristyn was a deity, and maybe he would have been if he hadn't also been dealing with Tessa the last several months.

"I told you not to coddle her," Luka replied in a bored tone as he made his way to the food spread. "She can see right through that shit."

"We need to draw her out of herself, not give her more reason to sink into her power," Blackheart retorted.

"You all act like she's going to go off any second."

"She *is* unpredictable. Do you not remember what happened at the Pantheon when Theon left?"

A warning growl rumbled from his chest at the mention of that day. As if he needed any sort of reminder of what had happened. He relived it every time he closed his eyes. Every time he slept, which was only when she was sleeping, he hoped Tessa would draw him into her dreams so he could see what exactly was going on in that mind of hers, but it never came. She clearly didn't trust him anymore, and the feeling was pretty fucking mutual. The problem was that since he wasn't pulled into her dreams, he instead relived the nightmare of that day repeatedly.

Of watching his best friend, his *true* brother, walk out of that chamber. Of Tessa thrashing in his arms. Trying to talk to the others over her shrieks of fury and her power that flared more and more. Gritting his teeth against the shocks of energy that rippled off her, sinking into his being and power, trying to latch onto anything it could. It had wanted to take, and she had let it do whatever it wanted. His power hadn't been enough to counter it, just as Theon's had never been enough by itself. Razik had helped, the power of two grandsons of Sargon at least containing her, but it had taken the addition of both Tristyn and Cienna to finally stop her.

And stop probably wasn't the best word to use.

The siblings had combined their gifts from their father, Pax, the god of peace and calming, and their mother, a powerful witch. They'd managed to put Tessa into a deep sleep, and Luka had felt a twinge of guilt the moment she'd gone lax in his arms. And while Tessa may have been in a magic-induced coma of sorts, he could still feel her magic thrashing in her soul.

Angry.

Vengeful.

Chaotic.

Everyone else had wanted to leave right then and there. Eliza was already at the mirror preparing to summon her queen when Luka had stopped her. He was the real reason they hadn't left Devram yet. He was the reason they were still here two weeks later. Everyone thought it was because of Tessa, and it was in a way, but he was admittedly dragging his feet on this.

He'd initially argued it would be a mistake to take Tessa from the only world she knew when she was already volatile. She'd wake up in unfamiliar surroundings in a new world, reeling from everything that had been said in that chamber, and her power would consume her. It might have been true; it might have been an exaggeration. Either way, everyone else eventually agreed, more afraid of her than they needed to be. And while it drove him mad she hadn't uttered a single word to anyone since she woke a day later and all the days since, he hadn't had to argue about staying when she was displaying just how unstable she was at the moment.

His arguments may have been about Tessa, but in truth, he was trying to think of a way out of this. He knew Theon's orders, but the idea of leaving his best friend behind in a world that would be destroyed? His family? His brothers he'd been raised with? Suffered and survived with? All those years of plotting and planning? He wasn't sure he could live with himself if he didn't at least try.

But he'd come up short and patience had clearly run out. This morning, every single person, including his father, had said it was time to go. They'd tried to include Tessa in the decision, and Luka had hoped she'd finally argue, but of course, there'd been nothing from her. Just her watching, listening, and learning everything she could.

Still following Theon's orders to this day.

Except she'd learned to be just as cunning and vicious as the Arius Heir too, and while it made her a bigger pain in his ass, it also made the dragon in his soul want her even more. Once again, he was at odds with the thing, especially now that they'd had a taste of what could have been with her.

"You have nothing to say?" Tristyn demanded as Luka layered deli meat onto slices of bread.

"What is there to say?" Luka countered, annoyed that now they suddenly wanted his opinion, when for the last two weeks they'd been arguing with him.

"Are you even trying to help her?" the male snarled. "Do you even care at this point?"

Of course he fucking cared.

That was the entire godsdamn problem.

He cared about Theon.

He cared about Axel.

And damn it all to the Pits of Torment, he cared about Tessa when he absolutely fucking shouldn't.

He'd gone in a godsdamn circle. Wanting her and denying himself, forced to spend time with her, finally having her, and now back to not wanting to want her.

The Fates were cruel.

"Tristyn makes valid points."

Luka turned to his father, finding him standing across the room on his own. Razik wouldn't give him the time of day, and Eliza, while not blindly loyal to her mate, was still standing firmly beside him. Cienna and Gia had claimed seats on the sofa now that Tessa had left, and Luka took a bite of his sandwich, waiting for the male to go on.

Xan crossed his arms, mirroring Razik's stance and one that Luka often found himself in. "She's too quiet. Chaos is never quiet."

"This is information that would have been helpful a couple decades ago, Xan," Tristyn bit out, pulling a roll of lull-leaf from his jacket pocket and lighting it up before dragging a hand through his hair that immediately fell back into his eyes.

His glowing sage eyes.

"We didn't know. Nobody knew what she would grow to be. Everyone has been waiting and watching," Xan replied.

"But you had to have had an idea," Tristyn argued.

"Everyone had ideas, including Rordan and Valter," Xan retorted. "You've seen firsthand how they tried to prepare for what she could be. We all failed in this the moment we lost her."

"We lost track of her. They lost track of her. The fucking Fates lost track of her," Tristyn said, blowing out a plume of smoke. His entire body was already relaxing, the tension bleeding out of his limbs. "But the day you placed that babe in my arms, you—"

The sound of a plate clattering to the table interrupted whatever Blackheart was saying, and all eyes turned toward Luka, where his half-eaten sandwich was now on the table.

"Surely I misheard the two of you because it sounded like *you,*" he pointed at his father, "brought Tessa to Devram, and then handed her over to *you.*" He finished, moving his finger to Blackheart. When both males remained silent, he said, "We all came here because of her?"

"Let me guess," Razik cut in, his words dripping with disdain. "You weren't abandoned in another realm because you were *needed.*"

"Needed for what?" Luka asked, turning to his brother to find him smirking in derision.

"The same thing I was abandoned for. A direct descendant of Sargon? The son of Temural's Guardian? Nothing is more important to him than fulfilling our *duty,*" Razik said, glowing eyes holding Luka's.

"I was always supposed to be hers," Luka muttered, repeating words she'd whispered to him more than once. She'd known, her soul had known, but he'd always thought it meant . . .

He turned back to their father. "Is that true? Is that the reason I was brought here?"

Xan sighed, his arms dropping to his sides. He winced a little when the collar at his throat jostled. The collar they'd tried countless times to remove without success.

"It's not just about a Guardian bond. Yes, your Wards are safer with you, but *you* are also safer when bonded to another. Bonds are more complex than simple words and magic tricks. Surely you all realize that by now," Xan said.

Luka glanced at Razik, his brother's features back to stoic, but Luka saw the slight head tilt that told him Eliza was speaking down their bond. And while he suddenly found himself with even more questions, the one that came from his mouth was, "Does Tessa know?"

"Know what?" Xan asked.

"That you brought her here. That you handed her over to Blackheart. That I was . . ." He trailed off, not sure how to phrase everything he was trying to wrap his mind around.

"Valter told her I brought her here, but she never asked me about it," his father answered, shifting on his feet. "I expected her to. Waited for the question every time she found her way to my cell, but she never did."

"And you?" Luka pressed, looking at Blackheart.

"I never told her," Tristyn said. "I was trying to gain her trust, and that didn't seem conducive to that goal. I always planned to. It just . . . never came up."

"It never came up?" Luka repeated. "She's been searching for answers for months, her entire godsdamn life, and it never fucking came up?"

"We can only interfere so much," Cienna cut in.

Luka had forgotten she was there, but not anymore. He rounded on her next, his lip curling back and baring his teeth. "You knew this entire time. All of you fucking knew and never said a godsdamn word."

"If we interfere too much, we don't answer to the Legacy or the gods," Cienna snapped, her words icy and hard. "The Fates come for us. Interfering too much would have led them straight here."

"We came here, and Tristyn met us on the other side. In the—" Xan started but Luka interrupted him.

"No," he snarled. "You're not telling me these details now. Not without her here. She deserves to hear it all from the three of you, not secondhand from me. I'll see if I can get her back down here."

He didn't wait for a reply as he stormed from the room. Everyone and their godsdamn secrets. Hoarding information for leverage. Blackmail and having the upper hand. It was all this fucking realm knew. Moves and countermoves.

And Tessa had learned that strategy as well as she'd learned everything else.

He knew that was why she'd kept the knowledge of his father from him. She'd gone from the Arius House to the Achaz Palace. She was in the perfect position to learn any and all information, and she had sworn to destroy the Arius bloodline. Why would she have told him anything when he showed up on the Achaz doorstep? Of course she was suspicious. She'd told him numerous times she didn't want him there, and even though he'd told her his loyalty was to her, words meant nothing to her. How often had pretty words been used to manipulate her?

No, Tessa only understood actions. Words fell on deaf ears and emotions betrayed her.

She understood being shoved into cupboards and locked in wine cellars.

She understood someone getting her flip-flops and sitting under the night sky with pizza.

She understood being forced to share a bed and dropping to a knee in obedience.

She understood someone being at her side when she woke from an assessment.

She understood someone giving her the gift of music and playing Chaosphere on a makeshift field.

She understood the two people who swore they never would, walking away from her, one in anger and one in an attempt to save her.

In the end, he couldn't blame her one bit for sinking into her power. It was the only constant she'd ever had.

He paused outside her door. Or maybe it was their door? He didn't sleep anywhere else, and he didn't have another room here. The few things he did have with him were all in that room too. He couldn't hear her moving around, but he could hear . . . humming?

Not quite ready to deal with whatever he was going to find on the other side of the door, he pulled his phone from his pocket and dialed the same number he'd been dialing nearly every hour for two weeks. And just like every other time, it went straight to voicemail.

Theon hadn't answered a single phone call. The godsdamn bond was clearly fractured, and Tessa . . .

Blackheart thought he was being apathetic, but it was the opposite actually. He was trying to get under her skin. He was doing anything he could to get a reaction out of her, and that was something *he'd* learned from Theon. All those months ago when he'd first brought her to Arius House and she'd withdrawn into herself, Theon hadn't let her be. Luka told him to leave her alone, but he'd pushed and pushed. Finally, he understood why. It wasn't entirely obsession and control issues. Sure, it was mostly that, but in the end, he always got her to react. In the end, he pulled her back from the edge. He craved her snark and her ire simply because it meant she was feeling *something*.

He understood now because he'd felt utter relief when Tessa had slammed the bathroom door in his face a few hours ago. For the first time since that chamber, she'd shown emotion. It was fleeting, and when she'd emerged from the bathroom, she'd been back to apathetic, but it had been there.

Theon was the one for this. Not him.

Sighing, he slipped the phone back into his pocket, idly wondering if it even mattered. Would the new world they went to have phone technology? Razik and Eliza wouldn't even touch the things. A stupid thing to be contemplating right now really, but he was just delaying the inevitable.

He didn't bother knocking as he turned the knob and pushed the door open. He'd taken all of one step when he went still. Tessa was lying on her back on the bed, still in the clothing she'd put on after her shower. Her head hung over the side of the bed so she was looking at the world upside down, the ends of her golden hair brushing the floor. One hand rested on her stomach, her finger tapping a beat to her humming, while the other hand was raised, toying with her power in the air. A swirling mass of energy, lightning flickered among it, and . . .

He stepped fully into the room, shutting the door behind him.

A damp mist hung in the air, as if it was seconds away from raining *inside*.

And all the while, she just lay there humming.

Humming that stupid Revelation Decree song.

"Tessa," he said, his tone sharp. A command that usually made her pause, but there was nothing this time. She didn't look at him. No blink or start. "Tessa," he tried again. "There is a discussion happening downstairs that you need to be a part of. Information you deserve to know."

She still didn't acknowledge him, that storm in her hand growing, and Luka had never felt so godsdamn helpless. He was the grandchild of the god of war and courage; he didn't know how to accept defeat. But that was exactly what he felt was happening as he crossed the room and sank to the floor.

He tipped his head back, resting it on the bed beside her and listening to her hum. As much as he hated it, his entire being relaxed a little. Just being next to her was like taking a drag of lull-leaf. Whether it was the bond he'd been dragged into or something else, he didn't know, but he let himself revel in it just for a moment. Tonight everything was going to change forever, and he selfishly wanted this last bit of peace.

He didn't want to think about how he'd failed in his duty as a Guardian. There was no other word for it when his Ward was welcoming his own destruction with open arms. He didn't want to think about how, for the briefest of moments, he'd had everything. Family. Acceptance. Love. He didn't want to think about how it had all shattered so quickly, and he didn't want to think about all the conflicting emotions that came with that. How he'd given in to his fury. A controlled recklessness.

"I don't know how we recover from this," he said, his eyes falling closed.

She never ceased her humming, but he knew she was listening. He wasn't even sure what he was saying or why. Maybe because the two people he used to talk to were being left behind, and he had no one else.

It's a lonely club being the grandchild of gods, but we don't have to be alone anymore.

Her words from days that felt like a lifetime ago flitted through his mind, his chest aching at the memories of it all.

"We're going to a new world, Tessa, and all we'll have is each other," he said into the room, his eyes still closed. "I don't know what that looks like. I don't know how we do that after the betrayals we've faced here."

Because in the end, that was what he felt. Betrayed by Tessa. A thousand times over. But he also felt betrayed by Theon. For thinking he could walk away from him after decades of surviving together. How that betrayal was what ultimately made him feel like a failure. He was just as furious with Theon as he was with Tessa.

"I know he's the one you need right now. I don't know how to be that. He's the one who's always protected us from ourselves, and I know you need him. You hate it, but you know it too." He fell silent, the seconds stretching on filled only by her humming. Then he said in a voice so low he didn't even know if she could hear him, "I don't know how we live without him."

He'd realized it before they did. Theon might have understood it in the end. Tessa was still figuring it out, but the three of them were so intertwined, surviving without a piece of them seemed impossible. And it wasn't because Theon had pulled him into the warped Source bond. The Fates could only control so much, and no one could control Chaos.

It was only then he'd realized the humming had ceased, the entire room going quiet and still.

Luka opened his eyes and lifted his head to find her staring at him. The small smile on her face was one he could only describe as terrifying madness.

"Tessa . . ." he said carefully, unsure of what to say or do as her power consumed her more and more. Knowing that with each passing day, they were losing her, and it only made the path ahead that much more uncertain.

She rolled onto her stomach, her hair falling over her shoulder. So close to him now, her breaths fanned across his cheek. He turned too, keeping his eyes trained on her.

Never turn your back on a predator.

Her head tilted as she watched him, and he waited for her to speak, to blink, to do *anything*.

He jolted, nearly shifting to his dragon form when her hand shot out, reaching for him, yet her touch was soft as her fingers danced across his lips. And when she opened her mouth, finally speaking to him, her tone had that eerie ring that made the hair on the back of his neck stand on end.

"You ask the wrong questions, Luka Mors."

In the next blink, she was standing on the bed before leaping lightly to the floor. Her humming once again filled the room as she moved to the windows, her fingers sliding along the glass as she paced the length of the room.

Back and forth.

Back and forth.

The drizzle in the room had stopped, but so had the raging winter weather outside. It was completely still outside. Not a breeze or stray snowflake.

Unease filled his gut as he stared at her. Bare feet. Hair wild as the fingers of her other hand wound into the strands. Eerie humming. Power echoing and mirroring her every move.

A calm before a storm.

A darkness before a dawn.

That was what he was staring at.

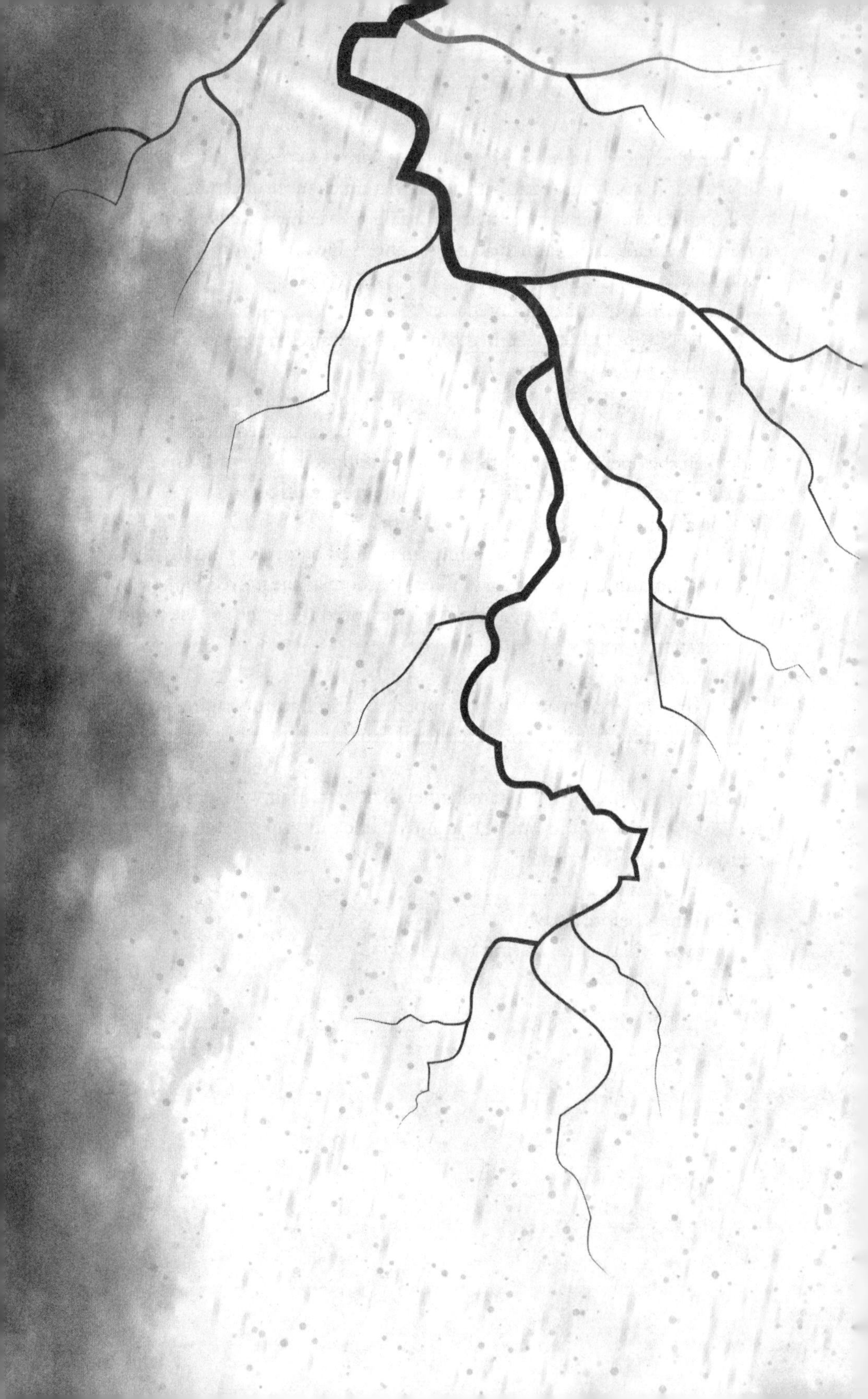

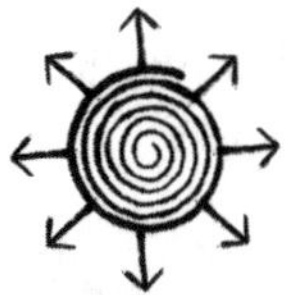

3
TESSA

"You need shoes, Tessa," Luka said from the main foyer of the penthouse.

She looked down at her bare toes, brow furrowing.

"It's been snowing for days, and I know it's stopped, but now the sidewalks and roads are icy," Luka continued, dropping a pair of boots on the floor in front of her. "More than that, we have no idea what we're going to step into when we go through the mirror gate."

She wasn't really worried about that.

He pressed socks into her hands, and she looked up at him, wrinkling her nose in disgust.

"You can't wear flip-flops," he chided, crossing his arms, and she rolled her eyes as she plopped down on the floor and slid the socks onto her feet. Then she pulled on the black boots, working the buckles and laces. The things came nearly to her knees. She would have preferred a dress, but she was in fitted black pants and a form-fitting top. Clothing very similar to Razik and Eliza, who were clad in what she assumed they had arrived in this realm in.

A hand appeared in her line of vision, and she slipped her fingers into Luka's palm, letting him pull her back to her feet. Then he dropped a stocking hat on her head, and she scowled at him. He ignored her, reaching to take a cloak that Tristyn was passing out. All of them would wear the cloaks the Keepers wore. An extra layer of disguise everyone was hoping they wouldn't need.

She hadn't come back downstairs until everyone was ready to leave. Luka had said they were discussing something important and had tried to convince her to come listen to it all, but the truth was, she didn't care. Nothing anyone said was going to change anything, and any information they had could be told to her after this night.

"Everyone have everything?" Tristyn asked, and Tessa watched him slowly take in the space around him. A place he'd lived in for centuries.

Razik reached to take a pack from Eliza, shouldering it with his own. Cienna and Gia had bags she assumed held potion ingredients and books. Tristyn had two bags stuffed full, and Luka had a backpack along with a duffel bag.

She had nothing.

The bow Auryon had left her was back at Luka's cave. Her phone was in Faven. The book Rordan had given her was hidden. She had nothing, just like she'd gone to the Arius Kingdom with.

She had nothing, but all that was about to change.

Luka reached over, pulling the hood of the cloak up and tucking her hair in. Taking care of her like Theon had instructed. His new assignment.

With another last look around, Tristyn pressed the button for the elevator that opened directly into his main foyer. They all stepped in, the ride to the first floor quiet, and they stayed that way as they stepped out onto the street, taking a side door that emptied into an alley. The door behind them hadn't even closed completely when two large shapes stalked from the shadows, glowing orange eyes locked on her.

Tessa smiled as Roan came to her side, rubbing against her legs. Her fingers sank into his silver fur while Nylah prowled a few feet in front of her, dark as the night. There would be little doubt who they were if they were spotted, but few would dare to do anything. She was powerful. Her wolves were dangerous. Her company was violent.

It was the start of everything that was to come.

Tristyn took the lead along with Xan, Nylah with them. Luka stayed on her other side. Behind them were Eliza and Razik, and Tessa idly wondered how they kept their footsteps so light. Cienna and Gia took up the rear.

The world was still around them, as if the entire realm was holding its breath, and Tessa inhaled deeply. Fresh cold air filled her lungs, and she wished her bare feet were leaving prints in the snow rather than her boots.

Sticking to the dark streets and staying in the shadows, they made their way to the Pantheon. The trek took three times as long as it should have, but they couldn't exactly pull up in a car at the front doors.

From the corner of her eye, she saw Luka pull his phone from his pocket multiple times. For the most part, he appeared to simply be checking the screen. A few times, his thumb moved as if typing a message.

It was over two hours before Tristyn was leading them through the hidden door and down passages in the Pantheon. Roan dropped behind her, the passage too narrow for him to stay at her side, and she heard Luka cursing at the wolf for separating him so far from her. Soon enough, they were all spilling into the chamber, everyone pulling back their hoods and breathing a collective sigh of relief.

Or everyone else was.

Tessa kept her hood up, coming to a stop just inside the chamber. Her eyes swept over the room, vividly remembering every breath and step, every word spoken and tear that had fallen.

A kiss, soft and tender and full of sorrow.

Tessalyn Ausra, I would sacrifice all the realms and all the stars for you. You are perfectly wild. Perfectly untamed. You were not made to be caged, nor were you made to be a sacrifice for a realm that does not deserve such a gift. You were made to live in the light. Go live, little storm.

Thumbs swiping at her cheeks.

And fury.

So much fury as he had walked away from her.

"Stay with us, Tessa," came a low murmur, and she blinked, finding Xan standing in front of her. He had a knowing look on his face, sapphire eyes searching hers. "Let him help you. The deeper you sink, the harder it will be to pull you back."

Her lips pulled up at the corners. "Maybe I want to drown."

If he was surprised she'd spoken, he didn't show it, and he didn't balk at her words either.

"I know that's easier," he said with a nod. "It's easier to give in, but in the end? That's all it will be. An end."

Then he moved away as Luka approached, eyeing his retreating father suspiciously. "Are you all right?" he asked, still watching his father. When she didn't reply, he finally turned to face her fully. "Before we go, Tristyn and Cienna need to remove the enchantment that was put on you when he freed you from the cells. We don't know where we're going to end up, and we need to be able to Travel in case we find ourselves somewhere unfavorable."

She nodded because it would be nice to have the enchantment removed. It made her feel caged not being able to portal anywhere, and she didn't like feeling trapped. More than that, they could have all simply Traveled here rather than walking these last few hours. Roan nudged her hand, his nose wet and cold where he sat beside her. Nylah was pacing the perimeter of the chamber.

"It is easier to remove here," Tristyn said, coming to Luka's side. "Especially down here, where magic is stronger and more prevalent."

"Why?" she asked.

Tristyn blinked, unable to conceal his surprise like Xan had, but a pleased expression quickly replaced it. "Because the Pantheon is located at the center of the continent. It is already a more powerful location because of its position as a nexus. Beyond that, this chamber is the center of the Pantheon, making it more powerful still. That is why the cells you were in could contain you. There is more magic here."

"You mean more Chaos," she supplied, her fingers winding into Roan's fur once more.

Tristyn nodded slowly and almost seemed to hesitate before he said, "Yes, and because of that, I do not know how you will be affected. It will be easier for *us* to remove the enchantment, but I fear it will be harder on *you*."

"What does that mean?" Luka demanded, edging closer so he was partially blocking her from view.

She almost scoffed. She didn't need physical protection. Only protection from those who tried to take from her. Control her with pretty words. Use her.

"She is already . . . immersed in her power," Tristyn said. "Undoing this enchantment will require us to draw on the magic here, and her magic is drawn to . . ."

"Itself," Tessa supplied, slipping past Luka and venturing deeper into the chamber. She kept her back turned to the passage she'd watched him walk down, leaving her behind. Instead, she focused on the mirror, where Eliza and Razik were speaking in a low tone.

"Stand in the center," Cienna said in her usual harsh tone, and Tessa moved to the middle of the room. She reached up, pushing back her hood and removing the stocking hat Luka had given her, tossing it to the side where everyone had placed their packs of belongings.

She could feel it. The power Tristyn had referred to. It buzzed in the air, frenetic and enticing. Or maybe that was her own power? It didn't really matter. They were one and the same. But the magic in her veins was seeking. The thing in her soul was stretching. She could feel it all. Everyone's power.

The dragons and the fire. The calming that Tristyn was pushing on her. The magic of the realm and the stars beyond.

The power of that mirror.

Cienna was circling her, drawing Marks on the ground as she went. Tristyn was standing before her, concern etched deep into his features.

"Luka will be here, wild fury," Tristyn said, trying to muster his cocky smile. He truly was worried about this. How interesting. "As soon as we're done, he'll be here to pull you back."

Her head canted to the side. "Back from where?"

"The madness," Xan supplied. "Temural would often have to do so for your mother."

Tessa blinked. For the first time in two weeks, she actually *wanted* more information. Despite her parents abandoning her, she was still curious. She didn't know how she'd react if she ever met them. Would she be cold and distant like Razik? Or would she be tentative and open like Luka?

Probably more like Razik. He'd been intentionally abandoned; Luka had been a victim of this realm.

"Ready?" Tristyn asked, looking more nervous than Tessa had ever seen him. He was always cool and collected, snapping at Theon and putting people in their place.

Tessa nodded, once again wishing she'd taken her boots off before they did this. She curled her toes, hating the feeling of the socks.

"He can't be in the circle with you," Tristyn said. "You need to listen for his call."

Tessa glanced at Luka, who stood with his arms crossed. Holding her stare, he said, "I will come for you, Tessa."

One would think he'd felt her hesitation and uncertainty about that statement, but she knew that wasn't the case. The bond was broken. It had broken the moment Theon had left this chamber. All three of them were broken, and there was no fixing them anymore.

Luka took a step towards her, lips parting as if he was going to say more, but Cienna started reciting something in an old tongue. Tristyn joined her, and the moment was lost. Luka's lips pressed into a thin line, but she couldn't focus on him. Not as she felt her power rush to the surface, that thing inside of her screaming with excitement. Not as she felt power surround her, her magic stretching and yanking to greet it.

She heard Tristyn falter, but Cienna snapped, "We keep going, Tris. We don't even know if she can leave this world with the enchantment in place. Do not stop."

Tessa's head tilted as she watched the siblings, both eyes glowing a soft sage, his with russet undertones, hers with violet. They resumed their incantations, and her eyes fluttered closed as she felt the push and pull and call of what she was.

It swirled around her, and she gasped, her eyes flying open. Light *and* dark flared at her fingertips, wound up her arms. Sparks of gold and embers of silver fluttered among it all. Her feet lifted off the ground, and her hair fanned out around her as if caught in a windstorm. Maybe she was because rain and snow were falling around her, and *gods*. She hadn't been worried, but this *hurt*. As if the magic of every world was trying to rip her apart to get at the power she held. It wanted to take and take and take. It was that same feral craving she always fell into when she let her magic have its way. They'd warned her. Told her it would take everything from her if she let it, and this—

This is what they'd meant.

Tessa!

Her name echoed in her mind. Maybe Luka had yelled it. Maybe the emotion was strong enough to filter through a splintered and fractured bond.

It didn't matter.

When she opened her mouth, a scream erupted from her.

The scream of her magic.

The scream of her pain.

The scream of chaos and fury.

A fierce roar mingled with her cries, but she couldn't focus on anything as power wrapped her up in a whirlwind of Chaos. She thrashed among it, trying to find a way out, a way to free herself, but the power gripped her tighter. As if the enchantment had been doing more than just keeping her from portaling and Traveling. As if the enchantment had somehow caged her power too, and now it was angry. It was taking what it wanted, and she would be the cost.

She screamed again. Her knees cracked against the stone floor of the Pantheon chamber.

And she fell into Chaos.

It was like watching the mirror as worlds and stars swirled around her, held together by the Chaos it all came from. No order. No structure. No balance.

She couldn't breathe, but she also didn't know that she needed to in this space. She didn't think it was the After. Maybe it was the Beginning.

Maybe it was nothing and everything at once.

She was tossed around, and yet . . .

Despite the Chaos, she felt calm.

How odd.

She stopped struggling. Stopped flailing and just let herself be.

She watched.

She listened.

She learned everything she could.

And then she was standing in an opulent room. Gold and white, black and silver. Marks she knew and symbols she didn't glittered on the walls, the floor, the ceiling. In the center of the floor was a vast chasm that seemed to swallow the light yet illuminate the room all at once.

"Thank the . . . Well, not the gods. Because frankly, fuck them and their failures. The Fates? But that would be awkward, right? Considering—"

"There is not time for this," a male voice interrupted the female.

Tessa had spun at the voices, and it had taken her several seconds to find the female figure slinking through the shadows. All in black, she wore a cloak, the hood up, but an ashy-blonde braid was snaking out and down her chest. And by the gods, she had so many weapons strapped to her body, Tessa wasn't sure how she could even move.

More movement had her attention shifting to the male. Tall and broad with deeply tanned skin, he had the arched ears of the Fae and Legacy. His black hair was tied up atop his head, eyes the color of a thunderstorm fixed on her. But it was the brown feathered wings that arched over his shoulders that had Tessa's eyes narrowing.

He was the same as Dex, Oralia, and Brecken.

The female pulled her hood back while simultaneously pulling a dagger from her hip, spinning the point against her gloved finger. She smiled, the tips of fangs visible, and the smile held a tinge of madness that Tessa recognized as honey-colored eyes connected with hers.

Her head canted to the side in a predatory manner while she said to the male, "I was beginning to think she'd gotten the date and time wrong."

"You don't trust my sources?" came yet another female voice that had Tessa spinning again.

"Depends on which one it was," replied the first female, still spinning her dagger.

The newcomer breezed into the room, carefully closing the door behind her. Arched ears were just visible through her long dark red hair, and Marks peeked out of the wide collar of her long-sleeved top. Tessa also suspected the nose piercing wasn't her only one, and once again, honey-colored eyes settled on her.

"I know it's calling to you," she said to Tessa, moving farther into the room, her white sneakers quiet on the gleaming floor.

Tessa remained quiet, watching them all and trying to figure out what was going on in yet another vision she didn't understand. The Chaos wasn't driving her mad; these godsdamn glimpses of everything and nothing were going to be what pushed her over the edge.

"How long do we have?" the male asked, planting himself between Tessa and the hole in the center of the room. His feathered wings flared wide, as if creating an additional barrier, and she could tell just by looking at him he was a trained warrior, perhaps even more so than Razik.

"Anala is doing her part. Again," the dark-haired female said bitterly.

"We can't help it if she's his favorite," the first female said.

But Tessa had stopped listening to them as the thing in her soul yanked her forward. She stumbled a step, the male going rigid as she got closer.

"Em . . ." the male warned.

"I've got it," the dark-haired female snapped before focusing on Tessa once more. "Listen for his call. Don't go deeper."

"I don't know what you're talking about," Tessa said, trying to peer around the male as the first female slunk to his side, a dagger in each hand now. As if they anticipated a fight was about to happen. Maybe it was because her power wanted . . . It just wanted.

"Resist it just a little longer," the female—Em—said. "If you go to it, he'll find you and the balance will never recover."

"There is no such thing as balance," Tessa retorted, taking another step forward.

"There is," Em insisted. "But if he finds you, he'll just add you to his collection that keeps him in power. Is that what you want?"

Tessa faltered, unsure of who or what they were talking about.

"That's what he does," Em went on, noticing her hesitation. "He finds. He creates. He cages. He will keep you."

"I am no one's," Tessa hissed, her power flickering at her fingertips.

And the floor shuddered.

"Shit," the male muttered. "He'll have felt that."

"I thought you said you had this under control," the other female snapped, stepping to Em's side. "That we just needed to keep her distracted for a minute or two."

"That's what he said," Em retorted.

"This is why I don't trust your godsdamn sources."

The door being thrown open had them all turning as an ethereally beautiful female strode in. Her red-gold hair hung in loose curls down to her waist, amber eyes honing in on Tessa.

"We are out of time," the female said, her voice fire and power. She never slowed, coming right up to Tessa. "You must go. Find the one who chose Death. She has your answers."

Then her hand thrust out, her palm, wrapped in flames, slamming into Tessa's chest, and she fell into Chaos again.

The stars tumbled. The worlds fell.

And then she was standing before a cell.

She'd been here before, and knew when she turned to the window, she'd be below the sea.

The same female was behind the bars, her fingers in her lanky black hair, tugging at the ends. Bright violet eyes snapped to Tessa, the female lurching forward, careful not to touch the bars.

"Did he send you?" she asked, sounding more than a little mad. "Is he finally coming for me?"

"I . . . don't know who you are," Tessa answered slowly, her head tilting as she watched the female slowly back away, shaking her head.

"But you do, child. But you do. We are one and the same," the female said. Then she tipped her head back and laughed as she shot forward, wrapping her hands around the bars of her cell.

Power rippled out, slamming into Tessa, and again she fell.

But it was faster this time.

Glimpses of visions as if looking through windows. Her soul being pulled in so many directions she wished it would simply tear apart.

A silver-haired female in a chamber surrounded by books. It took a minute to recognize Scarlett, worry etched on her features as she frantically flipped pages. Three males stood in the doorway, watching her. One was Sorin. All three shared a look of concern as her shadows coiled around her.

Another female with silver hair, a white snake around her shoulders as she slipped into the shadows of night.

The land in the sky.

A child with blonde curls and blue eyes, laughing as she ran before she shifted mid-step into a small feline.

A female with hair as golden as her own sitting on a balcony railing, legs swinging in the air and smiling as if she could see Tessa.

A male with long black hair tied at the nape of his neck. Wolves walked at his sides, a black eagle screeching in the sky above him. Pine green eyes homed in on Tessa, as if he, too, could see her.

As if Tessa was straddling two worlds. All worlds.

The thing in her soul whined, begging to be set free. The female tipped her head back, laughing to the dark clouds above her, while the male clenched his jaw, the wolves at his sides tipping their heads back and howling to a clear sky.

A land once pristine and now rubble, a male with black hair and piercing emerald eyes. Her feet finally found the ground again, rocks crunching beneath her boots. He palmed her cheek, his thumb stroking gently. "Go home, Tessa. He's calling for you," he said.

And before she could say anything in response, before she could tell him she didn't have a home, he bent, pressing his lips to her brow. Everything in her soul settled, even as she fell into Chaos yet again.

"Tessa? Open your eyes, Tessa!"

Her name was a growled command, her shoulders shaking as her eyes fluttered open. Luka stared down at her, relief filling his face. He was kneeling on the ground, her body cradled in his arms, and she rolled from his hold, bile rising up her throat.

He reached over, gathering her hair back in case she vomited, but it never came. Her arms trembled as she stayed on her hands and knees, trying to reorient herself.

"Did it work?" Luka demanded.

"It worked," Cienna replied.

"How can we be sure?"

"It worked," Tessa said, lifting her head as the nausea subsided.

"What the fuck happened?" Luka asked, his attention on her now.

But Tessa just pursed her lips, sitting back on her heels. "I saw things."

"Visions," Luka clarified.

"Kind of. It was like I was falling through them in a way. They went so fast. Different worlds. Different times. Two worlds at once. I . . ."

She trailed off, shaking her head and trying to clear it. Luka released her hair, withdrawing from her, and the calm that had settled over her immediately left. Her power rushed to him, latching on, and she heard him suck in a sharp hiss. His own magic scrambled to protect him, and then it was her sucking in a breath as their power intertwined.

"Enough," Luka gritted out.

"Just give me a minute," she rasped again, trying to push to her feet but immediately dropping back to her knees.

"What do you mean, you fell through visions?"

Tessa looked up to find Eliza standing over her, grey eyes narrowed.

Tessa shrugged. "That's what it felt like."

The Fae looked up at Razik, who was at her side. "Doesn't that sound like . . . ?"

Razik rubbed at his jaw. "It could be similar," he agreed.

"Someone fill us in. Again," Luka snarled, getting to his feet and helping Tessa up as he did. She swayed, and his lips pressed into a thin line as he held her steady.

"Scarlett wasn't born what she is," Razik said. "She found the power of the world walkers."

"She found it," Luka repeated dubiously.

"It had been contained and hidden," Eliza cut in. "When the war between the gods and world walkers ended, that was the cost. They didn't want that power lost, so it was contained. The World Walkers were still beings of Chaos."

"And Scarlett obtained that power, essentially becoming one herself. And Tessa is . . . something similar," Razik finished.

"So you are saying she, what? Walked the worlds?" Luka asked.

"Not like Scarlett can, but something similar, perhaps," Razik agreed.

Luka took her shoulders, spinning Tessa to face him. A finger under her chin had her head tipping back, forcing her to meet his gaze. "What did you see?"

She should tell him. They should be past keeping secrets, but she couldn't make any sense of anything she saw. They weren't alone here, and she was just getting used to working her shit out with another person or two. Not a whole godsdamn room.

His nostrils flared with an exhale, faint traces of smoke appearing when she remained silent. He leaned in, his voice low as he said, "This conversation isn't over, Tessa, and Sargon help me, you're going to tell me. You're going to have to figure this out because I don't have near the patience Theon does."

He released her, stalking to the other side of the room to grab his bags. She stared after him, her hands curling into fists. She'd just . . . needed a moment. She knew he was pissed at her—had every right to be—but fuck.

"Easy, Tessa," Xan said, trying to calm her, but his voice was too much like his son's. Tears burned the back of her eyes. She wished she could say they were tears of hurt, but it was fury.

It was always fury lately.

The only time it wasn't eating at her, her power was clawing at her insides. She just needed a minute to breathe. A minute to think. A minute to—

"Summon her. Let's get on with this," Luka snarled, snapping Tessa out of her spiral.

Everyone else had gathered their belongings. Eliza and Razik were waiting near the mirror.

"Wait!" Tessa cried, lifting a hand to stop them, but power ricocheted around the room. Energy and light bounced around, curses sounding.

"Control it, Tessa," Luka barked, and she slid her gaze to his, her lip curling back in a sneer.

He was pissed, but so was she.

"I am," she said, and this time everyone stilled because her voice was too soft. Too calm. "I'm controlling all of it."

She made her way to the mirror, Razik pulling Eliza into his side as she approached.

"We can call her," Eliza started. "She gave us a way—"

"I'll do it," Tessa interrupted, pulling a gold dagger from a swirl of magic. Ignoring protests, she sliced her palm, curling her fingers to keep the blood from dripping to the ground as she looked over the symbols and runes surrounding the mirror.

"She won't have a symbol," Razik said. "That's why we were given a way to contact her."

Tessa looked over her shoulder, her smile wild and wicked as she said, "I know."

Then she pressed her palm to the Mark she'd been seeking.

An eight-pointed star.

Find the one who chose Death.

"That's not the right—" Tristyn started, reaching for her, but she lifted her other hand, magic shoving him back. Light swirled, keeping the others at bay as the mirror flashed with worlds and scenes, just like the visions she'd fallen through. She was so godsdamn tired of everyone thinking they knew what was best for her. Of telling her to do as she was told. Go with Luka. Leave this world. Tell me what you saw. Control it. Stop fidgeting. Just give in. Try harder. Be more. Be less.

The mirror swirled faster, moving too quickly for her to make out anything, until it slowed and a female came into view. Silver hair flowed over her shoulders and past her navel, a crown of white flames as bright as starlight atop her head. Thick kohl lined her eyes, her lips as red as blood. Her black gown was nearly sheer, and slithering along her torso and around her shoulders was a white python, stark against her bronzed skin.

Glowing silver eyes settled on Tessa, and her voice was as ethereal and cold as the voids between the stars when she said, "I've been waiting for this since the moment I learned of your existence."

"Everyone knows who I am, yet no one cared to tell me," Tessa replied, her hand dropping to her side, her magic having already healed the cut. "But I'm told you have answers for me."

The female stood too still. She didn't even look like she was breathing.

Maybe goddesses didn't have to breathe.

"What answers do you seek?" she asked.

Fingers brushed her arm, wrapping around her elbow as if to pull her back, but she shook them off.

He'd told her to control it.

That was what she was doing.

"You chose him. Chose Endings over Beginnings," Tessa said. "Why?"

The female's eyes softened a touch as she looked at Tessa, never breaking her stare. The snake moved, its tongue flicking in and out as it tasted the air. But no one spoke. There was no other sound, and the silence stretched on for so long, Tessa was wondering if she was going to reply.

But she would have her answers one way or another, and the goddess seemed to understand that when she said, "To start a genesis."

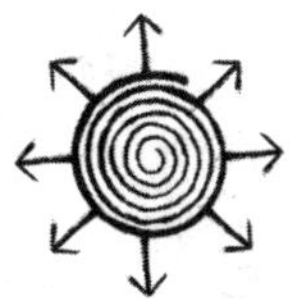

4
LUKA

She'd summoned a godsdamn goddess.

Serafina, the goddess of dreams and stars. The consort of Arius. Tessa's grandmother.

Luka stared at Tessa as she squared off with a First Goddess. He should be furious with her. He *was* furious with her. She'd once again, single-handedly, altered their plans. But by the gods, he was also so fucking proud of her as she lifted her chin, waiting for the goddess to answer her. It was going to fuck up everything. He could feel it in his bones. She was about to do something wild and uncontrolled, and he was probably going to fight with her about it later, but in this moment, his chest swelled with pride.

"To start a genesis," the goddess finally answered, her eyes softening a fraction as she held Tessa's gaze.

A genesis?

The term nudged at something in the back of his mind, but then there was a hissed, "*Mors!*" from Blackheart that had him turning to his right.

Only to find the male on a knee. Cienna and Gia were in the same position. Looking at his father, he found him, Razik, and Eliza on a knee as well. The same way the Fae knelt for the Legacy Lords and Ladies.

Because they were the gods in Devram.

Luka had never had to do such a thing. It made sense, being in the presence of an actual First Goddess, but he didn't like the idea of being on a knee with Tessa being so . . . unpredictable right now. More than that, why in all the realms would he kneel before a being that had abandoned their world, leaving it to become what it was? He'd kneel before someone he was loyal to, and that certainly wasn't a fucking goddess.

Silver eyes slid to him as if she could hear his thoughts. Her facial expression didn't change. Her body language remained still. That snake continued to glide around her. He wouldn't kneel before her, but he did give her the courtesy of being the first to break the stare, dropping his eyes and bowing his head as he would to a Lord or Lady.

Until the goddess said, "Xan, it has been some time."

Luka's head snapped back up, looking at his father.

"It has, Serina," Xan answered.

Serina?

His father was on a first-name basis with her? Not only a first-name basis, but a familial name of endearment?

"Sargon is growing anxious," Serafina said.

"Understood, my lady."

What did he understand? He'd been so worried about Tessa and Theon these last weeks, he hadn't had spare time to sit down and talk with his father about anything. When they did talk, it was all of them trying to convince him they needed to go and stop wasting time. Or rather, it was them trying to tell him he needed to deal with Tessa and convince *her* it was time to go.

A few more seconds of tense silence passed before the goddess said, "You all may rise." Her gaze moved over them again, stopping to his right. "Tristyn Blackheart, your dealings do not involve me, but I can still see your deepest desires and dreams. Taika will be interested in this report of events."

Luka watched the male's jaw tense, his fingers curling into fists at his sides, but he said nothing. His father was a god. What sort of dealings did the male have with another goddess? This was all getting too messy, and quite frankly, he didn't care about their dealings or the mysteries of the gods. The only thing he wanted an answer to was what she'd meant by a genesis and why Tessa was asking this of her in the first place.

Tessa was apparently in agreement because the bands of light at her wrists were glowing and snaking up her arms, only now there were flecks of darkness among the light.

"Enough," Tessa snapped, stepping closer to the mirror once more. "This isn't a reunion with souls who found their way to a realm you care nothing for. What did you mean 'to start a genesis'?"

That's our girl.

Luka thought it before he could stop himself.

Godsdammit.

Serafina refocused on her granddaughter, lifting an arm so the snake could coil around it. "Devram was created millenniums ago," she said. "Much has happened since that world was cut off from the rest." Silver eyes scanned the room again. "And much history has been forgotten. If not forgotten, altered, depending on who is telling the tale."

"Then how am I to believe anything you say?" Tessa demanded, her hands flying to her hair.

He wanted to step forward and stop her, but he hesitated, unsure why. He could say it was because she hadn't asked for his help. That he was letting her do this on her own unless she asked for him, but he knew that wasn't the only reason. His dragon knew it too, snarling internally.

She's not ours, he snapped at the creature in his soul. *She betrayed us.*

Of course the possessive dragon side of him didn't care. Once it claimed something, there was really no going back.

Which just made her an even bigger pain in his ass.

"You do not have to believe me," the goddess was saying to Tessa. "But you summoned me for a reason, so I would gather you will, at the very least, listen to what I have to say."

The power winding up Tessa's arms flared again, but then Roan was there, rubbing along her legs, and her fingers sank into his fur. Grounding her. Giving her something to latch onto.

Luka ignored the guilt coiling in his gut.

Serafina's eyes dipped to the wolf, a small smile lifting on her lips. "One of my son's own," she said.

"Roan is *mine*," Tessa retorted. "As is Nylah."

"Because you are of him," the goddess answered simply.

Luka heard the scoff from Tessa before she said, "Tell me your version of history then, goddess."

Serafina's smile morphed into something tight and cold. A smile he'd seen on Tessa's face more than once. "Careful, child. Family or not, I am still a goddess."

"I do not care," Tessa said. "I have been forgotten and discarded, used and abused. You think I have any care for what you are? For my own wellbeing at this point? I have nothing to lose anymore. I've already lost it all. I am the villain in everyone's story, including my own. I am the excuse for everyone's actions, and I am the power everyone seeks. I stand at a crossroads. Salvation or destruction. So either tell me why you chose your path or leave. I will make a choice either way. You can decide if your knowledge is valuable enough for me to consider before I take that next step."

Serafina didn't move. Didn't blink as she studied Tessa. And Luka found himself drawing closer. He hadn't even realized his feet had moved, but he needed to see her face. He wasn't entirely sure what he'd been expecting, but it wasn't the cool iciness that he found. There was no hesitancy. There was fury, but when wasn't there anymore? And her words? She'd once said things so similar, but she'd been different then. Beat down by a world full of the wicked. She was a villain because this realm had turned her into one.

The difference was now she didn't seem to care. She was embracing all that she was.

Wild and untamed.

Chaotic and uncontrollable.

Powerful and vengeful.

"So much like your father. Wild and stubborn," Serafina murmured.

"He abandoned me. I could not care less about him," Tessa spat.

The goddess leaned in, as if she wanted to whisper into Tessa's ear. "You are powerful, but you are not immune to my gifts, Tessalyn. Is that what you believe happened? That he wanted nothing to do with you? That he left you to the Fates?"

"Worse," she sneered. "He left me alone. Everyone did. It is what I have lived and what I know. Alone in a damned world. Wishing someone would care . . ."

She trailed off, waiting for Serafina's response, and Luka glanced at the goddess. Her lips were pursed, eyes glowing even brighter now, as if they were starlight themselves. Silver flames flickered in them. The same silver flames Scarlett could wield.

"Arius and Achaz used to be quite close. Like brothers," Serafina said. "The first to emerge from the Chaos, they worked together in harmony, as was always meant to be. Keeping the balance."

"You would have tipped the balance either way," Tessa said.

Serafina's answering smile was anything but joyful. "We were not the only beings to emerge from the Chaos. Arius and Achaz may have been the first, but other beings emerged after them. Some before the rest of us."

"You speak of the World Walkers," Razik cut in, drifting closer. The draw of new information pulled him in like a moth to a flame.

"The World Walkers were one of them, yes," the goddess agreed.

"Who else?" Tessa asked.

"The dragons. The seraphs." Her gaze moved from Xan and settled back on Tessa. "The Fates."

"Are there more?" Tessa pressed.

"They are the main players," Serafina replied. "We all emerged with our own strengths. We were all meant to be a balance, but . . . We created. New stars. New worlds. But the World Walkers were the ones who could move most freely among the realms. The rest of us could do so, but there are costs for magic that is not inherently yours."

"What does any of this have to do with choosing Arius over Achaz?" Tessa cut in.

"The World Walkers were just as powerful as the gods. While we had our own powers, so did they. They could also create worlds, and they could shift forms at will. The Fates warned of a coming imbalance, and as happens when one tries to figure out fate, destruction befell us all. War erupted between the gods and World Walkers."

"The Everlasting War," Eliza clarified.

Serafina nodded. "We were losing, and in our desperation, we thought if we could create a powerful child, stronger than any other being to exist . . ."

"You and Achaz were going to create . . . Why didn't you?" Tessa asked, inching a little closer.

"It is a long tale. One we do not have time for this day," Serafina answered. "But there came a time when we disagreed with Achaz. He was consumed by victory and power. We knew the balance was going to tip either way. The Fates stepped back and provided a choice."

"Salvation or destruction," Tessa murmured, her hands opening and closing at her sides.

Serafina nodded again. "Two could come together and change the course of history. A terminus and a genesis. It was left up to them to choose it. Since that time, there have been other crucial moments offered to two souls that could alter history. Some chose the genesis. Some did not. Some do not realize they have even chosen it. But the Fates do not intervene beyond ensuring their paths cross."

"It was always more than a bond." Tessa's words were so quiet, Luka was sure no one else had heard them. She had taken a small step back, her hands once again in her hair. Then her eyes flashed to him. "He knew?"

"I don't . . ." Luka started, still trying to wrap his mind around things, but an image flashed in his mind. A term circled over and over on a sheet of paper in Eliza and Razik's rooms.

Genesis bond.

He slowly slid his gaze to Razik. "*You* knew. Did you tell him?"

"It was a term we'd come across. We were still researching, but we suspected," his brother answered in the same apathetic tone he always spoke in.

"You son of a bitch," Luka seethed.

"We cannot interfere," Razik retorted.

"The Fates cannot Travel among the worlds?" Tessa asked suddenly, looking back at Serafina.

"When the World Walkers lost at that point of the Everlasting War, we did not want their power lost to the ether," Serafina replied. She lifted her arm once more, the snake sliding back up. "The power was taken from the most powerful and contained, but it also created gateways for us to move among the realms."

"Like this one," Tessa clarified.

"Yes."

"And these mirror gates are the only way the Fates could come here? That anyone else could come here?"

Serafina hesitated, her eyes narrowing on Tessa once more, before she answered carefully, "There are always work-arounds. It is a matter of if one is willing to pay the cost. The gateways are simply the easiest and fastest."

"And the Fates will come for me?" she pressed. "Because I am an imbalance."

"I cannot say the intentions of the Fates or their prophecies. I deal in dreams and desires."

"And I deal in Chaos," Tessa said, and that fucking eerie ring in her voice had Luka snapping to attention. "Do you regret your choice?"

The goddess had taken a step back too, as if Tessa could somehow affect her from this side of the mirror. It probably had something to do with the light and dark curling around Tessa and rolling off her like a fine mist. Or maybe it was the sparks of gold and silver that flickered among it. It could have been the energy, streaks of lightning flashing through it all. But it was probably the storms brewing in her palms. Rotating vortexes. One of brightest white and the other of darkest black. A push and pull between the two that Luka could feel in the air.

Serafina swallowed thickly, as though she knew her answer was going to set something into motion. But her voice was power and strength when she said, "No. I would choose Arius a thousand times over."

Before anyone could blink, let alone move, Tessa lurched forward. Her palms landed on the glass, cracks and fissures immediately spider-webbing out from her fingertips.

"Tessalyn, no!" Serafina gasped, the white snake lifting its head in interest as the goddess stumbled forward. "You do not understand the cost of this! I don't—I don't know how this will alter things!"

Tessa's head tipped to the side as magic poured from her hands, the cracks deepening and spreading farther. The mirror was starting to swirl violently, the same magic Tessa was spilling across it sparking and bouncing around the chamber.

"Neither do I," Tessa replied. "I never know what's going to happen. I suppose, for once, we'll all be on the same playing field then, hmm?"

She lifted her palms, her feet coming off the floor as her power swelled all around her, and her hands slammed back onto the glass again. The goddess opened her mouth, but they'd never know what she was going to say because she disappeared as the pieces of glass started to fall to the ground.

"No!" Razik bellowed, lunging for her, but Luka was there first. Not to stop her, but to shove his brother back. His wings ripped free, shredding his shirt, and Razik snarled in response.

"Do not touch her," Luka warned.

Razik's eyes had long since shifted, vertical pupils filled with fury. His body trembled, telling Luka his brother was fighting the shift just like he was.

"That is our only way home," Razik growled. "If you think I'm going to let her destroy it and strand us here forever, you—"

But he didn't get to finish that statement. Not as the floor beneath them shook, making them both stumble. Not as small pieces of rock and debris rained down on them. Razik turned, an arm snapping out to haul Eliza into his side, and Luka spun, finding Tessa with power still rolling off her. It spread, snaking across the floor. Up the walls. Through the ceiling.

"Tessa, what are you doing?" Luka cried, but he was certain she couldn't hear him. She was too deep. How the fuck was he supposed to pull her back from *this?*

"We need to get out of here!" Tristyn yelled. "She is bringing this chamber to ruin!"

"Make her stop," Razik snarled again. "That is our only way home!"

"It's already done," Tessa said in that eerie ring that had them all spinning back to her.

Her entire being was glowing with an aura of . . . chaos. Light and dark. Energy and embers. Beginnings and endings.

"The mirror still stands," Razik argued.

"Not for much longer," she replied, starting for the chamber exit. Each step left a bootprint of dark power, magic radiating with every footfall.

"Let's go!" Tristyn said, racing to lead them out of here.

Everyone else fell into line, grabbing their packs from the floor and scrambling to follow. Luka grabbed his own and rushed ahead until he realized Tessa wasn't in front of him. Skidding to a halt, he looked over his shoulder, trying to figure out where she'd gone. When he finally found her, he didn't know what to think. While the rest of them were clambering to get out of here, she had moved to the perimeter, dragging her fingers along the wall. Fissures spread from beneath them, seeping into the foundation. Tristyn hadn't been wrong. She was going to bring the chamber to ruin, but this . . .

This would bring the entire Pantheon down.

He rushed for her, grabbing her other hand. "Tessa, we have to go," he said, tugging her along.

But even as he pulled, she didn't appear to be in any hurry. Her hand never left the wall as he dragged her along. Down the passages they moved, cracks spearing in all directions. Nylah had prowled ahead like she normally did, but she kept circling back because they were falling behind. Roan was behind Tessa, nudging her forward with his nose.

"Tessa, we need to move faster," Luka gritted out as the debris that was falling grew bigger, large chunks of stone and marble crumbling when they hit the ground. He could hear the others ahead of them, yelling to people they came across to run and get out of the Pantheon, but Tessa only smiled. Her eyes were nearly wholly black save for rings of violet on the edges glowing bright. Trying to avoid the obstacles of the quickly narrowing passages, they finally made it to the steps that would take them up to the main floor.

She'd started humming again, that damned Revelation Decree song, and he was done with this. Scooping her up in his arms, he raced up the broken stairs and emerged into mayhem.

Priestesses were screaming and running, arms full of supplies and books. No one paid them any mind, which was good. His cloak had been shredded when his wings had appeared, and while he'd made them disappear, he was still shirtless and recognizable. Not to mention Tessa was well known by everyone now, no longer the wild Fae trying to blend in with the world.

With the crowd, it was too hard to carry her, and he was forced to put her back on her feet. Nylah had circled back yet again, and her wolves made sure people stayed back from them. Still, Tessa walked calmly through the main floor of the Pantheon. Energy continued to emanate from her, and her magic *took*, taking down Priestesses as she moved. With every body that hit the floor, he felt her power increase, and he finally understood how she refilled her reserves.

Life must give, and death must take.

She hadn't taken in weeks.

He just needed to get her outside. Once they were outside of the Pantheon walls they could Travel, assuming Tristyn and Cienna had indeed managed to remove the enchantment.

Luka spotted the others up ahead as they neared the main doors. Sentinels were pouring in, trying to help evacuate the Priestesses. It was only then he realized there wasn't a single Fae to be seen. He whirled back to Tessa, and she only smiled at him, dark and wicked. Finally embracing that she was life and death, and today she was channeling the latter.

"You planned this all along," he said in disbelief as she moved past him.

She said nothing, only lifted her hands in front of her and threw arcs of light ahead of them. The heavy wood doors were blasted off their hinges, exploding out into the courtyard. He followed, bounding down the twenty steps that led up to the building where the others were waiting for them. But they were staring past him, and he turned, not knowing what he would find anymore.

There were no words as Tessa sat on the top step removing her boots. The Pantheon was swaying behind her, as though it would fall at any moment, and she didn't seem to care.

Because she was in complete control.

Two sentinels raced for her, but her wolves were there, their screams cut short by massive jaws. Tessa tossed the boots behind her as she stood, and only then did she descend the steps. Light swirled in one hand, while darkness hovered in the other. Energy skittered out with each step, the stairs crumbling to nothing as she left each one behind. She still wore her cloak, and it billowed behind her as the winds picked up. The clouds above them thundered, lightning striking far too close.

She reached the bottom, and her eyes slid to the left. Luka turned to see what had captured her attention, only to find the Achaz Lord and the four Ladies standing before them.

Shit.

But Tessa only tilted her head as she slowly lowered to the ground and placed a single palm flat on the stone. All they could do was watch as a final crack speared from her hand, back up the rubble she'd left behind and straight into the heart of the Pantheon.

The realm shuddered as the first streaks of dawn pierced the sky.

And then the Pantheon caved in on itself, the fall rippling and radiating power outward as it came crashing down.

Dust and ash filled the air so thickly that even with his eyes shifted, Luka had trouble seeing what was happening. He stumbled forward as the ground continued to shake beneath them, finding Tessa standing upright once more.

"We need to go," he growled, clasping her shoulder and spinning her to face him. He took her chin, forcing her face up to his. "You made your point, Tessa. Now we need to go and regroup. Figure out what we do from here."

Tristyn appeared, a hand covering his mouth to keep from breathing in the wreckage. His eyes were glowing brightly as they settled on Tessa. "We have to get beyond the courtyard. That's where we'll be able to Travel."

Tessa nodded, turning to peer through the storm of chaos. The wind shifted just enough to clear the air and give them a perfect view of the Achaz Lord and the Ladies once more. Rordan's gaze was fixed on Tessa, and she stared right back. There was no mistaking what was passing between them. Tessa had announced her intentions to the entirety of Devram. Something was coming, and this was the only warning.

Then she spun, turning her back on all of them, and barefoot, she walked away from the ruling families of Devram. She'd burned their godsdamn castle to the ground.

Luka moved to her side, and he felt the others fall into a formation of sorts behind her. Tristyn and Cienna were done hiding. His father was free and choosing their side. Devram was about to be divided.

Chaos was about to reign.

"The Fae are safe," she said suddenly, not seeming to care about the rubble they were maneuvering through. It had to be slicing up her feet.

"What do you mean they are safe?" he asked.

"I sent word ahead of time. To make sure the Fae were removed from the Pantheon before we arrived. Only Legacy went to the After this day," she replied.

"How?"

She shrugged. "I watched. I listened. I learned everything I could."

"You just declared war, Tessa," Luka growled. "Without consulting anyone. There will be consequences. They will retaliate."

"I will not live in a realm where Fae are forced to serve. This world deserves a war. Devram deserves a reckoning," she bit out as they crossed out of the courtyard.

"And you believe that is your call to make? To pass such judgment?"

She stopped, turning to look up at him. "I believe my purpose is a genesis. More than that, I believe my purpose is to at least try when no one else is doing a godsdamn thing."

He blinked at her, unsure how to respond to that, but before he could say anything, Tristyn and Cienna approached.

"We cannot return to my penthouse," Blackheart said. "We made a statement following Tessa out of there."

"I'm aware," Luka muttered, still eyeing Tessa. Her eyes were still too dark; she was still too lost to her power. And he couldn't decide if it was her magic talking or her.

"Do we go to the Underground?" Tristyn pressed.

"It is the first place they will look," Cienna said. "We need some place few know of."

His head whipped to her, finding her piercing gaze fixed on him. "No," he growled.

"We need some place where we will not be disturbed. We need a plan, and she needs to be brought back from the brink," the Witch countered.

Godsdammit.

He knew she was right, but by the gods, did he fucking hate it.

"Fine," he grumbled, an arm winding around Tessa's waist and pulling her in close. For once, she didn't fight him. He held out his other hand, Cienna taking it. Making sure they were all connected, Luka Traveled them to his cave to try to figure out how they were going to survive when there was no way to control the uncontrollable.

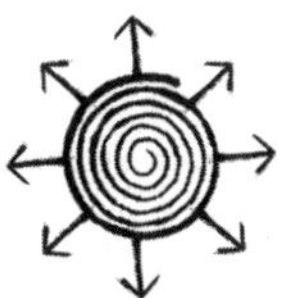

5
THEON

He was working on borrowed time.

He knew that.

Not only from the Fates, but from his father.

Luka had told him his father had been freed when they'd rescued Xan. He'd told Luka they didn't need to come up with a plan, that the Fates would take care of it, but who knew when that would be. While the warnings from the prophecy all seemed to be aligning, indicating that it would be sooner rather than later, soon could be days or decades for immortal beings. Theon was certain the only reason he hadn't run into his father yet was because he was off searching for Eviana. He didn't know the specifics of why he couldn't find her. There'd been no time for detailed explanations before he'd left them all at the Pantheon. If he'd waited any longer to leave, he was sure he wouldn't have been able to do it. Tessa's screams had echoed down the passages as he'd left, and now they haunted him. Waking. Sleeping. It didn't matter. He heard them all the time.

Theon had been staying at the penthouse in Rockmoor, trying to formulate some semblance of a plan. And he had one. Sort of. He'd tied up some loose ends, moved funds around in accounts, and stocked up on blood rations, because without a Source, he was going to need them. More than that, he'd purchased a new phone, shutting off his old one. He couldn't risk being tracked, and Luka kept trying to contact him. A male could only resist temptation for so long. This needed to be a clean break. The only thing he couldn't control was the bond between the three of them, and wasn't that ironic? The thing was broken, and he was both grateful and irritated by that.

It was a double-edged sword. He wanted to know if they were all right, but he needed to let them both go. He'd entrusted her to Luka, and he couldn't interfere with that. Not anymore. Besides, they should be long gone from the realm by now. It'd been two weeks. It was the last thing he'd asked of Luka.

But now he was ready to track down Axel in the Underground. He needed to fill his brother in on what was happening, and honestly, he wanted to be with the only two people he considered family with Luka and Tessa gone. If their world was going to end and he was going to meet Arius, he wanted the remaining time to be spent with them. So he'd watched Arius House from afar for the past several days, making sure his father hadn't returned. Once he was certain only the staff remained, he'd gone in under the cover of night.

Theon methodically worked through his father's study, packing up books and maps. Anything that might prove valuable. He wished he could just move this entire room, along with the library in Arius House. Countless hours were spent poring over these volumes. Sometimes with Luka. Sometimes with Axel. Usually by himself. But he had to travel light. He couldn't take all of it as well as his personal effects. Not to mention some of Tessa's belongings he wanted to keep.

That red dress she'd dropped the night she'd taken control with one hand.

The fleece blanket she often wrapped herself up in on the balcony.

The necklace she wore the first time they faced his father as a united front.

The coffee mug with the cracked handle she favored.

The godsdamn bright purple flip-flops.

He was on a rolling ladder searching the top shelves when he heard the footfalls. Immediately tensing, he slowly descended, setting aside the three books he held and sliding his hands into his pockets. The footsteps drew closer, and he tilted his head in interest. These weren't the heavy steps of his father or the hesitant and quiet movements of the staff.

"Hello, *Mother*," he sneered when the door opened, Cressida standing in the doorway.

How foolish of her considering they'd learned she'd been working with Cordelia and Rordan for years now. Not to mention she'd helped set a trap for Tessa to bring her to heel and ruin.

"Oh. It's you," Cressida sighed, her disappointment evident. "I thought your father had finally returned home."

"You mean the male you've been double-crossing for . . . How long has it been?" he replied, his tone cold and dark. "From the very beginning?"

But his mother only smiled in return, something just as icy. "You think you have this all figured out, don't you, Theon? The academic and the clever one of the family."

She moved deeper into the room, her long black dress clinging to her figure. It was a casual piece, but she still wore her heels. They clicked loudly with every step until she reached the desk, picking up a decorative paperweight. She spun it in her hand, gaze fixed on the object as if she wasn't worried about her son's calculated temper in the least.

"I think I have a pretty good grasp on things at this point," he finally gritted out when she only continued to toy with the decor.

"Always researching and scheming," she went on, as though she hadn't been waiting for him to speak. "Digging into things you needn't have bothered with. If only you could have done as you were told. Been what your father had tried to train you to become."

He went utterly still. How many times had he said such similar words to Tessa?

She sighed dramatically, "This would have all been taken care of if you hadn't insisted on Selecting that wretched cu—"

She didn't get to finish. Theon was across the room before she could blink. His hand wrapped around her throat, he cut off her words and shoved her back into the desk.

"Do not *ever* speak of her like that," he snarled. "Then again, you won't be speaking much longer. You set her up. You worked with Cordelia to break her and cage her. You fed information to Rordan to take her from me. Did you really think I would never find out?"

She choked out a gasp, and he loosened his grip to let her speak. With a derisive laugh, she said, "You're just like your father, Theon. Too wrapped up in your own agenda and power to notice what's going on around you. You didn't even realize the female wasn't Fae until it was displayed to everyone at the Emerging. For someone so clever, you miss what's right in front of you every single time." She paused, then added, "Although, I suppose that's not entirely your fault. Considering what you are."

His hand tightened again, and a sharp gasp slipped past her lips when his power seeped from his palm, adding to the pressure. "Tell me everything, or I kill you right now."

"You . . . can't," she choked out.

His darkness wound up from beneath his hand, crawling along her jaw and making its way to her parted lips.

"You think I care because you are my mother?" he asked. "You've never been affectionate towards me. You've never cared. You are my mother by title only, and you hurt her. Tried to take her from me. The cost of that transgression is your life."

She sputtered, and his power eased a fraction. "I raised you," she rasped.

"Caris raised me, and then Pen when she was murdered. Try again," he sneered, removing his hand altogether to let his power do the work.

Her lip curled into a sneer of her own. "I raised you even though you weren't mine. You won't kill me, Theon, because killing me will kill the one who actually birthed you. Then you will never have answers to questions you didn't even know you had."

"What are you talking about?" he demanded.

She shifted, and he felt a hand brush his thigh. Looking down, he found her pulling up the skirt of her dress. He lurched back a step, his darkness keeping her pinned to the desk. "What the fuck are you doing?"

She said nothing as she pulled her dress higher. Then she shifted just enough to show him where a Mark stood stark against the flesh of her inner thigh. It was in a place few would ever see, and certainly not him, and it was one he'd never seen before.

"What does it do?" he asked sharply.

"It binds my life to hers. Consider it my . . . safeguard," she rasped out, his power still coiled at her neck.

"I would have never known if you hadn't said something," he countered.

"Not a safeguard from you," she replied, straightening as he loosened his power even more. "From your father."

"Who else knows?"

"No one," she replied. "At least not that I have told. He bound me with a Secrecy Mark, but it faded when he was not the Arius Lord for a short time." Lifting her bare arm, she showed him where a Mark had once graced her flesh above the crook of her elbow for the entirety of his life. True to her word, it was gone. He'd never questioned it. His father forced others to take Secrecy Marks all the time. He'd had some of the same Marks on his flesh at various times in his life.

"If she still lives, then where is she?" he asked, narrowing his eyes.

"Now why would I tell you that?" Cressida asked, a smirk lifting at her newfound leverage.

"And Axel?"

"Axel is mine," she said fiercely.

That made sense. She always favored him, while she seemed to tolerate Theon. She would sometimes intervene on Axel's behalf, leaving Theon to fend for himself against his father. Axel had the auburn undertones to his dark hair thanks to Cressida's dark red locks, while Theon's hair was the pitch black of his father's. But still . . .

"We look nearly identical," he argued.

"Genetics are powerful," she said simply. "Your father made sure his Match . . . had certain characteristics."

He shook his head. "I don't believe you."

"Believe me or don't," she said with a shrug. "That's your prerogative."

But he did believe her. That was the problem. The female before him now was cunning and creative, just as her bloodline was known for. For decades she had put on a persona. A female who only cared for frivolous and superficial things. Being invited to the best gatherings and having the finest dresses and jewels. When in reality, she had been scheming, harboring her own grudges and vendettas. Just like everyone else in this damned realm, she'd been plotting her own power moves.

Her smile grew as she watched him come to the realization she spoke the truth. Even if she wasn't his mother, she had watched him grow up. More than that, she'd paid far more attention than he thought she had. She would know his tells and mannerisms.

"How would this have been hidden from the other ruling families?" he asked. "They approve Matches and verify all pregnancies."

Her features darkened. "That is enough questions for today," she snapped.

He fought his own smile now, finding a weakness. "But you were so willing to tell me all about my mother, *Cressida*," he crooned, stepping closer. Towering over her, it forced her to tip her head back to look at him.

"This is bigger than you and your little Source," she bit out.

He tsked. "But she's not my Source. You know that. Have always known that."

"I didn't know *what* she was."

"Valter *and* Rordan kept you in the dark? Maybe you're not as valuable as you believe," he replied with a sharp smile. She brought a hand up to slap him, but he caught her wrist before she even got close. "What am I to do with you now?" he mused. "Lock you up until I can verify your claims?"

"Verify them all you like," she retorted.

"And how am I to do that?" he asked, cocking his head to the side and watching every intake of breath and twitch of her eyes. Watching for the lie.

"You know nothing of what it is like to be a female in this house. In this kingdom. In the realm," she hissed. "The only value we have to our families is to help them move higher up in society, closer to a Lord or Lady, and then only if we can bear a child. Do you know what would have happened if I hadn't borne Valter a child? And not just any child. My contract was *very* specific. I was to produce a son, and your father had insurance."

"How could he have insurance against something like that?" Theon asked, trying to keep her talking. She was angry. People revealed all kinds of information when they were in that state of mind. It was one of the basest forms of manipulation.

She looked him up and down with a bitter laugh. "You were it," she said. "At least, that's what he told me. But I suspect the outcome would have been the same even if my first child had been a male."

Theon blinked at her, not grasping what she was saying. Or rather, not wanting to believe it, but he knew full well the lengths his father would go to in order to ensure the outcome was what he wanted. Still, if Cressida wasn't his mother, who was? What other bloodline ran in his veins?

All the Matches for Lords, Ladies, and heirs had to be sanctioned by the sitting rulers. It was a way to ensure balance and make sure one kingdom didn't become more powerful than another. His father had been required to petition for their approval prior to Theon signing the Match contract with Felicity. Had his father initially wanted a different Match of his own, and it had been denied? More than that, how in the realms had they hidden the fact that he wasn't Cressida's?

Still holding her wrist, his darkness snapped out, wrapping around her throat once more. She gasped, surprised at the sudden attack. Her other hand slapped onto the desk behind her, searching for something to use against him, but the only thing she found was the paperweight. She threw it at him, but the toss was weak and he easily caught it.

"I will give you a choice, Cressida," he said, tossing the weight aside. "You can either tell me where my supposed mother is being held, and I will have you locked up somewhere with daily food, water, and weekly blood rations.

You will be . . . somewhat comfortable until I can deal with you properly. Or you can continue to keep your leverage to yourself, and I will make sure you are absolutely miserable for the rest of your days."

Cressida glared at him. "You are not yet the Arius Lord, Theon St. Orcas. You do not have the authority to lock up a Lord's wife. Someone will come for me."

"If they can find you," he said coldly. "Are you willing to wager your comfort on that? The gods know you've become accustomed to the finer things Devram has to offer."

He watched the debate play out in her emerald eyes. Eyes he'd once thought he'd gotten from her. He saw the uncertainty flash, wondering if he was bluffing, and he gave away nothing. Only stared hard and cold back at her.

"You're wasting my time," he snapped after several seconds, lifting a hand and letting more of his power appear.

"Wait!" she cried, trying to push off the desk. His darkness shoved her back again, and a small cry escaped her lips.

"I don't have time to wait, Cressida," he replied, his power sliding up her throat again.

"I can't tell you exactly where," she said, panic entering her voice.

"Then I fail to see what use I have for you at this point."

"You cannot kill a Lord's wife!" she tried again.

"You're incredibly confident for someone who knows the things I was forced to do for said Lord," he mused.

Inky black skated under her chin, a tendril slipping into her mouth, and she whimpered, feeling the sting of it.

"I cannot tell you! I am bound!" she gasped.

"That Secrecy Mark has faded," he countered. "You showed me yourself."

"He keeps her where he keeps all things he does not want found," she wailed as more darkness slid between her lips, ready to end her.

He stilled, taking in her words.

Gods-fucking-dammit.

He knew exactly where she was talking about.

With a flick of his fingers, his power moved once more, wrapping around her wrists and wrenching her arms behind her back. He left the box of books and things sitting on the floor. He'd be back for it in a bit. Now he had something else to take care of.

Fishing his new phone from his pocket, he clicked on one of the few numbers he had stored as he started for the door. His power yanked, dragging Cressida along behind him. He heard her stumble, scrambling to keep her feet under her. The clicking of her shoes told him she was all but running to keep up with him, and he inwardly winced at how often he'd made Tessa do the same in heels.

"Where are you taking me?" Cressida asked. "I told you what I could."

He didn't bother looking over his shoulder at her. He didn't bother even replying to her as he made his way through the house. Not as the call connected.

"Yes?"

"I need a favor," Theon said, taking the stairs two at a time and not caring if Cressida fell down the damn things.

There was a pause, then a sigh. "You are accruing quite a debt of those."

"Can you meet me outside Arius House? I need you to hold something for me."

"Right now? The sun still slumbers, Theon."

"I wouldn't ask if—"

"Just say you're desperate."

He gritted his teeth at the truth of that statement, knowing full well they wouldn't help unless he said those exact words.

"I'm desperate," he ground out.

"Be prepared when we come to collect on all these favors."

The line went dead as they reached the main foyer. Before he led Cressida out into the night though, he stopped, turning to her.

"If anything you've told me is false, you will wish for death," he warned her.

But she only gave a humorless huff of laughter. A sound he'd heard from so many in this realm. It was why he didn't doubt her when she replied, "As if I haven't wished for that in the past." Then she lifted her chin, emerald eyes hardening. "And when I couldn't have it, I found ways to make my life bearable here and strike back in ways he'd never see coming."

Theon didn't reply. Only let his darkness seep into her just enough to render her unconscious. His magic wrapped around her as he pulled the door open, making sure no staff were lingering in the shadows. Moving quickly through the grounds, his power carried Cressida behind him. It took nearly ten minutes to reach the main gates, and another fifteen to move beyond the wards.

"You could have told me you were going to take the scenic route," the female waiting for him griped.

"Thank you for coming, Tana," Theon said, greeting the Anala Heir.

"Don't thank me yet, Theon," she replied. "You're the one who will need to explain *that* to my mother." Her amber gaze moved beyond him to where the limp form of Cressida was floating on a mist of darkness.

"I just need her to be kept imprisoned. She can't know where she is. Daily food and water. Weekly rations. I'll send payment. Doesn't need to be luxurious by any means," he replied. "I'll explain when I can. I—"

The ground lurched beneath his feet.

No.

The entire *realm* seemed to shudder, as if a piece of the world had died.

Theon stumbled forward, and Tana's Source lurched to catch her as she was knocked off her own feet by the force.

"What was that?" she asked, eyes narrowing on Theon as if he was the cause.

"I don't know," he answered, taking in the surrounding trees as the first light of dawn cast an ethereal glow on them.

"What do you mean you don't know? This is your kingdom," she retorted.

"And we've never had quakes here in all my years," he shot back.

A phone rang, the sound loud in the now still daybreak. Tana's Source retrieved a phone, glancing at the screen before handing it to Tana. "Your mother," he said.

"Yes?" she answered. Then her eyes went wide, landing on Theon. "I understand." She hung up, her hand clenching around the device. "Gatlan, take Cressida. We need to get back to Idalia."

"What happened?" Theon asked, stepping closer while Gatlan moved to retrieve Cressida.

Tana's lips pressed into a thin line as a fire portal appeared, her red hair glimmering in the flames. "The Pantheon has fallen."

Theon blinked once. Twice. "That isn't possible," he finally managed.

"I do not know the specifics. My mother will fill me in, but I must go. I will be in touch."

With that, she disappeared through her portal, Gatlan right behind her, and Theon was left standing by himself. If the Pantheon had fallen . . .

Perhaps he didn't have days or months or decades.

It appeared the Fates had already come to rip their world apart in search of Tessa.

He spun, racing back through the courtyard to gather his things. He needed to get to Axel. Needed to see him and explain before he never got the chance. Needed to be with the only family he had left if their world was truly coming to an end.

In record time, he was pulling into the small portal station in Castle Pines. The one his father never let anyone use. The one he still technically had access to because no one really knew who was running the kingdom at this point, and the sentries there didn't want to risk pissing off their possible Lord.

With a duffel bag across his chest, his computer bag over a shoulder, two smaller bags in one hand, and a box of books and maps under his other arm, Theon hurtled through the portal and to the Underground.

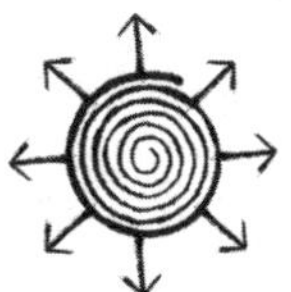

6

AXEL

Balancing precariously on a step stool, he reached for a leather case on the top shelf. It was a canister, and when he finally grabbed hold of the thing, he twisted off the cap as he leapt down to the floor. Inside was a map of the Underground. He could have looked at one in various books, but this map was large and would span the entire work table across the room from the desk.

Axel carefully unrolled it, placing weights in the shapes of skulls on the corners, and then he stood over it, studying the thing. This was Theon's place, not his. Theon could stare at a map for hours, days even, and when he finally came out of his scholarly stupor, he'd have a fully formed plan. Axel knew that would never be the case for him. He could study this thing all he wanted, maybe even come up with some half-formed plan, but in the end, he operated more on instinct. It had served him well as he'd navigated the Underground for his father. He wasn't entirely sure why he was contemplating changing tactics now.

Probably because he'd implied the Underground was his kingdom and had all but started a war for it.

Fucking reckless, but there was no going back. He refused to pledge fealty to Bree, and he'd seen the way she'd looked at Kat. Or, more precisely, at Kat's belly.

While trying to formulate a plan had certainly been part of the reason he'd come to this study today, it wasn't the only one. His rations were low. Too low. Pretty much depleted. He'd never thought it necessary to keep a large stock. He could have gotten blood anywhere in the Underground until

Bree had struck the first blow before he'd even realized it. She'd come to his home that day already having cleaned out the blood suppliers.

This was different from when he'd needed the blood to fill his power reserves. Blood was needed to *survive* now. He wasn't entirely sure what happened when a vampyre went too long without, but he wasn't too keen on finding out. He'd already experienced the craze of bloodlust. If it was even close to that, he couldn't risk it. If it was *worse* than that, he couldn't fathom it.

But his mouth was already starting to feel too dry. He'd been limiting himself, and he was feeling the effects of it. His senses were heightened even more than a Legacy's, particularly when it came to smell. He could scent Kat's blood from the floor above, and it made him grip the table so tightly his knuckles were white. He'd finish off his rations in the next day or two, and then what the fuck was he going to do?

Stretching his neck from side to side, he tried to ward off the need to feed. How did Night Children learn to control this anyway? The only time he'd ever felt fully satisfied was when he'd taken far too much from Kat. Then again, maybe he'd simply been too lost to the bloodlust and the curse. Too much had been happening in that moment.

Focus.

He needed to focus on what he was going to do.

Picking up a mug of coffee, he studied the map, trying to ignore how the hot liquid was very much *not* blood. How it wasn't quenching any thirst or hunger or need. How it was—

Focus.

He set the mug down, swiping up a glass of water instead as he forced himself to study the map.

They were at one end of the Underground. Bree and the Night Children occupied the Dispensary District on the opposite side. That left a lot of territory in between and a lot of potential allies that could be swayed either way. People who had been stuck here for decades. Centuries even. Many of them hadn't seen the sun or the sky in just as long. It was one of the things he was missing most. Fresh air. The air down here was musty and dry. Not that he could go in the sun anyway. Not anymore.

Focus.

Who did he go to first? He had relations with all the Districts, but that was as an Arius Heir. Now he was one of them. They might turn on him out of pure spite, and he couldn't really blame them. The other three Night Child Houses wouldn't turn on Bree. They still hadn't replaced

Henry. Rayell was too entertained by dramatics. Cade would listen and hear him out, but he would ultimately decline to side with him in the end because the male would see him as a threat to his own position of power.

Which led him back to the remaining territories. He was on good terms with many Fae in the Apparel District, but they were still Fae who had a grudge against the Legacy. Again, for good reason. The Shifters in the Leisure District would be ideal. They were fickle beings who refused to be on the losing side, putting the victory above all else. Which was good if they were on your side.

It was devastating if they weren't.

And they always chose carefully to ensure they were on the winning side. Which meant he needed to have other allies already on board before he went to the Alpha and Beta.

Which left the Apothecary District and the Witches.

He would probably have good luck there. His relationship with Cienna had put him on good terms with many of the Witches. Miara was the leader of the District, and she would be the most logical one to approach. He couldn't just keep hiding out in the Charter District, especially with his blood stores nearly depleted. More than that, he refused to cower before Bree.

"I woke to a cold bed. Again."

His hand clenched around the water glass as her scent hit him a moment before her voice filled the room. Carefully, his hand shaking a fraction with the movement, he set the glass back on the table. He glanced to the doorway, finding Kat standing there. Her hand resting on her stomach, the babe was growing more every day. Her coils of black hair were piled on top of her head, and her warm dark skin seemed to glow in the low lighting. She wore one of his shirts and her own pair of lounge pants with her feet clad in slippers they'd purchased in the Apparel District last week.

Looking back at the map, he gripped the edge of the table. "I slept—"

"I know where you slept, Axel," she interrupted sharply.

"I would have heard you if you'd needed anything," he replied, staring at the map but not really seeing it. The territories were all blurring together before him.

"I need a husband who sleeps in my bed with me," she retorted. "Or was that just a 'heat of the moment' thing?"

His head snapped up. "You know that's not the case, Katya."

"I clearly do not know that, or I wouldn't have suggested it," she said, folding her arms across her chest. The Union Mark on the back of her hand was visible now, and he glanced at his own, along with the onyx band on his finger.

"I've given you no reason to doubt my intentions," he argued, picking up the water glass again. Then he hissed, the glass slipping from his grasp as it became too hot to hold. It hit the floor and shattered, shards of glass flying everywhere and scalding water splattering.

He slowly lifted his gaze back to her. She was glaring at him, not an ounce of remorse on her face. In fact, he could see the faint flames flickering in her eyes from here, and those were wisps of shadows floating around her, courtesy of the child in her belly. If he wasn't riding an edge of his own right now, he'd be gathering her up in his arms. He loved it when she got like this. Would purposely irritate her because she came out of her shell so much more like this. But now wasn't the time.

"I'm protecting you, Kat," he replied. "I'm on the last dregs of rations, and you're *right here.*"

She rolled her eyes, and Axel straightened at the action. Did she truly not grasp the severity of this situation?

"You are just like Theon," she chided. "Thinking you have to do everything yourself. I'm *right here*, Axel. Instead of talking to me and coming up with a plan together, you—"

He snapped to attention, moving fast and suddenly in front of her.

"Stop doing that," she gritted out, shoving at his chest. Not that it mattered. He didn't even stumble.

But he gently took her shoulders, pressing a kiss to the top of her head. "Someone crossed the wards. They're on their way up. Stay here. Please."

"Axel—"

"Please stay here," he repeated.

Her mouth pressed to a thin line as she held his stare for another few seconds before she looked away from him, dipping her chin in the barest of nods.

"We'll talk more," he promised.

But he heard her mutter, "Somehow I doubt that," as he left her standing in the study doorway.

This wasn't how this was supposed to go. It wasn't how anything in his life was supposed to go. Then again, that seemed to be the way of fate for an Arius Heir.

He bounded down the stairs to the main floor, moving to stand several feet from the lift doors. Security hadn't called up to ask about allowing someone passage. So either they forced their way through, or this was someone with unfettered access to the penthouse. If it was his father, he was fucked. He had no desire to see his mother, but he'd placate her. If it was Tessa . . . They weren't exactly on the best of terms right now, and Theon and Luka had their hands full with her. In the end, he had no idea who to expect when those lift doors opened, but it certainly wasn't Theon laden down with arms full of shit.

His brother strode into the room, immediately looking him up and down. Always worried about those he viewed himself responsible for before himself.

Looking beyond him as the lift doors closed, Axel's brow furrowed. He was alone.

"What are you doing here?" he asked, following Theon with his eyes as his brother moved to hang his computer bag on the hooks nearby. The habit had been ingrained in him since he could walk. Leave nothing lying around just in case their father showed up. Their father had to have known all the times Theon covered for Axel. Theon was too meticulous and controlled to make such frivolous mistakes, and yet he took the blame for them time and time again. Axel hadn't realized just how often until he was well into his second decade of life.

He set the box down on a side table, placing his large duffel bag and smaller bags beside it. One of them clinked as he set it down, and Axel zeroed in on it.

"Did you feel the quake a few hours ago?" Theon asked, removing his suit jacket and hanging it beside his computer bag.

Still focused on the bag, Axel replied, "What quake?"

"The one that was apparently felt across the realm," Theon said. "Although, I guess not in the Underground. The Pantheon fell."

That had his gaze whipping to Theon. "What does that mean?"

Theon had unbuttoned his shirt cuffs and was rolling his sleeves back as he said, "Exactly what it sounds like. The Pantheon was reduced to nothing but rubble. The Tribunal building as well."

"How the fuck did that happen?"

"That's part of the reason I'm here," his brother answered, his hands slipping into his pockets now.

Axel waved his hand impatiently. "Well, spit it out."

"I don't . . ." Theon started, trailing off. A hand came up, pushing through his hair before he dragged it down his face. He cleared his throat. "I figured out the Revelation Decree or prophecy or whatever you want to call it." Axel only blinked, waiting for him to get the fuck on with this. "The decree was never meant to be instructions on how Devram should be ruled. It was a prophecy. About Tessa and the downfall of Devram."

"And?" Axel asked.

"She's an imbalance," he went on. "Achaz and Arius. Light and dark. Beginnings and endings."

"Achaz *and* Arius," Axel said. "We knew all this."

"Yes, but we didn't realize how much. She's the granddaughter of Achaz, Arius, *and* Serafina. Her mother is still a mystery, but her father is a god and she's more but—"

"Theon, get to the fucking point," Axel interjected. He truly didn't care how he had figured out whatever this was. He just wanted to know what new fuckery had just been dumped on them.

"The Fates will come here looking for her," Theon said, straightening at Axel's tone. "To end her and fix the balance."

Axel shrugged. "Sounds like that would fix a lot of our problems considering she's looking to end our bloodline."

Darkness churned around Theon at the words, and Axel couldn't bring himself to care. He had bigger things to worry about than the Fates coming for Tessa. She was Theon's to worry about, not his, and she certainly didn't care about him. She'd made that perfectly clear when she could have found him and didn't. If she would have, maybe everything would be different.

Maybe he wouldn't be terrified of sharing a godsdamn bed with his wife.

"You're serious," Theon gritted out when Axel didn't add any sort of caveat to his statement.

Axel only shrugged again, crossing his arms. "Look what she did to you, Theon. Even if you might have deserved some of it for being an absolute dick most days. And yeah, it'd be great if she could rid us of Father, but all Arius Legacy? There are innocent people in our kingdom who have nothing to do with her or any of this."

"I know," Theon said, and something shifted in him. Axel couldn't quite pinpoint it, but it was almost an air of regret or resignation that filled the space.

When he didn't continue, Axel said, "So, what? You think this quake that happened is another omen?"

"I think it was the Fates coming here," he said.

"For Tessa," Axel clarified.

Theon nodded slowly.

"What aren't you saying, Theon?"

He shoved his hand through his hair again, tugging at the roots. "Tessa's not here."

"I'm sure she's in Faven," Axel deadpanned.

But Theon shook his head. "She's not here, Axel. I figured all this out, and I sent her away with Razik and Eliza. Luka went with her. She's not in this realm. And when the Fates cannot find her, Chaos will reign. They will destroy this realm in search of her to correct the balance."

Axel could only stare at him because he couldn't wrap his mind around what Theon had just said. He couldn't possibly have heard him right.

An entire minute passed before Theon said, "Can you say something?"

"Can I . . ." Axel trailed off, huffing a humorless laugh. "What do you want me to say?"

"Something. Anything."

"Let me get this straight," Axel started, taking a step forward. "You knew the Fates would come here looking for her, so you sent her away? Condemning an entire realm to death for her? The female who had no qualms about sentencing an entire group of people to destruction simply because of the blood that ran in their veins? A kingdom of people *you* are responsible for? A *realm* of people who have nothing to do with any of this?" His voice rose with every word as he advanced on his brother. "What the fuck were you thinking, Theon?"

"I was thinking she doesn't deserve any of this," Theon retorted, that darkness drifting across his irises and thickening around him. "She didn't ask for this."

"Neither did we!" Axel yelled.

"This realm made her what she is," Theon shot back. "Just like it made us what we are. We're not innocent here, Axel."

"We might not be, but there *are* innocent people here, Theon. Forget the Legacy. There are Fae here. Mortals. There is an entire Underground of people who have nothing to do with the politics of Devram. None of them deserve to pay penance for her!" Axel snarled, shoving at Theon's chest. "I cannot believe you. You're as reckless as she is."

"You think I did this without thought? That I was impulsive?"

"Of course not," Axel scoffed. "That makes it all the worse, Theon. You *did* think about it. Knowing you, you spent countless hours weighing options, and you still came to the conclusion that this was what needed to be done. Sacrificing an entire realm for her."

"I would sacrifice every realm for her! She is mine to protect!" Theon bellowed.

"Then you'll understand that I will slay any Fate or god that comes here to protect what is mine," Axel spat back. "Even if that means going to war against *you*."

"He'll go to war for us. Fight the Fates and the gods, but he can't be bothered to speak to me or even be in the same room as me."

They both turned at the sound of Kat's voice, finding her descending the stairs. His gaze collided with her amber eyes, her anger still glaring back at him, before she moved on to Theon. Her chin lifted as she stared down at them, and gods, she was a vision, despite being in sleep attire. He couldn't even be upset with her for not staying upstairs like he'd asked. Why would she? She knew Theon wasn't a threat to her, but Theon didn't know about . . .

He turned back to his brother, finding him staring at her. Or more accurately, at her stomach. But even that wasn't true. His gaze was bouncing from her stomach to her hand to his, as though he had just now noticed the Union Mark and ring on Axel's hand.

"Kat . . ." Theon started, but he trailed off, swallowing thickly.

"Hello, Theon," she said, the edge gone from her voice and a softness to it that had Axel raising a brow. She'd told him she had spent hours researching beside Theon these past months, but apparently they'd also become . . . friends.

Theon shifted on his feet, and that had Axel even more surprised. He'd never seen his brother be anything but the in-control, emotionless, and calculating Arius Heir. Except when it came to Tessa, but that was an entirely different matter.

"You're . . . The two of you are—"

Theon had taken a step towards Kat, but he stilled, going silent when Axel moved in front of her. Emerald eyes met his, and there was something there that Axel had never once seen in all his years.

"Don't look at me like you're hurt," he spat at Theon. "You just told me you willingly sacrificed this realm. You think I will let you near my wife and unborn child?"

Theon said nothing. He only stared back at him for a long moment before taking a step back, creating more distance between them.

Tension filled the space, thick and heavy, until Katya was the one to break it.

"Theon isn't going to hurt us, Axel," she said softly, her hand brushing down his arm.

Her mere touch was everything. Gods, he missed her, but he was as big a danger to her as Theon was.

He stiffened at the thought and heard her sigh as her hand fell away.

"Since you're here," she said, stepping to the side so she could peer around him and see Theon. "We were discussing a problem—"

"Enough, Kat," Axel interjected.

"No," she snapped. "You need help, and this is what a relationship is, Axel. Helping each other."

"What's wrong?" Theon asked, new concern filling his features.

"Nothing that will matter when the world ends," Axel retorted.

Kat swatted his arm. "Stop being petulant," she chided.

She stepped closer to his side, and a low growl rumbled from his chest as he glared at his brother.

Theon arched a brow at the warning. "I was under the impression that the twin flame bond would no longer exist once . . ."

"Once I turned into a vampyre?" Axel finished for him.

"Well, yeah," he admitted, pulling on the back of his neck as he studied him with new interest.

"It doesn't," Axel said harshly. "We lost that, but we chose each other anyway."

"I see," Theon said, waiting for one of them to go on.

"He has turned completely," Katya offered. "But that isn't the problem. The problem is Bree."

Theon didn't seem surprised by this in the slightest. He only nodded for her to continue, but Axel was the one to speak with a sigh.

"You know she was the one keeping me for a time. She let me go under the assumption the bloodlust would cause me to kill Kat, and I would have if you hadn't been there," he admitted. "Bree thought I would kill her, then return and pledge loyalty to her House. She wants to rule the Underground."

"And now?" Theon pressed.

"She showed up here when she'd heard I'd returned. She saw Kat, and there were words exchanged. But she already knew. Before she came up here, she had the covens clear out all the blood stores in the Underground. The only place to get blood is the Dispensary District." He paused for a moment, wincing as he added, "I may have also insinuated I was going to be the one to take the Underground, which may have started a feud."

Theon snorted a laugh, scratching his brow with a finger as he absorbed all the information. "How much blood do you have left?"

"I'm almost out. That's why it's not safe for Kat to be around me," he answered, looking down at his wife.

She scoffed, rolling her eyes and crossing her arms. "I still do not believe you will do anything to me. Besides, I have fire *and* shadows at the moment. If you would use your head and think logically, you'd realize I can defend myself."

"Shadows?" Theon asked, his brows shooting up. "From the babe?"

Kat nodded as Axel said, "It happened before I sent her with Tristyn."

"You didn't say anything," Theon said, looking at Kat.

"I couldn't," she replied, a hand dropping to her stomach and rubbing along the side. "Eliza helped me hide it. I didn't know who to trust. A Fae carrying a Legacy's child? And an heir at that? I had to protect him."

"Him? It's a male?"

Kat nodded, a small, soft smile filling her face.

Theon turned away then, striding to the bags he'd hauled in with him. Picking one up, it clinked lightly. He didn't come any closer than he'd been previously, keeping a healthy distance and respecting the boundary Axel had drawn. He placed the bag on the ground, then stepped back from it as he said, "It's rations. Several bottles. Take them."

Axel's eyes went wide, going from the bag to Theon and back. Then he lunged forward, unzipping the bag to find more than two dozen bottles. He snatched one out, drinking the entire thing in seconds, and he nearly sank to the ground in relief. Warmth filled his veins, and for the first time in nearly two weeks, he felt normal. He didn't feel like he was on edge or out of control. He felt sane. He felt powerful. It hadn't tasted great, nothing like what he craved from Kat, but it had done what he'd needed.

He recapped it, tossing it aside as he turned back to Kat. Her eyes went wide when he was before her in the next breath, and before she could scold him about moving so fast, he'd taken her face in his hands and planted his lips on hers.

He swallowed her gasp of surprise as she melted into him. The blood still lingered on his taste buds, but he could also taste her. Hot and fiery. Lucious and perfect. Her hands landed on his torso, fingers tracing lines beneath his shirt. If Theon weren't standing mere feet away . . .

Forcing himself to pull back, he didn't go far, touching his brow to hers. "I'm sorry, kitten."

"I've missed you," she whispered.

"I didn't want to hurt you."

"I know," she murmured.

"I wouldn't be able to live with myself," he said, a thumb swiping along her cheek.

"Can you please let me help?"

He huffed a rueful sound. "It sounds like we have to fight the Fates."

Her hands came up, fingers wrapping around his wrists where he still held her face. "That sounds like we'll need an army."

He stilled, pulling back to study her, and the way she was looking at him? Gods, it made him feel like he could do anything.

His lips brushed hers again before he tucked her into his side and turned to his brother. Theon's hands were in his pockets, eyes looking anywhere but at them as he tried to give them this moment. He may have become resigned to the world's demise, but Axel wouldn't go down without fighting. They deserved a future. His *son* deserved a future.

Sensing his attention on him, Theon lifted his head.

Holding his brother's stare, Axel said, "I need your help."

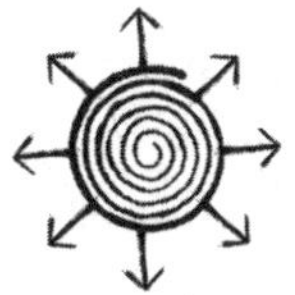

7
EVIANA

"No," Lange said, shaking his head adamantly. "We are not stealing a boat."

Eviana said nothing from the front seat of the vehicle. Her hands folded in her lap, she sat perfectly still and stared straight ahead, watching the small marina.

Corbin's hands flexed on the steering wheel he was gripping tightly. "He's right," he said. "We already stole a Lord's vehicle, disobeyed direct orders from a Legacy, essentially stole a Lord's Source, and—"

"You are detailing quite a list," Eviana interrupted. "What difference will it make to add one more transgression at this point?"

"Because it is never just one more with you," Lange griped from the back seat.

She supposed he had a point, but she was tired of doing nothing. Not that they'd been doing *nothing* exactly. They'd taken a day to pack supplies—food, clothing, and the like. She'd pilfered several rooms of the Raven Harbor manor knowing they'd need to sell items for coin and bribe others for their silence. But they'd also needed to travel light. Eventually, they'd have to leave the vehicle behind and that day had come.

They'd driven west for a few days, staying south of the Night Waters, but for the last week, they'd been stuck here, on the outskirts of a small marina town on the edge of the River of Endings. The border between the Serafina Kingdom and Arius Kingdom was only a few miles to the south of them, and for the last several days, she'd been trying to figure out how to cross the border. Fae couldn't cross kingdoms without proper documentation.

Corbin could forge it, of course, but everyone knew who she was. More than that, everyone knew Valter was looking for her. Her Master being inadvertently set free had definitely added another layer of difficulty to this.

"I still think it's best to call Luka or Theon," Corbin said carefully.

He paused, waiting for her to dismiss the idea—and she would—but she'd let him speak. She wasn't really listening anyway, too focused on the plan forming in her mind.

"They will help us," Corbin rushed on when she didn't reply. "We've heard the rumors, Eviana. The Pantheon has fallen. We felt the echoes of that. We need their protection."

She nearly scoffed. Their protection? The Legacy only cared about protecting the powerful Fae to use them. The only protection they would receive would be punishment for trying to run, followed by being locked away to make sure they never did so again.

"We're going to steal a boat," she finally said.

"By the gods," Lange muttered, throwing himself against the back of the seat in exasperation. "And do what, Eviana? Sail our way into the Serafina Kingdom?"

"Yes," she replied, studying the few sentinels patrolling the docks. "There are no guards in the middle of the river."

"I'd say you can't be serious, but I know you are," he replied, sitting up now to lean between the seats. "The sentinels will still spot us in the middle of the river. They'll sound an alarm, and whenever we come to shore, they'll be waiting. Or they'll send boats out to us and detain us there. *Or* we'll never be able to get to shore, and we'll wind up in the Dreamlock Woods."

"Correct," Eviana replied.

For the last two days she'd been debating which boat they were going to steal. There were only three large ships owned by elite Legacy. The other vessels were not nearly as grand, but they'd be comfortable. She didn't know how to steer a boat, and she was certain Corbin and Lange had never even been on one. But she was also certain they'd adapt quickly. Neither of them had known how to drive either, but Corbin had picked it up with little effort. Adept with technology, he quickly figured out the screens and various components of the vehicle. They were survivors that had been adapting to change their entire lives. That was the life of Fae in Devram. They'd figure it out.

"Just for shits," Lange continued, "let's say we were fine with that. We still have to get the boat. What's your plan there?"

"A distraction," she answered.

"I'm afraid to ask what the distraction will be," Corbin said.

"Me," she said simply. "I'll be the distraction while you two get the boat. I'll meet you there."

"We can't—That's not—No," Lange sputtered. "That will never work."

"No?" Eviana countered. "Did the winds tell you that?"

"You keep saying that shit, and I still don't know what you're talking about," he retorted.

She finally turned to look at him. His sky-blue eyes were bright with fury as he glared at her. Pale blond hair fell into his face, features twisted into a determination that would eventually break and become resignation. She was the one in control here, and everyone in the vehicle knew it.

"If you are the distraction, we may as well just turn ourselves in," Corbin cut in. "The minute you are recognized, every kingdom will be notified. There is no doubt we will be followed to detain you, and Lange and I will be immediately killed for kidnapping a Source, despite that not being the case."

She had considered that, but she was banking more on a sentinel wanting something of a Lord's. It was definitely a risk. Corbin wasn't entirely wrong. If they were detained before they were killed, their lineage would be discovered. They certainly wouldn't be killed then, but punishments and imprisonment would still ensue. Despite that, she hadn't been able to think of any other options. She'd debated going east and stealing a boat to use the sea to enter the Serafina Kingdom, but unbeknownst to her travel companions, the plan was indeed to enter the Dreamlock Woods.

"There is a much simpler solution," she offered, not looking at either of them.

"I'm sure it's simple," Lange scoffed.

"Remove my bands. I can easily take care of the few sentinels here. Then we can simply walk up and take a boat."

"Until we cross the border and are spotted by Serafina sentinels," Corbin shot back. "Then we're back to the beginning. You're trapped, and we're dead."

"We need to get into the Serafina Kingdom," she replied. "Once we are on the other side of the border, I know secrets that will keep us safe. We just need to get there."

"If you'd bother to clue us in on what we're doing, we might be more willing to help," Lange drawled from the backseat.

She hadn't really considered that. Her entire life had entailed watching her Master and others keep their secrets close. When someone knew your secrets, they had leverage over you. No one freely gave up information; just like no one trusted one another. You got what you wanted through coercion and force. Not by simply asking. The mere idea was madness.

"All you need to know is that we need to get into the Serafina Kingdom," she finally answered, her fingers flexing the smallest amount where her palms were flat on her legs.

"Why?" Lange pushed.

"Either come up with another idea, or we are stealing a boat," she replied, a hand sliding to the dagger she had stashed in her coat. The same coat Tessa had brought her when she'd been held in Faven. "Unless you are willing to remove my bands."

"We're not doing that," Lange snapped. "But we're not inept. We have power of our own, you know."

Of course she knew that. She had just assumed they wouldn't be willing to help her. Even the insinuation now had her suspicious.

"I know what you're thinking," Lange went on, his head tilting as if he heard something. "Why trust us, right? But the truth is, you've dragged us in too deep. If we go back now, we'll be killed. If not for running, they'll say we kidnapped a Source. No matter what, we're fucked. We have as much to lose in this as you do now."

That wasn't entirely true, but she wasn't ready to reveal her true motives to them yet. Perhaps they had a point, but they would need to prove themselves. She couldn't just blindly trust them. Anyone could use words to make something sound shiny.

"You would use your magic to aid in this situation?" she asked, eyes narrowing as she watched for any tell he was lying.

"Will we use our magic to ensure we don't end up dead?" Lange drawled, rolling his eyes. "Yeah, *bellana*."

"Don't call me that," she said, turning to face forward once more.

"You blackmailed us and endangered our lives. I'll call you whatever I like," he retorted.

"Lange," Corbin sighed, rubbing at his brow, but Eviana's head had tilted at Lange's words.

"Don't scold me," Lange replied, once again flopping back in his seat. "I'm tired, I'm hungry, and it's been ages since we've had a good fu—"

"Lange!" Corbin barked.

"I've never stopped you from receiving pleasure from each other," she replied plainly, once again focused on the patrolling sentinels.

Lange muttered something under his breath that she couldn't quite make out. She also couldn't quite process what was happening here. No one ever spoke so candidly around her. Except that wasn't true. Legacy spoke as if she wasn't in the room unless she was being used for something. Fae never spoke to her. All of this was rather confusing.

"A plan," Corbin said through gritted teeth. "We need a fucking plan."

"Yeah, yeah," Lange grumbled. "I have one of those."

"Do share," Corbin said, sounding exasperated.

"We enter the Serafina Kingdom through the river," he replied simply.

"We already discussed why we can't steal a boat," his partner countered.

"I didn't say anything about stealing a boat. I said we use the river. You have water magic. I have wind," he said, as if this was obvious.

"You want to enter *through* the river," Corbin said in understanding, but Eviana still had no idea what he meant. "We could go a few miles upstream where the river isn't guarded. Slip in there."

"Precisely," Lange said. "We can go as far as we can before our magic runs out, and we need to come up for air."

Everything clicked into place then as Eviana said, "You mean to enter the kingdom underwater where we will not be detected."

"Exactly," Lange said.

"How long will your magic hold?"

"We haven't been using it much," Corbin supplied. "Our reserves are full. We should easily be able to get into the kingdom before we need to surface. The river current will be a factor though."

She nodded as she listened. It wasn't the time to tell them they needed to make it to the Dreamlock Woods. She would wait to reveal that bit of information until they were well inside the territory.

"I think this plan is sound," she finally said.

Lange snorted a laugh from the backseat. "None of what we are doing is sound, *bellana*."

She frowned at the nickname again, but said nothing. She supposed it was fitting he referred to her as the plant that was stunning on the outside and produced poisonous berries. They tasted delicious but rendered one lifeless within an hour of eating them. Instead, she only nodded once at Corbin's questioning look before he started the vehicle.

They rode in silence for several minutes until they were far enough upriver with no one and nothing around. Parking in a somewhat sheltered area of trees, he shut the vehicle off, and Eviana wasted no time exiting and rounding to the back where their supplies were. They wouldn't be able to take everything, and she methodically began moving items to a backpack. She felt Lange and Corbin approach, and they silently began doing the same.

Within minutes, they were hoisting the packs onto their shoulders, and Corbin reached up to close the back hatch. Sharing a look with Lange, he turned to Eviana and asked, "Are you ready?"

Eviana only nodded, adjusting a strap.

"When we get to the water, I'll use my magic to create a dome of sorts. We'll enter it to keep us dry and protected. Lange will supply the oxygen. Once we're submerged, I'll take us down, and we can walk along the bottom of the river," Corbin explained. "I'll do my best to mitigate the current."

She nodded again, clasping her hands before her as she studied the churning water. A crystal blue, it was the opposite of the Night Waters. Even still, she was sure beneath the surface it was just as dark. She'd been forced to keep others submerged beneath water on Valter's orders numerous times. Twice, he'd done the same to her, and while she feared nothing after everything she had endured, her heart rate still picked up at the idea of willingly going beneath the river.

"Eviana? Are you all right?" Corbin asked, pulling her from the path she had started to spiral down.

A little girl in the Serafina Kingdom. That was what she needed to focus on. She would and could do anything for that tiny soul.

"Yes," she answered primly, stepping to the water's edge. She felt more than she saw the two males exchange another look before they stepped to her side.

Corbin stood between them, and he lifted a hand. Water immediately rose in tendrils at the same time as the lapping waves split, as if flowing around a large boulder. He wove the tendrils higher until they indeed formed a dome, just as he'd said would happen. The water's edge jutted out now, muddy earth sloping down the farther out it went.

"Let's go," Lange said, stepping forward and looking at Eviana.

She followed, the boots Tessa had given her sinking into the silty river bottom. Pausing for a moment, she sucked in a shuddering breath, closing her eyes. Then fingers were wrapping around hers, and her eyes flew open, finding Lange holding her hand. Corbin had moved to his other side, his face twisted in concentration.

"We've done this before," Lange said quietly, as if trying to coax a spooked animal.

"You've moved beneath a river?" she questioned, taking another step as he gently tugged her forward.

He huffed a laugh, pulling her along another step and another as he said, "Not here, *bellana*. But we got into our fair share of mischief, especially when we had more freedom at the Acropolis after the Emerging Ceremony."

"That's fitting," she murmured, tension easing as he guided her farther and farther into the center of the river. Walls of water towered over them on both sides as they made their way deeper.

"Why is that?" Lange asked, and she could swear there was a teasing note to his tone.

"No reason," she replied, glancing at Corbin. His hazel eyes were brighter, as if they had shifted some.

"Ready, Lange?" Corbin asked.

"Yep," Lange answered, the air around them thickening when the male rotated the fingers of his other hand as though calling the winds to him.

"Eviana?" Corbin questioned.

She glanced at him once more. "What?"

"Are you ready?"

"It is a little late to turn back now, don't you think?"

He gave her a small smile. "That it is," he answered, and as he lowered his hands to his sides, the water closed in.

As if encased in an enormous bubble, the water closed in around them, and she stumbled as the river current took hold. But Lange was still holding her hand, and he let go only to snake an arm around her waist and tuck her into his side.

"Sorry," Corbin muttered, and Eviana could feel his magic around them working to keep the water at bay.

Everything around them grew darker and murkier. The river was swallowing them up, and there was beauty in the depths. What she could make out anyway. The light was quickly fading, unable to reach so deep. Fish swam by in schools. Various creatures skirted around them. The water plants beckoned and called to her magic, even if she couldn't see them fully. She knew they were there. If only these godsdamn bands were gone.

Flexing her toes in her boots, she slipped her hands into her pockets, fingering the makeshift weapons in one side and the dagger from Valter's desk in the other. Next to it was the phone she'd forced Corbin to give her. They didn't know it, but she'd kept it charged. It was powered off, of course. She didn't want to leave any possible opening for Valter to track her.

"How long do we have?" Eviana asked, feeling Lange's grip loosen as they all got their footing. She turned in a slow circle, taking everything in, but it was far too dark now. Only faint traces of sunlight filtered this deep, and she squinted, trying to adjust to the darkness. Sound was muffled, and the dome of water did nothing for the chill this far down in the water.

"Corbin's reserves will wane faster than mine," Lange answered. "It takes more power for him to keep us below the surface, fight the current, and keep us dry."

"But you must conjure air," Eviana countered. "Out of nothing."

"Not out of nothing," he said, moving to the edge of the dome and dragging a finger through the water. "There is oxygen in it. I just have to draw it in."

"How long do you think we can make it?" she asked again, pulling the coat tighter around herself. She needed to figure out how to prepare for their next moves, and to do that, she needed an idea of where they were going to surface inside the Serafina Kingdom.

Lange glanced over his shoulder as Corbin came up behind him, wrapping an arm around Lange's waist and resting his chin on his shoulder. "I should be able to last a couple of hours. As long as we keep moving, we should make it into the Serafina Kingdom. I'll let the current push us without overwhelming us and sweeping us away. I don't want to lose control."

"How deep into the kingdom?" she pushed, already knowing it wouldn't be nearly as far as she wanted to be.

"I think we should just start moving," Lange said. "We can all agree we want to get as far as possible. None of us want to be discovered, *bellana*."

She rolled her eyes at the nickname the male had apparently latched onto, but he had a point. While she'd had decades to learn her limits and could tell them exactly how long her power would last, they were still discovering theirs. They were still figuring out the depths, and from the brief time she'd spent with them, she knew not only had they not discovered their full capacity, they also didn't understand just how powerful they were. That was fine. She'd force them to learn it. She'd drag it out of them, because they would all need to be at full strength to survive the Dreamlock Woods. But again, they'd learn that soon enough.

She let them have this moment of peace as they started moving along the river bottom. Half listening to the two males discuss a Chaosphere game, she wished she had the capacity to care about something so trivial. Truly she did.

Unfortunately for them, the Fates had made their paths cross, and she was a poison that spread to everything she touched. Maybe *bellana* was a fitting name after all.

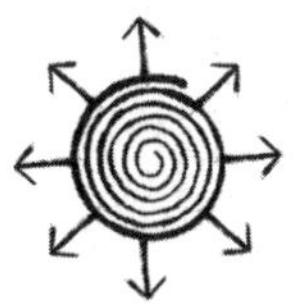

8

LUKA

"Stop touching things," Luka growled, coming back into the main living space of his cave.

Everyone was here. *Everyone*. There were too many people near his things.

"I'm not touching anything," Razik retorted, arms crossed over his chest. He tilted his head and leaned closer to a small square tin. "How old is this?"

Luka stalked over, swiping it up. "Stop looking at things," he snapped, heading to the kitchen and setting it on the counter. Away from his brother.

"It's not even a bowl, Raz," Eliza drawled from where she was sitting on the sofa. She'd found a book somewhere, the pages open in her lap. "Stop antagonizing him."

"And I suppose that bowl just disappeared on its own?" he shot back.

"You probably just misplaced it."

"I don't *misplace* things," he snarled, smoke furling on his exhale.

She rolled her eyes, going back to her book, and Razik moved along to study the wall of empty frames. Luka tensed, eyes narrowing as he watched his brother. They'd been here a whole two days, and he was hating every fucking second of this.

Forcing himself to tear his eyes away, he moved to the fridge, pulling out various items. Cienna, Gia, and Tristyn had Traveled to Castle Pines and stocked up on food, spare clothing, and other necessities. None of them knew how long they were going to be hiding up here. More than that, Theon seemed to have gone into hiding too. He couldn't be reached by phone, and the bond wasn't an option anymore. A part of him wondered if he'd used a

Mark to block the bond somehow like Eviana had and that's why it wasn't working properly. As for Eviana, he hadn't been able to get in touch with Lange or Corbin either. That didn't bode well, but it wasn't as if he could be in three places at once. He wasn't exactly sure when this had all become his responsibility.

Placing eggs in a pot of water, he turned the burner on to hard-boil them. While they cooked, he sliced up vegetables, deli meats, and cheeses along with some fruit. There were chips and nuts he dumped into bowls, all the while keeping his brother in his line of sight to make sure the male didn't touch a single godsdamn thing.

He was just rinsing the eggs when Razik came over to the food spread, although he didn't fill a plate. He only straightened to his full height and crossed his arms as he said, "Where is she?"

Luka glanced at him before returning his attention to what he was doing. "Xan is with her."

"And you're just going to keep her from me until . . . when?"

Setting the bowl of hard-boiled eggs down with the rest of the food, he mirrored his brother's stance. "Until I know you're not going to attack her the moment she steps foot in the same room as you."

"She's not your Ward," Razik sneered, his lip curling up in disgust.

"I'm aware."

"And she doesn't appear to be *yours* anymore," he continued.

"What's your point?" Luka snapped, his dragon snarling internally at those words.

"That it's not your place to protect her," Razik retorted. "She needs to answer for her actions. Fucking Fates. What is with that bloodline thinking they can do whatever the fuck they want without consequences?"

"The Arius bloodline?" Luka asked in confusion.

"Arius. Serafina. Their godsdamn grandchildren," he grumbled. "The point is, it no longer appears it is your place to stand beside her and her choices."

Luka ground his teeth, staring back at the arrogant challenge in his brother's eyes. As if the male could see the war raging in his soul, he smirked, waiting to see what Luka would do. And what could he do?

When it became apparent he wasn't going to respond, Razik took a step forward, his arms dropping to his sides. "She destroyed my way home," he snarled.

"I know," Luka said.

"I do not want to be stuck in this realm."

"And what, exactly, do you want me to do about it?" Luka retorted. "I cannot rebuild the Pantheon, and I certainly don't have the ability to world walk. So what are you hoping to accomplish? More than that, what do you think *she* will be able to do?"

"She *is* Chaos," Razik snapped. "There has to be something she can do."

Scoffing, he said, "Because she's clearly in a position to be thinking about world walking. She's so deep in her power, she grows more mad every day."

"Madness is how we dream."

They both turned as Tessa's voice floated into the room, that eerie ring to it. It hadn't left. Since the day she'd brought the Pantheon to ruin, that eeriness had been there. It was the most telling thing that betrayed how much control her power had over her right now. But there were things the others didn't notice as much. The way she always had to be touching something, usually the wall. Her hands always in her hair. The humming. But her mannerisms were growing more erratic, and everyone was taking notice of that.

She moved deeper into the space, her bare feet leaving footprints. They weren't ashes like Auryon had often left behind, but they were similar. Tessa's were more silver and gold wisps. Luka glanced at his father, who sent him a grim look where he leaned against the back of the sofa Eliza was sitting on, her focus still on her book as though she hadn't heard the unstable female who had entered. Luka knew better though. There was little that female didn't notice.

Razik glared at Tessa as she passed him, but she didn't seem to care. She only swiped up an orange before hopping up onto the opposite counter, her legs swinging as she peeled the fruit. No one said anything because what was there to say at this point?

Her golden hair fell around her shoulders in soft waves, and he watched her fingers tremble slightly as she pulled at the rind. Her fitted dress was casual, with long sleeves and slits up both sides that went to the tops of her thighs. The wide neckline allowed a view of the Mark over her heart. The one that had started all of this. That had pulled him into something he'd tried to deny himself.

"Where were you?" Luka asked.

Tessa didn't answer, didn't even acknowledge them as her feet continued to swing.

"I took her outside," Xan answered.

He turned to his father. "Outside? Why would you do that?"

"She needs to see the sky," he replied. "There are certain things that will ground her. Things she associates with safety and security. Things she associates with—"

He cut off abruptly, and when he didn't continue, Luka asked, "And the sky does that for her?"

"There are better options," Xan said pointedly. "But it is something until she can be pulled from the depths of chaos."

"And the better options?" Razik inquired, but his stare was pinned on Luka. It took everything not to flip him his middle finger.

"For Akira, a person was always best," Xan said carefully. "Tessa may be different . . . I am simply trying to help her find something, and Akira likes to see the sky."

She wasn't different. Luka knew that.

Stay where I can see you.

He glanced over his shoulder to find she had finished peeling the orange, but now she was picking at the pith of the fruit. He could see the juice dripping down her fingers, and her lips were moving as she murmured to herself. With a sigh, he closed the space between them, and as he neared, he could make out the mutterings.

"Xan is right, but he doesn't want us. No one wants us. We did that. Me. You. We just lie and deceive, but they can't see—No one can see . . ." she trailed off, a hand coming up. Luka caught her wrist before her sticky fingers went into her hair.

She startled, apparently not having realized how close he'd come. Slowly she lifted her gaze to his, the violet in her irises piercing through the swirling silvers and golds. They didn't speak, but some words passed between them in that stare. More words than they'd spoken since they'd come here.

He watched her throat bob with a swallow, and he took the orange from her other hand as he felt her power reach for him and try to draw him closer still. The band of light around the wrist he held wound down around his fingers and up his arm instead of hers. The power in her eyes settled some, more of the violet shining through, but more than that, there was a glimmer of emotion. He couldn't feel them down the bond, but he could see it in her eyes.

Desperation.

Determination.

Regret.

Resignation.

Failure.

Fury.

"Come with me, Tessa," he said, wanting to take her away from the stares of everyone. Where he was going to take her, he didn't know. There were plenty of rooms, and she had her own space, but they never left her alone for long.

The last time they'd done that, she'd plotted and carried out a plan to decimate the center of the realm.

She tugged on her wrist, trying to pull it from his grasp. "You can't see," she whispered.

"Can you show me?" he countered, fully aware of everyone watching them.

She held his stare as she slowly shook her head. "You don't want to, and I understand."

"Razik is angry with you," he tried again.

Her head tilted, hair slipping over her shoulder. "I didn't ask you to catch me this time, Luka. I understand I no longer have that right."

He still held her, was still touching her, and this was the most coherent she'd been in two days. If he hadn't already known his father was right, this was all the confirmation he needed. It wasn't enough to pull her back completely, but it gave her a solid footing, if only for a brief reprieve from the lull of the magic.

Luka let her go, her power clinging to him long after he'd taken a step back. Picking up another orange, he began peeling it, keeping himself between her and Razik as the male stepped closer. Luka expected Razik to be the one to speak first, but it was Tessa.

"You have something to say to me?" she asked. And gods, Luka could swear the air in the room thickened with tension.

He turned back to Tessa to find she'd shifted so that she now sat on her knees on the counter. Her power had wound up her arms, a gold mist hovering as she studied Razik.

"You destroyed my way home," Razik growled.

"I destroyed the way in for the Fates," she countered.

"And my way home," he reiterated.

"Surely you knew that was a risk when you chose to interfere here in the first place?"

Luka almost laughed because she wasn't taunting him. It sounded like a genuine question.

"Of course I knew it was a risk," Razik snapped.

"Then you should be upset with yourself, not me," she said simply, her fingers dragging along the countertop.

"Serafina told you there are other ways in. You accomplished nothing but trapping us here."

"If there are other ways in, there are other ways out," Tessa replied with a shrug of her shoulders. Then her lips tipped up in a small, unnerving smile. "But I'll find those too. I'll destroy every avenue."

"You want this world to have a reckoning," Eliza said, coming up beside Razik. Her grey eyes were pinned on Tessa. "Why not simply leave and let the Fates do just that?"

"Because the innocent here deserve to have justice, not die alongside those who only saw their value in how they could use them," Tessa hissed, power bouncing from her fingertips.

Eliza nodded, far calmer about this entire situation than her twin flame was. "You want to dismantle the Legacy."

"Do you not think the Fae here deserve to have the freedom you enjoy in your own world?"

"I do," Eliza agreed.

"Excellent answer," Tessa said, her gaze sliding to Razik as a smirk curled on her lips. "Seeing as you are now stuck here for the foreseeable future."

"You're lucky I don't—" Razik started, but he snapped his mouth shut when her power thickened, coiling into a whip in her hand. Light and dark crackled, sparks of energy and embers of something other flaring off it.

"Tell me," Tessa crooned. "Tell me all about the *luck* I have, Razik Greybane. Is it the abandonment at birth? The time spent in small spaces to *think?* The *friends* who used and deceived me? The Lords and Ladies who did the same? Or was it the not knowing what I was, having no way to figure it out, while you had all your books and teachings? Then you come here and act as if we are beneath you for not having the knowledge you were so freely given."

"Tessa," Luka said quietly in warning, stepping towards her as her power swelled more and more around her. Phantom winds swirled, the food platters clanking and some flipping to the floor as thunder cracked somewhere outside.

But Tessa ignored him. Instead, she moved fast, no one expecting it as she leapt from the countertop and landed in front of Razik. The male cursed, shoving Eliza behind him at the same time that Luka wrapped an arm around Tessa's waist and hauled her back against his chest, the orange plopping to the floor, forgotten. Her power bit into his skin, and his flames rushed to the surface, to meet her magic or protect him, he wasn't entirely sure.

"Or am I the lucky one because despite promises and gentle touches, I let myself believe I'd finally found a home, only to learn that's not my fate in the end?" Tessa went on, venom dripping from each word, but Luka felt her body tremble slightly as she spoke. "I think the lucky one here is *you*, Razik Greybane. You have a home you will do anything to return to. More than that, you have people who *want* you. People who want you despite you not returning the sentiment. I'd be careful with that. Eventually they stop trying and stop wanting you, and you realize too late you wanted them all along."

The room had gone utterly silent. Eliza was peering around Razik's body, her hand gripping his forearm. There was no doubt the pair was communicating down their bond, but Eliza appeared ready to intervene should her mate attempt anything.

Not that she would need to. Luka was positive that if he let Tessa go, she'd be more than capable of holding her own against the male with her magic so volatile right now. As the silence stretched on, Luka slowly lowered her back to her feet. She smoothed her hands down her dress, then she reached for her hair before stopping herself.

She straightened, all her power disappearing into her aside from the light bands at her wrists. Then she lifted her chin, holding Razik's stare as she said, "I don't have the luxury of luck, and the Fates are determined to end me. I will not apologize for fighting for my survival, nor will I apologize for not allowing others to become a sacrifice for me. And I certainly will not ask forgiveness for—"

She snapped her mouth shut, clearing her throat as she looked around the room. "In all things, there must be balance, but how does that come to be when one race rules all? Keeping others locked away in the dark beneath them? They tell us Achaz is wrong, that he wants to rule the realms, but then it stands to reason we must resist him. If we are to resist him, then it must start here."

With that, she wandered away, as if there hadn't just been a confrontation that had nearly ended in magic being thrown around. Her fingers trailed along anything she could touch—the sofa, a side table, the walls—and she started humming as she went, making her way towards a passage that would take her to the guest rooms. The opposite way from his own room.

Luka waited until she disappeared from view before he followed, easily catching up to her with his long strides. She was muttering to herself, and he couldn't make out the words until he was nearly on top of her.

"We damn one to save hundreds. We damn ourselves to save them. That's what we do when we love . . ." She trailed off, flattening her palm against the wall, watching darkness seep from her fingertips. Except it wasn't darkness. It was swirling black mist and gold embers. Then she nodded to herself. "This is what happens when you let yourself be loved. That's what they taught us. No. Yes. I can't . . ." Her hands wound into her hair, pulling at the roots.

"Tessa," Luka said, something in his chest aching at seeing her like this, but he shoved the feeling aside.

She whirled, and he could swear there were pools of silver glimmering in her eyes as she stared back at him before she blinked them away.

"You didn't eat anything," he said when she didn't speak. Her head tilted, but she didn't reply. "Have you tried to reach him?" Luka asked, taking a different angle at talking to her. Her gaze darted to the side at the words. "He won't deny you," he added, reaching to pull her hands from her hair, but she lurched back a step.

"He already has," she retorted, lightning flickering in her irises. "He's . . . perplexing," she murmured.

"I think the feeling is mutual, little one."

If she'd lurched back before, she stumbled back now as if he'd struck her. He knew why. Knew she remembered what he'd told her about that particular pet name. But he needed to remind himself. He couldn't trust her. She'd kept him in the dark about his father. Hadn't told him of her plans for the Pantheon, not that he could blame her on that one. Every one of them would have attempted to stop her. But he needed to keep a distance between them, even if he would wind up being her Guardian in the end. He would do that. It had been Theon's last request of him, and he would do that because it was the duty of his bloodline and his family.

She nodded to herself again, and he found himself wishing he could hear her thoughts. Wishing everything wasn't so fucking broken. But he wasn't sure he'd ever feel whole again, even if things were different with Tessa. Not without his family. And he didn't mean the blooded family out in the main room.

"Tessa, I—"

"Where is my bow?" she interjected.

Luka's brow furrowed in confusion. "What?"

"My bow. From Auryon. It's ours."

"Ours," he repeated slowly.

She nodded, bouncing on her toes. "She left it to us. Said it was our birthright."

"Tessa, maybe you should get some rest. When was the last time you slept?"

She shot forward, pushing onto her tiptoes as she spoke inches from him. "Do you know what I see in my dreams, Luka?"

"No, Tessa," he said carefully. "I don't know what you see in your dreams. Not anymore."

She fell back, moving to the wall and dragging her fingers along the stone. "I see all the things that will never be. They torture us," she murmured. "Light and dark. Beginnings and endings. My dreams haunt us. They are nightmares. I do not like it there."

"You still need to sleep," he insisted. "I know you just filled your power reserves, but you still need to rest. If you're not taking care of yourself, it's easier for your power to take control. It is why Theon was neurotic about your diet and schedule."

She whirled at his name, lightning flickering in her eyes. "He no longer wants me."

"Tessa, that isn't—"

"There you are," said a male voice that had both of them spinning as Tristyn came into view down the passage.

"Keeper of Lies and Deceit," Tessa greeted, her eyes narrowing.

"Wild fury," he answered in kind, a mocking note to his tone. Thank the gods he'd finally stopped coddling her.

"I'd ask where you were, but you'd simply lie about it," she replied with a sneer.

He sent her a smirk as he slipped his hands into the pockets of his leather jacket. There was a faint sage glow to his russet eyes, making them appear almost hazel. The male may have dropped the coddling act, but he was still prepared to face Tessa as the deity he was.

"Where are you off to?" Tristyn asked, looking around the passage as though he wasn't monitoring what kind of threat she was in this moment.

"Shouldn't you know the answer to that?" Tessa sang, dancing back from them to press a palm to the wall once more. Her power snaked out of her, winding along the rock, and Luka reached out, yanking her hand away.

"The gods help you if you destroy this cave, Tessa," he growled.

She didn't even look at him as she said, "The gods never help me. I don't see why they'd start now."

Tristyn cleared his throat, sending a warning look to Luka as he said, "I think you're confusing me with my sister, wild fury. She's the one who can see the ever-changing."

Tessa hummed, pulling her wrist from Luka's grip. Her hands fell to her sides, where she fisted them in the fabric of her dress. "Then what do you want?"

"I'm glad you asked," he said with a hint of mischief. He pulled his hands from his pockets, opening one before her. In the center of his palm were two rolls of lull-leaf.

Her eyes narrowed as she met Tristyn's gaze once more. "Is this how your father keeps the peace as well?" she asked, picking up one of the rolls and twisting it between her fingers.

Blackheart's eyes darkened. "My father views peace as optional in most cases, and he decides when it's a weapon to wield."

She only hummed once more. "Then what is this? A peace offering?"

"Without pizza and *agaveheart*?" Tristyn scoffed. "What kind of a peace offering is that?"

Seconds ticked by, the passage falling eerily silent until she held the lull-leaf back out to him. "I don't trust you, Tris," she said with a sigh.

The male's arrogance faltered, but only for a moment, before he took a single step forward. "What do I need to do, Tessa? I've sworn loyalty to you. What can I give you in penance?"

In the next breath, her entire face lit up as she said, "A story."

Tristyn's face paled at the words. "I think stories are more your thing, wild fury. Not mine."

She stumbled forward, somehow tripping on the length of her skirt. Luka moved to catch her, but she was already clutching at Tristyn's arm, crushing the lull-leaf roll in her hand. "You have to tell me a story," she insisted, panic and mania creeping into her voice. "We're the same. You are alone. And I'm alone. And you survived. I need to know how to survive being alone. We were alone for so long, and then I thought . . . And then we weren't, and now we are. And I know it's my fault, but—"

She stopped speaking abruptly when Tristyn reached up and ran a hand down her hair, hushing her with a soothing sound. "All right, Tessa," he said softly, and Luka knew he was using his gifts on her right now. "I'll tell you a story." She nodded, her body still too tense even with his power. Meeting Luka's gaze, Tristyn said, "I've got her. Take a break, Mors."

"Take a break," Tessa murmured. "He doesn't want us. We struck too deep. We chose destruction." Before he could say anything in response, her head snapped up. She lurched from Tristyn's hold, suddenly in front of Luka. Her hands fisted in his shirt, and she clung to him, saying, "But I saved him for you."

There was a pleading in her voice he didn't understand as he clasped her upper arms, trying to ease the white-knuckled grip she had on his shirt. "Saved who, Tessa?" Luka asked.

But she was shaking her head, back to mumbling. "He can't see." Lifting her gaze to his, grey was peeking through the violet and gold that often hid the color from them these days. "You can't see."

"See what, Tessa?"

Her smile was small and sad as she released him, slowly backing away. Shaking her head, she murmured, "He can't see."

Then she was drifting down the passage away from him, back to humming and sliding her hand along the wall, her fingers and bare feet leaving a trail of magic behind her.

"I've got her. Seriously, Mors. Take a break for a while," Blackheart said with a grim smile.

"She's in too deep," Luka said.

"I know," was all the male replied before he turned to follow the fury of chaos.

Luka stayed rooted to the spot long after they had disappeared. He wasn't even sure where they'd end up.

You can't see.

Stay where I can see you.

I saved him for you.

Saved who? His father? He'd done that. He was the one who had gone to get his father after learning where he was. Not her.

Gritting his teeth, he turned and went back the way he'd come. Reaching the main living space, he found Eliza had disappeared somewhere, leaving him with only his brother and father. Which was great. He'd been hoping they all would have fucked off somewhere after the confrontation with Tessa.

Xan was in the kitchen cleaning up the food spread that few people had touched. Luka suspected it was simply to have something to do. It appeared sitting around doing nothing wasn't something their bloodline was accustomed to. All three of them were restless and itching to act. To do *something*. It wasn't in their nature to hide. It was in their nature to protect and fight for those they viewed as theirs.

"Apparently she didn't need you to protect her from me after all," Razik drawled from the sofa, sitting in the same place Eliza had been.

"I don't think Eliza needs your protection either, yet you still shoved her behind you," Luka retorted, stalking past him to help their father.

"Eliza doesn't need me to protect her," his brother replied, an arm draped along the back of the sofa as he watched them over his shoulder.

"Yet you do so anyway."

"She is mine," Razik replied simply. "She comes before all else, including myself and my Ward." With a glare in their father's direction, he begrudgingly added, "She is, indeed, my inevitable."

Luka ground his teeth, turning away only to put himself in the path of his father.

"She's not wrong, you know," Xan said. "Achaz looks to conquer and divide individual realms. It's what he's been doing for centuries. The only way to survive it is for a realm to come together and resist him."

"You think I don't know that?" Luka ground out, bracing his hands on the counter's edge, his head falling to his chest.

Xan moved to stand beside him, leaning against the counter and crossing his arms, wincing as the collar bit into his skin. Guilt washed over Luka at the realization they still had done absolutely nothing to even attempt to remove the thing.

"What do you wish she would have done? Left?" Xan pushed.

Luka didn't know how to answer that. Leaving is what would keep Tessa safest. It was what he should want, but . . .

He wasn't upset. He should be, but he wasn't. He wasn't even entirely sure he would have tried to talk her out of it. If he was upset about anything, it was that she hadn't included him in her plan. Irony at its absolute finest.

"Can I speak plainly?" his father asked, pulling him from his thoughts.

He glanced at the sofa to find Razik gone. The only reason he nodded was because they were alone. He had a feeling this wasn't a conversation he wanted anyone else around for.

"An inevitable bond is not forced, Luka," Xan said. "There is a pull you both feel. It is overwhelming, but it is not like a twin flame bond. It is not something destined by the Fates. It is as wild and untamed as the Chaos it comes from, and it only appears when two souls need it most. But in the end, it is still a choice."

"And you think I would be foolish not to choose it," Luka said bitterly. "That I would be throwing away something others will only ever long for."

"You put words in my mouth, son," Xan said, pushing off the counter. He paused, gripping Luka's shoulder and squeezing. "I think you have experienced much loneliness, loss, and torment in your short years, and it has shaped how you view the world and what you value. And I think the hardest part of all of this for you is that you know she is the same. A mirror of what you are. The hardest part for you is that if you fault her, you must also fault yourself." He squeezed his shoulder once more before releasing him. "You still care, and that eats away at you. You feel out of control, drawn to something you don't want to want, but torn between what you believe is your duty. So I will say this: remember the bond only comes to be when two souls need it most. It is a bond born of Chaos."

He left Luka standing in the kitchen, crossing the room and making his way to the passage that would lead to the cave entrance. But he paused before he disappeared from view, turning back to Luka once more.

"For what it's worth, she still claims you," he said. "In the only way she knows how."

"She doesn't know what it means to claim someone," Luka retorted scathingly.

Xan's only answer was a resigned nod that made a sense of shame crawl up Luka's spine. He could tell his father was disappointed, but he didn't understand. He let Razik hold his grudge, but faulted Luka for *this?*

With a growl of frustration, he stalked towards his room. He needed to fly. He needed to breathe. He needed to talk to his godsdamn best friend.

And he needed to get away from the temptress that had upended his entire world.

She wasn't the one for this. Just like he'd said all along.

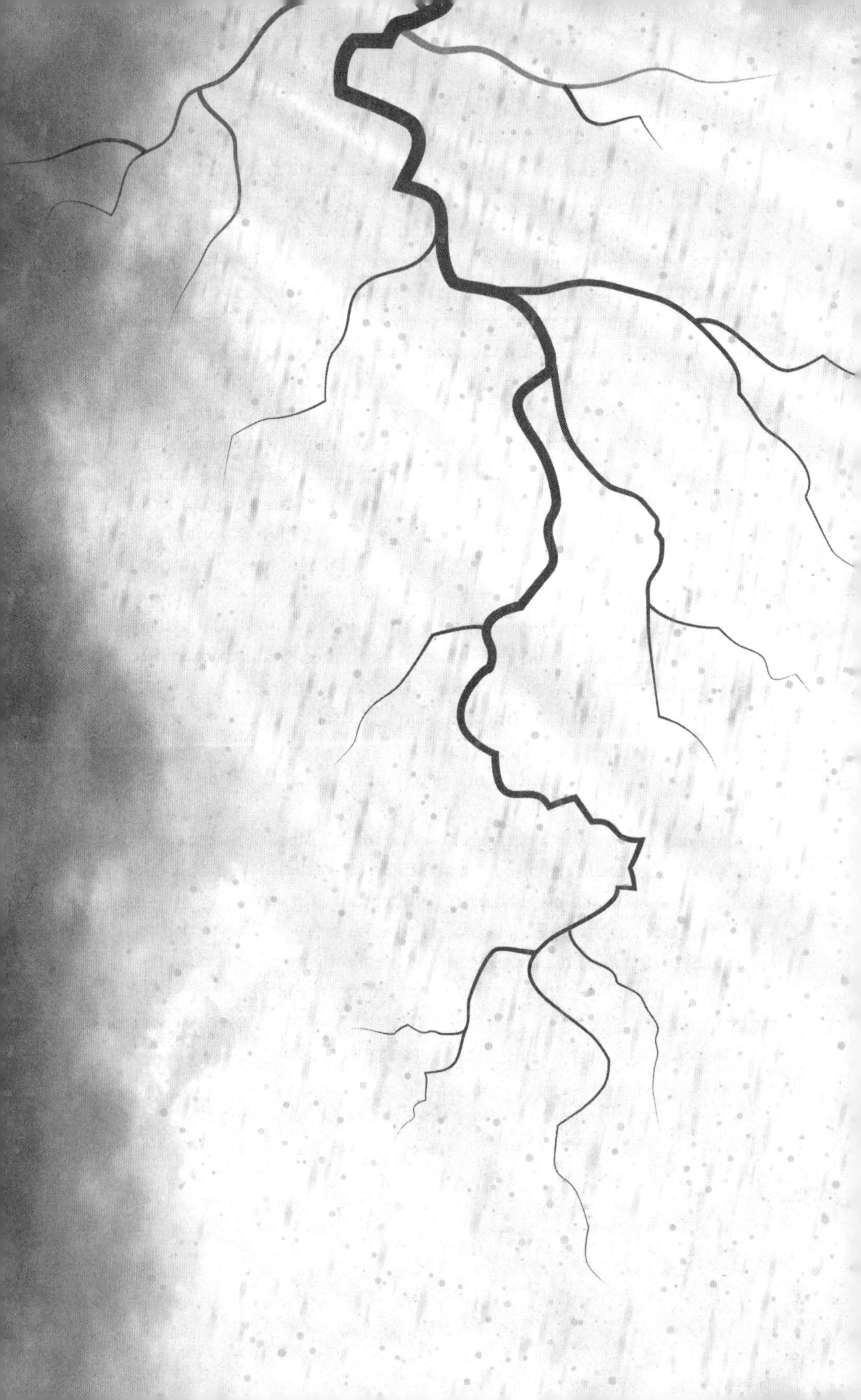

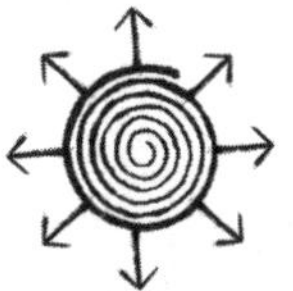

9
TESSA

"I don't need you, Keeper," Tessa said as she followed Tristyn farther down the passageway.

"Of course you don't," Tris replied over his shoulder with a smirk. "You don't need anyone, right, wild fury?"

She frowned at his words, pausing for a moment, and her fingers flexed against the wall, her light winding around the digits like fine threads.

"That's not what I said," she finally retorted, resuming her pace. She wasn't trying to keep up with Tristyn, but she couldn't . . . stay still. There was too much . . .

There was just *too much*.

It thrummed in her veins, the power constantly seeking more, and with so many powerful beings around her all the time now, it took every piece of her to keep it at bay. In retaliation, it had sunk its claws deeper into her, dragging her down and holding her in this perpetual place of feeling like she was going to crawl out of her skin. Of wanting more and pushing them away. Of needing but not being able to have. Of knowing eventually she wouldn't be able to keep it confined. Not without a balance.

Knowing that in the end, the prophecy about her would come true, and Chaos would reign.

Neither of them spoke again as he continued to lead her along. Xan always took her outside, which she appreciated, but Tristyn was leading her deeper into Luka's cave system. She hadn't ventured beyond the spaces he'd shown her—the main living space and the guest rooms. There were far more rooms and passages, but she'd already shattered his trust in her. She wouldn't disrespect him further by intruding on his space when he clearly didn't want her here in the first place.

A duty.

A burden.

A constant reminder of betrayal and what she'd stolen from him.

That was all she was to him now, and in the end, she wouldn't let him bind himself to her to become her Guardian. Xan had told her how that bond worked and how it was created. She'd refuse and give him the freedom from her he so desperately craved.

Despite Tristyn leading her deeper into the mountains, the path was sloping upwards rather than down. Somehow being here, it didn't bother her quite as much that they were underground. She still longed to see the sky though, and as far as she could tell, there were only two ways into the cave. There was the main entrance and a secluded balcony off Luka's room.

"Pick one," Tristyn said, coming to a stop with two rooms on either side of the hall. Neither had a door, and she came up beside the male and peered into them.

The one on the left was a game room of sorts. Paddles and a ball sat atop a table for table tennis. Over in a corner was a green felt-topped table with a deck of cards and playing chips. A TV hung on the wall, a few gaming consoles connected, and Tessa knew without a doubt that this room was mainly for Axel when he came here. If she were to look, she was sure she'd find a phone somewhere that was connected to the sound system to play his music.

Crossing the passage to the other room, she stopped in the doorway. The decor here was the same as the rest of the cave. Overstuffed leather furniture. A cozy hearth. A rug to warm the space. A round table off to the side with a few chairs while a long, low table sat among the furniture. This space was for Theon, and she'd taken several steps into the room before she'd even realized she had moved. The low lighting Tristyn had turned on cast a soothing glow around the room, and she made her way to a lamp on an end table. She turned the switch, and it illuminated the space further to allow for reading.

"I had a feeling this was the room we'd end up in, but I didn't want to assume," Tristyn said, sliding around her and plopping onto the sofa.

"You know what happens when we assume," Tessa murmured. Gods, she could swear she could still *smell* Theon in here. And Luka. Both of them. Together.

This was her new favorite room.

Tristyn huffed a laugh at her comment as he pulled a lighter from his pocket and lit the roll of lull-leaf he'd placed between his lips. All Tessa could think about was how ridiculous it was that a deity had to use a lighter. Then again, she would have to do the same, she supposed.

"Sorry I crushed the other one," she said.

"As if I don't have more," he replied with a wink, reaching for the remote on the end table.

She thought it was for the television, but when he clicked the power button, the fireplace sprang to life. Her head snapped to the flames, and she lurched forward. Crouching down, she didn't stop until her face and hands were less than an inch from the glass.

"Fucking Fates, Tessa," Tristyn yelped, suddenly at her side and trying to pull her back.

But she shrugged him off, instead dropping to her hands and knees as she crawled along the expanse of the fireplace.

"Always trapped," she murmured, the flames licking at the glass. At each other. Oranges and reds. Yellows and blues. Writhing in every direction trying to find a way out. But if they escaped, there would be nothing but destruction as they devoured and fed and took and took and took.

There had to be a balance.

Tristyn had sat back on his heels, watching her, and when she stopped crawling around only to roll onto her back and stare up at the ceiling, he took the spot beside her, doing the same. Their shoulders butted up against each other, and Tessa gritted her teeth as the thing inside her sat up straighter, inching closer to the surface.

Shoving it back down with a shudder, she reached over, plucking the lull-leaf from his lips and taking a drag. It was a terrible idea. If she became too relaxed, her control could slip. Or worse, she'd fall asleep.

"You owe me a story," she sang while the plant did its job, the tension easing from her limbs.

"I was hoping you'd forget," he muttered, taking the lull-leaf back from her and sucking in another deep drag.

"I don't forget anything," she replied.

"That's not true," he answered, a grim note in his tone. "But that's not entirely your fault."

Unsure of what that meant, she stayed silent, her fingers winding into the fabric of her dress.

"I've been waiting for you for a very long time, but when you—"

"That's not how stories start," she interrupted, lifting a hand and letting power pool there. That gave her more relief than the lull-leaf did.

She could feel Tristyn watching her magic, could feel him tensing despite the lull-leaf in case he needed to counteract her gifts. Or try to at least.

And still she waited because he knew what she meant.

She heard him swallow thickly before clearing his throat. "In all things there must be balance. Beginnings and endings. Light and dark. Fire and shadows."

"The sky, the sea, the realms," she whispered in kind.

"I'd been waiting for you," he continued. "Not to use you like you believe, but because you are the ticket to my salvation, Tessa. That is not the story I wish to tell you though. I wish to tell you a story about *you*."

She hummed, contemplating, but finally she nodded. As much as she wished to know his story, she wanted these answers more.

"Your arrival in this realm had been prophesied for centuries," he said, settling in once more. He took another pull from the lull-leaf before passing it to her. "And whenever someone finds their way to Devram, they are met by a Keeper."

"I know this story," she cut in.

"I assure you, you do not," he said gently, almost sadly.

She fell quiet once more, passing over the lull-leaf to let him take the final drag. He put it out, setting the butt aside before clearing his throat once more.

"You know there have been many Keepers over Devram's life. Some have gone to the After, some have vacated the role but still live, and some have deviated from their purpose. But the fact remains that a Keeper greets everyone who enters the realm through a mirror gate."

"Wait," she interrupted yet again, pushing onto her elbow to look down at him. "There is more than one?"

He nodded slowly. "You destroyed the main one, but each kingdom houses a mirror gate, Tessa. They keep them hidden and guarded. It was meant to keep power balanced, but like all things in Devram, the purpose has become twisted."

"Hmm," she hummed, lowering down once more.

"That's all you have to say to that?"

"This is a dreadful story," she replied, again toying with her power. "And I am beginning to believe you are stalling, Keeper of Lies."

It was Tristyn's turn to sigh, and she knew she was right when he cleared his throat again. He was nervous about whatever he was going to reveal.

"Cienna and I were met by Keepers, just like Xan was when he arrived with you in arms, his son and wife at his side."

"His wife," Tessa murmured. "Where is she now?"

"That is a question for Xan. A story for him to tell," he answered, and she tsked under her breath.

"The problem with that is that everyone keeps their stories a secret until they are forced to reveal them—"

"I was the one who met them," Tristyn interrupted.

The power in her palm expanded at the words. Light and dark spiraling upwards and out, seeking to sink its claws in and take as her fury grew once again.

"*You* met them when they arrived here," she said, too calm. Each word too even. "And you are just now telling me this? If you knew who I was, how the fuck did I end up at the Celeste Estate? If you knew who I was, how was I so godsdamn lost for years? You were waiting for me? For what? To watch me waste away in neglect and abandonment? Why didn't you fucking do something?"

She had no idea when she'd gotten to her feet, but she was standing over him as he scrambled to his own. A sage glow eclipsed his russet-colored eyes, and he reached for her before wisely shoving his hand through his hair instead.

"I couldn't do anything. You *were* lost, Tessa," he insisted. Pain and regret lined his features, but she couldn't trust it. She couldn't trust anyone in this godsdamned realm. "Xan handed you to me when they arrived. You were my purpose here, but when the mirror gate let them in, others took the opportunity to come here too. They'd been waiting, just as I was."

"Who?" Tessa snapped. "Who else came here?"

"Seraphs sent by Achaz."

"You mean Dex. And Brecken. And Oralia," she seethed.

"There were others."

"And again I ask, why are you just now telling me this? When you have known this entire time?"

"Because I haven't known this entire time," he answered, a bite of irritation creeping into his tone now too. "I know you have every reason and right to jump to the worst conclusions, Tessa, but let me explain. Then you can decide how long to continue hating me."

She glared at him but bit her tongue on her sharp retort, instead crossing her arms and jerking her chin at him to continue.

"I wasn't the only one waiting for you," he said, moving for his jacket to retrieve another roll of lull-leaf. "Like I said, your arrival here had been prophesied for centuries. Some say since the world was created. At one time, the kingdoms had all worked together, before the current rulers took their thrones. But relations between the Achaz and Arius Kingdoms had started to erode well before Rordan and Valter, even if they worked together for some time. Valter was trying to regain their place in Devram, and Rordan professed he was vying for peace among the kingdoms. But Rordan left The Augury, abandoning Valter, as you know. What we didn't know was that Rordan hadn't been working for peace at all. He has eyes everywhere and working alongside Valter gave him access to information that the Arius Lord learned. You arrived, and they arrived, having made arrangements to enter through the Achaz Kingdom."

"Then where was the Keeper to meet them?" Tessa interrupted.

His smile was all teeth when he answered, "Killed the moment they stepped through the mirror gate, despite having pledged loyalty to Rordan. He took no chances."

Her breath stalled, but she didn't react otherwise, waiting for him to keep going, because none of this answered how she had gotten lost among the realm.

"I met Xan at the mirror gate, and the plan was to take you to my place until Xan and Aiyana could acclimate to the world and culture. They were to be your legal guardians, and there were plans in place to integrate all of you into the Arius Kingdom. But we never made it out of the Pantheon," Tristyn went on. "We had scarcely left the inner chambers when they appeared, charging down the stairs. Xan had already handed you off to me, shoving Luka to my side while he and Aiyana fought, but neither of them could shift inside the tight spaces. They killed several of the seraphs, but they had been a diversion. Rordan was waiting with four others, stronger than an average seraph, along with Elowyn."

"Stronger than an average seraph?" Tessa asked, her head tilting at this information.

Tristyn nodded, relief crossing his face at her willingness to hear him out. "Yes. They are called Maraans, and they are stronger than a seraph in the way a Sargon descendant is stronger than a dragon shifter. Both the dragons and the seraphs emerged from the Chaos, but—"

"Achaz and Arius made some stronger and more elite, playing like the gods they are," Tessa sneered.

"Yes and no," he answered, tipping his head from side to side as he debated what to say. Or maybe how to explain it. "Sargon and Arius were always close, from my understanding. When Arius deflected from Achaz in the Everlasting War, that was when the Guardians were created. Achaz answered with the Maraans, but that is not the point of this story. The point is, they let Xan and Aiyana weaken fighting the seraphs. I was using my power to keep you and Luka safe, and by the time Rordan and the Maraans appeared, we were all low in reserves. Before we could properly act, Elowyn cast an enchantment, but she did so at the same time that Xan struck down one of the Maraans. The enchantment collided with his power, and the effect caused the enchantment to hit people it wasn't supposed to. While I suspect it was meant to make us forget who you were specifically, the power collision made the enchantment unbalanced. It did make us forget, but it also made other memories and knowledge murky and distorted.

"The next thing I remember was being in that passageway surrounded by the destruction of the fighting. We couldn't remember what you looked like, and we didn't know what had happened. I didn't even remember the Maraans being there until recently, only the seraphs. Elowyn's enchantment was to modify memories, but it hit her and Rordan too. None of us could remember who you were and what happened, but all of us knew you were here. None of us knew how to find you or where to begin looking."

"So only Dex, Oralia, and Brecken knew where I was?" she asked, new fury simmering in her gut.

"I can't say for sure, but that's my guess," he said, familiar pity filling his face now. Pity she didn't want or need. "Because for over two decades I was searching, Valter was searching, and Rordan was searching. It appears Rordan learned of you first, enacting a plan of his own that obviously didn't go accordingly."

Tessa had gone silent, letting all the new information settle in her soul. Repeating it and turning it over in her mind.

"I was trying, Tessa," Tristyn said after several full minutes of silence. "Every moment was spent trying to find you. I became obsessed, leaving Cienna to deal with . . . everything else. Every second was spent working to recover lost knowledge and creating new spells in attempts to find you."

"But you didn't tell me when you *did* find me," she argued, hands driving into her hair. "You didn't tell me anything!"

"I hadn't pieced it all together yet. How was I supposed to explain myself when I couldn't give you the answers you were so desperately seeking?" he said. "By the time I could, Rordan already had his claws so deep in you, you wouldn't have believed me anyway."

"I want to be alone," she said suddenly, turning away from him to face the fireplace once more.

"Tessa—"

"Leave, Tristyn," she bit out.

It took another full minute before she heard him pick up his discarded jacket and leave the den. She had a feeling he wouldn't go far. Or someone else would come relieve him of babysitting duty. She knew they were all watching her closely.

Dropping down, she sat in front of the glass pane and wrapped her arms around her bent knees. The flames danced with each other, always fighting. Pushing and pulling. Hating but needing each other all the same.

She'd been right.

That had been a dreadful story.

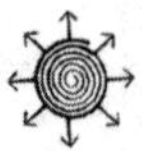

She didn't know where she was.

Definitely Devram. That was where she'd wanted to go when she'd stepped through the mirror gate, but this wasn't where the Pantheon had once stood. Then again, she'd destroyed that mirror gate before they'd left this world. This was obviously one of the other mirrors she hadn't destroyed in her quest to decimate them all before the Fates could get here. She'd run out of time in the end anyway.

Rubbing her arms against the chill in the air, she turned in place, recognizing she was in a city of some sort. It was run down, but not in complete ruin like she would have expected if the Fates had come searching for her. Buildings still stood, the streets empty, and she started walking, the pavement freezing beneath her bare feet.

She walked for several minutes, turning up and down streets. There was nothing here she recognized, but that didn't mean anything. She hadn't seen much of the realm beyond the Arius and Achaz Kingdoms. She could be anywhere, but based on the cooler weather, she guessed the northern part of the world.

Entering what was clearly a residential district of the city, she was about to turn another corner when a voice had her stilling and slowly turning.

"Hello, clever tempest."

Theon stood several feet away, his hands in the pockets of his suit pants and his hair stirring in the slight breeze. He watched her, and the smallest of smiles tilted on the corner of his mouth.

Her heart fell.

He was still here. That part of the future hadn't changed despite actions she'd taken to alter things. Despite her trying to alter this outcome. It had driven her mad, and she'd still failed in the end.

He looked up as the first raindrop fell, the sky quickly turning from sunny to grey. Then he looked back at her. "Why so sad, little storm?"

"You are still a phantom," she said with a frown, watching him drift closer.

That small smile tilted a little more. "Worried about me?"

"Yes. No." She reached for her hair, fingers getting caught. "You are infuriating."

"Where is Luka?" he asked, reaching for her hands and gently untangling them.

She shrugged, reveling in his touch. She'd stopped trying to figure out how, didn't really care. Not as half her soul settled at feeling him near.

"I have not seen him since he left," she answered while he switched to the other hand.

His brow furrowed. "What do you mean?"

"I . . ." She trailed off, trying to remember. The dreams got confusing with memories from now and those of the future that might never be memories at all. This part she remembered though. It was something she'd been contemplating for days. "He didn't want me," she finally answered, her voice nothing but a whisper.

"You are all he wanted," Theon said tightly.

She shook her head again. "I was too much. Did too much. I set him free. That's what we do for those we lo—Care about, right? That's what you did. That's what we do. That's how—"

Her words stalled as he finished with her hair, a large hand cupping her chin and tilting her face up to his. "He left you?"

"Yes. I mean, not yet. But in this time . . ." She trailed off, too lost in emerald eyes with darkness swirling, calling to her own power. "I hurt him."

"And we hurt you," he said tightly, releasing her chin and taking her hand.

"Where are we going?" she asked, letting him pull her along. She welcomed it. No decisions to make. Nothing to think about. Just letting him take all that from her. Not forever. Just a reprieve. As if he knew it was what she needed right now.

"Out of the cold," he answered over his shoulder, climbing a few steps and pushing open a front door.

Everything in the house was covered in a thick layer of grime and dust, but the bones of the structure were still good. A whip of darkness wrapped around a wooden chair, snapping it into pieces before depositing them into the wood-burning fireplace.

"A little help?" he asked, looking at her expectantly.

Her brows pinched. "I do not have fire magic."

He still held her hand, and he tugged her forward so she stood in front of him, clicking his tongue in disapproval. "I've seen that lightning of yours start more than one fire, clever tempest."

"And if I start the entire house on fire?" she countered.

A palm landed on her shoulder before sliding down the length of her bare arm. Gooseflesh was left in its wake as he folded his fingers around her hand. "You can do this," he murmured, speaking softly into her ear. "Let us help you."

"I don't know how to trust anyone anymore," she whispered.

His movements paused, his breath making the fine hairs by her ear flutter against her temple.

Finally, he said, "That's fair, Tessa. Then trust yourself."

"I don't trust her either. She's too—"

"She's perfect," he interjected. "Too many people have tried to change her and use her and take from her."

"And now?" she asked, her voice wavering as she waited for his answer.

"And now she is free to become whoever she wishes to be," he replied, once again lifting her hand. "She gets to decide who is worthy of her. The only reason you don't trust yourself is because you were constantly told you weren't enough."

A fine mist of darkness hovered, waiting, and she sucked in a sharp breath as she let her power rush to the surface. Lightning arced, just as he'd said it would, and that darkness guided it to the hearth, flames jumping to life.

And she stared as the fire danced, free yet controlled.

Wild yet content.

Fierce yet balanced.

Then she spun in his hold, looking up at him once more before she was pushing onto her toes as high as she could. He met her halfway, sounds of desperation coming from both of them. It may be a dream, but her body and soul felt the separation of decades.

Breaking the kiss, her hands slipped behind his neck, linking together as he pulled her impossibly closer. With her head on his chest, she could swear she could hear his heart beating. Phantom or not, she didn't care right now. Not as they began swaying in an empty house among the ruin of a realm.

Not as she danced with a ghost of what could have been and would never be.

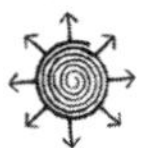

Her eyes snapped open, and she gasped for a breath.

On the floor.

She was on the floor in the den. Sitting up, a blanket pooled in her lap. Someone had covered her and dimmed the lights so only the glow of the fireplace illuminated the space. It wasn't until she ran a hand down her face that she felt the tears on her cheeks.

This was why she couldn't let herself sleep. Because she could still feel him. His arms tucking her in tight. His lips on hers . . .

Nightmares that haunted her. Just like she'd told Luka.

She needed to get out of this room. It smelled like them and lulled her into a false sense of security.

Quietly stepping from the den, she made her way back down the passage, passing several rooms with doors closed. Everyone must have gone to bed for the night.

The sitting room was empty and still, and despite knowing she shouldn't, she crept to Luka's room. As delicately as she could, she turned the knob and pushed the door open. He was there, in the middle of his nest of blankets and pillows, and she felt two more tears slip free at the memory of being in that bed with him.

Of being in a bed with *both* of them.

Tiptoeing into the room a little more, she made her way to the closet where she found the shirt he'd worn that day. Shoving her arms into the sleeves, she didn't worry about rolling them up just yet. She'd do that once she was out.

Steeling herself, she kept her footsteps light as she slipped from the room and quietly shut the door behind her, never once acknowledging the glowing sapphire eyes that tracked her every step.

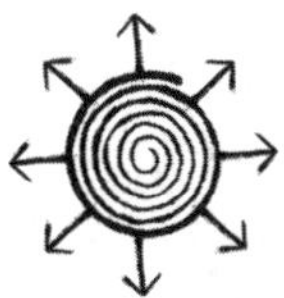

10

AXEL

"I really don't like this," Axel said from where he sat on the edge of the bed.

Kat poked her head out of the ensuite, her toothbrush in her mouth and her brows knitted. "Like what?" she asked around the brush.

"You know what," he grumbled.

She gave him a small smile before returning to the bathroom, but he knew she was annoyed with him. It had been a week since Theon had shown up here, and like he'd known he would, Theon had set about laying out all their options and overthinking everything. Yes, Axel needed his brother's help, but overthinking wasn't how things were done in the Underground.

Unless it came to his wife.

Then *he* was the one overthinking things.

Katya returned, wearing only one of his shirts. Her belly was too large for her own clothes at this point, and while he had purchased her maternity wear from the Apparel District, she said his shirts were more comfortable to sleep in. That might be true, but he suspected it might also have something to do with the scent of him that lingered.

She stopped before him, resting her hands on his shoulders. His fingers trailed up bare thighs as he spread his legs and tugged her between them, needing her closer. He could swear his canines tingled as he inhaled her scent, despite having drank plenty of blood that day. Theon had given him all the rations he'd brought, not keeping any for himself. He insisted he could go get more when they needed it, but gods, that trek there and back would take at least a week. Theon couldn't Travel, and without a Source, he couldn't shadow walk like their father either. But that wasn't what had him worried currently.

"I don't suppose I can convince you to stay behind tomorrow?" he murmured, his fingers brushing up and down her soft skin.

A small, coy smile formed again. "It hasn't worked yet," she answered. "What makes you think it will work now?"

He sighed, his fingers tightening around the backs of her thighs. "It's dangerous, Kat. The Shifters are—"

"Cunning and fickle," she interrupted. "Yes, I'm aware. I have met them before."

"I could kill Theon for taking you there," Axel snarled, dragging her closer still until her protruding stomach bumped against his torso.

"I was as determined to find you as he was, Axel," she said, reaching up and pushing her fingers through his hair. "I insisted."

"Because you are stubborn," he muttered. "It puts you and the babe at risk."

"So your solution is to leave me here alone? How is that any safer?"

"Stop being so logical," he grumbled with a scowl.

But her smile only grew. "Stop bringing up the same argument every few hours," she countered. "Give me something new to work with."

She slid onto his lap at the words, her knees going to either side of his hips and her hands looping around his neck.

"You've worked with that plenty," he grumbled more as she settled over him and ground down.

"So grumpy," she chided, peppering kisses along his jaw.

"I'm being serious, Katya."

She pulled back with a sigh, now visibly irritated. He held her hips, supporting her weight and helping her stay balanced as her arms dropped to her sides.

"We truly must have this argument again? Fine. What do you propose, Axel? Are you sending Theon by himself so you can stay with me? Are you leaving me here by myself for Bree to find? Is Theon staying and you're going to deal with the Alpha and Beta alone? Which option do you choose?" she demanded.

"I know there aren't any good options," he argued, his own irritation climbing.

"There *is* a good option," she insisted. "It involves the *three* of us going as a united front. It involves showing you are already different from your father and other Legacy by taking a Fae for a wife."

"You're not a fucking bargaining chip to parade around and be used to further an agenda, Katya," he interjected.

"So you would relegate me to a position of being quiet and docile? Doing what I am told and staying hidden from the world?"

"That's not fair. You're pregnant, Kat. If anything happened to you . . ."

She took his face in her hands, forcing him to hold her stare. "Have you considered for one moment that I feel the same? That perhaps I am just as possessive and overprotective as you are? I lost you once, Axel. I refuse to do so again," she said, flames and shadows flickering to life in her eyes.

"Kitten," he breathed.

"I love you, Axel, but in this matter, I am stronger. I have my fire *and* your shadows. Theon has his power."

"And I am nothing," he said, feeling the sting of that statement in his soul.

"No," she insisted, holding firm when he tried to turn away from her. "You are *everything*. And you have knowledge, Axel. You know the Underground better than anyone. Knowledge can win over sheer power if wielded with the same finesse. It is what makes Theon so dangerous; he is a powerful being who covets knowledge. Your worth lies in more than your magic. You taught me that. But if you go into that meeting tomorrow thinking you are less than what you are, they will see it. They will see it, and it will be all they need to see. They will not follow someone who does not believe they aren't the most powerful in the room. Who does not think he is worthy to lead."

"Am I?" he asked, completely vulnerable in front of the one person who could bring him to his knees.

She leaned in so her words feathered across his lips when she whispered, "Axel, you weren't born to live in the dark. You were born to bring your people out of it."

"Gods, I love you," he breathed before his lips were on hers, his hands sliding behind her head to hold her to him.

"What are you doing?" she gasped when he released her.

"Kissing you," he answered, his lips gliding along her jaw.

"I know that," she said, already sounding breathless. "But you . . ." She shook her head before dropping her brow to his. "You keep doing this," she said, her eyes falling closed, but he saw the tears pooling. "You do this and then stop."

"You know why, kitten," he said softly, tucking stray hair behind her ear. "I don't want to hurt you. Ever. And if we . . . I could lose control."

"Then don't kiss me and look at me like you do," she snapped.

By the gods. He loved her feisty side, but this was more than that. Navigating when to push her and when to back the fuck off while she was pregnant had been more than a little challenging. One minute she was upset about orange juice, and the next she was perfectly fine and going about her day.

Or in this case, one minute she was making him feel like he could conquer the Underground, and the next, she was making him feel like an asshole for trying to keep her safe.

"Look at you how, kitten?" he finally asked carefully.

"Like you want something from me, but won't give it to me. It's making both of us miserable. And by Anala, I *need* you to *want* me right now, Axel. I just . . . need," she sighed.

His entire body went rigid, and he took her chin, forcing her face up to meet his gaze. "You think I don't want you, Katya? You think I don't want to touch you, taste you, feel you around me? Because I know what it's like to feel you come apart on my cock, kitten. I think about it all the godsdamn time. You think I don't remember what it's like to worship you?"

"Stop saying things like that," she seethed, and gods, he was a dick because her eyes were clouding with desire just at his words.

"Katya, if I hurt you—"

"I'll burn you and restrain you with your own shadows," she cut in. "Just please—"

"No," he growled, dropping small kisses on one corner of her mouth and then the other.

He felt her shoulders slump, and he knew she wouldn't argue with him about this again tonight, but the word hadn't been meant to stop this.

"You never need to beg me to want you, kitten," he murmured, his voice low and full of the darkness that ran in his blood. "I'm sorry you thought you did."

She sucked in a gasp as she pulled back, amber eyes searching his own. "You're not going to stop?" she asked, and fuck, she was already trembling slightly beneath his fingers.

"Not as long as you promise to stop me if I—"

He let out a soft chuckle as she dragged her fingers lightly down his bare chest before gently shoving him backwards onto the mattress. Then the chuckle turned into a hiss as her hands slid lower, down his abdomen to the waistband of his pants. She was teasing him though, as she moved them back up, sliding them over the planes of his stomach at the same time she repositioned herself.

It was then he realized she wasn't wearing undergarments beneath his shirt.

"Clever kitten," he crooned. "You planned this."

"Knowledge and wit can win over sheer power if wielded with the same finesse," she said breathlessly, moving over him, seeking and searching.

His hands landed on her hips again, helping her keep her balance. "Tell me what you need," he said gruffly, mesmerized as he watched her move.

"I need you to stop protecting me and start needing me in the same way I need you," she answered. "I need to know you love me. That it wasn't an in the heat-of-the-moment decision. That it's not just because I'm carrying your child. That it's not because we were supposed to have a bond." A tear slipped free, even as she continued to move over him, her bare center moving along his hard length over the thin material of his pants. "I need to know you still choose me, Axel."

The last words were a whisper, and they shattered something in his soul. Because she'd tried to tell him. Tried to tell him all of this, and he was so concerned with keeping her safe from him, he'd missed being what she actually needed him to be. He hadn't meant to, but the lessons ingrained in him his entire life had taken over, doing exactly what she'd accused him of. Relegating her to a place of doing what she was told, only he'd convinced himself it was to keep her safe.

Her hand slipped lower again, and he almost let her go. Almost let this new bold side of her slip that hand into his pants and pull him out, but he halted her movements where he still gripped her hips. More tears slipped free, but these were angry tears of frustration.

"You said you wouldn't stop me," she said, the words threaded with defeat and exasperation.

"I'm not stopping you, kitten," he said, gently moving her off him and scooping her up. "I'm controlling the pacing."

"What?" she asked, the irritation morphing into confusion as he deposited her properly onto the bed.

But he didn't answer. He slowly slid his shirt over her body, letting his fingers scrape and drag lightly along her sensitive skin. Watched her chest hitch with a stalled breath at the touch. Felt his own mouth go dry at having her bare skin waiting for him. Taunting him. Testing every bit of his self-control not to taste her blood, although that desire was there. If he hadn't drunk an entire bottle of blood this evening, there was no way he'd be letting himself do this, but she was right. She deserved more than being protected behind closed doors and glass windows.

She deserved to be worshipped.

He said nothing when he pushed his pants down over his hips, kicking them off. Then he crawled in beside her, gently rolling her to her side. She went willingly, this sudden give and take between them more intoxicating than anything. Anticipation of when she'd take control again lingered just beneath the surface, and he loved it.

He loved her, and damn him to the Pits of Torment for ever letting her doubt that.

Lifting one of her legs and spreading her perfectly for him, he nestled in behind her. Her head fell back against his shoulder, a soft moan falling from her lips as she pressed back against his cock.

"This isn't going to slow down anything," she rasped.

"No?" he teased, pressing a kiss just below her ear.

She shook her head, grinding back against him again. "Nothing will slow it down. I'm too close. I've been . . ."

"I know, kitten," he whispered, running his nose along her jaw and down her neck. Breathing her in.

Then he let his fangs scrape the barest amount along her throat, and she froze.

"Axel . . ."

"I won't," he rasped, doing it again. "I won't unless you let me. And not until I'm sure I can control it."

She was silent long after he pulled back, running his fingertips down her bare arms, back up, along the side of her full breast. Feeling the gooseflesh he left in the wake of his touch.

"After the babe comes," she finally breathed.

"Gods, you're fucking perfect," he murmured, gently kneading her breast in his palm, pulling another moan from her that went straight to his cock. "Are you throbbing yet?"

"Wh-what?" she gasped as he plucked at her nipple.

"I can feel how wet you are," he said, rocking his hips against her ass.

"But if you're not throbbing here," he continued, sliding his hand down her stomach and brushing his thumb along her clit, "I have some work to do."

"Please, no," she whined. "Just fuck me."

"Such filthy words, kitten," he chided, and she let out an honest-to-the-gods growl. "I'm not going to just fuck you, Katya," he said, turning serious and pressing a kiss to the juncture between her neck and shoulder. "You said you needed me to prove myself to you—"

"I didn't mean . . ." she panted, her words trailing off as he brushed along her clit again before dragging his hand back up over her stomach and between her heavy breasts.

"You did, and you're right," he said. "So no, I'm not just going to fuck you, Katya. I'm going to worship you. I'm going to feel you, and you're going to know that I am yours and you are mine. In this life and the next." His hips rolled again, his tip nudging at her center but never entering, and her already short breaths quickened even more. "So tell me, kitten. Tell me how to love you."

"I . . . *Axel.*"

His name was a whine as he gently cupped her breast, and her hand flew up to clutch at the back of his neck.

"Yes, kitten?" he said, smiling against her neck as he rolled a nipple between his fingers.

She arched against him. "You love me when you truly see me," she gasped out. "When I'm not just something to protect. When I'm not just a Fae—"

"You were never just a Fae, Katya," he said sternly.

"You make me believe that," she said, panting now and her fingers flexing on his nape. "I need you to trust me to know when I need to be protected."

"I do, kitten. I don't trust myself."

"But *I* trust you, Axel," she said, arching again when he turned his attention to her other nipple. "You love me when you let me help you and don't insist on doing things alone. You love me when you *see* me," she said again.

He paused his ministrations, and she turned her head, letting him capture her lips. She was the one who demanded entrance with her tongue, and he gladly let her, growing impossibly harder with every swipe against the heat of her mouth.

"I hear you, Katya," he said when they were both gasping for breath. "I see you."

Her head fell back against his shoulder again. "You love me when you give me what I need," she said between panted breaths. "And right now, I need you."

He didn't bother saying anything as he slipped inside her. He was done prolonging this as much as she was over it.

"Yes," she moaned at the same time he hissed, "Fuck."

It was the first time he'd been inside her since before he'd handed her over to Tristyn.

Months.

It'd been months of being terrified to properly love what was his. Never again would someone take something from him that wasn't his choice to give. Never again would he be at the mercy of someone else. Not his father. Not Bree. The only one he'd go to his knees for was the female currently taking her pleasure from him, and for her, he'd give away his soul.

He thrust in again, and she hadn't been lying. She was already there, teetering on an edge.

"More," she whined, arching into him and guiding his hand back to her breast. "Touch me, Axel. Everywhere."

No problem there.

His hands roamed, cupping breasts, sliding over hips, brushing along the crease of her thigh. Within minutes she was clenching around him, forcing him to follow her into the depths of ecstasy. She muffled her cry into a pillow while blinding pleasure ripped through him.

He waited a bit for them both to come down before he helped her clean up, and when they were back in bed, his naked body curled around hers, he dropped a kiss to the top of her head. Her breathing had already shifted, and he could swear she was asleep before her head had even hit the pillow.

He skimmed his hand over her belly, holding his palm flat. He could hear the babe's heartbeat, the rhythm strong and steady.

And then there was the smallest of flutters beneath his hand.

"Kat?" he whispered.

"I know," she murmured, clearly not as asleep as he'd thought she was. "You could have felt him a while ago."

"You didn't say anything."

"I tried," she said around a yawn, pressing back into him. "You were too . . . consumed. You wouldn't talk to me."

"Never again. I promise."

She hummed, pressing even farther back into him as she slipped into a truly deep sleep. He meant those words. Meant that promise.

And as he slipped into dreams of his own, he made another promise. This one to his unborn son.

He promised him he would see the stars.

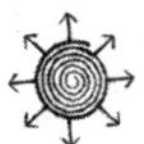

He kept his head held high as the doors of the make-shift throne room thudded shut behind them. Katya's hand was clasped in his where she was to his left, while Theon stood to his right. But while Theon was dressed in his usual suit and tie, Axel had opted for something a touch more casual. He'd ditched the suit coat and tie, wearing only black pants with a black button-down, leaving the top two buttons undone. Something to show he wasn't here as a Legacy to lord over them, but that he was still someone to reckon with. And the female at his side?

Gods, Katya was stunning in a black dress that hugged her figure and accented her belly, eliminating any possible doubt. Long sleeves and a high neckline that reached to her chin may have hidden flesh, but the deep slits of the sides that went to the tops of her thighs made up for it. Her flat sandals were gold with various colored gems along them, and the band on her finger shimmered in the low lighting of the room. She'd piled her ebony curls atop her head, a few of them framing her face, and if anything, he wanted this meeting over with so he could take her home and have a repeat of last night.

None of them faltered as they strode to the front of the room, stopping before the chairs that were clearly meant to portray thrones. They stopped as one, none of them even so much as dipping their chins as they met the stares of the Alpha and Beta.

The Beta was the first to speak, her chin propped in her manicured hand. A nail filed to a sharp point tapped her chin as she said, "I don't know if you are aware of this, Theon, but this is your brother. Not our missing Shifter prince."

Without missing a beat, Theon said in a tone that betrayed nothing, "It appears I didn't need your assistance after all. I always find a way to get what I want, Giselle."

Giselle's light grey eyes narrowed on him, her wine red hair swaying above her collarbone. "Here I thought this was going to be a cordial visit."

"It certainly can be," he answered, hands sliding into his pockets. "I suppose that's up to the two of you."

"Enough of this," Kylian cut in harshly. "You do not get to disrespect us in our own house, Arius Heir."

"I have done no such thing, and I won't need to as long as we can have a . . . productive discussion."

"About?" the Alpha ground out.

"Allegiances," Axel said, taking over for Theon.

His brother was here as support, but these needed to be his negotiations. Theon had offered to take over, and Axel could tell it had taken all his self-control not to do just that. But Theon's place wasn't in the Underground; this was Axel's domain now. He needed to earn their loyalty.

"We are loyal to the Arius Kingdom, of course," Giselle said in her ever-sensual lilt. "Where else would our loyalties lie?"

"You are loyal to the Arius Kingdom because you are forced to be, but I am not speaking of the Lords and Ladies who leave us to rot in the dark," Axel replied.

"Us?" she asked, her full lips tilting up into a wry smile. "I did hear a rumor you had joined us for good, young . . . vampyre, is it now?"

"It is," he said without so much as a wince. "So now I ask again, where does your allegiance lie?"

"Surely you are not asking us to turn against your family?" Kylian said, arching a brow, but Axel had spent enough time with them to know he was pushing for Axel to reveal his hand.

"Maybe not today," Axel said with a shrug.

That had both the Alpha and the Beta sitting up straighter.

"Explain," Giselle hissed. Gone was her lilt. Instead she sounded like the giant python she preferred to shift into.

"If anyone could negotiate with them about us being allowed to see the sky, I would think it would be a familial relation," Axel said. "I will not be relegated to the dark the rest of my days, and I certainly won't raise a child who never knows what the fucking sun is."

Each word grew shorter and darker. He might not have his shadows anymore, but he was still a godsdamn St. Orcas. He'd still been raised to command a room. Still been prepared to rule. He'd hated his father for it, but fuck him to the After and back, he'd been raising him for exactly this. Now he'd take all those lessons and use them, just not in the way his father had planned.

Both of their eyes flicked to Katya, where she still held his hand, their fingers intertwined. But while Kylian's gaze lingered on her belly, it was Giselle who said, "We'd heard you had taken a bride, but I didn't truly believe it until you walked in here with her." She settled back in her chair, once again resting her chin on her palm. "A St. Orcas son taking a Fae as a wife. Whatever did your father say? Or is that why you were sentenced here in the first place?"

His lip curled back, baring his fangs. "I wasn't sentenced here," he snarled. "I came here willingly."

She huffed a sharp laugh. "Oh, you naïve thing. No one comes here willingly."

"Naïve?" Axel repeated, stepping forward. He released Kat's hand, but she moved with him. His brother, however, stayed back, letting him do this on his own.

It should have terrified him. Theon was always the one to take care of him. To shield him. But maybe they'd both finally learned that it couldn't always be that way. That eventually he needed to find an identity outside of the family. Outside of Luka and Theon. And Theon needed to let him.

But he wasn't alone.

Not as shadows slowly drifted across the floor, threads of flame weaving among them.

The Alpha and Beta were both wide-eyed, and Kylian's knuckles were white where they clutched the arms of his chair as he said, "The babe is an Arius Legacy."

"The babe is a St. Orcas," Kat said, chin held high. "And is currently next in line after Theon."

"That means nothing," Kylian said. "The Arius Heir will have an heir of his own. He already has a Match."

Axel felt Theon's power swell at the words. It was subtle, but he knew his brother's magic when he felt it. Knew his brother was working to keep it leashed.

"You can take that chance," Kat said. "But everyone knows that even if that is the case, Theon and Axel are close. You truly think Theon will allow his nephew to remain here? That he won't *negotiate* when he takes the Arius throne? And whose side do you wish to be on when that time comes?"

"You are a clever little thing, aren't you?" Giselle said, studying them both with newfound interest.

"What do you wish of us?" Kylian asked.

"Your allegiance," Axel said. "I'm sure you have heard whisperings of Bree's plans. I wouldn't even be surprised if she had already been here asking the same thing of you I am."

Neither the Alpha nor the Beta moved or gave any indication that what he'd said was true, but he knew it was. While they'd been holed up putting together their plans over the last week, Bree had been planning this coup for decades, if not centuries. Fuck, the Shifters could even be part of it, but he had to try. For Kat. For their son. He cared more for these people than Bree ever would. She'd made it clear she wanted all of Devram, and the Underground was just her stepping stone.

"If she enacts her plans and we are forced to stand against her, I want assurance you will be on our side," Axel continued.

"On the possibility of you negotiating our freedom with your brother someday *if* he holds the Arius Kingdom throne?" Kylian said with a scoff. "That could be decades from now, and with the way the kingdoms are divided at this moment, the Arius Legacy might very well not even have a kingdom in the coming days."

"And what has Bree promised you?" Kat asked. "Power? Freedom? You think she will give you any of what she takes? You will be in no better position than you are now."

"We will always answer to someone," Giselle said. "Whether it be a Lord, a god, the stars themselves. We will not be faulted for choosing our alliances to ensure the best for our people. So what is it, exactly, that you are offering?"

"A choice," Axel said. "Something rarely given to anyone in Devram. You're right. I can't guarantee a godsdamn thing, but I can vow to never stop trying." He pulled a small knife from his pocket, slicing the blade along his palm and letting his blood drip to the floor. "Whether or not you join me, I vow to never stop fighting for the freedom of people who don't deserve to be locked away in the dark. You are a threat to everything they have built. They know that. Bree knows that. She wants to use you for it; I want us to fight for the freedom to simply live among them. Not as beings beneath them, but as people worthy of that simple right."

"Under your rule, then?" Kylian interjected.

"I have no desire to rule," Axel said. "But I will certainly help lead if I am asked to fight for justice, and I'll pursue it even if there's no one at my side. I've spent more days these past years in the Underground than I have with my family. And yes, I was forced to at my father's hand, but I wouldn't trade it either. Because I've seen what they fear. A people capable of changing fate if not kept in cages.

"I don't require an answer today. You know where to find me," he said, once again taking Kat's hand as he turned to walk away. He'd said all there was to say, and he wouldn't beg, just as he'd never beg at Bree's feet. Never again.

"What was the purpose of bringing your brother here for this exchange?" Giselle called after him. "Intimidation?"

Axel paused, looking back over his shoulder. "No, actually. He has his own matters to discuss with you, and until I know where your loyalty lies, I don't suppose I have any reason to intervene on your behalf, do I?"

Her eyes went wide as they snapped back to Theon. Axel didn't know what business Theon had with them. His brother had only asked him to trust him on this, and he would explain everything after the day was done. Axel had agreed. His only request was that Theon didn't use coercion to force them to agree to an alliance. An alliance made by force wasn't an alliance at all, and it would break at the first test. He needed the Shifters to *choose* this. True loyalty was born of choice, but in the end, he was still a St. Orcas. He was still death, but he was resourceful in a way his brother never would be, because he'd been forced to survive here long before he'd been forced to hide here.

He was still a villain; the Shifters could decide if he was going to be theirs.

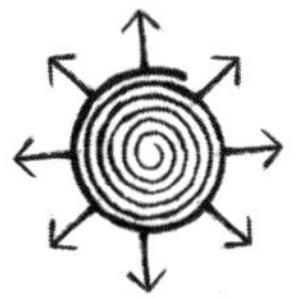

11
THEON

The doors hadn't even finished closing behind Axel and Kat before Giselle said, "Our bargain still stands, Theon. Bold of you to come here for something more when you haven't even fulfilled your other obligation."

"As already discussed, it turns out I didn't need your bargain anyway," he replied. If there was any other piece of furniture in this room, he would have sat down, but they kept it sparse on purpose, forcing their visitors to stand before them while they lounged in their wannabe thrones.

"Yet a bargain Mark remains," she said, relaxing in her seat and crossing a leg over the other.

"It does," he agreed, sliding his hands back into his pockets. "And I will honor it. I will continue to look for this missing Shifter and report any of my findings, even though I no longer require the information bargained for to find my brother."

"I know there is nothing benevolent about a Legacy," Giselle drawled, tilting her head as she watched him. "So what shall be the cost?"

She wasn't wrong, and he had come here with a purpose.

"I still require the location of my father's holdings in your District," he answered.

Kylian scoffed. "Then the bargain stands."

"It does not," he answered. "The bargain was worded specifically that information would be provided to find my brother. The fact that I need the same information does not affect the terms of the bargain in the least."

"We have the leverage here, Theon. Not you," the Alpha said with a cold sneer. "You are not in a position to be setting terms."

"That's where you're wrong," Theon said, finally letting his power out. He'd been holding that darkness in, keeping it locked down while his brother did his own bargaining. "I did not come here on my brother's behalf. Your dealings with him are separate from your dealings with me. Although his wife spoke truth, I will be the Lord you will eventually deal with. But you were also correct," he continued, moving a few steps closer. "The timing of that inevitability is unclear. It could be tomorrow. It could be several decades. Unfortunately, the Seers of the realm seem to be in disagreement about that."

"I am failing to see how any of that is leverage," Kylian said, the temple of the shaved side of his head resting on his fist.

"That is not my leverage."

Kylian's brow arched in a silent command to continue.

Theon only smiled back—cold, dark, and wicked. "My leverage is being the most powerful in this room."

Before either of them could move, let alone shift, his power had them wrapped up tight and secured to the chairs they both loved so much. Giselle gasped when his power squeezed tighter, winding up her throat and pressing on her windpipe. They may be stuck in their human forms, but his shadow wings were flared wide behind him. Kylian's eyes had shifted to feline pupils, and Theon held his stare knowing his own eyes were wholly black.

He ignored Giselle's outraged whimpers, but they all knew what was happening here. Theon knew how the Shifters worked. Anyone could challenge the Alpha and Beta for their positions. The beings were wild and untamed after all, and they followed many of the ways of their animal kin. The strongest one held the title. Theon was just making sure they remembered who that person truly was in a way they would understand.

Kylian lowered his eyes, then his chin in submission, but Theon still didn't release him or his mate. Not until he had what he came for.

"Tell me where the house is, Kylian," Theon said, the calm order promising pain if denied.

"I can't," the Alpha answered tightly. "But release Giselle, and I will tell you what I can."

Theon laughed. "You think I will release her only to find a snake at my throat? I think not. Tell me what you can, or she will find the little bit of air I am allowing her suddenly unavailable."

"We don't know where the holdings are," Kylian spat. "We have an idea, but—"

"If you don't know where it is, how were you planning on fulfilling your end of the bargain?" Theon interrupted.

"As you just reminded us, our side of that bargain involved us giving you information to find your brother. It did not specify the exact location be disclosed."

"You fuckers," he snarled.

"You were so distracted with Blackheart and your absent Source, you let yourself be taken advantage of. That is no fault of ours," Kylian growled back. "It is the way of Devram, Arius Heir. Even those of us in the Underground know that."

Theon yanked on his power, pulling Kylian from his seat and forcing him to stand where Axel had just stood. Then he casually walked around him and climbed the steps to the makeshift dais, sitting in his chair and staring down at the Alpha. "New plan, Kylian," he said, resting his temple on his fist and mirroring the male's earlier pose. "Tell me some information worthy of saving the Beta's life, and make it fast. I don't have time to waste on games and tricks."

"Your Source is still here," the Alpha said tightly, and that was the very last thing he'd expected the male to say. Kylian must have mistaken his shocked silence as misunderstanding though, because he added, "One of my guards reported hearing you and Axel discuss the female leaving the realm on your way here. You believe she is gone; she is not."

"I told you not to lie to me," Theon said, Giselle's high-pitched whimper the only indication of his growing irritation.

"I'm not lying to you," Kylian insisted, trying to lurch forward, but Theon's power held him tight in its grasp. "There have been inquiries from the kingdoms. You know they all have their own spies here. She was seen at the destruction of the Pantheon by the rulers themselves. A handsome bounty is being offered for her whereabouts."

Theon sat quietly, letting that information simmer and trying to decide if he believed it or not. The gods help him if it was true, and Luka hadn't taken her from this realm.

But also, the gods help *them* if Tessa had truly brought the Pantheon to ruin.

"And my father's holdings?" Theon asked, deciding to debate the merits of the prior information when he wasn't in the middle of negotiations.

"I cannot tell you where they are," the Alpha said again. "We are paid coin, but it's never directly from him. And we have our suspicions about the area, but nothing we've ever been able to substantiate. We suspect wards."

"And the suspected area?"

"The northwest part of the District. Near the border."

Of course it would be near the border of the Charter District. His father would never stray too far from his own safe territories.

Pushing to his feet, Theon released both the Alpha and the Beta. Kylian lunged for Giselle as she leapt for Theon, rage emanating off the female in a palpable wave. But Kylian pulled her back into his chest, murmuring low in her ear while Theon paid them no mind, only buttoning his suit jacket before straightening his shirt cuffs.

"This did nothing to help your brother," Giselle spat.

"Our dealings have nothing to do with my brother," Theon said. "He has asked me to stay out of his . . . confrontations in the Underground."

"Then why are you here with him?"

"I thought he made that clear. I had my own purposes for meeting with you," Theon answered, striding for the door. But he stopped beside them, looking them each in the eye as he added, "But should he summon me for aid, I will answer. Consider whose side you wish to be on should that happen when you deliver your decision of allegiance to him."

His footfalls echoed in the room as he continued making his way to the exit.

"We will remember this encounter, St. Orcas," Kylian called after him.

"Please do," he answered, not even bothering to turn back to them. "It will serve you well in the future."

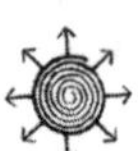

"Tell me again how attacking the godsdamn Shifter leaders isn't going to affect their decision," Axel said, descending the stairs back into the living room.

Theon was waiting for him, holding out the glass of whiskey he'd poured while taking a sip of his own.

"We already discussed this extensively over dinner," he answered, Axel snatching the glass from his hand and downing half of it in one gulp. "Where's Kat?"

"Asleep," Axel answered, dropping unceremoniously onto a sofa. "She'll never admit it, but this was a lot for her today."

He'd changed while he'd been upstairs, now in sweatpants and a

Chaosphere tee, while Theon was still in his suit pants and shirt. Granted, he'd lost the tie, and his shirt was unbuttoned.

Theon took a seat on the other end of the sofa, crossing an ankle over his knee and resting his drink on the sofa arm. "How has she been feeling?"

His brother swiped a hand down his face. "She's . . . strong. Her moods can be unpredictable, but she's fucking strong, Theon. She did the first half of this alone, and I don't have experience, but even I know that Fae and Legacy pregnancies are brutal."

"It'll get worse," Theon added. "As the babe and his power grow. She needs to rest."

"Yeah, well, tell her that," Axel grumbled, glancing over at him. "What?"

He'd caught Theon with a small smile on his lips, watching him. "It's odd to think about, isn't it? You, the younger heir, married with a child on the way. More than that, you're married to someone you love and truly care for. Not a Match forced upon you for the sake of continuing our bloodline and maximizing power. But something pure and . . . I'm happy for you, Axel."

"This isn't exactly what I pictured though, you know?" Axel said, his gaze fixed on his drink as he toyed with the glass. "No powers. A vampyre. Hiding in the Underground, trying to keep my wife and unborn son from a power-hungry centuries old Night Child."

"Same game, different location and different players," Theon said grimly.

"Yeah, I suppose you'd know all about it with Tessa. Minus the child part."

They both fell silent, several seconds ticking by before Theon said, "Kylian said there are rumors she's still here. In Devram. That she never left."

"Wouldn't you be able to feel her down your bond?" Axel asked, bringing his drink to his lips once more.

"It's too broken," Theon answered, knocking back the rest of his own liquor. "The three of us . . . We're too damaged by what this world has turned us into. Products of a realm run by the same power-hungry villains. Pawns in the centuries' old games of the gods."

"Would you have been able to handle it in the end?" Axel asked. "Sharing the bond with Luka? Inevitably sharing *her* with Luka?"

"I handed a world over for destruction for her," Theon said, watching the ice slowly melt in his glass. "In the end, it has nothing to do with what I want, but what she needs. But even that . . . I think in the end, it wouldn't be the same without Luka. The three of us . . ."

"Balance each other out," Axel finished for him. "Take one away, and the whole thing implodes."

"Yeah," Theon murmured, thinking over those words.

Take one away, and the whole thing implodes.

"At least the co-dependency between you and Luka serves a purpose now," Axel added.

Theon's head snapped up, finding a smirk on his brother's face.

"Dick," Theon muttered, flicking his glass in Axel's direction and letting the ice cubes fly towards him.

Axel batted them away with a laugh, and it was strange to hear it. It'd been far too long since they'd just sat and talked. If Luka were here, it'd be just like old times, plotting and scheming into the late hours of the night.

Several minutes had passed, a comfortable silence settling over them, when Axel broke it, saying, "So about this property you felt the need to torture our potential allies over . . ."

Theon sighed, knowing this conversation needed to happen. He wanted to wait until after they'd met with the Shifters so Axel could be wholly focused on his task while they were there.

Getting to his feet, Theon set his glass on the side table and retrieved the liquor bottle. He didn't bother refilling their empty tumblers, instead opting to take a pull straight from the bottle before passing it to Axel.

"This doesn't bode well," his brother muttered before taking a drink of his own.

"Cressida showed up at Arius House before I came here," Theon said, reclaiming his seat.

"Ah," Axel said, tipping the bottle up again before handing it back to Theon. "And you're going to tell me you killed her for her treason and her part in trying to kill Tessa."

"I wish that was what I was telling you," he replied grimly, taking another drink before resting the bottle on his knee. "She made a compelling argument as to why I couldn't kill her."

Axel slowly turned to look at him. "Which was?"

"That killing her would kill my mother," he said bluntly, not knowing any other way to say it. "My true mother."

Axel blinked once. Twice. His mouth opened and shut a few times before he finally said, "And you believed her?"

"Again, she made a very convincing argument," Theon replied before proceeding to fill him in on the conversation, what Cressida claimed, and where he suspected the female was if it was true.

"You're telling me I was being held somewhere with your *mother* when I was lost to blood lust?" Axel said, both hands going through his hair. "You're telling me we're not actually brothers?"

"No," Theon said firmly. "We *are* brothers. Even if we only share a father, we *are* brothers. The same way Luka is our brother."

"Yeah, but . . ." Axel pushed to his feet, starting to pace and stretching his neck from side to side.

Without a word, Theon got up and went to the kitchen, returning with a small glass of blood. The relief on Axel's face was tangible as he took it, and Theon had to give him credit for not drinking the whole thing at once.

Theon gripped his shoulder, squeezing it tight and keeping him in place. "You are my brother, Axel. This changes nothing, but I do need you to know that when I am able, I will kill Cressida."

Holding his stare, Axel swallowed thickly and nodded. "I understand, Theon. She's a threat and a liability. To everything and everyone."

"You won't hate me for it?"

"We all know she wasn't motherly," he answered, some of the tension leaving him as he absorbed the initial shock of the information. "Sure, she favored me, and now we know why, but she wasn't . . . I'll feel *something*. I don't know what it is yet, to be honest, but I won't hate you for it."

Theon nodded, squeezing his shoulder once more before returning to the sofa and picking up the bottle of whiskey.

"So did they tell you then? Where this house is?" Axel asked, nursing his glass of blood.

"Kylian said they don't know. There are wards or some shit," he answered with a sigh. "They have suspicions I can look into, but there might be something more pressing."

Axel arched a brow in question, and Theon was almost more anxious to circle back to the topic of Tessa than he'd been to discuss Cressida, considering how he'd reacted to news of Tessa when he first got here.

"I need to look into this claim of Tessa still being here. That she never left Devram," he said.

"Rumors are rampant in the Underground, Theon. Doesn't make them true. You know that."

"I do, but again, when there is a compelling argument—"

"You overthink and don't sleep and become unnecessarily obsessed? *Especially* when it involves Tessa?"

"Fuck off, Axel."

He shrugged, gesturing to the liquor bottle. "Maybe instead of thinking tonight, you should drink the rest of that, and just . . . not think. For once in your godsdamn life."

If only it worked like that.

"But I know you're not going to do that," Axel sighed. "So what's the plan here, Theon?"

"I need to leave the Underground for a bit. Find out if it's true. I'll get you more rations while I'm gone too," he added.

Axel nodded but remained silent.

Theon hesitated before saying, "I know you're going to, but know that you don't have to stay here, Axel. We can find someplace for you and Kat to stay that isn't . . . here."

Axel huffed a derisive sound. "As it stands, if I leave here, I'll be in hiding. Me, as a Night Child. Kat, as soon as it's realized whose child she's carrying. At least here, we don't have to hide. And I know you don't know the people of the Underground well, but the vast majority of them don't deserve to be shunned away from the rest of the world simply because they exist. Yes, there are the truly wicked who deserve to be locked up, but you know where most of those people are? In the kingdoms. Sitting on advisory boards and on the seats of power themselves."

Theon tapped his fingers on the sofa arm, staring up at his brother, into emerald eyes that mirrored his own. Silent seconds ticked by, turning into minutes.

Axel was just finishing the last of his blood when Theon said, "So we topple the whole godsdamn thing."

His brother choked on the blood, coughing for several seconds before he could get out, "I'm sorry, but it sounded like you just said you wanted to upend the entirety of Devram."

"You just said the people who deserve to be locked up are running everything. For the most part, the people of the Underground are innocent. Many of them were born here. Generations of families who have known nothing else. And out there? It's the same."

"Says the male who just put on a power display to get what he wants from the Shifters," Axel said flatly.

"To get necessary information."

"For personal gain."

"Fair point," Theon muttered. "But if what Cressida said is true, we do need to find her, Axel. Why was Valter hiding it? He does nothing without purpose. There is an entire half of my lineage I know nothing about."

"If you find Tessa, you can ask her how that feels."

"Gods, you're snarkier since becoming a vampyre," Theon muttered.

Axel flipped him off, setting the drained blood glass next to the empty whiskey tumbler. "I'll follow you on this, Theon," he said. "But I have conditions."

It was Theon's turn to arch a brow. Axel had never been so . . . dominant. He could command a room, sure, but always in answer to an order he'd been given. This was different. This was a male who had found something worth fighting for. This was a male who found himself with something to lose. This was a male who was going to command a room not because of his last name or the power that had once run in his veins, but because he was going to be worthy of the loyalty of the people who followed him.

"Name them," Theon said.

"You keep us in the fucking loop. None of this waiting to fill us in until you have every minute detail figured out. You tell us information as you learn it," Axel said, crossing his arms and staring down at him.

"I can agree to that."

"You can't upend an entire system on your own. You have to include us, and you can't be an arrogant asshole about it."

"Anything else?" Theon gritted out.

"When hard decisions need to be made, we make them together and for the betterment of all the people we're fighting for, not just one. Not just me or Luka or Tessa. We don't sacrifice entire populations for one person, Theon," Axel said pointedly.

"You wouldn't do the same for Kat and your unborn child?"

A muscle feathered in Axel's jaw. "You're right. I would," he finally conceded. "But that doesn't make it right. We can't deem entire people as less valuable simply because we don't know them as intimately. We protect those we believe to be our responsibility, and if we do this, Theon? They are *all* our responsibility."

Silence fell again, and after a few minutes ticked by, Axel rapped his knuckles once on the end table before heading to the stairs, presumably to join his wife in bed.

"Think on it, Theon. Tell me before you leave in the morning," Axel said.

"Who said I'm leaving in the morning?"

"It's Tessa," he answered. "I'm surprised you're not already gone."

He waited until his brother was halfway up the stairs before he called out, "Axel?"

He paused, looking back. "Yeah?"

"Purpose looks good on you."

The smallest of smiles tipped on the corner of his mouth. "Get some sleep, Theon. Apparently, we're going to start a godsdamn revolution."

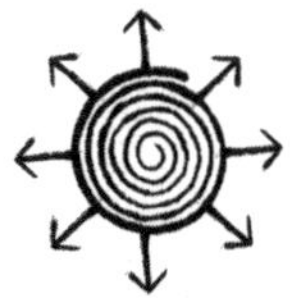

12
EVIANA

Sky-blue eyes slammed into her the moment she entered the tiny room above the tavern they'd been staying in the last several nights. Corbin was downstairs waiting for the food they'd ordered, while Eviana had come back upstairs to pack up their few things. As soon as they were done eating, they were going to be on their way.

They'd made it over the border and a few miles into the Serafina Kingdom before Corbin's power had started to give out. It was exactly what they'd expected given he was having to expend more to keep them dry and fight the current. They'd slowly come to the surface, doing their best to watch the shoreline and make sure they weren't spotted. Then they'd all donned sweatshirts with deep hoods to hide their faces, walking until they came to a decent-sized city. Passing two small towns along the way, they kept moving. Gossip spread like wildfire in small towns. No, they'd needed a small city large enough that they wouldn't be noticed. Where they could easily slip to the seedier parts of the city and bribe someone for silence, room, and board so the two could recover their power reserves. For a moment, she'd thought she was going to have to figure out a way to drag them up the two flights of stairs because they were so exhausted. If she could feel anything anymore, she probably would have felt guilty for making them expend their power then walk for hours. They both collapsed onto the only bed before she'd even shut the door. Lange had slept for two days straight. Corbin had slept for four.

And she'd sat in this tiny room, in a chair next to the window, planning their next moves.

They'd stayed a few extra days to allow them to recover as much as possible. There was still a ways to go to get to the Dreamlock Woods, not that the males knew that yet, and once they got there, they'd need every bit of that power they'd just spent the last days restoring.

"Where's Corbin?" Lange asked tightly.

"Waiting for our food," she answered, already striding for her pack.

"You left him down there alone?"

"Can he not handle retrieving food and bringing it up the stairs?"

"That's not what I mean," he gritted out, standing from the bed.

For the first time since this had started, Eviana felt a trickle of . . . something. She didn't know what, but Lange was imposing as he towered over her. His eyes were narrowed, pale hair falling into his face, and the air in the room stirred, despite the window being closed.

"I don't know what the worry is then," she replied, turning back to her packing. "Unless you know something I don't?"

She waited for him to answer, but he said nothing. She wasn't surprised, but she was disappointed. Or perhaps more irritated than anything.

"If you're packed, you should pack his things," she said, double and triple checking all the various weapons she'd stolen. "We leave the moment—"

"I'm going to help Corbin," he said tightly, and she spun, finding him already striding out the door.

Interesting.

Maybe she didn't need to be disappointed after all.

Zipping her pack shut, she hoisted it onto her back. Then she finished packing Corbin's few things before picking up the packs Lange had left behind. If her suspicions were correct, they wouldn't be coming back up here.

She took her time descending the stairs, but Lange grabbed her arm, dragging her out the door and into the small alley where the entrance to the rundown establishment was. He shoved her up against the wall, no one around to pay them any mind. Even if there was, no one would do anything, but all Eviana could think about was the casual way he touched her without thought. No one touched a Source. The sensation was jarring.

"What did you do?" Lange hissed, mere inches from her face.

"I don't know what you're talking about," she replied calmly, holding his stare.

"Bullshit," he spat, shoving her lightly again before stepping back and running his fingers through his hair. "Corbin is *gone*, Eviana. I know you did something."

"How can you possibly know that?" she asked, her tone bored as she set the other two packs down before straightening her coat and readjusting her pack. Toeing Lange's bag on the ground, she added, "Here. I grabbed these for you."

"Just when I think we're developing some sort of odd trust—"

"Don't ever think that," she interrupted. "The only person you can trust in Devram is yourself, and even then, it's all lies you tell yourself to make it to the next day, hour, or minute."

He stared at her, and she had no idea what he was thinking. To be frank, she didn't care.

"I know you had no one in that fucking house," Lange finally said, each word sharp and filled with a fury she hadn't known he was capable of. But she saw it now. She felt it as the wind picked up with every syllable that fell from his lips. "I don't know what horrors you've experienced. I probably can't even fathom them, and I've faced some pretty fucked up shit, Eviana. But by the gods, you can't assume every single person who crosses your path is out to hurt you. You could have a friend if you tried. We're not the fucking Legacy."

Her head canted to the side at his words, and she didn't know what he saw on her face, but he took a step back from her.

"Take that fucked up shit you've experienced, little wind-walker, and multiply it by fifty," she replied, lacking the venom of his tone, but he straightened anyway. "Then do it every godsdamn day for decades. I considered it a good day when it ended with blood on my hands rather than my own blood being spilled. I hoped for the days that found me on my knees rather than on my back. I breathed a sigh of relief when it was Valter whose bed I shared at night rather than another's. You speak of friends? They'll sell you out the moment they believe it will gain them something, even for something as small as extra rations at a meal. Ask me how I know that. Ask me why you were moved to the Celeste Estate. Ask me which of your *friends* knows what you truly are."

He stared at her, mouth pressed into a thin line, until he finally said, "If there's not even an ounce of trust between us, after all these days you've forced us to spend with you, then you're no better than the Legacy who did those things to you."

"You're right," she answered simply. "I'm not. Now, we should go before we're too late to save your lover."

"I'm going to kill you when this is over," Lange muttered, stalking past her and snatching the two packs she'd dropped from the ground. "I'm going to kill you and dump your body in the river and make Corbin bury it in the bottom so not even the fish can eat it and become poisoned."

"Surely you can be more creative than that," she said, having to take two steps to his one to keep up with his long strides.

"Give me time, *bellana*. Give me time," he muttered, stopping for a moment as a gust of wind swirled around them. "Which way do we go?"

"What did the winds tell you?"

"You keep saying that shit—"

"And you keep feigning ignorance," she interrupted. "I would love to hear another delightful monologue from you about the merits of trusting people, but I'm afraid Corbin's life depends on you proving me right."

"A dagger. Multiple stab wounds," he muttered, as he stretched his neck from side to side, summoning another gust of wind.

"I recommend deep into the thigh. It is one of the most painful, but I will stay awake for the repeated stabbing."

"Or in the ass so you feel it every fucking time you sit down," he snarled, turning left and leading the way.

"Much more creative than just killing me and sending me to the bottom of the river."

"You are . . ." He shook his head, never finishing the thought. Instead he became quiet and focused, following silent instructions that only he could hear.

She was pretty sure he didn't know exactly what he was, but she'd guessed he was getting a grasp on his powers now that he'd finally had time to actually sit with them. Selection years were chaotic. It was when Fae were supposed to master their magic, but they were never truly given the chance to discover their depths. Their classes were kept to the basics, and even the advanced courses kept them busy mastering only specific skills. And once they were assigned to their kingdom and duties, they were kept busy in other ways. Why would the Legacy want a Fae to understand what they were truly capable of?

Only those who became sentinels were given that kind of training—other than Sources, of course—and the privilege of that training came with chains of its own. The average Fae didn't know that sentinels were forced to bear loyalty Marks that gave a Legacy complete control over them. Not quite as extensive as a Source, but . . .

Lange had been destined for that life. Valter had already been planning it as soon as he'd learned of the male's heritage. Corbin's fate, on the other hand, hadn't been decided yet. Valter had still been debating what to do with him.

But with days of sitting in the Raven Harbor house, the days in the car, the river, the tavern, she'd given them that time to let their magic breathe. She needed them to tap into all of that power to survive the Dreamlock Woods and what would come after, and if she had to push them to their limits to get them there, then that was what she would do.

Lange started to turn another corner before he was suddenly lurching back and shoving her hard into the wall. She swallowed her cry of surprise, glaring up at him, only to find him glaring at her.

"I am going to ask you this one time, Eviana," he said, his words too controlled. "Did you sell Corbin out to the Serafina Kingdom?"

Shock and dread slithered down her spine, but she showed none of it when she asked, "What?"

"There are Serafina sentinels up and down this entire street," he hissed. "And if I'm right, Corbin is in one of the transport units. So I'm asking you again: Did you sell him out to the Serafina Kingdom?"

"You said you were only going to ask once."

"I swear to every one of the fucking gods—"

"No, I did not sell him out to them," she snapped. "Why would I do that?"

"I don't know, Eviana," he drawled. "I don't know what we're doing, why we're here, or anything else that goes on in that fucked up head of yours."

"This was not what was supposed to happen," she said, ignoring his barbed words. "I paid the male at the tavern to kidnap him and take him to a truck that would take us farther into the kingdom. The coin should have been more than enough to buy his silence. I just needed you to find him so we could sneak into the truck too. None of us want to walk that far and getting the three of us in there would be noticed."

Lange stared at her. He just . . . stared, and then he started laughing, pressing his lips tightly to keep the sound from slipping out.

"Why is this amusing?" she asked. "If Corbin is caught—"

"If?" he said in disbelief around his huffs of silent laughter. "Hate to break it to you, *bellana,* but he's already caught."

That male at the tavern had sold them out.

"That fucker," she snarled.

"Somehow, I know exactly how you're feeling," Lange replied dryly.

"This is not the time for your whining," she replied, shoving up her sleeves. "I need you to take these off."

Lange looked from her to the bands on her wrists, then back to her again. She watched him debate it. Could see him warring with himself.

"If we have any chance of saving Corbin, you have to take them off," she said, lifting her hands a few inches higher.

"You've repeatedly told me not to trust you."

"You shouldn't," she agreed. "But you can trust the winds."

His lips pressed into a thin line. "You keep saying that like you know something, but the winds know everything and nothing."

"The way I see it, you can leave these on me and know for sure you will never see Corbin again. Or you can take these off, perhaps have the same outcome, or maybe have another night with him by your side," she said.

"I have a feeling I'm going to regret this," he muttered, reaching for the band on her right wrist.

"Undoubtedly."

"That's reassuring."

"It wasn't meant to be."

He shook his head, mumbling something she couldn't make out as he slipped the band over her wrist, then did the same with the other.

And Eviana took her first full breath in months.

Her eyes fell closed as she felt her magic rush to the surface. The tips of her fingers tingled, and the power in her soul yanked and thrashed to be set free. She could hear every rustling leaf on the boulevards and feel every root of every tree and flower and everything in between.

Rolling her shoulders back, she opened her eyes to find Lange staring at her, and he made a show of slipping the bands into her pockets.

As if she'd ever let him put them back on her. It would be the last thing he'd ever do.

She slipped past him, peering around the corner. He hadn't been lying. There were dozens of sentinels and at least ten transport units.

"What are they all doing here?" she asked, more to herself than to him as she debated their options.

"They were tipped off we were here," Lange said quietly at her side.

"By who?"

"That I don't know."

"Do you know which vehicle he's in?"

He was silent for several seconds, and she let him concentrate as she watched the sentinels. It wasn't until she saw Lev, Lady Isleen's Source, that true dread set in. If the Serafina Lady was here, they had definitely been discovered. Which she'd anticipated, but she hadn't anticipated the Lady getting here so quickly. She'd thought they'd have more time. A miscalculation on her part.

Unless she sent Lev ahead of her.

Then they might have a chance.

"I don't know which one exactly," Lange whispered, sidling closer to her. It was such an odd sensation to have someone so near that she hadn't been instructed to pleasure or torture. "But it's one in the middle of the bunch, which makes sense. It's fucking surrounded."

"I have a plan," she said.

"I'm afraid to ask what it is."

"The same one from before," she replied. "I'll be the distraction. You find the truck."

"Eviana, no—"

But she was already striding out from around the building they'd been shielding themselves behind. Within seconds she was surrounded, and despite her power straining with the need to protect her, she let them come. Because she was still a Source, and even if she was perceived to be on the run, everyone knew touching her, *hurting* her, without her Master's permission would still result in unfavorable consequences.

"Show your Markings," a sentinel barked, already pulling a set of black bands from his hip.

She showed him the only one that mattered: the Arius symbol on the back of her hand.

"You're to be detained by order of the Lords and Ladies of Devram until your Master can come collect you," the sentinel continued, taking a step towards her.

"*I* will handle her by order of Lady Isleen," came a sharp, low command.

The sentinels stiffened, all eyes staying on her except for the one who had been speaking. He turned as people parted to create a path for Lev to stride through, giving him a wide berth.

Stunningly attractive, as all Sources were, his blond hair was perfectly styled around his arched ears. Sharp features added to his allure, and he wore a wool coat and scarf. While it got warmer the farther south they went, the winter chill still reached them here. Deep blue eyes swept over her, and his lip curled in disgust.

"The Arius whore in our kingdom," he sneered. "My Mistress will be very interested to speak with you before your Master gets here."

"It will be a waste of everyone's time," she replied. "We all know I cannot betray my Master's secrets, no matter how much she tortures me in my dreams."

"Are you going to come with me willingly?" he asked, a dagger of ice forming in his hand.

Eviana glanced at it, unimpressed. "I'm surrounded, Lev. It's not as if I can go anywhere else."

"I'll take her from here," he said, jerking his chin in a command for her to come to his side.

And like the good little Source she was expected to be, she did. She fell into step beside him, and it wasn't anything new. How many times had she walked beside other Sources a step behind their Masters and Mistresses? The new Sources were still figuring it out. She'd watched them gang up on Tessa. She'd watched their pettiness as they shared words with one, only to backstab the same to another. But the Sources of the rulers? They'd shared tables at events for decades at this point. They'd sat in Tribunal meetings and stood behind thrones for hours. There weren't friendships by any means, but there was an . . . understanding that could only come from experiencing many of the same things. It forced a different kind of bond, although one that was just as unwanted. They'd faced horrors together, which is why she wasn't surprised when the moment they rounded a truck and were away from prying eyes, Lev turned to her and looked her over far more carefully.

"What the fuck are you thinking, Eviana?" he hissed.

"Is Maya here?" she asked.

He shook his head. "She sent me to collect you. Something to taunt your Master about. We are to bring you to Sanal."

"Is Valter there?"

"I suspect he will be by the time we get there."

She nodded, clasping her hands in front of her. "Do you know where he is now?"

"If Maya knows, I was not privy to the information, but I cannot be a part of whatever this is, Eviana," he said, sliding his gloved hands into his pockets.

"I understand."

"And if you attempt to escape, I will have to stop you."

"I would expect you to try. I will not ask you to lie to your Mistress, Lev," she said.

"I want to know nothing of your plan."

"I wouldn't tell you anyway."

His smile was flat as he held her stare, then he dropped his voice to scarcely more than a whisper. "I don't know why you think you will not be caught. The punishment for this . . . Will you even survive it?"

"Maybe that's the whole point," she mused. "None of us truly care about survival anymore, do we?"

"I can't help you," he said again.

She only nodded.

"There were reports of two Fae traveling with you. We have one detained."

She said nothing, but she held his stare, telling him everything he needed to know.

His voice a touch too loud, he said, "You'll ride in the transport truck with the other. No use wasting numerous vehicles and sentinels when it's just the two of you." He paused then, and she could only assume Lady Isleen was speaking to him down their bond. "Your third companion. Where is he?"

"Trying to break the other one out," she answered.

"By Serafina," he muttered. "Come on."

She followed Lev past four more trucks before they went to the back of the one in the center, where they indeed found Lange trying to figure out how to open the back doors. She hadn't bothered to tell him the truck was warded and it would be impossible.

"May as well join your friend," Lev said darkly, removing a glove and slicing his palm with his ice dagger. Pressing his bleeding hand to the door, it sprang open.

Corbin sat inside, his eyes going wide when he spotted Lange and Eviana. "Fuck," the male muttered with a sigh.

"In, Fae," Lev barked.

Lange was muttering curses under his breath as he climbed into the back of the transport unit, sitting on the bench seat next to Corbin.

"The unit is warded against magic, so your power will be useless. There are bands in the bins beneath the bench. Have them on before we get to Sanal. If they're not, the consequences will be unpleasant," Lev instructed.

Then he turned to Eviana. "Enjoy the ride. I have a feeling it will be the most luxurious thing you'll experience for quite some time."

"Fuck off, Lev," she snapped, ignoring his outstretched palm and climbing up into the transport unit.

"It's cold back here," Lev said, holding up the glove in his bare hand. Then he tossed it at her feet as she sat opposite Lange. "Stay warm," he added with a sneer.

She held his stare as she made a show of placing her boot atop the glove and grinding it into the unit floor.

Lev smirked, slamming the door shut, and she immediately relaxed, tipping her head back against the wall of the truck and letting her eyes fall closed. She knew the males were watching her, but she didn't care. Not as the transport unit started, everything vibrating around her.

He hadn't taken her pack.

It wasn't until the vehicle lurched forward that one of them broke the silence.

"So we're dead, right? That's how this ends?" Lange said.

Eviana sighed, opening her eyes as she slipped the pack off her back. She bent, picking up the glove. She'd scented the blood immediately, and she turned it over in her hand until she found the smear of red she was looking for.

"It's a possibility, but it always has been," she said, carefully placing the glove in her pack. She wouldn't need it for a while yet.

They were still quite a ways north of the Dreamlock Woods. The transport unit wouldn't go through them. Instead, they would go around the woods, passing by the Serafina Estate on their way to the Serafina Kingdom capital. They still needed to enter the Estate through the woods, but now they could get so much closer. This was actually safer for all of them. It meant less time being hunted by their nightmares.

"And I needed to remove your bands, why?" Lange asked.

"You did *what?*" Corbin demanded, twisting to gape at Lange.

"You'll be grateful you did when we get there," Eviana replied, dropping her head back and letting her eyes fall closed again.

No one said another word for nearly any hour.

"About the stabbings," she said suddenly. "Another good place is the lower back where the kidneys are. Even a Legacy feels the lingering effects for days."

"By Sefarina," Lange muttered, shaking his head and letting it drop back, his eyes falling closed this time.

"Do I even want to know what this is about?" Corbin asked, looking between the two of them.

"No," Lange said, sitting up once more and rubbing at his brow. "You do not."

"Then what's the plan now?" Corbin asked as Lange settled into his side.

"Now we rest up and fill our reserves," she said, flexing her fingers as her power ached to be used. "We're going to need every last bit of them."

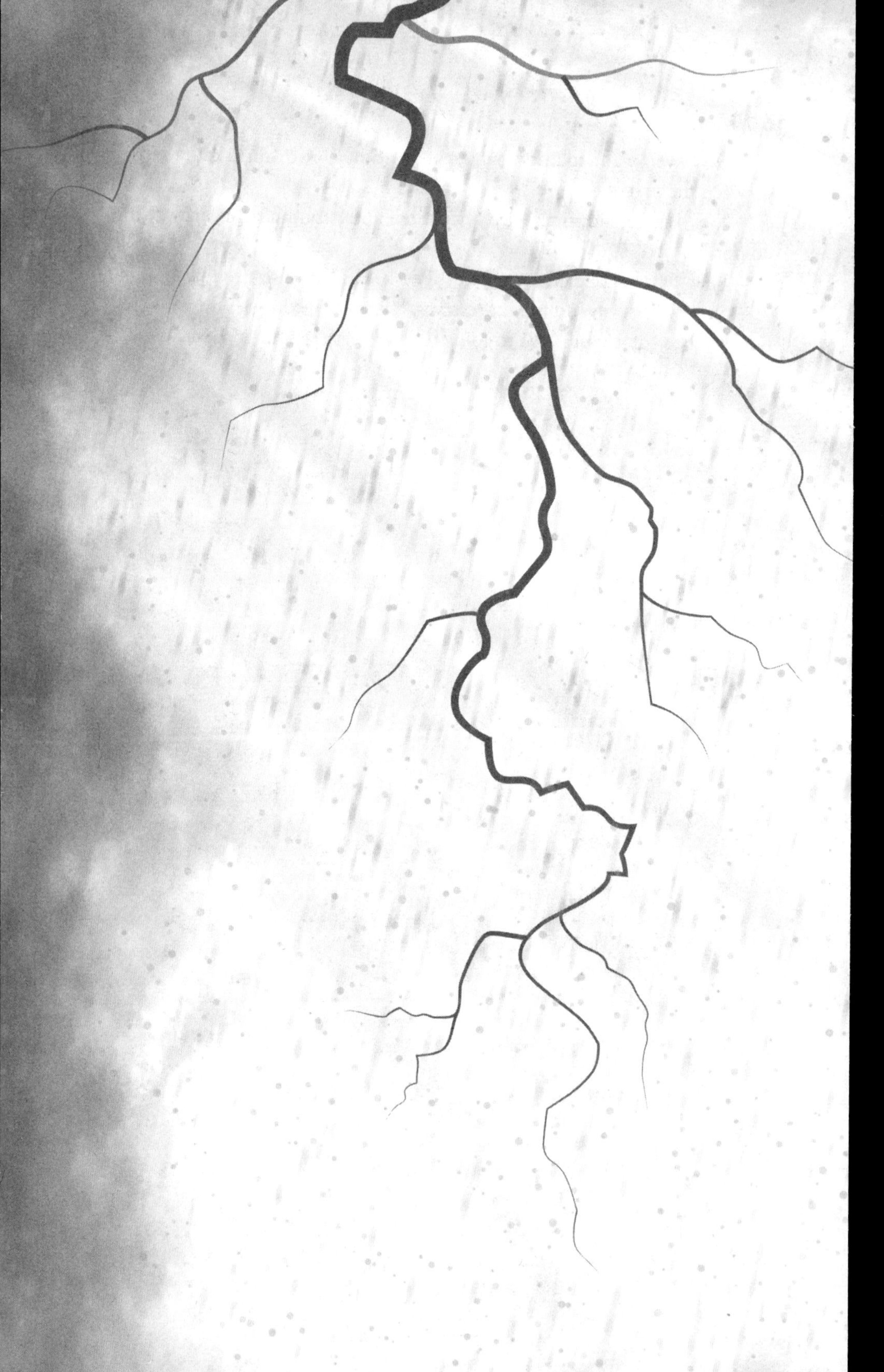

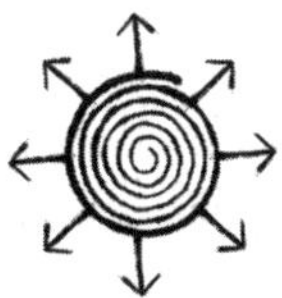

13
TESSA

"Use your hips and your hit will be more powerful."

Tessa spun at the voice, finding Eliza standing in the doorway.

"I've never seen you in here before," the female said, striding deeper into the training room until she came to a stop a few feet away from where Tessa had been throwing punches at a giant bag of sand that was bigger than she was.

"I wait until the room isn't in use," Tessa answered, her hands clenched at her sides. They were wrapped the way Luka had taught her, but it had been quite some time since Luka had trained her. She was just in here trying to avoid falling asleep, and if she was doing that, she may as well continue her training on her own. Which was stupid because she had no idea what the fuck she was doing. She mainly tried to go through drills that Luka had taught her, but if her form was off, there was no one here to tell her.

Until now apparently.

Eliza nodded, pushing her red-gold hair back over a shoulder. The female was in looser pants than normal and a low-cut tank top. Clothing Tessa rarely saw her wear. It felt too . . . modern for the clothes Eliza favored. Despite that, there was still a dagger shoved down the side of her boot.

"Your form is decent enough, but you need to swing more from your hips. Not just your torso. Use your whole body. Your hit will have more force," she said, crossing her arms and jerking her chin.

Tessa stared back at her, unsure of what to say because was she . . . giving her an order?

"Well?" Eliza said irritably.

"Well, what?" Tessa asked.

"Are you going to try it? Or is this a waste of my time?"

"I didn't ask you to come in here," Tessa said, utterly perplexed by this entire interaction.

"Just try it. And don't tuck your thumb," she added.

"Yeah, yeah," Tessa muttered. Luka had drilled that into her as much as he'd drilled her stance into her.

Planting her feet in the proper position, she readied herself, inhaling deeply. Then, twisting from her torso *and* hips, she punched out, keeping the path of her fist straight. And, yeah, all right, there was more force behind it.

"Good," Eliza said. "You learn quick."

Tessa turned back to her, hands dropping to her side. "I'm sorry, but what are you doing here?"

"I brought you something. Or rather, I stole you something. But I hear it's yours anyway, so is it really stealing?"

There was a bright burst of flames that had Tessa twisting away, but when she turned back, the female stood there with a bow in her hand. Memories of the last time she'd held it clawed up from the dark places she'd locked them away, and with them was her magic as her control slipped the smallest amount.

Auryon's bow.

Her bow.

"You stole this?" Tessa said, reaching tentatively for the weapon. "From Luka?"

Eliza nodded. "I'm sure he'll be pissy as fuck when he realizes it's gone, but I've dealt with plenty of dragon tantrums."

Tessa took the bow, feeling the weight of so much more than wood and string as she held it in her hand.

"I don't even know how to use it," she whispered, but gods, her power was buzzing inside her. Frenetic and forceful, it was drawn to the bow in the same way it was drawn to power, and she wasn't entirely sure what to make of that.

"No better time to learn," Eliza said. "We can go outside."

"It's the middle of the night," Tessa argued. "I won't even be able to see anything to shoot at."

"And I'm a fire Fae," the female retorted, lifting a palm where flames sprang to life. Flames that were allowed to breathe and dance and had purpose.

"Tessa?" Eliza asked when she didn't respond.

"Sorry," Tessa murmured, still transfixed on the fire before she shook her head to clear it. "I get . . . Wait, where is Razik? You two are never apart."

The female huffed a laugh. "We are, in fact, often apart. My Court is on one continent; the king he serves is on another."

"That seems inconvenient."

Eliza shrugged. "We make it work. Are we going outside or not?"

Truthfully, breathing fresh air and seeing the sky sounded like the perfect distraction, so Tessa nodded, falling into step beside Eliza as she looped the bow across her chest.

"You are his Source, right?" Tessa asked, keeping her voice low since the rest of the cave slept.

"I am," she answered.

"By choice."

"Yes."

"Why?"

Eliza glanced at her before looking ahead again. "That is a long story."

"Is it because you are his twin flame?"

"No. I actually hated that for quite some time and refused to accept that bond."

Tessa tripped on air at those words. "You . . . What?"

"Razik figured out what we were before I did, but he never pushed for it. He'd experienced someone trying to force a bond on him, and he swore he'd never do that. He . . ." Eliza sighed, the next words sounding pained. "He would have let me go if I had wished for it."

"But you chose him."

"I did."

"And he chose you."

"Obviously."

"And you don't regret it?" Tessa pushed as they stepped into the fresh air.

Eliza was quiet for a long moment before she answered, "No, I don't regret any of it, but that doesn't mean it's right for everyone. Only you can decide if it's the right path for you."

"Right," Tessa murmured, tipping her face up to the sky.

Within seconds, there was a rustle before Roan and Nylah appeared, climbing over the rocky terrain. It was not that they couldn't come inside the cave. They just . . . didn't. Roan appeared in there every once in a while, but for the most part, they stayed outside. Patrolling and guarding, apparently finding her safe enough when inside. But they were always here when she ventured out with Xan.

It was cloudless tonight, revealing all the stars usually kept hidden. The moon was waning though, only a sliver of it visible, allowing the dark to obscure those wanting to stay hidden. A part of her wanted to just sit here and soak it in. It was peaceful, as if a piece of her soul loved the dark and night.

Or maybe it just made her feel closer to him.

It didn't matter in the end. Not as flames erupted in a large perimeter, burning nothing and lighting up the night. The heat warmed her skin, and Tessa wished she was in a tank top like Eliza rather than the fitted long-sleeve training top she wore, even if it did leave her torso exposed.

With a flick of her wrist, another pillar of fire sprang to life, twisting and writhing until it took on the shape of a large and broad male. Then Eliza turned back to her, motioning impatiently to the bow slung across Tessa's chest.

"You can't shoot it that way," the female chastised.

"I know that," Tessa grumbled, her fingers winding into Roan's soft fur while Nylah sat near the perimeter. "I'm not going to be shooting anything without arrows. Auryon always just . . . had some."

"Yeah, I know someone like that too," Eliza said. "I found these though when I was looking for that bow."

Another burst of flames receded, and she held a quiver.

"Where did you find it anyway?" Tessa asked, lifting the bow over her head.

Eliza pulled an arrow from the quiver before setting it aside. "He hid it in one of the narrow passages off the gallery.

"What gallery?"

"The one with all the empty frames on the walls. So maybe not a gallery? I don't know, but it was in a narrow tunnel off that." When Tessa only blinked back at her, Eliza said, "You didn't know about that space?"

"No. I . . ." She trailed off before clearing her throat. "This is only the second time I have been here, and the first time I didn't exactly get a tour. I try not to intrude on his space . . ."

She trailed off again, trying not to think about what had transpired the first time she had been here. It was why she kept herself busy, and she suspected it was also why Xan often took her outside. But now that she was thinking about it, she had to actively work against the onslaught of emotions she was trying desperately to keep locked away. Her magic thrived when she was . . . Well, when she was unbalanced.

"There's no such thing as balanced," she murmured, dragging her fingers along the smooth curve of the bow.

Streaks of her power were left in their wake, curling around the wood before seeming to sink into it. It warmed beneath her touch, and more power rushed from her so suddenly, it took her a moment to wrestle it back into submission.

Tessa's head snapped up, her gaze locking onto Eliza's grey stare where the female was watching her cautiously. "The stars and the realms are obsessed with the balance, but there's no such thing. We are all wasting our time. How do we find something that doesn't exist?"

Eliza seemed to weigh her words before she finally said, "Maybe balance isn't something to be found or fixed or rectified. Maybe balance is something to be created. Maybe *we* get to decide what that balance looks like."

"For the realm? We decide that for everyone? For the spaces in the voids and the stars that cease to shine? For the kings and the forgotten? For the magic wielders and the mortals?"

Each word was more panicked, coming faster and faster.

"That can't be right," Tessa went on, her heart beating too fast. An agitated growl rumbled from Roan where he sat a few feet away, his glowing eyes glimmering brighter with the flames.

"It's not up to one person to decide what balance is for the realms, Tessa," Eliza said. "But you do get to decide what balance is for *you*. Just because the world is trying to tell you what it should look like doesn't make it true. What is balance for me may not be balance for you."

"But you gave in to your balance," Tessa argued. "You accepted a bond you didn't want."

"It was something we both grew to want over time. It wasn't instantaneous like I've witnessed with other twin flame bonds. It's different, and we wouldn't trade that because it's *ours*. We made it what it is, and your balance will look different from what everyone else thinks it should look like. Fuck what others think. It's still a choice. *Your* choice. No matter what this realm has tried to convince you of otherwise. You get to decide what your balance is and who you choose to bring into that balance," Eliza said with such fierceness it had Tessa blinking in surprise as her words rolled over in her mind.

"And the rest of the realms? What does balance ever really look like?" she mused. "Or do we just leave that up to the gods?"

"I don't know that it should be left up to any single being," Eliza said, stepping closer and turning Tessa to face the other way. "I think it is the responsibility of those with the most power to ensure those with the least are cared for and treated the same as those with plenty. It is no fault of a mortal that they were born with no magic in their veins in a realm with Fae or Shifters or others."

"Or a Fae born in a realm ruled by Legacy," Tessa murmured.

Eliza paused for a moment, her gaze flicking to Tessa once more before returning to assessing her form. "Yes," the female agreed. "Or that."

Tessa hummed as Eliza tapped the ground with her toe, showing her where to plant her feet. There was no more talk of balance or stars, kings or mortals. She didn't want to think anymore, so she focused entirely on what Eliza was telling her.

"Stand straight, and don't lean back," she was saying as she adjusted Tessa's fingers on the weapon. "Square your shoulders, keep them directly over your hips, and keep your feet shoulder-width apart." Tessa adjusted slightly before Eliza said, "Good. Now, lift the bow in front of you. Your arm holding it should be mostly straight. Only a slight bend in the elbow. No, that's too much bend," she said when Tessa shifted.

The female stepped forward, straightening her arm more.

"Like this," she said. "You want the bones in your arm to hold the weight when you draw the string back, not your muscles." She tapped her other arm. "We call this one your draw arm. Keep it high when you draw back. A little higher," she said when Tessa pulled back on the string. "At least as high as your nose. When we add the arrow, you want the crease of the elbow on the same level as the arrow or above the line of the arrow at full draw."

Tessa nodded, trying to absorb all the information as Eliza handed her the arrow, showing her how to nock it. She got back into position, a thrill zipping through her at learning this. She didn't know why. She'd never had any desire to shoot a bow, but something about Auryon telling her it was her birthright . . . It made her feel connected to *something*, even if she had no idea who or what that was.

"Pull back on the string," Eliza instructed. "The string should touch the tip of your nose without leaning your head forward or backwards. Stay standing straight and relax."

"I can't relax after everything you just told me," Tessa snapped, irritated when Eliza stepped behind her and tugged on her shoulders, proving she was leaning forward.

The female ignored the retort. "Take a breath and focus on your target. When you're ready, release the string."

Tessa inhaled deeply, trying to force her body to relax. It was pointless. She hadn't felt relaxed in weeks. Her muscles were always tense; her body strung too tight. But she tried anyway, inhaling once more before she released the string, mainly because it was becoming too difficult to maintain the draw.

She heard the arrow whistle through the air as it was released.

And then it hit to the far right. It didn't even touch the flaming target.

"Good," Eliza said, already handing her another arrow.

"Good?" Tessa repeated. "I didn't even hit anything."

"I would have been thoroughly impressed if you did."

"You expected me to miss."

Eliza gave her an incredulous look. "It was your first time shooting a bow. Of course I expected you to miss. To be honest, I'm surprised the arrow even went as far as it did."

"You could have warned me."

"Warned you that you were going to be terrible at this the first time you attempted it? Why did you expect otherwise?"

Tessa pursed her lips, snatching the next arrow from Eliza's hand and nocking it to the string. "Tell me what to fix."

The next two hours went on in the same way. Tessa would shoot until the quiver was empty, Eliza correcting her and giving her tips after every shot, and then they'd go collect the arrows and start all over again. At least she was hitting the target now—most of the time—but never where she was actually aiming.

Eliza held out the quiver as Tessa deposited a handful of arrows she'd gathered before they both continued to search for two that were missing. Even with the fire, there were still areas cast in shadows. And gods, Tessa was *hot* with all these flames. It was like when she slept next to Luka.

Glancing up at the sky as she swiped up another arrow, she turned back to Eliza, finding her with the other missing one. Tessa closed the space, dropping the arrow into the quiver before they turned to head back to the shooting line.

"You have a lot of Marks," Tessa said, because with the female in a sleeveless shirt, she could see them all. Some on her arms, across her chest. There were even a few on her back.

"I do," she agreed.

"What are they for?"

"Some have a purpose for strength and abilities. Some are loyalty Marks to my Court. A couple are bonds."

Tessa nodded, trailing her eyes over them and stopping at the one atop her heart. The same place she bore a Mark.

"I thought there was only one Source Mark in your world," Tessa said.

"There is," Eliza answered, tapping a Mark on her forearm.

"Then what is the purpose of this one?" Tessa asked, brushing her fingers over her own heart.

Eliza stilled, one hand coming up to cover the Mark on her skin before she dropped her hand again. Her hands curled into fists, and Tessa wasn't sure what to do or why the question had elicited such a reaction.

"Not all my Marks were given by choice, just as not all of yours were," Eliza finally answered.

"But I thought you were free there?"

"We are free in that we are not forced to serve another, yes, but we are not free of injustice and moral failings," she replied tightly. "There will always be those who believe they deserve more or are superior simply because of the blood in their veins, the family they descend from, and in some cases, because they have a cock between their legs."

Tessa took an arrow from the quiver that Eliza held out, nocking it to the string. "Then isn't leaving here pointless? You are simply exchanging one realm's problems for another."

"Every realm has problems, Tessa. Just as every kingdom, every family, every relationship has problems. None of them are perfect, but there are those who try harder to thrive despite those imperfections. Widen your feet."

Tessa adjusted her position before pulling the string back.

"Keep your spine straight, including your neck," she added.

Tessa took a deep breath, releasing the arrow. It hit lower than where she was aiming, but at least it had gone straight.

Lowering the bow, she turned to face Eliza. "Do you like stories?"

"What?"

"Stories," Tessa repeated. "Do you like them?"

For whatever reason, the female became very cautious when she answered, "I don't particularly care for them, but I know of one who loves to tell stories."

Tessa took a step forward, excitement coursing through her. "Are they good ones?"

"No. They're dreadful, but a few find them enlightening."

"Oh," was all Tessa said. Then her head tilted. "You will not tell me the story of that Mark?"

"No, she will not," came a dark, lethal voice.

But Tessa paid him no mind, reaching for another arrow as Razik came prowling closer to them.

"It's fine, Raz," Eliza said, although there was something new in her tone. A hint of sadness maybe? "She doesn't know."

"It is not something you need to share if you don't want to," he retorted.

So protective.

She'd had that once.

That was what Tessa thought to herself as she silently placed the arrow on the string.

"It's a Curse Mark," Eliza said, shoving around the dragon who'd planted himself between her and Tessa. "The male I believed to be my father for a time put it there because I was born with fire magic rather than earth magic like he had."

Tessa slowly lowered the bow she had raised. "But you cannot control that."

"As I've already said, my world is not free of injustice and moral failings. It simply looks different there," she replied. "He had plans for me, and those plans were destroyed because of who, or rather what, I turned out to be."

Well, if anyone could understand that, it was Tessa.

"In retaliation, he cursed me with this Mark before he abandoned me. Live or die, I was no longer his concern," Eliza went on. "But he made sure I could not have children of my own to 'disappoint him further,' as he worded it."

Tessa's power was writhing in her soul, and she knew there were streaks of light flickering in her eyes when she asked, "Does he still breathe?"

"No," she answered.

Tessa's gaze flicked to Razik. "He avenged you?"

"I avenged myself," Eliza retorted.

Razik was quiet, his arms crossed over his broad chest, but the glare he was aiming at Tessa told her he wasn't happy this was being discussed.

Too bad for him Tessa didn't care what he thought.

"But you still bear the Mark?" Tessa asked.

"It is forever," Eliza answered, jerking her chin in an order to get back to practicing.

"Perhaps not forever," Razik cut in.

Eliza rolled her eyes as she reached out to lift Tessa's drawing elbow a little higher. "Razik thinks he will find a way to remove it."

"Because you want children?" she asked, glancing at the dragon shifter.

"Because she deserves to make that choice for herself," he replied. "It has nothing to do with me."

That was a valid reason, she supposed. Actually, the reason gave her a new kind of respect for the male altogether.

Inhaling deeply, she released the arrow, and to her shock, it hit just to the right of where she was aiming.

"Good," Eliza said, handing over another arrow. "Again."

Several minutes later, Tessa released the last arrow in the quiver. "I don't understand how Auryon could shoot three of these at a time."

"Agreed," Eliza said around a yawn. "Our Fire Court Second can manage two at a time, but there is another in our world who can fire three. No idea how."

"There is a Huntress in your world?" Tessa asked, looping the bow over her chest while Razik went to retrieve the arrows this time.

"She is not a Huntress," the male answered from across the makeshift archery range. "At least, not fully. We are unsure what she is."

Another thing Tessa could relate to.

Razik was back in far less time than it was taking her and Eliza to retrieve the arrows. He placed them into the quiver as Eliza yawned again.

"You need to rest, *mai dragocen*," he said, with far more gentleness than he ever showed anyone else.

"I know," she grumbled. Turning to Tessa, she asked, "Are you ready to head inside?"

"You two go ahead. I'm going to stay out here a little longer," Tessa answered, Roan reappearing at her side and rubbing along her legs.

"My flames will go out. It will be dark," Eliza said, her brow furrowing.

Tessa clasped her hands in front of her. "Yes, I'm aware."

Eliza glanced up at Razik, uncertainty on her features. "I don't think it's a good idea to leave her out here alone, Raz."

"She's not alone. The two of you haven't been alone this entire time, and I do not mean the wolves," he answered, his eyes darting to the sky.

"Luka is out here," she said in understanding.

He nodded, his hand dropping to her lower back as he guided her inside. "She'll be fine."

Tessa wasn't sure if *fine* was the word to use, but she'd also known Luka had been out there the whole time. With the waning moon, he wasn't visible against the night sky, but she knew. She always knew when they were near, bond or no bond.

So it was no surprise when a giant dragon appeared moments later, settling down on a ledge above her. His glowing eyes seemed even brighter with Eliza's fire gone. They were the only thing illuminating the night now.

"Do you want to hear a story?" Tessa called out as she sank to her knees, the cold earth biting through her thin training pants.

He didn't answer, and she knew he wouldn't.

"In all things there must be balance," she started. "Beginnings and endings. Light and dark. Fire and shadows. But in bids for power and answers to challenges, we are never happy. We always want more and more and more. Guardians were created," she murmured, and she heard him creep closer down the side of the mountain as her voice lowered. This story was more for her anyway. "Maraans were his answer. Hunters were created, and in turn, the Huntresses were brought into existence. And I . . ."

She picked up an arrow, slicing the arrowhead along her palm before she gripped the bow in blood. She'd wanted to be alone for this, and with Eliza gone, in a sense, she was.

"I am both, aren't I?"

Luka roared in warning at the same time she recited the words Auryon had told her. Magic rolled out of her. Threads of light and dark. Glowing golds and silvers. Life and death. It all wound around the bow until she felt like it was a piece of her.

Innate.

Intrinsic.

Hers.

"Tessa, just wait," Luka said, having shifted at some point and landing several feet away. Now he was taking long strides to reach her.

She looked up to find him shirtless, his wings still splayed, and gods, when was the last time she saw him like this? When they spent their time here, forgetting about the world for a few precious hours? But she remembered. Her body remembered. She knew every dip of his abdomen. Knew what his fingers would feel like when they touched her. She remembered when they'd needed to drown in each other because no one else understood.

She remembered what it was like to have him look at her with something other than the hard indifference staring back at her now.

"You do not need to be here, Luka," she said, gracefully rising back to her feet. "I am not your Ward."

"But you will be," he countered.

She shook her head as she murmured, "You still don't see."

"I see just fine, Tessa," he replied, snatching up the quiver as she reached to grab an arrow.

"You do?" she asked in relief.

"I see you out here doing something incredibly reck—"

His words died as she lifted a hand. Her power swirled, and when it receded, she held an arrow between her fingers.

"Tessa," he breathed, and *gods*. There was a reverence in her name that she hadn't heard from him in weeks.

He stepped closer, examining the arrow, because while it looked exactly like the arrows she'd been shooting all night, she knew it wasn't. Knew Luka could feel it was something *other* too.

"What did you do?" he asked, leaning in close to inspect the weapon.

His scent assaulted her, and she could feel his heat, warming her soul in a way no fire ever could.

"Something wild and reckless," she answered.

"How did you do it?"

"I don't know. I never know."

"We'll work on that," he answered, his fingers brushing over hers as he gently took the arrow from her.

"We . . . We will?" she asked, knowing better than to let the hope trying to blossom in her chest bloom.

"Yes. This is another power you need to understand. Need to control," he replied, handing the arrow back to her.

"Oh," was all she said, reaching for the arrow.

"But not tonight. You need to rest too."

"No," she said simply.

No sleeping.

Sleeping made it worse.

So much worse.

"Tessa—"

"In all things there must be balance," she murmured, nocking the arrow before raising the bow. "Beginnings and endings." She took aim at a dead tree in the distance. The trunk was half gone, and the bare branches were brittle. "Light and dark." She inhaled deeply, holding the breath for one second. Two. Three. "Fire and shadows," she whispered on the exhale, releasing the arrow.

It struck true. She knew it wasn't her skill, but this new *thing* guiding the arrow.

And the entire tree was nothing but the same gold and silver ashes of her power moments later.

"By Sargon," Luka said, awe ringing in the words.

The same way he'd once said her name.

She looped her bow over her chest, turning away from him and heading back to the cave entrance.

"Tessa?" he called after her.

"I'm not your Ward, Luka," she called back. "We're not yours to worry about anymore."

But suddenly he was there, having Traveled to block her path. "You are mine to worry about. Theon entrusted you to me—"

Her harsh bark of laughter cut him off, and she couldn't blame him. It bordered on hysterical.

She *felt* hysterical.

She felt out of control.

She felt unbalanced.

"Okay," he said calmly. "Okay, Tessa. Just . . . Take a breath."

It was only then she realized her power had surrounded her. An armor between him and her.

"Let's just take a moment," he said. "We'll figure all this out."

"There is nothing to figure out," she said, her words cold and void of all the emotions she was feeling. "He doesn't want us. You don't want us. The only ones who want us, want to use us. *I* will figure it out. I am not your Ward."

"But you will be," he insisted. "We need to figure out how that will work."

"We do not," she replied, pushing past him. "I am not going to become your Ward."

His brow furrowed. "Of course you will."

"No, I won't. I saved him for you. Or I'm trying to. But even if I hadn't, I wouldn't bind myself to someone who doesn't want me. I would never force you into something you do not want."

He reached out, trying to grab her elbow to stop her, but then he hissed a curse as her power bit into him. She felt his eyes on her long after she'd disappeared into the depths of the cave, and she kept her magic in place just as long.

A barrier.

A physical blocking as much as an emotional blocking.

It was the only way she was going to survive this. She'd fucked up. She'd hurt him, but she didn't deserve to be treated like a burden. And she'd meant what she'd said. She wouldn't force him into a Guardian bond because he thought it was his duty.

She was more than a duty. She was more than her power. She was more than the blood in her veins and the beings she descended from. She was no longer a pawn in the games of the Legacy, the gods, or the Fates.

Lifting a hand, her power swirled again, this time leaving a gleaming gold dagger in her palm. But it wasn't just gold. There were silver and black etchings down the blade. Marks and symbols she'd never be able to read but knew what they said.

No, she wasn't a pawn.

She wasn't a Source.

She wasn't a Queen or a Lady or a god.

But she was a reckoning.

She was vengeance.

She was chaos and fury and everything in between.

And even if she could choose it for herself, there was no one left to be her balance.

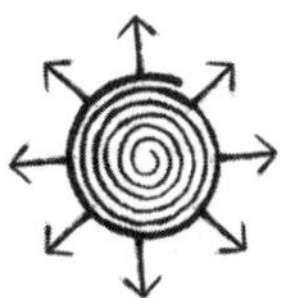

14
THEON

He'd made it from the Underground to the portal station in Castle Pines in record time, and no one had questioned him when he'd demanded an immediate portal to the Acropolis. He wasn't sure how to substantiate the claim of the Alpha and Beta, but he figured there was no better place to start. More than that, he wanted to see the Pantheon for himself. If Tessa had really done what the rumors claimed, he wanted to see the devastation with his own eyes.

"Arius Heir," a portal agent greeted with a small bow the moment he appeared in the Acropolis station.

But this wasn't his normal greeting. Beyond the agent stood a handful of Celeste sentinels, those that patrolled the Acropolis, but there were more mixed in. A sentinel from each kingdom, save for Arius, stood among them.

"Arius Heir, your presence has been requested by Lord Jove and the Ladies of Devram," said the Achaz sentinel, taking a step to the front of the company.

Adjusting his shirt cuffs, Theon sent him a dark glower. "You can tell them I decline the request. I do not have time for their frivolity today."

Several of the sentinels shifted uneasily, but it was none of them who answered. A female voice floated from behind them, the large bodies stepping aside to make a path for her.

"We both know a request from the rulers is never refutable, Theon," Tana said, her tight red curls piled atop her head. "But in this case, consider it fulfillment of one of the *many* favors you owe my mother's kingdom."

She came to a stop in front of him, her amber eyes daring him to deny her. And how could he? She had come to his aid without hesitation and was now keeping Cressida a prisoner on his behalf. He did owe her, no matter what had brought him here.

"Fine," he ground out, gesturing for her to lead the way.

Turning on her heel, Tana fell into step beside Theon. Gatlan, her Source, was only a few steps behind, and the Anala Heir waved off the company of sentinels.

"I've got it from here," she said dismissively. "A lot of help you were anyway."

"My Lady, your mother—" started the Anala sentinel, but he stopped speaking the moment her head snapped in his direction.

"Are you questioning me?" she demanded.

"Of course not, my lady," he said, bowing his head. "Only attempting to spare your mother's wrath."

"I will handle it if needed," Tana said, striding through the security gates and entering the bustling lobby of the portal station.

The sentinels stayed behind, and as they made their way through the crowds of the station, travelers gave them a wide berth. However, it wasn't until they were ushered into a waiting car that either of them spoke.

"What is this about, Tana?" Theon asked, settling into the leather seat.

Tana shifted, taking the glass of water Gatlan handed her and passing it to Theon. "What it's always about these days," she answered.

"Forgive my ignorance, but many topics have been discussed at the meetings I was part of."

"As I understand it, you often had 'better things to do' than attend the meetings. As it stands, your father is hunting for a Source that has deserted him, and your duty calls once more," Tana replied, taking a sip from her own glass. "But you need to prepare yourself. This meeting is, once again, to determine the fate of your not-Source."

He couldn't stop the sharp laugh that fell from his lips. "They wish to determine Tessa's fate? It appears she does not care what they say if the rumors are true."

"See for yourself," Tana said, lifting a hand and gesturing out the window.

Theon twisted, peering through the tinted glass, and if it hadn't been beaten into him to keep his composure at all times, his features would have betrayed the shock that he felt in the depths of his soul.

Where the Pantheon had once stood overlooking the entire Acropolis, there was nothing but chunks of stone and marble. The columns and the steps, the statues and the glass, everything was in ruin, and it wasn't just the

Pantheon. They were on the street at the bottom of the hill, and her destruction had eviscerated all the surrounding buildings. It had stretched in a radius wide enough to encompass the Tribunal building.

And all he could think about was how he wished he'd been there to see it—to see *her*—bring it all down. Gods, she must have been an utter vision. Wild and fierce. Untamed and stunning.

"Casualties?" Theon asked thickly.

"Only the priestesses and some Legacy," Tana answered. "Not a single Fae."

He glanced at her before returning his attention to the destruction.

"And where, exactly, are they meeting with the prominent buildings nothing but rubble?" he asked.

"The Celeste Manor," she answered. "After a ridiculous and lengthy debate, of course."

"Of course," he said with a smirk, settling in once more. If that was the case, they had a twenty-minute drive at the least. "And you were sent to fetch me because?"

"My mother convinced them I would have the best chance of persuading you, but they were not opposed to force if necessary."

"Obviously," he said dryly, fingers flexing around his water glass. "There are reports they saw her there. Jove and the Ladies."

Tana nodded. "My mother reported what she saw herself. Tessa and Luka. Tristyn Blackheart. Three other females and two males. They are in an uproar, Theon, and while they are debating her fate, they also debate yours."

"Mine?" he repeated, taken aback.

"She is your Source."

"That was taken from me," he snarled, familiar fury stirring in his gut.

"They need to hold someone accountable," she said. "They have to show the kingdoms they are doing something."

"So you are taking me to my own godsdamn trial?"

Her lips pursed, but her silence was answer enough.

"I did not realize the payment of my debts would be to stand trial for another's failings," he added, his jaw clenching with the words. He did not have time for this shit.

"Another's failings?" Tana asked.

"Tessa was taken from me. Even your mother agreed it would be better for her to remain with me, but Rordan insisted. He was the one who let this happen. She was under his care when all this shit occurred, yet *I* am the one who has to answer for it?"

"You chose her as a Source," she said carefully.

"I didn't know what she was. The people sitting on those thrones cannot say the same," he spat.

"Are you . . . Are you saying they knew all along?"

"Rordan did for godsdamn sure. The Ladies? I don't know that they knew *what* she was, but they sure as fuck know the Source Marks given are gross manipulations of other, more sacred, Marks."

Tana went quiet, and at least five minutes ticked by before she said in a hushed tone, as though she was afraid of being overheard even here, "Are you saying you disagree with how things are being run in Devram?"

"I don't . . ." He swiped a hand through his hair, then cursed himself for messing with it before he was about to go before the realm's rulers. Should he really admit this to a rival kingdom's heir? In the end, did it matter? He was plotting a rebellion with Axel anyway. It was going to come out eventually. So he inhaled deeply, locking eyes with her as he said, "Yeah, I guess I am."

The car pulled to a stop, and Tana placed a hand on Gatlan's thigh to halt him as he reached for the door. "Tread carefully today, Theon. Survive this, and perhaps we can continue this discussion."

He didn't have time to question what she meant. Gatlan pushed open the door and climbed out before helping Tana from the vehicle. Theon followed, slipping into the role he'd been trained for his entire life. Cold. Dark. Indifferent.

The Heir of Death.

Fae escorted them in, taking Tana's coat from Gatlan before leading them down a hall to a grand sitting room. He fought the urge to roll his eyes when he found the room arranged with six cushioned chairs to one side, the heirs and their Sources seated on sofas along the perimeters, and one lone high back armchair in the center of the room. Theon strode right past it and took a seat in the empty cushioned chair that was for the Arius Kingdom.

And he stared Rordan Jove in the eyes the entire time.

"That is no longer your seat, Heir St. Orcas," the Achaz Lord said tightly.

"Since my father is still unavailable, I think it is," he answered, sitting back and spreading his legs wide as he got comfortable.

"It wasn't a request."

"And my response wasn't a suggestion. I was accosted at the portal station and brought directly here, disrupting my day and my own business."

"You forget your place, Arius Heir," Jove said, light flickering in his eyes and sparking at his fingertips.

"And maybe you've grown complacent and overstayed yours."

"Respect is still required, Heir St. Orcas," the Falein Lady cut in.

A retort lingered on his tongue, but he swallowed it down. Verbal sparring with the Achaz Lord wasn't going to speed this process along. So instead he said, "To what do I owe this undeniable summons?"

"Your Source is out of control," the Serafina Lady said sharply.

"My Source," Theon repeated dryly. "I was under the impression she was no longer mine. In fact, those were Rordan's—"

"Watch it, boy," the Achaz Lord cut in sharply.

But Theon's smile was just as sharp when he said, "*Your* exact words were 'she is no longer yours.' I was repeatedly reminded of this since you took her from me. You are the one who has failed to keep her under control. I warned you it was an impossible task. You insisted you were handling it. As such, unless I am missing something here, I believe it should be *you* in the chair before us answering for your failings to the realm."

The room was utterly still, but he didn't give a single fuck. They wanted to pull him in here and blame him for what was happening when he'd told them from the beginning that caging her wasn't going to work? That it would blow up in their faces? Blame him for her bringing their most sacred spaces to ruin in a single godsdamn night?

Control the uncontrollable, or to fury they both lose.

He held Rordan's stare a moment longer before locking eyes with each Lady in turn. Serafina. Celeste. Falein. Anala.

And he could swear the Anala Lady was fighting a small smile when she calmly said, "Heir St. Orcas makes some valid points. Of course, we would never suggest putting a fellow Lord on trial, but I do believe we have questions. We were told she was being held beneath the Pantheon until decisions could be made, and yet . . ."

"And yet what?" the Achaz Lord snapped. He flung a hand in Theon's direction. "Ask the one who broke her out."

"I did no such thing. I have not seen her since the Sirana Gala," Theon replied, steepling a finger along his temple.

"Lies," Rordan hissed.

"In case you've forgotten, the female has a vendetta against my entire kingdom. My people were slaughtered. I've been tending to them while my father's fucked off to gods-know-where," he drawled. "My attention is on our defenses."

"Then why are you in the Acropolis today?" the Falein Lady asked.

"Supplies. As well as substantiating rumors," he answered. "As a fellow lover of knowledge, surely you understand desiring facts, proof, and truth before believing something to be true."

Lady Farhan nodded in agreement, just as Theon had known she would when he appealed to logic.

"And now that you have seen with your own eyes, what is your next course of action, young heir?" Lady Aithne asked, embers crackling at her fingertips as she held Theon's gaze.

He sat up a little straighter, his hand falling to the armrest. "I plan to do what's best for my people."

"And what do you believe that is?"

"To protect them from the dangers of the realm."

"Indeed," Lady Aithne said, and he didn't know what to make of the Lady's response. Her face was unreadable, and she turned away from him as she said, "His worries are valid, and he only seeks what we seek for our own kingdoms. I think his actions have proven such these last months during Valter's . . . absence. He has taken on immense responsibility far sooner than any of us did."

"What are you insinuating, Kyra?" Rordan gritted out.

"Valter has failed his kingdom," the Anala Lady said. "I move we allow Theon to take the necessary steps to take his seat and formally recognize him as the Arius Lord."

The fuck?

Theon sat up straight, shock rippling through him. That was the very last thing he'd been expecting her to say, and judging by the shock on the other rulers' faces, they hadn't anticipated it either. It clearly had not been discussed, but a motion had been made. It would have to be voted on. Theon wouldn't be allowed to vote, and this type of decision had to be unanimous. There was no way it would pass, but Kyra had planted a seed that would linger.

"Absolutely not," Rordan barked.

"That is not how this works," Kyra replied calmly. "A motion has been brought forth. Unless you are saying you have absolute power here?"

"Of course not," he gritted out from between clenched teeth. "But this has never once been discussed—"

"On the contrary. It has been discussed at great length since Valter went missing. Something none of us knew anything about, right?"

Oh, she was good. That was all Theon could think as he watched this play out. All the rulers were manipulators, but to watch them manipulate one another?

"We have all been paying attention to how Theon has handled matters, and while we were irked about his absence at meetings, he was tending to his people. That is the role of a Lord, is it not?" the Anala Lady went on.

"That is a valid argument," the Falein Lady said, clearly thinking deeply. "He has also offered to help with Tessa repeatedly. Would have taken responsibility for her once more if it had been granted. Comparing his time with the female and yours, Rordan, he did appear to have more control of her."

"That's bullshit," Rordan snarled, his face becoming red with rage.

"Is it?"

And Theon nearly fell out of his chair at the female that had asked that question.

The Serafina Lady's eyes were narrowed on Rordan. "We have lost the Sirana Villas, the Pantheon, the Tribunal, and the trust of our kingdoms while she has been in your care."

Two kingdoms that had always been steadfastly loyal to one another now on opposite sides.

All because of Tessa.

"And his people experienced a massacre of their own while under his care," Rordan argued.

"Because of *her*. While she was *your* responsibility," Lady Isleen snapped. She turned to the Celeste Lady. "Luna?"

The Celeste Lady appeared to hesitate, weighing her words, before she said, "We do have duties to our kingdoms to protect them. Their trust is how we maintain control, and we are losing that trust rapidly."

"Because of her," the Serafina Lady interjected. "Because no one can control her."

"But there were not massacres or buildings being destroyed when she was with Theon," the Falein Lady offered.

"Is that enough to offer him our blessing to proceed?" the Celeste Lady asked, looking among the Ladies, and Theon couldn't help but notice they weren't including Rordan in the discussion anymore. But they should be. Without his vote, none of this would matter.

"And what are we to do with Valter when he returns?" the Serafina Lady posed.

"He would have to answer for his absence and face such consequences," Kyra said simply. "But if Theon is the one caring for their kingdom while

Valter has seemingly disappeared, then concerns and meetings should involve him. Not Valter."

"That is logical," Lady Farhan agreed.

"And it is still his bloodline," the Celeste Lady mused.

"But he doesn't have a Source," Rordan cut in, his knuckles white where they clenched the arms of his chair. "We are giving an heir without a Source a seat? Anyone could overthrow him."

"Then I guess if Valter wants his seat back, that's what he'd need to do," Kyra said. "Besides, he does still technically have a Source."

"So we are making him a Lord *and* giving him the female?" Rordan demanded.

"Tessa," Theon interjected. "She has a fucking name."

At that, Rordan's golden gaze slid to him, and Theon knew that smile all too well. That was the smile of someone who was about to play a winning card or move a chess piece into checkmate.

"He has a Source, but what of a Match?" Rordan said.

"He has a Match," the Celeste Lady said, a crease appearing in her brow.

"But it is not official," Rordan countered. "A Match Ceremony has not occurred."

"It is a Selection Year," Theon retorted, struggling to keep his darkness in check.

"If we are making exceptions for you to take a kingdom seat, then surely we can make an exception here as well."

"What does me taking a Match have to do with any of this?"

"It is a sign you take your role seriously. A wife to produce an heir to keep the bloodline going, and by extension, the protection of your kingdom," the Achaz Lord said with a smile. "We all had Matches before we took our seats. Am I incorrect, Ladies?"

"He is not," the Falein Lady said. "But that is easily rectified if we are all in agreement."

"Wait," Theon said, forcing himself to stay seated and not lurch to his feet.

But what was his argument here? How was he supposed to argue against moving forward with his Match Contract? Especially with a fucking Bargain Mark still on his skin?

And when he locked eyes with Rordan once more, the Lord knew he had him backed into a corner.

"That is my stipulation," the Achaz Lord said. "I will agree to Theon taking over as the Arius Lord as soon as his Match Contract is fulfilled and he has a wife."

"That is agreeable enough," the Falein Lady said. "Anyone else?"

And one by one the Ladies agreed, with Kyra being the last as she turned to face Theon fully. "Are the terms agreeable to you? You will be recognized as the Arius Lord as soon as you take a Match?"

No.

Yes.

Fuck.

"Surely they are if this is about protecting your people and your kingdom?" Rordan said, a brow arching in question.

"And Tessa?" Theon asked, trying to keep his voice neutral.

"I think we can all agree the realm was safer when she was in your care. I propose she be returned to you until an agreement can be reached regarding her fate," Kyra said.

Begrudgingly, everyone murmured an agreement.

"Then we have an agreement," Theon said, rising from his seat and buttoning his suit coat. "Now, if you'll excuse me, I need to make a phone call."

He didn't wait for a dismissal. He strode from the sitting room, down the hall, and out the front door before he pulled his old phone from his pocket. Powering it on, he ignored the numerous texts and missed calls from Luka. He'd deal with that later.

Instead, he scrolled to a name and clicked it before lifting the phone to his ear. It rang only once before connecting.

"Theon? Thank Arius. I've been so worried," Felicity said, sounding genuine in her concern.

He didn't bother with pleasantries as he said, "How soon can you be in the Acropolis?"

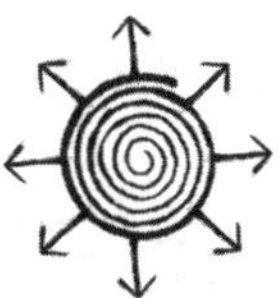

15
LUKA

"Why can't I just use my own arrows?" Tessa said with a scowl when Eliza handed her another normal arrow.

"Because your arrows are magic," she retorted. "You need to learn to shoot regular old arrows. What if you can't access your magic? Besides, we don't need you turning the mountain into ashes."

"They're not ashes," Tessa grumbled, nocking the arrow to her bow and taking aim.

Luka heard the crunch of boots behind him, but he didn't take his eyes from the females below. He was sitting above them on a ledge, his legs dangling over the side. They likely knew he was up here, but neither of the females had acknowledged him. Which was fine. It was better this way.

He could tell by scent alone who approached. His own blood mixed with fire.

"She's smart in how she trains her," Luka said, watching while Eliza adjusted Tessa's arm.

"She's been training warriors for decades," Razik replied. "She knows what she's doing."

There was a twinge at the words, and Luka realized a moment later it was jealousy. Jealous of what, he wasn't entirely sure. Her training warriors? Or maybe it was her just being around warriors when something like that was in his blood. A part of him wanted to ask Razik about it, but the male would probably just spout a smart-ass comment, reminding him yet again how much he didn't care that they were related. Which is why Luka was a bit shocked when Razik spoke again.

"Is it truly just you and Xan here? The only Sargon Legacy in the entire realm?" Razik asked.

Luka glanced at him sidelong, finding him studiously watching Tessa and Eliza.

"As far as I know," Luka answered. "Then again, I thought I was the only one until . . ."

Until Tessa revealed the secret she'd been keeping.

"And Aiyana?"

"Again, I assume she's dead, but I thought that about our father as well."

He stiffened at the words, but Luka was done trying not to piss him off. Xan was their father whether Razik wanted to acknowledge that fact or not.

"You are not the only one in your realm?" Luka asked.

Razik shook his head. "Tybalt is there. Xan's brother," he clarified. "We also have a cousin there. He is half-Witch and Scarlett's Guardian."

Another blooded relative. Or two, actually.

"But Sargon Legacy are rare to begin with. The god only had seven children, supposedly picky about who he sired them with."

"*Only* seven?" Luka said with a scoff.

"For a being that has been alive for thousands of years, that seems like a relatively small number."

"It's probably more," Luka said.

"Probably."

A few silent minutes ticked by before Razik broke the silence yet again. "So you've been alone."

It was a statement, and one that Luka stiffened at. "I had Theon and Axel."

"But you had no one to help you hone your power. You did that all on your own," Razik pushed.

"Why does it matter to you?"

"It doesn't. Eliza forced me to try to . . . do whatever this is."

Luka almost let the huff of laughter slip. "Are you saying your bonded forced you to try to bond with me?"

"Don't say it like that," Razik grumbled.

"What, exactly, do you want to know?" Luka went on. "My favorite color? Favorite food? Stuffed animal I had growing up?"

"Why the fuck did you have a stuffed animal growing up? Did you at least hunt it properly first?"

Luka finally turned to stare at him. "It wasn't a *real* animal. What is wrong with you?"

"You are the one who brought up stuffed animals."

"They are a child's comfort object. What do you have in your realm for children?"

"Not stuffed animals," he retorted.

Luka shook his head at the ridiculousness of the entire conversation, but some of it felt familiar too. Something stupid he'd argue about with Theon and Axel.

Knowing he really shouldn't bring this up, Luka took a breath before he asked, "I know you read a lot. Like Theon. So in all those books, have you come across something to remove the collar from our—from Xan's neck."

It was another few seconds before Razik answered, "Not yet."

"Yet? Are you looking?"

"I never said that."

"Right," Luka muttered, returning to watching the females. Tessa drew back the string on her bow, releasing the arrow a few seconds later. It missed her target, striking too low.

Neither of them spoke for another ten minutes before Razik said, "What are you going to do about her?"

Any tension that had bled from him returned, his back and shoulders stiffening. "What am I supposed to do about her?"

"You say she's not yours, yet you protect her like she is."

"Because I am to be her Guardian."

"But you're not yet, and it's more than that. I know the pull of a bond. How hard it is to ignore it. How impossible, even when it's all you want to do."

"You denied Eliza?" Luka asked, the fiery female watching Tessa with her hands on her hips.

"She denied me," he corrected. "I could never deny her a godsdamn thing."

With those words, Razik stood, leaving Luka abruptly alone again. Something he was all too familiar with, even if Theon and Axel had been constantly around. There was still a loneliness there. Something associated with being the only one of his kind. A loneliness that had been nonexistent since Tessa had come around.

He sighed as he saw Razik below, making his way the few hundred feet down the rocky terrain rather than simply Traveling. Something softened on Eliza's normally harsh features at his approach, and he leaned in, murmuring something in her ear that had her eyes filling with a desire Luka could see from where he still sat.

The female said something to Tessa, who waved her off, before taking another arrow from the quiver and nocking it. Apparently, she was content to keep practicing, but he knew that too. Knew she snuck into his training rooms inside the cave at night when everyone else was sleeping. Knew she went through all the routines she'd complained about when he'd been training her. Knew she was getting stronger, and not just with her magic. He could see it in the definition of muscles forming. In the set of her posture. In the quiet confidence that was growing more every day. He saw her. All of her. He both loved and hated it.

He waited until Razik and Eliza disappeared inside before he followed Razik's path, debating how to bring this up with Tessa. They needed to continue a conversation from the other night, and she seemed . . . Well, she didn't seem as consumed right now.

Luka knew she heard him approaching, but he moved with force anyway, making sure the crunch of rocks beneath his boots announced him. Tessa, of course, was barefoot. Eliza had argued with her about it, but had wisely dropped the argument after only a minute.

She stooped down to grab another arrow, not bothering to look at him when she said, "Xan can come out here with me if you feel the need to have me monitored."

"Tessa," he sighed, crossing his arms over his chest. "We need to talk more about this Guardian bond."

"There's nothing to talk about, Luka," she said simply, nocking the arrow, but he reached for her, halting her movements.

She stilled, gaze fixed on the spot where he held her elbow, and gods, he finally understood Theon's obsession with understanding her emotions. Luka had always been able to read her, but right now? He had no idea what she was feeling or thinking. She was stoic and cold, and he wished this bond wasn't so godsdamn broken. Then again, he wished a lot of things were different right now.

"Tessa," he said, his tone unintentionally softer, but it had her lifting her eyes to his.

Her head tilted to the side, as if she was trying to figure him out as much as he was trying to figure her out. Maybe this was the way it was always supposed to be. He'd always berated Theon for not being able to understand her, but maybe Theon had been doing it right all along. Working to build something on a foundation that wouldn't crumble to nothing with one choice.

Luka cleared his throat, dropping her arm and crossing his once more. But his dragon was preening at having her attention on him. She never looked at him anymore, and his magic was reaching, wanting. Apparently hers was too, but she didn't bother to leash it like he was. It flowed around her like a black and gold flecked mist. Light and dark. Power. And his dragon wanted that. His black flames wanted that. Wanted to tangle with her, draw her in.

His arms had dropped to his sides, and he hadn't realized he'd taken a step towards her until she took one back.

"We need to be able to be around each other," he said. She opened her mouth to argue, but he stopped her before she got the words out. "At least for now. While we figure out our next moves going forward."

They could worry about the necessary Guardian bond later. He just needed her to talk to him right now, and he knew pushing her on that topic was going to make her shut down immediately.

She studied him for a long moment, and he fought the urge to fidget. Gods, what the fuck was wrong with him? But her violet stare was penetrating and eerie as her magic swirled faintly in her eyes.

"I know your magic is a lot, and I know neither of us trusts the other right now. But I think we can agree we have a common goal," he tried.

"And what is that goal?" she asked, taking a step to the right. "To leave this realm?"

He moved with her as he answered, "If that was your goal, you wouldn't have destroyed our main way out."

She hummed, taking another step and forcing him to turn to keep her in his line of sight. "Then what is our mutual goal, Luka Mors?"

"To survive until we can figure out what the fuck we're going to do, and to do that, we need to work together."

She hummed again, still moving. "Everyone has plans. You. Me. Your brother. Rordan. Valter. Tristyn. I bet even your father has a plan. He knows things. I know things. Th—" She stumbled when she almost said his name, but then resumed her movements. "Everyone knows things."

"We're past the point of keeping secrets, Tessa. It could mean the difference between death and survival."

"Salvation or destruction?"

"Yes."

She hummed, still holding her bow with the arrow nocked at her side. "Would you have liked to leave here?" she asked suddenly. "Would you have preferred to leave with your father and brother?" The question caught him off guard, and when he didn't immediately answer, she added, "Should I not save him for you? I thought . . . What would you choose? If this world wasn't damned and tyrants didn't rule?"

"I would wish for my family," he finally said. "The family I chose and formed over the years, not by blood. If you are asking me to choose one or the other, I would choose those brought into my life by the Fates."

"The Fates want to kill me," she said simply. "You side with them."

"Don't put words in my mouth."

She was still moving, and he was still turning, and it was only then that he realized she was circling him. Like a godsdamn predator, footprints of her power left in her wake with each step. He felt his eyes shift at the realization, his power seeking and his dragon loving the idea of wrestling for dominance.

"All I am asking," he gritted out, "is if we can call a tentative truce."

"I was unaware we were fighting," she replied, finally ceasing her stalking, and her head canted to the side again.

"We both need each other right now, whether we like it or not."

Her brow furrowed. "I know you do not want me here, Luka. I have simply been giving you your space."

The dragon in his soul snarled at the words, and he swallowed down an audible growl. He thought she'd been avoiding him, but she had been . . . She thought this was what he'd wanted. And it was, wasn't it?

"We don't have to figure out everything at once. We just need to take this day by day," he offered, needing her to give just a little on this.

"One foot in front of the other? Just one step?" she asked, taking the smallest of steps towards him instead of continuing to circle him.

"Yes," he answered, relieved she finally understood what he was saying.

She worried her bottom lip, appearing to debate something, before she nodded once. Whether to him or to herself, he wasn't sure, but he'd take the small victory.

"Let's work with your bow," he said, jerking his chin to the weapon she still held at her side.

"We don't have to do this," she said, taking three steps back.

"I know Eliza has been training you," he said. "I've been watching, and she's smart to make you train without your magic. But you need to train *with* your power too, Tessa."

"Really?" she asked, a thread of excitement sounding as the bands of light around her wrists flared at the words.

He almost smiled, but instead, he reached for the arrow she had nocked, pausing for a moment to see if she would pull away from him. When she didn't, he took the regular arrow, moving to replace it in the quiver before turning back to her.

She was nearly bouncing on her toes as she let small tendrils of her magic free to float around her. If he was being honest, she'd learned a lot of control over these past months, even if it still overwhelmed her most days.

"Summon an arrow, and let's see what you can do," he said, a smile filling her face as she lifted a hand. There was a swirl of power before an arrow appeared, and he stepped closer, leaning in to study it. "Do you know what the markings are?"

Tessa shook her head, lifting her other hand and producing a dagger. "Do you?" she asked, holding the blade out to him.

He took it from her, the odd etchings bigger on the dagger, making them easier to see. But he didn't know what they were. It was on the tip of his tongue to say they would ask Theon, but he stopped himself right before the words left his lips. Instead, he ground out, "We could ask Razik if he knows. Or Xan. Even Cienna or Tristyn."

She nodded, worrying her bottom lip again and turning away from him to nock the arrow. They may not be in a great place right now, but he didn't need the bond to know what she was thinking in this moment. Because while there were plenty of people they *could* ask about the markings, they both only wanted to ask the one who wasn't here. And neither one of them was willing to say that aloud.

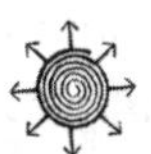

He shifted as he descended, his feet hitting the rocky ground a few seconds later. He'd needed the flight in the cool night air. Time to clear his head. He knew forcing himself to spend more time with her was going to have him questioning his resolve. His magic and the dragon in his soul were already pushing him back to her, but how could he possibly trust her, give her his loyalty, after she'd kept something so important from him? How did a person forgive that? Even if he did somewhat understand her reasoning.

He jogged down the stairs that led deeper into the cave. There was a small hall at the bottom, and he counted the empty frames on the walls to make sure they were still there. There were far too many people here who had overstayed their welcome.

There were also far too many dragons here.

He'd spent the rest of the afternoon working with Tessa on her archery, and then they'd all had a meal together. Which wasn't out of the ordinary. Everyone usually ate dinner together so that only one meal had to be prepared. But everyone else seemed to have sensed the shift in their relationship. There were curious looks and roundabout questions, but mostly, everyone seemed more at ease because Tessa's mannerisms were not as erratic.

Something that was confirmed when he stepped into the main living space to find his father on a sofa. He immediately stood when Luka entered, and Luka wasn't sure how to interpret his tone when he said, "She's been pacing around here for the last three hours."

The entire time he'd been gone.

"Everything seems to be in order," Luka replied, moving past Xan to grab a liquor bottle and pour a glass.

"She needs to sleep, Luka."

Yeah, he knew that too. He didn't need to be as close to her as he was today to see the lack of it wearing on her. Legacy and Fae rarely became sleep deprived. They didn't need it like the mortals of the realm did. The Fae needed deep sleep to restore powers. Another reason Theon had been over-the-top with her schedule when they'd all thought she was Fae. And while Legacy didn't need it for those reasons, as he'd told Tessa, they could only go so long before their magic capitalized on it and tried to take control.

Which is why he'd never said anything about her silently coming into his room at night and taking the shirt he'd worn that day. In fact, just like Theon used to do, he'd taken to leaving it out for her to find easily.

Luka sighed, taking a deep drink from his glass before he said, "Where is she?"

"She slipped into your room about twenty minutes ago, and she hasn't come back out," Xan answered. Then he hesitated, pushing a hand through his shoulder-length hair. "While Akira and I were not what you and Tessa are, I could help pull her back from the brink. She found solace with me, and that didn't need the same . . . connection."

"You mean you didn't end up fucking her," Luka said.

He was too tired for this. His father always tried to be delicate with these things while Luka was far more blunt like Razik. He supposed that was one thing he had in common with his brother.

Xan blinked once before something akin to disapproval appeared. "I'm saying that while you navigate what you want your relationship to be, you can still help her right now. Until something else can be figured out."

"And you appear to have more of a soft spot for her than your own children."

It was a low blow, but he was so godsdamn tired of everyone taking Tessa's side in this. Everyone subtly hinting that he was making this a bigger deal than it was. Didn't any of them realize Xan would likely still be in that fucking prison if it wasn't for him? Or if Tessa had told him sooner, he could have been out a lot sooner? So many things could be different.

Xan cleared his throat, the collar at his neck glimmering in the low flames hovering around the room. "I have a lot of regrets in my life, Luka. I simply do not wish for you to have to live with the same, but I will not bring it up again."

Luka said nothing, only knocked back the last of his liquor as he watched his father leave the room. One would think having the tension eased some with Tessa would put him in a better mood, but it was exactly the opposite. It was why he'd gone flying, but here he was.

With another sigh, he set the glass aside and made his way to his room. The door was closed, and it took him a long moment to find her in the dark room, forcing him to shift his eyes. When he found her, she was curled up in an armchair in the corner.

"Tessa?"

She said nothing, and he moved closer, finding her wrapped in one of his shirts and her eyes closed. Despite that, her hands were clenched around the fabric, magic flowing around them. Not letting himself think about it, he reached out, trying to pry them open, but he found her entire being tense and coiled tight. A soft moan of pure agony fell from her parted lips, and he told himself it was out of loyalty to Theon when he scooped her out of the chair.

She immediately melted into him, settling into his chest as he moved her to his bed, only opening her eyes when he pulled the blankets over her. Tessa blinked several times, her brow scrunching in confusion.

"Just for tonight," he said gruffly, turning away from her to pull his shirt over his head. He tossed it to the corner, knowing she wouldn't need it tonight, before he grabbed a pair of lightweight pants and changed into them.

She waited until he was climbing into the other side of the low bed before she rasped, "Why?"

"Because you need to sleep, Tessa."

She fell quiet, and Luka propped his hand behind his head, staring at the ceiling while he waited. Within minutes, her breathing changed, just as he'd known it would, and shortly thereafter, she was rolling into him. He tensed as she nestled into his side, a hand resting on his abdomen while a leg slid over his. Then he loosed a long breath, forcing himself to relax. He let his magic out, watching it gently wrap around her while he slowly did the same with his arm. His dragon gave a satisfied rumble.

It was just for tonight. If he gave her this, let her get some much needed rest, she'd be fine for a while. They wouldn't need to do this again for at least a week. Maybe two.

That was what he told himself over and over as sleep found him too.

That was what he told himself when he woke a few hours later to find himself curled around her. Her back to his chest. His arm keeping her held tightly to him. His face buried in her neck, her scent surrounding him. But even then, her arm stretched out, her hand seeking another that should be with them.

That was what he told himself when he jerked awake from his magic alerting him to someone crossing his wards around the cave. He was up and out of the bed, already half-dressed and working off pure adrenaline when he realized the bed was now completely empty. No blond hair fanned across a pillow or small form curled into a ball with the blankets thrown off. Apparently, they *both* slept more soundly when near each other. He knew that, of course, but that didn't mean he liked admitting it. Or seeing such blatant evidence of it.

Still, someone had crossed his wards who wasn't supposed to be here, and Tessa not being in his bed only had him hurrying to slide on his boots as he pulled a shirt on. He was nearly out the door when he saw the paper folded on one of the nightstands, his name scrawled across it.

Luka snatched it up as he left the room, reading as he went, but the more he read, the faster he moved until he was racing up the stairs and out into the crisp morning air. There was nothing here. *No one* here. Not her. Not her wolves. Not another living soul. Only a single off-white feather that he bent to pick up.

His heart beating far too quickly, the paper crumpled in his fist where he gripped it, reading the words over again.

Luka,

You once told me I don't know how to let myself be loved, and I think you're right. My entire life, I've tried to be what others wanted me to be. Mother Cordelia and the instructors at the Estate. Dex and Oralia. Then it was Theon.

You. Rordan. Achaz. All these beings with expectations and ideals of what they thought I should be and do and become. In the end, I don't think it's my fault for not knowing how to be loved because for so long, I never was. I didn't know how to recognize it. But you also told me I needed to find myself worthy and deserving. That I needed to fight for me, and because you taught me that, I know I don't want 'just for tonights.' I know that's all you can offer me now, and I understand why, but because of you, I know I can fight for more. That if no one wants wild and untamed and chaotic, then I am content to be alone now. Trying to conform to what this world, the gods, or the Fates think I should be is no longer something I wish to strive for. I simply want to be free of it all because that is what I'm deserving of.

I know I did this to us, and sometimes consequences are as lasting as our immortal lives. I won't ask for your forgiveness, because that is indeed not something I am deserving of. But I will say again, I am sorry, Luka. I am sorry I betrayed you so deeply. I am sorry we found each other only for me to be less than what you needed and expected. I am sorry I took so much from you. Being the grandchild of a god is lonely, and I'm sorry to leave you alone.

But while I don't know how to let myself be loved, I think I did learn how to love. How to give another freedom when it is what they desperately seek. How to sacrifice and hurt and bleed for another to allow them to live a life they deserve. It is all I have left to make amends with. While I know you have found your father and brother, I know that is not what you want. So I saved him for you. Or I'm trying to. I will. We will save him for you. We will save him, and then we will leave so the Fates can hunt us elsewhere and maybe the two of you can find a way to bring peace to a broken realm. If anyone can do it, it will be the two of you. You deserve a life of freedom as much as I do.

Thank you for trying to love me. Thank you for giving me the chance to be loved by you. Thank you for believing I am deserving of so much more. I'm sorry it took me too long to figure it all out. I'm sorry I was too late. But I don't regret our nights. Thank you for the time you did give me. Thank you for the training and the oranges and the flip-flops. I don't know how to let myself be loved, but I know I love you. Differently from him and yet somehow the same. Thoroughly. Completely. Forever.

Eternally Yours

He still held that godsdamn feather, and he turned, racing back inside, all but leaping down the stairs.

"Razik? Blackheart? Xan? Who's awake?" he yelled into the silence.

It shouldn't have surprised him his father was the first to appear, everyone else a few seconds behind him. It also shouldn't have surprised him Cienna was already in the kitchen, a cup of tea in her hands and violet eyes pinned on him.

"You already know," Luka said tightly, holding her stare.

"I do now," she answered.

He didn't have time for her vague answers. He turned to the others, holding up the feather. "Is this what I think it is? A fucking seraph feather?"

"Where is Tessa?" Xan asked instead.

"Answer me!" Luka demanded.

Razik stalked forward, taking the feather from him and examining it before he said, "That's what it looks like to me." He lifted his eyes to Luka. "Is she gone? Did she go back to them?"

She'd left.

And he didn't know if she'd willingly gone with them or not, but this sure as fuck looked like she had. Surely one of them would have heard a struggle. Been alerted to it. Her godsdamn wolves would have done something.

But he didn't know what her plans were or what she was thinking because he'd pushed her away too much.

More than that, he knew this was a crossroads. His own version of salvation or destruction. She'd given him an out. Now he was left to decide if he was going to take it.

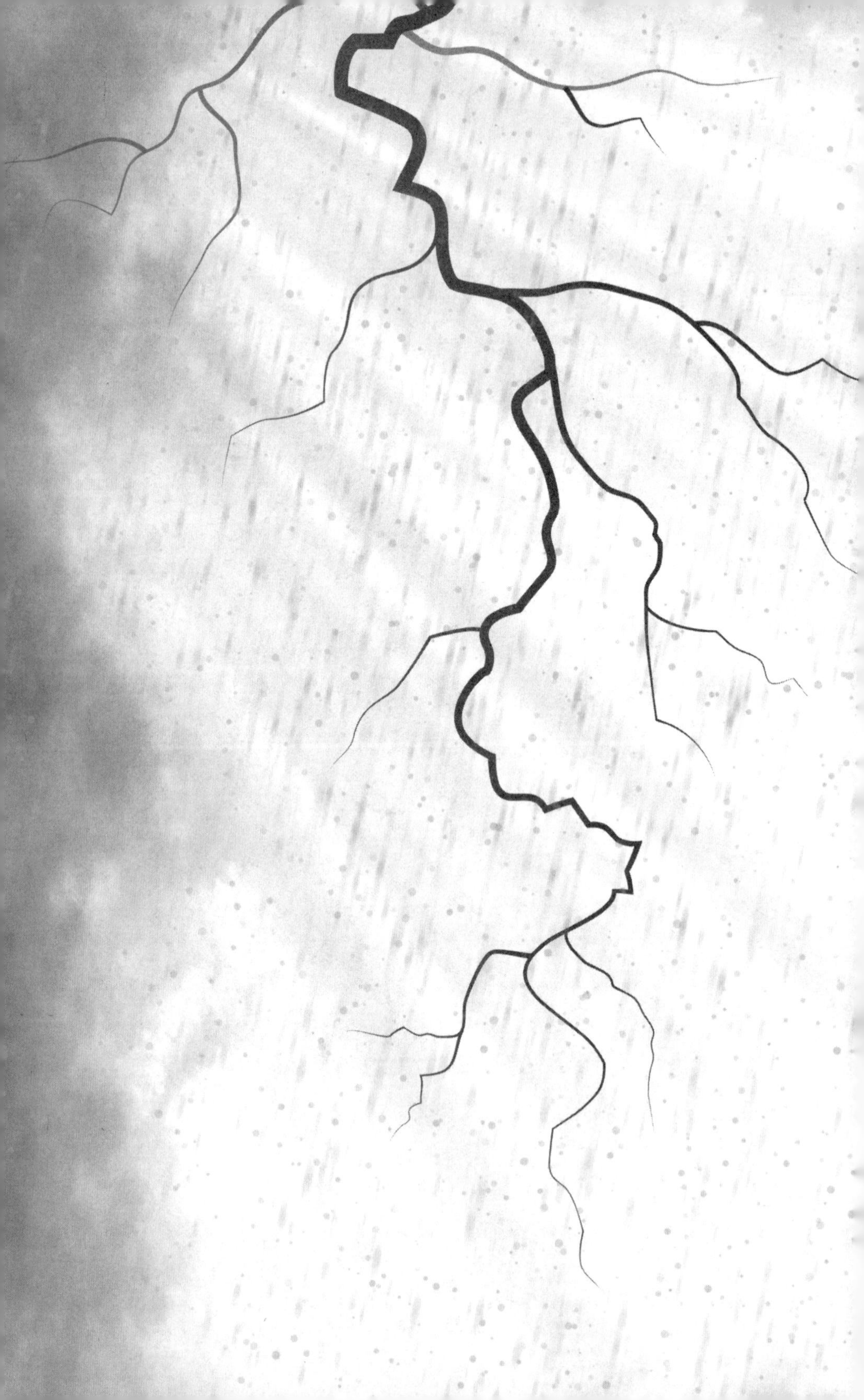

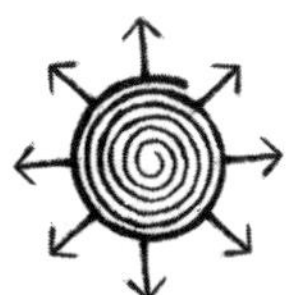

16
TESSA

Her bare feet sank into the soft ground on the river's edge as she watched the black waters merge with the clear, sparkling blue. It was hypnotic in a way; the dark swirling with the light. The black waters weren't murky like she thought they would be. They weren't thick or foreboding. They were just as crisp and clear as the other water, and she found herself drawn to the midnight river more than the rest, taking a step closer.

"They say the Night Waters have been a part of Devram since its inception."

She didn't turn right away, but the smallest of smiles pulled at the corner of her mouth. She'd been waiting for him.

"I was hoping you would come tonight," she said, her fingers twisting into the fabric of her dress.

"I will always come for you," he replied, and she finally turned to find him with a smile of his own. Emerald eyes were pinned on her, his hands in the pockets of his suit pants.

"The gods made some waters black?" she asked, slowly facing the flowing rivers once more as he came to stand beside her.

Nodding to the rushing waters, he said, "This is the Fractured Springs, where the Night Waters merge with the River of Endings. But I don't think a god did this."

"You don't think, or you know?"

He huffed a laugh under his breath. "I believe the waters turn black when an Arius descendant has an outpouring of intense emotions. When they feel so utterly helpless and broken, that all they can do is pour out their despair and sorrow, altering the world around them."

Her brow bunched in thought. "That doesn't seem right," she mused.

"Doesn't it? Does the weather not change when you are sad? Does a storm not scream its wrath when you are angry?"

She looked up at him, his attention fixed fully on her. She got a little lost in dark emerald eyes and black hair. In a small dimple and lips she'd kissed more times than she could count. Still he didn't reach for her. Didn't touch her.

Tessa cleared her throat. "So you think an Arius descendant turned the Night Waters into what they are?"

"It does stand to reason."

"So logical," she mocked with a sigh, turning back to the rivers. But when he didn't speak right away, she glanced back, finding him still watching her. "What?"

"It has been some time since I have seen you so . . . calm."

She sighed again, wrapping her arms around herself. "Can I tell you something?"

"Always."

She hesitated though. Saying this aloud was admitting it more to herself than to him. But did it matter in her dreams? In a vision that may or may not ever happen?

"I'm tired," she finally said, her voice scarcely more than a whisper.

He said nothing, knowing there was more. He always knew what she needed, but the patience . . . That was new.

"I'm tired of secrets. I'm tired of scheming. I think maybe I'm tired of trying to be the villain and the savior. I'm tired of hating you and missing you. I'm tired of being hated. I'm tired of fighting."

"Don't you dare stop fighting, Tessalyn. Do you understand me?"

"It's a constant push and pull," she continued as though he hadn't spoken. "My magic wants, and I desire. Power calls and fury beckons. A sea of freedom and a whirlwind of chains. How can it be all and nothing? How can I feel like I'm flying and falling all at the same time? I think maybe balance is as much of an illusion as hope in the end. I think—"

But she was cut off when large hands took her face, and those lips she'd lost herself in more than once took something she was finally willing to give. His mouth moved against hers deeply and thoroughly. She couldn't breathe, but she didn't care. She never wanted to come up for air. She could drown here, in this place. A piece of her soul still thrashed, but here, she was almost whole.

If only her dreams weren't fleeting.

He pulled back, and she whimpered. At some point, her hands had left her dress, instead fisting into the fabric of his shirt. She held on, keeping him near, and he kept her face in his hands as his eyes searched hers.

"I'm yours," he said, his voice husky with a need and desperation she understood all too well. "Every piece of me. And I will always come for you."

"In another life," she whispered, letting her light flow with the faint dark mist swirling around him in the same way the dark waters merged with the River of Endings.

"In every life, little storm."

Her smile was sad. "Still such pretty words, even as a phantom."

"Tessa—"

But he didn't get to finish as she pressed her lips to his once more, letting herself drown in memories.

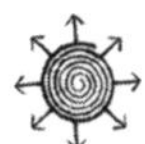

Her eyes fluttered open, and she reached up to brush hair from her face, only for her fingertips to find tears on her cheeks. For so long, she'd fought sleep, but here, she chased it. She used to use sleep as an escape. Maybe this wasn't so different. Her dreams were nightmares that would haunt her, but she found herself craving them as of late. It was all she had left now.

All she would ever have.

And while she'd made peace with that, it wouldn't stop her from seeking them out in her dreams, even with the risk of those visions being unfavorable. It was the only way she could know. The only way she could protect them now.

She sat up in the bed with a wince. It was a far cry from the beds she'd been sleeping on with Theon, in Faven, with Luka. It was smaller too. A single bed, she realized.

It took her a minute to remember everything that had happened. How she'd used her magic to keep Luka lulled to sleep, her power soothing his as light and dark coiled around her and gently extracted her from his hold. How she'd Traveled outside, having been practicing that skill as much as the others. Once she'd done it a few times, it hadn't been hard to figure out what triggered it and how to control it. With Roan and Nylah at her sides, she'd climbed down the mountainside in the still dark morning until she felt Luka's wards slip over her skin, stopping on the other side and far enough from the cave that it wouldn't be seen. Then she'd crouched down to speak to her wolves, telling them her plan. The only ones who knew. Perhaps the only ones who cared. Asking them to deliver a message for her when she was gone.

Then she'd sent a note to Dex with her magic.

The only light was of her own making while she'd waited for him. It took longer than she'd anticipated, but he came in the end, with all pretenses dropped, just as she'd requested. His off-white wings had been on full display, and he'd Traveled in himself, dark eyes narrowing when they fell on her.

"More games, Tessie?" he'd drawled, scanning the surroundings. "Where are your pets?"

"I'm done with games. I'm done with your lies. I want truth, and I want answers. You can give them to me, or I'll find them myself in much less . . . favorable ways," she'd replied, lifting a hand and letting her power surge until a small storm spun in her palm.

"So foolish," he'd sneered. "Trying to outwit a god when you are nothing but a child."

"And you?" she'd countered, taking small steps back until she felt the wards once again. "What exactly are you? Other than a lying, traitorous bastard. You're enslaved to that very god."

Then he'd smiled, and it had made her second-guess herself. Made her magic tense, ready to defend her.

"Oh, Tessalyn," he'd purred, slinking forward and following her path. "I may be caged, but you? You are the key to my freedom."

Something had shifted then, as if a veil was being lifted or a curtain pulled back. He wasn't alone like she'd thought he'd been. There'd been others with him. Not Oralia like she'd been expecting, but these were seraphs. At least a dozen. And while she'd been distracted by their sudden appearance, Dex had pounced. Before she could react, a cuff had clamped around her wrist before something had slammed into her head from behind and her world had gone dark.

With a growl of irritation, she adjusted the cuff, not even feeling the sting as she swung her legs over the side of the bed. This wasn't like Theon's bands. She couldn't take this one off, and it was preventing her magic from healing her. Her head was pounding from the hit, and her power was coiling in her veins, full of fury as she stalked to the single window in the small room. One look through the glass, and she knew exactly where she was.

The Celeste Estate.

She lurched back, stumbling over her feet. Why had he taken her *here*? She assumed he'd take her back to Faven. Not . . .

Breathe, she ordered herself, focusing on keeping control. It was more imperative than ever.

She was away from Luka and Xan. This is what she'd wanted. They were trying to get her to leave, and she was trying to . . . not leave. Not yet.

Taking a few more calming breaths, she looked around the room. Two single beds. Two small dressers. A dormitory.

She made her way to the door, surprised to find it unlocked. With a turn of the knob, she stepped into a hall she knew far too well. Counting the doors confirmed her suspicions that she'd come from Dex and Brecken's room. It only made her anger simmer more.

Within minutes she was crossing the courtyard and into the main building, ignoring the Fae who stayed back, trying to blend into the walls they pressed against. She had her sights set on one hallway, one door, and she threw it open when she got there.

Only to find Dex sitting behind the extravagant desk, a piece of steak halfway to his mouth. His surprise quickly disappeared, morphing into tolerance as he said, "Took you long enough."

"Where is Moth—Where is Cordelia?" she corrected herself.

Dex scoffed as he chewed his meat. "Hiding from you, of course. Everyone is so on edge with you running around, turning their precious buildings into piles of rocks. If I wasn't so irritated by it all, I'd find it humorous."

"Sorry to give you another mess to clean up," she sneered, taking in the office she'd spent so much of her childhood in while avoiding the small cupboard on the wall.

He waved her off. "I'm not so much irritated with you as I am with them. They focus on such trivial things here. Even Rordan seems to have forgotten the end goal."

"Which is what?" she asked absentmindedly, hating being in here and knowing that was exactly why Dex had chosen it.

"Getting you home where you belong, of course."

Her head whipped back to him, only to find him not even looking at her. No, he was busy cutting another bite of meat as though she truly was the dismissive nuisance she'd always felt like.

"I'm having a plate brought for you," he said. "Take a seat."

"Fuck off," she retorted.

He clicked his tongue in disapproval. "Is this not what your little letter demanded of me? No pretenses? Only truths and answers?"

"Take this off," she countered, lifting her arm to show the cuff. "Then we can chat all you want."

"Make a blood vow not to harm me, and we can discuss that," he countered. She scowled at him, and he smirked, knowing he'd won for now. "Take a seat, Tessie."

"Stop calling me that," she snapped.

He sighed, placing his silverware on his nearly empty plate and pushing the dish aside. "You summoned me, Tessa. With your erratic behavior as of late, can you really blame me for taking precautions? Oralia said you attacked her the last time you saw her."

"I did," Tessa said simply, starting to wander around the room. She let her fingers drag along the wall. "She is irritating."

Dex huffed a laugh. "I can agree with you on that."

There was a knock before the door pushed open and a seraph entered, carrying a tray of food. She watched the male move, feathered wings of a soft light grey rustling with each step before he set the tray on the other side of the desk.

Dex nodded to the male in dismissal, and the male gathered the dirty dishes before heading back to the doorway.

"Thank you," Tessa said tightly when he passed, and the male paused for only a second. Hazel eyes met hers, an expression she couldn't read lingering in their depths.

"That is all," Dex said coolly.

The seraph took the hint, continuing on his way and the door snicking shut behind him once more.

"Sit and eat, Tessa," Dex said pointedly. "Before it gets cold."

She glared at him, but she *was* hungry. It wasn't as if she couldn't eat while she was here and carrying out her own plans. With an irritated huff, she crossed the room and dropped into the wooden chair, immediately sitting still and proper as if Cordelia were the one sitting across from her.

Refusing to let her nerves or discomfort show, she picked up a piece of bread and took a bite. "So what's the plan, then, Dex? I don't trust you. You don't trust me. Are either of us going to believe a word we say?"

He smiled that smile he used when he was reassuring her he would fix whatever she'd fucked up. "I have a proposal."

"Which is?"

"A truth agreement. You can specify the time frame."

Luka had told her of this. How he'd made one with Rordan when he'd come to Faven to ensure neither of them could lie to one another during negotiations.

"An hour for now," she replied, picking up her fork and steak knife. "For the next hour, neither of us can speak a lie to one another."

"Do we have an accord?" Dex asked, arching a brow.

Her smile was all teeth when she answered, "It's a bargain," before taking a bite of her own steak. She felt the bargain Mark settle, this one along her left ankle. It would be gone before she left this room. "I'll go first," she said after she swallowed and began cutting another piece of meat. "How did you get here?"

"Through a mirror gate, the same as you," he answered, folding his hands atop the desk while he watched her. "In the Achaz Kingdom. We bided our time and came at the same time Xan brought you so our presence wouldn't be felt as strongly when we entered."

"How did you know when I'd be coming?"

"It's my turn for a question, Tessie," he mocked. "Are you fully bonded to Theon St. Orcas as his Source?"

"No," she answered, picking up her bread once more to hide her trembling hands at this name. "The Source bond never worked right. My power rebelled against it."

"But some aspects did work, right?"

"My turn," she said with faux sweetness. "What, exactly, is the power you stole?"

He blinked, seemingly surprised. "I see Xan has been running his mouth," he muttered. Then he sighed as he said, "While there are only elemental Fae in Devram, there are other types of Fae in other realms. They are known as cognitive Fae, and one of their gifts is being able to alter or mask reality."

"You can . . ." She trailed off as piece after piece fell into place. "Like when you met me in the mountains? You made it seem like you were alone. That's how you hid the other seraphs with you?"

He nodded. "What are the names of all the people who were with you when you destroyed the Pantheon?"

She took another bite to stall, but there was no way around that very specific question. His dark eyes watched her, tracking every move and breath, but she held his stare as she finally said, "Luka, Xan, Tristyn, Cienna, Gia, Razik, and Eliza. I'm going to go out on a limb and guess you are far older than I am, so why did you wait so long to come around?"

Dex shifted in his seat, one arm falling to the armrest while the other stayed on the desk. He tapped his finger a few times, appearing to stall just as she had. "I didn't wait," he gritted out. "The more I have to alter, the more draining on my power. I can only hold an illusion for so long. Small illusions are easy enough, but larger ones—appearing to be younger, for example—take more power. I simply ensured you were . . . not around when I came here when you were younger or when my power was low."

Her utensils clattered to the desk, bouncing off the glassware to the floor. "You are the reason . . ."

Of course he was, but it still hurt to have it confirmed. It all made perfect sense. Tristyn said he was there when they were attacked. Dex and the others were the ones who'd taken her from them. He'd known where she was the whole time, keeping his secrets from everyone else, including Rordan. Not even Cordelia knew what she truly was. Dex had kept her hidden, letting her grow up. Breaking her. Grooming her to be what he wanted—meek and submissive. Completely reliant on him. Looking to him for comfort and answers.

"Don't look at me like that, Tessie," he scoffed. "You were too young to understand the intricacies of all the moving parts. You are still too focused on this realm. It's one of hundreds. You are meant for more."

"You let me endure years of abuse!" she cried, lurching to her feet. "You—"

"I taught you how to survive," he snarled, smoothly rising to his own feet. He braced his hands on the desk, leering towards her. "'Be what they want you to be now, so you can be who you were meant to be later.' That's what I taught you. How to blend in in a world that would seek to use and destroy you. How to make them see what you needed them to see so you could sneak around and cross wards. We needed them to believe you were Fae, so we needed *you* to believe it too. Until it was time."

"You're lying," she spat.

His smile was chilling. "We are under a truth agreement, Tessa. I can't lie to you right now. Isn't this what you wanted? Truth and answers?"

Yes.

No.

She needed a moment. Even with the cuff on, she felt her control slipping. Her power surged, snapping and lashing out, trying to break free. Dragging her down.

"How are you any different?" she asked, her voice shaking. "You want to use us as much as they do."

He'd rounded the desk at some point, and now he stood directly in front of her. His hand cupped her chin, forcing her to look into his dark eyes. "I'm not seeking to use you, Tessa. I'm seeking to set you *free*. I'm seeking to see you at your rightful place."

"You said so yourself, I was the key to your freedom."

"And you are," he confirmed. "But you are also the key to *yours*." When she didn't immediately reply, he leaned closer, letting his hand slide from her chin to tuck her hair behind her ear. "Give me a week, Tessie. Give me one week to prove to you I've always been on your side."

"What could you possibly show me in a week that could convince us of that?"

His lips tilted in a knowing smile. "You, of all people, should know how much one's perspective can change in a single day, hour, let alone a week." Taking a step back, he pulled a phone from his pocket, glancing at the screen. Then he added, "I think you will find even your presumed allies only have their own interests in mind."

"What does that mean?" she demanded.

"Come. We have visitors."

Tessa had little choice but to follow Dex from Cordelia's office. She stayed at his side, refusing to trail him like a Fae or a fucking Source. She knew where they were going anyway. Taking a left instead of a right, they stepped into the grand foyer of the main estate building.

"Who are we waiting for?" she asked in irritation.

"The Arius Lord and his wife."

"Valter and Cressida?"

"Valter is no longer the Arius Lord," Dex said.

"Then who is?"

"His heir, of course."

But if Valter wasn't dead, the only way he could be the Lord was if all the ruling Lords and Ladies had unanimously agreed. Rordan would never, but it was another word that had her lungs constricting.

Wife.

"It's a Selection Year," she said a touch too weakly, betraying her own emotions.

Dex glanced at her, pity on his features. As if talking to a child who had learned a hard lesson, he said, "It is my understanding an exception was made for an extenuating circumstance."

The door opened then, a male and female striding in. She took in the female first, wrapped in a long fur coat. Her chestnut hair was styled half-up, brown eyes immediately finding her and narrowing as she pointedly removed her gloves to showcase the Mark on the back of her hand.

"Arius Lord," Dex said, bowing deeply, but Tessa stayed rooted to the spot.

Her gaze slid to him, staring at his hands. On the back of one was the Achaz Mark, but on the back of the other . . . She couldn't tear her eyes from the Union Mark that stood out.

Dex stood straight once more. "What can we do for you and your wife this afternoon?"

Slowly, she let her eyes drag up his form. He waited until she met his emerald irises, swirling with darkness and already fixed on her, before Theon said, "I've come for what is mine."

PART TWO
BEGINNINGS

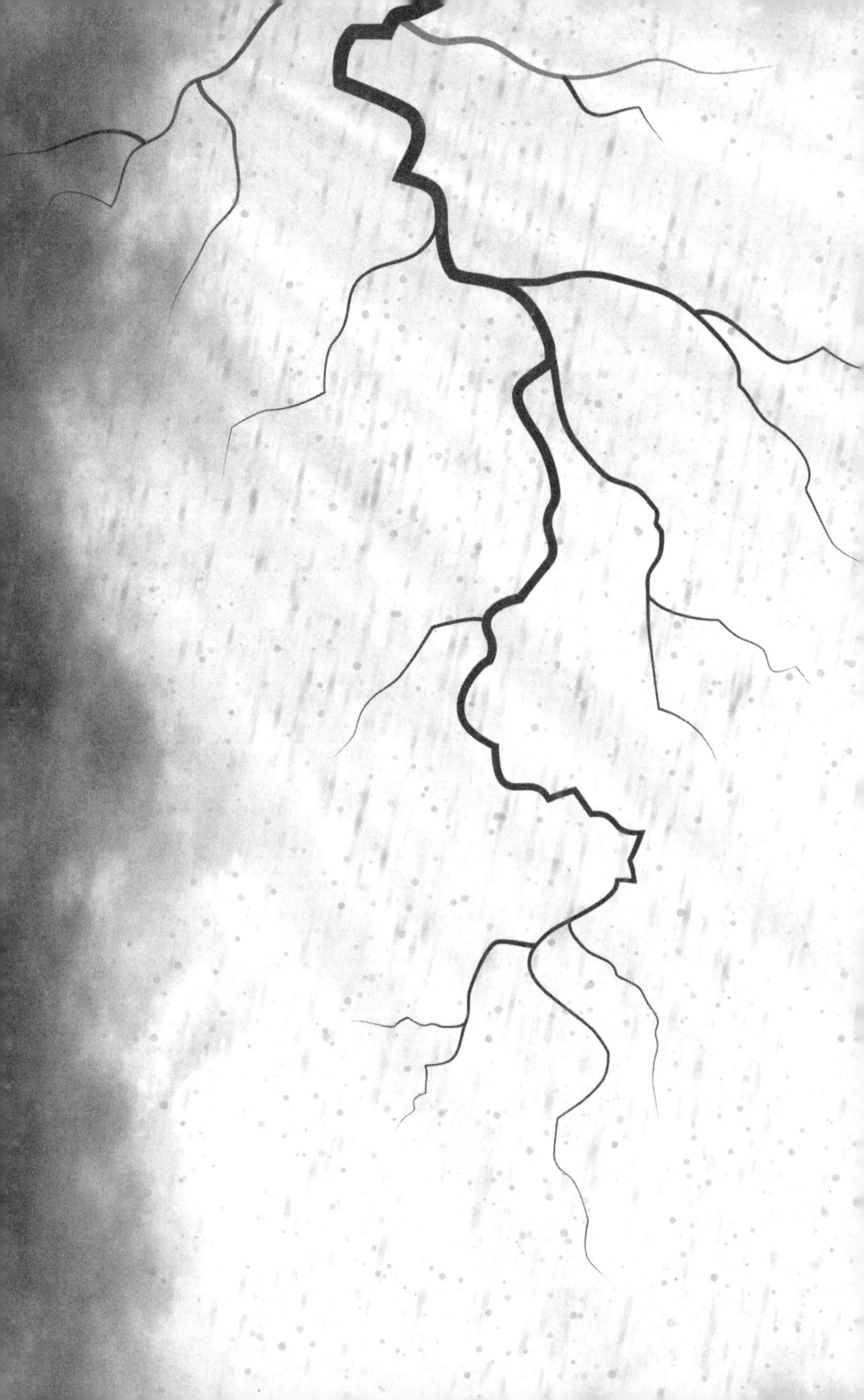

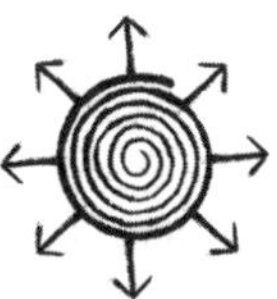

17
TESSA

"Thank you," Tessa murmured when a glass of wine was placed before her on the table.

The same seraph from Cordelia's office moved around the space, placing drinks before the three other people in the room. She'd never been in here. She'd never been *worthy* of seeing the second and third floors of the main Estate building. These two floors were Cordelia's private living quarters. But Dex had apparently been privy to these spaces all the time, and Tessa wondered when Cordelia had learned that he wasn't Fae at all. Had she always known? If not, when had Dex revealed it? How often was he in this very room while she'd been huddled in a small dark cupboard, her stomach aching for food?

The seraph left the room, and the tension was oppressive as it hung in the air. Theon hadn't looked away from her once, gaze fixed on her and watching her every movement. Felicity Davers sat to his right, across from Dex, who sat next to Tessa. The lounge they sat in was lavish, exactly like Cordelia's office. Rich fabrics, flashy colors. Everything to exude her importance, and now they sat at this table for six, somehow intimate yet formal.

"I have fulfilled the requirements for my lordship," Theon was saying, still focused on Tessa. "Prolonging this is only making me want to end your life sooner."

"I know this is hard for you to understand, as most things are for Arius and his lineage, but you don't get to have something just because you want it," Dex sneered.

"And yet that's exactly what happened for Arius and Serafina, is it not?" Theon asked, bringing his glass of liquor to his lips and taking a drink. Still holding Tessa's stare the entire time. "Is that not what this whole vendetta is about to begin with?"

"Such arrogant fools. All of you," Dex retorted. "As if Achaz would let the cunt of one female dictate the fates of all realms. This is bigger than Serafina and Arius. It always has been. They used to be part of it until they were swayed."

"The way Rordan and Valter used to work together until Rordan was swayed?" Tessa asked, glancing at the male she'd once considered her closest friend.

The male tipped his head from side to side, debating his answer before finally saying, "The Fates like to watch the different ways history could have played out."

Her brow furrowed. "What does that mean?"

Dex finally deigned to look at her, his features cold as he said, "Perhaps if you'd be who you were meant to be, you'd know the answer to that. Instead, you choose to throw tantrums and give yourself over to whoever gives you what you want."

"Watch it," Theon barked, his darkness snapping out like a whip and striking Dex in the chest. Felicity gasped, but Tessa only stared at the thin line of red that seeped into Dex's white shirt before dragging her eyes back to Theon.

To find him still fixated on her.

Her head tilted as she took him in yet again, and then her eyes narrowed when Felicity reached over, placing her hand on his arm and leaning in to murmur something. She couldn't hear it. All she could hear was the blood rushing in her ears as her gaze dropped to the Union Mark on the back of Felicity's hand.

The hand touching Theon.

The hand—

"Eyes on me, clever tempest," came the low command, but it had her gaze snapping back to his, a knowing look on his face.

"Eyes on you," she repeated slowly, reaching for her wine glass. It was the first words she'd said to him since he'd arrived at the Celeste Estate over an hour ago, and something akin to relief washed over him until she added, "Every time you say that it's followed by pretty words attempting to lure me into submission."

"Thank Achaz you finally recognize that," Dex said, swiping up his drink.

"Of course I do. It's all anyone does in this realm," she replied, holding emerald irises as she brought her wine to her lips. She took a sip, her tongue sweeping over her bottom lip when she finished, and she watched Theon's gaze dip to the movement. "Pretty words and extravagant actions to distract from true motives."

The clicking of a tongue sounded before Felicity spouted, "Always so dramatic."

Tessa's smile turned serpentine as she slid her gaze to the female. "What pretty things did he promise you, Ms. Davers?"

"It's St. Orcas now," she replied with a saccharine smile.

"Is it?" Tessa asked, swirling her wine. "It sounds to me like nothing is official until Rordan and the ruling Ladies arrive to confirm everything."

"Semantics," she gritted out.

Tessa tutted, mimicking her from seconds earlier. "You're to be a Lord's wife. You should understand that nothing in Devram is merely semantics, but I'm sure you'll figure it all out in time."

Red splotches appeared on her cheeks, and Tessa didn't miss how her grip tightened on her wineglass. "And did you figure it out, Tessalyn?" she asked, unable to hide the sneer from her voice. "Did you figure out your place?"

"I have," Tessa answered. "Pity you haven't figured out yours."

"I am his Match," she spat.

Tessa said nothing. Only smiled as she sipped her wine again.

"I am his Match," she repeated, spluttering the words. "And what are you? Other than something to be leashed and brought out when needed?"

Theon started to say something, but Tessa held up her hand to halt him. Her tone was tinged with a madness she knew they all could hear when she said, "I am salvation and destruction, beginnings and endings, light and dark. I am the secrets of gods and the sorrow of fate. I am wrath and vengeance, chaos and fury. But to you, *Ms. Davers*? I will only be your end."

Tension crackled in the air as Dex cleared his throat, signaling to someone for a refill of drinks, and when Tessa's stare slid back to Theon, his eyes were still on her. She knew they'd never left during that entire exchange, as if imploring her to understand something. She could swear there was even a faint, insistent tugging on the broken bond, but she wasn't sure she was ready to examine that yet.

"Take that cuff off her," Theon said, his tone low and dark, startling her back from her thoughts.

"I'm afraid not," came a voice that had Tessa inwardly flinching.

Rordan Jove strolled into the room, his Source a step behind him along with his heir, Dagian Jove, and his Source. Dex and Felicity got to their feet, bowing their heads, while Theon and Tessa stayed seated.

The last time she'd seen the Achaz Lord he'd been berating her for not fulfilling her purpose. She'd promised she would act, and it had all been a set up. She wasn't a fool. He'd organized the entire godsdamn thing, working with Cressida and Cordelia for the Augury attack, and knowing she'd summon the Hunters that would end in a massacre in the Arius Kingdom.

That was her fault, even if she was set up. It was still her actions that had ended in the deaths of hundreds. Just like Pen last fall.

Destruction. Not salvation.

"An agreement was made, Jove," Theon said tightly. "Are you not a male of your word?"

"I most certainly am," the Achaz Lord replied casually, taking a seat at the head of the table while Dagian took the other end. "I am also a male of tradition and policy. All Lords and Ladies must be present to recognize a new ruler."

"Then summon them. Now."

"I'm afraid Maya is a little preoccupied at the moment. Something to do with your father and his rogue Source she has detained," Rordan said, leaning to the side for a glass of liquor to be placed before him.

Tessa straightened at his words at the same time Theon said, "Eviana?"

"Indeed," Rordan mused. "She was somehow freed from my home." His stare slid to Tessa.

"What a shame," she said sweetly, reaching for her wineglass once again.

"It is," the Lord continued, picking up his own drink. "Our sources report two Fae helped her. They will all be sentenced to death for their treason, of course."

"What?" Tessa asked, nearly dropping her glass.

But before Rordan could respond, Theon cut in. "I do not care about my father's Source or what she's been doing. I care that I receive my title and what I was promised. I have completed all of your requirements. Make this happen sooner, Jove."

During his little tirade, Tessa managed to regain her composure, but she knew Rordan hadn't missed it. She needed to get out of this room. Off this Estate. She needed to see the sky and feel the breeze. She needed to talk to Lange and Corbin and make sure they were okay. If her actions ended in their deaths, she would never forgive herself. She'd let this world shatter, and she'd go down with it.

"We have other responsibilities, *Theon*," Rordan said. "If I recall correctly, you often had other things to tend to when we requested your presence at meetings. The Ladies will arrive when their schedules allow."

"And in the meantime?" Theon demanded.

"I suppose we wait."

"Great, I'll take what's mine and wait in the Arius Kingdom. Let me know when everyone has found time," he said, moving to get to his feet.

"Tessalyn will not be left alone with you until everything is official, St. Orcas. You are free to do what you wish, but she will stay here with Dexter until your lordship is finalized," Rordan said calmly.

"Bullshit," Theon snapped. "I'm not fucking leaving her here."

The Achaz Lord shrugged. "As I said, you are free to do as you wish. Leave or stay, it makes no difference to me. I'm sure you can work on . . . fulfilling your obligations as Lord with your new wife here or there."

Theon's features darkened. Or rather, his power did, darkness floating around him. "You have interfered with my personal matters quite enough, Jove. Try to do so again, and your heir may find himself in your seat sooner than planned."

"Are you threatening me, St. Orcas?"

"Was I not clear enough?"

"You can't even draw from a Source," Rordan sneered. "I suggest you get an heir in your new wife's belly before facing death."

"I *am* death," Theon retorted, his darkness swirling until his wings formed at his back.

"Be that as it may," Rordan said, light flickering around him, "you will still fall if you attempt to make good on that threat."

"No one is going to decide where I stay," Tessa cut in, standing so abruptly she bumped the table. Liquid sloshed over the rims of glasses, and her chair scraped lightly, nearly toppling over. "I am not a possession to be passed around. I am no one's to be used." Her eyes flashed to Felicity, and the female had the good sense to flinch back, inching closer to Theon. Tessa planted her hands on the table, leaning closer as she added, "Or *leashed*. And I sure as fuck don't need my power to remind you of *your* place, Ms. Davers."

She turned, stalking out of the room without looking back at any of the males who thought they could control her. Her bare feet padded down the stairs and out to the places she knew best. She didn't stop until she reached the park benches on the edge of the property, sinking down onto one and breathing in the crisp air. Her eyes fell closed, and she tipped her head back, letting the sun try to warm her face.

The winter months were waning. The snow was gone, and there were signs that spring was trying to flourish. Trying to find its way up from the frozen ground. Trying to find the beauty it knew it was capable of if winter would just lift its oppressive hand from its neck. Trying to grow and become something new.

"You have this knack for disappearing as of late," drawled a male voice. "It makes everyone so uneasy."

Tessa slowly opened her eyes, lifting her head to find Brecken standing before her. He seemed paler, but she supposed everyone did in late winter, not spending as much time outside. His brownish-blond hair stirred in the wind as his dark eyes took her in, his hands stuffed in the pockets of his jacket.

"What are you doing here?" she sneered.

"No one is letting you go off by yourself right now," he replied with a shrug. "You can't tell me they weren't watching you wherever you've been hiding these last weeks."

"So Dex sent you?"

"It was me or Oralia, and I need to keep up pretense. He's growing suspicious."

Tessa scoffed, closing her eyes and tipping her head back once more. While she didn't exactly trust Brecken, the male had helped her get all those Fae to safety at the Sirana Villas and when she'd destroyed the Pantheon.

She heard his footsteps before the bench jostled when he sat beside her. Her lips pressed together, keeping in the words she was longing to say.

But Brecken seemed to know exactly what she was thinking because he said, "Ask it, Tessa."

"There's nothing to ask really," she said, slipping her hands beneath her thighs to warm them while she toed at the ground. "I could ask why you never told me. I could ask how you could have known what was happening to me and didn't do anything about it. I could ask so many things, but it all comes down to survival. I can't fault you for that, but I also can't trust you because of it."

"That's understandable."

"Even the things you've helped me with, if you told anyone, you'd be implicating yourself. So it still comes back to your own basic survival. It's the way of Devram."

"It's the way of most realms," he said, stretching his legs out in front of him while clasping his hands behind his head.

"How old are you? And Dex? Oralia?" she asked, peering at him sidelong.

"Oralia is the youngest of us. Still under a century. Dex is the oldest."

She nodded, letting those truths settle. "And what do you have to gain from this? Or is it simply blind loyalty to Achaz?"

"We were created for a purpose," he said, staring out across the desolate courtyard. "From the time we could crawl we were taught that purpose: to serve Achaz. It isn't much different here for the Fae. We are born, complete our studies. Then we find our powers, studying beings the same way heirs watch the Sources here."

"And you killed an Arius Legacy?"

Brecken nodded, an arm falling along the back of the bench while the other fell to his side. "And I was rewarded greatly for it. It's what got me the spot on this mission."

"To find me?"

He clicked his tongue. "I told you once, your well-being was never my concern. You were always Dex's main priority."

"And you?"

"I was sent to aid him and the Achaz Legacy here, but I was given tasks of my own. So was Oralia," he said, and he sounded almost . . . sad.

When he didn't explain further, Tessa said, "How come you and Dex and Oralia can make your wings disappear, but it appears other seraphs can't?"

"There is a difference between the seraphs and the Elite seraphs, just as there is a difference between dragons and Guardians."

"So . . . you are a light guardian? Like Luka is to Theon?"

"Kind of. Only we're all bound to Achaz, not another individual."

She mulled that over in her mind for a few quiet moments before she said, "A few months ago, you told me your freedom depended on me being who I was meant to be."

"And it does," he said, turning to face her for the first time since he'd sat down. "There are so many paths before you. One path offers freedom to some while condemning others. Another path does the opposite. Some paths free many, while some paths bring only death."

"And who am I meant to be then?"

"Come now, Tessa," he chided, his signature smirk tilting on his lips. "I know how clever you are. I've watched you outwit the Achaz Lord and Dex these last months." He chuckled under his breath. "You've provided quite the entertainment for me."

"I'm so glad," she muttered in irritation.

"You're smart enough to know only you get to decide who you are meant to be. Isn't that what you've been doing since being Selected? Fighting back? Telling everyone they don't own you? That you can't be leashed or collared? And yet . . ."

"And yet, what?" she snapped, her power stirring beneath her skin before quieting once more.

"And yet I'm not entirely sure you've convinced yourself of that yet. It's why everyone continues to try to use you and trap you."

She stared at him, words failing to come to her in any kind of retort.

"Anyway, it became about more than survival for me long ago. Well before I found myself in this cursed realm," Brecken said. "Yet as cursed as this realm is, I'd rather stay in it than return to where I came from."

Startled at the revelation, Tessa said, "You don't want to go home?"

"That world stopped being my home when someone I loved was taken from me," he answered, getting to his feet. "It changed me. Much in the same way you've been changed. I am powerful, but you? You could destroy a world, and I think you would. You've been on the brink. It's why they fear you so much. It's why they keep trying to collar you and leash you. Because as soon as you fully believe in yourself and what you're capable of? That's when you'll be free."

There was a lump in her throat, and she swallowed around it as she peered up at him. "Why are you telling me this?" she asked hoarsely.

"So you can decide who you *want* to be," he answered. "Not for me or Dex. Not for Theon or Luka or Achaz or Arius. But for you, Tessa."

She looked away, trying to clear her head. Maybe it was more pretty words. Maybe it was him trying to gain her trust. It was all anyone had done her entire life. Become her lifeline so they could manipulate her. He wanted freedom, and she was his ticket to it. She wasn't sure there was anything he could do to prove otherwise.

Then again, she'd once thought the same about Theon.

"Do you know how to take this cuff off?" she asked suddenly, lifting her arm. "We hate it."

Brecken nodded slowly. "Those were designed to contain beings of Chaos during the Everlasting War. It requires the blood of three different First gods, or, in this case, their Legacy to remove it."

"I am the blood of three different First gods," she argued.

"Yes, but you're the one entrapped. Not only that, we all know what your blood can summon," Brecken pointed out.

The Hunters.

She'd been so careful not to call them forth since that day near the river.

"I can help you take it off, but it'll take me a little time to get what we need. But doing so will also mean I won't be able to be as . . . helpful," Brecken ventured.

"Because they'll know it was you who helped me," she said with a sigh, twisting the cuff around her forearm. At least it didn't bite into her skin like the other bands did.

"I'll help," he said again, getting to his feet. "Just give me a little time to work out a plan."

"And what am I supposed to do in the meantime?" she asked as he turned to walk away.

"What you've been doing all along, Tessa. Figuring out who you *want* to be. But fair warning, you're running out of time."

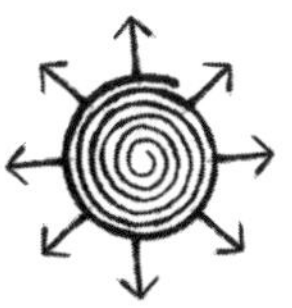

18
AXEL

"Everything's okay, right?" Axel asked, leaning against the wall with his hands behind his back.

It was taking all of his self-control not to snarl and shove the Witch away from Kat, despite knowing she wasn't harming her. The Witch knew Cienna, and she ran the Apothecary District. She was on their side, and yet watching her hands hovering over Kat's rounded belly with faint light flowing made him want to do incredibly violent things.

"Stop talking," Miara said, her tone as harsh and cold as all the other Witches Axel had ever encountered.

Her long dark hair hung in loose waves around her shoulders, stark against her pale skin, and her violet eyes were closed as she worked, tilting her head as though listening for something.

"Everything is fine, Axel," Kat said softly, her hands resting at her sides.

"She's taking longer than usual," he argued.

And she was. They've been coming to see Miara every week now, and the Witch never took this long to tell them everything was fine and progressing as normal. This wasn't some few minutes delay either. It'd been nearly fifteen minutes of them sitting in utter, anxiety-inducing silence.

"Axel, let her work," Kat said, her eyes closing. She could try to hide it, but he heard it. The thread of worry she was trying so hard to gloss over, and it was all he needed to push off the wall and step forward.

He bent over her head where she lay on the exam table, smoothing his hand over her hair. Pressing a kiss to her brow, he looked at Miara, not caring that she was still trying to focus. Katya being worried and stressed couldn't be good for the babe, but Axel just didn't like seeing Kat distraught about anything. She was the logical and sensible one. If she was worried, then everyone in the godsdamn realm should be worried.

"She's been more tired lately," he said to Miara, his hand slipping over Kat's and interlacing their fingers.

"I'm sure she has," Miara said, finally straightening and lowering her hands. "Fae babes grow rapidly, but the last months are the most taxing. She's managing her own power, which I'm told is vast, and now the babe's as well. That eats through her magic reserves rather quickly. It will not get better."

"It's going to get worse," Axel clarified unnecessarily, but he wanted all the facts laid out.

"She needs to rest. And eat," Miara added, moving to her worktable and sifting through vials of liquids and baskets of plants. "She also needs to be siphoning off that power. It will be exhausting."

"But the babe is fine?" Kat asked, pushing onto her elbows to watch Miara.

"He is well," Miara said, mashing some leaves with a pestle.

"But?" Kat pushed, and Axel's brow furrowed as he helped her sit up.

"But what?" he asked.

"She took a long time to examine him today, and now she won't look at us," Kat said, embers sparking in her eyes. "She's not telling us something."

He looked at Miara, finding the Witch's features pinched in annoyance. "I find you too clever for your own good."

"You do not keep things from me when it involves my son," Katya retorted, shadows appearing and drifting around her like an aura. "If you know something, you will tell us."

Axel blinked at her fierceness. She rarely displayed it, but gods when she did?

He slid his hands into his pockets, leveling Miara with a dark look. "You heard her. Tell us what you know."

"I don't *know* anything," Miara replied, dumping the ground plants from the mortar into a larger bowl. She reached for a few vials, adding their contents as she added, "The future is ever-changing."

"But you've seen something?" Axel demanded.

"All Witches have that gift. Some more than others. My premonitions are not nearly what Cienna's are. You should seek her out."

"Cienna is not here," Axel said sharply. "You are."

"We cannot tempt Fate. I cannot risk it."

"Then you are risking your life, and I will not be the one to end it," he said, with a pointed look at Katya.

The shadows had thickened around her, bright embers floating among the dark. Those same embers were in her dark hair, trickles of flames winding among the tight curls. A female who would stand between the world and her child. What a mother was supposed to be and do.

"Just say it, Miara," Axel said, bringing his hand to Kat's lower back.

"The babe cannot come before the sixth month," she finally said. "That is all I will tell you."

"But he is not due until the seventh month," Kat said, confusion replacing the menacing notes.

"He will not make the seventh month," Miara said, using a dropper to fill several vials with whatever she'd just created. "But if he does not make the sixth, you will not meet him until the After."

Katya lurched back. If his hand hadn't been there, she may very well have gone over the side of the small exam table.

"You just said yourself, the future is always changing," Axel said.

"And you insisted I tell you what may or may not happen," Miara said simply, striding forward while extending the vials she'd just prepared. "These will make your sleep more restorative. I will prepare more for next week when I see you again."

Kat took them from her. The tinkle of the vials was loud as they shook in her trembling hands.

"What are we supposed to do in the meantime?" Axel asked, immediately taking the vials from Kat and slipping them into his pockets before retrieving her shoes from the nearby chair. He dropped to a knee, sliding them onto her feet.

"The same thing you've been doing. Don't try to figure out fate. It will only lead to madness," Miara warned. "The Fates are crafty beings, keeping their secrets close. They wander about unknown and unseen. It is why we do not meddle. They are everywhere and nowhere."

"Now you sound like Cienna," Axel grumbled, pushing back to his feet and helping Kat from the exam table. "Or maybe Tessa and her nonsensical ramblings."

"Do not try to unravel their secrets," Miara warned again. "It is valuable time you will never regain."

Neither Kat nor Axel spoke as they left her place, located in the southernmost part of the Apothecary District. The District completely separated the Dispensary District from the rest of the Underground. He held Kat's hand as they passed the walls of her home, larger than the rest of the shops and homes in the District since she ruled over it the same way the Alpha and Beta did the Leisure District.

The same way Bree, Cade, and Rayell ruled over the Dispensary District.

The thought alone had his throat suddenly too dry.

He forced his mind to Kat, moving silently at his side, her other hand rubbing along her stomach.

"She's wrong," he said in determination.

But Kat just nodded, and he fell silent once more. He knew her well enough by now to know she needed to think this through. Needed logic and her books. She'd talk to him, but not yet. Not until she'd gone through all her knowledge and theories. So much like Theon in that way.

Shadows still clung to her, trailing her footsteps and drifting in the air between them. Axel swiped his fingers through the dark, suppressing a shudder as he remembered what it had been like to wield them. When they'd been an extension of him. When he'd been more than . . . this. When he hadn't been so utterly helpless to spare her from such worry and fear.

Now his wife and son would have something that he would only ever have memories of.

They were nearing the central road that ran from one end of the Underground to the other, and Axel was about to suggest they stop to rest when Kat spoke first.

"I need to talk to Theon."

Axel came to a sudden halt, forcing her to stop too. "What? Why?"

And why couldn't she talk to him? Why did she need to talk to Theon?

"Because Theon is the one who can get to Tessa, and Tessa has visions," she said.

His heart sank at her words. At her utter desperation.

He stepped forward, reaching to tuck her hair behind her ear as he said gently, "Kitten, I—"

"Don't look at me like that," she said, stepping out of his reach. "Tessa has visions, and she will tell me what the Witches won't. She doesn't care about the Fates or the gods."

"Tessa doesn't care about anyone but herself, Kat," Axel said, his voice hardening. "We are not letting her near our son."

"We have to try, Axel," she pleaded.

He shook his head, not knowing what to say. "None of what you are saying is logical."

Flames flickered in her eyes again, but tears glimmered there too, along with an unwavering resolve. "Find a way to get me in touch with Theon or Luka. Someone who can get me to Tessa. Or I'll do it myself."

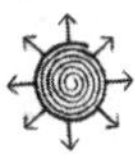

His throat was on fire.

No, *he* was on fire.

That was all he could think as he thrashed.

His arms, his legs.

His godsdamn throat.

It took him a minute to register someone was holding him down. Or attempting to.

He snarled, throwing all his strength into his burning muscles as he flipped the person off him, pinning them down. Everything was a blur. A haze that he couldn't see through.

But he could touch and taste and *smell*.

He could smell the blood now squirming beneath him. As if it could get away from him.

It was fire and shadows and power.

And it was *his*.

His fingers skimmed warm flesh, and it stilled beneath his touch. But he could hear the ragged breathing. The panting. Could feel a chest heaving as he walked his fingertips higher, along the hollow of a throat. The column of a neck. Until they stopped on a pulse, beating rapidly. Thrumming with something he'd been craving for days and days. Weeks. Months. Maybe his entire life.

He leaned in, inhaling deeply. Let his fangs drag along that pulse point. He inhaled again, ready to feast.

Then he was growling in pain and fury as he was thrown to the ground, landing hard on his back. The air was knocked from his lungs, but he didn't care as he tried to scramble to his feet to chase down what was his.

Only he couldn't move. Or, at least, he couldn't move his limbs.

"Axel."

The voice was far away, trying to break through his anger and bloodlust and want.

"Axel, look at me."

He snarled again, and whatever was keeping him contained burned. The snarl morphed into a bellow of pain, but broke through the all-consuming need. He blinked, everything coming into focus.

Including his wife standing over him murmuring, "I'm sorry. I'm sorry. I'm sorry."

Her hands were raised, flames in her palms while cords of shadows held him to the floor. She didn't look fearful of him, even though she godsdamn should be. Unshed tears were glimmering, but she wouldn't let them fall as she watched him.

"I'm sorry," she said again. "Axel?"

"I'm back, kitten," he said around the dry lump in his throat. "Let me up."

She eyed him for another few seconds, clearly gauging the truth of that statement, and he was glad she did. He wanted her to take every precaution. This was exactly what he'd been afraid of, even if she didn't appear shaken in the least.

Slowly, the shadows unwound, but she kept the flames in her hands as he got to his feet. He wanted to rush to her, but he moved slowly, giving her the time she needed to trust he was back in the right state of mind.

She was in one of his shirts, but it only hit her upper thighs now. He was shirtless, only in his undergarments, and he clenched his hands into fists, feeling the lingering burn at his wrists and ankles.

"I'm—"

"Do not apologize to me again, Kat," he interrupted, his tone dark and commanding. "You did what you needed to do."

"I know, but . . ."

"There are no buts. I told you this was what I was afraid of, and you said you could fight me off if needed. You did what you needed to do."

She nodded, the flames waning but still at her fingertips as she watched him. "You're not feeding enough."

"I have to ration myself," he said, forcing himself to stay rooted despite wanting to pull her into his arms.

"You have to drink enough to stay healthy, Axel," she argued. "You fret around here about how much I'm eating and sleeping. You have to do the same for yourself."

"When Theon comes back with more rations, it'll be different."

Her eyes narrowed, and the flames went out as she crossed her arms over her chest. "Did you contact him yet?"

"We just saw Miara a few days ago. I can't simply call him. You know that."

"I can send a fire message," she argued.

"Just . . . give me some time to figure it out. This needs to be a conversation. Not passing notes back and forth like we're in studies. He's busy, and—"

"No, Axel," Kat interrupted again. "I do not care what he is busy with. I want to talk to Tessa. Contact Luka if you don't want to bother Theon."

"Tessa wants to end our bloodline, Kat," he said, trying not to raise his voice. "That includes our son."

But she only glared back at him, unmoving in her resolve. He wasn't going to win this battle, and he knew if he dragged this out any longer, she would make good on her promise to do so herself.

He sighed, shoving a hand through his hair. "I have to go to the Underground entrance to use a phone," he said. "If I leave now I can hopefully be back late tonight provided there aren't any surprises along the way."

"I'll come with you."

"No," he argued. "You will stay here and rest. You hardly got sleep tonight. I'll send word to Miara to have a couple Witches come stay with you. I have some Legacy contacts in the District that owe me favors as well."

"I think I've just proven I can defend myself," she said wryly, but the underlying heaviness told him how accurate his assessment was. She was exhausted, and while she'd just expelled some power, it was draining on her too.

He left her standing there while he went to the large closet, quickly dressing and brushing his teeth. When he came back out, she stood in the same spot, arms still crossed.

Stopping a few feet from her, he asked, "Can I touch you yet?"

Her features softened, and she lowered her arms. "I'm sorry," she whispered again as he pulled her into him, inhaling her scent for an entirely different reason now.

"Stop apologizing, Kat," he sighed, resting his cheek atop her head. "If this is our new reality, we need to adjust. I'd rather you burn me every day as long as I still get to call you mine at the end of it."

She pulled back, peering up at him. "It will be different when he's here. You'll never have to worry about having blood."

"I'm not going to use you like that," he replied, cupping her cheek.

"You mean you'll feed from others?"

His brow furrowed. "No, I'll get rations like I do now."

"But . . . why? When I'm right here. Why would you take from someone else?"

"I'm not . . ." He paused, cocking his head at a realization that couldn't possibly be true. But he couldn't help the slow smirk that tilted on his lips when he said, "Are you jealous of me feeding from others, kitten? Even from a fucking glass bottle?"

"No," she said quickly, eyes darting away.

He couldn't swallow his huff of dark laughter quickly enough. He leaned in, his words fanning over her lips when he whispered, "Liar."

His hands dropped to her hips, walking her backwards until she bumped into the wall. Her breathing was ragged once more, only this time he liked what he was doing to her. She tipped her head back, biting her bottom lip as she stared up at him.

"Tell me, kitten," he said, his voice low and gruff. "Tell me you're jealous at the idea of me feeding from another."

Her amber eyes flared, that annoyance he loved to pull from her there, but something else he'd never quite processed was there too.

"I don't know why you're so surprised," she retorted, her hands flat on his chest. "Fae are known to be as possessive as Legacy."

"Is that so?" he taunted, reaching up to wrap a coil of hair around his finger.

"Yes," she snapped, that irritation rising. "You want me to call you mine at the end of the day? I'll call you mine every minute of it, Axel St. Orcas. You're mine as much as I am yours, and you'd rip apart anyone who tried to provide something so vital for me."

"Are you going to spill blood for me, kitten?" he asked with a smirk, not missing how her thighs clenched at his tone.

But her voice was steady and fierce when she pushed onto her toes to get closer as she replied, "No. I'll burn them to nothing, and then I'll burn the ashes to be sure they understand you're mine."

"Gods, you're so fucking perfect," he muttered before his mouth crashed into hers.

Her lips were already parted, and he wasted no time diving in, his tongue twisting and sliding against hers. A moan rumbled from him, and he fully regretted getting dressed now. There was a quiet fury behind her kiss that came out whenever he managed to rile her up enough. But this? This possessiveness?

It was a thousand times better.

Her teeth bit into his lower lip, and he nipped hers back in response, feeling her sharp gasp all the way down to his cock.

He pulled back, watching her chest rise and fall as he said, "I have to go, or we're going to end up back in that bed." She started to protest, but he put a finger to her lips, watching her eyes flare again at the action. "Someone wants me to contact my brother, and I can't disappoint her. She's likely to start something on fire if I do."

"You're such an ass sometimes," she muttered, but it was followed by a yawn.

"And you're exhausted," he answered, brushing his lips to her temple before guiding her back to the bed.

"Yes, but now I'm also needy."

And gods, it was almost a whine. He pulled the blankets up over her before leaning in close once more. "Rest, kitten," he said in a low voice. "When I get back, you can possess me all you want."

"Oh my gods," she muttered, snuggling down into the blankets. "You can go now."

He huffed another laugh, dropping another kiss to her brow before making his way out of the room. Stopping in the kitchen, he winced as he grabbed a bottle of blood. He hadn't been lying. The stock was diminishing. It maybe wasn't a bad idea to be getting in touch with Theon. Kat was right. He wasn't drinking enough, and he couldn't let anything like what happened earlier happen again.

And now, knowing how she felt, it made drinking this blood even harder than usual. She didn't realize how much he craved to taste her again. How much the memory of her life force sliding down his throat haunted him. Not because he'd almost killed her that day, but because it had been *divine*. He didn't particularly want to examine what that said about him as he grabbed a jacket from the hook near the lift and stepped inside, taking a long swallow from the bottle.

All he knew was she wanted this as much as he did, and that information somehow changed everything and nothing.

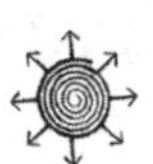

The trek to the main gates was uneventful, and he'd expected to run into Bohden when he got here. The entire way he'd been preparing for the confrontation, but his father's Commander-of-Forces was nowhere to be seen. There were the usual Arius sentinels about, but they wouldn't question him. Not without Bohden present.

He made his way into the main office, swiping an emergency cell phone before moving to a more private location, but he stayed outside. The clouds were blocking the sun, and if he wasn't so pissed at Tessa, he'd almost thank her for being miserable today to provide the cloud cover.

"Who is this?" came Theon's dark voice when he answered after the second ring.

"Who pissed in your coffee this morning?" Axel asked, watching the clouds drift across the sky. Taking it all in. Memorizing it.

"Axel? What's wrong?" Theon asked immediately.

What isn't at this point? he thought. But to Theon he said, "I need an update on a blood supply. Mine are almost gone, and . . ."

"And what?"

He sighed, rubbing at his brow. "It's not enough, Theon. I tried to feed from Kat in my sleep. She had to use her magic to fend me off, and the babe is already taking all her energy. She doesn't need to be expending it on this shit."

"Is she all right?"

"Yes, but that isn't the point. When are you able to come back?"

"I'm . . . not sure," he ground out. "Things didn't go as planned."

"They never do when Tessa is involved."

"Yeah . . ."

"There's more."

There was an audible sigh, but it wasn't irritation. It was a palpable heaviness.

When he didn't speak, Axel said, "Kat wants to talk to Tessa."

"What? Why?" he asked, the surprise carrying down the line.

"We've been seeing Miara every week for the babe, and she mentioned some possible futures a few days ago."

"Godsdammit," Theon muttered. "The future can change. Visions are only possibilities."

"I know, but she was pretty certain. Said we should talk to Cienna, which isn't exactly possible right now."

"Call Luka. He's with her."

"I'm calling *you,*" Axel retorted. "My wife wants to talk to Tessa, not Cienna. And while I hate the idea, and don't want her anywhere near Kat, she's insistent. If I don't come through on this, she's going to take matters into her own hands."

"She's smarter than that," Theon argued.

"She's a mother," Axel said. "She's logical about everything else, but the life of our son? Logic doesn't exist when it comes to a mother protecting her child. That's what it's supposed to look like. Not what we grew up with."

"Okay. Just . . ." Theon trailed off, and Axel could practically see him pacing wherever he was, shoving a hand through already disheveled hair. "I'm on a timeline here. I can't leave for at least two weeks."

"I won't last that long, Theon. I can't get any blood here."

"I know," he gritted out. "I'll send Luka."

"He's not with you?" Axel asked in confusion. "I thought you were going to find Tessa, and Luka was with Tessa."

"I found Tessa, but they aren't together. And I haven't been able to talk to Tessa alone. She's at the Celeste Estate. Rordan is here. Her fucking friends from the Estate are here. But everything else is going fine there?"

"I've locked in some alliances," he answered, scanning the area to make sure he was still alone. "The Witches are with us. I think we have the Shifters. We have a meeting with the Fae leaders in a few days."

"You're doing well, Axel," Theon said. "I'll make sure you get some blood."

"And Tessa? What should I tell Kat?"

"I'll bring her as soon as I can."

"She's not going to like that answer."

"It's the best I can do right now," Theon said. "Tell her I swear I'll be there as soon as I can."

"Yeah, all right," Axel grumbled, not convinced in the least.

"Axel."

"What?"

"We're almost there," Theon said. "When I come there with Tessa, I'll be the Arius Lord. Tell her that. Tell her we're almost there."

The line went dead, and Axel looked down at the phone.

He would be the Arius Lord? What the fuck did that mean?

He pondered the possibilities all the way back to the Charter District while also marveling at not having any trouble this entire trip. It was unheard of in the Underground. But when he entered his building, he knew immediately something was wrong. The doorman was inside, stationed where the building managers usually were.

Axel didn't bother asking. He raced for the lift, jamming the button repeatedly, even while ascending to the penthouse. The moment he stepped into the foyer, Kat was there. Her face was pale, and there was genuine fear in her eyes as she clung to him, trembling. She hadn't feared him that morning. Had faced him without flinching. Whatever this was, it was bad.

"What the fuck happened?" he demanded, taking in everyone in the room. The building manager was here, yes, but so were the two Legacy he'd called in favors with and three Witches, including Miara.

"You had a delivery," Ajax, one of the banished Legacy, said grimly.

"A delivery of what?"

"I think it was more of a message," Miara said tightly, motioning to one of the other Witches.

The female stepped forward, a canvas bag in her fingers.

A canvas bag stained with blood on the bottom and dripping onto the marble floor.

She reached inside, and Axel pressed Kat farther into his chest, shielding her face.

Because that was Bohden's severed head in the Witch's hand.

And he had no doubts who had sent him the Commander-of-Force's head.

Bree Fucking DelaCrux.

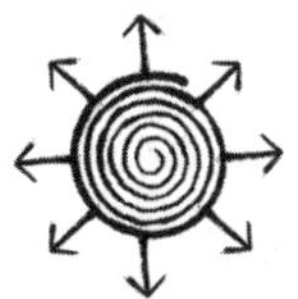

19
EVIANA

"Motherfucker," Lange grumbled when the vehicle lumbered over a large pothole in the road. Everything not secured rolled all over the back of the truck. Corbin grabbed him, keeping him from rolling off the bench where he was stretched out, his head resting on Corbin's thigh. "Every fucking time I'm asleep. You'd think they'd be able to keep their roads in decent condition."

He was grumpier in the truck. Or maybe it was just her effect on him. When Eviana had first met Lange and Corbin, Lange had been the more carefree and easygoing of the two. But with each passing day, he became snarkier. Darker. A little meaner. She should probably feel bad about it, but truthfully, it was a good thing. He'd need that grit for what they were about to face. Sunny dispositions got you nowhere in Devram.

Even if she was starting not to mind his stupid nickname for her.

"How can you sleep, *bellana*?" Lange muttered, something hitting her in her face.

She opened her eyes, stretched out on her own bench, and glared at Lange, brushing the crumpled napkin onto the floor. "I'm not sleeping with your constant commentary," she retorted.

"Like you could sleep in these conditions anyway."

"I've slept in far worse, wind walker. At least we've been alone these last several days."

She could feel eyes on her, and she glanced at Corbin, finding him watching her far too intently. If Lange was the carefree one, Corbin was too observant and introspective. Which wasn't surprising. She was sure it was an instinct based on what he was, but it didn't mean she liked it.

"Do you think we're close?" Lange asked around a yawn, trying to stretch out a little more. Corbin's hand fell to his chest, fingers brushing down his torso and back up. Lange relaxed some under the comforting touch, and Eviana suddenly wondered if she'd ever find a touch comforting like that.

Probably not.

"I don't know," Corbin answered. "We've never been to the Serafina Kingdom."

"That means we're once again reliant on you, *bellana*," Lange drawled, and Eviana shrugged, pushing to a sitting position.

She climbed onto the bench, pushing onto her tiptoes. It allowed her to just see out of the small rectangular window. Nothing had changed since the last time she'd looked out, and she said as much when she answered, "Still just trees."

"They're not just trees," Lange said, sitting up himself and reaching for a bag of food they'd been given. It hadn't been much. Deli sandwiches. Fruit. Cheese. Water. He fished out a small bag of carrot sticks, opening it up.

"The trees aren't the problem," she replied, leaping lightly off the bench before beginning to move from one end of the space to the other.

"Stop doing that," Lange muttered. "It makes me uneasy."

"That's unfortunate for you," she said, not ceasing her movements.

She knew exactly where they were though. Just as she'd predicted, they'd traveled around the Dreamlock Woods. Actually, they'd given the woods a larger berth than she'd thought they would, adding more days to this trip than she'd anticipated. They'd stopped in cities along the way so the transporters could rest and eat. That was when they were allowed to use restrooms, under supervision of course. They had to put bands on whenever they left the truck, but the moment they were locked behind the warded doors again, they removed each other's.

But the Serafina Estate was maybe a day's travel away now, and they needed to get out of here and into the woods before they passed it.

"How many times have you been here?" Corbin asked, his hazel eyes tracking her progress back and forth.

"Why does that matter?" she replied.

"Just trying to gauge if we have any idea what to expect. I'm from the Anala Kingdom. Lange is from Falein. We were both at Celeste and then Arius. All the kingdoms are different, and this is the only one we've never stepped foot in."

"The Serafina Kingdom is—"

But she went still, sucking in a sharp breath. Frozen. She felt entirely frozen for several seconds, unable to breathe out. As though she was being attacked by a water and an air Fae at the same time, but this wasn't that.

She moved with purpose then, leaping back onto the bench to peer out the window. The Source bond and all its facets were still blocked, but she didn't need a bond to know the oppressive shadows drifting about like a fine mist were Valter. She'd know his magic anywhere.

"We need to get out of here," she said tightly, stepping back down from the bench.

"If we could do that, we would have done so already," Lange said dryly.

"It wasn't time until now," she replied, efficiently packing up the backpack. She slipped a couple sets of bands into the bag and pulled out the glove Lev had slipped to her. "You two need to create a diversion. Get them to stop the truck."

They stared back at her as though she'd just spoken in an ancient language.

"Get them to stop the truck, and I'll get us out," she said, her power thrumming with excitement at the prospect of being unleashed after weeks and weeks of being trapped.

"You'll get us out," Corbin repeated, those intuitive eyes narrowing. "You've been able to get us out this entire time?"

"Not while the truck is moving."

"But you can . . . Why did you wait?"

"Because she set this all up," Lange said, venom in every word as he got to his feet. He prowled forward, and that darkness she'd been contemplating earlier spiked. He looked more like a predator as he towered over her, his teeth bared.

He looked like a primal Fae, the way they were always meant to be. Not submissive beings who answered to the Legacy of gods. Not tamed creatures, bowing and serving.

She started when he reached out and took her chin between his thumb and forefinger, holding her stare as he said, "She set you up to be captured back in that town. I couldn't figure out why until now. You're trying to get somewhere."

Eviana scowled, shoving his hand away from her face, but Corbin was there too. Both of them advanced until she was up against the wall of the truck. They hit another bump, and she stumbled, falling into Corbin's chest, but Lange shoved her back hard enough that the back of her head slammed into the truck wall.

Lange gripped her chin fully now, his fingers squeezing in an all too familiar way. Each word was laced with a quiet fury as he said, "You've put our lives at risk. I know you don't give a single fuck about anyone else, but you're going to tell us what exactly we're giving our lives for, Eviana. You're going to tell us now, or we're not doing shit."

"Lange," Corbin said, a low sternness to his tone.

"No, Corbin," Lange retorted. "She had you fucking *kidnapped*. They could have killed you right then and there. She didn't care. She's after something, and she's using us to get it. We deserve to know what we're about to die for."

But Eviana said nothing as she held his malice-filled stare. She knew her eyes were just as hard, revealing nothing, and Lange released her face with a mirthless scoff.

"You're just as bad as the Legacy," he sneered.

"I don't know why you ever thought otherwise," she replied flatly, still not daring to move. Corbin still stood before her, even with Lange stalking a few paces away.

"If you told us, we could help," Corbin said quietly.

"Don't bother, Corbin. I already tried," Lange spat, kicking a discarded water bottle to the other end of the truck. "She's a selfish cunt that poisons everything and everyone who comes in contact with her. We should help deliver her to Valter. Maybe then he'd spare our godsdamn lives."

"Lange!" Corbin barked, his head snapping towards his lover. "What the fuck is wrong with you?"

But Lange didn't answer. He just shook his head before dropping back onto the bench, staring resolutely ahead.

Corbin slowly turned back to Eviana, and she saw it then. The subtle shift in his eyes. She'd been waiting for it. The larger pupils. The change from hazel to a pale gold. The shape even became a little more almond shaped.

More feline.

His hands landed on either side of her head, caging her in as he leaned down. His voice was soft and cold, so low she wasn't sure even Lange's Fae hearing could pick up the words. "You're changing him. Whatever the fuck you're doing is changing him. So this is what's going to happen." Each word was accompanied by a low, fierce growl. "We're going to get this truck to stop. You're going to get us out of here, and the moment it's safe, you're telling us *everything*. If not, we'll do exactly what Lange said and turn you over to your Master."

"He'll still punish you," Eviana said evenly.

"As long as you're back under his control and unable to even breathe without his consent, I don't think I give a fuck."

She stared up at him because for the first time in decades, something stirred in her chest. An emotion she hadn't paid any mind to for years and years. An emotion that never served her.

But she felt a trickle of fear. They meant it. They would give her back to Valter, who was currently far too close for comfort, and then she would never save the only person who truly mattered to her. She could understand their anger in that regard. They cared for each other in the way she cared for Priya. Would kill and torture, burn and endure for each other.

She let them see none of that though. Right now she needed to focus on getting into the woods, far from Valter. Once she'd gotten to Priya, gotten the girl to safety, she'd gladly turn herself back over, as long as Priya was no longer an option for him.

So Eviana gave Corbin a sharp, curt nod, and he pushed off the wall. She stayed rooted to the spot, watching him approach Lange. Watched as he reached out and tilted the male's face up to his own. Watched as some silent exchange happened between them before he bent down, brushing his lips against his.

Then he held out a hand, pulling Lange to his feet. She wasn't sure what they were doing as they stood on one side of the truck before rushing to the other. Back and forth they went, throwing all of themselves into the sides.

And the truck started rocking.

It was like they were on a godsdamn boat with the full strength of two Fae males going back and forth. Eviana stumbled, dropping to her knees at one point, splitting them open, but she scrambled back to her feet. Grappling for the glove, she crouched near the doors, trying to keep her footing.

Someone in the truck cab pounded on the box, a muffled order to "Knock it the fuck off," carrying to them, but they didn't stop. Even when the truck slowed, pulling off to the side. Even when they were panting with exertion, they didn't stop.

And when the truck stilled completely, Eviana pressed the bloodied glove to the doors, hearing the latches click. She pushed a door open and hopped out, moving quickly. The sentinels weren't even fully out of the cab yet when she conjured vines and snapped them out, wrapping around their necks and yanking them to the ground.

She dropped low, pressing her hand to the asphalt. Her power delighted as it called up roots from the nearby trees, the streets buckling under their strength and the cement exploding around them. Fragments of rock rained down, but the roots rose up like a dome, keeping her protected. Wrapping around the bound bodies. Dragging them down through the rubble to the earth below, strangled cries dying out.

The escort vehicles were screeching to a halt, and she knew they had only seconds. Eviana whirled back to the truck, finding Lange and Corbin wide-eyed.

"Holy fuck," Lange murmured.

She quickly made her way over to them, reaching into the truck and grabbing the pack she'd left just inside. Pulling out her makeshift weapons, she passed one to Lange, keeping the dagger she'd taken from Raven Harbor for herself.

"Are the winds warning you of anything we can't see?" she asked, pulling the pack onto her back while they jumped down to the rubble-strewn ground.

"Why do you keep asking that?" Lange demanded. "And why didn't you give Corbin a weapon?"

"You have your powers, but Corbin is more. You know it. I know it," she retorted, moving to Lange's side. "We need a shield to buy us time. Now."

Lange didn't argue, throwing up a hand and creating a hard shield of wind. She watched the sentinels struggle against it, one with air magic trying to counter Lange. He was more powerful though, even if he grunted softly at the exertion.

"Valter is nearby. I need you to find out which direction," she said, using her magic to draw up more tree roots. The element of surprise was gone now though, and they were actively combating her too.

"I don't—"

"Do it, Lange," Corbin cut in.

Lange was quiet, his jaw clenching before he said, "I can't do that and keep this shield in place. I haven't had enough practice. It's too much."

"Then your lover will need to shift," she said simply, tightening her grip on the dagger as the sentinels moved closer. "But mark my words, if Valter gets to us first, death would be a kindness. He knows what you both are. He has plans. You wonder why I am the way I am? You would find out firsthand how I became one of the monsters."

"If we do what you say, then what?" Lange countered. "We're still fucked."

"We go to the woods. They won't follow, and even if they do—"

"We are *not* going into the Dreamlock Woods," Corbin interjected.

"Then we may as well let them take us to Valter," she replied. "Choose your nightmare."

Corbin cursed under his breath, shoving a hand through his hair. "Apparently you're my fucking nightmare," he muttered, straightening again. He glanced at Lange, so focused on holding that shield in place, before he said, "What I said in the truck stands. Get us out of this, and then you tell us everything."

Eviana didn't bother answering, drawing up her magic to the tips of fingers in one hand and tightening her grip on the dagger in the other. It was the only weapon they had that could actually kill a Legacy, but she didn't want to kill them. She wanted them incapacitated so they could slip bands on them. If they couldn't use their magic, they would be no match for her, Lange, or Corbin. The problem was they were outnumbered and only had so many sets of bands.

Which is why Corbin needed to shift.

"I need to know where Valter is so I know which direction to go," Eviana said. "If Lange needs to lower the shield to focus on that, we need to be ready. At our strongest."

"Yeah, yeah," Corbin muttered, stretching his neck from side to side. "You ready, Lange?"

The male nodded, small beads of sweat at his hairline.

"Protect him like you care for him," Eviana said.

"I love him," Corbin snapped.

That would do. She assumed that meant he would do whatever was necessary to keep him safe.

With a nod, Lange lowered his shields. The sentinels wasted no time, power racing for them. The earth magic wasn't an issue. She was stronger than anyone here. More than that, she didn't *need* the roots and plants around her. Using them simply didn't drain her reserves as quickly.

The water attacks were harder to dodge. Snares of water and knives of ice. Corbin was able to fend off most of those, although she felt the sharp slice of magic more than once as they fought.

"Where is he?" she demanded, needing Lange to hurry the fuck up.

"He's trying," Corbin snapped, freezing a whip of water while Eviana struck out with her foot, shattering the ice.

"He needs to try harder," she retorted, rallying her magic. Her palm face-down, she raised her arm. The rocks and rubble around them rose with it, hovering in the air above their heads. The sentinels panicked, covering their heads, but they didn't veer away. Too close. They were too close.

With a surge of strength, she brought the debris closer, concentrating it above the closest two before letting it fall. One sentinel went down, buried beneath the asphalt pieces. The other took a hit to the head, a wide gash cut down the side of his face, now dripping blood.

"You fucking bitch," he seethed as she planted her feet, needing him close to plunge her dagger into his heart.

Until a giant mountain cat appeared, mauling the male and taking him to the ground.

About godsdamn time.

Sleek and powerful, the mountain cat's jaws clamped around the male's throat. An Anahita Legacy, daggers of ice appeared in his hand, but they became water before they could be plunged into the cat's side. Apparently, Corbin could control his water element while in his shifted form.

Interesting.

Eviana whirled to Lange, finding him with his eyes closed. She opened her mouth, ready to berate him for not knowing yet, but he held up a hand.

"Don't say a fucking word," he muttered, brow pinched in concentration.

Corbin prowled over, his massive paws silent on the rubble, and he planted himself between her and Lange. His feline eyes narrowed, a faint golden glow pulsing around them.

"We don't have time. We're out of it," she said, knowing more sentinels would appear any second. Not to mention Lev.

"He's to the south. Waiting," Lange said, his eyes snapping open.

"He won't once he learns we've stopped and there's been an incident," Eviana said. "We need to run. Now. To the woods."

They took off, Lange snatching the pack right off her back, allowing her to move faster while he carried that weight. Corbin went ahead, taking down a sentinel while she combined her power with a gust of air from Lange, rubble slamming into another sentinel so violently, he was thrown feet into the air.

The males were faster, their strides longer, but she pushed herself harder. Once they made it past the tree line, they could slow. She could tell Corbin was holding back to stay by Lange's side, and they were so close.

But not close enough.

She could see the shadows thickening. Knew Valter had been told what was happening.

Then she was crying out as she was lifted from the ground before she was choking on a lungful of water. Lev was walking calmly towards her, one hand raised and the other in his pocket, and she was trapped in a fucking orb of water.

Corbin and Lange skidded to a halt, spinning back to see what was going on, and she wanted to scream that they were being idiots. That they needed to keep going, keep running.

But then they did just that. A look passed between them, and they turned, racing for the woods and leaving her behind. It was what they should do. Every person for themselves and all that. It was the way of Devram, and yet . . .

Pushing down whatever it was she was trying to feel, she focused on Lev. Her features became impassive and unreadable as she stared back at him. Her lungs were burning now, unable to pull in oxygen, and she ground her teeth, refusing or unable to show her discomfort. She wasn't entirely sure. She'd spent too many decades training herself not to show the pain but to endure it silently. Too many of the people she was forced to spend time with got off on inflicting pain, including her Master.

Deep blue eyes held hers, and he rotated his palm, the orb she was in spinning with the movement, making her disoriented.

Fucking prick.

Then she was falling, crashing to the ground hard enough to feel it in all her bones. She heard rips as various portions of her clothing tore on the sharp rubble scattered about, and she'd bitten her tongue so hard, she spat blood as she glared at Lev walking towards her. Her clothing was soaked, weighing her down, and the boots Tessa had given her were filled with water.

Curling her fingers into the rocks and dirt, she felt tree roots shuddering as she called them to her, the ground shaking.

"Don't," Lev snarled, a dagger of ice pressing to her throat. "I told you I would have to stop you if you tried to escape."

"And I told you that you could try," she replied, her voice a little hoarse.

And before he could say anything else, the roots exploded from the ground. Four found Lev, and he was on his back before he could fully process what was happening. The rest wound around her, soaking up some of the water from her coat and pants as they placed her gently on her feet. A single vine unfurled, slithering up like a snake to present the dagger she'd dropped at some point, and she took the hilt in her hand.

Taking the few steps to his side, she stared down at Lev. His eyes were hard as he struggled against the tree roots, but not even his ice weapons could slice through them.

She lowered to a crouch, the roots pulling back enough to reveal a space on his chest.

Directly over his heart.

"Do it then," Lev gritted out. "What was it you said? None of us really care about survival anyway?"

"I . . ." Her fingers tightened, the dagger still at her side.

"Maya will punish me for losing you," he said, his head dropping back in defeat.

"Would you prefer that? Would you prefer to live and face her wrath?" she asked, her tone as flat and cold as the Witches of the Underground.

His jaw flexed as he ground his teeth, and it was answer enough. None of them could ask for death. None of them could end their own misery. And she was already fucked if caught, so what would it matter if she added more to her punishment?

"You could come with us," Eviana said, not sure where the words had come from or why she was offering it.

"No, I can't," he said, his voice thick. "We both know it. However you're keeping Valter from finding you won't work. I would be a beacon right to you, Eviana. I don't know what you're doing, but I meant what I said. I don't want any part of it."

Eviana nodded, looking around at the destruction. At the shadows that were only growing. She was wasting time. Another sentinel could appear at any moment, and she'd used so much of her power too fast. They were out in the open for anyone to see, anyone to find.

She heard the rocks crunching under boots, saw the mountain cat in her periphery. Then a large hand wrapped around the one that gripped the dagger, and Lange lowered down beside her. They hadn't left her, and that realization made her *feel* something. Something that was too much with what she was facing.

"You are sure about this?" Lange asked, his voice low and soft.

She didn't know if he was asking her or Lev, but they both nodded. Corbin sat, tail switching and keen eyes observing, as Lange lifted her hand and guided it, the blade hovering over that cleared spot on Lev's chest. It would still be her hand that did it. That gave Lev mercy. Her hand that spilled his blood, not the Fae male's. They wouldn't be punished because it was her giving this to someone as tired and as tortured as she was. Who understood that to continue living this life wasn't living at all.

The dagger came down.

It sliced through flesh and muscle and bone.

And the only sign of pain was a small wince from Lev, because even in death, they knew better than to show emotion. Than to betray themselves or their Masters.

Blood dribbled from the corner of his mouth as Lev whispered, "Thank you, Eviana."

And then his eyes closed forever, and her eyes fell closed too, wetness clinging to her lashes.

The last time she'd cried was the day they'd taken something small and innocent from her.

"We have to go," Lange said too gently for someone that had just helped end a life.

Eviana nodded, yanking the dagger back to herself. Lange took it from her hand, wiping the blade on Lev's coat before handing it back to her. She shoved it down the side of her boot before standing.

"I'm sorry," Lange said when she turned away.

"Don't be," she replied coldly. "Let's go."

They were silent as they hurried to the trees, slipping into the Dreamlock Woods. They couldn't go too deep yet, but they needed to get deep enough that they'd be nearly impossible to find.

Somewhere along the way, Lange had swiped the pack he'd dropped. It was slung over one shoulder, and Corbin stayed in his mountain cat form for whatever reason. She didn't have it in her to wonder right now.

So no one spoke.

No one spoke when she finally stopped, too tired to continue. No one spoke as they coaxed a small fire to life, eating protein bars and apples. No one spoke when she curled up on her side to sleep. No one spoke, but they stayed closer than they ever had before.

Corbin lay down near her head, and Lange stretched out beside her, his head resting against Corbin's flank. He wasn't touching her, but she could feel his body heat. Inches away, the comfort was an offering if she chose to take it.

She didn't.

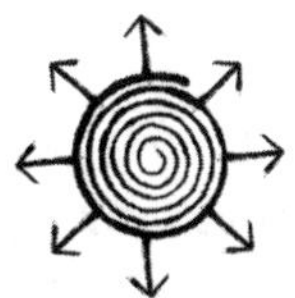

20
THEON

Finally.

That was all he could think as he sucked in a sharp breath. This always happened when he found himself here. It took a moment to orient himself, although it was getting easier each time. The hardest part was figuring out where in Devram he was and where he'd most likely find her.

Still in his suit from dinner, he turned in a slow circle. Everything was in ruins, as it always was. Partial buildings covered in moss and decay. Rubble and the-gods-knew-what else under his feet. The black waters rushed and flowed, but this wasn't the Night Waters because this wasn't the Arius Kingdom. Which meant it was likely the Wynfell River. It was the only other place with black water because he'd turned them black himself. There was the possibility that someone at some time had turned some waters black in the future, but he didn't have time to contemplate the odds. He never knew how long she'd keep him here.

He started moving, his pace brisk, keeping an eye out for the only other person he ever saw here. She always kept her distance, and he was still trying to figure out what her presence meant.

There were trees far off, and it didn't take long to realize he was close to Faven. Or what would have been Faven. Decades in the future, it was as desolate as everywhere else, the Fates having come just like he'd said they would.

Just like it'd been prophesied.

But she'd survived. These visions proved that, and that was all that mattered.

He turned, about to head toward what would have been the capital city, when he spotted the glimmer of gold as the sun's rays caught on her hair. Forcing himself not to run, he made his way to her, rounding a small bend to find her standing at the river's edge, arms wrapped tightly around herself.

He stopped a few feet away, knowing she heard his approach, and he slipped his hands into his pockets, always letting her take the lead on these encounters.

"You have a wife," she said, her gaze fixed on something across the river.

"I am required to take a Match to get back to you," he answered. "Everything is always for you, little storm."

"Always with the pretty words," she muttered, her light coiling around her with those brilliant new black and gold embers and sparks flitting among it.

"I tried to tell you last time," he replied.

Those words finally had her turning to him, a look of puzzlement staring back at him. "Last time?"

"The last time you pulled me to this place."

The confusion stayed for a few seconds before it morphed into surprise. "Pulled you in . . . You're not a phantom? You're . . ."

She trailed off as he came closer, eating up the space between them in a few long strides. Lifting a hand, he cupped her cheek, and she tilted her head back to look up at him. He took in every piece of her. The bright violet eyes, suspicious yet with a glimmer of hope. The golden hair, unbound and drifting in the soft breeze. Her soft skin beneath his fingertips. The light and dark flowing around her. Courting her. Calling her to go deeper, to let go, to give it control. Finally understanding, after all this time, what she needed.

"Where is Luka, Tessa?"

She frowned, immediately tensing. "He doesn't want us, so we let him go." She stared up at him, earnest and imploring, when she said, "That's what we do, right? When we love someone? We let them go when they don't want us? We set them free and let worlds burn to nothing to make sure they are happy? It's what . . ."

She trailed off as his thumb brushed along her cheek, a simple soothing motion that she leaned into. Her eyes fluttered closed for a few seconds, and when she opened them, tears clung to her lashes.

"He's not here because we're all too broken," she whispered.

He leaned down, pressing his brow to hers. "Maybe we're all broken, but maybe together we can form something new. Something whole."

She was quiet, her eyes closing once more. Something flitted across her face, an expression of wanting something that was impossible to have.

But she was wrong.

He'd swore to always give her everything she needed. He'd failed on so many counts in delivering on that promise, but he would not fail in this.

"Look at me, Tessa," he said, the order low and rough.

And like she always had, she obeyed. Her eyes fluttered open, holding his. Misery and desperation stared back at him in a rare show of vulnerability.

"I am yours. Every piece of me. In this life and all the ones to come," he said. "I'm sorry it took me so long to figure everything out. I'm sorry, but we'll fix it."

"We?"

He nodded, still cupping her cheek, while his other hand tentatively fell to her waist, tugging her a little closer. Forcing himself not to groan at the contact, he said, "We. Because it's not something I can do on my own."

She bit her bottom lip as she thought. Then her eyes narrowed when she said, "How do I know this is real? That I can trust you?"

He couldn't help the smirk that pulled at his mouth, admittedly something smug and satisfying. "How do you think I am here, clever tempest? You only pull people into your dreams that you trust implicitly."

"I . . ." She trailed off, still uncertain. Still wary. And he couldn't blame her after everything she'd experienced these last months. The entirety of her life.

"You're not alone, Tessa," he murmured, brushing his lips across hers in the lightest of kisses. He still felt her shudder at the contact. "Wake up, and I'll prove it."

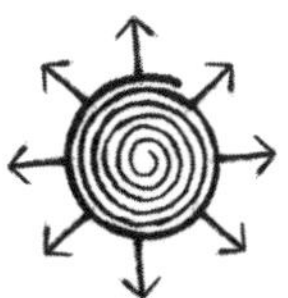

21
THEON

He was on his feet before he was fully awake, still completely dressed from dinner earlier this evening. For days he'd been waiting for Tessa to pull him into her dreams. He hadn't been able to get a moment alone with her. Rordan and Dex made sure she was never by herself, and at night, her room was guarded by seraphs and warded. Up until this moment, he hadn't even been sure she *wanted* to talk to him.

He hadn't lied to her. He'd tried to warn her about what was going to happen the last time she'd pulled him into a dream. But then she'd kissed him and he was powerless when she did that. When she clung to him like it was the only way she could survive. When she wasn't fighting him and they were both grasping to keep something so fleeting and impossible.

Theon shrugged off his suit jacket and loosened his tie before taking that off as well, tossing it to the sofa. He'd never stayed at the Estates before. He'd never even visited them really. Luka had always gone and done the scouting, his father wanting their plans kept a secret. What nobody had realized was that Theon had been keeping *his* plans a secret from his father too, and while Luka was visiting estates on his behalf, he was dealing with his father's attempts to get him to fall in line.

Still, with the Ladies not "able" to come here for two godsdamn weeks, he'd become more than a little acquainted with the Estate these last several days. It was spacious, much like the academic campuses he'd read about and even attended occasionally, although he was never gone from Arius House for more than a few months at a time. The main building housed the foyer, dining hall, a few small meeting rooms, the Estate Mother's office, and other inconsequential rooms. The second and third floors were her private living quarters. There were dormitories for the Fae, segregated by age, and at the southernmost part of the estate was a grander complex designated specifically for when Legacy were visiting. Rordan was staying in Cordelia's living space. Seraphs roamed the halls of the complex, and he'd been given a suite on the second floor while Tessa was being watched and sequestered in a suite on the top floor.

Now he just needed to figure out how to get into it.

"Are you finally coming to bed?"

Theon turned to find Felicity in the bedroom doorway, a silk robe tied loosely around her. Her long hair was flowing over her shoulders, and she tugged at the sash of the robe as she sauntered into the room.

"I don't know why you're asking that," Theon said tightly, rolling back his shirt sleeves to his elbows.

"Because part of the Match contract involves me conceiving an heir, Theon," she said, frustration seeping into her tone. "I can't exactly do that if you won't even sleep in the same bed as me."

"I don't need to share a bed to fuck you, Felicity," Theon said darkly. "But even with that being the case, you will never carry my child because we will never fuck, let alone share a bed."

"I understand you're just using me to get to Tessa," she said, her tone going sultry once more. She came closer still, the robe falling open. "But you understand you can have us both, right? Keep the female, Theon. I don't care. I'm only here to help. She can't carry your heir. The other kingdoms would never stand for it."

She stood directly in front of him now, the robe hanging off her shoulders revealing full breasts and the flat planes of her torso. Long legs led up to the apex of her thighs, as bare as the rest of her. She brought her hands up, her palms landing on his stomach. They slid up to his chest, the robe slipping down her arms, and she pushed onto her toes.

And then he felt her power pressing against him. A power that could increase conflict or deflate it. It pulsed around him, emanating out from her palms as her lips brushed his jaw.

"Use me, Theon. I'm here to make your life easier as your Match. It's my role as a Lord's wife," she murmured against his skin, getting braver when he didn't stop her. One of her hands slid around the nape of his neck as she moved from his jaw to his cheek, getting ever closer to his mouth.

Her lips were a mere inch from his when she gasped, eyes going wide. She tried to lurch back, but his power had wound around her throat, keeping her still. Darkness thrummed as he took a step back from her, wanting her to understand every bit of this rejection.

"I am not fucking you, Felicity. Not ever. We will never share a bed, and Tessa will never be required to share me. Your side of the Match contract is not my concern," he said coldly.

"But you need an heir—" she rasped, gasping for air when his darkness tightened at her throat.

"Which is not your concern," he replied. "Here is what *is* your concern though, *Ms. Davers:* if you ever attempt to use your magic on me again, my power won't just be wrapped around your neck. It will snap it. Do you understand?"

She nodded frantically. Well, as much as she could anyway.

"Good," he said, making his way to the door. "The only thing I need you for right now is to ensure I get what I came for. You've always known what this is, and you'd do well to remember it. Do not leave this room tonight."

He slipped out the door, letting it click shut behind him before he released her from the grasp of his magic. He didn't know if she'd obey his order or not, but even if she didn't, she wouldn't leave right away. She was as manipulative as the rest of the realm. She had motives of her own. Her father may have agreed to the Match Contract in negotiations with Valter, but Felicity had wanted it. Wanted the status. Wanted the power that came with the title. She wouldn't risk that. Not yet. But he saw the desperation seeping into her actions. Like tonight.

He probably shouldn't have had that confrontation quite yet. He needed her compliant until that Lordship title was his, but then again, if things went as planned, he wouldn't need her for that either.

He took a side stairwell rather than the main, knowing it wouldn't matter much. The moment he crossed the wards, someone would be alerted. A plan would be better, but the only plan he could come up with was to deal with whoever tried to stop him.

The building was only five floors, and the moment he stepped foot on the staircase leading to the fifth, he felt the wards. He didn't slow, continuing up and coming face-to-face with one of Tessa's so-called friends. Not Dex or Oralia. The other one.

He had a roll of lull-leaf between his lips, and his dark eyes looked him up and down as he leaned against the doorframe of the stairwell.

"It's about time," he drawled, pinching the roll between his fingers. Then he added, "That won't be necessary."

"Somehow I doubt that," Theon replied, his magic coiled tightly in his palm, preparing for the fight that was sure to come.

"I know you haven't talked to her much as of late, but I'll take you to her. Let her explain."

"You're going to take me to Tessa?" Theon asked skeptically. "What's your name again?"

"Brecken," he answered, putting the lull-leaf back between his lips. Suddenly in front of him, a hand landed on Theon's forearm before he felt the pull in his stomach. The fucker could Travel.

In the next breath, he stood in a suite grander than the one he'd been given. It took up half of the fifth floor, and he wasn't sure how many rooms there were. A main bedroom for sure, along with the formal living room they were standing in.

And there she was, pacing back and forth before the unlit hearth. No lights were on. There was only the moonlight streaming in as she muttered to herself in the dark.

"We have a purpose," she was saying softly, never ceasing her back and forth strides. "They could help? No, no. It's too broken. I'm broken. They're broken. The realms and the gods. There can never be a balance."

Each step had her power trailing, the chaos echoing around her in a faint pulse. Not even that cuff could fully contain it. Her hands came up, fisting in her hair and pulling, and her face twisted in an agony that had his chest hurting. It *pained* him to see her like this.

"You going to say something?" Brecken asked flatly.

But his throat was dry, the words a hoarse rasp when he said, "Little storm?"

She shook her head. "Wasting so much time. We save him, and then we leave. They can be together. Happy. And I can—"

"Tessa, look at me," he said, the words sterner, clearer. Breaking through whatever she was battling internally.

Her head snapped up, violet eyes latching onto his, and her mouth dropped open. "You . . . You came?"

"One day, Tessalyn Ausra, you will understand that I do not lie to you," he said, rooted in place as she stared back at him. "I will always come for you."

She worried her bottom lip, one hand drifting back up to her hair as her gaze slid to Brecken. "You brought him here?"

"I did tell you time was running out," he replied, the lull-leaf between his fingers. "But I suppose I also am trying to prove something to you for some reason."

She scoffed, the smallest of smiles tugging at her lips, and while Theon was certain he didn't need to be, a minute part of him was jealous that she'd only smiled at the seraph since they'd appeared here.

Theon cleared his throat. "He said you would explain why we don't have to worry about him telling anyone I'm in here."

She was still staring at Brecken when she said, "He has been helping me. At the Sirana Villas and the Pantheon. He helped ensure the Fae were out of harm's way before I . . ."

"Then you believe we won't have unwanted interruptions tonight?"

Her eyes flashed to his, lightning flickering in their depths. "Where is your *wife?*"

He smiled then, a dark smirk that had her eyes widening slightly, but she held her ground. "That will be all," he said, keeping her attention on him as he dismissed Brecken.

He heard the seraph's chuckle under his breath before he Traveled out, and for the first time in months, he was alone with Tessa.

"Are you jealous, tempest?" he asked, one hand sliding into his pocket while the other came up, his thumb pressing to the corner of his mouth as he watched her.

"No," she sneered.

"Still with the lies," he chided.

"Enough," she snapped, both hands back in her hair, getting caught as she pulled. "I thought—You said—We came back to—" She was pacing in a small circle, nearly spinning in place, and then she whirled back to face him. "You said I could trust you. That you'd prove it to me. That you were mine. You can't be mine and hers. You can't . . ."

"I am only yours, Tessa," he said, his voice low and clear. "In this life and all the ones to come."

"You have a *wife*, Theon!" she cried. "How can you say that to me? I mean, I know I'm . . . I know I wanted . . . I know there's you and there's Luka, but this isn't that. I know it's not, and I can't—I won't . . ." She trailed off, shaking her head as she stumbled over her words, fury and agony behind every single one.

"She's not my wife," he said when she fell silent, her chest heaving with her emotions.

And she went so preternaturally still, he wasn't even sure she was breathing. Even her power had stilled, specks of gold and silver, white and onyx, frozen in the air around her, tangled with her hair. She looked fucking ethereal.

"She's not my wife," he repeated. "She thinks she is. Everyone believes she is. The priestess who performed the rite and gave the Union Mark was Gia. It's incomplete and not binding. At least not in that way."

"What does that mean?" she demanded.

"Gia wove a binding Mark into this one. Disguised it, I guess you could say. If Felicity learns the truth, she will be unable to betray me," he replied.

"Then she is bound to you."

"Until I decide to free her from that oath, yes. I suppose she is."

Her lips pursed, and he gave her a minute to process everything.

Finally she said, "I don't like her."

A huff of laughter burst from him. "I gathered that, little storm."

She nodded again, rubbing her fingertips together at her sides. Then her eyes snapped back to his once more. "You left me behind. You *left* me."

"I stand by what I said. I would let a realm become nothing but rubble for you. Let the Fates destroy every living, breathing thing in this world if it meant you could live. I do what must be done and have no regrets," he replied, taking a single step towards her. His head tilted as he studied her. "But you didn't leave. Why?"

"Because you are his family," she answered, that sharp tone faltering at the words.

"Luka?"

She visibly flinched at the name, but she nodded. "He doesn't want me, Theon. He wants you and Axel. His family. So I . . ."

"You what?"

"I wanted to save you for him. Then I will leave, and maybe the two of you can save Devram from itself," she said in a rush.

He tsked, taking another step closer. "Do you really think I will not follow you?"

"You weren't going to," she retorted, that anger flaring once more. "You sent me away like I was no—"

"Don't you dare say that," Theon interjected, his own fury flaring just as hot. "Do not imply that you are nothing to me when you are *everything*. I will do whatever is necessary to ensure you are safe. That you are protected.

And if that means I have to send you to another realm with a dragon, that's what I will do. As long as you are free and happy—"

"But we won't be happy without you!" she cried. "You always think you know what's best for everyone. Me. Luka. Axel. But we get choices, Theon! You don't just get to *decide* what makes us happy. You don't get to *decide* where I go, what I do. And you sure as fuck don't get to tell me to leave the fucking realm when you've made me lo—"

Her mouth snapped shut, eyes darting to the side, but there would be none of that. They were back in the place where they thrived. A push and pull. A constant battle. Uncensored words and heated actions.

"Don't go quiet now, Tessa," he purred, prowling forward and closing the distance between them. He took her chin between this thumb and forefinger, tilting her face up and forcing her to look at him. A stuttered breath fell from her lips, frustrated tears pooling in endless depths of violet while her power swirled among it all, trapped and unable to do anything more.

His other hand came up, fingertips running along the planes of her face. Her brow. The bridge of her nose. Tracing her upper lip.

"Say it," he said, a low command.

She tried to turn away, tried to free herself from his hold, but he held firm. Not now. Not this time.

"Say it," he growled again.

She swallowed thickly, one frustrated tear spilling over. It trailed down her cheek, and before he could stop himself, he pitched forward, catching that salty drop with the tip of his tongue and tracing its path. He heard the pained sound she tried to swallow down, and his lips brushed her flesh as he dragged his mouth to her ear.

"Say it," he whispered, the words low and dark and full of sinful promises. One finger found the hollow of her throat, dragging down between her breasts, along her stomach, lower. "Say it, and I will give you everything you want, clever tempest."

"Yours," she gasped out, her head tipping back with the single word. "I'm yours. Every piece of me. As much as I am his."

"That's right, you are," he growled, another gasp escaping her as he gathered her roughly into his arms.

"Theon!" she cried in outrage, but he wasn't waiting, making his way to a bedroom. The main bedroom. A spare bedroom. He didn't particularly care.

She'd finally said it. Those words he'd begged for. Longed to hear from her lips, and gods, he was glad she'd never lied about it. Never said them to appease him. Because her saying them when she meant them?

If he hadn't been irrevocably hers already, that would have done him in. He'd drop to his knees for her. Crawl for her. He'd give up his kingdom, this world, his very soul for her. And he needed her to understand, needed her to realize all of that.

For all the roughness of moments ago, he lowered her gently to the edge of the bed, leaning over her. His brow pressed to hers, just like in her dreams, and she lifted a trembling hand, sliding her fingers into his hair.

"You said it. In my dreams. But I need to know—"

"Yours, Tessa. Only and solely yours. You never need to question it," he said before his lips found hers. He tried to keep it soft and gentle, but that wasn't them. It never had been.

Her lips parted wider, and he took advantage. His tongue sank into the hot silk of her mouth, and he groaned when she nipped at his bottom lip. Her back arched, her need palpable, and he would never deny her. He palmed her breast through her shirt, only then realizing what she was wearing.

"This is his?" he asked, pulling back to look down at the black button-down shirt.

"It smells like him. It's my last one," she said, each breath harsh. "I would have found a way to steal one of yours. It makes the nightmares bearable."

"You're not alone, Tessa. Never again. I swear it."

She nodded, but he could see the uncertainty in the movement.

"How can I prove it?"

"I don't know," she whispered. "So much is unknown right now. I keep trying to change fate, and it's not working. Nothing is working. I'm broken, and we're broken. And what if that's how it's meant to be?"

"I refuse to accept that," he replied vehemently. "If that's what the Fates want, they can go fuck themselves."

"I spoke to Serafina, and she said—"

"You spoke to Serafina? The *goddess* Serafina?" he interrupted, unable to help himself.

She looked at him curiously, but then a tiny smirk pulled at the corner of her mouth. "Are you jealous?" she mocked.

"Fuck yes, I'm jealous," he said, palming her breast once more. "What did she tell you?"

Tessa sucked in a gasp, her eyes starting to glaze with lust. "She said . . ."

But she trailed off when he began teasing her nipple through the fabric of the shirt. "She said what, Tessa?"

"I asked her why she chose Arius over Achaz," she gasped again.

Theon hummed, bringing his mouth to her neck. "And what did she say?" he asked against her skin before latching onto it.

Tessa moaned, her fingers tightening in his hair. "She told me what you wouldn't." He nipped at her delicate skin as he growled at her answer. "Or maybe what you knew but didn't realize you knew," she amended with a quick inhale.

He pulled back then, her hand slipping from his hair as understanding donned. "She told you of the genesis bond."

"Not that exact term, but yes," she said, her breathing unsteady. "But *you* didn't tell me."

"I figured it out shortly before they put you in that cell, but I . . . Tessa, I didn't want you to be forced into another bond. Not if you didn't want it. I didn't want to put that pressure on you." Her eyes fell to her lap, where she was wringing her fingers together. "Please tell me you understand my intentions."

"I do," she whispered before lifting her gaze back to his. "I do because it's the same freedom I gave Luka."

Another lone tear slipped free, and she reached to swipe it away, but he caught her hand before she could. Intertwining their fingers, he stepped closer to the edge of the bed, between her legs. Releasing her hand, he slowly started working the buttons of the shirt she wore, slipping it down her arms and tossing it to the side.

With the tip of his finger beneath her chin, he tilted her face to his once more. "I promise we will fix all of this, Tessa."

She nodded mutely, uncertainty shifting to something more heated as her hands came up. They followed the path another's hands had trailed in another room. Up his torso to his chest, erasing all of it and leaving only her.

"But tonight, I just need you," she whispered as she returned the favor and undid the buttons of his shirt.

"Tessa," he groaned, her fingertips barely grazing his bare skin as she moved. Within moments, he removed the rest of his clothing and climbed onto the bed with her as she scooted farther up, her hair fanning across the plush pillows.

He stared down at her, and he found himself wondering if he was still dreaming because this . . . This was what dreams were made of.

"Mine," he whispered, running his fingers along her side, tracing her ribs, grazing her breast, along her collarbone. His hand trembled faintly, and he realized he would be content with this for the rest of the night. Marveling at her willingly beside him. Naked and glorious and waiting to be worshipped.

"Please, Theon," she said, the words bordering on a whine, breaking through his trance, and the reverence quickly turned into something wilder. Untamed. Feral.

Sliding on top of her, he sat back, touching and groping, because it had been far too long since he'd had her beneath him. He cupped a breast, her nipple peaked and hard, and another growl rumbled from him as he bent down, taking it in his mouth.

Tessa writhed, her hips seeking and searching. Aroused. Sensitive. His favorite way to have her.

"Patience, little storm," he chided, sitting back and running his thumb over her nipple again. "I know what you need."

"And I'm still questioning that," she retorted.

His laugh was soft and dark as his hand skimmed up to her throat, gripping loosely. "We both know that isn't true. We both know that I know exactly what to do when you're needy and wanting. And we both know you'll take whatever I give you."

Releasing her throat, he slid back off her, settling onto his side and propping his head on his fist.

"Then what are you doing?" she demanded, once again breathless.

One of her hands came up, skimming along her skin, kneading her own breast, but there would be none of that.

His darkness unfurled, wrapping around her wrists—and that godsdamn cuff he'd be getting the fuck off her—and pulling them above her head, keeping them there.

"As if I'm going to let you touch what's mine," he said with a soft snarl. "Do you have any idea how much I've missed touching you? Sleeping beside you? Sliding my cock into your tight cunt and feeling you come undone?" Her breath hitched at the words, and when her thighs rubbed together, he reached down, pulling one away. "I'll be the one to give you all your pleasure tonight, Tessa. Only me."

"Then get on with it," she retorted.

Or she tried to.

It was definitely a whine, and he chuckled again, leaning down to run the tip of his nose along the length of hers.

"Keep them open," he said in a dark command as he ran his fingers up the inside of her thigh. "Or I'll do it for you." She sucked in a sharp breath, but then she relaxed, her legs falling wider in obedience that she only ever gave him here. When she needed someone else to make the decisions, to make her feel good, to let her exist without expectations.

Trailing his fingers up, he brushed by the spot he knew she wanted him to touch. "You can be so good when it serves you," he said, leaning down to kiss along her jaw, down her neck. He nipped at her collarbone, her chest, dragging his mouth back to her breast. "You know you drive me mad, right?"

"Yes," she rasped, squirming to try to get his fingers where she wanted them.

He smacked her inner thigh, a cry coming from her lips as he rubbed his palm on the same spot, soothing the ache.

"I'm glad you realize how crazy you make me," he went on. "Because then you'll understand why I want to see you just as undone, just as crazed, as you make me."

"Theon," she gasped when he sucked her nipple into his mouth once more, swirling his tongue around it before moving to the other side. He didn't stop there though. He finally gave her what she'd wanted, circling her clit fast and hard. Her whimpers and gasps were a symphony he wanted to memorize. The only music he ever cared to listen to again.

He planted kisses between her breasts, down her torso. Gods, he was painfully hard, and all he wanted to do was climb on top of her and fuck her until they were so bonded, no one would ever doubt who she belonged to again. There was only one other who would have her like this, and if he walked away, he was a fucking fool.

"Are you as insane as I am yet, little storm? Do you understand what you do to me yet? What I crave and need and have to have?"

"Yes," she gasped, bucking against his hand.

"Are you sure? Because I don't know that you deserve to come until you do."

Her eyes had fallen closed, but they snapped open at that, lust and fury glaring back at him. "I always deserve to come."

"Is that so?" he smirked, watching that confidence falter just a little as he rolled back over her. He kissed her once, twice, before tracing the seam of her lips with his tongue. His cock slid against her wetness, and she chased him yet again, grinding up against him. "How do you plan to convince me not to drag this out? Because I'll admit, it's a sight to see you so needy for me."

She went still for the briefest of moments before her legs wrapped around his waist, pulling him closer. Pressing his dick against a hot and ready cunt.

"Fuck," he hissed, but she wasn't done.

Even with her wrists suspended above her head, she managed to lift up, pressing her bare breasts against his chest as she licked a path up his neck. He was chasing her now, leaning in, following her lips. Her teeth grazed below his ear before her tongue flicked his earlobe. Then her throaty voice rasped, "Please fuck me, Theon. I'm yours. Every piece of me, so claim me."

He cursed again as he shifted, lining himself up and sliding into a paradise that he was sure was better than the After. He felt her stretch around him, inch by inch, and he went as slow as he could, wanting to savor every second of having her. *Truly* having her. But his self-restraint was too frayed, and he was sliding in to the hilt, his eyes rolling back as he settled fully against her.

There was a soft sigh from her as her legs tightened around his waist, and he lifted his head, his lips brushing over her closed eyes. Brushing his nose down the length of hers. Taking her lips with his own.

"Perfectly wild," he murmured, kissing her again. "Perfectly untamed." Another kiss. "Perfect."

A soft cry sounded in her throat, and he felt her yanking at his magic. He obliged, freeing her wrists, and her arms immediately wrapped around his neck, keeping him close.

He tried to move slowly, sliding nearly all the way out before thrusting back in, but her heels dug into his back, urging him to go faster, harder.

"More," she keened, her back arching with every thrust. "You know me, Theon. You know what I need, and it's more."

Well, fuck. She didn't have to tell him twice.

Her hands slid across his back to his shoulder, nails digging into his flesh as he picked up his pace. Every thrust had more heat pooling at the base of his spine. It intensified every time he slammed back into her. It was base and primal, and the need to claim her just as she'd demanded was blinding.

There was only them. Her pants and moans, his grunts and curses. There was only her rolling her hips to meet every thrust. Only the feel of her around his length, hot and slick and *everything*.

"This is it. You realize that, right?" Theon ground out, leaning back to grip her hips, angling them up to hit deeper, harder. "There's no going back, Tessa. No more running."

"No more," she agreed, nodding her head frantically.

"No more," he repeated, over and over. It was a chant he wanted to drive into her as hard as he was fucking her.

And when she started spasming around him, so godsdamn close, he reached between them, rubbing until she was arching off the bed, her head thrashing from side to side as she chased bliss.

"Eyes on me, Tessa," he commanded, violet irises immediately finding his. "Good girl. Now give me what's mine."

And she did. She clamped down around him so tightly, he had no choice but to follow as she held him tight against her with her legs still wrapped around his waist. Falling forward, he caught himself on his forearms, not wanting to crush her beneath him, and her teeth sank into his shoulder as she cried out. Pulse after pulse coaxed every bit of release from him, and she was clinging to him like she'd never let him go.

By the gods, he prayed she'd never let him go.

He stayed hovered over her long after they both came down from their highs. He brushed the hair from her face, fingertips tracing and memorizing. She lightly dragged her nails up and down his back. Only when she shifted beneath him did he pull out of her. He rolled to the side, his hand splaying across her stomach because he couldn't not touch her. Not anymore. Not with her here beside him.

"How long have you known? That I was pulling you into my dreams," she clarified.

"Not long," he answered. "Well, I guess that's not true. I figured it out in one of your dreams when you said you don't know how to trust anyone. But I haven't been able to get back to you to explain. I was going to last time, but I ran out of time."

She nodded, reaching up and sliding her fingers through his hair, along his jaw, across his lips, but she didn't speak again.

Eventually they forced themselves out of bed to clean up, and Theon went to the small alcohol cart to retrieve them water, handing her a glass when she emerged from the bathroom. He didn't need to tell her to drink it. She did so without fuss, draining the whole thing before setting it on the nightstand and crawling back into the bed.

He followed suit, and she propped herself up on her elbows. The moonlight fell across her face as she said in surprise, "You're staying?"

"Do you want me to go?" he asked, halfway into the bed.

"No," she said quickly. "I sleep better with one of you with me."

"I'm staying, Tessa," he said, settling in and rolling onto his side. He reached across the bed, pulling her to him, her black flush against his chest.

Quiet seconds ticked by before she said, "What if they catch us?"

"They won't."

"How can you be certain?"

"I have a plan," he murmured, pressing a kiss to her temple. "Sleep, Tessa. We'll discuss it in the morning."

She tensed before relaxing against him once more. "You don't lie to me," she whispered.

"Not once."

She nodded, and minutes later she was asleep, her breathing soft and steady. Theon dragged his fingers up and down her bare arm, reveling in the fact she was giving him this. That she was his, and he was hers. And if it weren't for the moonlight, he would have missed the cords of black and gold that were trailing his fingers, chasing him.

He stilled, his fingertips still pressed to her flesh, but those cords caught him, winding around his fingers, his hand, his arm while doing the same to Tessa's arm. Winding together until they couldn't be separated. A beginning and an ending. Light and dark flared brightly before dimming and settling once more.

Repairing something broken or maybe creating something new altogether.

And he felt her.

All of her.

The defeat and the resilience.

The wild and the untamed.

The uncertainty and the fierceness

The broken and the healed, but not quite whole.

He pulled her tighter to him, burying his face in her hair. "We'll fix it, little storm," he whispered. "I swear to you we'll fix it all."

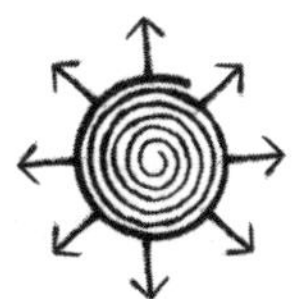

22
LUKA

"Now you can call me, you fucking prick?" Luka seethed, answering the phone after the third ring.

"Good to talk to you, too," Theon replied, and Luka could hear the godsdamn smile in his voice.

"You are an ass. Where the fuck have you been? I've been trying to reach you for weeks, Theon."

"I know," his friend said, turning serious. "I was . . . trying to stay out of things. I know you and Tessa weren't on good terms when I left, but I was hoping the two of you would figure it out. On your own. You needed to learn to exist without me, and I needed to try to do the same."

"And you didn't think that something possibly went wrong—that things didn't go as planned—when I kept calling?" Luka growled. "Oh, wait. How could you when you didn't have your phone on? Fuck, Theon!"

With nothing else to do, he hurled black flames off the balcony of his room, wishing he had something to throw or hit. He would go to the training room after he finished this phone call. Or flying. No, not flying. He wanted to destroy something.

"Did you get that out of your system?" Theon asked dryly.

"No, you dick," Luka retorted. "For weeks, I've been trying to figure out what to do. How to find you. What to do with Tessa. She's been . . . She didn't speak to anyone for days, Theon. Not a single word. Do you have any idea how godsdamn unnerving that is?"

"I am well-versed in Tessa not speaking to me, yes."

"And then she destroyed the Pantheon."

"I heard."

"After she summoned a fucking goddess!" Luka continued. "She *summoned* a goddess, Theon. Not just any goddess. Serafina." He was pacing now, long strides back and forth on that small, hidden balcony. "Destroyed the Pantheon and the mirror, so we couldn't leave like you said. And where could we go? Not back to Tristyn's penthouse. Not to the Underground. No. Our only option was my cave. There are too many fucking people here, Theon. They keep touching my things. I'm missing a small bowl."

A snort of laughter came down the line, and Luka wanted to throw the phone over the balcony. Or throw it to the ground and stomp on it.

"This is not funny, jackass," he growled, his dragon as irritated as he was. Irritation he'd been dealing with since he woke up to that letter. "My brother is here. My father. One wants nothing to do with me, and the other is trying. Cienna comes and goes. Gia's been gone for days now. And Tristyn left after Tess—"

"After Tessa left," Theon finished for him.

Luka stilled, turning to look out over the mountains spread before him. "You found her then I take it."

"Of course I fucking found her, Luka," he retorted sharply. "Did you even try?"

"We've been formulating a plan," he answered tightly. "We know seraphs took her—"

"To the Celeste Estate," Theon ground out.

"What?"

"You heard me. They took her to her godsdamn Estate."

"Why?"

"Because they're desperate to keep control of her, and what better way than taking her to the place where all her nightmares started?"

Well, fuck.

He pushed his hair back before swiping a hand down his face. "But you have her now?"

"Not fully," Theon said, his tone one Luka knew all too well. "We have to wait until the Ladies get here next week to approve me taking the Arius Lord seat."

"But Valter's not dead."

"There's lots to fill you in on," he answered. "But all I need to know from you right now is what you're planning to do. She told me she left. That she wasn't holding you to anything."

Luka said nothing, his grip on the phone tightening. Some part of him was jealous that she'd gone straight to Theon. It had always been the other way around. Theon driving her away, and her coming to him. He supposed this was his fault, but she'd pushed him to this point.

"Luka?" Theon said, his tone getting shorter. "What do you plan to do?"

"I don't know, all right?" he snapped. "She said she was going to leave, and—"

"And what? You thought I wouldn't follow her if she left this realm alone? The only reason I was able to let her go to begin with was because I knew you would be with her, Luka," he retorted.

"She knew where my father was for months and didn't say a fucking word, Theon!" Luka yelled into the phone. "How the fuck do you expect me to move past that?"

Silence greeted him, stretching on for a full minute before Theon finally spoke again.

"She was doing what everyone in Devram does, Luka. She was doing exactly what we'd taught her. She trusted no one—"

"She trusted *me*," Luka cut in. "I was the one she was pulling into her dreams. I was the one she was making concessions for. And yet she couldn't tell me *this*?"

"Did you ever ask her why?"

"Of course I did," Luka retorted, but when only silence greeted him once again, he let himself really think about it. She'd tried. She'd tried to explain and apologize, but he wouldn't hear it. And since then . . .

Since then he'd made it clear where he stood, and she'd done nothing but accept the boundaries he'd drawn.

"I'm not going to tell you what to do here," Theon finally said. "You're my family. My brother. The one person I trust without question. We have things to do, and I can't do them without you. But she's not going anywhere. Take the time you need. Figure your shit out, but when you come to find us, you best have your mind made up one way or the other. Don't make her wonder, and don't give her hope if there isn't any."

"Anything else?" Luka gritted out.

"Yeah. I fucking miss your broody ass," he retorted.

And the line went dead.

Luka stared at his phone, the Firewings logo staring back at him from the home screen. He was no closer to knowing what he was going to do than he was when he'd found that letter. But that wasn't entirely true either. She'd said she was going to leave, and then what would he do? She would leave the realm, and the choice would be made for him. It was the coward's way out. He was well aware, and the Fates had fucked him over anyway.

If he wanted to stay with Theon, as his Guardian and family, she would be there. Theon had made that perfectly clear, and he was right. He needed to decide and have that conversation with Tessa, so there wasn't any misunderstandings or confusion about where they stood. Then they could both move forward.

Sighing, he slid his phone into his pocket and made his way out to the main living area. He paused when he found Razik and Eliza at the counter eating sandwiches. Razik glanced at him before resuming his meal without a word.

Luka didn't speak either, continuing to the kitchen and grabbing the supplies still laid out to make a sandwich of his own.

Eliza cleared her throat, setting down her food. "Do we have a plan yet?"

"Well, I know where she is, so I guess that's a start," Luka muttered, spreading mayo and mustard on some bread.

"Okay, well—"

"Can I ask you something?" Luka interrupted.

Eliza blinked in surprise, wiping her fingers on a napkin. "What is it?"

"Razik said you didn't want the bond right away," he started.

"She told the Shifter Beta in our world to come to my room when we stayed there. Tried to offer me up on a silver platter," Razik said, taking another bite of his food.

"I did not!" Eliza cried in outrage. "That is not what happened that day, and you know it."

"Did you not tell Arianna my room could be in her wing?" he challenged.

"That is not the same as telling her to come calling for a fuck," Eliza argued.

"Who said anything about fucking? Although, since that's where your mind went, it proves what I said was correct."

"It proves shit, Razik Greybane," she retorted, smoke drifting from her palms where they were now flat on the countertop.

And Luka saw it then. The smallest twitch of his brother's lips. Eliza saw it too, her eyes narrowing.

"She is very possessive," Razik continued in a mock whisper, reaching for an apple, but Eliza's hand shot out, snatching it up before he could. Then she whipped the fruit at him, hitting him in the temple. The male was unfazed, picking up his water glass instead. "And extremely violent."

"Oh my gods," Eliza gritted out.

"Anyway," Luka interjected, gaze bouncing back and forth between the two of them as she seethed and Razik continued to eat his food. "You tried to reject it at first, right?"

"Yes," Eliza gritted out.

"Why?"

She looked down at her plate, pulling her hands into her shirt sleeves and fisting her fingers around the ends. "I had my own misgivings and past to deal with. It wasn't him. At least not entirely."

"Every bond will have its own trials."

They all turned at the voice, finding Xan in the doorway at the base of the steps. The last Luka had known, he'd been outside getting some air. The collar was still stark against his skin, a constant reminder of how much they were failing. Although Xan, oddly enough, didn't seem phased or anxious about it.

"Now you're eavesdropping?" Razik muttered.

"Raz," Eliza hissed, nudging him with her knee.

"Not eavesdropping," Xan replied, coming deeper into the space. "Just returning to the inside. You are all talking in the open. It stands to reason you will be overheard in public spaces."

This time it was Eliza trying to hide her smirk while Razik narrowed his eyes on his father.

"All I am offering is that you cannot compare your potential bond to theirs, Luka," Xan continued, ignoring his son's obvious displeasure with his presence. "Each pairing is unique, and up to the two of you. No one can make the choice for you. No one can guide you. It's your own path, with or without her."

"Are you speaking from experience?" Luka asked, not even thinking about the question. He was just so lost to his own inner turmoil that he'd spoken without thought. It took him a few minutes to notice the sudden silence that had fallen among them.

Eliza had her food halfway to her mouth. Razik had sat back in his chair, fully invested in the conversation now, and Xan was frozen, if not a little stunned.

But then their father sighed, pulling out a stool and taking a seat at the island. He left one stool between him and Eliza, folding his arms atop the counter.

"I shouldn't be surprised. I assumed this conversation would happen eventually," Xan said, angling himself so he could look between Luka and Razik. "Yes, Aiyana and I share an inevitable bond. We faced trials of our own. Had choices laid before us." His sapphire eyes flicked to Razik. "Forced to make sacrifices that nearly broke us."

Razik said nothing, but he stiffened. Eliza immediately reached over, resting a hand on his arm. All of their earlier bickering was gone as she leaned closer, giving her strength to her bonded. Luka was sure she was speaking down their bond, and something in him stirred. Something he acutely recognized. Something he'd often feel watching Theon with Tessa in the beginning.

"We didn't accept the inevitable bond until after Razik was born. Until after we'd had to leave him with my brother," Xan continued.

"Is that what we're calling it?" Razik cut in, each word dripping with venom. "Because I call it abandonment."

"I can understand why," Xan said, sorrow and regret filling the air around him. "It was never supposed to be that long. Nothing went the way it was supposed to. Aiyana . . . She hated me for that. For a long time, she resented me. I can understand why you would do the same."

"And yet she forgave you?" Luka asked, desperate to know how and why. Wishing she was still alive so he could ask her.

Xan's smile was small and sad. "She did. As I said, we faced trials of our own."

"You left me there for centuries," Razik interjected again.

"Your world was locked. No one could get in," Xan replied.

"Others found their way in."

"At great cost."

"I wasn't worth the cost. Glad you could confirm what I've wrestled with for decades," Razik sneered, pushing to his feet. "You know what? It doesn't fucking matter. Tybalt is my father. Not you, even if it is your blood in my veins. I survived centuries without you. I sure as fuck don't need you now."

"Razik!" Eliza called, scrambling off her stool to go after him, but he was gone before she'd even taken three steps. She turned back to Xan. "I'm sorry. He . . ."

"You do not need to apologize, Eliza," Xan said. "This is my penance to pay, and I have faith that someday, we will break through this. Someday, he will be ready to hear me out. And if not, it is deserved, but I will never stop trying."

"Please don't," she whispered, and then she left, going to find Razik so she could be whatever he needed in this moment.

The quiet settled over the room once more, and Luka cleared his throat. "Did you eat?"

"No, but I can . . ."

Xan trailed off as Luka passed over his untouched sandwich before beginning to make another.

"I know the inevitable bond is sacred and you think I'm a fool for considering not accepting it," Luka said, eyes fixed on what he was doing.

"I have never said that," Xan replied. "I wouldn't have blamed your mother if she had never given in to it. However, I can also tell you she doesn't regret it. Perhaps someday she will be able to tell you the same herself."

The knife he was using slipped from his hand, bouncing off the counter's edge and clattering to the floor. Luka slowly lifted his eyes to his father, sure he couldn't have heard him right. Sure this wasn't fucking happening again.

"She's alive?"

A snarl laced his words, but Xan didn't appear alarmed in the least. Stoic and calm as always.

"She is," he answered.

"Where the fuck is she? Is she chained up some place like you were for over two decades? Why are we just sitting here? Why haven't you said anything until now?" Luka demanded.

And what the fuck was wrong with him? First Theon, now his father. He was never the one to lose his cool. He'd always been as calm and collected as his father.

Until she came along.

"She is safe, Luka," his father said, getting up and retrieving the knife. He placed it in the sink before getting a new one, continuing to make the sandwich. "We arrived here when you were scarcely five years. You and me, Aiyana and Tessa. You've learned what happened. How we lost her, but you have yet to learn the rest. There has been so much happening, I don't blame you. One can only process so many things at any given time."

"It's no excuse," Luka cut in, watching his father finish making him a sandwich. "I should have asked, but you should have said something."

"You are a Sargon descendant through and through," Xan said. "You value duty and loyalty. You are a Guardian, but you are first and foremost a dragon. You fiercely protect what you consider yours. We all do. It's what we've always done.

"I was protecting Razik when I left him with my brother. I was protecting my Ward's daughter when we came here, and I've been protecting you and your mother each day I sat in that cell. It wasn't a burden to be tortured and locked up to keep you safe. It is our honor to do such things. I know you feel the same about Theon, and I know you feel the same about Tessa. This is why this choice wars within your soul. It goes against your nature to deny it, but it also goes against your nature to accept it."

And somehow, in a few simple sentences, his father had put into words everything he'd been feeling. All the thoughts he'd lain awake at night trying to sort out. All the rage and uncertainty he'd spent hours and hours in the sky attempting to shake off.

"Then where is she? My mother," Luka clarified as Xan placed a plate with the freshly made sandwich in front of him before returning to his own seat.

"The Anala Kingdom," Xan answered. "You were young. The enchantment that altered our memories of Tessa had lingering effects, but it affected you the most. Younglings already don't store all their memories, and the enchantment increased that. It's why you have so few and remember so little of your earliest years."

"I don't understand. She's just been in the Anala Kingdom? This entire time? While I was . . ."

And he suddenly understood exactly how Razik felt about their parents. Because how could she have been one fucking kingdom away this entire time? For over two decades?

"I know what you're thinking, and you are wrong," Xan said, his voice sterner than Luka had ever heard it. "Your mother cares for you deeply. It has destroyed her knowing you were so close, yet impossible to reach. Returning to you would have resulted in her immediate death."

"Was this before or after you were detained?" Luka asked, trying to remember something, *anything*, from that time, but he came up blank. The first real, concrete memory he had was Valter telling him of his parents' deaths.

"Before, but not by much. A day to be exact," Xan said, both of them having long since forgotten their food. His father shifted, almost appearing nervous about what he was going to say. "When we arrived, and after we lost Tessa, we went to the Arius Kingdom. It was only natural. As the son of Sargon, it is in my blood to protect Arius's bloodline. We can sense them, although you have likely never realized it growing up around them your entire life.

"Anyway, Valter was thrilled to discover what we were since the Sargon

Legacy of Devram had experienced a genocide centuries earlier. He immediately made me part of his council, giving me the singular task of finding Tessa. Of course, that proved to be far more difficult than any of us imagined it would be, but during that brief period, I spent a lot of time with Valter and his other advisors."

"Julius and Mansel," Luka said, his lip curling back.

"Among others," Xan said, shifting in his seat. "Your mother and I kept our distance, and we kept you away as much as possible, despite Valter pushing you and Theon together constantly. But one day, we discovered you with another. A female. Same age. Dark red hair. Emerald eyes. She was said to be Mansel's daughter, but your mother insisted she wasn't. I knew she was right. I could scent it. Not just the Arius lineage, but the St. Orcas lineage."

"What are you talking about?" Luka asked, not understanding. Because how could the child be a St. Orcas but also the same age as him and Theon?

"It took some time to figure it out. I kept working with Valter while Aiyana searched for answers," Xan continued, but then he hesitated.

"What? I swear to the gods if you keep any more godsdamn secrets from me," Luka said on a growl, smoke appearing on his exhale.

"No, you're right," Xan said. "I won't keep it from you; it's just going to come as a shock. The female was Cressida's daughter. With Valter. Cressida is not Theon's mother."

The truth hung in the air between them as Luka stared back at his father, unable to say anything.

"Her name is Kasdeya," Xan said, his tone a touch softer. "I don't know the specifics. I don't know why she was being raised in Mansel's house rather than his own. But I had learned quickly what kind of male Valter was. I knew he was using the child to lord over Cressida, and I knew she was likely being kept and groomed for much more sinister things."

He wasn't wrong. Luka knew that. But all of this . . . That child was *Axel's* full blooded sister, unless Cressida wasn't his mother either?

"It is in our nature as Sargon Legacy to protect the Arius bloodline," Xan said again. "And while Aiyana is not born of Sargon, she is still a dragon. Kasdeya may not have been hers, but she was an innocent child caught in the middle of things that were not her fault. Much like Tessa.

"We agreed to leave. To take you and Kasdeya and regroup. Your mother went first, but she couldn't take both of you. She took Kasdeya, and I was to follow the next day with you. Except Valter learned of the betrayal, and he betrayed me in return, handing me over to Rordan in vengeance. And you?

You became as lost among it all as Tessa was. Different, yet still the same. Only you formed a bond with Theon. Something just as powerful as all the bonds in existence. Perhaps more so because it was chosen. And Tessa . . . Well, you know."

"Yeah," was all Luka could say.

He did know. She'd had no one. Was locked away in cupboards, forgotten and alone until Dex had shown up. Then he'd betrayed her. Her entire life was betrayal and manipulation. Sure, he'd given her a couple months of something more, but had he? She didn't know how to be loved, but nobody had let her learn either. Did it matter in the end? She could have still chosen something other than what her life had been. But he hadn't been enough to sway her. Whatever was between them hadn't been enough.

And maybe in the end, that was what was keeping him from letting go of this. From being unable to move forward. His entire life he'd strived to make sure he was worthy of his lineage. The last remaining Sargon Legacy. He'd strived to be good enough.

And he hadn't been enough to keep her from going over that edge.

"She's still in the Anala Kingdom?" Luka asked, finally picking up his sandwich, mostly so he had something to do with his hands.

"She is. As far as I know. I do not have reason to believe otherwise," Xan answered. "Although this collar blocks magic, including my bond with her. But I know they made it safe. I know she lives because even this collar wouldn't have saved me the agony of my soul losing her. Beyond that, I do not know.

"Why there? Does the Anala Lady know?" Xan asked.

"Lady Kyra knows a great number of things," his father answered, picking up his own sandwich. "Like everyone else in this realm, she has simply been preparing and waiting."

"For what?"

"A beginning or an ending. No one really knows."

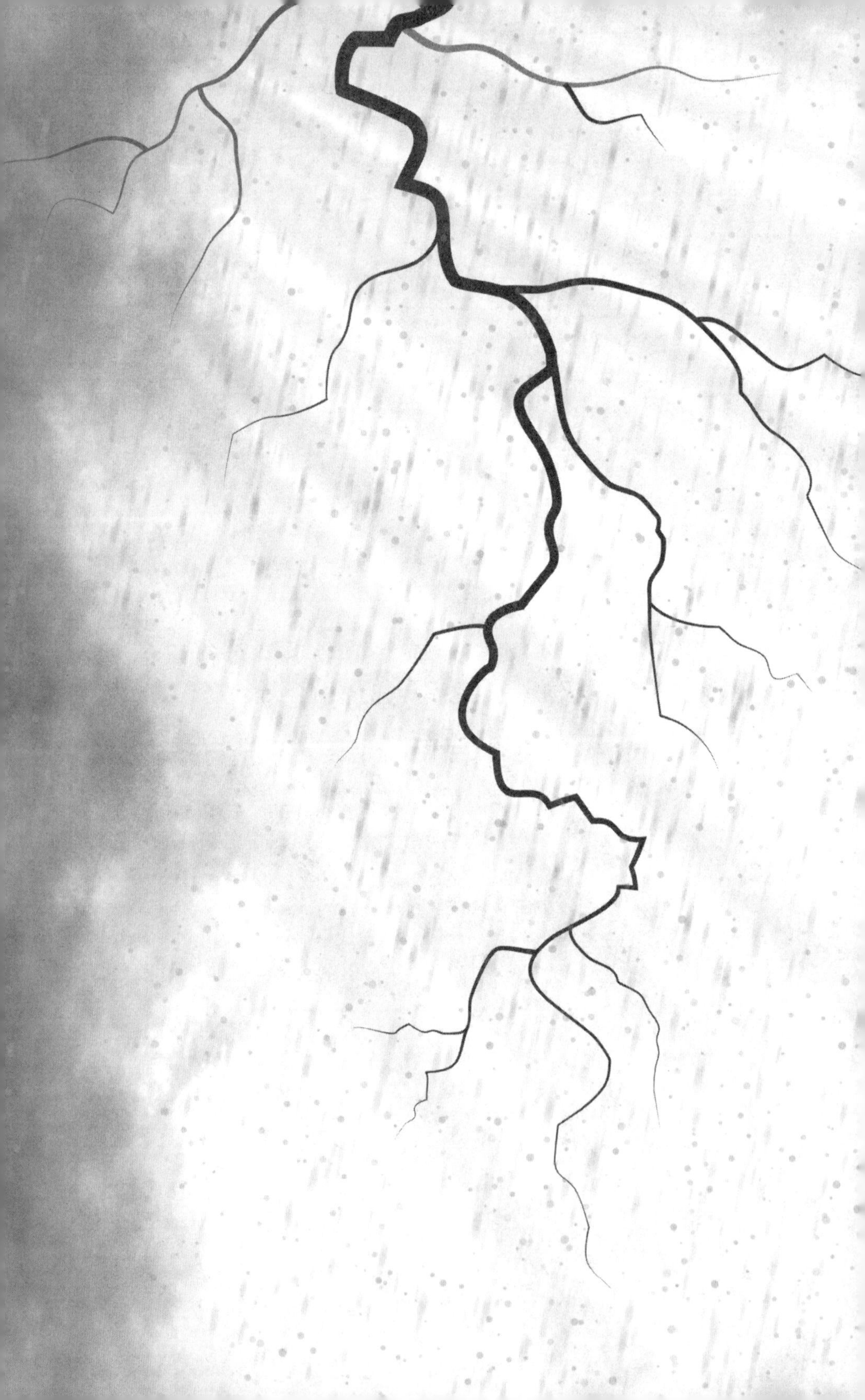

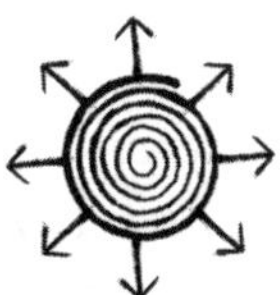

23
TESSA

She could feel him. It was strange. She could feel him, but they couldn't hear each other's thoughts. It was as if only two of the Source Marks were working. Maybe they wouldn't all work because they were missing a piece of their whole. Maybe it would forever be fractured, a constant ache that they'd become numb to but that would never really go away.

Tessa stretched an arm out, feeling the bed still warm from where he'd vacated it moments ago. He'd called Luka three days ago, but he hadn't had much to say apparently. That was okay. The Ladies were supposed to arrive tomorrow. They would all approve of Theon's new role as the Arius Lord, and they could leave this place.

This place full of haunting memories. This place with Dex or Rordan around every godsdamn corner. All the seraphs and too small spaces, even if she'd been given this suite. Every day she was ushered to a room with either Dex or Rordan, where she was forced to sit in their presence, because what else was she going to do? They had to know Theon was finding his way to her. Couldn't they scent it?

She inhaled deeply, the smell of him enveloping her. It was on the sheets, the pillows, and she burrowed deeper into the blankets. These past nights she'd actually *slept*. Not as deeply as she once had, but enough to not feel utterly exhausted each and every day.

"Glad to see some things haven't changed."

His voice carried to her, and the smallest of smiles tilted on her lips. Not that she'd let him see it.

The bed dipped, a large palm smoothing down her hair, then down her back, and she rolled over, looking up at him. He was staring at her like *she* was the phantom now, as though he couldn't believe what he was seeing.

She shoved hair off her face, the cuff tangling in her golden strands. "I want this off," she said, her voice still raspy from sleep.

"I know, Tessa," he said. "One more day. After tomorrow, it's off. Never again."

"We've said that before," she muttered.

He leaned in, his face inches from hers. "In one day, everything will be different, and you will be untouchable. Not from anything I did, but because you are the most powerful being in not only Devram, but in all the realms. Not even that cuff can fully contain you."

He had a point. Her power still managed to escape. Not a lot. Embers here. A little light there. Nothing like what she should have access to. No, she couldn't access it, but she could feel it all. That thing that prowled in her soul, furious at being caged yet again. It clawed at her, and until Theon had found his way to her, she hadn't been sure she would survive it. She dreaded the mornings when he had to leave, for more reasons than one now.

"Where'd you go, little storm?" he murmured.

"My power is angry," she said simply, tracing the etchings on the cuff. "We don't like this."

"We," Theon repeated.

"It traps us, and we don't like being trapped," she went on as though he hadn't spoken. "And when we are free again? We will seek out the ones who did this. It has been a long time since we took, and we are starving."

"Tessa, look at me." His tone was an order, and she blinked up at him in confusion.

"What?"

"I told Luka to take his time, but we are out of it," he muttered, more to himself than to her. Then he cupped her cheek, his thumb swiping along her skin. "One more day, Tessa. I need you to hang in there one more day."

"Rordan is cunning," she said suddenly. "Remember that."

His eyes bounced between hers, searching as he asked, "Do you know something I don't?"

She shook her head. "No, but I lived with him for a time. He never fully confided in me, but he told me enough to make me feel important."

"You are important."

"You know what I mean," she said, waving him off. "I know I have this power—"

She started when he took her chin between his thumb and forefinger. "*You* are important, Tessa. Not your power. Not your bloodline. *You.*"

Her throat clogged, and she swallowed against the sudden onslaught of emotions.

"I'm sorry for ever making you feel otherwise," he added, releasing her chin and letting his fingers skim her jaw. She gasped, and his eyes widened in alarm. "What is it?"

"I can't decide if this is a dream," she answered, and his brow furrowed.

"It is not a dream, Tessa."

"Then you truly just apologized to me?" she asked with a wry smirk.

"You are a brat," he muttered, leaning in once more to brush his lips along hers, but she kept him there, fisting his shirt to hold him in place. Deepening the kiss. Tasting him and taking what she could, knowing it would never be enough to get her through this day.

He pulled back, a low groan coming from his chest. "I have to go, Tessa. We need to pretend for one more day."

"One more day," she repeated, but her gaze lingered on his lips because this damn bond was more than excited about what had been transpiring. *That* part of the bond was back to working just fine.

He tapped her chin, forcing her eyes to his. "You do not regret last night?"

She shook her head.

He smiled. "I'll see you at dinner," he said, pressing one last kiss to her brow before going out to the living room to meet Brecken at the allotted time. Every morning before sunrise.

It was gross to be awake this early, so she rolled over, determined to sleep a little longer. But it never worked. She could never fall back to sleep, and if she did, it was fitful and not worth it in the end.

Grumbling, she flung back the blankets, showering and getting ready for the day. Of course, she'd only been provided with bright white and gold clothing, and she spent a good hour "altering" a dress into something she could actually wear and move in. Deep slits up the side. Hollows at the waist so she could breathe properly. She couldn't find anything black to add, not even a curtain or sheet she could cut up, so when her power lingered, faint and weak, she sent it to the dress. Silver and onyx settled against the white garment, accenting with gold, and she smiled as she twisted to look at it from all angles in the mirror. Even she could see the madness in that tilt of her lips.

Her gaze fell to the cuff, and despite having tried it every single day since speaking with Brecken, she sliced her finger with the scissors, careful not to let a drop of blood hit the floor. Instead, she smeared it across the cuff, watching the thing pulse faintly, the red absorbing into the thing, and then . . . nothing. Just like every other day.

With a sigh, she pulled her sleeves down, covering her wrists, and made her way to the living room with two minutes to spare before there was a knock on the door. Pulling it open, she flashed a dark grin to the seraph who stood waiting for her.

"Are you always so punctual?" she asked, tilting her head and studying the male.

Eyes that were a few shades darker than his soft grey wings stared back at her. His raven hair was neatly trimmed around his ears. He was handsome in that warrior way with muscles that showcased how intensely he trained.

Stepping to the side, he gestured for her to go in front of him, and she sighed. "So where are we going today?" she asked, her bare feet silent on the marble floors as he brushed past her to lead the way.

Of course, he didn't answer her. She'd never heard him speak.

She watched his wings rustle slightly as he walked, back straight and head up. Not for the first time, she wondered what being the male had killed and what magic he now possessed. She hadn't seen him use any power. Not that such a thing mattered. Dex had been using his power around her for years, and she hadn't realized it.

They crossed the courtyard to the main estate building, and it wasn't until they turned down an all too familiar hall that she stopped.

Digging her heels in and stepping back a few paces, she said, "I'm not going in there."

The seraph stopped, turning to look her up and down before arching a brow. Tessa only crossed her arms, glaring at him. He'd have to throw her over his godsdamn shoulder and haul her to that office himself.

"Go tell Rordan or Dex, whichever one is waiting for me, that I will not be joining them there," she said, the magic on her dress swirling in her agitation.

The male noticed it though, cocking his head and peering closer.

"Go tell them," she repeated.

The seraph shrugged, turning away and continuing down the hall to the end. She watched him push the door open and gesture in her direction, and for the first time, she wondered if he actually *couldn't* speak.

Then Rordan appeared, casually strolling down the hall in his dark navy suit, blue eyes pinned on her in disapproval.

"Come, Tessalyn," he said, stopping a few feet from her. "Breakfast is waiting, and we have sensitive matters to discuss."

"I am not sitting in that room for hours today," she replied, unease prickling in her gut at his words. "Pick somewhere else."

"Everything is already set up and prepared. It will be a waste of everyone's time to move things now."

"That is not my problem," she retorted, turning on a heel and going in the opposite direction. She ignored his barked command, making her way down another hall to one of the formal meeting spaces, where she plopped her ass in a chair at the head of the table.

When Rordan finally appeared, her elbow was on the table, chin in her hand. "I knew you'd see it my way," she said, her tone dripping with faux sweetness as the seraph appeared behind Rordan, laden down with a tray of breakfast items. "Thank you," she added when he placed it on the table before her.

She immediately reached for the coffee carafe, pouring herself a cup and adding cream and sugar while Rordan stiffly set up his own things to her right, a few chairs down.

Studying the tray, she found it contained a platter of three doughnuts, all of them with chocolate frosting, a bowl of strawberries, hard-boiled eggs, and a small bottle of orange juice.

Ignoring the doughnuts, she pulled the strawberries closer before picking up a hard-boiled egg and taking a bite. She knew Rordan was watching her, but she ignored him, instead twisting to look out the window.

The youngest Fae were outside, running and playing. Too young to recognize and grasp what their lives were truly to be. She envied them and their innocence. Born into a world that valued their power more than who they were. She couldn't fathom choosing to bring a child into this world on purpose. Certainly not a Fae child, although now she understood that so many of the Fae were forced into existence. Then again, even if things were different in the world, she didn't think she could be a mother.

"We need to discuss your plans, Tessalyn," Rordan said, pulling her from her thoughts.

She dragged her eyes back to him, picking up her coffee mug. "I don't think I'll be discussing anything with you."

He tsked in annoyance, as though she were an irritating child. "I understand we've had our differences—"

"Differences?" Tessa interrupted. "You set me up, Rordan. You used me to orchestrate a massacre in the Arius Kingdom, then stood by while I took the fall."

"Sometimes we must take drastic steps to push in the right direction," he said factually, picking up a pen to write in a notebook sitting beside him. "Dexter said those are your favorite. Are they not?"

Tessa blinked at the casual dismissal and sudden change of subject. Glancing at the doughnuts, she looked back at Rordan. "When do the Ladies arrive tomorrow?"

"Whenever they choose to," he retorted. "We don't answer to you."

"Then who do you answer to?" she countered. "Certainly not your people. Who holds *you* accountable?"

His smile was tight and cold. "As rulers, we hold one another accountable. It's why I am here. Because the Ladies blame me for your obstinance, as if I have any control over the less becoming traits of your heritage."

She scoffed, popping a strawberry into her mouth.

"But back to the matter at hand. We need to discuss your current predicament. I've bought you enough time," he continued, settling back in his chair and pinning her with a stare.

"And what predicament is that?" she asked, picking up another strawberry.

"Come now, Tessa," he chided. "If something isn't done, Theon will attempt to take you with him tomorrow. You were once so desperate to be rid of him."

"You promised to free me of him, and yet I still bear his Marks."

"Because you've been so cooperative," he said with a slight sneer.

"Because you've been so forthcoming with your motives," she countered.

Rordan huffed, something between a laugh and annoyance. "You are quick-witted and clever, I'll give you that. Are you not eating those?" he asked, gesturing to the doughnuts again.

"Would you like one?"

"No. There was simply extra care in ensuring you were offered something you enjoy," he said.

Tessa hummed, glancing at the pastries once more before selecting another hard-boiled egg, watching Rordan carefully. Seeing the small twitch as he ground his molars. The irritated flare of the golden rings in his eyes. The single tap of his index finger on the arm of his chair.

"The way I see it, we have two options here," Rordan said when she didn't answer. "I can arrange for you to leave with me."

"But you have a deal with Theon and the Ladies," she argued.

"That can easily be taken care of," he answered dismissively. "But the other option is more appealing to me. You can go with him. I need information that he has."

"Which is what?"

He clicked his tongue. "I am attempting to be—What was it you wanted? Me to be more forthcoming? I am attempting to do that, but I won't simply tell you my plans without proof of loyalty, Tessalyn."

"I am loyal to myself," she retorted.

"Aren't we all," he replied, picking up his coffee mug. "But I am willing to show you *my* loyalty."

Her brow arched, admittedly somewhat intrigued about what a show of loyalty from the Achaz Lord could possibly be. "I'm listening."

"Unfortunately, this is why I wanted to meet in the other office. It is too cumbersome to haul down here, so you will need to go there," he replied, turning back to his laptop. "Your choice, as always, Tessalyn."

As always.

She nearly scoffed at the absurdity of that statement.

Rordan clearly sensed her skepticism though, because he sighed, closing the cover of his computer. "I am trying, Tessalyn. I procured your favorite breakfast. I have ensured you have the nicest amenities while here. And I have yet another show of good faith waiting for you."

"Forgive me if I don't believe a word that comes from your mouth," she said dryly.

"I can escort you myself."

She debated it. Knew this was likely a trap. Knew Rordan was cunning.

But so was she.

She also wasn't alone anymore.

"Grab a doughnut, and let's settle this," the Achaz Lord said, pushing back his chair and standing.

"Are you sure you don't want one?" Tessa asked, standing as well and leaving the pastries untouched. "You seem overly concerned with the doughnuts this morning."

"I simply do not want you to go hungry," he replied, but she heard every bit of the lie in those words.

Tessa said nothing, waiting for him to open the door for her. She knew it rubbed him the wrong way to do something that would equate to being beneath him, but that was exactly why she did it.

The seraph was standing in the hall, presumably a guard, and he stepped aside, bowing his head to Rordan when they walked past.

"Does he have a name?" Tessa asked, the seraph staying behind.

"Illithor," Rordan said. "He serves Achaz and thus me."

"But how did he get here? How did any of them get here?"

"How did *you* get here?" Rordan countered.

"How silly of me. Did the enchantment affect your memories so much that you don't remember attacking Xan when he arrived with me?" Tessa asked with faux dramatics.

Rordan glanced down at her, his features tight. "So the dragon does remember. I knew he did, despite his words during our various discussions over the last two decades."

"You mean while you tortured him."

"There were still words exchanged," Rordan said simply.

They'd reached Cordelia's office, and she once again let Rordan get the door. She wasn't really sure what she was expecting, but it sure wasn't Felicity fucking Davers sitting on a small settee beneath the window in that office.

The female rose quickly, eyes wide as they bounced between her and Rordan.

"What is the meaning of this?" Felicity demanded, taking a few steps backwards and nearly falling over the settee she bumped into.

"I'm glad you received my summons," Rordan said, closing the door behind them.

"I cannot refuse a Lord," she answered. "At least not until my husband is crowned one."

Husband.

The word grated on Tessa's ears, her face twisting in distaste.

"True," Rordan said, moving deeper into the room while Tessa stayed rooted to the spot, trying to figure out what his angle was here. Rordan stopped at the desk, leaning against the front and bracing his palms on the edge behind him. "You are not nearly powerful enough to deny anyone, are you, Ms. St. Orcas?"

"Davers," Tessa said sharply.

Felicity's smile was sinister as she lifted her hand, showcasing the Mark on the back. "It doesn't matter how many times you say it. He is still mine."

And despite the cuff, her power flared. Not like it should, and it was almost immediately snuffed out, but her point was made. Felicity's smile faltered, and she turned away, facing the Achaz Lord.

"What can I do for you, my Lord? I truly cannot stay away from him for long. My husband has needs that must be met," she said, the last words ringing in Tessa's ears.

"Oh, did I not mention? You are not here for me, my dear," Rordan said, his eyes sliding to Tessa. "You are here for *her.*"

"What?" Felicity said with a gasp, spinning to Tessa once more. "What did you do?" she hissed.

Tessa ignored her, her entire focus on Rordan. "How is this any show of loyalty?"

"It is a peace offering," he replied, pushing off the desk and returning to her side. He moved behind her, leaning in to speak low in her ear. "You heard her. She knowingly took something you covet. And *he* allowed it. I have brought you what you crave most, Tessalyn. I have brought you vengeance."

And gods, she liked the sound of that. She wanted her power to sink into Felicity's manipulative soul to feast. Wanted her to feel every moment of her wrath at thinking she could touch what was hers. Wanted her to recognize her mistakes when it was too late to do anything about it.

But she couldn't.

Not only because of this godsdamn cuff, but because Theon had a plan. He'd told her everything, and they'd spent these last nights changing details and making it perfect. Doing this now would ruin all of it.

The words stuck in her throat, but she forced them out. "She is not mine to deal with."

"You are saying she is his?" Rordan asked, circling to her side.

"No," she said quickly.

"Then . . . ?"

"I . . ." But gods, her power was thrashing, wanting to take from her. From him. And it was trapped, and she was trapped. And she felt hollow and empty. "We don't want her," she choked out, her power clogging her throat. Trying to stop the words from escaping because they absolutely did want her. It was famished, and that ache was so much worse than when she was starving for food as a child.

"Pity," Rordan said, reaching out and twirling some of her hair between his fingers. "Then just to ensure I am understanding correctly, you are rejecting this offering?"

"What offering? How does she show your loyalty?" Tessa asked, watching Felicity, who was obviously panicked.

"I think Theon should be here for this," the female said, her voice shaking.

"Don't say his name," Tessa snapped, her power once again flaring and winking out in the same breath. She was failing. She was supposed to be playing a part. Be civil at dinners. Be indifferent, but she couldn't. Never had been able to. Not only that, but Theon had offered to let a realm die for her. *That* was a show of loyalty.

Turning her back on the female, she faced Rordan, repeating her question. "How does this show any type of loyalty?"

"Sweet child," he said, his smile too wide, too full of delight, as he reached out and ran a hand down her hair. "Did you think I was showing my loyalty to *you*?"

He turned his back on her, pulling open the door to the office once more.

Everything was suddenly too loud and too quiet all at once.

And she couldn't breathe, couldn't move. Couldn't do a godsdamn thing as Mother Cordelia strode into the office.

"My loyalty is *always* to Achaz," Rodan said coldly. "And you? You are simply his insubordinate grandchild at this point. But I tried, Tessalyn," he said, faux sympathy dripping in his voice. "I gave you one last chance to come back to his side. All you had to do was end the female. With his Match dead, he wouldn't be able to take the Arius seat. We would have still let him take you though. We need information from him."

"What information?" she rasped out, unable to pull her gaze from Cordelia.

The female was as formidable as ever. Her dirty blonde hair was pulled back in her signature tight bun at the back of her head. Dark navy eyes filled with loathing held her own, and her sharp features were more prominent since Tessa had seen her last.

"He has hidden Cressida somewhere," Rordan said simply. "We desire her back."

"I don't know anything about that," she said, sweat already beading on her nape and trickling down her neck. She hated that the Estate Mother still had this kind of power over her, and her magic was locked down, unable to defend her.

As if reading her thoughts, Cordelia smirked. "Not so tough without that abominable magic, are you?"

It tried. The thing in her soul clawed at her, her knees nearly giving out as it howled and growled and screamed. Her hands were in her hair, tugging and straining. Because it was too much, and Cordelia was here, and she'd only needed to survive this one more day.

One more day.

One more hour.

One more minute.

One more second.

One more song.

And it wasn't her power screaming. It was her soul. It was the sound pouring from her own lips a moment before her air was stolen, Cordelia taking what she always had.

It was her dropping to her knees on the ornate rug beneath her feet. It was Rordan crouching before her and tipping her chin up, mock pity on his face as he said, "I tried to help you, Tessalyn. You did this."

"Don't worry, Rordan," Cordelia said snidely, coming to his side and staring down her nose at Tessa as she struggled to take in a breath. "I know somewhere we can keep her until we can figure out how to get her under control. I have experience with her unruliness."

Tessa shook her head frantically, clawing at the cuff on her wrist, but Cordelia gripped her elbow, dragging her to her feet. And Tessa dug in her heels, slamming her elbow up and back, just like Luka had taught her. She heard Cordelia curse, her hold on her magic loosening, and Tessa sucked in a breath. But then it was more than her air being stolen as light wound around her. Binding her wrists.

"Help her," Rordan ordered Felicity, and the female didn't hesitate. Gone was her hesitancy, replaced with contempt. Tessa could feel more than that as she neared though. Could feel her power winding around her, trying to soothe her into cooperation. But Rordan had been right. She wasn't nearly strong enough.

She managed another gasping breath before Cordelia's magic struck again. She was tugged towards that small, dark space she'd avoided looking at when she'd been in here with Dex. Felicity rushed forward, pulling open the cupboard door.

But a different door was banging off the wall as it was thrown open. It had them all spinning, Cordelia dropping Tessa back to the floor.

And that was Theon standing in the doorway with darkness swirling all around him. His wings were out, a dark backdrop behind him, and his emerald eyes blazed with a fury she recognized. A fury she felt in her own soul because she was feeling her wrath mixed with his.

She had bound herself to death, and he had come for her.

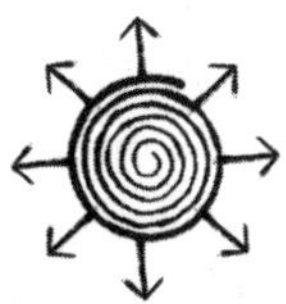

24
THEON

Darkness clouded his vision, and all he could see was Tessa on her knees. Her face was flushed as she sucked in breath after breath. That fucking cupboard door was open, but he hadn't needed to see that to know what was happening here. He'd felt every bit of her panic. Every bit of her helplessness. Every bit of her fury.

"Cordelia," he said coldly, stepping into the room and shutting the door firmly behind him. "What an unexpected yet opportunistic surprise."

"Theon—" Felicity started, but she snapped her mouth shut when he held up a single finger.

"Now, correct me if I'm wrong, but did we or did we not have a discussion about your involvement with Tessa?"

The Estate Mother clicked her tongue. "That was well before everything was revealed, young heir. You no longer have the power here."

Theon only smiled. It was all he needed to do to make her falter. He didn't need to have his darkness thicken around him. Didn't need to have it drift along the floor like a dense fog that devoured. Didn't need to, but he did.

"Rordan," Cordelia said tightly. "Ask him. Make a trade for the information."

"What an excellent idea," the Achaz Lord said calmly from where he'd drifted to the desk, leaning against it. "Give me the location of your mother, and I will leave you to . . . handle matters here."

"What?" Cordelia said in outrage, spinning to face the lord. "You can't leave me here with them!"

Theon crossed the room, holding a hand out to Tessa because he couldn't think properly with her on her knees when everyone in this room should be on their knees before *her*. Her fingers shook as he wrapped his hand around them, pulling her to her feet. He wanted to do more than that. Wanted to pull her into his chest. Shield her from Cordelia and Rordan and everything they would face in the coming days. Even knowing she didn't need to be shielded from anything, it was still instinct. Keep what he loved safe. It was what he'd done his entire life.

"I don't know where my mother is," Theon said, facing Rordan once more while his power wound around Tessa. He felt her anxiety ease, and she lifted a hand, letting the dark drift around her fingers.

"Lies," Rordan hissed.

Without missing a beat, Theon drew a dagger from his magic and sliced his palm. Tossing the blade aside, he let his blood drip to the floor. "I swear on my blood and the god I descend from, I do not know where my mother is. Feel free to challenge my integrity."

Rordan studied him for a long moment, everyone in the room seeming to hold their breath before he pushed off the desk. He drew a dagger of his own, slicing it across his palm before clasping Theon's hand.

"Speak it again, and let your blood reveal a lie," Rordan said, low and vicious.

"I swear on my blood and the god I descend from, I do not know where my mother is," Theon repeated.

Rordan gripped his hand, and Theon knew he was waiting for the blood between their palms to spark with lies, but all he would find was truth.

After several seconds, Rordan dropped his hand with a sneer. "This isn't over." Then his gaze slid to Tessa. "You deny everything you were meant to be. Achaz will see to it you pay for that betrayal."

Bright light flared, and he stepped through a light portal.

"Rordan!" Cordelia cried, trying to follow, but Theon's magic snapped out, wrapping around her throat and yanking her back.

She cried out—or tried to—but that darkness tightened. Cordelia sank to her knees, fingers clawing at the power.

"I know her death is yours to claim, little storm," Theon said darkly. "But I am going to ask your permission to claim it on your behalf."

Tessa looked up at him, and he could feel . . . something he didn't know what to do with down the bond. It was twisted and wicked, but also warm and light.

"Will you make it torturous?" she asked, that eerie ring back in her tone as she tilted her head, watching her former Estate Mother struggle to breathe.

"I will make it as torturous as she made your childhood," he answered, and Cordelia's eyes widened. She abandoned her attempt at trying to claw at his magic, instead scrambling away from him.

The room shook as wind blew violently around them, trying to do the same thing he was and steal their air, but he'd been prepared for this. A shield of dark power was wrapped around him and Tessa. She was a fool to waste her reserves on this, but he'd let her do just that.

"Theon," Tessa breathed, something sinfully nefarious on her face as she watched Cordelia panic and scramble on the floor, only able to suck in short, minuscule breaths.

"No one is allowed to touch you without permission, Tessa," Theon said, removing his suit jacket and proceeding to roll his sleeves up to his elbows.

"*Your* permission?" she asked with a defiant sneer.

He paused, slowly turning to her. Then he reached out and took her throat, tugging her closer so his words fanned over her lips when he said, "No, Tessa. *Yours.*" Her eyes flared before that power winked out. He'd take care of Cordelia and then that godsdamn cuff. "Now be a good girl and get me that dagger."

She gave him a sardonic smile before pulling out of his grasp, his power keeping her protected from Cordelia's desperate and sloppy attacks. He strolled forward, coming to a stop beside the female, staring down at her. Her mouth opened and closed like a fish out of water, and Theon loosened his grip on her enough to let her gulp some air. She coughed and spluttered, gasping dramatically.

"You can't do this," the Estate Mother panted, her waning power feebly attempting to do something and failing.

"Of course I can," Theon said, Tessa returning to his side, dagger in hand. "You are beneath me. That's how this works, right? You tortured Tessa when you thought she was beneath you?"

"She is uncontrollable," Cordelia said, malice-filled eyes swinging to Tessa. "She needed to learn control."

"I would say the same for you," Theon said coldly. "Because every time she is in your presence, *you* can't seem to control yourself. So by your logic, that requires some discipline, no?"

"This is my estate!" she cried, her voice becoming too high-pitched as dark, thin tendrils began creeping up her torso, her chest. "You can't—I'm an Estate Mother! I was promised protection!"

"And I am giving you that," Theon said calmly, his power crawling up her neck. "I am currently protecting you from *her*. Aren't you grateful for my mercy?"

Those inky strands rose up, hovering over her mouth, and Cordelia's eyes were wide and frantic. Her terror was palpable, and Theon glanced down at Tessa. She was impassive as she watched her Estate Mother on the ground, but he could feel her. Could feel the wicked delight at the retribution. Could feel the feral need for vengeance. Could feel the tentative awe at someone caring enough to give her this, let her watch this, because it was all for her.

"I asked you a question," Theon demanded, and Cordelia jumped at the harsh tone. "Aren't you grateful?"

"Her power is locked down. She is nothing without it," Cordelia sneered, and then he felt Tessa flinch inwardly. It wasn't something anyone would see because she was a master at keeping her emotions out of sight, but he *felt* it. And any leash he'd been keeping on his self-control snapped.

Those tendrils struck, going up Cordelia's nose, and when she opened her mouth to scream, they went down her throat. He moved slowly, letting that darkness burn hotter than any dragon fire as it slowly seeped into her bloodstream. Death ravaged, slowly tainting her blood and letting it flow through her body. Her veins became stark, first an ashy grey, then slowly becoming black webs across her body.

And on the outside, he was making sure she couldn't scream, couldn't breathe, couldn't see, couldn't move. His power moved as an extension of him, forcing her limbs to twist and contract, not caring as bones snapped to force them into the positions he wanted. Small. Confined.

Able to fit in a fucking cupboard.

But he wasn't nearly done. He crouched beside her, the female's tears trailing down her face as she arched in agony. Theon grabbed her jaw, wrenching her face to the side.

"Look at her," he demanded, nodding at Tessa. "Look her in the eyes now."

The words were feral and wild and untamed because this female had taken and taken from Tessa long before she was his.

Theon shifted so he could peer up at Tessa as well. Everything about her was cold and uncaring as she stared down at Cordelia. "Anything you want to say to her, tempest?" Theon asked, because this would be her last chance.

"She's too much of a hassle," Tessa said flatly, his darkness drifting around her and winding through her hair, around her arms, doing what her light couldn't do right now.

Those words were all he needed, and he turned back to Cordelia, pale and writhing. "Keep your eyes on her," he said. "I want to make sure she's the last thing you ever see."

Cordelia's eyes somehow went even wider, but his hand covered them. That onyx mist sharpened, becoming palpable and pointed, stabbing deep into her eye sockets to ensure she was trapped in the dark, just as she'd trapped Tessa in dark spaces for years. He loosened the grip on her throat just to let Tessa hear her screams, and when he quickly glanced at her to make sure she was all right, he found her smiling. Wrapped in his dark power, she looked every bit like the Chaos she was.

"Is this sufficient, tempest?" he asked, death pumping more fiercely through Cordelia's body with her racing heart.

"Nothing will ever be enough, but I don't want to waste another second on her," she said, holding out the dagger.

His smile was as dark as hers, and he took the blade. Gripping the hilt tight, he leaned closer so he could speak directly into Cordelia's ear.

"Arius is her grandfather. We'll make sure he knows of you to ensure you receive a special place in the Pits of Torment," he said.

Something gurgled came from her throat, but it was cut off when he sank that dagger into her chest, directly into her heart. His power followed, delivering death to an already black heart.

Then it was still and quiet.

Theon slowly pushed to his feet, leaving the blade lodged in Cordelia's chest. The adrenaline of everything was coursing through him as he turned to face Tessa fully. She stared up at him, violet-grey eyes full of things he'd never seen directed at him before. He opened his mouth to speak, lifting a hand to reach for her, but then he was blinking in confusion as another was blocking her from view.

"By Arius, Theon, are you all right?" Felicity cried, pushing Tessa aside to throw her arms around his neck. He stiffened at her touch, too high off the vengeance he'd just wrought to fully comprehend what was happening. He'd forgotten the other female was even in this room.

She pulled back, sliding her palms down his chest and looking him over as if searching for injuries, and then she froze when Tessa's voice filled the space.

Cold.

Maniacal.

Deadly.

"You really need to learn to stop touching things that aren't yours."

Felicity looked over her shoulder, and Theon could hear the sneer in her voice when she said, "This doesn't involve you. I will touch my husband whenever I want."

"Is that so?" Tessa asked, her head tilting to the side, and Theon had to use all his self-control not to hide his smirk.

Violet eyes flicked to him, and he only gave her one small nod before sliding his hands into his pockets and taking a step back.

"Yes," Felicity retorted, missing all the things he could see.

Tessa's fingers flexing at her sides. The way she started moving, circling, forcing Felicity to spin to keep her in her line of sight. Gone was the victim of the Estate Mother and in her place was a predator. In her place was someone freed of a burden that had held her down. In her place was a huntress about to claim what was hers, and fuck. It did something to him to know that *he* was the prize, even if she'd given him everything last night.

"And tell me, *Ms. Davers*, has he touched you?" Tessa asked, her voice lethal, and Felicity somehow missed that too.

"Of course he has. You've seen us together at functions."

Tessa's lips tilted, and she hummed. "Yes, a hand on your back for appearances is certainly the same as having him pin you against a wall while muffling your cries of pleasure."

"Some of us have class," Felicity retorted. "I can't be found fucking in a dark corner. I'm a Lord's wife. There are expectations of a Match, Tessalyn, which I understand might be hard for you to comprehend."

Tessa's laugh was dark. "But you're not a Match. You're not a wife. And you're not a St. Orcas."

Felicity tsked, still turning as Tessa continued to circle. "Once again, Tessalyn, you saying something doesn't make it true."

"While I am an excellent liar, this time I speak truth. Ask him," Tessa said, her smile growing.

Felicity spun to him. "Theon, I know she is your Source, but something needs to be done here."

"Something is being done," he answered, pulling his hands from his pockets, a small vial in one of them. He moved past Felicity and went to Tessa, taking her arm and pushing back the sleeve. Removing the stopper, he poured a few drops of blood onto the cuff, the contraption snapping open.

"How?" Tessa breathed, her eyes fluttering closed as her magic appeared, light flooding the space around her before flaring out again.

"Brecken," he answered in a low voice, replacing the stopper and sliding it and the cuff into his pocket. The male had warned him not to leave the cuff lying around, and until they could figure out how to destroy it, he'd have to keep it with him.

Tessa lifted her palms, her brows pinching together as she studied them. "Something is wrong."

"What do you mean?"

"It's not . . . Something is wrong," she said again.

"Of course there is something wrong," Felicity snapped, coming up beside them. She placed a hand on Theon's forearm. "That's what I've been saying. You're—"

But then she cried out as Tessa's fist snapped out, connecting with her face.

"Stop touching things that aren't yours," she seethed, and while something might be wrong, there were still faint traces of light wrapped around her fist. And that power had left its mark on Felicity's cheek, crackling and sending jolts of energy with each pulse.

"You can't treat me like this!" Felicity cried, clutching her face. "I am a Legacy—"

"As if I have ever cared about that," Tessa seethed, and Theon lightly gripped her upper arm when she took a step toward her. "You care about power, like every other Legacy in this realm. That's the only reason you signed that contract. Tell me, what did you and Cressida scheme to do these last months?"

"That is none of your concern," Felicity flung back, and Theon could feel her power trying to wind around Tessa.

And he could tell when Tessa let her chaos bite back because Felicity flinched, a small cry sounding as her power retreated.

"Theon!" Felicity cried. "I know what you said before, but you still need me. You need a wife to become the Arius Lord."

"And I have one," Theon answered. "But I am curious. What *did* you and Cressida discuss?"

Her eyes widened, and she took a small step back. "She was guiding me. She's been a Lord's wife for decades. I've only ever wanted to be what you need, Theon."

"How did she guide you?"

"She gave me advice on my role. Devram politics. How best to serve you and fulfill my duties," she said, and now she was shuffling forward. She lifted her arms as if to reach for him, but she glanced at Tessa, and her features hardened again. Her hands dropped back to her sides, clenching into fists.

"Fine. You want to know what your mother and I discussed? You are difficult, Theon. I was trying and offering myself to you, and all you wanted was *her*. But she can't produce your heir. We've talked about this. So, yes, she gave me ideas on how to procure that."

A harsh bark of laughter came from Tessa. "Are you saying you went to Cressida for advice on how to seduce her son?"

"He's my husband!" she shrieked, her irritation peaking. "If I do not conceive an heir, I become nothing."

"Then it is about the power," Tessa said.

"It's always about power," Felicity sneered. "I was raised for this, yes, but I also *want* it. I want the status and the notoriety that comes with the position. I'm willing to do anything for it."

"So you cozied up to Cressida?" Tessa asked. "Do you even realize Theon does not care for her?"

"I do not care," she spat back, and Theon suddenly realized what Tessa was doing. Felicity was so riled up, she was speaking without thinking. Revealing secrets. Something he'd done to Tessa more than once. Clever, clever tempest.

"Theon wouldn't give me the time of day, so I went to his mother," Felicity was ranting. "We tried everything, but he never took the drinks I offered him. I made you think we were fucking until I could make it happen. Did whatever Valter and Cressida asked of me to make that happen. He never gave in, even when I presented myself bare and willing. I told him days ago he could have you and only use me to carry a child. I only needed him to give in once to bind him to me."

Her brown eyes went wide as she realized what she'd said. A trembling hand came up, covering her mouth.

"Repeat that," Theon said coldly.

"Didn't you hear her?" Tessa asked, that unnatural delight creeping into her voice. "She was trying to trick you into a binding. I'm dying to know what *that* would have entailed."

"I just meant that I thought once he could see how good we were together, he would see that I am an asset, not a hindrance," Felicity said, her voice trembling.

Tessa shook her head, pulling her arm from Theon's grasp. "The thing about liars is we easily recognize our own," Tessa purred, stalking closer. Her power skittered, far weaker than what it should be, but it was enough to make Felicity lurch back.

"I am a Lord's wife," Felicity said. "You can't touch me."

"No, *I* am a Lord's wife," Tessa retorted. "I warned you. Months ago we sat at a table where I told you he was mine. Then when you came here, I told you to figure out your place. Moments ago I told you that you were not his Match, and yet you still continue to touch what is not yours."

"You're delusional."

"Ask him," Tessa purred again.

And it seemed to finally sink in as Felicity slowly slid her eyes to him. "Theon?"

"I told you the other night you'd do well to remember what this is. What I came here for," Theon answered. "But I am curious to know how convincing me to fuck you would have bound me to you. A child? After one fucking? The odds are astronomical."

Felicity was shaking her head, tears pooling in her eyes as she held up her hand. "I don't understand. You're my husband. It's a Union Mark."

"He's *my* husband," Tessa hissed, whatever power had lingered from her earlier hit flaring again on Felicity's cheek, making her cry out. "But there is the issue of you being bound to him and the bargain with Valter."

"Tell me about this binding, Felicity," Theon ordered, and she flinched when his power appeared, drifting towards her.

"Valter said . . . He had a way to ensure an heir would be born. That he'd done it before. As long as we slept together once, I didn't need to conceive that night. We just needed to make *you* believe I was with child. Then he would take care of the rest," she confessed, tears sliding down her face.

"The fuck?" Theon said. He should be shocked, but he wasn't. His father had always ensured he got exactly what he wanted. After all, wasn't he proof of her statement? Everyone had believed he was Cressida's child.

"I'm sorry, Theon," she said, fear and panic filling her voice. "I didn't mean—"

"You're not sorry," Tessa cut in, back to circling her. "You're only sorry you got caught."

"That's not—"

"You are a terrible liar," Tessa said with mock pity. "But that's what you were after? Trapping him with a child?"

"A child would ensure my place of power. It's all I've ever wanted," she retorted. "I didn't care if it was Theon, Axel, or an heir in another kingdom." Then her glare swung to Theon. "And now you've fucked yourself. They'll never accept her as your Match *and* your Source. It's an imbalance among the kingdoms they will never allow. You've thrown away everything, just like your mother said you would. If you were half as smart as you think you are, you'd turn her over and be rid of her. Let Rordan deal with her so the realm can move on and get back to business."

Tessa moved then, and Theon's eyes widened in surprise. Because she didn't attack with her power. Not right away. No, this was all physical as she tackled Felicity to the ground. Felicity shrieked, trying to throw Tessa off her, but that training with Luka had clearly paid off. Tessa's hand wrapped around her throat as she straddled Felicity. Her power flickered in and out, and she was right. Something was wrong. But she didn't seem to care at the moment.

She swung her fist, marring Felicity's other cheek. "That's for being in our fucking room all those months ago," she sneered, and everything in Theon heated at watching her. Feral and unhinged and possessive of *him*. She leaned closer, a few of her embers of power drifting around her. "Truthfully, I don't care what you have to say about me. Your opinion matters as much as Cordelia's rotting bones over there. But you kept fucking *touching* him."

She lifted a palm, and Theon had no idea what she was doing until a staggered swirl of her power formed, leaving a dagger he'd never seen before in its wake. Felicity tried to scream, and Tessa loosened her grip a touch.

"You're insane," Felicity rasped.

"Indeed," Tessa hummed, twirling the dagger in her hand. "It happens when people keep trying to take what is ours. We don't like it."

"Tessa," Theon cut in, recognizing the spiral she was about to go down.

Tessa sighed, her fingers tightening on the dagger hilt. "But you are still bound to him, and I don't like that. Especially not after learning you tried to trick him into having a child with you. But more than that, there is a bargain with Valter that all comes back to . . . you."

"I have nothing to do with that," Felicity said, squirming beneath Tessa's weight.

"You have everything to do with it," Tessa hissed. "And I know what it is to be trapped and confined and bound when you don't want to be. Surely you can see the conundrum here. Because I know people like you. You'll never stop until you get what you want, and unfortunately for you, that's a problem for us."

"You have the dragon!" Felicity cried. "You can't have them both. It doesn't work that way."

Tessa reared back a little at her words, and Felicity took advantage. She twisted, throwing Tessa off her. In her surprise, the dagger came loose, and Felicity snatched it up, scrambling to where Tessa was pushing to her knees.

"If he won't do what needs to be done, I'll do it myself," Felicity said, determination filling her features. "You'll be gone. The realm will be safe, and he'll be *mine*."

Theon lunged to stop her, his power lurching, but he didn't need to. Tessa lifted a hand, her light wrapping around Felicity's wrist and snapping it as Felicity brought her arm down. The dagger had been inches from Tessa's chest, but it clattered to the floor.

"Stop touching my godsdamn things," Tessa snarled, swiping up the dagger and slashing it across Felicity's throat. Blood sprayed as she plunged it into Felicity's chest. The female gasped, a hand reaching for the hilt as she fell onto her side, and Theon watched in fascination as she faded to embers that matched Tessa's power before fading away altogether.

"You've been keeping secrets, Tessa," he chided with a dark purr, striding to her and extending a hand. Her fingers slid into his, smears of blood gracing his palm as he pulled her to her feet. He gripped her chin in his other hand, forcing her eyes to his. "You are stunning," he growled.

"Say it," she rasped, the words harsh and rough as the high he'd experienced moments ago flashed in her violet irises. He knew what she wanted to hear.

"Yours, little storm. Only yours. Every piece of me."

"I don't regret killing her."

"We do what needs to be done, and we don't have regrets," he replied.

"Am I a villain now?"

"I don't give a fuck if you are. I'll still sacrifice every star in the sky for you," he said, reaching for her arm and pulling her sleeve back to reveal a brand new Mark.

It wound around her wrist, just below her bands of light. It was a Mark he'd never seen before, but after his meeting with Rordan and the Ladies—when they'd laid out his lordship requirements—he'd called Felicity.

Then he'd contacted Cienna.

He'd needed a fake Union Mark, yes, but he'd also needed something more. He'd needed a Union Mark to bind him and Tessa, and last night, Brecken had brought the Witch with when he'd taken Theon to Tessa's rooms. Tessa had agreed to his plan. He would never have forced her. Would have come up with something else, but she'd agreed. A binding of her own choosing with conditions of her own. Conditions Theon had never imagined being even remotely agreeable to, but ones he hoped would eventually come to pass.

But that wasn't up to him

He swiped his thumb along the black and white loops and swirls that wound around her wrist, matching the one on his.

"Are you all right?" he murmured.

"Something is wrong with us," she said, lifting her palms and studying them.

"With your power?"

She nodded. "It's like it's . . . empty. There are only dregs of it in my soul, as if it can only appear in short bursts. It's never been like this."

"But you just killed Felicity," he said. "Isn't that how your power refills?"

"Yes, but my power didn't take. That was . . . something else."

"I'm going to need you to fill me in on that, or I can't help, Tessa."

Before she could reply, light flared, and it wasn't hers. Theon shoved her behind him, but she didn't stay there, because of course she didn't.

Not as Rordan stepped from a portal with Dex at his side.

"What are you doing back here?" Theon demanded, his power immediately winding around Tessa.

"I see you figured out how to remove that cuff," Rordan answered, gaze sweeping over the mess of Cordelia's corpse on the floor. "Dexter thought you might have. So we have come to make a bargain. Give us the cuff and the two of you can leave."

"Just like that?" Theon asked doubtfully.

"I'm sure we will meet again soon enough."

"And if we refuse?"

"Ah, then we will have to detain you for murder," he answered. "And kidnapping? Where is your wife?"

Neither he nor Tessa answered that question, but Theon said, "And what makes you think you'll be able to detain us?"

Rordan smiled something truly sinister. "I know her power is not what it should be. Not with that cuff absorbing her magic for the last two weeks, even if I couldn't convince her to eat a pastry this morning to make it slumber even more. Beyond that, you are not yet a Lord. Even if you were, your Source is weakened. You are not strong enough to take me on, but aside from all that, I also have them."

As he said the words, seraphs appeared in the room. Some Traveling in and some bursting through the office door. More than a dozen of them. Some had power swirling at their fingertips; others had weapons.

"You disappoint me, Tessie," Dex said, cold and harsh as he glared at her. "I tried to give you everything. I would have taken you home when this was all over."

"Achaz would never let me live," she answered. "He would use me to do his dirty work, then kill me for the Arius blood in my veins."

"And now he will simply kill you," Dex replied. "Stupid, reckless child." With a jerk of his chin, he commanded, "Get me the cuff, and bring her to me."

The seraphs converged, coming for them, and Theon didn't know what he was doing as he tugged Tessa into his chest. Darkness wrapped around them, swallowing them whole. He didn't know how or why, but it was instinct to take a step, shadow-walking through the dark.

But he'd never done this before, and he didn't know where they were when they appeared beside a body of water. Trees surrounded them, and clouds obscured the sun.

"Lake Moonmist," Tessa said, taking in their surroundings. She looked at him in concern. "We didn't go far enough, Theon. This is right next to the estate."

"I don't even know what I did or how I did it. I don't know . . ." He trailed off, feeling helpless and out of his element. He *always* knew. Always had control of his power.

And then the seraphs appeared.

Tessa was nearly powerless, and they were alone.

Fuck.

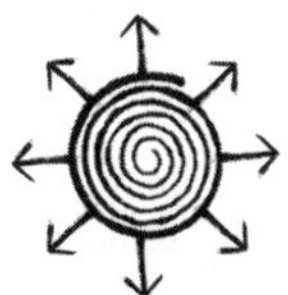

25
LUKA

"This is where Fae are raised?" Eliza asked in a tone that told Luka exactly what she thought of that.

"Most of them," Luka answered as they approached the Celeste Estate main gates. "There are four estates. Some Fae have homes in the cities after they are assigned to kingdoms. But all Fae children are sent to an estate for academics by the age of six."

"And the Fae just . . . allow that?"

"It's how things are done," he answered.

"It's cruel."

"I don't disagree," he answered. "But when it's how it's always been done, eventually everyone stops questioning. It's just . . . normal." Stopping at the gates, he added, "Devram is on the edge of a reformation. The Lords and Ladies are trying to incite panic to control the masses, but . . . I don't think things will stay the same. Change is coming either way."

"That's the hope," Eliza grumbled. "How are we getting in there?"

Luka had used the Tracking Mark that still connected him to Tessa to make sure she was still here. Assuming Theon wouldn't leave her again, two days ago they'd Traveled to Arobell, the Celeste Kingdom capital city, with Razik and Eliza. They'd all agreed they should leave the cave for a while. Not because anyone could access it with his wards, but because Tessa had clearly been taken from there. There were likely seraphs lingering as spies.

Cienna had taken Xan to the Underground while Razik and Eliza had come with him. At this point, any extra power wouldn't hurt. They had no idea what they were going to come up against. So they'd rested up in

Arobell, letting their reserves fill fully, before they ventured to the estate, being dropped off at the end of the long drive they'd just walked up.

"We could fly over the gates," Razik offered, a slyness to his voice that Luka didn't understand.

"Why are you saying it like that?" Luka asked at the same time Eliza said, "Absolutely not."

Luka glanced between the two of them. "Did something happen when you were flying?"

"No," Eliza retorted.

"How could it when her feet have never left the ground?" Razik added.

Luka looked back at Eliza in surprise. "Never? You've never gone flying with him?"

"Has Tessa?" she asked in irritation.

"Yes," Luka answered. "Granted, those were life or death situations, but she's not averse to it."

"If I were meant to fly, I would have been given wings," she said. "Figure out something else."

"Why aren't there guards out here anyway?" Razik asked, stepping closer to study the tall metal gates.

It was a good point, and a question Luka didn't have an answer to. He'd come to get Theon and Tessa out of here; then they could all regroup. He'd clear the air with Tessa. He'd be back with his Ward, and things could move forward.

Pushing on the gate, it swung open easily, and everything in him went on high alert. Something was very wrong here. Not even the wards around the property were active.

"Be prepared for anything," Luka said in a low voice, shifting his eyes to see everything more vividly.

"Don't expect me to protect you if we have to fight, *mai dragocen,*" Razik said, walking at Eliza's side.

"The only one who's going to need protecting is you. From me," she grumbled.

He chuckled low, and Luka could swear her lips twitched, hiding a smile.

They were an odd couple.

Pulling his attention back to the estate, he wasn't entirely sure where to go. He'd only been to this estate once. The only thing he had to go on was the Tracking Mark that was guiding him deeper into the estate grounds.

They stuck to the shadows, trying to stay out of sight. Rounding the main building, they all went still. In the center of the courtyard stood the Anala Heir and her Source. A fire portal was open, and they were ushering Fae children through as quickly as possible.

"What the fuck?" Luka said under his breath.

"What is happening?" Eliza asked.

"I don't know," he answered, watching Gatlan move among the children. More than once, he crouched before a scared child, wiping at tears and saying words Luka could just make out. Telling them everything would be okay. They'd be safe soon.

Tana somehow sensed them then, her golden eyes connecting with his. She said something to Gatlan, who nodded, calling to a few others Luka had missed. One was Brigid, Tana's younger sister, who was closer to Axel's age. The others were clearly related as well with their various shades of red hair.

Tana moved in their direction, and when she was halfway to them, a seraph Luka recognized fell into step beside her. Luka immediately went on high alert. It was Brecken, one of Tessa's so-called friends. The same one that had helped her at the Sirana Villas. Luka didn't know whose side the male was on, and seeing him here with Tana was a little bit of a mindfuck.

"Based on conversations and debts currently owed by Theon, I'm going to trust you will not speak a word of what you have seen here today," Tana said tightly, flames winding up her arms and into her hair.

"I don't know what I'm seeing," Luka said. "Where are you taking them?"

"Where we always take those who are no longer safe," Tana answered. "But our resources are growing sparse, particularly space. We need to know where Theon stands. We've been watching him. Tessa has . . . changed him in many ways."

"That's one way to put it," Luka muttered.

"Who are they?" Tana asked.

"Razik and Eliza."

Tana eyed them, amber eyes narrowing, but before she could say anything further, Brecken cut in.

"We have limited time, Tana. We could be discovered any moment."

"I thought you took care of the guards?" Tana answered, glancing to where Gatlan, Brigid, and the others were continuing to guide the children.

"I did, but I'm not as worried about them as much as I am about . . . *her*," Brecken replied, dark eyes boring into Luka's.

"Isn't Theon with her?" Luka demanded.

"He is, but it won't be enough. Dex and Rordan went after them with a small company of seraphs."

Panic and anxiety settled in. Theon was powerful; Tessa was more so. Brecken knew this. If he was worried . . .

"Where are they?" Luka asked.

"I can take you," Brecken said, glancing at Tana, who nodded. "But they will know I have been betraying them this entire time. I need to know I can leave with all of you."

"Done," Luka answered without hesitation. "Take us to them now."

Within moments, Brecken Traveled the four of them to the edge of a lake, leaving Tana to finish with the Fae younglings.

"Well, this looks familiar," Razik grumbled under his breath. He was already pulling his shirt over his head and summoning his wings. Glancing at Eliza, he added, "If I kill more than you, I win that sword."

"Fuck off," she scoffed, her elegant sword already in her hand with flames twisting around the blade. She was bouncing on her toes, and if he didn't know for a fact she didn't, he'd swear she had Sargon blood in her for as much as she liked to fight.

Razik reached over, tightening some of the straps on the leather armor she favored. "Because you know you're going to lose?"

She shoved his hand away, grey eyes scanning the scene before them. "Theon and Tessa are by the edge of the lake," she said, pointing in their direction, but Luka had spotted them the moment they'd appeared here.

Theon had Tessa shoved behind him. His darkness was a writhing swarm around him, shadow wings wide and flared. There were at least two dozen seraphs in the sky, which explained why Theon hadn't hauled her up there. Where else was there to go?

"Why isn't Tessa using her power?" Luka asked, that familiar adrenaline coursing through his body, preparing to fight and protect what was his.

"She's drained. I don't have time to explain," Brecken said. "She needs to take, but her power is too drained to do anything."

"So it's just Theon?"

"It *was*," the male drawled.

Everything around them seemed to still, as if even the world was holding its breath, and then it was chaos. Seraphs attacked from all sides, diving for Theon and Tessa as power and magic flared.

"Fuck," Luka muttered, already running. Eliza was at his side, while

Razik launched into the sky with Brecken, the male's cream wings a stark contrast to Razik's black ones.

"Keep them out of the sky as much as possible," Eliza was yelling as they ran. "Only fire truly kills them. Mine. Yours. Doesn't much matter. If you get ambushed, incapacitate them to keep them down. Snap wings. Slit throats. Cut off limbs. Knock them out. We can come back around and finish them off later. And for the love of Anala, don't waste all your power right away."

Then she was jumping into the fray, that beautiful blade swinging. By the gods, she was every bit the war general they said she was. Not only that, her power was vast.

Wings went up in flames while her blade swiped through torsos. She ducked and flipped, trails of fire and blood left in her wake. Daggers of pure flame went before her, distracting her victims so she could come in from behind, and above them, her bonded was doing the same. Razik had shifted to his full dragon form, and seraphs became encased with dragon fire before becoming nothing at all.

He should be up there, doing the same, but not until he got to Theon and Tessa.

"Nylah! Roan! Now!"

Tessa's cry carried to him above the din of battle, and something twisted in his gut at her crying out for her wolves for help instead of him. It only spurred him on faster, shoving seraphs aside, dodging attacks, and when all else failed, using a short sword he summoned to incapacitate them just as Eliza had said. It was stupid and went against all his training to be singularly focused on the two of them, but Theon was his Ward. Of course he was the priority. And Tessa was—

Howls rent through the air, and seconds later the wolves appeared. One light and one dark. Growls sounded and jaws snapped, teeth sinking into wings and flesh as they moved towards Tessa.

And then there was Theon, his twin short swords in hand as his darkness devoured. He looked every bit of the dark god he descended from, all lethal grace and not letting a single seraph near Tessa. She had two of her daggers, but why the fuck wasn't she using her bow?

Tessa spun suddenly, as if knowing he was there despite their fractured bond. Her eyes went wide, mouth parting slightly, and Luka was about to yell at her to look out.

But he didn't need to.

She spun as the seraph with water magic appeared behind her, walking atop the water of the lake. Her golden hair was a wave behind her as one dagger went into the left side of his chest and the other went into the right side of his gut. She slid the blades, slicing wide, more than blood spilling from the body cavity, and then she lifted her leg, planting a bare foot in the center of his torso and shoving him back. Just like with her arrows, the seraph seemed suspended in time for a few seconds before he dissolved into the embers and ashes that were her power, slowly drifting and floating away in the water.

She was godsdamn magnificent, and he understood his brother's fascination with his bonded on an entirely different level.

Roan appeared at her side, her fingers drifting into his fur and her eyes fluttering closed. Where had the wolves been before she called them? Why hadn't they been with her this entire time?

He closed the last of the distance, saying fuck it and letting his power obliterate three seraphs with one mighty burst of black flames.

"What's the plan here? Travel out?" Luka asked, finally making it to Theon's side while reaching over and pulling Tessa in between them. He heard her suck in a sharp breath, but he ignored it.

"And go where?" Theon asked, dark mist springing up to block an onslaught of attacks from above.

He had a good point. Luka would bet there were seraphs waiting around the cave now. And who could they trust in the kingdoms? Arius House was questionable, but even if it gave them a few hours to regroup and come up with a plan, it might be worth it.

"What happened to your power?" Luka asked, glancing down at Tessa.

But Theon answered, pulling some kind of cuff from his pocket. Thicker than the usual bands, it resembled a vambrace. It was white and black with gold and silver etchings he didn't recognize. "They had this on her. Apparently it was absorbing her power."

"How?"

"We didn't really sit down and have a conversation about it," Theon growled, his power converging to snap wings clean off a diving seraph. The being's cries echoed as Roan pounced, teeth tearing out the female's throat.

Luka took the cuff, examining it and debating if he could get Razik's attention. If the cuff had absorbed her power, there had to be a way to get it released. Right?

"Incoming!" Theon yelled, a handful of seraphs rushing them.

Luka passed the cuff to Tessa, saying, "Stay between us."

"But I—"

He didn't hear what she was going to say as he engaged with a seraph. Black flames wreathed his fists, blocking a hit with his arm while landing a punch to the male's ribs with the other. The seraph grunted, but he didn't go down. His next hit landed, wrapped in ice, and Luka swore as he absorbed the blow to his jaw.

The seraph was trying to circle him, but he'd had enough of this. He lunged, the seraph clearly surprised as he scrambled to shield, but Luka wasn't aiming to land a hit. His fingers closed around soft, dark brown feathers, and he yanked hard, hearing several snapping sounds. So much like his own wings, but also different.

The seraph let out a bellow of pain, an ice dagger appearing in his hand, but Luka caught his arm a second before the blade pierced his skin.

And then a dark dagger was in the male's throat as Tessa practically climbed Luka, using his arm as a step to jump and reach the male's neck. She leapt, landing in a low crouch while the seraph crumpled and blood sprayed, splattering her golden strands.

"I had it under control," Luka grunted, watching Theon take down another.

"Never tell me to stay back and safe between the two of you again, Luka Mors," she retorted, pushing to her feet.

He blinked at her. At the female who'd wanted exactly that when he'd escorted her to a stage to be claimed as a Source. And now . . .

Now she was a fierce thing of chaos and fury who'd taken control of her own destiny. Who'd kept training, not because she was forced to, but because she *wanted* to. Who'd found another way when he'd so often dismissed her. On her own. With Eliza. Both in combat and with her magic.

She'd found herself worth fighting for.

"Why aren't you using your bow?" he demanded, watching her lips purse in annoyance at his dismissal of her command.

"Why aren't you using your fucking power?" she shot back.

"Because someone is going to need to Travel us out of here," Luka retorted. "If I'm too drained, then we're stuck here—Fuck!"

His hand snapped out, grabbing her and yanking her into his side as three seraphs came from the sky. He *was* using dragonfire then, two of them nothing but a few drifting ashes before they made it to the ground.

But the third . . . had disappeared?

"Dex is here," Tessa said in cold fury. "He's using his magic to make us see things that aren't there. This whole thing could be an illusion."

"He's *that* powerful?" Luka asked.

She shrugged. "Maybe. They want this cuff."

She still held the thing in her other hand, keeping a tight grip on it.

"We need to go," Theon said, out of breath as he came up beside Tessa. "More seraphs just arrived. Even with Razik and Eliza, it's a deathtrap to stay here."

"How do we get us all in one spot to Travel out?" Luka asked, looking to find Razik engaging seraphs far off to the left. He could only assume that was where Eliza was. Razik would never stray far from her.

"They want this," Tessa said again, studying the cuff. "So let's give it to them."

"What?" Theon asked. "Tessa, we can't–"

"Of course she can," sneered a voice, Dex appearing a few feet away as though he'd been there the whole time.

"I told you he was nearby," Tessa whispered, her face paling as she clutched the cuff to her chest and raised her dagger.

The cuff, Tessie," Dex said in a cold command.

"No," she retorted, eyes darting around as seraphs closed in, waiting for an order from their apparent leader.

"But you just said you were going to hand it over. It's the smartest thing you've said all day," Dex went on, taking a step towards her. He extended a hand. "Give it to me, and I'll fix everything."

Something about his words made Tessa go eerily still.

"Tessa?" Theon said softly. "Give me the cuff."

He reached for it, but she clutched it closer.

"You're surrounded, Tessa," Dex said sharply. "You're surrounded and out of power. Your lovers have been using theirs, but they won't last forever. They'll die, and it will be your fault. I won't be able to clean up that mess for you. I won't—*No!*"

Dex was yelling, wings ripping free as he launched into the sky.

But he was too late.

Tessa had moved so godsdamn fast, throwing the cuff with everything she had far out in the lake behind them. It hit the water, sinking below it.

"You have no idea what you've done!" Dex bellowed, his face full of shock before he Traveled out.

Then the ground shook beneath their feet.

It was a faint tremor that made them all stumble at first, and then it was a violent jolt. Ripples spread across the water, transforming into waves that became as brutal as the trembling ground beneath their feet. There wasn't time to think or come up with a plan. There wasn't time to get everyone together to Travel anywhere.

Luka grabbed Tessa, wrapping an arm around her waist as he yelled to Theon, "Get into the sky!"

They both launched up, getting as high as they could, but it was too late.

Power exploded from the lake, and the water went with it, as if the cuff had been transformed into some kind of explosive.

"Luka!" Theon bellowed, from several feet above them. Darkness reached for him, trying to wrap around them, but it wasn't enough.

That surge of power shredded through the darkness, and all Luka could do was hold Tessa as tightly as he could, wrapping his wings and his magic around her as they plummeted to the ground. The water from the lake fell around them, pelting and stinging like razor blades. And the power? Gods, that explosion of magic rippled through him over and over, a never-ending current of energy and pain.

She didn't scream, didn't cry out. Tessa only clung to him just as tightly. He should have shifted long ago. He should have Traveled her and Theon out and come back for the others. He should have done so many things differently.

That was all he could think when they hit the ground hard, rolling several feet. He felt various parts of his wings snap and tear, the pain excruciating, but still he kept his hold on Tessa tight until they finally stopped. He couldn't draw in a full breath. Whether from the hard landing or the pain wracking his body, he wasn't entirely sure. And for a moment, the world was quiet as both sides tried to recover from whatever the fuck had just happened.

Tessa moved first, stirring against him, and he grunted as she pushed a wing off herself as gently as she could. She had injuries of her own, a dark bruise already forming on her cheek. Scratches everywhere. With her magic so depleted, she wouldn't heal herself as quickly, if at all, but she seemed relatively unharmed. Good. That was good.

He blinked, his vision going in and out of focus, and his dragon was trying to claw its way out. Was trying to protect him. But he couldn't. Something was wrong with him. His dragon. Nothing was working right for some reason.

"Luka?" Tessa whispered, eyes wide as she took him in.

She lifted a hand, as if to touch a wing, but she pulled it back. So tentative and worried. Scared. Of him? Why was she scared of him?

"Are you . . . What do I do? I don't know what I—" Then she was crawling to him and shoving at his chest. "Why did you do that?" she demanded, ignoring the low growl of discomfort. Tears filled her eyes, and he didn't know if they were sad or angry. Pushing hair out of her face, red was left in the path of her hand. Blood dripped down her forearm from another injury, flowing over a new Mark around her wrist. "Why did you do that? You didn't have to come! And now you are—Because of me. And I don't know what to do!" Looking around frantically, she cried, "Theon? Nylah? Roan?"

He could hear movement, the rustling of wings that told him the surviving seraphs were starting to recover. Pushing past the pain, he thought he might have enough reserves to Travel her out. He tried to push into a sitting position, to reach for her, but he couldn't move his body right. Then she was wrenched away from him, a cry of surprise sounding.

"You wild and reckless child," Dexter snarled, hauling her to her feet by her hair. "You truly ruin *everything*, don't you? And once again, I have to clean up your mess."

Luka didn't understand what was happening when he grabbed her arm, but Tessa clearly did.

"No!" she cried, yanking and pushing and trying to break his hold.

It didn't matter. Dex tipped her arm, her wound dripping to the ground, and Tessa screamed, not in horror but in utter fury as a Hunter appeared.

"You called, your grace?" the Hunter said, his eerie voice wrapping around Luka's bones like ice. So much like the voice Tessa could have, yet different.

"No," she said, shaking her head wildly. "I didn't. Leave. You are not needed."

But more and more Hunters materialized, even as she spoke the words.

"Hold her," Dex sneered, passing her off to the Hunter.

"Dex, no! Please no!" she cried, but he didn't stop.

The male moved to stand over Luka, a sneer of disgust on his face. "Another one of Sargon's heirs fails his duties." His booted foot came down hard on a battered wing, the male grinding all his weight atop it. Tessa cried out again, and Luka was fighting the urge to vomit at the excruciating pain. "The thing is," Dex continued, "a Hunter's blade doesn't do much to your kind since your fire burns away the poison. This blade, however . . ."

The seraph smiled, pulling a long, thin dagger from his belt. The hilt was gold and the blade itself was pure white with gold etchings.

"It was created especially for your kind," Dex said, dropping to a knee beside him. "Achaz created it just for Sargon and Arius and their little pets. We use it in weapons." He flashed a dark smirk. "Or collars. Which I did debate for you. We could use a replacement for your father, but I think this will break her more." He leaned closer, his voice merciless. "And I need her fucking shattered."

And Luka could do nothing but watch as he raised his arm above his head and sank the blade deep into his chest.

If he'd been in pain before, it was nothing compared to this, because he was dying.

No.

His dragon was dying, thrashing and keening in his soul. He'd never survive losing that piece of him.

Tessa was screaming, and his dragon was dying.

He tried to speak, holding her horrified stare. Willing her to understand the words he was mouthing.

Keep . . . fighting . . . baby girl.

And the last thing he saw was lightning flickering in endless violet depths before his dragon let out a defiant roar, and the world went dark and silent.

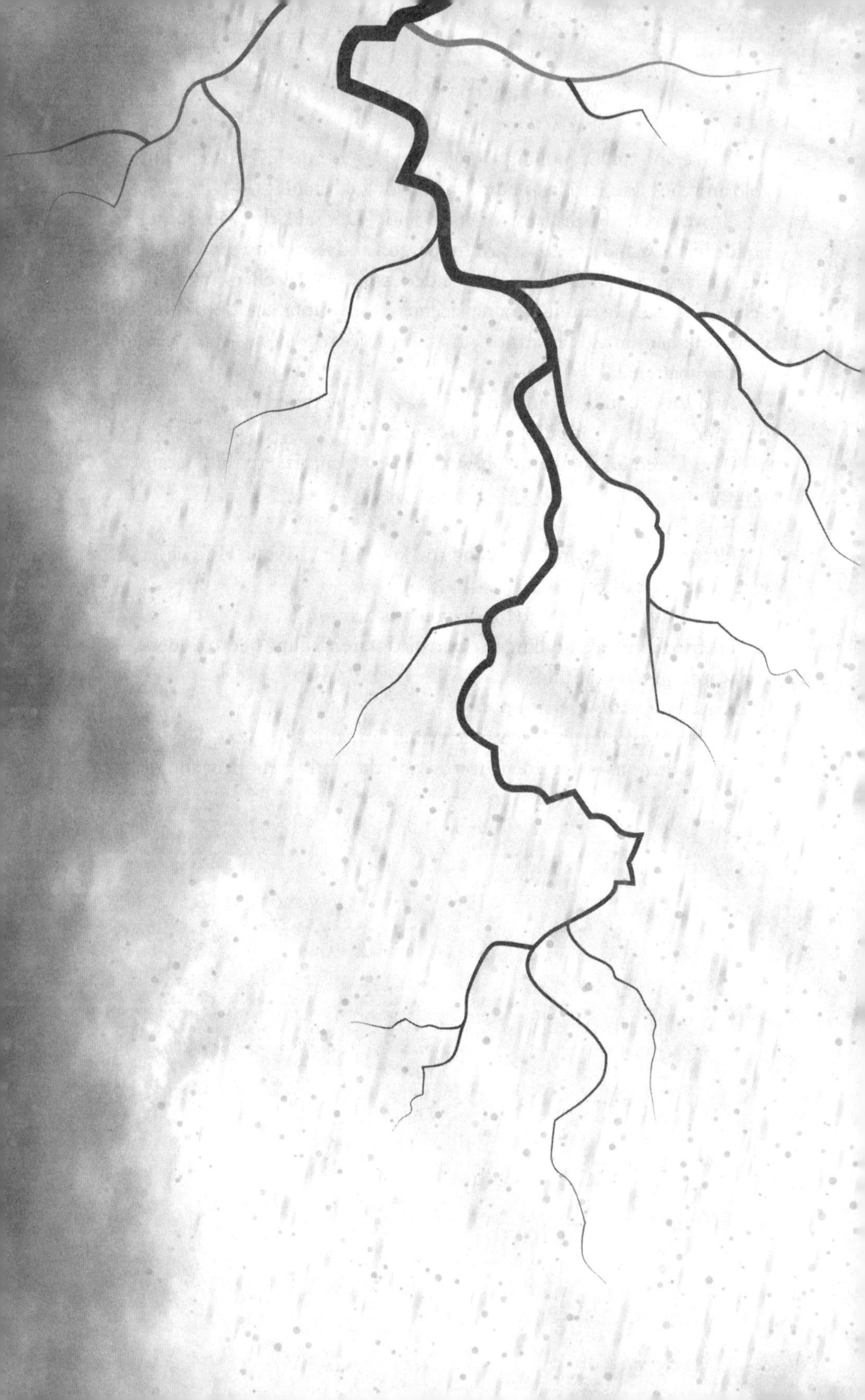

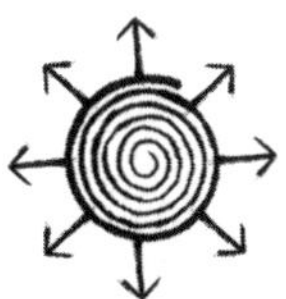

26
TESSA

The world was too quiet.

Or maybe sound was just muted?

There was a faint buzzing. A low din in the background that wouldn't stop as she stared and stared at that dagger lodged in Luka's chest. Because he wasn't moving. And why wasn't he moving? He was a dragon. *A dragon*. He couldn't just . . . stop moving.

And there was something in her that was breaking. A fracture that was deepening. Splitting her apart. And it was all she could feel. She couldn't breathe. There was no one to tell her to put one foot in front of the other. No one to guide her through the dark. Who was going to continue her training? And tell her to get over her shit? And tell Theon when he was being an ass?

Who was going to buy her flip-flops?

And why was she thinking about flip-flops when he wasn't fucking moving?

Because being the grandchild of a god was lonely, and she had just saved Theon for him, and now he was not moving?

No.

No, no, no.

Her hands were in her hair, pulling at the strands, but she couldn't feel the pain that would usually ground her because all she could feel was her soul breaking. And her chest burned. And the back of her neck. And—

No!

She looked down to find the Source Mark over her heart flaring and fraying, as if it too was being pulled apart. Because he was part of that, and he was not moving.

And then she heard him.

Felt him.

His bellows of agony broke through the drowning silence. She moved so violently the Hunter holding her wasn't expecting it, and she spun, searching. Theon was maybe twenty feet from her on his knees and curled in on himself. His face to the ground and hands on his head as if he was dying too. As if he was being ripped apart as much as she was.

"The death of a guardian is excruciating for their wards," came Dex's whispered words in her ear, one of his hands pulling her hair over her shoulder. "But you know all about that, don't you, Tessie?" A finger ran down her nape, directly atop her third Source Mark. "Still, it will be worse for the Arius heir because you never accepted your bond with the dragon. A regret for both of you, I'm sure. Now that it will never come to be."

Another cry of pure torture came from Theon, and he was *crawling*. Theon was dragging himself across the ground, trying to get to Luka. But Hunters were converging and closing in around him, drawn by his Arius blood, and they no longer answered to her. But they didn't attack. They just continued to circle, eyes keen on their prey as he stopped and cried out again.

And she could feel his agony mixing with her own, and it brought her to her knees. Gods, she wouldn't survive this. None of them would survive this.

"They won't kill him yet," Dex said, crouching beside her. "I won't let them. I want him to feel every ounce of that fucking bond dying. Only then will I let the Hunters have him."

Her Source Marks were like a hot brand now, as torturous as when she'd received them.

The Source Marks.

Slowly, she lifted her hands, turning them over. The Arius Mark on one hand, but the other . . .

She only needed enough to take a little.

Lifting her head, she could see Theon through the faintly translucent Hunters. He was still clawing at the muddy ground, trying to get closer. Strangled grunts and cries coming from his chest in a way she'd never imagined. He was always so sure, exuding power.

And she looked back over her shoulder at Luka's unmoving form. He was always strong and broody, never taking anyone's shit.

"I tried to do this nicely, Tessie," Dex whispered. "Your actions caused this, just like they did all those years ago in this same place. I had to clean up that mess too." She slowly turned to face him, his dark eyes glittering with triumph. "All you had to do was do as you were told."

Why can't you just do as you are told?

Too wild.

Too much to deal with.

Not worth the hassle.

Nothing.

All the things that had been hurled at her for two decades resounded in her head. He'd known the entire time. Had used all of that to manipulate her. Control her. Get her to trust him. He'd played into it, always *fixing* mistakes and *cleaning up* her messes. Because she was just a helpless, uncontrollable thing that needed saving and protecting.

Except she wasn't any of those things.

No one controlled her.

She wasn't too wild. She was the daughter of the wild and untamed.

She wasn't too much to deal with. She'd only needed to understand how she was different to find her balance.

She wasn't too much of a hassle. She'd just needed to learn what real love felt like and how to accept it.

She wasn't nothing.

She was Chaos.

Holding Dex's stare, he started at whatever he saw on her face when she said in that eerie, maniacal tone, "I'm going to kill you." She slowly rose to her feet. "You're going to run because you're a coward, but I will hunt you down. It won't be too much of a hassle. I'll enjoy it. Knowing you're constantly wondering if today will be the day I find you and make such an awful mess. I'm going to kill you, and I'm going to enjoy every second of it."

Then she tugged on that bond, yanking and pulling on everything that connected her to Theon until she found his magic. It was trembling and writhing, and it was depleted from the fighting. She felt terrible about taking it from him, but she just needed enough to take.

So she wrapped her light around it and called it to her, and she felt him jerk at the pull.

"I'm sorry," she whispered before she yanked harder, forcing it to follow. The thing in her soul drank it up, starved and feral. His darkness merged with her gifts, becoming what she was as he became *her* Source of power.

It took Dex far longer than it should have for him to realize what was happening, but he was on his feet and stumbling back from her. "No," he said, shaking his head in disbelief. "Not possible. It's not . . . You're *his* Source."

Tessa lifted a hand, light and dark appearing. Golden embers and silver ashes. All of it circling and spinning together. Everything and nothing. Chaos in the palm of her hand.

"I will not fail in my tasks," Dex gritted out.

"Today you will," she replied, and her power struck, Dex Traveling out a second before it landed.

With Dex gone, the other seraphs scrambled, as if unsure what to do. Lightning arced from her palm, chaos following, and a seraph screamed when it found its mark.

And her magic took.

She did the same thing, again and again, until she could stop drawing from Theon because her power was feasting.

And Theon—

She spun, the Hunters closing in with no one here to rein them in.

Tessa summoned her bow, letting her power have its way with the seraphs while she nocked arrows and took down Hunters. Hunter and seraph. Seraph and Hunter. It didn't matter.

Chaos does not choose.

It devoured, and when it had taken enough, she didn't stop it. She let it have her, lifting her off the ground until she was hovering feet above them. Only then did she yank on her power, wrestling with it. Trying to take back some control.

"Not them," she hissed. "We don't hurt them."

It pulled and snapped, trying to buckle under her one command.

"Everyone else. Not them," she repeated.

Then she let it go once more, watching it pour out of her and spread like a net. It wrapped around the seraphs fleeing in the sky and those running for cover in the surrounding trees. It wound among the Hunters, down their throats and squeezing whatever life-force from their beings. It took life from the trees and the water and the wind, but it did not touch Theon or Luka. It did not linger near Nylah or Roan.

But she felt it all. Could feel the power from her toes to the tips of her fingers. Could feel it swirling in her eyes and flowing in her veins. This *thing* she'd always known was there but could never control.

Because Chaos wasn't meant to be controlled.

Chaos was meant to reign.

And when they were all gone, when only those she loved remained, she drifted back down, already running as her bare feet hit the ground soaked with water and blood. Because her reserves were full after taking so much life, and Luka still wasn't moving.

She dropped to her knees beside him, all the pain and grief mixing with her fury and chaos. He wasn't gone yet because she could still feel the bond in her soul splintering, on the precipice of snapping altogether.

"Tessa, there's nothing—"

But she twisted with a snarl when someone touched her shoulder, finding Brecken standing over her, and he yanked his hand back.

Holding his hands up in supplication, he said, "Okay, Tessa. Okay. I won't touch you."

Movement caught her eye, and she found Razik and Eliza with Theon, helping him over to where they were. He couldn't even stand, let alone walk. She didn't have time to wait though. Twisting back to Luka, she didn't know what to do.

His wings were ripped to shreds in some places. He had open wounds everywhere with small pools of blood forming. He had a dagger in his chest.

Her power snarled at the thought, and she let herself sink into it. She had no idea what she was doing, but she was light and dark. Life and death. Beginning and endings. If she could take, she could give too. Right?

She clasped the dagger, yanking it out. Blood immediately poured from his chest, running along his flesh. Lifting a trembling hand, she let her power pool there. Let it swirl and grow, pouring everything she had into it. Then she sent it to Luka, straight into the wound on his chest. Her palm covered the wound, trying to keep blood in.

Just like when she took, her power raced through him. It wrapped around bone and muscle, seeped into his blood. It twisted around his lungs, taking shallow breaths too far apart. It encased his heart, infusing the organ that was scarcely beating.

That fluttered under her magic.

Then stopped beating altogether.

"No!" she cried, pushing up on her knees to hover over him, her face inches from his. "No, Luka Mors. You stubborn, broody ass! You do not get to leave me here. Do you hear me? I said I would let you go, set you free to live a life you wanted. I didn't let you go so you could . . . No!"

Someone tried to grab her, but she threw them off.

"We need to leave this place," someone—Razik—was saying. "It's out in the open, not to mention enemy territory."

"And go where?" Eliza asked.

"The Underground," Razik answered. "It's the safest space."

"And warded," she argued. "We can't haul Luka through those tunnels, and Theon can't even stand."

"But Tessa can cross wards without issue," Brecken said suddenly. Then she felt him shift, presumably kneeling down beside her because he sounded closer when he said, "Can you Travel us, Tessa? All of us? I'm told Axel is in the penthouse. Then we can . . . figure all this out. Can you do that?"

She gave a sharp nod, her eyes still closed as she continued to pour herself into Luka.

"Now, Tess," Brecken whispered.

And she did just that, pulling them all through space and depositing them in the main living room of the penthouse.

"What the fuck?" Axel barked, crashing sounds echoing around her.

Tessa opened her eyes just in time to see Axel rushing toward them, but she lifted her other hand, a burst of energy sending him flying backwards. No one was getting close to him. Not until his heart was beating.

"Somebody tell me what the fuck is going on right now," Axel demanded, a dark command that made her power pause for the smallest of moments. Her eyes were already closed again, trying to focus.

"Tessa," came a rasped voice at her side, and she shook her head. Because if she looked at Theon right now, it was over. If he told her it was over, it was too real. Because Theon never lied to her, and if he said it, it was true, and she refused to accept that.

There were noises, people talking, but she wasn't listening. Didn't care what they were saying. Because this wasn't how they ended. She refused to accept this.

Her power was still wrapped around Luka and everything he was, and she just needed his heart to start beating again. Energy flared, a shock of power that she felt ripple through him, but it still did nothing.

A touch to her back, a touch she knew. Darkness and control. She still refused to look at him. But his power was there, and she heard him grunt as she pulled on it again. If she wasn't enough, she'd use Theon's power too. If that wasn't enough, she'd find more power to take.

"Tessa, stop," someone else was saying. "Not like this."

But it would be like this because something had to work. Something had to fix this.

"Tessa—"

She didn't know who was trying to talk to her, but her answer was a feral scream of utter fury and anguish. This was *not* how this was going to end.

Chaos erupted around her. It wasn't destructive like it had been beside Lake Moonmist. No, this Chaos settled onto Luka like an armor before sinking into his being. She felt it in the power she already had laced through his body, in his veins, and around his bones. It fused and merged, and she could feel it all racing throughout his being.

And then his heart beat.

Once.

Twice.

Nothing once more.

"No!" she cried, resting her cheek against his chest. She could feel the sticky blood on her skin, but she couldn't feel him. She couldn't . . .

"I know you don't want me anymore, but I still want you, Luka. Please don't . . . I still need you. It only works if it's the three of us. I can't . . ."

Tears were flowing down her face, mixing with the blood on his chest, and she couldn't breathe. Her chest wouldn't expand, and still she pressed her hand atop that wound over his heart, right next to where she lay. As long as she didn't move her hand, there was still hope, and she had to believe hope wasn't as useless as she'd once thought.

"What is that?" someone—Axel—asked, his voice low and somber.

"That is going to be a problem," Cienna said.

"Tessa, I don't know what you're doing, but I don't think . . ." Theon started, but he trailed off when Luka's chest rose and fell. Then she felt his heart beat, pulsing beneath her magic as she held him together with all that she was.

One. Two. Three.

Just like when she was a child passing the time in a dark cupboard, she counted those heartbeats, and she kept counting each one.

One hundred sixty-three, one hundred sixty-four, one hundred sixty-five.

Not until she hit three hundred did she dare to open her eyes. Lift her head. See his chest rising and falling, slowly and too far apart, but it was moving.

"Cienna," Theon said. "What is happening?"

"She is bartering with the gods and the Fates," Cienna muttered. "Move her so I can work, Theon. Tris, I need you. Gia too."

"Come, Tessa," Theon said, gently taking her shoulders and pulling, but she still refused, clinging to Luka. What if everything changed when that connection was broken?

"Tessa, look at me. Now." The last word held a bite, and she slid her eyes to his while still holding her hand in place. "Good girl," he said, cupping her cheek, his thumb sweeping across her skin. "Now really look. If he was still dying, I would not be standing or forming words. I felt all of that, just like you did. I felt . . . I don't feel that anymore. It's fading. You feel that, right?"

She nodded, unable to speak as tears continued to trail down her face. That made sense. Was logical. But still . . .

"We need to let Cienna work, beautiful," Theon continued, cautiously reaching for her wrist. His fingers closed around it, directly over the Mark that bound them together. Slowly he pulled her hand away, her fingertips dragging across flesh that was covered with blood. Then they both stilled.

Because the wound was gone. The space she'd refused to move from was healed, but left behind was a Mark. One she'd never seen.

"What is it?" Tessa asked, her voice hoarse from screaming and crying.

"I don't know," he answered, pulling her into his chest before standing and gently moving her from Luka's side. "We'll figure it out though, Tessa."

"There will be a cost for this," Eliza said, arms crossed as she watched the Witches work.

"We will pay whatever it is," Theon said tightly.

"That's just it," she replied somberly. "You don't get to decide who pays it. Fate will do what it must to keep the balance."

"Fuck the balance," Tessa said. "If they want something from me, they can come and claim it themselves."

"You can't defy Fate," Eliza argued.

"Watch me," was all she said, eyes fixed on Luka until movement caught the corner of her eye.

Then her mouth went dry as she found Kat tucked into Axel's side, the male's hard emerald eyes narrowed on her. He tried to move in front of Kat, but there was no way to hide it.

"Don't look at her like that when you told me you planned to kill my entire bloodline," Axel said coldly. "Don't look at her at all, Tessa."

She nodded, turning back to Luka, but she heard Kat's whispered, "Axel, stop."

"I don't like her here. You know that," he replied.

She couldn't blame him. He'd tried to come to her for help, and she'd sent him on his way with only promises of death. Of course he didn't want her here when he had a child involved. At least, she assumed the child in Kat's belly was his. With the depravity of Devram, she couldn't rule anything out.

"One thing at a time, Tessa," Theon said softly, leaning down to speak in her ear. "Luka first. Then we'll worry about Axel."

She nodded again, but she would leave if that was what Axel wanted. As soon as Luka was well enough, she would go.

Lifting a hand, her fingers wound into her hair. Her power was free, pacing in her soul, yet somehow content. It was only then she realized Theon's darkness was drifting around her, brushing along her skin and soothing her restless magic. Calming her anxious soul.

"You are truly all right?" she asked him, still watching as Cienna examined a wing and Tristyn's hands hovered over a wound on Luka's side.

"Feeling him . . ." he started, and she felt him shudder against her. "It was an agony I didn't think I would survive, but that faded and continues to do so with each passing minute."

"You weren't hit by anything?"

"I was higher up," Theon said. "The others said they Traveled out, but I couldn't . . . I watched the two of you fall and knew I wouldn't be fast enough to do anything."

"Do we know what happened?"

"You destroyed a mirror gate."

They both turned at the sound of Brecken's voice. He had a few battle wounds himself, but he was already healing. His wings were gone, and he stood off to the side, away from everyone else. As though he wasn't sure where he belonged. Something she thoroughly understood.

"What do you mean I destroyed a mirror gate?" Tessa asked.

"Each kingdom has a gateway into the realm. The Celeste Kingdom's was in Lake Moonmist. There is a tunnel that leads to a chamber beneath the lake. Or there was," he explained. "When you threw that cuff into it, the power it had absorbed from you sought out the power from the mirror gate."

No one spoke, all of them falling silent as Cienna continued to instruct Tristyn and Gia.

Her plan had always been to destroy a mirror gate. It was why she'd sent a note to Dex and let him take her. Granted, she'd expected to be taken to the Achaz Kingdom. She'd had an idea of where to look for the mirror gate there, but when she'd found herself at the Celeste Estate, she'd thought her plans had been thwarted. She'd just assumed the mirror gate was in Arobell where Lady Candra resided. She'd assumed the ruling Lords and Ladies would keep their mirror gates close, but that was apparently not the case.

Tessa broke the silence, trying to keep her mind busy because why was this taking so long? There were *three* Witches working on him. They had gifts of healing. All three of them. It shouldn't take this long.

"Do you know where the other gates are?" she asked, Theon's fingers toying with the ends of her hair. Simple touches to keep her grounded.

"I've been searching. When I would go to find Fae for Dex, I would search while I was gone," Brecken answered.

Tessa nodded, her breath stalling as Cienna stood and came toward them, features tight and emotionless as always.

"He'll live," she said. "But you already know that."

"I didn't," Tessa retorted, a breath whooshing out at the words 'he'll live.'

"You must have," Cienna replied, the words short and harsh. "He lives because of you."

"I didn't . . . I don't know what I did," she managed to stammer. "But if it saved him, then I don't regret it."

"There's always a cost, and you are playing with life and death."

"I *am* life and death," she said, an eeriness settling over the room as her power flared.

Cienna took a small step back, but that was the only sign of unease she let show. "You say you are prepared for the cost, but there are things far worse than death, daughter of wild and fury. Best you remember that in the coming days."

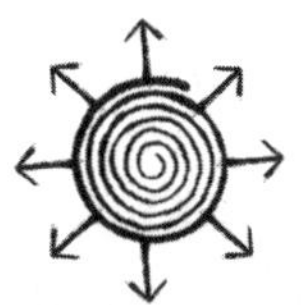

27
AXEL

"What are you doing?" Axel asked, stopping short when he entered the kitchen to find Theon rustling around in a cupboard. Random food was spread out on the counter, the sounds of pots and pans clanging filling the room.

"Looking for a knife," Theon answered, still digging.

"For what?"

"To cut something, Axel," he retorted in irritation.

"But why?"

Finally admitting defeat, Theon slammed the cupboard door shut and straightened. "I need to make Tessa some food. She hasn't eaten since we got here."

Axel huffed a laugh. "*You* are going to make food? Do you even know how?"

"As well as you do," his brother shot back, that muscle in his jaw feathering in annoyance. "I can make a sandwich."

"Somehow I doubt that," Axel replied, forcing Theon to move aside as he came up beside him, surveying the ingredients. Or lack thereof. "You don't even have bread out, Theon."

Turning away from him, he went to the refrigerator and pulled out cheese, sliced ham, pickles, and a container of leftover soup. Depositing the items on the counter, he grabbed some bread before he pulled out a pot and dumped the leftover soup into it to reheat.

As he was spreading mayo on the bread, Theon said, "I can make a sandwich, Axel."

"Right," he said with a smirk. "Like I'm sure you could make wild rice soup," he added with a nod to the simmering pot.

"You didn't make that," Theon said with a scoff. "Dumped it out of a can maybe."

"I absolutely did make that," Axel retorted. "You forget I have a pregnant wife. When she wants wild rice soup, I find a way to make that happen."

He finished prepping the sandwich before grabbing another pan, turning on a burner to heat it to toast the ham and cheese.

"So . . . you've learned to cook?" Theon asked, watching him work.

"I mean, I kind of had to here," Axel replied, stirring the soup. "I know I could pay for anything, but I also wanted to get to know the people even more. What better way to do that than asking them to help you make the best wild rice soup when at the market? Asking for advice on other things? I'm trying to prove I'm on their side. It's a lot easier if they see me as one of them instead of as someone who wants to rule over them." When Theon didn't immediately respond, Axel glanced up to find his brother staring at him. "What?"

"Nothing," Theon said quickly, his pointer finger tapping once on the countertop. "What can I help with here?"

With a smirk, Axel slid the pickle jar to him. "Can you handle fishing a pickle out of there?"

"Ass," he muttered around a laugh before doing just that and grabbing some grapes to add to the plate.

And then he added a piece of chocolate.

"Someone has grown," Axel said mockingly.

Theon flipped him his middle finger as Axel took the sandwich from the pan, cutting it in half before filling a bowl with soup. But as Theon reached for the dishes, Axel swiped them up.

"I'll take them to her," he said, balancing the plate as he tucked a bottle of water beneath his arm.

"I don't think that's a good idea," Theon said, the ease of a moment ago gone as he eyed Axel.

"You don't get a say here, Theon," he replied simply. "This is my domain. My space you all just dropped into. Kat wants to talk to her, and we need to reach an . . . understanding before that can happen."

"Then I'll come with."

"Nope," Axel said simply, brushing past him. "And if you try to interfere with this, we're going to have a problem. This needs to happen. You know that."

"I agree, but I still don't think you should be alone with her."

"You think I'll hurt her?" Axel asked, the corner of his mouth turning up.

"What if I do think that?"

"Good," he answered. "That is my wife and child she threatened."

"And it's *my* wife you're threatening," Theon retorted.

Axel nearly dropped the dishes of food as he held his brother's stare. Not knowing what else to say, he blurted, "Does Luka know that?"

Theon shoved a hand through his hair. "Not yet."

"Idiot," Axel said with another huff of laughter. "You couldn't just let me have this, huh? You had to go get a wife too?"

"By Arius, you are a prick," Theon sighed, beginning to clean up the mess on the counter.

Axel kind of wanted to ask what his plan was from here. How this was all going to work with Luka now. But he was also more concerned with talking to Tessa about Kat and the possibility of the babe coming early. He'd leave Theon to deal with his own shit for now.

"Don't follow me," Axel called over his shoulder as he left the kitchen.

He climbed the stairs to the second floor. He and Kat had taken over the third floor primary bedroom so someone had Traveled Luka to Theon's suite. And thank the gods for that. There was no way they would have been able to haul the male up the stairs. He would have had to stay on the living room floor.

Pushing open the door, he didn't bother keeping quiet. Luka was going to wake up when he was well enough to do so, and he didn't care if he woke or startled Tessa. As it happened, she was curled up in an armchair next to the bed, a blanket draped over her as she slept. Rounding the bed, he kicked the leg of the chair, making it shake, and Tessa jolted awake.

Her attention immediately went to Luka, and when she found him still sleeping, her gaze slid to Axel, eyes widening in surprise. He unceremoniously dropped the plate with the sandwich, fruit, and whatnot into her lap, a few grapes rolling to the floor. Then he let the water bottle drop beside her. Not wanting to clean up spilled soup, he opted to set the bowl on the bedside table.

"Thanks, I guess," Tessa said, eyeing him as she reached for the water bottle.

His laugh was humorless and dark. "Oh, baby doll, don't thank me quite yet," he purred. Moving quickly, he was beside her chair once more, one hand braced on the back, the other on the arm as he leaned in.

She jumped, the water bottle crashing to the floor, but she managed to keep the plate in her lap. "Gods, Axel," she snapped.

Ignoring her, he said, "The last time we spoke, you told me you were going to kill me and my entire bloodline. But I've also just learned you're my brother's wife. Seems a little counterproductive. What's changed?"

She glared at him, securing the plate in her lap. "A lot has changed," she grumbled, immediately unwrapping the chocolate, breaking off a piece, and taking a bite.

"I'm going to need more than that, Tessa."

"I thought it was my purpose," she answered, eyes on her lap. "I thought . . ."

"You thought it was your purpose to *kill* my entire bloodline?" he demanded. "Look me in the face and tell me that."

Her head snapped up, eyes hard and glowing. "You know what? Yes, Axel. I thought that was my purpose. When you're told something often enough, you start to believe it. I was told I was nothing. Worthless. Then I was told I was only valuable because of my power. So when someone came along and said I had a purpose that was more than being a vessel to funnel power, I believed them." The plate had clattered to the floor, the food forgotten as she twisted onto her knees so she could be face-to-face with him. "This world taught me to hate. This world taught me how to seek vengeance. This world taught me that being the most powerful in the room is how you get what you want. So yes, I went where I could have all of that. I would have done anything to keep it."

"And what the fuck changed?" Axel pressed, his tone as harsh as hers. "What's stopping you from using that power you have and ending my existence right here and now?"

She sat back on her heels, her hands on either side of his on the chair arm. "No one controls us," she hissed. "No one uses us. Not Theon or Rordan. Not Achaz or Arius. What do you want me to say? That I was weak enough to be constantly manipulated? That I was desperate enough to believe pretty words and lies because it made it hurt less? That it was easier to let them have control because fighting for myself is hard, and I didn't know if I was worth it? Because all those things are true."

"None of that answers what has changed," Axel snarled. "None of that is enough for me to let my wife and unborn child near you."

"It's because of your wife and child I'm still here," she spat back, lurching forward and once again in his face. "It's because of the Fae, forced to kneel and serve. It's because of the children just like yours, who when discovered, will be handed a fate worse than a Fae. It's for everyone forced to stay in the Underground simply because they don't fit in the kingdoms. It's because injustice shouldn't be tolerated simply because that's the way it's always been done. Injustice wrapped in pretty words is still injustice thousands of years later. I claimed my power. Now I will use it for those who have none. Is that what you want to hear?"

"Is it true?" Axel asked, with a smile so dark and wide, the tips of his fangs showed.

She answered in kind, her power filling her eyes. "Every word."

"Then, yes, baby doll. That's exactly what I wanted to hear. I want to know that when I emerge from the Underground with Kat and my son, you'll fight for them with all that power," he answered. "But so we're clear, if any of that was a lie, you'll be my next meal."

Her nose scrunched up. "Did you just threaten to eat me?"

"Yes, and not in the good way. You can get that from Theon," Axel retorted, straightening.

"I do," Tessa tossed back, uncoiling like a cat from the chair and stretching.

Axel huffed a laugh as she bent to pick up the food that had spilled everywhere, breaking off another piece of chocolate as she did. She piled it all back on the plate, setting it on the end of the bed before retrieving the water bottle and taking a drink. As she recapped it, the small bit of mirth between them dissolved, and she focused on Luka once again, worrying her bottom lip.

"I am sorry, Axel," she said quietly. "I did learn how to hurt and hate from this realm, but I learned what true friendship could look like from you." She turned her head to look at him. "I truly am sorry, but I know pretty words don't mean shit."

"In this case, they do, Tessa," he said, far more gently than their previous words had been.

She nodded, looking back at Luka. "Did you really marry her?"

He huffed a laugh, moving closer. Shoving his hands in his pockets, he said, "Yeah, I did. Did you really marry Theon?"

It was her turn to huff a laugh. "Yeah, I did. You're going to be a father."

"Glad to see we're continuing to state obvious things."

She glanced at him, giving him a weak smile. "I can't imagine that was planned. Was it?"

Axel sighed. "No, it wasn't, but it is something we need to talk to you about."

Her brows arched. "Me? I don't know anything about children. Even when I was one, I was never really around them."

"It's not about raising them or anything," he said with a wink. "But rest a bit. Eat some food. Kat is sleeping, but I know when she wakes, she will want to speak to you right away."

"I don't know what kind of help I'll be, but I can try."

"That's all I ask," Axel replied, taking a step toward the door. Then he paused, turning to walk backwards as he spoke. "I have an extra phone and earbuds. I'll bring them to you."

Her smile was small but there when she answered, "I'd like that very much."

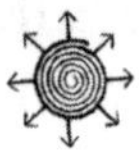

"I've never seen a Mark like that," Razik was saying when Axel and Kat came into the room a few hours later.

"But you've been alive for . . . a long time," Tessa argued. "You could have seen it in passing at some time, right?"

"These two are older than I am," Razik said dryly, gesturing to Cienna and Tristyn. "I don't see you questioning their lack of knowledge."

"Have any of you seen anything similar?" Theon cut in, standing next to the chair Tessa was curled back up in. "Or do any of you have any idea what it could be or do?"

"I'm well-versed in Marks, wild fury," Tristyn said. "That is one I've never seen before."

"So it just appeared? That's not possible," Theon said in frustration.

"Of course it's possible," Eliza said from where she perched on the end of the bed. "Scarlett can create new Marks because of what she is. Why wouldn't Tessa be able to?"

"But I didn't," Tessa insisted.

"That you know of. Maybe you didn't know what you were doing," she countered.

"Cienna?" Theon asked, looking at the Witch.

"It is a new Mark we've never seen before," Cienna replied. "Tessa is unlike any other. It would make sense that she can create Marks unlike any other."

"I've only ever drawn one Mark," she argued, all eyes on her now. Her fingers dug into the fabric of the armchair, and Theon sat on the arm, taking one of her hands in his. Some of her tension eased, but even Axel could see it was still present.

"Be that as it may," Tristyn said, "the fact remains you are one of a kind, Tessa. I suspect you will continue to discover new facets of your gifts throughout your immortal life."

"But as for that Mark," Cienna said, gesturing to Luka's still form. "We won't know what it does until he wakes. And even then, we may not know right away. Magic is volatile, and a debt is owed."

"And when will he wake up?" Tessa gritted out.

"When he's ready. My answer to that has not changed," Cienna answered.

"Let's table this for a bit," Theon said, locking eyes with Axel and Kat where they still stood just inside the room.

"Is this a good time?" Kat asked tentatively, because of course she did. Axel didn't really care if it was a good time or not.

"Of course, Kat," Theon answered with a reassuring smile.

"Here. Sit," Tessa said, already rising from the chair.

"I'm fine," Kat started, waving her off.

"Sit, kitten," Axel insisted, a hand on her back to usher her forward.

She sighed in resignation, letting him guide her around the bed, trading places with Theon and Tessa.

"You can sit on the bed, Tessa," Theon was saying.

"I'll stand," she replied, sliding her hands into the front pocket of the oversized sweatshirt she was wearing. One of Theon's, Axel assumed.

When they were situated, Axel cleared his throat, "While there have been some developments here since I saw you last, Theon, we have something more pressing to discuss."

"Your visions," Kat interrupted.

Theon's brow arched, and Tessa blinked in surprise. "My visions? You mean my dreams?"

"But that's what they are, right?" Kat asked. "You see potential futures?"

"Sometimes," Tessa replied cautiously. "But I can't control them. I can't *ask* to be shown a possible future. I just . . . am."

"And they change?"

Tessa nodded slowly. "Yes. Often. What is this about, Kat?"

"We have been going to see Miara every week to monitor Kat and the babe," Axel explained. "The last time we saw her, she was rather ominous about when the babe would come. She said he would not make full term, but if he came too soon, he wouldn't survive."

The room fell silent, Kat's hand rubbing along her stomach. Axel was certain she didn't even realize she was doing it.

"I just wanted to know if you've seen anything, Tessa," Kat said quietly.

Tessa shook her head, and Axel believed her when she said, "I'm sorry, Kat. I haven't had any dreams with the two of you in quite some time. And when I have, you've never been with child."

"But visions can change, right?" Kat persisted, a quiver to her voice that had Axel wrapping an arm around her shoulders where he sat on the arm of the chair.

"My visions change often," Tessa said gently. "But I think my dreams are different from what they see."

She motioned to Cienna and Tristyn with her last words, and Axel locked eyes with the Witch. A female he'd known his entire life and who he had some sort of relationship with.

"Cienna?" he asked, feeling Katya tense beside him.

"The future is ever-changing," Cienna said.

"That's not what I'm asking."

"I know what you're asking, Axel," she replied. "And I do not have the answer you wish for."

It wasn't the first time he'd heard that before. She'd been the one to warn him he was close to turning. She'd been the one to tell him it was too late to turn back. Why wouldn't she be the one to tell him there was nothing they could do about this projected outcome?

"And what have *you* seen?" Axel asked, not breaking her stare. But when she didn't speak, it was answer enough. "You've seen the same as Miara and didn't say anything?"

"This is exactly why," she answered, her tone going sharper than usual. "How many days have you spent worrying? Trying to figure out an alternative? How many nights have you lost sleep trying to come up with a way to change a possible future? Ensure it doesn't come to pass? There is every possibility these exact actions send you down that path."

"So your proposal is to do nothing?" Axel charged. "You expect us to sit back and just let whatever happens happen?"

"We do not tempt the Fates, Axel."

"No, *you* don't tempt the Fates, Cienna. You don't get to make that choice for the rest of us," he shot back.

"Live your lives, Axel. Trying to trick Fate is a waste of your days."

"I will waste them all if it ensures my son survives."

The look that crossed her face was almost pained as she said, "I know. That's what I fear."

The silence that settled over the room was palpable. Kat had tipped her head back against the back of the chair, her eyes closed, and Axel knew she was trying to keep in tears.

"If I dream of him, I will tell you," Tessa said quietly. "I have altered more futures than one. I can try."

"Thank you," Kat whispered, her eyes remaining closed.

Tessa looked at Axel, and he nodded in appreciation. "While we're discussing dire situations, we need to discuss Bree."

They listened while he and Kat recounted what had transpired after they'd learned of the babe—when Axel went to call Theon and returned to a delivery of Bohden's severed head.

"I know we all assume it is Bree, but do we have any proof of that?" Theon asked after they'd caught everyone else up on what had been happening in the Underground.

"I'm considering the invitation that came the next day to be proof enough," Axel answered.

"Invitation for what?" Theon asked. He'd taken a seat on the edge of the bed, but Tessa still refused, standing a few feet away from him and listening.

"For dinner. At the House of Four," Axel replied. "All the Underground Leaders were invited."

"When is it?" Theon asked. "I can go with you."

"That's the thing," Axel said, scratching the back of his head. "It was addressed to me and Kat."

"Who gives a fuck?" his brother replied. "This has gone on long enough. Bree is not taking the fucking Underground."

"If you go, it will undo all the work we've put in here these last months," Kat cut in. "We've built trust and relations largely on the fact that Axel chose a Fae as his wife."

"She's right," Axel said. "In fact, I'm certain she's the only reason the Apparel District tentatively aligned with us in the first place."

"So the two of you are going then?" Theon asked, reaching out and tugging Tessa to a stop as she started to pace.

"No," Axel said at the same time Kat said, "Yes."

He sighed. They'd been arguing about this since the day the invitation had arrived. Well, maybe not since that day. Kat had waited until the next morning to ask him what she should wear to this dinner. He had informed her she absolutely was not going, and then it had been a continual argument that had gone nowhere since.

She twisted to look up at him. "You just said I was right, Axel."

"I said you were right about Theon not going. Not that *you* should go. I can go myself," he replied.

"But all the reasons you just listed are the same reasons I need to go with you," she replied, fire and shadows appearing in her amber eyes.

"It's the timing of it all, Kat," he said, once again trying to appeal to logic. "That dinner is in the middle of the fifth month. We need to get to the sixth month. We need to be cautious until then."

"Me going to a dinner will not affect the babe," she said, clearly exasperated.

"If she wasn't with child, would you be opposed to her attendance?" Eliza asked, eyes narrowed.

Axel hesitated, because yes, he would be. He didn't want her anywhere near Bree. The Night Child had already tried to have her killed once. He was certain she wasn't done, and he couldn't shake the feeling this dinner was more than that.

"It's a trap," he finally said, avoiding Eliza's question. He turned back to Theon. "Bree has plans that have been in the works for years. Decades. You know this is all part of that."

"You won't let anything happen to her, Axel," Tessa said from where she now stood between Theon's legs. His hands on her hips, thumbs moving in slow circles.

"Of course I'll do anything in my power to keep her safe, but we all know that isn't always enough. Look at the past year. How many times were you hurt or taken?" Axel argued.

"Thanks," Theon grumbled.

"You know what I'm saying. If Tessa was pregnant, you'd feel the same way, Theon. You can't deny that."

His brother fell silent, but Axel didn't miss the way his fingers flexed on Tessa's hips.

"This is ridiculous," Eliza snapped. "Why must I keep reminding you that just because she's pregnant, it doesn't mean she's suddenly fragile and incapable. She can attend a godsdamn dinner and sit in a chair and debate politics. She is clever and observant, and I'd argue you need her there to help not be caught in a trap by the Night Child."

"This is not your world," Axel shot back. "Things are not the same here."

"But we're trying to change things," Tessa said. "Continuing to do things as they were will not push change. And isn't the Underground different anyway?"

He could not believe they were all arguing for Katya to attend this with him. None of them understood. None of them had children or babes on the way. And he couldn't do this anymore. He couldn't sit here and let them argue with him about willingly taking his wife and child straight into a web with a spider waiting to strike.

"It seems I'm not needed for this discussion since everyone else appears to be in favor of letting her walk right into danger. I'll leave you all to discuss the logistics," Axel said, his tone icy as he rose and crossed the room.

"Axel, that's not what we're saying," Theon tried.

He didn't stop, didn't even slow. He was halfway down the stairs when her voice carried to him.

"Don't you dare walk away from me, Axel St. Orcas."

He did pause then, mid-step with a hand on the railing. Then he turned, watching Kat descend the stairs, her features full of anger.

"Please be careful," he sighed, waiting for her to reach him before resting a hand on her back to guide her down to the main floor.

They moved to the kitchen, neither of them speaking, and he poured himself a glass of liquor. Although he desperately wanted blood. But he was still barely getting by, and he couldn't risk running out.

Liquor it was.

He knocked back the first glass and immediately refilled it.

"When will it end, Axel?" Kat finally asked, breaking the standoff. "After he is born, will you then argue I should not attend things because he will need one of us? Will you again try to convince me to stay home from an outing because there is a minute possibility of getting hit by a car?"

"That is not the same thing, and you know it," Axel charged, taking another drink. "This is too dangerous. We are being irrational to even entertain it."

Kat rounded the counter, taking his glass and sliding both it and the liquor bottle to the side. Then she reached up, taking his face between her hands. "Everything we are is irrational, Axel. Our relationship has been dangerous from the start. And every time we have survived. We have come out on top. But only when we do things together."

"It's terrifying, Kat," he said, his throat thick with emotion. "All I can think about when we talk about this is having to send you away with Tristyn.

How terrified I was and doing what I needed to do to keep you safe from my father and this fucked up realm."

"And I was just as terrified when I didn't know where you were," she replied, her hands dropping to his chest. "But look at what we have done together. You told me I'm more than a Fae. Please don't force me into the background simply because we have a family."

"I don't want that, Kat. You know that. You have spent the last days worrying about the babe coming early, and this is . . ."

He trailed off, not knowing what else to say. How else to argue his points.

"We can be scared, Axel. We can be scared and do it anyway. That's what I want this child to grow up knowing," she said, one hand running over her stomach. "Fear and courage go hand in hand. Tessa is here now. She'll be watching, and she won't keep things from us like Cienna and Miara. I know she won't."

"We're putting our hope in Tessa now?" he asked, arching a brow and pulling her closer. "I think she's truly a little mad."

"Seems to be serving her well," Kat said with a sly smile.

Axel huffed a laugh as he dropped a kiss to the top of her head, then he turned serious once more. "I hate this."

"I know," she replied, leaning into him. "But I refuse to stay in the background. I want him to know I did everything I could to ensure he was brought into a better world than what we know. Please don't deny me that, Axel."

He sighed again, pulling her close and wondering when she'd figure out he would never deny her anything.

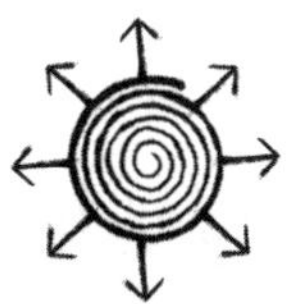

28

EVIANA

"So obedient," Mansel crooned as he cupped her chin, his thumb swiping across her lower lip. He glanced over the top of her head. "You trained this one well, my Lord."

"That I did," Valter said, and she didn't need to look over her shoulder to know he was seated in his over-large leather chair, likely with an ankle on his knee and cigar in hand. "She's beautiful, of course, but when she's on her knees . . ."

"She's exquisite," Mansel finished, that thumb swiping along her bottom lip again as he reached for his zipper with his other hand.

She was prepared to do what she must. It wasn't anything new, which is why she was surprised when Valter said, "Wait."

"My Lord?" Mansel asked, hands stilling on his belt buckle.

"I have something to ask of you," Valter said, and she heard him rise.

"Of course, my Lord. Name it."

Everything in her went on alert, but she didn't dare move as Valter approached. His hand smoothed down her hair before he began gathering it one hand, and if she didn't know better, she'd believe his gentleness was out of affection.

"I would like to borrow her to you for a few days," he started, and Eviana fought to keep her emotions in check. This wasn't new either. She'd been given for a night here and there to seal deals, but Mansel wasn't someone Valter needed to negotiate with. If Valter told the male to turn around and bend over, he'd do it without question. Which also meant whatever Valter was about to ask him to do was going to be something terrible.

"I struck a deal with Desiray," Valter went on, still holding her hair in one hand. The fingers of his other hand were skating up and down the column of her neck. "I agreed to one of her experiments, provided I get to keep the outcome if favorable."

Bile rose in her throat, and she fought to keep it down. She knew well enough what Desiray did at the Sirana Villas. She'd visited them several times with Valter, but she was still unsure of what this had to do with her.

"I want you to sire the product," Valter said to Mansel.

"You want my child?" Mansel asked, a groove forming between his brows.

"You won't know if things are successful or not," Valter replied. "You will spend a week in the Villas, and after that, you will know nothing else of the matter."

"When do I need to decide by?" the male asked, Eviana momentarily forgotten on her knees before him.

"The next hour," Valter answered. "That's when I will leave to deliver Eve there."

She wasn't thinking when she whipped her head around. Or she tried to. Valter still held her hair, gathered in a fist at the back of her head. He held it tight, keeping her facing forward, and she swallowed down the cry of pain.

My Lord? *she asked down the bond.* I do not understand.

It is not your place to understand, *he snapped, a sharp yank of her hair accompanying the words.*

"You want me to get your Source with child?" Mansel asked in surprise, but she didn't miss the thread of excitement in his tone.

"That is exactly what I want," Valter said. "Do you accept?"

That other hand was still on her neck, and now those fingers slipped along her jaw, forcing her head up. Mansel's tongue darted out, running along his bottom lip, a hunger in his eyes.

"Give me an hour to make arrangements at the manor," Mansel said, his eyes raking over her.

"Done," Valter said, dismissing him.

The male was already lifting his phone to an ear as the study door closed behind him. Only then did Valter release her hair. But she didn't rise from her knees. No, she wouldn't do that until bidden, but she did risk speaking.

"My Lord? Have I displeased you?" she asked, trying to think of anything she might have done to set him off. To deserve this type of discipline.

"Of course not, my flower," he said, coming around to stand in front of her.

"Then . . . why?" she asked, willing the tears not to pool in her eyes. He hated when she cried. It showed too much emotion.

"What is the one and only thing I ask of you?" he asked, his tone hardening at her continued questioning.

Her eyes dropped to the floor, bowing her head. "Obedience, my Lord."

"Exactly. You will do this because it is what I want from you," he snapped, the sound of his zipper reaching her ears. "Now, give me your mouth before we go."

She gritted her teeth at the slice of pain, looking down to see the knife still deep in her flesh.

"You always cut too deep," Lange snapped, snatching the knife out of her hand.

These godsdamn Imps. But pain was the only way to be pulled from their grasp. The Imps made one relive the nightmares of their past, only freeing them when they made an offering of pain.

They all kept knives on them right now for this very purpose, and it was fine. They all healed fast enough, and she'd take the Imps over the Sprytes or the Dread-Nymphs.

"What was it this time?" Lange asked, eyeing the gash on her arm that was still heavily bleeding.

"Nothing," she replied, holding out her hand for her knife.

"Sure. Just like every other time," Lange said flatly, ignoring her request.

Eviana just shrugged. It wasn't her fault they couldn't keep their misery to themselves when they experienced their worst memories. The gods knew the Imps had plenty of material to choose from in her case.

They kept walking, the forest floor crunching under their shoes and boots as they went. Corbin had shifted back to his Fae form the morning after they'd entered the woods. They hadn't moved much those first few days, instead taking the time to rest and refill their reserves. The Imps had let them be until the third day. Now they were a daily nuisance.

"Maybe if you talked about it, it would . . . help," Lange trailed off when she sent him a dubious look.

"Does talking about your past help?" she retorted dryly.

"Yes."

She tsked under her breath, rolling her eyes. Lange didn't push further, which was just as well. She had no plans to tell him about the night Valter *borrowed* her to Mansel for a week. How, even though she knew it was pointless, she still asked the Lord not to make her do it. How she was obedient in the end, but Mansel was still so *creative* in his efforts at the Villas. How she begged the gods and the Fates that she wouldn't fall pregnant. How she'd tried to cry when it was confirmed, her face buried in a pillow while Valter took what he wanted from her, but she'd trained herself not to shed tears long ago.

Talking about any of that wouldn't help anything, though Lange and Corbin were constantly speaking with each other as if it would. Their voices were always low, especially after an Imp got to one of them. Gentle touches and soft kisses. A comfort to each other.

But she kept quiet, leading the way and letting them follow. She knew it was only a matter of time before a Dread-Nymph found them. Then they'd realize how little *talking* about it helped.

Slowly the light filtering through the trees started to fade, the woods becoming cooler with each passing hour. They always held out as long as they could, but when they estimated there was perhaps an hour left of light, that was when they would find a place to stop for the night. Being in the Dreamlock Woods was risky enough. Moving about in the dark was downright stupid.

Corbin went off, just out of sight, to gather sticks and wood for a fire. With his Shifter senses, he was the most capable of finding his way back and sensing danger on his own. She and Lange worked on clearing a space for the fire and trying to put together some kind of meal. One would think they'd at least be able to hunt wildlife, but living creatures of all kinds were sparse in the woods. The animals that were here hid their presence as much as they were trying to keep their own quiet.

"He's been gone longer than usual," Lange said, facing the direction Corbin had gone.

"He only left a few minutes ago," she replied, returning to her task.

"A few minutes? He's been gone for nearly an hour," Lange retorted, a breeze blowing through the area with his agitation.

She glanced up at him from where she was fishing various items out of the pack. "You're being overly dramatic."

But truly, it had only been five, maybe ten, minutes. Not anywhere near an hour.

"I'm not being dramatic," Lange bit back, taking a few steps toward the trees. Then he stopped, cocking his head. "Did you hear that?"

"I can't hear the winds' chatter," she muttered. "That is unique to you, Wind Walker."

"It's not the winds," he growled, the breeze becoming gusty now. The water bottles blew over, rolling a few feet away, and Eviana snatched up the packs of food before they were carried away too.

"Lange, stop!" she snapped. "Where are you going?"

Because he was suddenly sprinting, and she didn't understand what the fuck was happening.

"They found him, Eviana!" he yelled, nearly to the tree line. "Gods, how heartless are you? Can't you hear him screaming? They're killing him, and we're just sitting here!"

"Lange, there's nothing—"

Godsdammit.

She pressed a palm to the dirt, the tree roots immediately responding and shooting up to snag Lange's ankle wherever he was beyond the tree line. She'd just lost sight of him, but she heard him cursing as her power dragged him back.

"You planned this too, didn't you?" he bellowed, clawing at the dirt.

"I didn't—"

But she didn't get to finish because a violent burst of wind hit her square in the chest, sending her flying through the air. Her power tried to help her, branches and leaves reaching for her, but she still slammed into the trunk of a tree too hard. Her head snapped back as her spine collided with rough bark, and then she dropped to the forest floor. On her hands and knees, she tried to suck in a breath after getting the air knocked out of her. The spots in her vision didn't help, and she blinked rapidly, trying to dispel them.

"Corbin!" Lange bellowed, and he really needed to shut the fuck up. One Dread-Nymph was already here. He was calling more to a godsdamn feast.

"Lange," she hissed, crawling forward and pushing to her feet. She swayed some but kept going, watching him wrap his power around the tree roots keeping him tethered. Then he released his grip on the wind, and it snapped the roots before twisting around Lange like a funnel and lifting him into the air.

Good gods. No wonder Valter had been in a good mood after receiving his files the night Theon had claimed the male. She knew he was powerful, but this was . . .

This was a godsdamn nightmare.

She couldn't spend her time trying to reason with him. She needed to find the Dread-Nymph before he disappeared into the woods. They would never find him, but Corbin would never stop trying. Then she'd be alone—not that she cared—but survival was easier in the woods with others. She just needed them to help her get to the Serafina Estate and get away with the girl. Then they could all go their separate ways.

"Corbin!" Lange yelled. "I'm coming!" He looked down at Eviana, his expression cold and murderous. "I'm going to kill you for doing this again. Every time I think maybe you're not a cold-hearted bitch, you prove just how wrong I am."

The words sliced through her, and she hated it. Because words shouldn't have any effect on her, but for some reason, those did. Those did, and she couldn't let them.

"Where is it?" she whispered, crouching down to press her palms to the dirt once more. "Where is it? Where is it? Where is it?"

Then she felt the tiniest of flutters against her palm. She lifted one to find a sapling poking up from the ground. Another sprung up a few feet away. Then another. She stood following them, moving farther and farther away from the campsite. Away from Lange. All the while knowing he was going in the opposite direction, and where *was* Corbin? Couldn't he hear all the commotion? What if something really was wrong?

What if—

"Hello, my flower."

She froze, his voice an icy chill that settled into her bones.

He stepped from behind a tree. His dark hair and deep emerald eyes. His shadows a swarm around him, trailing each step. His perfectly tailored suit.

No. He couldn't be here.

She reached for her knife, wanting the pain to draw her out, but in her rush, she'd left it behind.

Shit.

Shit, shit, shit.

"I am so incredibly disappointed in you, Eve," he sighed in mock dismay, but she knew better. There was little Valter enjoyed more than discipline and *correcting* behavior. "Although you did make your punishment so much easier by bringing me all the way to the Serafina Kingdom, didn't you?"

He was before her now, and she could do nothing. Clasping her hands in front of her like she'd done thousands of times, she dropped her eyes to the ground. But long fingers wrapped around her chin, forcing her face back up.

"None of that now, Eve," he said coldly. "You thought you could *leave* me? You thought you could *hide* from me?"

His grip on her face was bruising, and she forced herself not to wince.

Not to react. Forced herself to shove down all the emotions and become the same nothing she'd always been because it was the only way to survive.

Valter's other hand came up, petting down her hair. "The only way to be free of me is by death. Is that what you wish for, my flower? Death?"

Yes. She couldn't say that, but she would take death a thousand times over before going back to Arius House with him.

He knew though. Even without the bond, she'd shown her hand the day she'd blocked their bond and ran. All her cards were on the table, so what was there to even try to hide now?

That hand on her hair turned into a fist, grasping a handful of strands and yanking hard. "Death would be a kindness, and you have lost any affection I had for you," he hissed.

Pulling on her hair again, he forced her to her knees. If only this was the worst he would do, she would survive it easily. Cocks and cunts were nothing anymore, but she knew this wouldn't be it. She would pay for this betrayal for the rest of her immortal years.

A small tendril of green brushed along her thigh, tiny leaves and flowers unfurling from the vine, and it was only then she remembered she was in the woods.

The Dreamlock Woods.

Whipping her head to the side, she saw it. Tall and lithe, her white eyes glowed in the darkening forest. Lanky black hair flowed down her back, tangled in the branches that were part of her. Her gown was decaying leaves, and her fingers were sharpened twigs. A walking spirit of the forest, the Dread-Nymph smiled, all her teeth as sharp and pointed as a Night Child's fangs.

She hadn't realized they could ensnare more than one victim at a time. Either that or there were two here. But she couldn't harm it with her power. The Dread-Nymphs were part of nature. A grotesque anomaly, yes, but part of nature nonetheless. Her power was the earth and plants and everything the Dread-Nymphs were. That was what made them so godsdamn difficult. All Fae gifts were powers of nature. But none of the three of them were *just* Fae. They all had other blood flowing in them that she had hoped would help.

Foolish.

So godsdamn foolish thinking she could take on the Dreamlock Woods.

And now she stood at an impasse and the creature knew it. Her wicked smile widened, those razor-sharp teeth gleaming in the dying light, ready to devour. And maybe a piece of her was ready to let it.

But not until she saved that child.

She turned on her heel and ran, racing back the way she'd come, praying to anyone but the fucking gods that she was going the right way. The trail of saplings was still there though, and it led her right back to her pack. She frantically dug through it, throwing items to the side without thought until she found the dagger she'd taken from Raven Harbor. Then spun, ready to hunt down the creature, but she didn't have to. It had followed her.

So had her nightmare.

"You can't kill me, Eve," he sighed, reaching for her. "You are mine. My Source of power. Mine to do with whatever I please." Those long fingers wrapped around her wrist while his other hand reached for the weapon.

But then she cocked her arm back and threw it.

It sank into the Dread-Nymph's torso, just below her heart. She tipped her head back, a screeching wail coming from her mouth that had Eviana dropping to her knees and clamping her hands over her ears. It did nothing. That piercing cry tore through her, nightmare after nightmare flashing before her eyes.

Mansel at the Villas.

Correction with Valter.

Torturing innocents.

A babe being snatched away from her.

She didn't know if it was the creature's wails or her own screams anymore, and gods, it was never going to end.

It felt like hours when it stopped. Her throat was on fire, and she could feel scratches on her face from her own nails. She was curled into a ball on the ground, mud and debris in her hair, and any daylight was long gone. There was no fire. No stars.

Only two glowing feline eyes staring down at her.

Corbin.

With a soft flash of light, he Shifted, thankfully still fully clothed. The male crouched down, arms resting on his bent knees.

"I think you killed it," he said somberly.

"I think it tried to take me with it," she bit out, pushing up onto her knees.

"No more splitting up," he said, standing once more and stretching out a hand to her. "They know we're here now."

Her eyes darted from his face to his outstretched hand and back again.

Corbin sighed. "I'm helping you stand. That's all. There's no debt to be owed. It's a simple kindness."

"Nothing is simple in Devram," she retorted.

"Nothing is simple with *you*, nightmare," he said, but there was no bite to it. "I just watched you thrash on the ground, screaming to the Pits of Torment, for nearly ten minutes. I doubt you can stand by yourself."

She huffed, but he had a point. So she placed her hand in his, letting him pull her to her feet. Then an arm slid around her waist when her legs nearly gave out.

"See? Help isn't so bad," he said, a teasing note to his voice as he led her back to the clearing. When had she even left it? The last she remembered, she'd been here throwing things out of the backpack.

"It's rather pathetic that I can't even stand properly," she replied flatly.

"You look pathetic," Lange said from where he sat beside a small fire, feeding it more kindling to help it grow.

"Thanks," she rasped, slowly lowering beside him with Corbin's help. Her entire body ached.

They were silent as Corbin continued to set up for the night, and she and Lange just sat, lost in their nightmares. Because that was what the Dread-Nymphs did. Forced you to live out your greatest fears. Paralyzed you so they could devour you.

It was only after Corbin had passed her a cup of hot water heated over the fire that she said to Lange, "So, one of your greatest fears is that I will betray you."

It wasn't a question; she'd witnessed it with her own eyes. Heard the words he'd hurled at her.

Neither of the males said anything, but she saw the look they exchanged. They were right not to trust her, but . . .

But if they did, even a little bit, maybe it wouldn't have been a weakness for the Dread-Nymph to prey on.

"Was there another one? Or just the one I killed?" she asked, watching the flames flicker before them.

"Just the one," Lange answered, sounding as exhausted as she felt.

"That's uncommon. They normally only prey on one at a time."

"I think it did," Lange said. "When it found you, it let me go."

"I think Eviana found it," Corbin said, passing around some dried meat he'd heated over the fire.

"You went looking for the thing?" Lange asked in surprise.

"You were yelling and alerting every Spryte, Imp, and Nymph in the woods to our presence," she muttered. "I needed it to let you go."

"I see," Lange said, biting off a chunk of meat. "No other reason then?"

"What other reason would there be?"

"None at all, *bellana*," he said. "None at all."

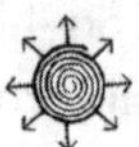

They stayed in that same spot for the next two days. She and Lange were too exhausted, and it seemed none of the other creatures wanted to venture too close to a space where a Dread-Nymph had met its end. So they'd spent the days resting, foraging for food, and resting some more, but tomorrow, they really needed to be on their way.

It was dark, the sun having set a good hour or two ago. She was stoking the kindling with a long stick when Corbin said, "You owe us some answers."

She looked up, the two of them seated across from her. Lange had an arm resting on a bent knee, leaning back on his palm. Corbin had his legs stretched out, leaning against Lange's side.

When she didn't say anything, Lange's eyes narrowed. "That was the deal, *bellana*. We get to these gods-forsaken woods with you, and you tell us what you know. Are you going back on your word now?"

"You should know by now that my word means nothing," she muttered, once again focused on the fire.

"No," Lange snapped. "I won't accept that. You owe us this, Eviana. You've dragged us all over the fucking realm. We deserve to know what we're likely going to die for."

She pressed her lips into a thin line, and Lange scoffed. But when he started to say something else, Corbin cut him off.

"Let her be, Lange," his lover said. "She's made it clear we're only along to be used. It's what we're for, right?"

Eviana looked up, meeting his hazel eyes narrowed in challenge. And she hated it. She hated his words had such an effect on her. Hated that either of them affected her. Hated that the words Lange had hurled at her when trapped by the Dread-Nymph played over in her mind at night when she was trying to sleep. Hated that she was making moves to ensure they stayed with her. Hated knowing the reasons she constantly recited to herself were excuses she refused to acknowledge.

Setting the stick aside, she brushed off her hands. "Have either of you been to the Sirana Villas?"

She could feel the surprise coming from them, but she didn't look at them. If she did, she might stop, so she kept her gaze fixed on the fire.

"No," Corbin finally answered. "We've never been to the Villas."

"You don't remember," she agreed. "But you were both born there."

"What?" Lange asked, shock resounding in that single word.

"The Villas are where the Legacy *experiment*. Yes, they breed the Fae there to keep their world running smoothly, but like all powerful things, they crave more. Any way they can gain an advantage over one another. Of course, it's all under the guise of advancing the realm," she went on.

"I'm not quite following," Corbin said.

She nodded. "Deals are made. Some in the shadows. Some in the light. But the rulers of this land want stronger Sources and more powerful Fae under their control. You know the Legacy take what they want from the Fae. Of course Fae became pregnant from their greed, and for a long time, those pregnancies were terminated. Until they weren't.

"Some of those babes lived. The mothers tried desperately to keep them a secret, but they were discovered. And those babes were more powerful than the average Fae, piquing interest. So the Mistress of the Sirana Villas was allowed to start arranging pairings. I am the result of such a pairing." She finally lifted her head, locking eyes with the males. "So is Lange."

Corbin looked horrified—the poor innocent thing—but Lange was shaking his head. Denial could be as powerful as fear.

"How can you possibly know that?" Lange asked.

"Because I've seen the files," she answered. "You know we all have records. It's how I knew you could hear the winds. It's how I knew what both of you were."

"No," Lange said, having sat up straighter. "If any of that were true, why weren't we claimed right away? Why weren't we tagged to be Sources?"

Her smile was humorless and bitter. "I was born to be a Source," she answered. "Valter picked out the pairing for my parents himself. His Source was killed when I was of age to be Selected."

"He wouldn't kill his own Source," Lange said.

She only stared back at him. He could cling to that denial all he wanted, but she wasn't going to feed into it.

"His question is valid," Corbin said. "If this is all true, why weren't we claimed right away?"

"Because complete files aren't released until you are claimed," she answered. "It's supposed to keep things somewhat fair between the kingdoms. Even the heirs don't get full access to files when they are scoping out potential Sources. It's why they do such extensive assessments of the possibilities. No one truly knows what's going to be revealed at an Emerging Ceremony."

"So you're saying the Lords and Ladies can handpick replacement Sources, but they can't do the same for their heirs? That's ridiculous," Lange argued.

"Everything with the Lords and Ladies is ridiculous," she replied. "But yes. As I said, it was an agreement in an effort to keep the power balance fair. Of course, they've all lied and cheated, but it's why Fae go through such extensive training and trials during Selection years. They watch for anything that might indicate that a Fae is more than."

"So then I'm what?" Lange demanded.

"Wind Fae and Sefarina Legacy," she answered simply.

"And you?"

"Earth Fae and Silas Legacy."

"And Corbin?"

She paused then, drawing in the dirt with her finger. "He was a surprise, and one that Valter was delighted with when he received the documents. And while you would have certainly been sent to the Sirana Villas to breed your power, Lange, Corbin . . ."

"Just say it," Corbin said tightly.

"Your father was a Water Fae, but your mother was a Shifter. The Shifter part shouldn't be a surprise considering what you know, but with the Shifters confined to the Underground, it was unexpected," she said. "He was still debating how he wanted to use you."

The silence that settled was deafening, but it was fine. Let them digest all that new information. The quiet didn't stay for long though.

"While that information is . . . enlightening," Corbin said, "it still doesn't explain where we're going and what we're doing."

"We're going to the Serafina Estate," she said simply.

"Why?" Lange asked.

But Corbin had the answer. Observant, introspective Corbin, who was always watching her with that penetrating stare.

"She has a child there," he said, his voice barely more than a whisper.

"Is that true?" Lange demanded. "You have a child? That's what this is all about?"

She could hear the disbelief in his voice, and she couldn't blame him. Imagine her, the cold-hearted bitch who didn't care about them and constantly told them not to trust her, as a mother. It was preposterous, and she agreed.

"She is to be my replacement," Eviana said quietly. "Valter is simply waiting until she is of age. Then I will meet my end like my predecessor, and he will take her. Break her. Make her what I am. I can't . . ."

She trailed off, looking up at the sound of rustling and footsteps. Lange had pushed to his feet, rounding the fire before dropping next to her. Then he wrapped his arms around her, pulling her into his chest, and she stiffened, not knowing what was happening or why he was touching her. Because the only touches she'd known for so long were greedy ones.

And still Lange held her to him when he asked softly, "Do you know her name?"

"Priya." And why did she practically choke on the name? Why were her cheeks wet? Why was she leaning into him and letting him gently rock her back and forth? Why was her chest heaving?

Corbin had moved at some point as well, coming to sit next to them. He reached over every once in a while, swiping tears away from her face.

"I don't know where I'll take her," she whispered into Lange's shirt, unsure when she'd fisted the fabric in her hands. "But she can't end up like me. I'm a terrible, unfeeling monster, but she doesn't deserve that."

"You're not a monster, *bellana*," Lange said gently.

"I am," she said. "And I'm okay with that. Because I'll be a monster for her so she doesn't have to become one herself."

"Then we'll become monsters too," he replied, a chaste press of lips brushing the crown of her head.

She should tell them no. They were too innocent to become what she was. Should tell them she couldn't stomach the idea of plunging a dagger into their chests like she'd done for Lev to put them out of their misery when they could no longer live with themselves.

But she'd tell them that later because this touch was comforting, and she didn't know it could be like that. She didn't know she could be touched and held and not have to give anything in return.

She didn't deserve what they were offering her, but in the end, she was still a monster. If they wanted to accompany her into death, she wasn't going to stop them.

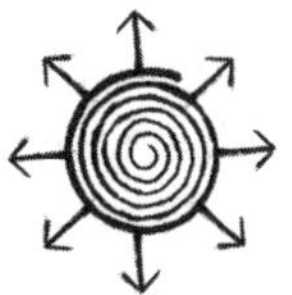

29
LUKA

Luka had woken up, finding the room empty other than Tessa. Her steady breathing was the only sound filling the space. The blanket draped over her was no doubt courtesy of Theon, and for her to be sleeping that deeply, Theon hadn't left the room all that long ago either. She'd looked different. Rested. Unharmed.

Unlike him.

His entire body ached, even if all of his wounds were mostly healed. He felt like he'd fallen out of the sky, and his wings were still tender. He could banish them, but he hadn't. Not yet. He wasn't doing anything to them until he talked to Cienna, just to make sure he didn't fuck something up.

Everything felt off yet somehow right, and he couldn't explain it. Someone else would need to explain it to him because he didn't know how long he'd been sleeping, or how they'd ended up at the Underground Penthouse, or what was going on in the realm. The last thing he remembered was Tessa's tearstained face before his world had gone dark. He'd expected to wake up in the After, not the Underground.

So he'd let Tessa sleep and made his way to the bathroom, taking a long shower. He let the warm water soothe aching muscles, and when he was done washing, he just stood in the spray. He shouldn't have survived, yet here he was.

When he'd woken, he'd immediately recognized the room as Theon's, and with no clothing in there, he went across the hall with only a towel wrapped around his waist. Finding training pants, he didn't bother with a shirt. Opening the door to go back across the hall, he stopped short, finding

Theon leaning against the opposite wall, waiting for him. Neither of them said anything. They didn't need to when they'd spent nearly every day together their entire lives. Then Theon reeled him in, careful of his wings.

"You almost fucking died," Theon said, his voice thick with barely restrained emotion.

"I feel like I almost died," Luka replied, his voice hoarse from lack of use. Pulling back, he crossed his arms, Theon resuming his position on the wall. "How long have I been out?"

"Nearly three godsdamn weeks," Theon answered, the disapproval heavy.

"Sorry about that," Luka drawled. "I'll try to keep it under two next time."

"There won't be a next time, you prick. What the fuck were you thinking? Why didn't you Travel out?" Theon demanded.

"I was thinking I couldn't leave you behind," Luka retorted. "I know you did it, but I couldn't. Maybe that makes me weaker than you, but fuck, Theon. I couldn't leave you there to die."

"But you did nearly leave me," Theon growled. "That was . . . Did you know if a Guardian dies, the Ward feels every excruciating piece of the bond dying too?"

Luka blinked. "What?"

"Yeah," Theon said tightly. "I didn't know that either." He shoved a hand through his hair, clearing his throat. "Tessa was screaming, and you were dying, and I was . . . I was trying to get to both of you, and I couldn't even drag myself across the fucking ground. If anyone was weak, it was me, Luka. Not you."

They both fell silent, Theon shoving his hand through his hair again. The sleeves of his shirt were rolled up to his elbows, leaving his forearms bare, which is the only reason Luka's gaze caught on the new Mark around his wrist.

"Did you make another Bargain?" Luka asked, jerking his chin in reference.

Theon froze, looking at his wrist, before clearing his throat again. "Something like that. You should eat. Come on. Axel can cook now."

"I'm not eating anything Axel has made," Luka said dryly, following him down the stairs. He knew Theon was moving slowly for him, and it grated against his pride, even if he was thankful for it.

"Just you wait," Theon muttered.

"She'll be all right? Alone in that room?"

The corner of his lips quirked in a small smile. "She'll find us when she wakes."

The rest of the penthouse was quiet as they made their way to the kitchen, and when Theon went to the fridge to retrieve leftovers, Luka asked, "Where is everyone?"

"Everyone is out. Eliza was going stir crazy, so Razik and Axel took her to wander. Brecken too. Cienna and Gia had matters to tend to. Tristyn too. Xan's with them. Kat is upstairs resting," Theon answered, loading up a plate with what appeared to be ham, potatoes, gravy, and vegetables. He glanced up as he worked. "Kat is pregnant."

"Fuck off," Luka said, eyes widening.

Theon huffed a laugh, placing the plate in the microwave. "Early in her sixth month."

"Axel's . . . right?" Luka said, taking a seat at the counter.

Theon nodded, filling a glass of water and sliding it to him. "Yeah. It's Axel's. There's a lot that's happened since we were separated. Axel and Kat are married."

Luka stilled, the glass halfway to his mouth. "They're married too?"

Theon nodded, now focused on repackaging the leftovers. "Yeah. Bree is trying to steal the Underground. I killed Cordelia. Tessa killed Felicity. Cressida isn't my mother—"

"How'd you learn that?" Luka interrupted, setting his glass down after taking a long drink.

Theon's eyes narrowed. "Why aren't you surprised by that?"

"Xan told me. Shortly before we came to the Celeste Estate," Luka said, and then he told Theon all about his own mother, Axel's potential sister, and more.

Theon stared at him, the leftovers forgotten now. The microwave had beeped long ago, but neither of them had bothered retrieving the reheated food. Not until Luka was done speaking, and then he was pretty sure it was only because Theon needed something to do while he processed everything.

"So your mother is supposedly with my half-sister in the Anala Kingdom?" Theon said. "And Kyra and her kingdom have been harboring Fae and kindling a rebellion for decades? That's why they're so stringent on who they let in?"

"From the sounds of it, yes," Luka said, not realizing just how hungry he was until Theon placed the plate of food in front of him. He needed to pace himself, but fuck, it smelled divine. "What else?"

"What do you mean 'what else?'" Theon asked, watching him carefully, because of course he was. Always worrying about those he viewed as his.

"What else do I need to know?"

He went quiet, and Luka glanced up in between shoveling mashed potatoes into his mouth. His friend's hands were braced on the countertop, head hanging down as he clearly debated how to say something. Luka was about to tell him just to spit it out, but then his dragon stirred in his soul and he could have cried. Because he'd felt his dragon dying, and somehow it was still here. It hadn't moved, and Luka had been too afraid to try to summon it because what if it had been gone? But something else had summoned it. Or someone. And he didn't need to turn around to know who was standing in the kitchen doorway. Just like he didn't need to see the look on Theon's face as his attention went there too.

"Sleep well, beautiful?" Theon asked. She must have nodded because he followed up with, "Are you hungry?"

"No," she said softly. "I won't stay. I just wanted to . . . see."

"You don't have to go—"

"It's fine, Theon," she interrupted. "I just needed to see."

Theon clearly waited until she was gone before his eyes slid back to Luka. "You need to talk to her."

"I just woke up. She was sleeping. Haven't really had time," Luka muttered, stabbing at some squash.

Theon sighed. "I know. It's just . . . There's a lot happening right now, and we can't have this hanging over us. It will interfere. I'm assuming you made a decision, and that's why you'd come to find us?"

"I said I'll talk to her," Luka growled. "Can I finish fucking eating first?"

Theon nodded, tapping his index finger on the counter. Once. Twice. Three times. Luka dropped his fork to his plate.

"Say it," he said, crossing his arms and watching his friend.

"Say what?"

"Whatever it was you were about to tell me before Tessa appeared. Whatever is eating at you so we can move past that too."

Theon straightened, that hand going through his hair again as a muscle ticked in his jaw. "Jove and the Ladies gave me a path to the Arius seat," he said. "You asked how I could be the Arius Lord with my father still alive. They gave me a way to do that."

"Which is?" Luka asked, bracing his forearms on the countertop.

"If I had a formal Match, they would all agree to appoint me."

"You have a Match. Or had one. Didn't you say Tessa killed her?"

Theon nodded. "I did. They wouldn't release Tessa to me until I had the Match Ceremony performed. Felicity was with me under the guise of being my wife. Even she didn't know it wasn't real."

"And now you have Tessa and no wife," Luka surmised. "How do you plan to take the seat now?"

"That's the thing," he said, holding Luka's stare as he lifted his arm. The new Mark wound around his wrist. "I do have a wife."

Luka didn't blink. Didn't look away. All he could think to say was, "Did she agree to this?"

Theon's brow furrowed. "Are you asking if I forced her into it?"

"You did force her into a bond. It's not far-fetched," he replied plainly.

"Fuck off, Luka," Theon retorted. "If you can't see things have changed, then I don't know what to tell you. I asked her to do this for me, and she agreed with stipulations of her own."

"Which were what?" Luka ground out.

"Ask her," Theon answered with a cruel smirk. "Sounds like the two of you have a lot to discuss."

Then he grabbed Luka's plate and turned away, apparently done with the conversation. Which was fine. If the fucker was going to dismiss him, he didn't need to sit here in awkward silence.

He pushed back from the counter, his stool scraping on the kitchen floor.

Theon grumbled about "dragon tantrums," and then he huffed a laugh when Luka snarled under his breath. But just as he reached the kitchen doorway, he called his name.

Luka paused, not looking over his shoulder, but stilling all the same.

"Not that it should matter, but if it does, know that I agreed to her stipulations," Theon said. "I just need you to know that."

He didn't ask what he meant. Maybe it wouldn't matter in the end. Maybe what he had to say wouldn't make a difference now that Theon had what he'd wanted all along. While he wasn't surprised, he was . . . something. His dragon was up, trying to pace in his soul at the thought of someone else having what he'd claimed, and while Luka was grateful to feel the thing, now was not the time to have it trying to drive his actions.

Climbing the stairs, he didn't bother knocking when he reached the door to Theon's room. She was bent over something on the small sofa, and she straightened at the sound of the door.

Wide violet eyes landed on him, looking him up and down, before she turned back to whatever she was doing.

"I'm sorry," she murmured. "I was trying to be out before you came back."

The door clicked shut behind him, and he crossed his arms. "What do you mean, 'out?'"

Packing. That was what she was doing. She was putting odds and ends into a small bag.

"Eliza and Razik have been staying in the room across the hall. That's your room, right? They've been staying there. Axel and Kat are upstairs. You need a room—"

"So do you," he interrupted.

"I don't need a room," she said. "I can sleep on a sofa just as well."

"I doubt your *husband* will allow such a thing," he retorted, and yeah, the word sounded a little bitter.

Tessa froze for a moment, slowly setting down the items in her hand before she turned to face him. "He told you already?"

"Thank the gods he did. You probably would have kept it from me for months."

Her eyes dropped to the ground, and gods. He was a fucking prick, but he was also still furious with her.

He said nothing else, watching her struggle with what to do. Finally, she turned back to the sofa, returning to packing that fucking bag.

"I just need to grab a few more things, and I'll be out of your space," she said.

"This is Theon's room."

"But you are still healing, and now that you are awake, I won't . . ."

Luka glanced at the chair where she'd been sleeping, then back to her. "Did you sleep there for the entire three weeks?"

"I'm sorry I was asleep when you woke," she answered. "I didn't mean to be."

"That wasn't what I asked you."

She zipped the bag then, turning to face him once more as she lifted it over her shoulder. "Yes, I did. I just needed to see . . ."

"See what, Tessa?" he demanded.

"I needed to watch your chest rise and fall because it didn't for a time, Luka," she said, tears already pooling in her eyes. "You weren't moving, and your heart wasn't beating, and I needed to see you wake up. Even if I missed that part, but I needed . . ." She cleared her throat, wiping at the tear that had slipped free. "And now I have, and I know you don't like me in your space, so I will leave."

"Go back to the way things were in the cave," he said flatly.

"I mean, I know it will be different, and maybe eventually things will be—I don't know, Luka. I don't know what you want me to say or do. I don't know what you want from me right now," she said, her hands coming up and reaching for her hair.

"Don't you dare," he growled. "We agreed you weren't doing that anymore."

She froze, but her eyes flashed. "We agreed to a lot of things that aren't happening," she retorted. "So again, I ask you, what do you want from me? Because I'm tired of trying to figure it out."

And there she was. This was the tiny thing of fury he could pick a fight with because that was what he actually needed right now. He wanted to punish her for what she did, and he couldn't do that when she was docile and submissive. He wanted her fiery and bratty; he wanted her ready to push back.

"You slept in my bed, and then you left me with nothing but a note," he growled, low and menacing as he reached behind him and locked the door.

"You made it clear I wasn't what you wanted anymore," she shot back, lifting her chin. "I deserve more than 'just for tonights,' Luka, and you deserve not to be bound to someone you can't stand to look at."

"Is that what you think? That I can't stand to look at you?" he asked, slowly prowling toward her, but she stood her ground, her grip tightening on the strap of her bag over her shoulder.

"I don't know what else I'm supposed to think. When I entered a room at your cave, you looked away. When you spoke to me, it was short and to the point. Even when I came downstairs to find you awake, you didn't even turn to look at me. I'm incredibly adept at knowing when I'm not wanted. I don't need it spelled out," she said, her breathing erratic now.

"Are you done with your little fit?" Luka asked.

"Little fit?" she spluttered, her light flaring, illuminating the Mark around her wrist that matched Theon's.

His dragon snarled. Or maybe that was him.

He was close enough now he could reach out and touch her if he wanted, and he was still debating what he was going to do next when she threw her hands in the air.

"Forget it. I've apologized. I've given you space. I've asked how to make amends. If you can't forgive me, I understand, but I won't sit around and let you play mind games with me," she snarled, already taking steps toward the door. "I'm sorry I bothered you."

His hand snapped out, gripping the back of the zip-up sweatshirt she was wearing. "Can you stop being so godsdamn mouthy all the fucking time?" he growled, yanking her back. She stumbled over her own feet, the bag dropping to the floor.

"Why? You can't seem to stop being a prick for even a minute," she snapped in response. "Let me go."

"No."

She scoffed, reaching up and unzipping the sweatshirt. "I made a mistake. A big one. I fucked up," she ranted. "I've tried to apologize. You rejected me. That's your right. But you don't get to continue to make me feel like a fuck up just because I'm in the same room as you."

She spun around, shrugging out of the sweatshirt he still gripped in his hand before she stalked toward the door. She was left in fitted leggings and a tank top that exposed her midriff.

"Come back here, Tessa," he barked, tossing the sweatshirt aside.

She looked over her shoulder as she parroted him from seconds ago with a smirk. "No."

Then her eyes went wide as he lunged, and she screamed, darting the other way, leaping onto the bed and down to the other side. He let her run, prowling behind her, because now she was trapped.

Or she would be.

As he rounded the bed, she made to climb back over it again, but he lifted his hand, black flames springing up to stop her. She cried out again, lurching back and straight into his chest. Luka spun with her, shoving her forward and pressing her against the windows, the curtains open wide so they could see out over the Underground below.

"Let me go, Luka," she growled.

"Not a chance," he growled in kind, his fingers threading into the back of her hair. "We need to talk, and we can't do that if you insist on being an incessant brat."

Her lip curled in a sneer. "I already said I don't need it spelled out for me. I got it, okay?"

"Apparently you do need it spelled out for you," he retorted. "By Sargon, you are infuriating. It drives me half crazy."

"Join the club," she snarked back. "So what's the plan here, Luka Mors? You need to make me suffer?"

His cock twitched at the thought, because yes, that was exactly what he wanted to fucking do.

"What if I do?" he replied, his voice going low and dark as he leaned in to speak into her ear. "What if I need you to suffer for keeping something so important from me? What will you do?"

Her laugh was sharp and slightly unhinged. "I'll take it and ask for more just to piss you off."

His grip on her hair tightened at the words, and she gasped, pushing onto her toes to relieve the pressure. There was no twitching of his dick now. It was fully hard, and his dragon was completely on board to remind her who the dominant one was in this relationship.

She arched against him, her breasts pressing to the glass and nearly spilling over the low cut of her top. His hand in her hair shoved her forward a little more, forcing her to turn her head so her cheek was against the pane. Her ass pressed into him, and his other palm landed on the window next to her head.

"Stop that," he snarled into her ear. "Tell me why you kept my father from me."

Her breathing stuttered, her fight stalling for a few seconds. "I didn't trust you," she admitted. "You were only there because Theon told you to be."

"Not in the end. You knew that," he retorted.

"And what was I supposed to do?" she cried. "Bring it up after we fucked the first time or the second? 'Thanks for the incredible sex. By the way, your father is being held in the cells in Faven. Let me check with Rordan and see if we can visit before we go for another round.'"

"This fucking mouth," he snapped, spinning her roughly around so her back was to the window now. She stared up at him, defiant as always, while her power flickered in her eyes. "Loyalty is everything to me," he said, low and controlled. "You betrayed that."

"I know," she said. "And I'm sorry. I don't know what else I can do or say. I wasn't keeping him from you. I was keeping him for me. I didn't know . . . I was trying to figure out who I was. He was a link to my past, and until I decided which path I was going to take, I needed that secret, Luka. I'm not saying it was right. I'm not trying to excuse my actions. But I—"

"Do you regret it?" he interrupted.

"What?"

"Do you regret keeping it from me?" Her eyes darted to the side, but he took her chin, guiding her gaze right back to his. "Answer me."

"I regret it hurt you, but . . ." She took a deep breath, and those were tears in her eyes when she admitted, "I don't think I'd change my actions. He was the only one I had when I was alone. If that makes me selfish, then I own it, Luka. I had no one until you came along, and then I was so afraid of losing you . . ." Her eyes fell closed, and she tipped her head back against the window. "It didn't matter in the end. I suppose I lost you either way."

He slid his hand back into her hair, threading it through his fingers and gripping once more, keeping her in place. "You pissed me off," he said. "The betrayal gutted me, and yes, I needed time to think. Yes, I wanted you gone. Didn't want to be in the same space as you." She stiffened at the words, screwing her eyes shut even tighter. "But no matter how hard I tried to hate you, I couldn't. Not because of some Marks or some supposed bond, but because you, Tessalyn Ausra, have worked your way under my skin. I'm as obsessed with you as Theon is, and we have time to make up for. Nights to claim and trust to rebuild. You didn't lose me, baby girl. You may not be my Match or my wife, but you are my light. You are *mine*."

Her eyes fluttered open, holding his for seconds that seemed to drag on and on, and then she was pushing up onto her toes, finding his mouth. His lips melted into hers, tongues taunting and teasing while they battled for dominance like they always had, likely always would.

"You can make me suffer now," she whispered onto his lips, and the growl that rumbled from him was all dragon as he pushed the straps of her top down her arms, freeing her breasts.

He palmed one, savoring the gasp from her as he kneaded the flesh, still gripping her hair in the other hand. Brushing a thumb over her nipple once more, he took her hand and tugged her with him.

Sitting on the edge of the bed to not agitate his wings, he pulled her between his legs. She stared at him, her breasts spilling out of her top, and her chest rising and falling erratically.

Hooking his thumbs into the band of the leggings, he tugged them down as he ordered, "Undress."

Her lips pursed, but for once she didn't argue. She took over, slowly peeling the leggings down her legs, stepping out of them and kicking them aside. Then she pulled the top over her head before shimmying out of her undergarments.

"Anything else?" she asked with a smirk while his heated gaze slid over her. He said nothing, only reached for her hips and pulled her back to him, forcing her to straddle his lap. She frowned, her fingertips brushing along his chest. "You're still partially dressed."

"And?" he asked, relishing the feel of her touching him again.

"It's not fair."

"There's nothing fair about suffering, temptress," he replied, leaning in to capture her lips. Her tongue swiped against his, and she sighed into him, relaxing in his hold. His hands ran over her ass, squeezing the soft flesh, and the sigh turned into a moan. Her hands were roaming now, and he knew she was growing hungrier.

But when she rocked against him, rolling her hips against his cock, he nipped her bottom lip at the same time one of his hands left her ass, only to come back with a sharp *smack*.

She gasped, lurching back and giving him an accusing look.

"We're not even close to doing that, baby girl," he said with a low chuckle as he smoothed his hand over the same spot. Her lips pursed, but that was intrigue in her eyes as she held his stare. "Theon said you killed Felicity."

Her brows crashed together. "What does that have to do with anything?"

"Why did you kill her?"

"Because she kept touching Theon," she answered.

Luka hummed, his hand still smoothing over her flesh. "Maybe you need to learn to share."

"Absolutely not," she snarled vehemently.

He smacked her ass again, leaning in to swallow her gasp while he soothed the spot with his hand, feeling her relax into him once more.

"How did you kill her?" he asked when he broke the kiss.

"I punched her in the face," she said, that now familiar madness creeping into her features. "She kept touching my things. Theon. My dagger. So I sliced it across her throat and then shoved it into her chest."

Another smack and that had a low moan slipping past her lips. "Luka . . ." she said breathlessly.

"You know I like seeing you covered in the blood of victory," he chided.

"It's not my fault you weren't there," she shot back, only to have his hand connect with her ass again.

"There's that bratty mouth again," he chastised. "What are we going to do with that, hmm?"

"Luka," she whined, squirming atop his lap as she clutched at his shoulders.

Another smack.

"Stop grinding against me, Tessa," he warned.

She was panting now, her hands turning frantic as she ran them over his arms, his chest, and she wasn't fucking listening anymore. Seeking and wanting. He hadn't been lying. He was going to reclaim her, but she was going to suffer first.

His hand smacked her ass twice more before he pushed her off his lap. The whine that came from her was downright pitiful, and he chuckled darkly, shoving her toward the chair.

"Is that where you've been sleeping, baby girl?" he asked.

"Yes," she said petulantly as she eyed him. "I didn't think you'd want me in your bed."

"Take a seat."

"I don't want to sit there," she replied, lifting her chin as if she would defy him.

"Too bad," he retorted, his power pushing against her and forcing her ass into the armchair.

"Luka," she cried again, already trying to stand.

"Stay there, Tessa," he warned. "I'm not above calling on your *husband* to keep your ass planted."

She stilled, and yeah, he knew exactly what those words did to her. Saw the subtle clench of her thighs. The intrigued tilt of her head. Another time, maybe, but this time—this reclaiming—was all his.

"Don't move," he ordered. "If you can't sit still, then you'll have to watch."

"Watch wh—"

But her words cut off when he stood and shoved his pants down, taking his cock in his hand and stroking it up and back down. He'd just needed some godsdamn relief because he was hard as fuck.

"Theon said you had stipulations about your newfound marriage," he said, continuing to stroke himself.

"What?" she asked, distracted and breathless.

"Focus, baby girl," he chided. "Tell me your stipulations for agreeing to become Theon's wife."

Her tongue darted out, gliding along her bottom lip as she watched him. And fuck, she couldn't be doing something like that right now.

"Tessa," he snapped when she didn't answer.

"I . . ." She shook her head as if trying to clear her thoughts. "It was a new Mark. Something Cienna created, I think?"

"And your stipulations?"

"It wasn't so much a stipulation as an open-ended opportunity," she replied, her hand drifting down her stomach.

"Don't you dare touch what's mine, Tessa," he snarled, smoke accompanying his exhale as the dragon in his soul strained, more than ready to take.

"Luka, please," she said, tipping her head back in frustration.

"What happened to making you suffer?" he mocked, working his palm over the head of his dick. "Tell me about this open-ended opportunity."

She bit her lip, and he was so godsdamn close to just hauling her up and sinking into her. He'd spent the last weeks in his cave doing everything in his power to deny himself and her, and while she was suffering, so was he.

"Tell me, Tessa," he ordered. "Or I'm finishing on you instead of in you, and you'll be left wanting."

Her eyes flashed to his. "You wouldn't."

His smile was cruel. "I liked seeing myself on your tongue. You think I wouldn't like it just as much seeing myself on your skin? I would absolutely leave you wanting, and I'd make sure Theon didn't come to finish the job."

She scowled up at him. "Asshole."

"Brat."

She ground her teeth, shifting in the armchair and rubbing her thighs together. So needy and wanting and *fuck*.

"Tell me, Tessa," he barked.

"I only agreed once I knew the Mark could be added to," she blurted, watching him as if he was going to rebuke her.

"What do you mean, added to?"

"I'm not . . . I'm different," she said, and that neediness was turning into something else.

Something he didn't like.

Uncertainty.

"I'm wild and untamed. I'm an imbalance," she went on. "But with you—and him—I can breathe. I can sleep. I'm not so uncontrollable when you're both . . . It's unconventional, I know, but I need you both. I can't fight it anymore. And if that was something you eventually wanted . . ."

She trailed off, shrugging a shoulder as she turned her head to look away from him. His hand had stilled, dropped to his side as he stared at her. Her stipulation to becoming Theon's wife was that . . . she could be his too? If that was something he wanted?

A cry of surprise came from her as he hauled her up, back out of the chair, and spun her around as he sat back on the edge of the bed. He couldn't risk the healing of his wings, so this would have to do for now. Pulling her back onto his lap, her back against his chest, he spread his legs wide, forcing hers wide in turn. He pushed on her back, making her lean forward some as he used his other hand to line his cock up with her more than ready center.

He thrust up as he pulled her down, sliding into her with one quick move. Hot and tight and godsdamn *everything*.

"Fuck," he growled, and she made a sound as she reached behind her, grappling for something to hold on to.

"Please, Luka," she gasped, but he was already moving.

Gripping her hair once more, he pulled, forcing her to arch her neck back so he could taste her as he pulled out and thrust deep once more. Something between a sigh and a whine came from her, her fingers twisting in the bed covers.

"More. Please," she moaned.

She didn't need to ask twice. It was hard and fast. A clear fucking as much as it was a reclaiming. Her head fell back against his shoulder, and he let her take over sliding up and down his cock as she took from him. His hands roamed, fingers tracing down her sides, up the planes of her stomach, between her breasts. His lips never stopped exploring her neck, biting and sucking.

And when he felt her tightening around him, he stood, pulling out and ignoring her disgruntled growl. He was already twisting them around, pushing between her shoulder blades, and forcing her chest to the bed. Kicking her feet wider, he sank back into her, thrusting deeper and harder.

She buried her face in the blankets, trying to muffle her moans, but he wanted to hear every sound. Gathering her hair in a hand, he pulled, making her back arch as she pushed back against him.

"Yes," she chanted. "Yes, yes, yes."

He leaned down as he continued to pump into her, making sure she could hear him when he said, "Never tell me you are too wild, too untamed, or too uncontrollable again. Do you understand?"

Tessa only moaned, her arms stretched out above her head as she clenched the comforter in her fingers.

His hand smacked her ass once more, that moan becoming more as she started to clench around his length.

"Say it, Tessa," he growled.

"I understand," she gasped out, breathless and completely at his mercy.

"No more sleeping in a fucking armchair. You sleep in a proper bed with me or Theon," he grunted, his balls drawing up tighter as he came closer and closer to tipping over the edge.

"Yes," she rasped, and he reached around her, finding her clit. He knew it wouldn't take much more, and he was right. "Please, Luka," she moaned again, grinding against his hand.

"You don't need my permission, baby girl," he growled. "You take what you want."

"*Gods*," she cried as she fell apart. Her body tightened, a spring ready to snap, and she shuddered as her pleasure ripped through her. Her breathing was erratic as she rode out her orgasm before going limp.

He released her hair, gripping her hips to pound into her, pulling her back into him harder and harder. Then he reached his own release with a final thrust, spilling inside of her as he clutched at her hips, a sheen of sweat on her back.

It took a minute for his own breathing to regulate, but he peppered kisses up her spine as he went, not wanting to pull out of her just yet. Her skin was salty, and she sighed, her fingers finally releasing the comforter. It was only then, with her drowsy and sated beneath him, that he noticed the faint cords between them. A faint midnight blue intertwining with gold so tightly there was no way to tell where one started and the other ended. It flared, hovering between them for a few seconds, before settling into them. Something he felt in the depths of his being. Something his dragon gave a snarled *'mine'* over.

They cleaned up before she crawled beneath the blankets, stretching like a cat and rolling onto her side to face him. He was lying on his stomach, hoping Cienna would stop by sometime soon. Turning his head, he found her eyes on him and her teeth worrying her bottom lip.

"You're okay with this?" she asked. "Me and you and me and him?"

"I knew what I was getting into, Tessa," he answered. "Theon was the one who needed to get on board."

She nodded, reaching over to run her fingers through his hair. "I want you to know there's no pressure. About the Mark. It's your choice. I never want you to feel trapped."

It was his turn to nod. He knew she was likely wanting an answer, some sort of enthusiastic commitment, but he couldn't find the words to give that to her just yet.

"Why us?" he asked, not even sure where the question came from.

Her fingers stilled, brows pinching. "Why us what?"

"Why choose us? When we made your life a godsdamn nightmare?" he pushed. "More so Theon, but I did nothing to stop him."

She was quiet for so long, he wasn't sure she was going to answer. But her fingers resumed their movement through his hair, nearly lulling him to sleep. One would think he'd had enough of that after three godsdamn weeks.

It was minutes later when her soft voice drifted to him. "Both of you let me be who I was always meant to be, whether that's a villain or a saint. You accept me and all my chaos. Some hate the villains, but I joined them and learned how to love and to be loved. And maybe it's not how the rest of the stars love, but it's ours."

She drifted off to sleep, but he didn't follow her. When her breathing was soft and steady, Luka reached over and ran a finger along the Mark on her wrist.

Villain or saint, she was theirs.

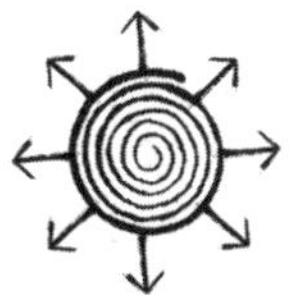

30
THEON

Tessa sighed where she was nestled into him. One of her hands rested on his chest, and he lightly toyed with her hair, waiting for Luka to come back. It was early, but he hadn't been surprised when Luka had slipped from the bed. He'd always been an early riser, and after sleeping for three weeks, he was restless. Adding on that his wings needed to remain out for a bit yet, and he'd be shocked if he got more than a few hours of sleep. He could only sleep on his stomach, and Theon knew the only reason he'd even come to bed last night was because that was where Tessa was.

The bedroom door pushed open, and Luka walked in, balancing a tray with three mugs, a coffee carafe, a plate of pastries, oranges, and juice. He set it down on the coffee table before picking up two mugs, carrying one to him. Theon was already carefully adjusting to sit up against the headboard while Tessa still slept.

Taking the mug, he asked, "How are you feeling?"

"Fine," Luka answered, but Theon narrowed his eyes. "I'm fine, Theon," he said again. "Sore. Annoyed my wings will take so long to heal, but it could have been worse."

"You mean you could have actually died?" Theon deadpanned.

Luka glared at him, but it quickly morphed into something else. His eyes drifted back to Tessa's sleeping form. "I thought . . . I'm pretty sure that dagger Dex used wasn't meant to kill *me*. Or maybe it was after . . ." He sighed a deep, shuddering thing. "I felt my dragon dying, Theon. That piece of me. That . . ."

Theon stared at him, not knowing what to say. Was that possible? To only kill the dragon piece of him? He couldn't imagine Luka not being able to shift, to fly. And would that take his power too? If his dragon was gone, would he have lost his dragonfire?

"But it didn't, right?" Theon finally said. "You still have your wings. Cienna said they will heal, and you can still feel your dragon."

"Yeah," he murmured. "I can still feel everything."

His friend didn't need to elaborate. Theon could still feel the Guardian bond being shredded apart. The excruciating agony. It was a phantom memory that he could feel as if it had happened yesterday. He wondered if it would ever fade.

"We monitor it," Theon said when the silence grew too heavy. "If anything feels off, we talk to Cienna right away. Or maybe Xan."

Luka only nodded, taking another drink of his coffee.

"Speaking of feeling off, that Mark on your chest . . ." Theon said, trailing off when Luka glanced down. He hadn't asked about it yesterday, which was surprising since he'd immediately asked about the new Mark on Theon's wrist. "Any ideas what it does?"

"Why would I know that? I didn't give it to myself," Luka said. "There was a lot to catch up on yesterday. I assumed it was something Cienna did to save my life, and someone would mention it if that wasn't the case."

"Not Cienna," Theon said with a pointed glance at the sleeping tempest. She'd hardly moved, nestling into his thigh when he'd shifted to sit up. Now her hand rested there, fingers grazing way too close to his dick, especially with her in only one of his shirts beneath the blankets.

Luka's brows arched in surprise. "*She* did this? How?"

"We don't know," Theon answered. "I was—I didn't see it all, and no one knows what that Mark does. Not Cienna or Tristyn, Razik or Brecken. They say Scarlett can create new Marks because of what she is. That's Eliza's theory. That Tessa did the same. The thing is, Tessa doesn't know what she did."

Luka's lips twitched as if he was fighting a smile. "Of course she doesn't."

"Cienna said we wouldn't know until you woke up, and even then, it might be a while before we figure it out. Until something activates it, I guess. Unless you've noticed anything?" Theon asked, but Luka only shook his head. Theon had figured as much, but he'd hoped it would be one thing that could be solved right away.

As if he couldn't help himself, Luka drifted closer to the bed, rounding to the other side, before taking a seat. Theon could see his fingers flex on the coffee mug and knew exactly what he was fighting—the urge to reach over and touch her.

"Did she talk to you about it?" Theon asked because this whole dynamic was something they'd never actually discussed. It had just sort of . . . happened.

Luka glanced at him. "You don't know?"

He knew they'd argued. He knew there'd been frustrations. He knew they'd fucked. Tessa's emotions down the bond had been a myriad of feelings he couldn't sort through fast enough. He'd forced himself to stay downstairs. Not to come up here and mediate, because they needed to figure their shit out first before they figured it all out together.

And he needed to know what Luka had decided. Sure, they'd fucked, but he knew as well as anyone that didn't mean anything. It could have been a "one last time" thing, or it could have simply happened with the height of emotions. But Luka coming to bed last night made him believe it was more than that.

"She told me her stipulations, yeah," Luka said, balancing his coffee mug on his knee. "But are you . . . Are we—We're really doing this? You're truly okay with it?"

"Did you tell her yes?" Theon asked, reaching down and smoothing back her hair without thinking.

"I didn't answer her," Luka admitted. "We had a lot to sort through, and adding that to the mix with everything else was a lot. But I also wanted to talk to you first."

"I already agreed to her stipulations," Theon said. "I told you that."

"But did you *want* to?" Luka countered. "You are the soon-to-be Arius Lord. I understand if we need to keep her . . . If she needs to be only—Fuck, why is this so difficult?" Luka muttered, brushing his hair from his face.

"She needs both of us," Theon said. "If these last months have taught us anything, it's that. One of us isn't enough to keep her balanced and in control."

"It's unconventional," Luka said. "We'll get pushback on this. That's why I'm saying if we need to keep the 'wife' title solely between her and you, I understand."

"The whole world is changing," Theon argued. "This can change too. Is it something I ever thought I'd be arguing for? Not in a thousand decades. I never imagined sharing. Never thought it would be something I'd agree to."

"Exactly," Luka said. "It's not in your nature."

"And it's not in yours," Theon countered.

"I'm more likely to share than you."

"Says the male who was ranting to me about too many people touching his things."

"That's different," Luka growled.

Theon huffed a laugh. "How is that different?"

"Because it's . . . It wasn't—I don't know how to say this without it sounding ridiculous," he finally managed to get out.

"We're discussing sharing a wife. Not sure it gets much more ridiculous than that."

"It's because it's you," murmured a sleepy, feminine voice. Then she stirred, languid and slow. She didn't even open her eyes when she added, "He doesn't care when *you* touch his things."

"Is that so, little storm?" he asked in amusement, lifting his gaze back to Luka.

He wouldn't look at him, instead already getting up to retrieve coffee for Tessa.

She rolled over, her ass and bare legs pushing against him now, and this was the part he wasn't sure what to do with. If Luka wasn't here, he'd already be between her thighs. His tongue first and then his cock.

Dammit.

Tessa turned and glanced up at him from beneath her lashes, a small quirk of her mouth telling him she knew exactly what he was struggling with. But if she thought he wasn't going to touch her, she was sorely mistaken. He might not fuck her right now, but . . .

As she pushed into a sitting position, he reached over and grabbed her throat, tugging her to him. His mouth landed on hers, and he swallowed her surprised gasp. That surprise quickly became something else, and her lips melted against his. Soft. Pliable. His tongue invading her mouth. Claiming and owning and taking something she was willingly giving him.

He pulled back first, more than satisfied by the dazed look in her violet eyes and the flush on her cheeks. "Good morning, beautiful," he purred, tucking hair behind her ear. "Luka has your coffee."

"Right. Coffee," she murmured, turning to Luka. She took it, glancing up at him and then back to her cup. She cleared her throat. "This is awkward, right?"

"You've woken up in a bed with both of us before," Luka said flatly.

"Well, yeah, but . . . Not . . . This is different, and you know it," she finally said, irritation creeping into her tone.

"How is it different? Did you not sleep well? Was coffee not delivered to you?"

"That's not—"

She saw the lip twitch at the same time Theon did, and Theon turned his head to hide his own smirk.

"Gods, you're such an ass," she grumbled, wrapping her fingers around her mug and bringing it to her lips.

Luka sat back down on the edge of the bed, taking a drink of his own coffee.

"It's new territory for all of us, Tessa," Theon tried. "But it's something we need to figure out how to navigate before we let the rest of the realm know."

"Which is why I'm saying if it needs to be just the two of you—"

"No," Tessa interjected, almost panicked. The bands of light on her wrists flared, illuminating their Union Mark, and those dark embers crackled at her fingertips.

"Easy, baby girl," Luka said, reaching over to brush his hand along her arm at the same time Theon ran his fingertips down her spine. "I'm not going anywhere. All I'm saying is it might be easier for both of you if my role in the relationship isn't advertised."

"You're not some secret fuck buddy, Luka," she said flatly.

"We're not hiding anything," Theon agreed. "Again, we just need to figure out things between the three of us. Then we can present it to the kingdoms, and they can fuck off if they don't like it."

"But maybe we should wait to share everything until after you've secured the Arius seat," Luka said. "We're already going to be up against opposition when it's learned you took Tessa as your wife. She's still technically your Source, and she's the most powerful being in the realm. Add this to it," he continued, gesturing between the three of them. "They're not going to like any of it, Theon."

He pulled on the back of his neck as he mulled that over. He had a point. A lot of really good points. If he suddenly showed up wanting to throw off every tradition and norm, they could easily fight him about it all and deny him everything.

"You might be right," he started, but he didn't get to finish.

"No," Tessa interrupted, shaking her head. "No. You knew my stipulations for this, Theon. I'm not hiding who I am. I'm not becoming less than because it's not what they want. I'm not . . . No. It's one thing if Luka doesn't want this, but if it's only because it will make things more difficult. No. I'll be as fucking difficult as I want to be."

Then she was passing her coffee mug back to Luka before she crawled—fucking *crawled*—to the end of the bed to climb off it. She stalked across the room, slamming the bathroom door behind her, and still all Theon could think about was the way her ass had looked peeking out from the bottom of her shirt when she'd crawled across the bed.

Luka's gaze was also on the closed bathroom door. "You're fine with this? Truly, Theon?"

"Is it what I envisioned? No," Theon answered honestly. "But none of this is. I thought I'd have a submissive Source that I could draw from to take down my father and be able to focus on our kingdom. Instead, we have this mouthy thing of chaos, who pushes back every chance she gets and is bringing the gods-damn realm to ruin."

Luka huffed a dark laugh. "I thought you'd get your Source and take over the Arius Kingdom. We'd take care of our own. Eventually you'd take a Match and so would I because it's tradition and required of us. Decades from now, we'd have children. Instead, Axel will be a father in a few months, and we're . . . sharing."

"Instead we're sharing," Theon echoed. When Luka didn't say anything, he ventured, "Does that mean you're accepting her stipulations?"

Luka sighed, setting his mug beside Tessa's where he'd placed it on the bedside table. Grabbing a hair tie, he pulled his hair back, securing it as he said, "A part of me wanted to rip her away from you when you kissed her."

"And the other part?"

"Wanted to join you," he replied, his voice low and thick with want. "I know we've shared in the past. I just never thought we'd end up keeping the same female."

They had shared in the past. Not often. A night here and there, usually after a brutal bout with his father when they were just trying to escape the reality of their fucked up lives. He supposed that was no different from the way Tessa would often try to drown herself in sex or alcohol for the same reason.

But maybe, in a way, it was all leading up to this in the end. He couldn't believe he was admitting it, but maybe the Fates had orchestrated something new and chaotic. Maybe all the little things had been leading up to and preparing them for this. Maybe it'd become a way out for all of them if they could figure out how to claim it. How to balance Tessa. How to redeem Devram. How two fiercely possessive beings could suddenly share something they both coveted and would shed blood for.

"Are you going to tell her?" Theon finally asked, glancing at Luka as he stood, picking up the coffee cups.

"Eventually," Luka said. "First, I need to shower."

"Tessa's showering," Theon said, extracting himself from the blankets. He'd heard the shower water turn on a moment ago.

"I know," Luka said, and Theon paused before he smirked. He was about to say something in return when there was a knock on the door and Axel poked his head in.

He scanned the room before he said, "Thank the gods. I didn't know what I was going to walk in on with the three of you. It could have been nudity or bloodshed. Or both."

"Fuck off, Axel," Theon said, moving toward the dresser where he'd returned all the clothing Tessa had packed into a bag. Thinking she would sleep on the sofa. As if he wouldn't throw her over his shoulder and haul her right back up here. "Need something?" he asked his brother.

"I don't, but Dagian does," Axel replied nonchalantly.

Theon whirled, Luka straightening. "Dagian? Dagian Jove?" Theon asked.

"The one and only. Sent a note asking to meet with you," Axel said, pulling a piece of paper from his pocket.

"Just Dagian?" Theon asked, grabbing the paper and skimming the words.

"Sounds like it. What do you want me to do?"

Theon glanced at Luka, then to the bathroom door. They were here. The Underground was their domain. If it was just the Achaz Heir . . .

"Set it up," Theon said.

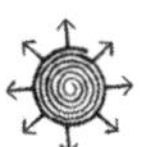

"Are we sure sending Razik and Eliza to collect him was a good idea?" Axel asked where he was standing near Kat, who was seated on the sofa.

"Yes," Theon answered. "No one knows who they are. If we'd sent Tristyn or Xan, they're easily recognizable and known well by the Achaz Kingdom. Until the Pantheon, Razik and Eliza being here was kept quiet."

"Yeah, but that's the point. They *were* seen when the Pantheon was demolished."

"It was our best bet," Theon said, watching Tessa, who was pacing back and forth a few feet away.

"How did he get here so fast? He just sent that request yesterday," she murmured, hands constantly drifting to her hair, but she'd stop herself before she touched the strands.

"He was insistent when I spoke to him," Axel offered.

"It's a trap."

He shrugged. "Probably."

"This is our territory he's walking into, Tessa," Theon tried. "The only person he was allowed to bring with him is his Source."

"Sasha," she murmured, then she shook her head as if clearing her thoughts. "I don't trust him."

"Neither do we," he replied. "No one said anything about trusting him. He'll be outnumbered. Look at everyone here. Even with his Source, he won't accomplish anything here."

Her eyes skimmed the room. Cienna and Gia. Tristyn and Xan. Even Brecken was here. She swallowed thickly, and he knew she was being haunted by memories of an assessment Dagian had infiltrated with the help of the Serafina Heir. No one knew what the Achaz Heir wanted, but Theon was more than intrigued.

Tessa started pacing again, light and ashes trailing in her wake. Violet eyes snapped to his, "We can't see the sun here."

He knew this was coming. The Underground, while open and not confining, still separated her from the outside world. Even Nylah and Roan didn't follow her here, choosing to stay in nature and the fresh air. They needed to leave soon. If anything, just to let her wild nature lose a little control for a bit. He chalked it up to her father's side—Temural, god of the wild and untamed.

"Go sit with Luka, Tessa," he said, and when she waved him off, muttering to herself, he sent a look to Luka.

He sighed, but then he crossed the room from where he'd been standing near the lift doors. She hadn't even noticed, and when she turned in her pacing, she nearly ran into his chest. He was already gripping her chin between his thumb and forefinger, forcing her to meet his gaze.

"Not that you need us, but he's not going to touch you, Tessa," Luka said, his voice low and brokering no argument. "You are the most powerful person in this room. Are *you* going to let him harm *us*?"

Lightning flashed in violet depths, the light on her arms immediately flaring as golden mist and silver embers danced in the air around her.

"That's what I thought," Luka said, and Theon could hear the smirk in his voice. "He is beneath you, Tessa. Not the other way around. No one controls you, which means no one gets to make you feel anxious or less than. Do you understand?"

Her throat bobbed with a swallow as she nodded.

"Verbal acknowledgement, little storm," Theon said, having drifted closer.

Her glare was cold, but not as icy as her words when she bit out, "I understand."

Which was fine. He was following Luka's lead and riling her up. It was a delicate balance with her—and yes, he found that ironic—but when she thought about things too much, it led to . . . this. When she let the fury drive her, she was a force to be reckoned with. She was a tempest capable of endings and beginnings.

"That's our girl," Luka said, his thumb swiping along her bottom lip.

If anyone in the room had questions about what was happening, they didn't voice them. Until the three of them navigated this thing of theirs, they'd leave everyone to wonder.

The sound of the lift ascending had them all turning to the entrance. Axel and Luka moved to the front, standing between the doors and everyone else. When they opened, Eliza gestured for Dagian and his Source to go first.

He entered the room with his head held high, ever an heir showing no weakness. He looked somewhat like Rordan with his golden blonde hair, but his golden eyes lacked the blue that Rordan's held, and those sharp cheekbones were all his mother. His Source was at his side, stunning with her bronze skin and brown hair. Neither spoke, but he saw the subtle tilt of her head, telling him they were speaking down their bond. That was an aspect of his own bond that hadn't been repaired. He could feel Tessa's emotions, but the mind-speak had never returned.

"Dagian," Theon greeted tightly, slipping his hands into his pockets.

"You assembled quite the greeting party, Theon," the Achaz Heir said casually, picking up a small knick knack from an end table and examining it as if the sheer amount of power in this room was nothing to him.

"We have an heir in our presence," Theon replied. "We wouldn't want him to be offended by the lack of welcome."

Dagian huffed a dark chuckle. "You always were an arrogant ass. Something my father says is an Arius trait."

He set the item back down, finally deigning to lock eyes with him. Theon said nothing, holding his stare.

Until that golden gaze slid to Tessa.

"Back where you belong, I see," he said, clasping his hands behind his back.

"Don't talk to her," Theon snapped, stepping between them. "Your business is with me, Dagian."

He scoffed. "And yet you have a small company here with you. Do you forget that without me, you would have been stopped before you fled with her to begin with? Now I *am* offended."

"That proves nothing," Theon retorted.

"What is he talking about?" Tessa asked, peeking around him before stepping to his side.

"Dagian was there the night Blackheart and I broke you out of the cells. He let us pass without alerting others we were taking you," Theon explained, a fact that had slipped his mind. It had been utter chaos that day, and Tessa had been lost to the same.

"Why?" she asked, her head tilting as she studied the Achaz Heir.

"Because while you are the catalyst, you are not what will eventually call the Fates to this world for destruction," Dagian answered, his attention solely on Tessa now.

"Of course she is," Theon said. "It's in the Revelation Decree."

"I said she is the catalyst," Dagian retorted, still watching. "She is part of it, has started it all, but she is not the thing that will drive the Fates to intervene. Not entirely anyway."

"You need to tell me exactly what you know, and you need to do it without your fucking eyes on her," Theon replied, letting his darkness loose to drift around him and her. Dagian only responded by letting some of his own power out. A gold mist to mirror the inky darkness.

Until similar light drifted among the onyx.

Theon clenched his jaw at feeling Tessa's power mingle with his own. It was euphoric and chaotic and *her*. He'd missed this, and so had his power, suddenly being pulled in two directions, because it wanted her too.

"Speak," Theon ground out, forcing himself to stay focused on the Achaz Heir.

"Tessa is not the only imbalance in Devram," Dagian said, wandering around the room, examining pictures and trinkets. His Source stayed rooted, but her eyes never left him. "My father has been . . . collecting power for a few decades now." He paused, looking over his shoulder. "Since she came and others followed."

They all turned, some looking to Xan and others to Brecken.

"Has that one told you what his job is in the realm?" Dagian continued.

"I'm assuming you're speaking of Brecken," Theon said.

"I'm certainly not speaking of the dragon. Those are Arius's pets."

"Watch it," Luka snarled, but he wasn't the only one. Low growls came from Xan and Razik as well.

Dagian only smirked. "Back to the matter at hand. I was sent here with a purpose, but it allowed me to pursue one of my own."

"Then spit it out," Theon said.

Dagian sighed dramatically. "Your bloodline really isn't known for its patience."

"And yours is?"

He cast him an incredulous look. "Achaz has plans that have been in the works for millenniums, and my father, well . . . That's why I'm here. He sent me to make some kind of meaningless bargain, as long as it included a matching ring to the one Luka bartered with."

Theon glanced at Axel, the ring with a square onyx stone in the center. His brother clenched his fist. Neither of them had any real attachment to them other than their father had asked where they came from and seemed to covet them himself. They became a symbol of defiance and camaraderie after Luka found them, but—

"How many are there?" Tessa asked from where she'd been observing at his side.

"Three," Dagian answered. "Either would do. He's not picky."

"But why? What are they for? Certainly not just to lord over them. They *do* something," Tessa pushed.

"So clever," Dagian mocked, and it was Theon's turn to snarl, echoed by Luka's low rumble. "Relax," he sighed. "I wouldn't be telling you all of this if I were here to betray you."

"How am I not the only imbalance?" Tessa asked, and then he had to work to control his surprise because her voice was cold and icy. Power and chaos, and he had no idea why until she said, "Why could I not feel you before?"

"What?" Theon demanded, that single word carrying violence.

"Not like that," Brecken intervened as Luka and Theon both took steps towards the heir. "It's not a bond of any kind. He is powerful. Tessa can sense that somehow."

"Power calls to power," Xan added, speaking for the first time. "Her Chaos is sensing his."

"But that would mean he has Chaos," Kat said, her furrowed brow telling Theon she was trying to work this out as frantically as he was.

"All beings with power have Chaos," Xan said. "There are beings of Chaos who emerged directly from the Chaos, such as the First gods and goddesses, but Chaos is the undercurrent of all magic. It is Chaos that determines how powerful one's gifts are. Legacy are powerful, but that power is diluted by mortal blood. Fae have traces of Chaos, created to balance the Legacy but never overpower them."

"But it could happen," Razik added. "We're seeing this in our realm. If two powerful Fae come together, their children could be . . ."

Xan nodded. "Yes. The Fae are monitored closely in all realms."

"In our realm, there is contention about powerful Fae joining," Eliza said.

"For good reason," Xan replied. "If children came to be, they would be sought from all the realms if they were powerful enough."

Eliza and Razik shared a look, but Theon didn't have time to try to decipher it. "Fine. We've established why Tessa can . . . *feel* Dagian, but how was it hidden?"

"Elowyn is skilled, just like your own Witches," Dagian said casually, casting a look at Cienna and Gia.

"A tonic then," Tristyn said, toying with an unlit roll of lull-leaf in his hand.

Dagian nodded. "But returning to your previous question," he said, his attention back on Tessa. "You are not the only imbalance because, like I said, my father has been collecting power. Power that one has been bringing to him."

He jerked his chin at Brecken, and they all turned to the seraph. Well, most of them. Luka kept his attention fixed on Dagian, not willing to give him any chance to catch them off guard.

"Brecken?" Tessa asked, her power lingering around her as she held his gaze.

"You knew this, Tessa," he answered solemnly. "You knew I was tracking down powerful Fae. Part of that was a search for you for a while, but after . . ."

"You knew this? That Rordan was taking their power?"

He nodded. "I saved as many as I could," he said with a pointed look at Katya.

Kat started, struggling to sit up straighter. "What do you mean, you saved me?"

"I wasn't supposed to take you to the Celeste Estate," he answered. "I was supposed to take you to Faven. Same with Corbin and Lange."

"Why didn't Rordan just come take them?" Tessa asked, drifting closer. It took everything in Theon not to reach out and tug her back. Tuck her behind him and protect her, but he couldn't protect her from truth.

"Once they entered the Celeste Estate and were processed as a completed transfer, it would have been too noticeable to move them again so soon," Brecken answered. "If they disappeared during transport, it was easier to cover up. There were other dangers, but that one, at least, was stopped. And then there was you. He wouldn't risk revealing himself before it was time. You became their safeguard."

"How is he taking their magic?" Razik cut in, studying Dagian. "The only way that can be done in our realm is if a goddess does it."

"Only a being of Chaos can transfer magic from one to another," Xan said. "The process is agonizing for the one losing their power, but if not willingly given, they do not survive."

"But the gods cannot come here," Axel interjected.

"There are other beings of Chaos," Theon answered, his attention back on Dagian. "Aren't you a being of Chaos, Xan? The son of a god?"

Xan shook his head. "My mother was mortal. As we discussed, that dilutes the power. To transfer magic, especially from someone unwilling . . . That would take a great deal of Chaos. A god or goddess. A Fate. A World Walker or a—"

"Seraph," Tessa said. "A seraph is a being of Chaos."

"Not all of them," Xan said. "Just like not all dragons are beings of Chaos. They didn't all emerge from the Chaos behind the gods, nor were they created from it like the Lessers."

"Does it really matter *how* he is doing it?" Dagian interrupted. "What matters is that he *is*. He is powerful. He's taken so much power, he cannot be taken down by the other Ladies. Or a Lord. Even Tessa will find it a challenge. She might be more powerful, but defeating my father will drain her to the brink of death. She might not survive it."

"Then we find another way," Theon said immediately. There was no way in all the realms he'd let Tessa get to that point.

A dark grin lifted on Dagian's lips. "I'm glad you say that," he answered. "Because that brings me to my proposal. I will help you, but I require something in return."

"What is it?" Theon asked, eyes narrowing in suspicion.

"When this is over, my life is spared, along with Sasha's. I want my family's home in Coveyll."

"You can have whatever home you like," Theon said. "If Rordan is out of the picture, you will be the Achaz Lord."

"I don't want it. I never have. More than that, for this to work, I won't be able to be the Achaz Lord anymore."

"And why, pray tell, is that?" Theon drawled, waiting for the catch.

"Because I'm offering you my power willingly," Dagian answered. "It won't be enough, but it will be a start."

The entire room fell silent as shock rippled through Theon. Surely he couldn't have heard the male correctly.

"You can't just give him your power," Tessa blurted.

"But I can," Dagian said. "I will. To stop my father. If he continues, he will not only call the Fates here, but the gods. They will not like him being as powerful as they are, and if the gods come here, Devram will fall. All accords will be broken, and the Fates will destroy it all to wipe the sins from the stars. None will be left standing.

"So I want to live peacefully in Coveyll on the shores of the Asning Sea," he continued, naming the city on an island in the Southern Achaz Kingdom. "I will give you my magic willingly in exchange. I will help and give any information I can."

"Anything else?" Theon asked tightly.

"Yes," Dagian said, his chin lifting a little more. "My mother will be left out of this."

Theon didn't care about Laila, Rordan's Match. She rarely attended any events, only accompanying Rordan when tradition demanded it.

"Fine," Theon said, pulling a dagger from a swirl of darkness. He sliced his palm. "It's an accord."

Dagian did the same, their palms meeting and the familiar tingle of a Bargain Mark marring his skin just below his shoulder blade.

"Now tell us how to transfer this power," Theon said. He would do this. Anything to protect his kingdom, his people, those he loved. Anything to protect what was *his*.

"You need to find a being of Chaos to do the power transfer," Dagian said again, wandering over to the alcohol bar and pouring a drink.

"Brecken?" Tessa asked, glancing at her friend.

He shook his head. "I'm not that, Tessa. Like Xan said, we weren't born of Chaos."

"Bring us whoever is helping your father," Theon said tightly to Dagian.

Dagian clicked his tongue. "We just agreed not to involve her," he replied, taking a drink.

"You said you would help in whatever way you could," Theon argued. "We just agreed to it."

"And we agreed not to involve her," Dagian said calmly, passing his glass to Sasha. She took her own sip, still watching them all. Sasha, who was Fae. Or perhaps had some Legacy blood, but she wasn't a being of Chaos, and the only other person involved in the bargain was—

"Your mother?" Theon asked in disbelief. "That's not possible."

"Yet here I stand," Dagian said.

"Bullshit," Axel interjected. "Your mother isn't a goddess or a Fate."

"No, but she is seraph," Dagian said, something fierce and violent filling his features. He took the glass back from Sasha, taking another drink as soft, feathered wings of golden mist appeared at his back. "One of the original angels from the Chaos. Achaz sent her here to help my father, and she is to be left out of this as agreed to."

"Then how the fuck am I supposed to take your power?" Theon demanded.

"That's your problem, but I would start with Chaos herself," he answered, tipping his glass towards Tessa.

"I don't know how to do that," she said simply. "And there is no one here to teach me unless Xan knows."

"I do not," the male answered, but when Theon turned to look at him, even he could tell there was something he wasn't saying.

"But?" Theon pressed.

Xan sighed, swiping a hand down his face. "The gods can't come here, and the Fates act first, examine facts later. Achaz keeps the original seraphs under strict security, and the dragons are in hiding."

"Scarlett could come," Eliza said tentatively. "She'd have to ask her mother how, but she could come."

Xan nodded as best he could around his collar, but Cienna interjected. "She cannot. There is a reason she sent you two and did not return herself."

"What other option is there, then?" Eliza asked. "Because from what I can tell, we're fucked."

"There is another," Cienna said, locking eyes with Xan.

"That would be disastrous," he said, shaking his head this time. "That would be—"

"Our only option," Theon cut in.

"We don't even know if Dagian's power will be enough. He said himself it likely wouldn't be," the dragon argued. "Doing this without certainty of the outcome is foolish."

"Let me worry about that. Let me figure out how to make this foolproof, but if I can, what are we bringing here and how?"

"The how we can figure out, but the what . . ." He trailed off, swiping his hand down his face again. "The what is Fury." Slowly, he slid his sapphire eyes to Tessa. "The what is your mother."

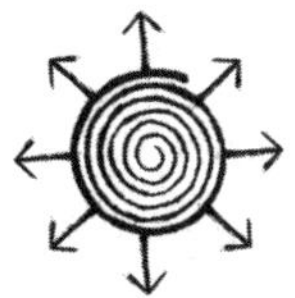

31
EVIANA

"Are there wards?" Lange asked in a low voice from her right.

"These woods are the wards," Eviana replied, scanning the younglings running around the courtyard. "We are taught of the horrors of these woods before we learn to walk."

"And yet you willingly dragged us into them," Lange muttered, and she felt his shudder. He'd had a particularly brutal run-in with another Dread-Nymph last night. If it hadn't been for Corbin shifting and tracking it, she wasn't sure they'd have ever found it to kill it.

"You grew up on the Serafina Estate?" Corbin asked from Lange's other side.

Eviana nodded, her eyes still on the children. Would she even recognize her if she saw her? Or would she look like all the other young females?

"What is the plan now, *bellana?*" Lange asked, sitting back on his heels. A small breeze rustled the trees, and he paused, tilting his head.

"What did they tell you?" Eviana asked, watching a young boy kick a ball to another. There was a group of females playing some kind of clapping game. A few stragglers and loners. None that she felt drawn to, but it was stupid to think she would be.

"Nothing noteworthy," Lange said.

"Everything the winds say could be noteworthy," she argued.

"Or it could be nothing," he sighed. "They are confusing and unrelenting."

"Maybe it doesn't seem important to you, but they could be telling you something vital," she retorted. "What did they just whisper to you?"

He sighed. "It was nothing, Eviana. Something about flowers growing in a flood and whispered nothings when shadows die and new beginnings arise. It doesn't even make sense."

"Right," she murmured. No one spoke for another few minutes before she said, "I'm going to check another angle. Stay here."

"I don't think we should be splitting up," Corbin argued, feline eyes flashing to her.

"You two aren't. I need you to stay here and alert me if someone is coming. Or if you spot her."

"We have no idea what she looks like," Lange said dryly.

"Just tell me if someone ventures too close."

After reluctant agreement, she crept back the way they'd come and then she headed to the east. If she circled around a cluster of trees, she would be able to see the Chaosphere field. Maybe she was over there.

Or maybe she was inside at a desk by herself, never allowed to be around others. Being kept solely for another.

Eviana gritted her teeth. This was why she was here. She wouldn't let that happen to her. She'd die before that came to fruition.

"Fucking Silas," she muttered when her braid got caught on some low hanging branches as she tried to quietly maneuver between the trees. The children wouldn't venture near, that was true, but disturbances in the trees still sometimes warranted an investigation by the Estate guards.

Finally freeing herself, she turned to continue on, then went still.

A young female stood several feet away. She couldn't be any older than seven or eight years. Her hair was more red than brown, and her turquoise eyes were hard as she narrowed them. She wore the same simple clothing as the other children. The grey color was stark against her skin tone, a shade lighter than Eviana's, and gods, she was beautiful.

"Who are you?" the child sneered, her lip curling as she surveyed Eviana.

The obvious disdain was a little jarring, but she didn't react. She was too well trained to show surprise. Instead, Eviana asked, "What are you doing in these woods? It's dangerous."

The girl's lips curled into something far too sinister for someone who should be innocent. "Is it?"

"Yes," Eviana answered. "So I'll ask again, what are you doing here?"

The child shrugged casually. "I'm not allowed near the other children so I come here."

"Why?"

She shrugged again. "It's safer."

That was an absurd statement.

"What are they protecting you from?" Eviana asked tightly.

"Oh, they're not protecting me from them," the child said with an eerie giggle. "They're protecting *them* from *me*."

"That's ridiculous," Eviana snapped, stepping closer. "You're a child."

"Am I?"

"Yes, you are, but you are in danger."

"The woods don't hurt me," she said with that dark smile.

"The Dreamlock Woods hurt everyone, child," Eviana retorted.

The child glided forward as though she were floating, her well-worn sneakers not even leaving prints behind. "What do you fear most? The Dread-Nymphs?"

"No," Eviana answered. "The Sprytes are worse. You do not wish to ever cross paths with one."

"Clever," the child mocked, stretching out an arm to glide her fingertips along the leaves of a fern.

"You should go back," Eviana said, the words making something in her chest ache. But she couldn't take her quite yet. She didn't have an escape plan in place. Lange had wanted to know what their plan was, and she didn't have that either. Then again, she hadn't expected the girl to simply walk up to her in the Dreamlock Woods.

The girl was drifting closer when Eviana asked, "How often do you come here?" Because none of this felt right. Something was off.

"Sometimes I am sent here. Other times I come here myself. I've been coming to these woods as long as I can remember," she answered.

"And you've never seen a Dread-Nymph? Or a Spryte?"

"Oh, I see them all the time," she answered, gesturing to her right.

Eviana stilled, her eyes falling closed. Of course this was all a godsdamn trap.

She turned slowly to see the towering woman. Her flowing dress was made entirely of greenery and florals. Antlers jutted out from her flowing hair the color of tree bark. Ivy wound around her head like a crown, and her eyes were red as blood.

A Spryte.

They were so much worse than the Dread-Nymphs. While the Imps preyed on your worst memories and the Nymphs survived on your fears and nightmares, the Sprytes were different. They stalked your dreams. Your heart's deepest desires. Your fears didn't paralyze you with a Spryte. No, they made you believe you were achieving your goals and desires. She'd been standing here, a willing target for minutes conversing with an apparition the Spryte wanted her to see. She could have been attacked at any time, too enamored with seeing the one thing that had kept her surviving and fighting.

Eviana reached for the dagger she had secured to her thigh, her fingers wrapping around the cool hilt. It was only then she realized she was trembling. Not out of fear, but because for these last minutes, she'd thought she'd been conversing with her daughter, and it had been nothing but bait. That tremble was from anger.

"Bold of you to reveal yourself before you had me bleeding," she sneered at the Spryte.

The Spryte only smiled, something just as sinister as the child's features had twisted into.

"And stupid of you to reveal your strategy. There's nothing left to lure me with," Eviana continued.

The Spryte lifted a hand, gesturing behind her.

Eviana glanced over her shoulder, where the child was still standing, watching her with interest. "The apparition is nothing anymore," she scoffed. "As I said, you foolishly gave up your element of surprise."

"She doesn't speak," the child said. "None of them do. Not the Sprytes or the Nymphs or the Imps. Not the trees or the flowers."

Then Eviana froze for an entirely different reason. Her blood went cold as she realized this truly was her, and she had . . . befriended the Dreamlock Woods? But why? And how?

The sound of leaves and twigs crunching had both the child and the Spryte spinning. The Spryte gestured once again to the child, and she nodded, turning and running back in the direction of the Estate. When Eviana turned back, the Spryte had disappeared just as Lange and Corbin came into view.

"I told you to wait," she snapped at the males.

"The children were all called inside, *bellana*," Lange said, scanning their surroundings. "What have you been doing? I thought you were going to see a different angle."

"I was. I mean, I am," she retorted, looking back the way the girl had run.

If that had truly been her . . .

How was she ever going to convince the girl to come with her?

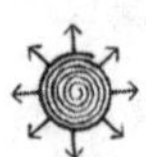

"We can't just snatch a child off the Chaosphere field and drag her into the woods," Corbin was arguing. "She'll be terrified."

"I don't hear you offering any better ideas," Lange retorted, popping some small berries they'd found into his mouth.

"And when she screams and cries? What's the plan then, genius?" Corbin deadpanned.

Lange shrugged. "Maybe you should just shift into a giant kitty cat and let her cuddle you."

"Shut up," Corbin muttered, kicking at him with his foot.

They were all seated around a small fire, trying to come up with something—anything—to move forward. The longer they stayed here, the more likely they were to be discovered. Maybe they already were. Maybe the child had already reported their presence, and they were already fucked.

The only saving grace in this right now was that Valter wasn't here yet. She'd know. Just like she'd known when he was close while they were in the back of the truck. Bond or no bond, she would know.

"We don't even know what she looks like," Corbin added, passing a piece of bread smeared with peanut butter to Eviana.

"True," Lange answered.

"Not entirely," she offered, taking the bread.

"That would have been helpful earlier," Lange deadpanned.

"I didn't know until this afternoon."

They both paused, and it was Corbin who was rubbing at his brow when he said, "Something you need to share, nightmare?

"She has reddish hair. More red than brown. Her eyes match mine," she answered, shifting where she sat. She hadn't shared about the encounter, wanting to keep it to herself for a little while. Why? She had no idea. But it was something that was hers. Hers and her daughter's. Theirs alone. Talking about it felt like she was letting too much in.

Letting them too close.

Providing a weakness.

"When did you see her?" Corbin asked, always too observant.

"This afternoon," she answered shortly.

"When, Eviana?" Lange growled, the flames of their fire dancing in the small gust of wind that fed it. When she pressed her lips together, he added, "We can't help if you keep information from us. Surely you've learned this by now."

She didn't say anything right away, debating what to reveal. She had to try, she supposed.

"She found me. In the woods," she finally answered.

"The fuck?" Lange said, sitting up straighter. "Why didn't you just grab her then? We could already be running."

"And go where?" Eviana hissed. "Where are we going to hide a child that Valter will be seeking as surely as he is hunting me? I can't take her until we have a plan."

"Maybe you should have thought of that before you dragged us all the way here," Lange spat back.

"Maybe you should go fuck yourself," she sneered.

"Everyone calm down," Corbin interjected. "Knowing what she looks like is helpful. We don't have to sit and watch the children for hours anymore trying to pick out which one is her. Now we just need to figure out our escape plan."

"And how to keep these cursed woods from preying on her," Lange muttered. "The three of us is one thing, but a child?"

The truth was, Eviana had been avoiding this part of the plan, hoping something would come to her on the journey to the Estate. But she'd come up short, and now it was fucking her over. Until they had a solid plan, they couldn't take her.

"Let's say the woods weren't an issue," Eviana ventured, interrupting Corbin and Lange's bickering. "Where would you suggest we go?"

"To Tessa," Lange said immediately.

"We have no idea where she is," Corbin countered. "Where do we even start?"

"Arius Kingdom, I suppose," Lange mused.

"Absolutely not," Eviana interjected. "I cannot set foot in Arius Kingdom. It's too . . . No."

"We could try Achaz Kingdom," Corbin said, pulling on the back of his neck. "With the rumors we've heard, I don't think she's there, but it is closer."

"Except we have to go deeper into the woods," Lange said flatly. "Not to mention cross the Wynfell River."

"Which wouldn't be an issue for Corbin," Eviana said, things starting to fall into place in her mind. "And I already told you the woods wouldn't be an issue."

"That was hypothetical, *bellana*. The woods will absolutely be an issue, and I still cannot go along with making a child endure them."

"She wouldn't be enduring them," she replied. "She has befriended them."

The two males stared at her, clearly not knowing what to say or if to even believe her. She couldn't blame them. For hours, she'd been trying to work out the same.

Priya would have powerful earth magic, just like her. Then there was Mansel's Nith blood. Earth and creativity. The Sprytes, Nymphs, and Imps were spirits of nature and dreams. Clearly her power made her connected to them somehow. If they could use that, they could easily go deeper into the woods. No one would hunt them there, and the child would be able to keep the woods at bay.

In theory, anyway.

She had no idea how deep that power went, but in the end, it was all they had to go on.

"We go to Achaz Kingdom," Eviana said in the silence that had descended. "From there, we figure out a way to get in contact with Tessa."

Lange was shaking his head. "This isn't a plan. This is banking on dreams."

"What better place to do that than in the Dreamlock Woods?"

"This place is nightmares and tricks," he retorted. "Not hopes and dreams."

"Then please share your superior plan," she said flatly, holding her palm above the ground and toying with her magic. Soil swirled, bits of leaves and debris among it.

Then it was swept away on a gust of wind.

She lifted her eyes, glaring at Lange.

"Let's sleep on it," Corbin said. "Let's get some rest, and discuss this again in the morning. Maybe something will come to us."

Lange muttered an agreement, but Eviana said nothing. She was taking the first watch tonight, and she remained silent as the males settled down beside each other. Corbin's arm looped over Lange's waist, keeping him close, and it didn't take long for them to slip into slumber. Even breathing and steady heartbeats. They always slept more deeply together.

Lange wasn't wrong. Tessa was probably their best bet. There was some kind of mutual understanding between them, with her visits at the Faven palace and the "gifts" she would leave behind. Eviana simply had no idea how to contact her.

With a sigh, she stood, stretching her legs and back, then she stilled at the sound of crunching leaves. Godsdammit. She was too exhausted to deal with a Dread-Nymph right now.

Retrieving her dagger, she made her way in the direction the sound had come from. She could handle the Nymph. Then she could rest while Corbin took over the watch.

Her steps were slow and tentative, trying to spot the Nymph in the dark. They blended in too easily, one with the woods and all that. So it was no surprise to her when she didn't find a Nymph, but instead was pulled into a nightmare.

"Eve," Valter purred as she rounded a small curve in the path she was trying to follow.

She swallowed thickly. *It's a vision*, she reminded herself. She just needed to play along and not get sucked in until she could find the Nymph.

"I will admit, you were rather clever with this whole thing," Valter went on. "Then again, I'm not surprised. You are my Source for a reason." He ventured closer, a flashlight in one hand that lit up the area around them.

Eviana scanned the trees, hoping the light would reveal the Dread-Nymph, but there was nothing. It had to be staying hidden in the shadows and trees, which was inconvenient and irritating.

"I had you bred especially for me," Valter continued, close enough now to wind strands of her hair around his finger. Then he yanked on them. "And still you chose to betray me. After all I have given you."

She hardly felt the pain in her scalp, too used to his mannerisms after decades. It wasn't real anyway.

"Yet a part of me always knew this day would come," he continued. "It's why I took . . . precautions."

Eviana gritted her teeth. Where the fuck was this godsdamn Nymph?

"I heard you met her today," Valter said, circling around her now, his fingers trailing along her shoulder and down her spine. "She is beautiful, isn't she? Just like her mother."

"Stop," Eviana hissed, unable to help herself. Even knowing this wasn't real, she couldn't sit and listen to this.

"Finally, a reaction," he crooned. "It has been so long since you've let those emotions slip. I've missed our time together correcting that behavior."

Eviana pressed her lips together, taking a few steps forward. She felt his hand slip from her back. She just needed to go deeper into the woods. The Nymph had to be hiding there.

"But after all these years, those behavior corrections wouldn't serve my purposes anyway, would they, my flower? I knew they would eventually become useless, so I took precautions for that too," he said from behind her.

She ignored him, making her way to the trees. Her hold tightened around the hilt of the dagger, and her eyes strained to see in the shadows.

"You can come out, my sweet Priya," he called, and Eviana paused as the child emerged from the trees down the path. She wore the same clothing as earlier today, her hair now braided in a plait over her shoulder. Her smile was wide and terrifying as those turquoise eyes landed on Eviana.

Valter stalked past her, and when he reached the child's side, he held out his hand. Priya slipped her little fingers into his palm without question, still holding her stare.

"You did well, my sweet Priya," Valter praised, squeezing her fingers in his own. "Thank you for helping me find her."

"What?" Eviana asked, breathing suddenly far too difficult.

Not real, she told herself. *It's not real. Find the fucking Nymph.*

She spun in a circle, frantically scanning the trees and bushes, all the dark and shadowed places. This was going too far. She should call for Lange and Corbin. She should—

She spun back, both of them watching her with matching amusement.

"Priya," she gasped, the name a breathy cry she nearly choked on. "Priya, you don't understand. He—He will hurt you."

"Hurt me?" Priya repeated, those innocent eyes going hard. "The Arius Lord would never hurt me. He's the only one who comes to see me. He brings me pretty dresses and food. He gave me these woods and the friends I have in them."

"He can't *give* you the woods," she snapped, dread and fear sinking into her bones.

"But he did," she insisted. "He lets me come here whenever I like, and now, because I helped him, I get to go with him too."

"No," she rasped, shaking her head. Then louder, she cried, "No!"

Spinning in a circle again, she searched for the Nymph. This death would not be quick like the last. She would drag this one out for making her live this nightmare. Its screams would wake the others and be a warning of what would happen if they came near her again.

"Why don't you go back to the Estate and finish packing your things, sweet Priya," Valter was saying, and Eviana glanced over her shoulder. He was crouched before the child, holding her slim shoulders. "We are leaving at sunrise, remember?"

She nodded, bouncing on her toes in excitement.

Valter pushed back to his full height, patting her head as he added, "Don't forget the extra sweets I brought for you."

The child giggled before she turned and ran, racing in the direction of the Estate. Eviana could swear the trees and flowers reached for her as she went.

Then she was left alone with Valter in the Dreamlock Woods.

"This isn't real," she gritted out. "But when I see you again, I will end you."

He sighed. "You cannot kill me, Eviana. The bond does not allow it, even if you have managed to block other facets of it." He slinked forward like the snake he was, and when he stood in front of her once more, he gripped her jaw. "And while I want nothing more than to wring your neck and watch the light fade from your eyes for your betrayal, I find that will be far too merciful, and I am not a merciful lord."

Gods, did she know the truth of that statement.

"Where are your companions?" he demanded in a low command.

But he was right. That bond was blocked, even in this nightmare.

"I don't know what you're talking about," she replied.

"It amazes me that such a short time apart can undo all the training I have instilled in you over the decades," he spat, his fingers squeezing her jaw tighter. "I know there were two with you. Where are they?"

"I left them long ago," she retorted, unsure why she would lie in a vision. "They were slowing me down and becoming a hindrance to my plans. Hopefully they died in the woods."

Those words made his lips turn up in a small, sordid smile. "Glad to see the viciousness is still there, my flower," he said, leaning in to run his nose along her cheek. "You'll need it to survive the rest of your immortal years."

Then his lips were on hers as shadows wrapped around her wrist, squeezing and bending. She cried out, Valter swallowing the sound as the dagger dropped to the ground.

The dagger she had been keeping to kill the Dread-Nymph.

The dagger that would have killed Valter.

But she couldn't kill him, just like he said. The Source bond was there, even if blocked.

And this wasn't a vision.

There was no Dread-Nymph.

This was a nightmare and not one she was going to wake up from.

Valter pulled back, her hands now wrenched behind her back and restrained by his shadows. He pulled something dark from his pocket. Metal that swallowed up the darkness around them before he lifted it and brought it to her throat. A thin chain that was freezing against her skin. He clasped it at her neck, and her power thrashed and howled in her soul before it was nothing.

Before she was nothing.

Helpless once more.

"Did you honestly think I would not find you?" Valter snarled, his finger slipping beneath the chain and yanking her forward. "Did you honestly think I didn't know exactly where you would go? That I have not been giving you crumbs of information about the child to ensure you cared just enough? You are predictable, Eviana. So godsdamn predictable. She was the one weakness I allowed you to have and all for this very purpose."

A tendril of his shadows coiled around the chain at her throat, and then he was yanking her forward by that too. By a godsdamn leash.

"You got what you wanted though, didn't you?" he said with a sneer as she was forced to follow him. Always a step behind her Master. "Now you will get to watch her grow up in my home, never able to tell her the truth. But you'll watch her adore me and love me the way you were always supposed to. You'll watch it all, my flower."

A tear had escaped, and she wished she could reach up to wipe it away. She'd be damned if Valter saw her cry. She tipped her head, trying to wipe it away on her shoulder when her eyes caught on feline ones in the trees. High up in the branches, a giant mountain cat was watching them. Soft glowing eyes were on her.

Stupid fools.

If they knew what was good for them, they'd leave her to her fate.

But she desperately hoped they wouldn't leave Priya behind.

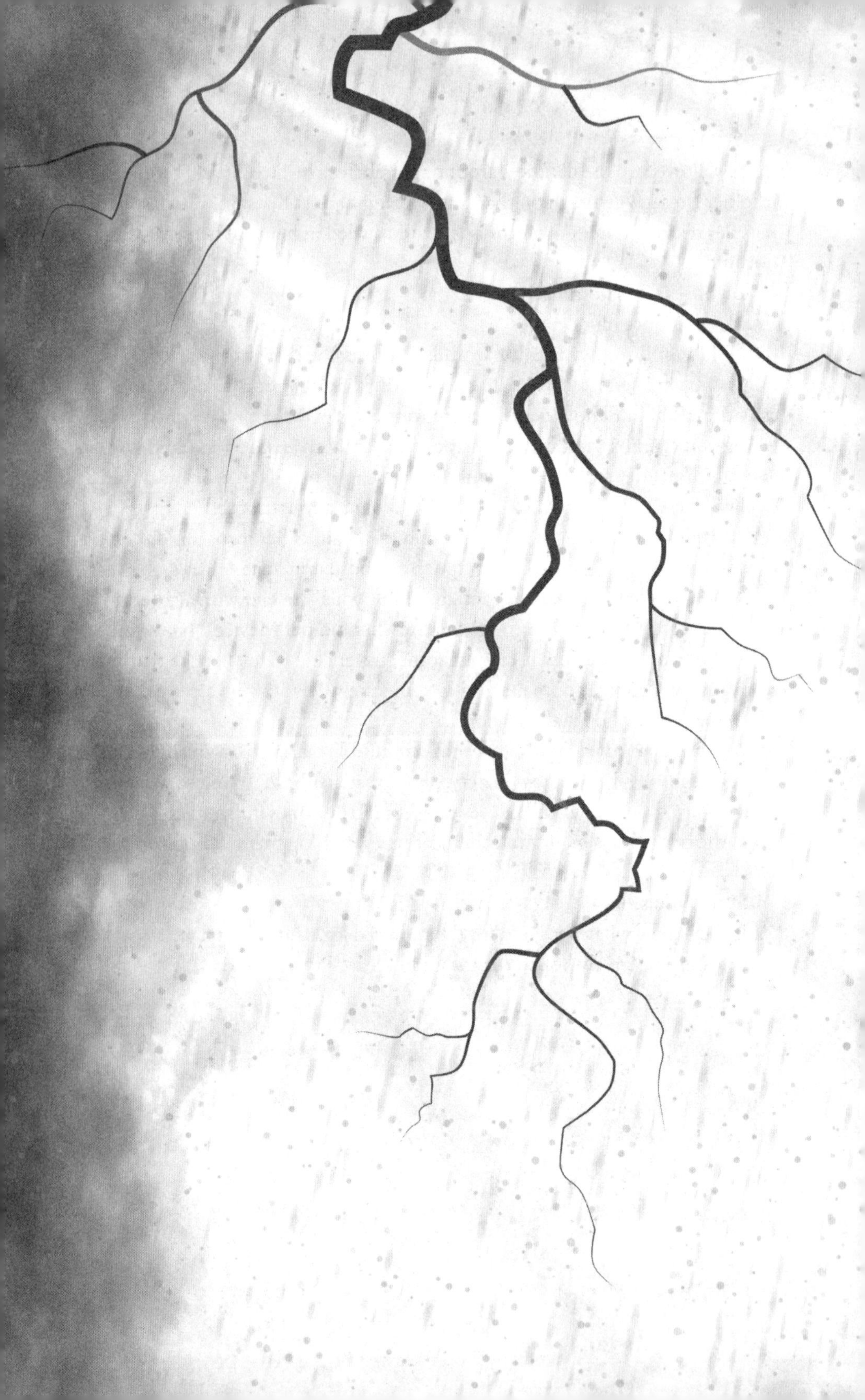

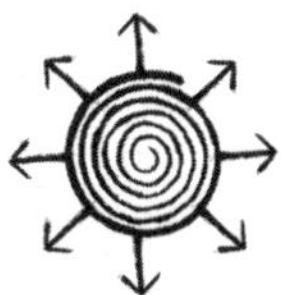

32
TESSA

"The day is finally here," Achaz said from a throne at the front of a great hall. Two others sat in thrones on either side of him. Tessa didn't know who they were. She didn't even know where she was.

Turning in her seat in the front row, she found floor-to-ceiling windows overlooking a sprawling city. It reminded her of the skyscrapers and the hustle-and-bustle of Rockmoor, but this wasn't Arius Kingdom. This wasn't even Devram. There were seraphs here, flying among the clouds.

She shifted, turning back to face the front. Others stood on either side of the dais. She scanned them, finding Dexter, his hands clasped behind his back and standing at attention. Down the line was another seraph she recognized. What had his name been? Illithor? And next to him stood another who looked similar. She was certain she'd seen him before too, along with the female that stood beside him. Her honey-colored eyes were locked on Tessa, a madness to them she resonated with. While the seraphs were all in armor of some sort, she was all in black, from her boots to the hood over her head, an ashy-blonde braid snaking out of it. The hood darkened her features, and she even wore gloves, as though she was a shadow herself.

"We have almost eradicated the last of the threats," Achaz went on. "We have nearly restored balance to the realms, save for one final task." Golden eyes flashed to another. "Bring them."

Then Arius and Serafina were being herded to the front of the room, gasps of surprise mixed with sharp mutters of disapproval. Arius took a step in front of Serafina as though to shield her, but she stepped to his side once more. Stronger together than separate.

"This is a waste of everyone's time, Achaz," Arius drawled, clearly not fazed by whatever was happening. "You cannot kill us. Killing a being that emerged from the Chaos requires more than magic and pretty words."

"Do not mock me, Arius," Achaz hissed, lightning flaring from his palms and skittering across the floor.

Instinctively, Tessa lifted her feet to avoid the shock, but she still felt it faintly through her chair.

"You think I do not know what is required to kill you both? You think I have not spent centuries planning precisely how to deal with your betrayal?" Achaz spat, gripping the arms of his throne. "One remains, and I have found it. Taken there millenniums ago by betrayal just as deep. Thanks to our granddaughter," his eyes flashed to Tessa, and she shrank back in her chair. What did she have to do with any of this? "Mirror gates still remain in Devram, and now that the last of a bloodline has fallen there, we can finally venture into that realm. I will find the last of the Requiem Swords. Then I will return and finally end this."

"You will not succeed, Achaz," Serafina said, lifting her chin.

Power hummed off her. Or maybe that was Achaz. Both? Either way, Tessa's power was growing restless with all the power in this room.

"What makes you think I will fail?" Achaz sneered.

"Your dreams are full of corruption and deceit," she answered, the silver of her dress glimmering in the low lighting. "While others dream of compassion and harmony." She spun then, her skirt flaring, and she looked out over everyone in attendance. "And as long as those dreams live on, there is hope. Not until dreams die is hope lost."

"Then I shall kill you last," Achaz sneered, pushing to his feet. "You speak of compassion and harmony when your very actions caused this in the first place."

"You forgot our purpose long ago," Arius interjected. "In all things there must be balance. We cannot take more."

"We are beginnings and endings!" Achaz bellowed. "We are *the fucking balance."*

Arius shook his head. "This is an Everlasting War, Achaz."

"It will be done with your own ending," Achaz replied coldly.

Arius turned his back on him then, emerald eyes locking onto Tessa. "Or a new beginning."

She gasped as she sat up, light and dark swirling around her as she choked down gulps of air. Sweat covered her, and her heart was beating far too fast.

"Easy, baby girl," Luka said from her right, rough fingertips brushing down her back. "We've been trying to wake you for the last five minutes."

Another hand cupped her chin, gently turning her head to meet emerald eyes.

Emerald eyes just like Arius's.

"You're okay, Tessa," Theon said quietly, his thumb brushing along her skin. "It was a vision."

His darkness was out too, hovering around him, and she glanced over shoulder to find Luka's black flames doing the same.

"We were trying to reach you any way we could," Theon explained, drawing her focus back to him. "Do you want to talk about it?"

She shook her head, pushing hair out of her face with a trembling hand. "I just want to shower. Rinse off," she said, pushing away from both of them to climb off the bed.

"Tessa," Theon called after her, but she waved them off, shutting the bathroom door behind her. Leaning against it, she let her head fall back, her eyes closing.

The mirror gates.

Those fucking mirror gates.

There was something here that Achaz needed, and he would use the mirror gates to come here and find it.

All the more reason to destroy them. She could destroy them all, save for one. Those who wanted to leave, return home, could go, and then she'd destroy that one too. The Fates wouldn't be able to come here, and neither would the gods. It would solve all their problems. She could do this. *This* was her destiny. Her purpose.

Lifting a hand, Chaos swirled, carrying a message to the only one who could likely help her.

It was fifteen minutes later when she stepped from the shower and a message returned. She plucked it out of the swirl of magic, reading the note:

Let's start with the Falein Estate. Tomorrow night. Meet in the kitchen when your bodyguards have fallen asleep.

Setting the note in the drawer with her things, she pulled a brush through her hair before returning to the bedroom. She wasn't surprised to find them both still awake, two sets of eyes watching her warily.

"What did you see, Tessa?" Luka asked as Theon pressed a bottle of water into her hand.

"Nothing important," she answered before she took several long swallows and replaced the cap.

"I find that hard to believe. You were trapped in that vision. Has that happened before?" Luka pressed.

She pursed her lips because the answer was no. She'd never been *trapped* in a vision.

Except she had.

During assessments. But this wasn't that. This was just her power being uncontrollable.

"Let's go back to bed. We can discuss this more in the morning," Theon said, his hand landing on the small of her back. He urged her forward, and she crawled back beneath the blankets.

Luka was immediately there, pulling her into him, his palm hot even through the thin material of the shirt she wore. Theon settled in behind her, his arm draping over her waist and resting on her hip. Normally this would settle her soul but not tonight. Tonight her power was hungry and wanting. Tonight she craved Chaos, and tomorrow she would have it.

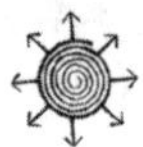

She crept down the stairs, her bare feet light on each step. It had taken Theon and Luka forever to fall asleep tonight, mostly because they were becoming more insistent about her telling them of her vision the night before. But they didn't need to be involved. She'd destroyed two mirrors now, and both times had been catastrophic. Last time, Luka had nearly died. She'd go in, destroy the mirror, and Travel back. She'd be back in bed before sunrise, and if they discovered she was gone . . .

She'd deal with that later.

She was under no obligation to report her actions to them. They didn't own her. No one did.

The faint glow of the light they always left on over the kitchen sink guided her to the room, and she found Brecken there, leaning against the counter.

"What are you doing here?" she asked, pausing in the doorway.

"I asked him to come with us, wild fury," Tristyn said, coming up behind her. He brushed past her, dressed completely in black like she was. He didn't have any weapons strapped to him, but she was sure he was armed. She had one of her gold daggers strapped to a thigh, while a black one with carvings etched into the blade adorned the other. "You sure you don't want to involve St. Orcas and Mors?"

Tessa nodded. She didn't want them anywhere near this. They'd done enough. Luka was barely recovered, only able to banish his wings again starting a few days ago, and Theon was the main reason she was destroying all the mirrors to begin with.

"You know where it is, right? It should be a quick trip," she answered.

"I don't know exactly where it is," Tris admitted. "That's where he comes in."

He inclined his head to Brecken, and Tessa's brows rose in surprise. "*You* know where the mirror gates are?"

"Not all of them, but some," Brecken answered. "Honestly, I'm a little offended you didn't think to ask me in the first place."

Tessa rolled her eyes. "I forget you're actually on our side half the time, and the other half I spend wondering if you're going to double-cross us."

Brecken sent her a fake smile. "I already told you: I have no desire to return to my home world. You destroying the mirror gates aids in my cause."

"Is that why you've searched for them?" she asked as the males crowded closer to her. "Were you trying to destroy them yourself?"

Brecken shrugged, taking her hand in his. "That was the hope. Some day. And it appears today is one of those days. Shall we?"

His smile had morphed into something destructive now, and she knew her lips mirrored his. She was bouncing on her toes in anticipation, not of destroying the mirror gate, but of getting out of the Underground. Seeing the sky. Breathing fresh air.

"Let's go," Tristyn said, grabbing her other hand.

One of them Traveled them all, and a second later, her bare feet were on cool, frost-covered grass. She looked around, pulling her bow from a swirl of magic did, and it took her a minute before she realized where they were.

Of course, the Falein mirror gate was on Ekayan Island.

She frowned, looking up at Brecken. "This is going to be a problem. How'd we even get here without the wards detecting us?"

"You, of course," he answered. "You and that delightful ability to cross wards without being noticed."

Okay, that made sense, but . . .

"Is the mirror in the catacombs? I can't destroy those, Brecken," she hissed. "Some of those texts predate Devram."

"We're on the opposite side of the island," he explained. "And to the north."

That explained the fog rolling along the shore and obscuring their view of the sea.

"Let's get on with this then," she answered, looping her bow across her chest. "Lead the way."

"It will be a bit of a walk," he replied, heading east. "I didn't want to take us straight there, just in case."

She nodded, bringing her hands to her mouth and blowing on them. He could have warned them it would be cold. She never thought of that anymore. Luka was usually with her, and she'd become used to him and his dragonfire always keeping her plenty warm.

They'd only been walking a few minutes when dark shapes prowled from the fog, and she smiled as Nylah and Roan came to her sides. Her fingers sank into plush fur, and Roan nuzzled into her knee, a soft huff coming from him.

"I've missed you too," she whispered, stopping to crouch before her wolves. They refused to come to the Underground, and she couldn't blame them. She was close to refusing to go back as she tasted the sea air and felt the night breeze kiss her face. She suddenly didn't care how cold it was. She was outside, beneath the stars, with her wolves at her sides.

She was free.

"Come on, wild fury," Tristyn urged with a soft smile. "Destruction first; play later."

She smirked, pushing back to her feet. They continued on, and with each step, she sank deeper into her power. She'd need all of it to destroy the mirror gate, and while she was certain there would be guards to take from, she couldn't bank on there being a lot of life to refill her reserves. To be honest, she wasn't entirely sure how she was going to keep refilling her magic wells. She couldn't simply go around killing people for her own gain. That was preposterous. And she couldn't take from Theon and Luka all the time. They'd have to drink Fae blood to replenish their power and would eventually face the same fate as Axel.

"Can you give me an idea of what we'll be facing?" Tessa asked into the night. "Is it under water like the Celeste Estate? Below ground like the Acropolis?"

Brecken shook his head. "I can't really explain it. You'll see when we get there. You'll probably sense it," he added. "You always could sense the one in Lake Moonmist."

"What?" she asked in confusion. "I had no idea that a mirror gate was there."

"Just because you didn't know what it was doesn't mean you couldn't sense it," he countered. "Why do you think Dex always deterred you from going there?"

She frowned, mulling that over in her mind. Dex had never outright told her not to go there, but now that she thought about it, every time it was suggested, he steered them in another direction.

Except once.

One time she'd been insistent, and Dex had finally relented. She didn't remember much of that night, and she'd always blamed it on drinking far too much during the excursion. But now . . .

"What happened there, Brecken? That night? Did I really lose control?"

Brecken sighed, casting her a pitying look. "Yeah, Tess, you did, but it wasn't your fault."

"What do you mean, it wasn't my fault?" she demanded, her power restless as emotion rolled through her. She tamped them down, not wanting Theon and Luka to feel the sudden shift. "There were . . . People *died*. Innocent people. Others from the Estate . . . Dex always said it was because of me."

"Your power may have caused it, but he knew it would, Tessa. He knew what taking you there would do," Brecken said grimly. "They were testing you. Seeing how strong you were. You were given the Mark to neutralize your power, just like the Fae are given upon birth. If not for that Mark, the Fae would come into their power around ten years, just like the Legacy do. It's another way they control them here. But you are not Fae, and as you grew, your power was likely angry at being trapped."

She'd always felt it. That thing inside her that would lift its head. That would thrash and make her feel something *other*.

"Anyway, they got you drunk. You already had trouble controlling what you didn't know you were. Intoxicated? It was worse. And then, having you by the mirror gate? Your power took over, much like it does now at times. It was what they wanted to see. They'd always known the Mark wouldn't be enough, but now they knew what it would take to contain you," he went on.

"But what happened that night? How did I . . ." She trailed off because how many times had Dex held that over her head? How many times had Oralia chastised her and reminded her of the messes Dex had to clean up because of her?

"Your power takes, Tessa," Brecken said gently. "It took before they could get you subdued. After that, they started mixing a tonic into your food, particularly your doughnuts."

She stopped mid-step, staring up at him. "They drugged me?"

"In a sense, yes," Brecken said, glancing over her head at Tristyn, who had remained silent during all of this.

Her gaze snapped to Tristyn, eyes narrowing. "You knew?"

"I suspected," he admitted. "I didn't know how they were keeping your power subdued, but that night, you were felt across the realm. They took a risk letting your power manifest like that."

"But you still couldn't find me?"

He shook his head. "We knew the general vicinity after that night, but we had to be sure. And even if we had figured out it was you, we needed a solid plan in place. You never would have agreed to simply come with us. You know that."

He had a point. Back then, she would have believed anything Dex said. If Tristyn, or anyone for that matter, had shown up and tried to tell her she was being used and kept hidden for something nefarious later, she would have laughed in their face. Mother Cordelia had done a superb job of convincing her she was worthless and good for nothing. Why would anybody bother hiding her away for something so grand?

It still stung that no one had even *tried* to get her out of there, even knowing all the facts. Knowing they had lost her. Knowing they'd been searching. Knowing she had been so groomed by Dex and Cordelia, and effectively Rordan, that it wouldn't have mattered if they had come for her anyway. No one had even *tried*.

Which led her back to thoughts of her parents. A god and a fury. Untamed and Chaos. And Xan had told them they needed to bring her mother here. She didn't know how to feel. She didn't know what to think.

Despite everything, even having Theon and Luka and the others now, she still felt so alone sometimes.

"We're nearly there," Brecken said, cutting into her thoughts.

"Nearly where?" Tessa asked with a slight frown, looking around. There was nothing different. No buildings or runes. Just the frost-covered ground, the rolling fog, and the sea beyond.

Brecken sent her a mischievous wink, gesturing ahead. "Surely you feel it?"

She was still frowning at him when she *did* feel something. When she felt that thing in her soul snap its head up in anticipation. When it pulled and tugged, her feet moving of their own accord. Her skin was buzzing. The gold bands on her wrists flared, while her power sparked at her fingertips.

A hand landed on her shoulder, gently squeezing and pulling her back. She looked up into russet eyes, Tristyn giving her a reassuring smile. "I can feel it too," he said. "Not like you, but as a deity, I can sense it."

Brecken had moved ahead of them, taking the lead, and her gaze bounced from him to their surroundings, studying the fog. "But can you see it?"

"Not yet," Tris murmured. "Are you cold?"

"A little," she admitted, and before the words had even finished leaving her lips, he was shrugging off his signature leather jacket and passing it to her. She gave him a small smile. "Thanks."

He nodded, pausing beside her and helping her slip it on. There was another violent lurch in her soul as her power sparked with excitement, that same spark flowing throughout her body. Her fingers and toes tingled, and she couldn't figure out where this damn mirror gate was. But . . . was the fog *rippling* like glass?

"Breck, you said we were close," she called to him.

He turned, walking backwards towards the fog. "It's just around—" But his eyes went wide, his wings appearing suddenly as he gasped.

"Brecken?" Tessa asked, her power swirling as she lost a little bit of control with the sudden panic. She already had her bow overhead, an arrow appearing in her hand. Nocking it, she started forward, her pace increasing. Then she was running as she saw blood flowing from the corner of Brecken's mouth, and he dropped to his knees, as if in slow motion.

Behind him stood another. Pale blonde hair glimmered in the moonlight. She wore all black as well, and she held Tessa's gaze as she placed her foot on Brecken's back and pushed him forward.

Oralia.

Brecken grunted, falling face first to the ground, and that was when she saw the blade sticking out of his back, right between his wings.

"What did you do?" Tessa gasped, trying to comprehend what she was seeing, but it wasn't connecting. She couldn't—This couldn't be happening.

"Taking care of a traitor," Oralia sneered in that too high voice. "I tried to tell Dex he was double-crossing us for years, but no one ever believed me." She bent down, gripping the hilt of the blade and twisting.

An agonized sound came from Brecken, and Tessa raised her bow, taking aim. But Nylah and Roan were already attacking, knowing what she wanted. Oralia snarled, moving to wrench the blade from Brecken's back, but she was too slow. Nylah reached her first, her teeth sinking into her forearm, while Roan tackled her.

"Don't kill her!" Tessa cried.

Not yet anyway.

"Tris, keep her here," she added as she ran the remaining distance, dropping to Brecken's side.

"Brecken? Brecken, don't move. Let me . . . We'll take you back," she said, her words becoming too jumbled as she watched the blood pour out around the long dagger. He turned his head, one arm moving and his hand seeming to search. She snatched it up, squeezing his fingers. "We'll come back another time," she tried to soothe.

Oralia started laughing. A high-pitched thing that grated on her ears as much as her voice did. As much as anything the female said or did.

Roan was pinning her to the ground, his massive paws on her chest. Nylah still had her teeth in her arm, and Tristyn was crouched beside her, a hand wrapped around her throat where a sage glow was emanating.

And she was laughing.

"What is so fucking funny?" Tessa demanded, her voice hard.

"You can't save him," she said between her laughter. "Not even the fucking Witches can save him. Look at his wings."

Tessa blinked, her gaze going to the feathered appendages, and she tried to swallow her gasp as the tips of the feathers turned deathly grey, slowly decaying and starting to disintegrate.

Brecken's fingers squeezed hers weakly, and she lifted her gaze to Tristyn, once again trying to understand.

He was somber when he said, "Just like there are special blades designed to end the dragons, Arius and Sargon answered in kind, creating blades to end the seraphs. It is absorbing the magic he stole while killing him from the inside out."

"No," she said, shaking her head. Not again. She couldn't be watching someone she cared about dying in front of her again. Maybe Xan would know. Maybe—

A fresh burst of laughter came from Oralia, and Tessa could see nothing but red.

She stood, striding around Brecken's body as he tried to push onto his knees. Looping her bow over her chest, she plunged the arrow deep into Oralia's side.

That laughter turned to a cry of pain.

"Stand her up," Tessa sneered.

Roan backed off, but Nylah still held her arm while Tristyn yanked her to her feet.

"What are you going to do, Tessa?" Oralia managed to taunt despite her gasps of pain. "Create yet another mess? Sooner or later, you'll fuck up so badly, no one will be able to fix it. Sooner or later, everyone will finally realize what a fucking *waste* it was to keep you so pampered and hidden. 'Go to Tessa, Oralia,'" she mimicked. "'Make sure Tessa isn't alone, Oralia.' 'Make sure Tessa isn't doing something stupid, Oralia.'" She paused then, her face twisted with hatred. "Why the fuck are you smiling?"

And Tessa was. The smile on her face was pure madness as she stared back at Oralia.

"Because I am going to kill you," Tessa said, the madness seeping into her voice. She was calm. Too calm. Even she knew that. "I'm going to kill you, and I'm going to enjoy every second of it. Then I'm going to leave the *mess* behind for Dexter to find. Let him clean it up and know that the same fate is waiting for him."

"They should have let me take your magic when Katya was taken from me. You are such an ungrateful, spoiled cunt—"

But her words became a garbled scream as Tessa pulled a sword from her power, the same dark blade and runes as her arrows and daggers. Tristyn barely moved out of the way in time as that blade sliced one of Oralia's wings clean off. It fell to the ground, and Tessa made sure to step on it when she raised her sword and did the same to the other.

Her screams filled the dark night; Tessa's smile only grew.

Oralia sank to her knees, her back pouring blood.

"How utterly *pathetic* to be so *weak*," Tessa said casually, dragging the tip of her blade on the ground behind her as she circled Oralia.

Tristyn had released her throat, but that strange glowing power of his was still wrapped around it. Nylah still held firm. Between the two of them, something was preventing Oralia from Traveling. The bitch wasn't going anywhere.

"Shut up!" Oralia snapped, catching herself on her hands as she fell forward. "They kept making me wait to take my power. They kept telling me that something better would come."

Her words were garbled gasps, and Tessa stopped in front of her once more. Pressing the tip of her blade beneath Oralia's chin, she tipped her face up. Tessa's head tilted to the side. "You were the back-up plan."

"You have no idea what you're talking about," Oralia snarled, blood dripping down her neck where the blade had pierced flesh.

Tessa smiled. "Without any power, you were easily controlled. They needed you powerless so that if things went wrong, if Dexter or Brecken were killed, they still had an option. It was never about finding you the perfect power."

"Fuck you," she spat.

"And now you will die as powerless as the day you were born. You got to watch everyone else get their gifts and learn to use them, while you were told to save yourself for something special." Tessa barked a humorless huff of laughter. "I know the feeling. I almost pity you. Too bad I don't."

Before Oralia could speak again, Tessa plunged her sword through her chest so thoroughly it protruded out of her back. Then she was dissolving into nothing but golden embers and darkest ashes that were scattering along the beach.

Her wings remained though.

And true to her word, she'd leave them for Dexter to find.

She turned then, rushing back to Brecken and dropping beside him once more. He'd managed to roll onto his side, but gods, his pallor was as grey as his decaying wings.

Wings that were scarcely there anymore.

"No," she breathed, her hands hovering over her face, his chest, trying to decide what to do. Something inside of her was breaking, the pain searing.

"There's . . . nothing . . . Tess," he gasped out, reaching for her hand.

His fingers were freezing and bony. Frail in her trembling hand.

"We can take you back," she said through tears. "We can take you back. Maybe Xan knows . . ."

But she trailed off as cracked lips tried to tilt up in his mischievous smile.

They never made it.

"I'm . . . fine," he rasped, his cheeks sinking in as she watched on.

"Brecken!" she cried, feeling Tristyn come up behind her. Gods, this *hurt* as if she was feeling his pain, his death. "I'm sorry. I'm so . . . This isn't how things were supposed to go!"

His fingers flexed in her hand again. "I'm fine," he rasped again. "I can face Arius . . . knowing I was . . . on the right side."

She shook her head, smoothing hair back from a damp brow.

Hair that fell out as she brushed it back, and she yanked her hand back.

"Breck," she cried again, his name a broken sob as that thing in her soul cracked even more. "I'm so sorry."

"Be . . . who you . . . were meant to be, Tessa," he gasped.

With tears streaming down her face, she looked up at Tristyn. "Give me some lull-leaf."

He didn't question her, crouching down to reach into the pocket of his jacket she was still wearing. He lit it, handing it to Tessa, and she brought it to Brecken's lips.

"A fucking . . . saint," he gasped, before inhaling a ragged breath.

One more.

And then he stilled.

Tessa tipped her head back and screamed. Another sacrifice made because of her. Another life taken because of her. She was beginnings and endings, and what good was it if she couldn't save those she loved? And why did she feel like she was dying right beside him?

"Um, Tessa? I know you're grieving, but we have another issue," Tristyn said, suddenly standing. He had two curved blades in his hands now, and her wolves were closing in, staying close, as inky darkness rolled along the ground, mixing with the dense fog.

She barely had a moment to panic before it caressed her, sliding up her body like a lover.

Then it tightened around her throat, and her magic bit back as Theon stepped from the rolling black mist.

He looked from her to Tristyn, then to the broken body of Brecken and the lone wings on the ground.

His voice was lethal when he said tightly, "I don't know what the fuck I'm interrupting, but we need to go."

"I can't—" Tessa started, the ache in her chest agony now, but Theon interrupted.

"Something is wrong with Luka. Cienna said he's dying."

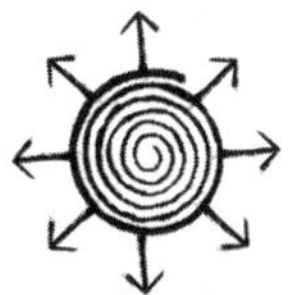

33
THEON

They didn't wait for Blackheart. Tessa grabbed his hand, Traveling them back to the Underground penthouse. Seconds later, Tristyn appeared with an unmoving Brecken.

He felt Tessa suck in a sharp breath at the sight of them, and Tristyn gave her a sad nod. "Go to Luka. I'll handle this."

Tessa nodded, swallowing thickly, and while Theon wanted to know what the fuck had happened, he was feeling too many other things to properly care right now.

"Upstairs," Theon said tightly, anger and fear mixing in his gut.

As if his voice broke her from some sort of trance, she took off, racing up the stairs. So godsdamn fast when she needed to be.

He followed, taking the stairs two at a time. Or trying to. Because he was feeling his Guardian dying all over again. It was only sheer adrenaline that had allowed him to go find her, and that adrenaline was waning.

By the time he made it to their bedroom on the second floor, Tessa was already on her knees at Luka's side, Blackheart's leather jacket hanging off her.

He and Luka had realized she was gone at the same time, her emotions down the bond jolting them awake to find no blonde-haired female between them. How she'd managed to crawl from the bed without either of them feeling her was still a mystery, but they were up in seconds.

"I'll check the kitchen," Luka had said as Theon had made his way to the bathroom.

He'd known she wasn't in there. The door was open, lights off, but he'd gone in there anyway. And thank the gods he had because just as he was turning to leave and go downstairs with Luka, he'd spotted the corner of a piece of paper sticking out of a drawer.

Yanking it open, he'd found a note mixed in with her hair things, a growl of anger escaping as he'd read it.

"Luka!" he'd yelled, his strides purposeful now. Something in his chest was writhing, and he'd assumed it was because Tessa was in the fucking Falein Kingdom. But then he'd found Luka, collapsed on the ground in only the lightweight pants he'd slipped into.

He'd realized then what was happening, his mind going back to Lake Moonmist when Luka had been stabbed and he'd been in so much agony, he couldn't function. Knowing what was coming, he'd braced himself, yelling for Razik and Eliza, who were in Luka's usual room across the hall. They'd gotten Axel, Kat, and Xan.

The Mark on Luka's chest had been pulsing a faint gold color, growing brighter, but then it had started to shift, growing darker.

Cienna had appeared, despite not staying at the penthouse with them while in the Underground. Her violet eyes had met his, and all she'd had to do was nod. "Go find her, Theon."

Because of course she knew what was happening.

It had taken every bit of his strength to shadow-walk and follow the Tracking Mark that still let him know where Tessa was. And now that he was back and she was here, he sank onto the small leather sofa in the room, trying not to vomit. Trying not to fall to his knees when he couldn't push down the utter agony of the Guardian bond dying once again.

Tears were coursing down Tessa's face as she stared down at Luka, her hands moving erratically as if she didn't know if she should touch him. Her head snapped up, lightning sparking in their depths when she found Cienna.

"Why are you just standing there?" she cried. "Do something!"

But the Witch just stood stoically to the side, keen eyes watching on. "There is nothing I can do," she answered simply.

"Nothing you can . . ." Tessa trailed off in outrage, her power seeping from her as she lost more control. "Then what good are you?" Her eyes swept the room in fury. "What good are any of you?" she screamed, her rage and helplessness flooding him down their bond.

But the agony in his chest was lessening, allowing him to think a little more clearly with each passing second. He watched her smooth her hands down Luka's face. Watched her push his hair back. Watched her lay her head atop his chest, right beside that Mark that wasn't pulsing quite so violently anymore. That was calming and settling back into a stagnant, pale white Mark on Luka's flesh.

"Where were you?" Cienna asked, watching them as carefully as Theon was.

"The Falein Kingdom," Theon answered, his voice steely.

"By yourself?" Cienna asked Tessa.

"With Tristyn and—Brecken," Theon answered, feeling Tessa's flinch down the bond at his name.

"Did they come back with you?"

"They're downstairs."

"Stop answering for me," Tessa snarled, glaring up at him. "Why does any of this matter? Why is no one doing anything?"

"Because *you* are the only one who can do something," Kat interjected.

And maybe it was because it was her, but Tessa tensed, clearly biting her tongue instead of snapping back a retort. Whatever it was, she was listening now, and Theon knew without a doubt that Kat had worked out the same thing he had.

Because everything in his soul had settled. The Guardian bond was fine. His bond with Tessa was humming in contentment at having her close once more. Luka's chest was rising and falling steadily.

Katya moved forward, awkwardly lowering to her knees on the other side of Tessa despite Axel's protest.

"He's fine, Tessa," she said softly. "Look."

Taking Tessa's hand, she shifted it so they could all see the Mark clearly. That perfectly calm and sedate Mark.

"I don't understand," Tessa rasped, wiping at her face.

Theon moved then, unable to stand seeing her in that godsdamn jacket a second longer. His panic and fear had subsided, and it was replaced by an anger that he was swallowing down with every breath. He strode around Luka's feet, coming to Tessa's side. Slipping his fingers beneath the collar, he slid it down her arms. In her own panic and confusion, she didn't fight, and he tossed it aside.

Katya glanced up at him, and he nodded in confirmation before he replied, "You gave him that Mark, Tessa."

"I know, but I don't know what it does," she said, having picked up one of Luka's hands. She looked up at Theon, worry there, but also an underlying grief she was pushing down.

"Neither did we until now," he answered. "But it appears you've bound his life to your presence in some way."

"That's not . . . What? I can't do that," she said, shaking her head.

"But you did," he answered. "You gave him life, and if he strays too far from that, death takes."

"No," she said, shaking her head in denial. "I would never do that to him without . . . No."

"It's the only explanation, Tessa," Kat said gently. "Since that day, you've never been apart—"

"We have," she argued. "Separate rooms. Out in the Underground."

"That's a small distance. Not two godsdamn kingdoms away and on an island," Theon said, trying and failing to keep the bite from his tone.

She shifted, her eyes dropping back to Luka.

"And after I found you and brought you back here, that Mark faded back to what it is now. I felt him dying, and now I don't. I know you felt him too," Theon continued.

"Yes, but I thought that had been . . ." She trailed off for several seconds. "Why isn't he waking up?"

"I'm sure nearly dying again takes a minute or two to recover from," he said dryly.

"Theon," Kat interjected in warning. "Now is not the time."

He knew that, and a piece of him was grateful to Kat for the small reminder. He was even more grateful nothing had appeared to change between them with his whole willing-to-sacrifice-the-world thing. They still spent hours going through books together, but now conversation was often lighter and more relaxed between them. The fact that she was carrying his nephew only strengthened their unlikely friendship.

Clearing his throat, Theon crouched beside Tessa, his hand brushing down her back. "We just have to give him a minute, little storm."

And gods, he hoped this wouldn't be the first lie he told her because the truth was he didn't know if or when Luka would wake up. None of them had any idea what this Mark did or the effects of it. Was it unlimited, or did a part of Luka die every time it was activated? How far could she stray from him? Could he go across the Underground? Was separate cities too far?

In the silent minutes that passed, Axel helped Kat to her feet before ushering her to the sofa. Razik and Eliza remained silent, always observing.

Tessa swiveled to look up at Xan, as if suddenly remembering he was here. "Do you know of this Mark? Or something like it?"

The male's sapphire stare was fixed on his son, and he seemed to be holding his breath as he answered, "No, Tessa. I do believe Eliza is correct. You created something entirely new. None of us know what comes with that."

She swung her gaze to the female. "Scarlett can do this, yes?"

Eliza nodded, her features always harsh and unnerving.

"Does she always know what they will do?' Tessa pressed.

"Scarlett has studied Marks extensively, and she has learned her own lessons about being sure to fully understand one before bestowing it," Eliza answered. "When she creates a new Mark, it is intentional. Deliberate. She may appear impulsive. However, she is anything but."

"How can she know?"

"I can't answer that. I don't have her abilities, nor have I studied them as extensively," Eliza said, looking up at Razik in question.

He sighed. "I don't know how she does it either," he said, his tone betraying how annoying he found that.

But before anyone could say anything further, a low groan sounded, drawing everyone's focus back to Luka. Tessa leaned over him, her breath catching, and Theon leaned closer too. It was another few seconds before his eyes opened.

He blinked several times before settling into focus on Tessa. Then he frowned.

"Are you covered in blood, baby girl?"

Her hand drifted up, fingertips touching her cheek. The blood that had been there had smeared with her tears, leaving red streaks behind.

"I . . . Are you all right?" she asked, dropping her hand back to his bare chest.

"Other than annoyed at missing out on *how* you became covered in blood, I'm fine," he grumbled, pushing into a sitting position. It was only then he realized a small audience had gathered in the room. Tessa was still touching him, refusing to break that connection, and his eyes slid to Theon in question.

"You don't remember?" Theon asked, watching him carefully.

"I remember waking up to find . . . *you* gone, but experiencing some kind of panic," he said, glaring at Tessa in disapproval. "Then nothing."

Theon nodded and quickly filled him in on what they'd worked out. Tessa was silent the entire time, avoiding eye contact as their theory about his new Mark was explained. When Theon finished, Luka studied her for a moment before saying, "Can you all give us a minute? We can discuss this more later."

Everyone nodded, trailing from the room, but when Theon made to follow, Luka stopped him. "Not you, you idiot."

Theon gave him a flat look, closing the door behind Xan. "I figured you wanted to—"

But Luka cut him off. "If the three of us are doing this, we're doing it together."

Theon nodded. They were still working out how to navigate this thing, but Luka was right. It needed to be done together. Something they needed Tessa to understand.

He slipped his hands into the pockets of his pants and watched as Luka reached over and tipped Tessa's face up with his fingers. "We have some things to discuss, but first, is this your blood or someone else's?"

"It's not mine," she breathed, tears welling in her eyes as the fear was replaced with grief.

Theon was moving then, reaching to pull her up before he grabbed Luka's hand to do the same. He swayed a little, a groove of annoyance appearing on his brow as he steadied himself.

"When I found her, she was with Blackheart and Brecken. Brecken was . . ." Theon hesitated.

"Brecken is dead," Tessa said softly, one of those tears breaking free, and all those tears brought Theon back to months ago when she was shedding tears for different reasons. Those reasons he could have fixed. Was trying to fix so many things, but this . . . He couldn't change this for her.

"How?" Luka asked.

"Oralia," she spat, and Theon went rigid.

"You saw Oralia?" he asked.

She nodded. "She was . . . She stabbed Brecken in the back."

"Where is she now?"

"The Pits of Torment."

"You killed her?" Luka asked.

She nodded again.

"How?"

It was a growled command, and Tessa's eyes flared at the order, her power appearing and snapping to attention.

"A blade," she answered, her tone dark and cold. "I cut off her wings one at a time, and then I shoved it all the way through her chest."

"So vicious," Luka purred. "You keep doing these things when I'm not around, temptress." His head tilted in a completely predatory move. "Which raises the question, what were you doing there? So far from us?"

"I . . . I didn't know this would happen," she answered, lifting her chin as that defiance that Theon both loved and hated crept in.

"I don't give a fuck that I almost died. Again," Luka growled. "I just want to know why you were there."

"To destroy a mirror gate," she answered coldly. "I asked Tristyn if he knew where one was, and he invited Brecken because he has—had—found some of the exact locations."

"And this goes back to the vision you were trapped in a few nights ago?" Theon cut in, putting the pieces together.

"Yes," she snapped. "I don't owe you an explanation."

"Wrong," Luka said in that same seductive growl, and Theon was glad he'd let Luka take the lead on this one. If Theon had done that, her defenses would already be too high, and she would have shut him down. "But that can wait. Right now, you need a shower."

"You don't—" she started in outrage, but then she paused. "What?"

"As much as I enjoy the sight of you covered in blood," Luka replied, taking her hand and leading her to the ensuite. "You need to wash it off. Then I'm assuming we need to deal with the aftermath of what happened."

"What aftermath?"

"Brecken," Theon said softly, seeing where Luka was going with this. "We need to deal with Brecken."

"Tristyn said he would take care of it," she answered, trying to pull her hand from Luka's.

"And we're going to take care of *you*," Theon replied. "You have to deal with this, Tessa. You can't ignore the grief and the pain. When you do, you lose control."

Luka dropped her hand to go turn on the shower, while Theon stepped forward and reached for the hem of her shirt, lifting it over her head.

"It's okay to feel things," he said softly. "You need to feel them."

"And you?"

"You know I feel things," he said with a dark grin, reaching to tuck her hair behind her ear. "From the very beginning. It's you we've never been able to read and figure out. Not even you know how to do that."

"Let's go, baby girl," Luka called, and they both turned to find him waiting.

Naked.

Her cheeks flushed as she hooked her thumbs in her pants and pushed them down. Theon followed suit, and they both moved to the shower. She reached for Luka, pushing onto her toes, but he stopped her before she went any farther.

"Just so we're managing expectations," Luka said, "there will be no fucking."

Tessa lurched back, crashing into Theon's bare chest, and he almost let a huff of laughter slip.

"What do you mean?" Tessa demanded.

"I mean exactly what I said," Luka continued calmly, but Theon knew he was anything but calm. She was naked, all that bare flesh on full display. Of course, they *wanted* to fuck her, but he also knew what Luka was doing.

Luka reached for her once more, and Theon nudged her forward. Guiding her under the water, Luka moved behind her, tipping her head back. "You need to deal with this, Tessa. Not by drinking. Not by fucking. Not by drowning in vices that push it down. Like Theon said, that's when your power takes control."

Then he was passing her back to Theon, where he waited with shampoo. He began lathering her hair, and even still, he could feel the tension rolling off her. "We know he was a friend, little storm."

"Stop," she gritted out.

"We won't stop," Luka said simply. "You need to learn to process your emotions, baby girl."

"Don't *baby girl* me," she snarled. She rounded on Theon, eyes hard. "And what about you?" she snapped. "You're pushing down emotions. I can feel you too, you know."

He knew his smirk was dark, and she faltered for the briefest of moments before steeling herself once more. Passing her back to Luka, he said, "Don't worry, Tessa. Our *feelings* about this matter will be dealt with when it's time. But right now, our focus is on you, not us."

She swallowed thickly as Luka guided her head back again, rinsing the shampoo from her hair. No one said anything else as they conditioned her hair and washed the blood from her skin. But they felt her. Felt her trying to shove down her sadness. Felt her starting to spiral. Felt her doing everything she could not to feel at all. Despite the heat from the shower, she was trembling when Theon held her to him while Luka quickly washed up. Then Luka did the same for him before stepping out and drying off.

It wasn't until Theon guided her out to Luka, waiting for her with a towel, that Luka said, "I'm sorry you lost someone else important to you."

"Don't," she snarled, sparks crackling at her fingertips.

"I know we just learned of his true loyalty, but he did a lot for you. For Kat. Likely for so many innocent people we will never know."

"Luka, stop," she said again, her sharpness cracking.

"I wish we'd gotten the chance to know him more. He seemed like a decent male. Arrogant and questionable, but decent in the end."

"Luka!"

He moved her to the side so Theon could step out, and he quickly dried himself off while Luka kept talking.

"I'm sorry you had to see his death, but it's not your fault," Luka continued.

"Of course it's my fault," she snapped. "His death is directly correlated to my actions. Just like Auryon and Pen. You and Roan nearly faced the same because of me."

Theon froze at the words.

Her hands were in her wet hair before either of them could stop her, and she pushed away from Luka as her power lashed out. Not at them, but just . . .

Theon watched as it coiled and writhed, snapping out before back in. It wound around her, then released her. Then it sprang back, moving up her torso to her own throat as if to—

"Tessa!" Theon barked, his darkness lurching for her chaos. Because it was lashing out at *her*. A reflection of her emotions she was trying so gods-damn hard to avoid. Her own self-loathing and guilt over her past—both things in and out of her control.

His magic did what he wanted it to, distracting her chaos. Luka must have recognized it too because his black flames were there, drawing her power away from her. They wouldn't allow her power to consume her rather than face this. Face herself.

"Did you get to talk to him before he died?" Luka asked, his tone bordering on harsh.

"Stop!" she snarled once more, taking a step back from them.

And what a sight this must be. The two of them with towels around their waists. Tessa naked, having pushed away from Luka's warmth, staring them down in the steam-filled bathroom with her fingers pulling on her hair. That madness lurked, trying to pull her under, while they did everything they could to keep her here with them.

"Brecken's death is not on you, Tessa," Theon said. She opened her mouth to argue, but he went on before she could. "There are more contributing factors than just you. The same was true for Auryon and Pen."

"But you said—"

"I know what I said," he interjected. "I was losing control, and you . . ." He swallowed, shoving a hand through his wet hair. "You were the easiest person for me to lash out against. But this? Tessa, you didn't even invite him. Blackheart did."

"And his own actions contributed too," Luka said, his tone softening. "He *was* a traitor to the cause he was sent here for. He got caught. That is not your fault, Tessa."

She shook her head, two tears slowly making their way down her cheeks. "He was . . . He told me truths when no one else would."

They were silent, letting her get her words out.

"He helped me figure out my true purpose. That I could decide what that was." She swiped at her cheeks angrily. "In a realm of villains, he wasn't one of them in the end."

"He knew the risks of his actions," Theon said gently.

"I'm the reason he was caught," she snapped, that anger returning.

"Give him some credit, Tessa," Luka said sharply. "He sacrificed for something he believed in. His death wasn't wasted. He saved innocent people. He was part of a revolution in Devram before we even realized there was going to be one. He helped start it. Don't do him the dishonor of cheapening his sacrifice."

"I don't want to talk about this anymore," she said suddenly, turning to leave the bathroom.

But Theon's power was faster, snapping the door shut before she'd even taken three steps. She whirled, the fury back, and the gold bands on her wrists flaring with it.

"You have to feel it, Tessa," he said.

"No, Theon. I don't," she retorted.

He only gave her a small, sad smile while Luka leaned back against the counter, crossing his arms.

Gods, he wanted to go to her and pull her into him. Take this from her. Protect her from herself, because that was what he'd always tried to do for everyone in his life. Craving control to keep those he loved safe, but he couldn't protect her from this. He couldn't take the pain or the guilt or the grief.

Neither he nor Luka dared to move yet, too afraid it would make her stop talking. Stop *feeling* everything she needed to face.

"We'll be here for it, Tessa," Luka said. "You're not alone anymore."

"It's easier to be angry," Theon added. "At me. At Dexter. At Rordan. The gods. The Fates." He paused before saying, "At yourself. That's easier than feeling the pain of a loss. You can busy yourself. You can let your power punish you. You can drink or fuck to try to drown it out, but eventually, it's going to consume you," he said again. "Eventually, it turns you into someone no one recognizes. Someone you swore you'd never be. Someone you were trying everything in your power not to become."

She swallowed thickly, finally pulling her hands from her hair, only to clutch them at her chest. Her power was still drifting, entranced by theirs.

And all that was left was for her to feel.

Shaking her head, more tears fell. "It hurts," she whispered. "I'm so tired of hurting. Of trying to be what I need to be, only to fail in the end."

Something wet landed on his cheek. Then another on his arm. The top of his foot.

And as Tessa finally broke, feeling things she'd trained herself to never acknowledge for years, it started to rain indoors. As if the steam itself were clouds of her own grief and sorrow.

Luka pushed off the counter, taking a towel with him. He wrapped it around her shoulders before scooping her up and lowering to the floor with her. Theon moved to them, sitting beside them as she buried her face in Luka's chest and cried. Sobs that made the rain become a gentle steady shower, seeping into everything, but he'd sit in the rain forever if it meant he could be one of the two people she'd let herself learn to feel with.

In the end, it was perhaps ten minutes before the rain subsided. Theon went to get fresh towels, drying themselves and her before they moved back out to the bedroom. Theon slipped one of his shirts over her head, and they all climbed under the covers. Tessa was asleep within minutes, tears still falling even while she dreamed.

Theon met Luka's gaze over the top of her, a silent understanding passing between them.

They'd give her time to process, time to grieve, but the matter of her going to Falein Kingdom without them would still be discussed. Luka was just as furious as he was. He could feel it down the bond.

They'd convinced her she wasn't alone. Proven it as best they could. Now she needed to understand that she was theirs as much as they were hers, and that meant she didn't fucking leave them behind.

They were hers in every way.

Lovers.

Equals.

Protectors.

And, when necessary, they'd still be her villains.

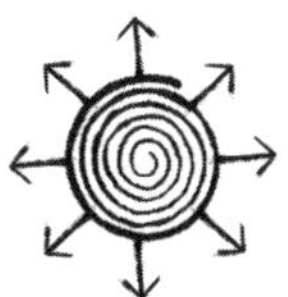

34
AXEL

"Do they know you're down here?" Axel asked.

Tessa glanced up at him, scowling. "Yes, they know I'm down here," she grumbled.

Axel hummed, walking around the kitchen island and opening the fridge. "Any particular reason you're down here instead of asleep?" When she didn't answer right away, he looked over his shoulder. Her face was slightly flushed as she stared down into her mug of tea, her hands clasped around the cup.

He smirked to himself. No one had spoken about it, but it wasn't hard to figure out the three of them had come to some sort of understanding. They all stayed in the same room, and he had no doubt they shared a bed. A part of him felt bad. The bed on the third floor was much larger and designed for three. The other part of him didn't give a fuck because his wife was pregnant, and her comfort mattered more than anyone else's.

"Well?" he prompted, nudging the fridge door shut after he grabbed milk, eggs, cheese, and a few vegetables.

She huffed, still not looking at him. "They think I need to learn to process my emotions instead of turning to my usual distractions."

He arched a brow as he laid everything out on the counter opposite of where she sat. "You wanted to fuck, and they kicked you out of bed?"

"They didn't kick me out of bed," she muttered. "They just told me to go drink some tea."

"Idiots," he muttered, because who in their right mind kicked a willing female out of their bed? Then again, they were right. Tessa did need to deal with her shit. "So, what are you attempting to avoid?"

"What are you doing?" she asked when he poured some milk into a small pot before placing it on the stovetop.

"Nice deflection," he replied, going to the pantry. Finding what he needed, he added a bar of chocolate to the pot before going back to the counter and picking up a red pepper.

"You're not going to answer?" she asked.

"You first," he said with a wink.

She huffed in annoyance. "I've been trying to teach myself about the Marks," she answered. "They are complicated. Part of me seems to innately recognize them, but I still . . . I don't want to fuck things up more than I already have by using one and not understanding the consequences."

"How not impulsive of you," he replied, moving on to an onion.

"Shut up, Axel," she muttered, and he smiled to himself. He'd missed this. Missed her.

"Have you asked Theon?"

"No."

"Because you're stubborn and trying to prove a point?" He glanced up to find her glaring at him. "You could ask Xan," he said with a shrug, moving to stir the pot before cracking eggs into a bowl.

"I'm avoiding him too," she sighed. "He wants to bring my mother here."

He paused for the briefest of moments. "Yeah, I could see how that would make you anxious."

"You do?"

"There's a lot there to unpack, baby doll," he said, beating the eggs. "Xan is clearly fond of her, and you maybe don't want to be fond of the female who abandoned you to this realm."

"Yeah," she whispered.

"But it might be nice to get answers directly from the source," he added.

"Maybe."

Grabbing a pan, he set it next to the pot, turning on the burner.

"And what if she doesn't regret it?" he continued.

Tessa didn't answer, but he didn't expect her to. He was simply naming the feelings she was obviously trying to avoid.

"What are you doing?" she asked again after a few minutes of silence.

"In about ten minutes, Kat is going to wake up craving an omelette," he answered. "Just getting it ready."

A small bark of laughter escaped her. "You're serious?"

"Sure am," he muttered. "Every night at the same godsdamn time. I'm so used to it now, I naturally wake up."

She huffed another laugh as he flipped the omelette.

"What's in the other pot?" she asked.

He smiled to himself, plucking a mug from the cupboard and filling it with the contents. Then he crossed to her, taking her mug of tea and replacing it. She looked down as he went back to finish the omelette.

"Hot chocolate?" she asked.

"Don't tell Theon," he said, throwing her another wink over his shoulder. "There's whipped cream in the fridge."

He heard her slide off the chair, then bare feet padding to the refrigerator. "I don't know the first thing about having parents," she said as she moved. "But I think you're going to be a great father."

"I don't know the first thing about *being* a father," he replied, sliding the omelette onto a plate and covering it with a lid to keep it warm.

"I think you have to care. Have to love. Deeply. The way you love Kat," she answered with a soft smile, nodding to the covered dish. "Did you *want* to be a father though?"

"It was just always something I knew would be required of me one day, I guess," he answered, leaning against the counter and crossing his arms while he watched her spoon whipped cream into her mug.

"That's not what I asked."

He smirked, but then turned contemplative. "Yeah, I think I did. Never thought it'd be this early. Figured it'd be decades from now, but . . ." He shrugged. "Sometimes the Fates surprise us."

"Fuck the Fates," she ground out, lifting the mug to her lips.

He smirked again, picking up on the sound of feet on the stairs. "We can have all kinds of plans, baby doll," he said, uncovering the plate and carrying it to the counter. "Some work out. Sometimes we're fucked over. And sometimes we didn't know we were dreaming the wrong dreams all along until we're living them," he said, smiling softly as Kat appeared in the kitchen. Sliding the plate across the counter, he said, "It's ready, kitten."

"I could have made it," she sighed, giving him a sleepy smile. She said the same thing every night. Glancing at Tessa, she asked, "Am I interrupting?"

She shook her head. "No, Kat. I think I'm the one interrupting."

Kat sighed again, picking up her fork. "Axel, can you—"

"Orange or grape tonight?" he asked, already opening the fridge.

"Orange," she answered, and he grabbed the orange juice carton.

As he poured the juice, he said, "Oh, and Tessa?"

"Hmm?" she asked, finishing off her hot chocolate.

"Maybe she has no regrets, but maybe she regrets every single day of the last twenty-four years."

She paused for a moment before getting up to take her mug to the sink.

"I'm still trying to decide if I care," she answered.

"Fair enough, baby doll," he said, wrapping an arm around her shoulders and pulling her into his side. "Fair enough."

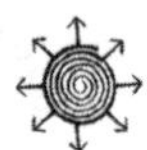

"I'm going to ask you one last time—"

"I swear to Anala, Axel, if you ask that question, I'm tying you up with shadows and going myself," Kat snarked, slipping her feet into gold sandals.

"You had me intrigued until the going by yourself part," he quipped.

She shook her head and turned away, but he saw the small quirk on her lips.

She looked stunning in a dress of burnt orange, a gold necklace at her throat, and his ring on her finger. Her hair was piled atop her head. Tessa and Eliza had helped her get ready, forcing him out of the room until minutes ago.

Moving to stand in front of her, he cupped her cheek, and she looked up at him in question.

"If at any time you feel uncomfortable, we leave," he said. "I don't care who is at that table tonight."

"It will be fine, Axel."

But she didn't know that. They had one more week until they were past the month Miara had warned them about. There was no way the timing of this dinner was a coincidence.

He bent, brushing his lips across hers. "Any discomfort, you tell me," he murmured.

She reached up, running her fingers through his hair. "I will."

Kissing her once more, he took her hand, leading her down the stairs.

"Ready?" Luka asked from the foyer.

Rather than walk across the entire Underground, Luka was Traveling them to the Dispensary District. They'd tested it earlier to make sure the distance didn't trigger his new Mark.

"Did you drink blood?" Theon asked, standing nearby with his arms crossed. "Do you need more before you go?"

"You know I drank extra today," Axel answered, grabbing his suit jacket.

"You sure you don't want me to go with you?"

"I've got it covered, Theon," he replied in irritation. Kat smirked up at him, and he pointed a finger at her. "Not a word, kitten."

"I didn't say anything," she said, amusement dancing in her amber eyes.

"Be smart. They're cunning," Theon warned as they stepped closer to Luka.

"I'm aware," Axel said dryly.

"He'll be fine, Theon," Tessa called from the sofa, where she was studying some books with Eliza. Apparently she'd gone to her instead of Theon for help learning about Marks.

"You've never met Bree," Theon replied curtly.

"No, but I've met Axel. He can be scarier than you when he needs to be."

"Thanks, baby doll," he said with a wink.

"Don't be stupid tonight," she replied, and he heard Eliza snicker.

"Kat, send a fire message if you need anything," Theon said, ignoring both him and Tessa.

"I will, Theon," she answered.

"So he can worry, but I can't?" Axel asked, reaching to grip Luka's shoulder.

"Oh my gods," Kat muttered as he slid his arm around her waist.

A moment later, they were standing just outside the Dispensary District. Kat swayed, and he tightened his grip. "You good?"

"Mhmm," she hummed. "Just need a second."

"Kat—" he started.

"Don't," she cut in, straightening her spine. "Let's go."

"You know what to do if you need us," Luka said.

"I'll let you know when we're done," Axel replied.

With a nod, Luka was gone, and they turned to walk to the House of Four. It was still a long trek, but as time does when dreading something, he blinked and they were crossing the bridge.

He'd thought this dinner would be held in the building the four Houses shared, but they were greeted and escorted deeper. His stomach dropped when he realized they were entering Bree's House, and his hand tightened around Kat's.

"Breathe, Axel," she murmured out of the corner of her mouth, and he forced himself to take several too shallow breaths as they took a lift.

He already knew exactly which dining room this dinner would be in. The same one he'd sat in while she'd delivered her proposition. And sure enough, those were the doors they were led to.

"Thank you," he said tightly to their escort before they entered.

They were only a step through the door when Bree was suddenly before them. Kat lurched back on instinct, and Axel hissed, baring his fangs.

"Axel, darling, relax," she said with a lilt of laughter. Those honey-colored eyes slid to Kat. "My apologies for startling you, poppet."

"Bree," he said tightly. "You remember my wife."

"Of course, darling," she purred, her gaze roaming over Kat, lingering on her belly.

Tugging Kat with him, he stepped around Bree dismissively. "Miara," he greeted, a part of him relieved to see the Witch here. At least if something happened with Kat, she was here, despite the warning having come from her in the first place.

A warning she still clearly felt as her violet eyes held his. "You tempt the Fates, young Lord."

"Not a Lord," he replied, guiding Kat to the table, but he stilled when Bree tsked at him.

"Your seats are here," she called, striding past him to the head of the table. Her smile was sharp as she gestured to the chair at her right.

Axel held her gaze as he continued in the opposite direction, guiding Kat to the chair at *his* right before taking the seat at the other end of the table. He leaned back, spreading his legs wide beneath the table. Propping his elbow on the armrest, he steepled a finger along his temple.

Bree's smile became forced. "This is supposed to be a cordial dinner, Axel, darling."

"And it is more likely to remain so if I am at the opposite end of the table," he replied, watching the vampyre carefully who placed a glass of water and a glass of wine before Kat. "She'll have cranberry juice instead," he said, and the vampyre glanced at Bree, who nodded once, before he took the wine and left the dining room.

Cade stalked in next, glancing once at them before he took the seat on Bree's right. The tension was thick with no one speaking until Rayell arrived, breezing into the room as if she didn't have a care in the world. The pink streaks in her hair were brighter, as though freshly dyed, and she dropped into the chair to Bree's left unceremoniously. Leif and Sevrin arrived, the Fae male partners who ran the Apparel District, and Kylian and Giselle arrived last, Giselle taking the chair beside Katya.

Light chatter had started, mainly at their end of the table while drinks were distributed. At least everyone else had been given beverages. The vampyres were last to receive anything other than water. When they were served, the clear goblets shimmered with blood.

"It's fresh," Bree said from across the table. Then she glanced at Katya before locking eyes with Axel once more. "I figured fire was your preference."

"It is," Axel agreed. Pointedly picking up his glass of water, he added, "But I prefer it direct from the source."

"That can be arranged," Bree said tightly.

"Not here," he said simply. "Unless everyone wants a show of where that will lead when I feed from her."

"You feed from her while she is with child? I somehow doubt that," Bree said mildly, picking up her own glass of blood.

"What we do and don't do is truly none of your concern," he said coldly, taking a drink of water and hiding his wince. Because he could smell the blood in the other glasses, and every instinct in him was on high alert the way it was. Leif and Sevrin were a chair away, not to mention Kat sitting right fucking there.

"If directly from the source is what you desire, you know I can provide that," Bree went on. "They are here by choice and well compensated, of course," she added for the Fae leaders' benefits.

They shrugged, and that was really all that mattered to them. They knew their blood was valuable, and as long as the Fae weren't being used or forced against their will, they didn't care. It was a bargaining power only they held, and they knew it.

If only the Fae in the kingdoms could figure that out as well, the entire system in Devram would change.

"Again, that is not necessary," Axel said curtly. "Can we get on with what this conclave is about?"

"All in good time, darling. Let's eat before we dive into business. You are guests in my—*our*—house after all," she amended when Cade shot her a look. Rayell didn't seem to care, sipping on her glass of blood. Axel knew better. She was paying as much attention as everyone else. There was a reason she was one of the clan leaders.

It was the longest godsdamn dinner of his life, and that was saying something. He'd sat through plenty of dull and uncomfortable affairs with his father, but this was over-the-top and ridiculous. Idle chatter and ten courses. Fake pleasantries and subtle temptations. More than once Bree asked if he'd changed his mind about having blood, and it didn't help that the vampyres at the other end of the table were drinking their own supply in no show of moderation. He'd been living on limited rations while they had this surplus.

A hand on his made him start, and he looked down to find Kat squeezing his fingers. He met her gaze, giving her a tight smile as he tried to focus on what Leif and Sevrin were saying. Something about contacts outside the Underground.

"I think we could do that, right, Axel?" Kat said, squeezing his fingers again.

"I'm sorry, what was that?" he asked, cutting a bite of the red velvet cake in front of him. All the food had tasted like ash tonight because all he wanted was blood.

"Leif is asking if we could arrange a meeting with the new Arius Lord to discuss a potential blood contract for rations," Kat said.

He frowned, trying to figure out what he'd missed. The kingdoms got their blood from the Fae assigned to them. It was part of their duties. The Fae blood from the Underground was considered contraband because it couldn't be regulated like the Fae blood in the kingdoms.

Taking the bite of cake to stall his response, he went utterly still. Because this wasn't just red velvet cake.

His gaze darted from his dessert to the others around the table. Bree, Cade, and Rayell all had the red velvet cake. Everyone else had chocolate. He hadn't noticed. Too distracted by his craving and trying to keep his shit together. He'd stopped caring about the food that had been placed in front of him after the third course when nothing tasted good.

But there was blood in this cake somehow, and holy fuck, was it divine. Powerful. *Hot*.

Blood from a fire Fae.

His eyes snapped to Bree, who was already watching him. Everyone else appeared to be oblivious to the silent battle of wills going on between them. She brought a forkful of red velvet cake to her mouth, taking a sensual bite. Her tongue darted out to lick a drop of frosting on the corner of her mouth, and then she smiled enough to show the tips of her fangs.

More.

He needed more.

He thought he'd learned restraint these past months. Had forced himself to practice it every fucking day, drinking only enough rations to keep himself in check. But there was blood just in reach, that goblet still sitting before him untouched. The cake. The Fae at the table. Kat.

Kat.

He turned to her, finding her engaging in polite conversation with the Fae, because of course she was. She was perfect and well-spoken. Beautiful. Divine. Powerful.

No.

A bead of perspiration slid down the back of his neck because now he couldn't focus on anything but the blood.

Just drink it. It's right there.

No.

It would have a cost. Bree wasn't just going to give him blood. She had a reason. She had to.

"Axel? Can we arrange that meeting?" Kat asked, and why did she sound far away? Muffled?

He'd drank plenty of blood before they came here. This shouldn't be an issue.

But if he didn't do something, this night would get a whole lot worse because he wouldn't be able to focus. He wouldn't be able to stay ahead of Bree and her games. Everything they'd worked so hard to secure these last weeks and months would be in jeopardy. All because he couldn't fucking control himself.

"Axel?" she said again, her voice a soft whisper. "Are you all right?"

And she'd shifted closer. Too close. Because all he could smell was her. Jasmine, citrus, smoke. Fire. Power.

He lifted a trembling hand, reaching for the goblet, but warm fingers wrapped around his wrist.

"No, Axel," she said, quiet and firm. "Drink from me."

He shook his head, at least still sane enough to do that.

"Is everything all right, Axel, darling?" Bree called from down the table.

"Everything is fine," he gritted out.

"Are you sure? You appear a little out of sorts," she continued.

"He is fine," Kat snapped.

"He looks like he's fighting bloodlust," Cade said flatly, everyone having picked up on the tension now.

"That is not surprising," Bree said, faux sympathy in her voice. "He has been a Night Child for a handful of months. He is a youngling. A mere infant, if you will. It takes years—decades—to learn to control the bloodlust."

"He controls it just fine," Kat said tightly.

"His restraint seems fine," Giselle said with a slight frown. "He hasn't touched his blood all evening."

"A fool's move," Cade said with a roll of his eyes. "Especially that newly changed."

"He just prefers his own," Kat cut in. "He thinks he needs to spare me in present company."

"Spare you? You are a Fae and his blood source."

"Watch it," Axel snarled, his vision going blurry. Why was everything taking on a red haze?

"He is honorable and respectful, unlike some of our present company," Katya retorted, and if he weren't riding this dangerous edge, he'd notice that endearing irritation creeping in.

Fingertips were at his chin, turning his face to hers. Shadows drifted in her eyes. So much power there for the taking . . .

"Axel, my love," she said softly, her touch leaving him as she moved her wrist to his mouth. "Drink. You can't hurt me."

And before he knew what was happening, his fangs sank into her. Warm fire slid over his tongue, coppery and divine. He drank deeply, forgetting everything around him. His entire existence was narrowed in on the life flowing into him.

Life must give, and death must take.

Pull after luscious pull, blood slid down his throat, a low groan sounding from his chest.

Until shadows wrapped around him and a slight burn prodded at the back of his mind. It flared a little more, enough to make him annoyed. Enough to make him snarl at whatever was trying to interrupt him.

He blinked as a lick of fire traced along his jaw. "Later, my love. We'll finish this later," she said, her voice breaking through everything.

And for the first time since he'd turned, he felt somewhat sated. Even though he still wanted more, needed more . . . But it was *her*. Nothing would ever be enough when it came to her.

A throat cleared down the table, and it was only then he remembered they were with a roomful of people.

It was only then he remembered the godsdamn snake at the other end of it.

Reaching over, he took Kat's chin, pulling her closer. He brushed his lips over hers. Once. Twice. Three times before he said in a low purr, "Thank you, kitten."

"Well, I think this little . . . issue is the perfect way to bring up the concern I've asked you all here tonight to discuss," Bree said, sitting back in her chair.

Axel's gaze slowly slid to her, his eyes narrowing. She was feigning concern, but he could see the touch of smugness beneath the mask.

"And what concern is that?" Kylian asked, picking up his glass of liquor and swirling the ice.

"I know tension has been high in the Underground. Alliances, both here and in the kingdoms, are being questioned. Some broken. New ones born," Bree said. "And let's not ignore the obvious. Everyone at this table knows of the escalating conflict between me and Axel."

"The conflict between us is personal, Bree," Axel said tightly.

"Exactly," she said, eyes widening. "And you are bringing others into a personal matter."

He barked a harsh laugh. "You cannot be serious. Everyone here knows you've been scheming to overtake the Underground. To seize control and power."

"Not from *them*," she argued, gesturing to the other leaders. "We don't deserve to be locked away down here."

"And I agree. That's why I am working with Theon to make changes. You know this."

She scoffed bitterly. "A Legacy cannot help us."

"Not alone, no," Kat interjected. "But Theon is not alone. Theon is different and so is she."

"Tessa is uncontrollable," Bree sneered. "You know that as well as I do."

"How can you possibly know that?" Axel asked. "You've never even met her."

"The Fates watch all the power players carefully," she returned. "The realm has been waiting for her. The Decree is proof enough of that."

"You're wrong," Kat cut in again. "But let's pretend you aren't. Let's pretend she is a potential problem. Theon is the best chance at controlling her. Theon is the best chance at seeing the Underground liberated. And Axel is the most logical path to Theon's ear."

"And what has he done as of late?" Bree countered.

"For starters, he is staying Theon's hand at retribution for sending us the head of an Arius general," Kat said simply, picking up her glass of juice. "If anyone is escalating tension in the Underground, it is you, Miss DelaCrux."

The room was silent for several seconds before Cade said, "I find it interesting your wife is speaking for you, St. Orcas."

"She is more than just my wife," Axel replied coldly. "If she wishes to speak, then she will. She is my equal as much as anyone at this table. As nearly everyone at this table can attest, I have no desire to rule over you. If we can work together and present a compromise of sorts to the kingdoms, we can start negotiations on different . . . living arrangements."

"And if they decline? What then?" Bree asked, clearly having collected herself. "When negotiations die and we are denied?"

"We deal with that if we must and not before."

She scoffed. "Going in without a plan is foolish."

"I do not want a war, Bree, but I never said I wouldn't fight if it came down to it. I think you know that better than anyone, wouldn't you say?" he replied, arching a brow.

"And we are to put our trust and faith in you? A scarcely turned vampyre who can't control his bloodlust? What happens if she isn't here next time? What happens when the other rulers overrule your brother?"

"What, exactly, are you hoping to gain here, Bree?" Miara cut in sharply.

"I am trying to understand how and why a turned Legacy has managed to overturn centuries of alliances and peace in the Underground in a matter of months," Bree snapped, her composure finally slipping completely.

"Perhaps it is because you came to me with a proposal to take control of the Underground and rule at your side. Perhaps it is because you want to control Devram altogether," Axel said coolly. "Perhaps I don't play games."

"Everything is a game," Bree sneered. "If you don't understand that, you are already dead. My point stands that you are unreliable and uncontrollable as evidenced moments ago when you couldn't control your bloodlust."

"Did he attack anyone?" Katya asked angrily. "Did he spill blood? Did he cause any kind of disturbance?"

"If you had not been here, it would have escalated to that point," Bree said.

"The fact that he allows himself to depend on others speaks to his ability to lead," Kat replied. "He does not pretend to know it all or be able to do everything. Everyone has weaknesses. He knows his and has taken measures to mitigate them. More than that, he knows his limits, which is why he understands the value of the alliances he has formed. If you cannot see that, Miss DelaCrux, it is you who are the foolish one at this table." Turning to Axel, she added, "I am tired and growing uncomfortable."

"Then we will take our leave," he said, immediately standing and extending a hand to help her to her feet. "Bree, I'd say it's been a pleasure, but I'm not in the business of lying for the sake of flattery. The rest of you, I apologize you were brought here for what appears to be a personal vendetta. I will be in touch to set up meetings with each of you soon. Enjoy the rest of the evening."

Kat's hand in his, they started for the doors, but they paused when Bree called out, "Safe travels home. I would hate for something unfavorable to befall you or the life you carry."

Axel slowly turned, but before he could say anything, everyone was gasping and shooting to their feet.

Everyone but Bree.

She was on her knees, shadows and flames at her throat, hissing in pain.

"If you ever threaten my husband or child again, you and I will start a game of our own, Miss DelaCrux," Kat said coldly.

"You cannot kill me," Bree gasped out. "You have no idea what you are dealing with."

Kat's head cocked to the side, and by the gods, she was terrifying as embers sparked in her curls and flames flared along the skirt of her gown. But her smile was all controlled rage. "The Fates are fickle, aren't they, Miss DelaCrux?"

And Axel could swear Bree paled.

"Good evening, everyone," Kat said. "Again, our apologies, but sometimes dramatics are indeed necessary."

Then she was grabbing his hand, and he followed her out of the dining room. Neither of them spoke until they were crossing out of the Dispensary District. Only then did he drag her down a side street and have her pressed against a building, his mouth on hers.

"You are so incredibly exquisite, kitten," he breathed before sliding his tongue into her mouth once more.

When they did finally break apart, he let his brow rest against hers. One of his hands was on her hip, the other at her nape, and he swiped his thumb along the pulse in her throat.

"You shouldn't have let me drink from you tonight," he said softly. "Are you all right?"

"Fine," she murmured, pushing her fingers into his hair. "Just a little tired.

The hand on her hip slid to her stomach. "And the babe?"

"He's fine too, Axel," she said with a soft smile.

"How could I be so weak that one taste of blood sent me into an uncontrollable bloodlust?" he muttered, his eyes falling closed in shame.

"You are not weak," she said firmly. "It makes you relatable to show that you don't have everything figured out. It shows you are like them and not above them. It makes us stronger."

"How are you so utterly perfect?" he asked, opening his eyes to stare into hers.

Tipping her head back against the wall, she gave him a small smile.

Brushing his lips over hers once more, he took her hand and tugged her to him. "Send Luka a message, kitten. Let's get you home."

But her brows pinched, a hand going to her stomach.

Axel immediately tensed. "What's wrong?"

"It seemed too easy tonight, right?"

"Nothing about that was easy," he said.

"I think I just thought . . ." She shook her head, giving him a too bright smile. "I'm sure it's nothing. Let's go home."

But he was still thinking about her words hours later as she slept beside him.

It seemed too easy.

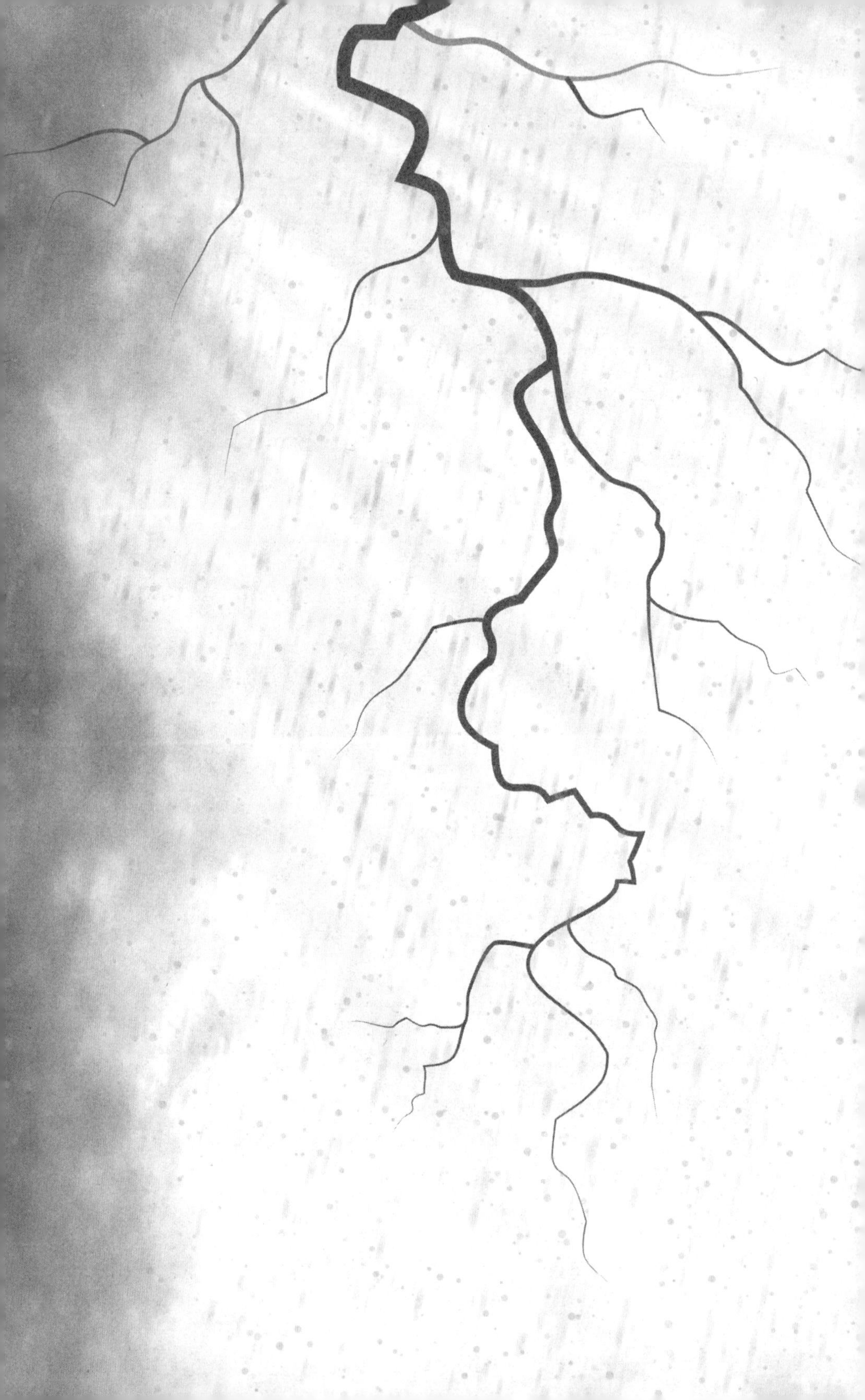

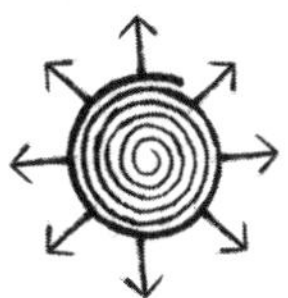

35
TESSA

Tessa lurched as her earbuds were plucked from her ears, spilling coffee down the front of her shirt.

"Up," Theon said, taking the coffee mug from her.

"Gods, Theon, could you be any more annoying right now?" she grumbled, getting to her feet. She'd known he was down here. She'd seen him walk into the kitchen, and even if she hadn't, their bond knew. Content to an extent but also wanting.

"You're in a mood this morning," he retorted with a hint of amusement.

"How do we even know it's morning?" she muttered. "There's no sun here."

But that wasn't the only reason she was in a mood. She was growing incredibly restless in the Underground. She needed fresh air and to see Nylah and Roan. Needed to see the godsdamn sky.

But she also *needed*.

True to their words, neither Theon nor Luka had touched her since Brecken's death.

No. That wasn't true.

They'd touched her. They'd held her and comforted her. Pulled her close and draped limbs over her in sleep. But there had been no sex.

And someone had removed all the alcohol from the penthouse.

And Tristyn was avoiding her because she would absolutely bribe him for some lull-leaf.

So yeah, she was in a fucking mood.

But . . .

While she would never admit it to them, she felt freer in a way. She'd taken a lot of freedoms for her own these past months. She'd left Theon and chosen her path back to him. She'd made choices and faced the consequences. She'd given Luka freedom, allowing him the choice to come back to her. She'd chosen her own destiny and purpose rather than what everyone else had told her she should be. Salvation over destruction, and in some cases, destruction over salvation. Her future was hers and hers alone.

But she'd also chosen to let herself love and be loved, and that had opened a door to something she hadn't expected. Other . . . emotions. Feelings she didn't know what to do with. She'd been just as trapped by emotions her entire life. Forced to shove them down to avoid punishment by Cordelia. Then forced to hide them because it meant unwanted attention. Until eventually, it had become second nature. It was easier to be nothing when you felt nothing.

Until she'd started letting herself love.

Then Luka and Theon had taken it upon themselves to make sure she learned how to feel every godsdamn thing.

She hated them for it.

And she loved them for it.

But it still fucking hurt.

On top of all that, she knew there was more to come. She could still feel their anger about her going to the Falein Kingdom over two weeks ago, and it had her on edge. For two people forcing her to confront her emotions, they were doing a fine job of avoiding their own. But every time she tried to pick a fight with them about it, they said nothing. Sometimes her own anger would flare because of it, and they'd let it. Sometimes she'd feel a sense of rejection, because if they were forcing her to be vulnerable with them, couldn't they do the same? Anger to sadness. Irritation to apathy. They were forcing her to deal with all of it. Never once leaving her alone, even when she screamed at them to do so.

"Go change," Theon said. "Luka is waiting for you upstairs."

"Change into what?" she drawled. "A different pair of leggings and another sweatshirt?"

He smirked but didn't reply, once again not rising to her bait for a fight.

She sighed, gesturing to the books she'd been studying. Razik had given them to her when she'd asked him for help in learning more about Marks. Maybe she could figure out this power transfer thing, and then they wouldn't need to worry about bringing her mother here.

"We need to figure out how to transfer power to you, Theon," she said.

"Not to mention trying to figure out Rordan's plans. Your father is out there. So is Eviana with Corbin and Lange. Then there's the Fates—"

"That's quite the list," he interrupted, sliding his hands into his pockets.

"Yes, it is," she snapped. "And instead of doing anything about it, we're sitting on our asses in the fucking Underground."

He smiled again, tilting his head.

"And you're being a dick. Both of you are. It's no wonder I went to the Falein Kingdom without the two of you." She planted her hands on her hips. "Come to think of it, I should get Tristyn and go again. I bet he'd be happy to, and he'd bring some lull-leaf and *agaveheart* too."

His features darkened, and his words were tight when Theon said, "Careful, beautiful. Get upstairs and change."

She rolled her eyes, instead plopping back down onto the sofa and reaching for her earbuds. "*You* go change. Then you and Luka can fuck off and go do whatever it is you're planning by yourselves."

"Gods, I forgot what an absolute pain in the ass you can be sometimes," Theon growled. And before she knew it, he was picking her up and throwing her over his shoulder, her earbuds dropping to the floor.

"Theon! Put me down!" she demanded, hanging upside down. When he ignored her yet again, she snarled, letting some of her power out. But he was prepared, his darkness already there and acting as a shield against her.

Then he sent that darkness to caress her own magic, and *gods*. Every part of her existence keened with need. Now he was just being intentionally cruel.

She felt him huff a dark chuckle as he kicked open the door to their room. Still hanging upside down over his shoulder, she couldn't see Luka, but she heard him just fine.

"I see her mood has improved," Luka said, and she knew without a doubt there was a smirk playing on his lips.

"Fuck off, Luka Mors," she spat. Then she was uttering more curses as Theon dumped her onto the bed.

"This godsdamn mouth of yours," Theon muttered as he stared down at her, loosening his tie and tossing it aside. "Will you please stop with your dramatics and get changed now?"

"My *dramatics?*" she repeated in outrage, scrambling up and standing on the bed so she was eye level with him. "I am trapped inside fucking mountains, Theon. No sky. No wind. It's suffocating. My power is—I'm—I can't—"

"We *know*, Tessa," he said firmly. "You think we can't feel you? That we haven't been monitoring your emotions these last weeks? Would you *look* at Luka?"

Her head whipped to the side, where she found Luka standing with a pile of clothing. It appeared to be . . . training clothes? And the look the dragon was giving her was clearly unimpressed.

Her eyes narrowed. "Where are we going?"

He shrugged. "If you'd stop throwing a godsdamn fit, we'd show you."

"Tell me," she countered, lifting her chin in defiance.

"Trust us," Luka threw back.

She glared at him, but he didn't back down.

"Either change or wear that. I don't really care," he said, dropping the clothing onto the coffee table. "But you look like a fucking mess."

"I hate you both," she snarled, leaping from the bed and crossing the room. With little fanfare, she stripped down, knowing damn well they weren't going to do anything about the hungry way they were watching her.

When she was done, Luka was there, handing her a hair tie. His hair was already up, and when she glanced at Theon, she found him in training attire as well.

"Now what?" she demanded.

"I'd tell you to put on shoes, but . . ." Luka said, arching a brow.

"No," she said simply.

"I figured as much," he said with a shrug, Theon coming closer. Then Luka grabbed her hand, Traveling them.

A moment later, she was outside. Instead of being under the mountains, she was in them. Inhaling deeply, she closed her eyes as the wind blew across her face. A few stray hairs fluttered against her cheek, and despite her foul mood, she smiled. That smile only grew when howls sounded seconds later.

"Where are we?" she asked, not bothering to open her eyes.

"In the Ozul Mountains," Luka answered. "This is a small outdoor training arena hidden near my cave."

She turned to look at him. "Why haven't you brought me here before?"

"Because I only bring people here I fully trust."

"What's so special about it?"

He held her stare for a few silent seconds before he said, "This place is where one of a handful of memories I have with my father is."

She nodded in understanding, a flicker of familiar guilt sparking in her soul. "Why bring me here now?"

"Because you needed to get out," Theon answered. "You're not made to be cooped up, are you, little storm?"

"No," she breathed, her eyes fluttering closed once more as she inhaled deeply again. The clouds parted, and she felt the warm sun on her skin.

But she snarled as black flames licked her flesh.

"What was that for?" she snapped, her magic yanking to be freed.

"Giving your power something to want," Luka said simply.

Theon was beside him now, his magic drifting around him and his shadow wings flaring wide. "You need to siphon off some power, tempest."

She smiled then. A real smile as she let her power free. It poured from her, racing to tangle with their magic, but also pulsing in time with her own heartbeat. For the first time in perhaps ever, she felt like it was a part of her and not a thing living inside her.

For the first time ever, she felt balanced.

She didn't know how much time passed as she played with her gifts, and they did too. Golden lightning and drifting black embers. Black flames and darkness. Chasing and tangling. Pushing and pulling.

And she laughed as the sun beat down on them.

Something deep and real.

She let herself *feel*.

Not grief or fury. Not defeat or pain. This was joy. This was serenity.

This was happiness.

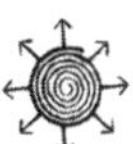

They didn't go back to the Underground that afternoon like she'd expected. No, instead, Luka had taken them directly to his cave. They were still worried about spies nearby, but Traveling directly inside shouldn't have alerted anyone. It had been several weeks now anyway. They just couldn't leave using any of the entrances.

She felt lighter than she ever had, and she hadn't stopped smiling since that morning. Theon and Luka had gone to shower. She'd done the same, surprised to find them still occupied when she emerged from the room she'd stayed in last time. They'd all showered separately, and she was okay with that, wanting to savor and explore this newfound lightness.

Wandering down a hall, she trailed her fingers along the wall, studying the large empty frames. Some were gold, some silver. Some were wood and others were inlaid with jewels. Such a bizarre thing to collect.

Continuing to the kitchen, she poured herself a glass of water before rummaging through the cupboards for something to eat. The sound of Luka's bedroom door opening had her turning and stilling as the two of them emerged. They were both in lightweight pants, and they were both shirtless.

And there was a tension rolling off them that instantly had her on alert.

She straightened, setting her glass aside as her eyes roamed over bare skin and muscles that disappeared below waistbands riding low on their hips.

"We need to discuss a few weeks ago," Theon said, his tone all cold fury.

Her gaze snapped to his. "What?"

"Falein Kingdom," he continued. "What were you doing there, Tessa?"

Even knowing they wouldn't hurt her, she took a step back from them as they prowled closer. "Looking for a mirror gate. You know this."

"Why?"

"To destroy it."

"Because?" he pressed.

She gasped as black flames suddenly licked at her skin. They didn't burn, but they made her *burn*.

"Tessa," Theon barked.

"If I destroy the mirror gates, they can't come here," she said, distracted by the way Luka's fire was teasing her.

"The Fates?"

"The Fates. Achaz. Any of them," she replied, lifting a hand to watch tendrils of black flames dance along her palm.

"Achaz can't come here," Theon said.

"What?" she murmured, that magic toying with the bands of light around her wrists.

"Achaz can't come here," Theon said again. "Unless you know something we don't?"

That had her eyes dragging back to his at the realization of what they were doing. That fascination turned to anger.

"Just ask me," she snapped. "You don't have to distract me."

"Apparently we do," Luka said, and she gritted her teeth when his magic suddenly tightened its hold, pulling her hands behind her back. "We tried asking you, temptress. Multiple times we asked you about that vision that trapped you."

"It had nothing to do with that vision," she retorted, yanking on the bindings at her wrists.

Theon clicked his tongue. "I know you're an excellent liar, beautiful."

She tugged at the magical hold again, but Luka's power only tightened. Then Theon added his too.

And she was somewhat weakened. They'd spent hours this morning in that training arena, and she'd let her power free to do what it pleased. She hadn't had time to rest, let alone time to replenish her reserves. She was still powerful, but so were they. Together more so, but still—

"This was a set up," she accused. "It had nothing to do with letting me siphon power."

"Of course it did, Tessa," Theon said, moving to stand in front of her and taking her chin between his thumb and forefinger. "We always know what you need. You needed to breathe. Needed to experience joy, and gods, were you a vision. Your laugh competes for one of my favorite sounds in all the realms."

"What's the other? The sound of your own voice," she snapped in irritation.

He smirked. "The sound of my name on your lips when you come."

Her stomach dipped at those words, and she internally scolded herself. This was not the time for *that*. She was too angry.

"You made me expend my magic so the two of you could overpower me to get information from me," she bit back.

"That's the thing, baby girl," Luka said, and she gasped again because when had he moved behind her? But there he was. A bare chest pressed against her back, her bound hands far too close to something she'd been wanting for weeks. His breath coasted over her ear as he said, "We shouldn't have to coerce information out of you. Not anymore."

"Unless you aren't ours as much as we are yours?" Theon said, drawing her attention back to him.

"You know that's not true," she argued, her knees starting to go weak at having them both so close and so . . . utterly dominant. She hated it, and she loved it. The idea of submitting made her want to rage, but the idea of not having to *think* made her want to fall at their feet just for a little while. After weeks of being forced to face emotions that had too much control over her—that made her hurt and grieve and rage—she wanted to feel *good*. Like earlier today.

"Then why did you go without us? Why not tell us? Why go to gods-damn Blackheart?" Theon demanded.

"I . . ."

"Speak, Tessa," Theon snapped, and she glared up at him because it would still always be a battle.

But before she could snap back, Luka was at her ear again. "Don't pretend to be upset right now," he growled. "Don't pretend you don't want to give him control in this moment. He's the one you need right now. Answer him, temptress."

She swallowed thickly, his low voice and Theon's penetrating gaze doing things to her. Things they'd refused her for weeks. Not to punish her, but to force her to learn to feel.

And now . . .

She stared up at Theon. "I was protecting you both. Because you are mine, and I am yours. You taught me that's what you do for those you love."

"We do protect those we love, but how are we supposed to protect *you* if you won't let us in? Secrets tear us apart. *You* taught me that," he countered darkly.

"I thought you'd try to stop me," she whispered, emotion clogging her throat. "And I . . . Achaz can't come here. That was the vision I had. There's something here he wants. Getting rid of the mirror gates would keep him out. The Fates too."

"Baby girl," Luka purred into her ear, "there's a balance here. You have to trust me to let you fly as much as you need to trust him to take control. We balance each other as much as we balance you. That's why it works."

"But not if you cut us out," Theon snapped, and she could feel all the fury he'd been repressing since he found her in Falein Kingdom.

She nodded, then she gasped again when Theon's fingers left her chin, instead wrapping around her throat and pulling her forward. His mouth hovered over hers, and she tasted the words when he said, "Say it."

"I'm yours. Both of yours. Every piece of me," she rasped.

His eyes fell closed at the words, some of the tension melting away. He still hovered over her mouth as if he was breathing her into his soul. It was with a start she realized she'd made them doubt her. She hadn't meant to, had only been trying to protect them, along with the realm, but she'd made them doubt her loyalty.

Again.

Shame and guilt slithered up her spine, and she tried to pull away. But Luka was still at her back, holding her in place.

"Do you trust us?" Luka asked, pressing into her more as one of his hands snaked around her torso, cupping a breast.

"Yes," she breathed.

"Do you? Because if you did, you wouldn't have left us behind, Tessa," he retorted, the soft caressing of her breast morphing into a harsh pinch of her nipple.

But the cry of surprise that fell from her lips instantly became a moan of pleasure as dark power skittered along her bare legs. Her power rose to meet it, greedy and wanting. A reflection of her own emotions, and she finally understood what they'd been trying to tell her all along. Why even when she'd learned to wield her power, she still couldn't always control it. Some of that was because it was pure Chaos, but a greater part was because she allowed herself to be the same.

Luka's other hand trailed up to her shoulder, gathering her hair and pulling it over her shoulder. His cheek nestled against her temple, his stubble chafing her skin.

"She says she trusts us, Theon," Luka said, a slight mocking in his tone that made her tense in irritation.

"She says she's ours," Theon replied darkly, head tilting as the furious emerald depths held hers. For the first time in a long time, she felt like the prey.

"Can we believe her?" Luka continued to mock, and her annoyance crept nearer to anger.

"I don't know," Theon said. "She's an excellent liar."

"That she is," Luka agreed, callused fingers dragging slowly between the valley of her breasts, down her stomach, lower and lower.

She was battling herself now. Her anger with her need, her hips tilting forward, trying to catch his fingers. But she was so crushed between them, the movement made her grind into Theon's thigh, and *oh*.

Luka chuckled darkly, and she realized that sound had escaped her mouth.

Dammit.

"So needy," he mocked again.

"Says the two insecure males seeking validation," she snarked back.

They both went too still, and she tensed, both satisfied with herself for pushing them the way they were pushing her, and also wondering what they were going to do about it.

"We're not the ones with something to prove here, little storm," Theon finally said, straightening and once more towering over her.

His hand slipped from her throat, and she swallowed the whimper that tried to escape at the distance it put between them. The dark curl of his lips told her he knew though. They both knew everything that was going on in her soul.

"You trust us. We're yours?" Theon asked curtly.

She nodded.

"Words, Tessa," he snapped.

"Yes," she bit out, Luka's hand now splayed flat on her belly.

"Prove it," Luka growled low in her ear, those two words so godsdamn sensual she couldn't help it when she clenched her thighs together.

His hands slid to her hips, grabbing the hem of her shirt and pulling it over her head, leaving her standing in nothing but her undergarments. She was staring up at Theon, his eyes dark with his power, anger, and lust.

Then Luka's hands were at her shoulders, and he leaned down to speak darkly in her ear once more. "Show him that mouth can do more than tell lies, temptress."

His hands slipped from her shoulders, their magic pulling away too, leaving her standing alone in the tension-filled air.

This was it.

She knew that.

They were proving a point, and she needed to prove her own. They were hers. Knew what she needed and were willing to do whatever it took to make sure she got it, even if it went against their natural instincts. They were giving her love and freedom and balance. All she wanted was to give them what they needed too.

Prove it.

The words echoed in her soul.

They weren't asking because they were insecure. She knew they'd stay by her side from now to the end of time. They were asking for her to give them something she'd never give to anyone else.

Control.

Loyalty.

Give it to them, and trust they wouldn't use it against her.

Never again.

Prove it.

Holding Theon's stare, she slowly sank to her knees before him. Saw his eyes widen the slightest amount, as though he hadn't thought she'd choose to do this. Heard the sharp inhale despite his features staying hard and cold.

Her hands slid up his thighs before her fingers dipped into the waistband of his pants, pulling them down. They slid to the floor, and he kicked them aside with a precise movement. Steady. Controlled.

Taking him in her hand, she stroked him once. Then, still holding his stare, she slowly wrapped her mouth around him, taking him down her throat in one fluid movement.

"Fuck!" he barked, his hips jerking forward and pressing in farther.

Luka's dark chuckle danced along her exposed skin, goosebumps popping up.

"I told you her mouth was made for this," Luka said, his voice all gravel.

Tessa pulled back slowly, gliding her lips, then sucking him down again. That hard mask he was wearing finally cracked, something almost pained flitting across his features.

She may be on her knees before him, but she was the one in control. Yet another point they were trying to prove to her.

Her head bobbed a few more times, her hands drifting up to brace herself against Theon's thighs. His muscles tensed and strained. Fists clenching and unclenching at his sides until, as if he couldn't take it anymore, a single finger slid along her jaw before tracing her lips wrapped around his cock.

Then another hand was smoothing down her hair. She felt Luka crouch beside her, his voice caressing every part of her when he praised, "That's our girl."

Gods. His voice. His words. All of it made her dripping core clench with need, reminding her just how empty she was right now.

"Look at him, Tessa," Luka went on, his fingers digging into her hair. "He'd let the world die for you, you know that, right? Would lay the ruin of the stars at your feet."

A throaty hiss escaped Theon as she dragged her tongue along the underside of his dick, circling the crown once before sucking on the tip. Then his hand was on the other side of her head, fisting her hair. Both of them pushing and pulling, guiding her up and down his cock.

"Your mouth is so hot. So wet. So fucking perfect when you're not throwing your bratty tantrums," Luka murmured, his other hand trailing up her thigh. She whimpered, another curse coming from Theon as the sound vibrated around him.

Her own desire was a thing threatening to swallow her whole as she started rocking slightly when Luka's fingers trailed higher.

"So fucking needy," he taunted, and she cried out when he smoothed his fingertips over her undergarments. "But you owe us, don't you, temptress?

For sneaking out. Leaving us behind. Putting yourself in danger without us." His other fist tightened at her scalp, yanking sharply, and she cried out again. "For not trusting us to let you be your wild and untamed self. We would never shove you behind us. Not anymore. But you did that to us, didn't you?"

And her eyes widened at *his* anger, understanding just how deeply she'd cut him once again.

"Fucking fuck," Theon gasped, his hips thrusting harder, faster, down her throat. She wasn't even doing much now, Luka holding her still so Theon could take his pleasure.

Pleasure only *she* could give him.

She felt him swell in her mouth, knew he was close.

"He doesn't need to see it, baby girl," Luka whispered darkly into her ear. "He just needs to feel you swallow him down. To know *he's* inside of you. A part of you. To know you can never get away from him."

Luka pushed her down, and Theon's hand was at her neck, feeling everything as he fucked her mouth. Then he stilled as hot spurts hit her tongue. Another hissed curse sounded as he thrust a few more times, making sure every last drop stayed with her and holding himself deep down her throat.

And she held his lust-crazed stare when she swallowed around him, constricting his cock one last time.

"So fucking perfect," he growled, pulling her up by the throat.

His lips were on hers, tasting himself as he licked into her mouth. He was still panting, each breath labored as he spoke against her lips, "Never wear his fucking jacket again."

She smirked at the reference to Tristyn's coat he'd found her in months ago outside of the hotel and then again a few weeks ago.

His fingers squeezed her neck in warning. "Never. Again. Tessa."

"Never again," she breathed.

"Good girl," he murmured, kissing her deeply once more.

Theon pulled back, his hand sliding to her jaw, and he turned her head. Her eyes widened to find Luka standing so close, sapphire eyes glowing with a promise of more. He'd lost his pants at some point, and he was hard and wanting. His muscles were coiled tight with restraint, and he was glaring at her when he said, "You belong to no one, but whose are you, Tessa?"

She knew what he was saying. What he was asking of her. "The two of you," she whispered. "Never alone again."

"Do you trust us?"

"Yes," she breathed.

"But can we trust you?"

She started, some of her lust-addled mind clearing. "What?"

"You heard me," Luka snapped, one hand fisting his dick. "Can we trust you?"

"Y-yes," she stuttered, watching the muscles in his forearm flex with each pass as he stroked himself. She was beyond needy at this point, and it wasn't until a dark tendril grabbed her wrist that she realized her hand was drifting to her cunt to relieve some of the pressure.

Luka smirked. "Like we'd let you touch yourself right now, temptress."

She pulled against Theon's magic, turning to glare at him. The curl of his lips matched Luka's.

"I might be the controlling one, beautiful, but I'm much more forgiving than he is," Theon said. Taking her chin, he turned her face back to Luka once more. "Better start working on that."

She shifted to face him fully, squaring her shoulders. "What do you want me to do? Crawl after you?" she said, not holding back her snark.

"I should make you do that," Luka growled back, his hand shuttling faster over himself. "I should make you crawl all the way to the bedroom, then have Theon restrain you while you watch me fuck my hand, paint you in cum, and leave your cunt needy and wanting."

She blinked at the horror of that idea. But her core clenched, because fuck, was his mouth dirty.

"Where's that bratty mouth now, baby girl?" Luka taunted.

She didn't know what he wanted from her. Theon was easy. Give him control, trust him to take care of you, and he would do just that. But Luka was different. He needed loyalty.

"I'm sorry," she whispered, not knowing what else to say.

Apparently that was the wrong thing, because a low snarl rumbled from him. He stalked across the room, and when she tried to step back on instinct, Theon lightly shoved her forward.

"Do not apologize to me for trying to protect what is yours, Tessa," Luka snapped.

Then *he* was dropping to his knees before her, and she didn't understand what was happening. Only knew she never wanted it to stop as Luka pressed his face to her center, his tongue making a long stroke. Over and over, stopping to suck on her clit every once in a while. There was no rhyme or reason, and it kept her on an edge. His tongue went deep, tasting and feasting, and her legs were trembling, threatening to give out.

"I've got you, little storm," Theon whispered darkly, bare skin suddenly at her back, and thank the gods, because she might have collapsed completely. His lips trailed down her neck, open-mouthed and sucking. One of his hands slid down her thighs before hooking under her knee. True to his word, he held her up as he pulled her leg, giving Luka better access to her, and *gods. This* is what Luka had been talking about.

I can only imagine what you'll do when we're both worshipping you.

She could feel Theon already hard again and pressing against her back. Her hand went into Luka's hair, still down from his shower, and she tried to hold him in place, tried to grind against his face as her orgasm shimmered just out of reach.

Theon huffed a dark laugh, his breath ghosting over her shoulder, as a hand reached around and tweaked a nipple. "You think it will be that easy with him?"

What was he—

Then Luka pulled back, getting to his feet. Her arousal glistened on his face, and she was fucking *dripping*. Dripping and on an edge and so—

A frustrated growl sounded, her power flaring and snapping out at him. Because now she was more than irritated. She got it. He was pissed, but was he really going to leave her like this? To prove a godsdamn point? He wouldn't . . . Would he?

"Are you angry, temptress?" he taunted, his black flames sinking into her light. She ground her teeth, fighting back, but the fact remained her reserves were lagging after this morning, while theirs . . .

"How?" she demanded, narrowing her eyes as she yanked on her power again. His flames only sank in more, and she grimaced at the dominance.

"We drank rations," he said with a mocking smile.

"You did *what*?"

"We drank rations," he repeated, once again casually stroking his cock while Theon still had an arm wrapped around her waist, holding her in place.

"You brought me here, tricked me into expending a large amount of my magic, and then drank Fae blood to restore your own so you could overpower me?" she seethed.

Luka sprang forward, gripping her face in one large hand at the same time Theon sank his teeth into the tender spot between her neck and shoulder.

"We did, and look at you right now. Easily overpowered," Luka sneered.

"I could draw from Theon," she snarled in return.

"And what if we weren't here?"

"What?"

"What if you went to another kingdom on a mission you didn't tell us about? What if there had been more than a powerless seraph waiting for you? What if you had expended your magic, only to find it a godsdamn trap, and you had no one to draw from? No power left to kill and restore your magic? What if Dex was waiting for you? Rordan? What if fucking Achaz had found his way here, and you had nothing left, Tessa? What then?" Luka demanded.

And oh gods.

That was all she could think as the true weight of understanding settled over her. As she felt not only their fury over her actions, but their *fear*.

He'd give her the freedom to do what she wanted; he only asked that she trust him to be at her side. Trust them not to force her to make herself smaller. Trust them to let her be wild and untamed. Light and dark. Trust them to let her run and be what she was always meant to be. Trust them to be at her side to catch her in the hard times.

They belonged to her, and she belonged to them.

A balance that existed after all.

She held his harsh gaze, the words crystal clear this time when she said, "I understand. I'm sorry."

"Godsdamn right you are," he growled.

Then he was grabbing her, her legs wrapping around his waist as he hoisted her up. His mouth slammed to hers, all teeth and dominance, and it wasn't until she was being dropped to a bed that she realized he'd moved. Carried her into his bedroom and climbed onto the bed, pushing her knees wide, and there was nothing gentle about it. Not this time.

Luka slid into her with one sharp thrust, and she cried out, but Theon was there, swallowing the sound with his mouth as he kissed her deeply. Thoroughly. Possessively.

"Ours," he snarled onto her lips.

And she nodded frantically, Luka pounding into her.

"Words," Theon snapped.

"Yours," she gasped, already back at the edge.

His mouth moved to her cheek, her jaw. Down her throat, nipping and biting as Luka's hands slid under her ass, tilting her hips up and allowing him to go deeper. Harder.

Theon was at her breasts now, plucking at one nipple while sucking on the other, and she was everything and nothing. There were too many sensations and not enough, and she couldn't have sorted her emotions if she'd wanted to.

And she didn't.

She just wanted to feel them. All of them. In every piece of her. As if this was what she'd been waiting for her entire existence. For them to find her.

"If another lie passes those lips when speaking to us—" Luka grunted, each word a labored pant as he drove into her again and again.

"It won't," she gasped, her hands grasping for something, anything. Theon shifted, nudging closer, and she found his cock, wrapping her fingers around it and stroking.

A groan came from him, and he started thrusting into her hand, his lips still roving. Tongue still licking.

"And no more fucking secrets," Luka snarled.

She nodded frantically, Theon still sucking and biting at her nipple, focused on his task. "I swear it," she gasped. "*Please*, Luka. Theon. *Please*."

Theon's hand snaked down her torso, his fingers finding her clit and circling as Luka shifted, hitting the spot that made her seize up. She tumbled into bliss, shuddering and tensing and clenching as Theon kissed her and Luka continued to thrust, cursing.

She went lax against the bed, trying to catch her breath as Luka pumped into her a few more times. But then he pulled out, and she started as Theon sat back on his heels.

"What are you . . ."

She trailed off when they both took themselves in hand, fists moving frantically.

"Help him out, baby girl," Luka ordered, the words a low rumble as he stroked and squeezed his cock, slick with her own orgasm.

She glanced at Theon. He was already moving towards her, seeking her mouth again, and she didn't care. Luka liked to watch, and she liked to have control over Theon. So she swirled her tongue around his crown, flicking it on the underside.

"Oh, fuck," Luka growled. "Just like that, baby girl. Keep that bratty mouth occupied."

"So fucking beautiful with my cock in your mouth," Theon ground out, his fingers gently stroking her brow, her cheek, her jaw. "So godsdamn perfect. I always knew you were meant to be mine."

Luka cursed again, and she felt the hot ropes hit her stomach as he came. Seconds later, Theon was pulling from her lips and doing the same. She should care, should hate every part of this, but she didn't. Because just like they knew what she needed, she knew what they needed. Two possessive, dominant beings. They needed to mark what was theirs. Remind her. Prove to themselves. See it with their own eyes.

They had both sat back on their heels, bodies glistening with perspiration and chests heaving as they came down from the intensity of what had just happened. Tessa didn't know who to look at, her gaze bouncing between them, so she let her eyes fall closed, basking in all that they were. For the first time in her entire existence, she felt completely at peace.

Completely balanced.

She needed to shower again.

"We all do," Luka grumbled, the bed shifting, and her eyes flew open.

"What?" she asked, watching him climb off the bed.

"Need to shower again. That's what you said."

Her eyes narrowed. *I didn't say that.*

Theon lurched forward, cupping her cheek and turning her head to him. "Do it again," he mouthed.

If you make me eat a salad after all that, I'm never doing it again, she sent down the bond.

"Burger and fries it is, little storm," he murmured right before he kissed her. Then another hand was turning her the other way, and her lips found Luka's.

This thing between the three of them finally repaired and as it should be.

"Go turn the shower on," Theon told Luka, scooping Tessa into his arms. "Let's get you cleaned up, tempest."

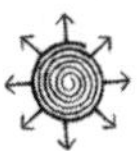

Hours later, they were sitting in the living room. Luka had Traveled to Rockmoor, grabbing them a pizza when she asked for that rather than a burger, and she was on the sofa, nestled into Theon's side and happily eating her third slice. He was scrolling through emails on his phone, and that muscle in his jaw ticked every once in a while. She couldn't decide if it was from the emails or from her eating pizza.

"Here, baby girl," Luka said, handing her a glass of wine before setting a tumbler of liquor down for Theon.

"Thanks," Theon muttered as Luka grabbed a slice of pizza and sat on her other side.

This was still . . . something, and Tessa idly wondered if she'd ever get used to it.

"It will become normal soon enough," Luka said.

She sighed. She needed to get back into the habit of blocking the bond so they didn't hear her every godsdamn thought.

Theon suddenly stiffened beside them, and they both paused, looking at him expectantly.

"What is it?" Luka asked.

"I've been summoned by the rulers. To update them on the status of my Lordship tasks," Theon said slowly.

Tessa set her pizza down, wiping her fingers as she shifted to face him, leaning back against Luka. She could tell by the look on his face he had more to say.

"And?" she prompted.

He hesitated before he ventured, "I've been working on a plan, but we don't do it if you don't want to."

"Me?" she asked, brows arching in surprise.

He nodded. "Yes, you. Not just for this, but for Dagian. Axel. Us. Everything."

Silence hung in the air as Tessa and Luka stared at him.

"I've been working it out for weeks," he added, studying them just as carefully. "But I can come up with something else if you don't want to do it."

Finally, Tessa said, "Tell us everything."

PART THREE

BALANCE

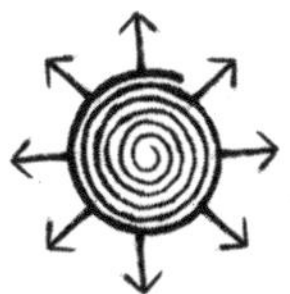

36
LUKA

The soft sound of her throat clearing drew his attention. His eyes connected with hers in the mirror he was facing while going through his morning training routine.

He'd known she was there. Even without that aspect of the bond, he could sense her. Apparently it had something to do with the inevitable bond they now shared, cemented into place when he'd nearly died for her. The only thing that seemed to differ from the bond she shared with Theon was that she could draw from him because of the true Source Mark incorporated with the fourth Source Mark of Devram. But he wasn't even entirely sure if that was true. He'd seen Razik and Eliza combine their gifts when they'd freed Xan. They said it was part of the twin flame bond, but a part of him wondered if it was more than that. Something he'd need to ask his father, he supposed.

He finished the pull-ups he was doing in the training room of his cave, dropping to the floor. She was still near the door, as if unsure if she should enter.

"Those aren't training clothes," he noted, eyeing the full-length silk robe she had cinched at her waist.

She rolled her eyes, crossing her arms. "Obviously."

"Where's Theon?"

"Making phone calls. Preparing for tomorrow," she said with a shrug, looking around the room.

"What's wrong?"

"Nothing."

"Then why won't you look at me?" That had her eyes snapping back to his before she looked away again. "Tessa," he said, the name a warning. "We just had a discussion yesterday about secrets."

She huffed a soft laugh. "Is that what we're calling it? A discussion?"

He smirked. "Sure. I think we should have another one today. I'll coordinate with Theon and let you know when and where."

She laughed again, a little louder, and his chest tightened at the sound. It was one they were hearing a little more with each passing day.

Taking a long drink from his water bottle, he made his way across the room, stopping in front of her. The lightheartedness had faded. She was clearly nervous about something. And despite everything that had been repaired these last weeks, he couldn't help the suspicion that coursed through him. Couldn't help but wonder if whatever she was worried about would be as devastating as the secret of his father.

"What's wrong, Tessa?" he said again, trying to keep that distrust out of his voice.

She shifted on her feet, tucking her hair behind her ear before crossing her arms once more. Toeing at something invisible on the floor, she said, "I need to ask you something."

"Go on."

"Are you . . . upset about the Mark? The one on your chest, I mean."

He looked down at the Mark in the very center of his chest. His eyes going back to her, she glanced up when he didn't say anything.

"Luka?" she asked, his name hesitant on her lips.

"Sorry, baby girl," he finally said. "I'm just trying to figure out why I would be upset about you saving my life."

"Because the choice was taken from you."

"If I was dead, it wouldn't matter, but I assure you, I would have chosen to live," he replied flatly.

"That's not what I mean," she said in frustration, a hand reaching for her hair. But when his eyes narrowed at the movement, she stilled, dropping it back to her side. "I mean you didn't get to choose the Mark. The fact that you have to—You can't—We have to be careful now."

Finally understanding where this was going, he set his water bottle aside before holding out his hand to her. Tentatively, she slipped her fingers into his palm, and he tugged her to him.

She tipped her head back to look up at him, something akin to guilt lingering in her eyes. "You didn't get to choose this," she whispered. "I know what it is to be forced into a bond you didn't want. Didn't get to choose."

He said nothing, only leaned down to kiss her. She melted into him, letting him take control of her mouth as he slid his fingers into her hair. Parting to let his tongue in, she sighed softly when he tugged on her hair and tilted her head for a better angle.

When he pulled back, he pressed his brow to hers. "I understand why this is hard for you, but I'm not upset, Tessa. You saved my life. Kept me here with you and Theon. If you're worried I'm upset that we have to be careful how much distance there is between us, I think we established yesterday that you shouldn't be going *anywhere* without us," he said. "If it means I must remain within a certain radius of you, I don't consider it a hardship."

"It's still a choice that was taken from you," she insisted. "Another thing that I stole from you."

"We're not doing that, Tessa," he said firmly. "We've dealt with what happened, and now we're moving on."

"You can't tell me this is a forgive-and-forget situation," she argued, her power sparking as her emotions heightened.

"You're right. It's not," he agreed. "But I think all three of us have learned from our past mistakes with each other at this point."

"I guess," she murmured.

"Not *I guess.* Last night we all agreed no more lies and no more secrets. If that isn't learning from our past mistakes, I don't know what is. It's that whole balance thing between us."

She gave him a weak smile that told him she still didn't quite believe him.

"Even though I didn't make this choice myself, I wouldn't change this. I would have chosen you. I *do* choose you. I was coming to tell you that day. To see if you still wanted me," he said. "This Mark on my chest makes no difference to me. We may as well call it our Union Mark for all I care."

"Okay," she whispered.

"That's not very convincing," he replied dryly.

"You realize that if something happens to me, if I die, you die too, right?"

"Considering that would put a great deal of distance between us, I understand that just fine. You are immortal, baby girl, and if there comes a day when you do go to the After, I'll follow you there," he said. "But we're immortal too, and Theon will fight death to keep you at his side, so I think we're pretty safe."

"Theon is death," she muttered, worrying her bottom lip. "Do you know he looks *exactly* like Arius? They could be twins."

"Don't say that," Luka said with a curl of his lip. "That would make the two of you far too related."

She huffed another laugh. "We've established multiple times that he is so far removed from Arius that is very clearly not the case. It's just . . . weird."

Luka hummed a response as his hand fell to the small of her back, and he guided her from the training room.

"You aren't going to finish your workout?" she asked in confusion.

He shrugged. "Cutting out early one day won't hurt."

"You never let me cut out early," she grumbled under her breath.

He pinched her side, and she smacked his hand away with a small smirk.

The truth was he could still feel her uncertainty. He might call her needy when they were fucking, but she was annoyingly self-sufficient. And as of late, she didn't crave anyone's approval. The fact that she was seeking his appealed to his nature of needing to care for her. If she needed reassurance, he was fine with that. He'd take the time to make it happen.

"There you are," Theon said when they appeared in the living room. "I was just coming to look for you. Are you all right, beautiful?"

"Yeah," she said with a sigh, making her way to the coffeepot. She pulled her hair up, piling it atop her head as she moved, then paused when she realized she didn't have a hair tie.

Luka was already moving, swiping up one from a tin on a nearby end table to hand it to her. His gaze connected with Theon's, and he gave him a questioning look that Luka just subtly shook his to in response.

They were all getting used to having one another in their thoughts again, and if they spoke down the shared bond, Tessa would hear it.

She gave him another small smile in thanks for the hair tie, pressing her lips to his jaw, before turning to pour a mug of coffee. Crossing the kitchen, she paused next to Theon, pushing onto her toes to do the same, but he turned his head, capturing her mouth instead.

"I'm going to get ready for the day," she said with another soft smile before making her way to the bedroom.

As soon as they heard the bathroom door click closed, Theon turned to Luka.

"What's wrong? Is this about yesterday and what happened with the three of us?"

"No," Luka said, going to get a fresh bottle of cold water. "It's nothing like that. It's a her and I thing, but it is something I need to address."

"Okay," Theon said, waiting for him to go on.

"I know we weren't planning on taking her back there for a while, but we need to go to the Underground. We need to talk to Cienna."

"Now?" Theon asked. "Can't it wait until after we meet with the Ladies and Jove tomorrow?"

"No," he said simply. "You won't be the only one who shows up at that meeting with a wife."

Theon's lips tipped up in a genuine smile. "It's about fucking time."

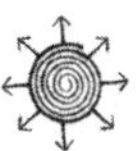

"It's dark down here," Tessa grumbled. "And musty. And dark. Too dark."

"We're not staying," Theon assured her. "It's just for a few hours. It's important, Tessa."

"Right," she sighed again, and Luka glanced over his shoulder to find her trailing along, her hand dragging on the wall. "We don't like it."

The passages were too narrow for the three of them to walk side by side, and Theon had slowed his steps to stay beside her as much as possible.

She looked up at him, eyes wide. "I like the dark, but I can't always stay there."

Theon reached over, smoothing a hand down her hair before dropping a kiss to the top of her head. "I know. It's only for a few hours, and we'll go back to Luka's cave. We can sit on his balcony the rest of the day."

"And after the meeting tomorrow?"

He hesitated, all of them having stopped now. Luka crossed his arms as they worked to convince her on this.

"It will depend on how things go," Theon finally said. "But my hope is to go to Arius House so we can figure out our next moves."

"It's dark there too," she said with a frown.

"It's not underground."

She shrugged, moving forward again. "Still dark."

They continued on, following the passages. Cienna had agreed to see them, but said they needed to do so at her place and not the penthouse. They'd all been irritated, but they'd learned the hard way not to piss off the Witch.

A half hour later, they finally emerged in her space, finding her at a work-table with Gia. The two of them had their heads together over something on the table, and neither of them bothered to look up at their entrance.

Tessa immediately started wandering, but at least she was contained here. She peered at various objects, chaos drifting around her fingers when she would pick something up. Cienna would have yelled at them for touching her things. Tessa apparently had a pass.

Until she came to a black orb, shadows seeming to swirl in its depths.

"Not that one," Cienna called, still not looking up from whatever it was they were studying.

Tessa frowned, her fingers still hovering over it.

"Theon," Cienna warned.

Theon went to her side, lacing his fingers with hers before drawing her away. "The faster we speak with Cienna, the faster we can leave."

"I'm not who you need to speak with," Cienna said, and Luka tensed.

"Then why make us come all the way here?" he asked, the words laced with a growl.

"Because I am the one who can tell you who you *do* need to speak with," she answered, finally deigning to turn and face them. With a pointed look at Tessa, she added, "Does she know why you're here?"

Tessa's brow furrowed. "What does that mean?"

Luka shifted on his feet. He didn't really want to do this in front of everyone, but apparently he was going to.

"Luka?" she asked, her confusion shifting to panic down the bond.

"You're worried about this Mark and me being upset," Luka said, gesturing to his chest. "I know we talked about it, but you're still unsure. I need you to understand that I would have chosen this. I do choose this. I choose you, not because I was forced to or because of some bond."

"Okay," she said, dragging out the word.

He pulled at the back of his neck. This was awkward as fuck.

Tessa's head tilted to the side. "I've never seen you so . . ."

"Nervous?" Theon provided.

Luka glanced at him, flipping him his middle finger when he found a smirk of amusement on his face.

"I know you prefer action over pretty words," Luka said, focusing back on her. "So I'm choosing a different Mark."

"You're . . ." Her eyes went wide, and she looked down at the Mark that encircled her wrist. "You're going to take the Union Mark?"

"If that is still something you want," he said, dropping his hands to his sides.

Her eyes came back to his, a smile lighting up her entire face. But not just her face. Her head, her arms, her aura all glowed faintly with her light.

"Of course I want that, Luka," she said softly.

Thank the gods that was over.

He turned back to Cienna. "Now tell us why we need to talk to someone else?"

"Because I can't perform the Mark you need," she said simply.

"But you did for us," Theon argued.

"Yes, for the *two* of you. Adding the third part makes it complicated. A new Mark had to be created," Cienna said.

"No one can create new Marks." But Cienna again looked pointedly at Tessa. "That's different," Theon gritted out.

"It's not, but she will have to bestow it."

"I don't know *how* to create Marks," Tessa said, shaking her head. "I won't put them in danger like that."

"You don't have to. You need to talk to the one who created the Mark for you," Cienna replied, already turning back to the work surface.

"And who is that?" Theon asked.

He'd told Luka that Cienna had figured something out for the Union Mark. Apparently, she'd had some help.

"Her cousin," Cienna answered.

"My cousin?" Tessa repeated. "You mean, Scarlett? She's not here."

"Obviously."

"And I destroyed the mirror."

"You destroyed *a* mirror. Two, I believe," Cienna corrected.

"So we need to find another mirror gate?" Tessa replied, her voice rising a little with her sudden panic and annoyance. "We don't have time for that."

Theon and Luka exchanged a look before Theon took her shoulders and turned her to face him. "Tessa, we know where a mirror is."

"You do?"

He nodded.

"The Arius Kingdom mirror gate?" she pressed. When he nodded again, she said, "Why didn't you tell me?"

"You never asked us," Luka cut in, probably more harshly than he should have. "You went about scheming without us instead."

She sent him a flat look.

We do not need to rehash this yet again, she snapped down the bond.

He held her gaze as he replied, *Do you want to get married or not?*

Now I need to think about it a little more.

Brat.

Ass.

The corner of his mouth kicked up before he crossed to her and took her hand.

"Thank you, Cienna," he called as they herded Tessa down the passageway.

The Witch just waved them off, already back to studying something with Gia.

"Where are we going?" Tessa asked, her voice breathy.

"Easy, baby girl," Luka soothed. "We just need to get out of this part of the cavern, and then we can Travel."

"Travel where? Where is the mirror in Arius Kingdom?"

"You know, now that I think about it, you already know the answer," Theon said, leading the way this time.

"I do?"

"Yep. I told you about it the week classes and trainings started for the Selection Year."

"You told me a lot of things at that time," she retorted flatly. "A lot of it was overshadowed by the fact that is also when you told me of your father's plans."

"Understandable you don't remember," Theon replied.

"I really don't need you to chastise me for not recalling every mundane and stupid thing you tried to make me remember back then, Theon. So perhaps you could just tell me again," she drawled.

"One would think you'd be in a better mood after fucking, pizza, and wine yesterday," Theon called back to her.

"One would think you didn't enjoy having your cock down my throat considering you're making me never want to do it again," she bit back.

Luka huffed a laugh. "Keep going, Theon. My cock will thank you every time I get to be in her mouth while you watch on."

"Fuck off, Luka," Theon retorted. Then he added, "It's in the Underground, Tessa."

Look how fast he changes his tune when you threaten to take away sucking his dick, baby girl, Luka said down the bond. *Tuck that away for later.*

She doesn't need any more ideas on how to get what she wants from me, Theon muttered.

She sighed. "Can we please just get out of these tunnels?"

The words brought them all back to the moment, and they hurried on. An hour later, they were back in the Charter District, but instead of going to the building that housed the penthouse. They walked past it. Continuing down a few makeshift streets, they came to another building. It wasn't as tall, and where all the other buildings in the District were onyx, this one was light grey marble with a wall around it of the same.

Tessa frowned, tipping her head back to stare up at it. "What is this place?

"My father's offices, along with the offices of those he leaves in charge here. Axel actually has an office here. He just never uses it. None of us do. Reception is shit everywhere here," Theon said. "Let's go."

They nodded to the security at the wall before striding in, then again to the sentinels at the entrance of the building. When they made it to the main foyer, they went straight through, going to the end of a long hallway where onyx double doors stood. Theon placed his palm on one, letting his magic seep into it, before they clicked open.

"They're not warded?" Tessa asked.

"Only the St. Orcas line can enter," Theon answered, striding in.

Luka ushered Tessa through, following behind her. She looked over her shoulder at him. "You've been here though?"

"A few times," he answered, closing the door.

She paused, taking in the dark tones of the room. It was just like Arius House. Blacks and greys and reds. One wall was windows, not that they could see much other than the wall across the courtyard. One wall was lined with bookshelves. The other had two doors, one leading to a bathroom and the other to a supply room.

"Where is it?" she asked, rocking up and down on her toes. She was fidgety, her eyes darting around the room, and Luka could feel her anxiousness down the bond.

Theon moved to the wall between the two doors. He stopped next to it, slipping his hands into his pockets. "That's where you come in, little storm. Normally only the Arius Lord can access it, but with your Chaos . . ."

"You think I'll be able to access it?" she asked. She'd started moving in place, small steps to the side and back.

"Are you all right?" Luka asked, his brow furrowing.

"Yes. I mean, no. I mean—" She lifted her hands, letting her power dance across her palms. "I can feel it. The mirror, I mean. Sense it. And my power wants it."

Luka immediately sent a tendril of black flames to wind around her arm, and Theon did the same to the other arm with his darkness. She shuddered, audibly sighing as the power distracted her own.

Balanced her out.

"You have to tell us these things, Tessa," Luka said.

"I know. I'm trying," she whispered, stepping forward. "I'm trying to remember you won't trap me or use me or betray me. That I can depend on you both, but I can't change it overnight."

"It's okay," Theon said. "We know what you need, and we'll make sure you have it."

She nodded, but she was thoroughly distracted now, studying the panel before them. "You've never seen it?"

"A handful of times," Theon admitted. "This is the mirror I first saw her in."

Tessa nodded, placing her palm flat against the surface. Her power gathered, spreading out across it as if the panel was cracking. Then it dissolved away, leaving a wall of glass with Marks and symbols carved around it.

"We destroy this one last," she murmured, already looking over the carvings.

One of her dark daggers appeared in her hand, and Luka caught her wrist before she sliced her palm. "You call Scarlett, Tessa. No one else."

She grinned up at him, that eerie, wicked smile that told him she was a little caught up in her power.

"How do we know which one it is?" Theon asked, leaning in to peer closer at the etchings.

"We don't," Tessa said with a shrug.

Before either of them could stop her, she slid the blade across her palm and smeared her blood, not on the markings, but on the glass itself.

"Tessa!" Luka barked, but there wasn't anything to be done now.

The mirror was crackling, swirling with gold and silver, light and dark. She stepped back, watching it all, and Luka and Theon stepped to her sides.

Luka was barely breathing because what had she been thinking? Anyone or anything could answer her call.

And it wasn't a silver-haired female that appeared in the mirror after a few minutes, but a white, silver-haired male. That hair reached just past his shoulders, silver eyes staring back at them. Beside him stood a female. She was quite a bit shorter than the male, and her black hair was long, reaching nearly to her waist. Her skin was darker, not as dark as Kat's, but a warm brown hue. Her amber eyes seemed to search for something, but they swirled a little. Just like—

"Auryon?" Tessa breathed, stepping closer.

"It's not her, Tessa," Theon said gently, placing his hand on her shoulder. "Her eyes are different."

"Who are you?" the male in the mirror asked.

"You first," Theon retorted, straightening to his full height.

"Not you," the female said dismissively. "You."

She was looking straight at Luka, and he stared back, stoic and unmoving.

The female didn't appear to care, peering up at the male. "It has to be him. They look too similar for it not to be."

"Wait, do you know Razik?" Tessa asked, stepping closer once more.

Both of their attention snapped to her. "Is he there with you? Where is he?" the male demanded.

"He's here, but he's not with us," Tessa answered. "You are from his world? You know Scarlett?"

The male stiffened, eyes narrowing. "What business do you have with her?"

But the female was lifting a hand, a swirl of ashes fluttering, and seconds later, Scarlett appeared, Sorin with her.

"Where are they?" Scarlett demanded, shifting as though it would help her see different angles beyond the mirror.

"Not here," Tessa said again. "Who are they?"

"My brother and his wife," she answered.

"They appear worried about Razik," Tessa said, eyeing them all.

"We're *all* worried about them," Scarlett replied. "It's been months."

The black-haired female stepped closer again. "But he is well? Can we see him?"

"I'm sorry," Tessa answered gently. "He's not here, but he is well. Both he and Eliza are well."

She nodded once, and the male slid his hand around her waist. "Soon, Lia. He'll be back soon."

"You keep saying that. I'm beginning to question if you know the meaning of the word," she replied.

"If you didn't summon me to send them back, then what do you need?" Scarlett asked sharply. "I cannot send you any more aid, and I—"

"I do not need you to send anyone else to this world," Tessa interrupted, her tone carrying that eerie ring. "When the gates open, more things enter than should."

Scarlett stilled. "Like what?"

"Like things that smell of the stars and stories yet to be told," Tessa answered.

Scarlett glanced up at Sorin, whose brows were pinched in thought as he listened and watched.

"We summoned you for a reason though," Theon interjected after a few seconds of awkward silence. He held up his arm, showing the Mark around his wrist. "Cienna said you created this Mark."

Scarlett glanced at it once, then back to Tessa. "I did."

"And now we need to add the third piece," Theon continued. "She said she couldn't do it because—"

"Because she doesn't have enough Chaos," Scarlett interrupted. "Yes, yes. You are okay with this, Cousin? It is what you want?" She glanced between them. "Two annoying, hovering males seems like an unnecessary pain in the ass."

"Scarlett," Sorin sighed, resting his hand on her shoulder. "Cienna explained this to us."

"Yes, but you know how I feel about the Fates trying to force our path," she replied with faux sweetness.

"It is my choice," Tessa cut in. "It was my stipulation about the Mark that required a new one be created."

Scarlett smiled. "I simply wanted to be sure. Having been to your world . . ."

"I understand," Tessa said, "but it is my choice."

"In that case, listen carefully and watch," Scarlett said. "You'll use blood mixed from the three of you for this, but it must be drawn precisely."

The next several minutes consisted of Scarlett drawing a Mark in the air with her starfire. Over and over again, while Tessa did the same on paper Theon had grabbed for her. And over and over again, Scarlett corrected it. A line that needed to curve more. Two lines that couldn't touch. Three lines that had to cross at a specific place. More than that, because it was going around their wrists, the curvatures had to be perfect too.

"Out of curiosity," Tessa ground out when Scarlett told her it was wrong yet again. "What will happen if I fuck this up?"

Scarlett shrugged. "Depends on which part you fuck up, I suppose."

Tessa tsked, rolling her eyes. Luka had felt her frustration growing and growing, and he knew she was reaching a tipping point.

"This is a waste of all our time. If this is something I'm supposed to be able to do, shouldn't my Chaos just *know*? It did for the Mark I gave Luka." She tossed her pencil aside, grabbing a new piece of paper. "I didn't need a scion or blood for that," she went on, slipping into that tone once more. "We just knew what to do. Knew what we wanted."

Her hand hovered just above the paper, thin streams of her power twisting and writhing.

"Tessa," Luka warned at the same time Theon said, "Tessa, stop."

"Let her go," Scarlett said, a hand pressing to the glass. "She's right, in a sense. She knows the Mark and what she wants."

"You can't tell me that's how creating a new Mark works," Theon retorted.

"Not entirely, but she's not creating a new Mark, is she?" Scarlett drawled.

Tessa was singing that godsdamn revelation song, and he was about to intervene when she lifted her head, and they both started. Her eyes were glowing violet, swirling with her magic. Slowly, she moved her hand, and on the paper was a Mark, shimmering faintly.

Theon tentatively reached for it, holding it up to the mirror, and Scarlett smiled darkly. "Perfect. Just like that, Tessa." She was still humming, one hand in her hair. Scarlett's smile faltered. "Did you ever learn her mother's lineage?"

Theon shook his head. "Achaz, obviously, but I don't know her grandmother on that side."

"She's trapped," Tessa said simply, spinning in a slow circle. "Locked beneath the sea." She stilled, looking over her shoulder and locking eyes with Scarlett. "For now."

Scarlett lurched back. "Tell Briar—"

"Already on it, Love," Sorin said, a fire message flaring and disappearing.

"What is going on?" Theon demanded.

"Nothing you need to concern yourself with right now," she replied with a fake smile. "Take your Mark, save your world, and send our family home."

Then she was gone, leaving them standing in the room with a humming Tessa.

"I won't take the Mark when she's in this state," Luka said sharply.

"I know, but what if she can't create the Mark otherwise?" Theon asked, shoving a hand through his hair. "We have to learn to help her control it, even when she has to give in to it."

Luka dragged a hand down his face, trying to figure out what to do.

"She's in there," Theon said. "She's a part of it as much as it's a part of her. So what if we use the bond to reach her?"

"Theon, this isn't the time for questionable theories," Luka sighed.

"Just listen," Theon said, that excited note seeping into his tone he always got when he was figuring something out. "We distract her power with ours and then use the bond to speak to her. Help her focus and control it."

"You're willing to risk getting the wrong Mark on this? What if it doesn't work? Or it gets fucked up?" Luka demanded.

"Do you want her or not, Luka? Theon retorted.

His dragon snarled at the implication, the sound rumbling from his chest as smoke wafted on his exhale.

"Then grow a pair of balls and do this," Theon snarled, his darkness appearing and already luring her magic.

"I don't think this is a good idea," Luka muttered.

"You said the same thing about me Selecting her."

This fucker.

With another deep breath, he called forth some dragonfire, letting it mingle with their magic. They gave it a moment before Theon said down the bond, *Tessa?*

They waited for several seconds, but no response came.

Tessa? Luka tried.

We need you to answer us, clever tempest, Theon added.

She was still humming, and Luka wanted to slap his hands over his ears. He shifted his eyes, knew they were glowing as brightly as hers when he sent down the bond, *It's lonely being the grandchild of a god, Tessa. I don't want to be alone.*

Her head cocked to the side a little, eyes settling on him.

There you are, my light, he coaxed. *You with us?*

She nodded slowly, glancing at Theon as he slid to Luka's side.

Eyes on us, little storm, Theon said.

And a few seconds later, her voice drifted to them. *Eyes on you.*

Good girl, Theon said. *We need your wrist.*

She raised her left arm, and they did the same, bringing them all together.

Are you sure about this, Tessa? Luka asked one last time.

It's the only thing I've ever been sure of in my entire life, she answered.

Then guide our magic, Theon instructed.

And she did, their power twisting and curving around their wrists. The threads of power becoming so entangled as she worked, Luka couldn't tell which Mark was being inked on whose skin. He felt her power cut into his flesh, stealing blood. Doing the same to her and Theon. Her Chaos absorbed it all, adding to whatever she was doing. She was breathing hard, and a tear slipped free.

This is too much, Theon, Luka ground out.

I can do this. We don't stop, Tessa insisted, her body starting to tremble.

Seconds later, those cords they'd all seen at one time or another sprang up.

The brightest gold.

The darkest black.

A midnight blue.

They were as entangled as the Mark she was bestowing. No telling where one ended and another began. Until they flared so brightly, Luka had to turn away and close his eyes.

Something pulsed through him, settling into the depths of his soul, and he turned back just in time to see their mess of power flare out.

Tessa stumbled forward, and Luka caught her before she fell to the floor.

"I've got you," he murmured, scooping her up and carrying her to the sofa in the office.

He placed her between them, and she slumped against his chest while Theon leaned in and cupped her face. "Tessa? Are you all right?"

She was still trembling, her head lolling against Luka's shoulder. "You're mine," she whispered, her eyes falling closed.

Theon lifted his gaze to Luka's, and they both raised their arms to see the intricate Mark wrapping around their wrists. It mirrored the one on Tessa's, and it was precise and perfect.

Looking back at Luka once more, Theon grasped his forearm and said, "Let's take our wife home."

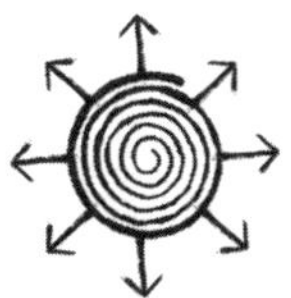

37
THEON

"You're sure about this?" Luka asked as they stood outside the Faven Palace gates.

"It's a little late to turn back now, don't you think?" Theon replied, adjusting the sleeves of his suit jacket. "Just make sure your wrist stays covered until the lordship is approved."

"They are never going to agree to this," Luka warned. "They're going to feel manipulated and tricked. All the relations you've worked on building outside your father's shadow will be broken and irreparable."

"Maybe," Theon agreed, straightening when the gates opened and five Achaz sentinels appeared to escort them.

But he was willing to risk it at this point. The kingdoms themselves were broken. Devram was irreparable. But his goals had changed. He didn't want to fix anything anymore. He wanted to start completely over, and that wouldn't happen without drastic measures and drawing hard lines.

Tessa was nearby, waiting until an agreed upon time. Having her there right away would be a distraction he didn't want right now. Not necessarily for him, but for the other rulers. But he could feel her down the bond, pacing and restless. He would have preferred her to stay at Luka's cave and Travel here when it was time, but that was certainly too far for her and Luka to be separated. They really needed to figure out the limits of that Mark soon.

None of them had realized what that Union Mark would cost her yesterday, or they would have waited to complete it. She swore there were no regrets, and she'd drawn from him this morning, refilling her reserves at least enough to get through the day. The Guardian Bond would draw from Luka for him if things escalated today, but there was no way they could bring Tessa here as drained as she was. That Mark had been as draining as the Source Marks had been, and it made sense. The Tri-Union Mark she'd given them tangled pieces of their souls together the same way the Source Marks did. The difference was the Tri-Union Mark was *meant* to do that. It wasn't some gross manipulation of other Marks. So while she'd been exhausted and drained, there hadn't been the physical side effects of pain and vomiting.

"Thank you," Theon said tightly when a guard opened a door to let him in, and the male's eyes widened momentarily before snapping back to attention.

Side by side, he and Luka strolled into the makeshift meeting room, and he loosed a small sigh of relief. A part of him had expected his father to be here, but the Arius seat sat empty. The Ladies were here, along with Rordan, but Lady Isleen's Source wasn't. That was odd.

His gaze slid among the rulers, holding the Anala Lady's stare for a second longer than the others, before he lowered into the Arius seat, sat back, and waited.

"Where is she?" Rordan asked coldly.

"I didn't know my Match would be required to attend to this summons," Theon answered, bringing his ankle up to rest on his knee.

"That's not who I mean, and you know it," the Achaz Lord retorted.

"But that *is* what this summons was called for," Theon said casually. "To update everyone on the status of my lordship. Although, I was a bit confused, considering you have known about the status for weeks, and I was waiting for all the Ladies to convene with us."

He saw Kyra's lips twitch in approval, and he knew his suspicions were right. They hadn't all needed to convene. She said nothing, letting the other Ladies voice their questions.

"What is he talking about?" the Celeste Lady asked. "All that was required was proof of a fulfilled Match Union. Everything was agreed to prior. We didn't all need to be present."

"Because of the extenuating circumstances involved, I thought it wise to ensure we were all part of the entire process," Rordan answered, his fingers tightening around the arms of his chair.

"I do apologize I missed our scheduled meeting," Theon said. "There were some complications."

"What meeting?" the Falein Lady asked.

"The one to confirm my Match and instate my lordship," he replied innocently.

"Rordan?" she asked, turning to the male.

"Times were turbulent," he snapped. "Maya was dealing with things in her kingdom. This wasn't pressing—"

"Wasn't pressing?" Theon interrupted. "The people in my kingdom have been in a state of uncertainty for months. I'm the one who's been taking care of things. I'm the one who has been pushing forward and making sure their needs are met. I am the one being summoned to these godsdamn meetings. The fact is, there are some things I can only do when I have that title attached to my name."

"This is easily rectified," Lady Kyra intervened. "You have taken a Match, Theon?"

"Yes," he gritted out.

"And where is Felicity?" Rordan asked, a knowing gleam in his eye.

"Unfortunately, I haven't seen Ms. Davers since the Celeste Estate," Theon answered, taking on an air of regret. "I believe you were away when the former Estate Mother appeared and attacked us. I know the Estate suffered greatly, and I am told there are a number of young Fae missing since that attack. If there is any way we can be of aid, Lady Candra, please let us know. As for Ms. Davers, she was terrified and was released from her obligations."

"How is that possible if she is your Match?" the Serafina Lady asked.

Theon turned his attention to her, and she looked . . . haunted. As though she was grieving and had no desire to be here. "Are you well, Lady Isleen?" he found himself asking.

"Of course I am," she retorted, lifting her chin. "Answer the question."

"While I had a contract with Ms. Davers, it was not carried through," he answered. "As I said, she was released from the obligation when it became apparent she could not handle the role."

"Then you do not have a Match as required," Rordan said with an air of triumph.

"I did not say that," Theon countered.

The Achaz Lord glanced at Luka where he stood off to the side. With a sneer, he said, "While I won't be surprised if you and Mors have finally admitted to involvement, unfortunately, that Match would not allow for an heir and will not fulfill your obligations."

If he only knew.

Theon replied with a flat smile, reaching into the inside pocket of his suit jacket and withdrawing a document. He passed it to the Anala Lady as he said, "Luka has taken a Match as well. Again an extenuating circumstance. But I bring the required proof of my own."

Kyra unfolded the piece of paper and held her palm above it, her power reading the magical signature that proved the document wasn't forged.

"Everything appears to be in order," Lady Kyra said. "A Match Union was done and proof has been provided. The terms are fulfilled as agreed. Congratulations, Arius Lord. We welcome you. May your rule be fruitful for those in your care."

The other Ladies murmured sentiments of the same, and Theon couldn't believe it was really that simple. After years of dreaming and scheming. The torture and determination. It was his.

The Arius Kingdom.

He was the Arius Lord.

He straightened, his foot dropping back to the ground as the weight of everything he was about to do pressed in on him.

We can still change the plans, Luka said down the bond, clearly sensing his conflicting emotions.

No, Theon replied. *We push forward.*

"He doesn't bear a Union Mark. Give me that," Rordan was saying in outrage, standing and ripping the document from Kyra's hand.

"It is done, Rordan," she said, her tone turning sharp and deadly. "All was agreed to before this moment. You signed the obligation along with the rest of us. It is legal and binding. As the kingdom in charge of upholding the laws and justice, you of all people should understand this."

Theon stood, removing his suit jacket and draping it over his chair. "Due to our . . . unique situation, we had to be a little creative. The common place for a Union Mark is taken by another Mark on my wife," Theon said, beginning to roll back the sleeve of his left arm.

Rordan's head snapped up, his power undulating and coiling around him. "She cannot be your Match. It is not acceptable."

"It is already done," Theon said.

Rordan whirled on the Anala Lady. "You accept this?" His eyes flashed to the others. "He has taken her as his wife!"

"What's done is done," Kyra said too calmly, her power slowly making an appearance while her Source stepped forward, adding flames of his own.

"Absolutely not," Rordan snarled. "It upsets the balance of everything we are."

"I have agreed to all your terms and jumped through every fucking hoop," Theon said, his darkness falling into place like armor, and Luka drifted closer.

Rordan rounded on the other Ladies. "He has taken his Source as his Match. You find this acceptable?"

The Celeste Lady's eyes went wide, while the Serafina Lady couldn't seem to find it in her to care. The Falein Lady tipped her head with interest.

Now, clever tempest, Theon sent down the bond as voices rose and arguments broke out.

A crack of thunder sounded so loudly it vibrated around them, and Theon smiled as everyone lurched to their feet. Luka also removed his suit jacket, draping it with Theon's on the Arius chair. The air was crackling with energy, and everyone's power in the room was vibrating with restraint and turmoil. Because Chaos always craved more, and the people in this room were among the most powerful in Devram.

But she was still more.

"What is happening?" the Celeste Lady demanded.

Theon slipped his hands into his pockets, rocking back on his heels. His smile was pure death and violence when he said, "Our wife is here."

The doors to the room were thrown wide, a swirling storm of glittering dark mist and light rolling in, and from the center of it strode Tessa. Her dress was a soft cream color, but that was just the base. Swirls of onyx and midnight blue adorned the gown, shimmering in the low lighting of the room. The fabric crossed over her chest, covering her breasts, leaving her torso bare, and gathering at her hips before flowing out for the skirt, where a deep slit up one side reached nearly the top of her thigh. Her hair was down, a mass of gold strands behind her, and her bare feet left prints of her power with each step. Her bow was looped across her chest, and Nylah and Roan prowled at her sides.

The room went utterly silent as she came to a stop before them, and even Theon was blinking twice because all of her Marks were glowing gold on her fair skin. Every single one, save for the Tri-Union mark on her wrist. That was shimmering white and black and midnight blue.

Her violet gaze slid over all of them, the Ladies tense and their power lingering. Lips curving into a slow smile, she stepped closer, and he could feel her. Feel her power wanting to take. Feel her giving it the smallest bit of freedom.

He sent a wisp of darkness to her, letting it curl around her ear, while dragonfire snared her wrist, pulling her closer until she stood between them. Her gaze went from Luka to Theon, a question lingering there.

Theon nodded once, taking her hand and bringing it to his lips to press a kiss to her fingertips. She inhaled a deep breath, and she turned to face the other rulers.

The three of them against the rest of the realm.

"What is the meaning of this?" Rordan demanded, finally finding his voice once more. "You suddenly need your Source here for a sense of dramatics?"

"I just sent him ahead to get the mundane things out of the way," Tessa said, slipping her fingers into Roan's fur where he sat at her side.

Rordan glared at her. "You have chosen the place of a mere Source instead of what you could have been. How disappointing."

"You must have misheard me," she replied, the power around her slowly drifting and sliding along her skin. "I sent *my* Source ahead of me."

The Achaz Lord scoffed. "He's your Source now?"

"Unless you want the job," she said, and Theon couldn't see her, but he knew she was smiling that dark thing that always brought him to his knees. She lifted a hand, a storm appearing and twisting into a whirlwind in her palm. "Chaos does not choose."

He felt the slight tug of her gifts, but so did everyone else. He could tell by the small gasps from the Ladies' lips, and the way Rordan's jaw clenched. Could she . . . draw from them? From *any* Legacy?

"Enough," Rordan snapped. "The three of you obviously came here with an agenda to deceive us. What is it?"

"I came as summoned," Theon replied. "The last time I tried to deny such a request, I was escorted by sentinels. More than that, the purpose of this meeting was the status of my Match and lordship, both of which have been addressed."

"In a deceitful manner," Rordan snarled. "You took your—She took her—Tessalyn cannot be your fucking wife. And *his*—It upsets the very nature of the kingdoms," he went on, stumbling over his words.

"Because she is powerful?" Theon asked.

"Yes."

"Because she is more powerful than most in this room?"

"Yes," he snapped again

"That is a valid point," Theon said. "Better fix that, clever tempest."

"Theon . . ." Kyra said tentatively.

He met her gaze, giving her a reassuring smile. "We are simply honoring the laws of Devram, my Lady, which state the most powerful of a bloodline shall hold the seat of that kingdom."

"In which case," Tessa interjected, her fingers flexing and straightening over and over in Roan's fur. "I challenge Theon St. Orcas for the Arius seat."

There were gasps from a few of the Ladies, but Theon was watching Rordan. None of them knew how he was going to react, and it had taken a little convincing to persuade Tessa to do this. She didn't want to rule over anything, but she did want to see change in Devram. He'd promised this wouldn't have to be forever. Just for now, as he'd explained more and more of his plan.

The room had fallen silent, and it was the Falein Lady who finally said, "What is your response, Lord St. Orcas? Shall it be a dual or concession?"

"I concede to Tessalyn Ausra," Theon said, stepping to the side. "Take your seat, my Lady."

She spun around, her gaze locking onto his.

He didn't drop his head or bow at the waist. No. That would never be enough. Theon lowered to one knee like the Fae did for the Legacy, and opposite him, Luka did the same.

Take the seat, Tessa, Theon urged down the bond as she stared at him.

Her gaze bounced to Luka. His expression remained impassive, but his voice drifted down the bond too. *You're not alone, my light. One foot in front of the other.*

She did just that, her chin lifted, and when she turned and lowered into the Arius seat, she held Rordan's furious stare the entire time.

"So you have chosen death," the Achaz Lord said, his tone murderous.

"And death has chosen me," she answered, and Theon felt her give a little more control to her magic. Watched those gold Marks on her skin flare brighter. Watched the Chaos in her eyes swirl faster. Watched her relax a little more.

Watched her take what was hers.

He and Luka pushed back to their feet as she propped her chin in her hand, watching Rordan. "Would you like to hear a story?"

"No," the Achaz Lord snapped.

"In all things, there must be balance," she continued, ignoring him. "Beginnings and endings. Light and dark. Fire and shadows. The skies, the seas, the realms. But what happens when one takes what he's not supposed to have? When he has deceived the realm he covets? When he calls the Fates here as much as I do?"

The Ladies all slowly turned to Rordan.

"What is she speaking of, Rordan?" the Serafina Lady asked.

"Something she knows nothing about," he retorted. "They have put a naïve child in charge of the Arius Kingdom."

"And a treacherous thief holds the Achaz throne," Tessa returned. Then she added with a sharp smile, "For now."

"You are not more powerful than I am," Rordan spat. "You cannot challenge me and win."

Tessa only smiled in return. "As a fellow Lady, I find it my duty to inform the other Ladies of your transgressions. Do they know where powerful Fae disappear to? How you mark babes from the Sirana Villas to hunt down later when their powers develop? Do they know you take what does not belong to you in preparation for taking from them next? That you were planning to use me to do the same?"

"And now what?" Rordan sneered. "You will take it all for *him?* All in the name of Arius, right? Now you will face the same fate that will eventually come for him."

Theon cursed as blinding white light flared, and he dove for Tessa at the same time Luka did. But she was on her feet, her power shielding them *and* the Ladies. The light faded, and Theon blinked, trying to regain his vision.

"Fuck," Luka muttered, clearly having shifted his eyes and seeing what he couldn't yet.

Theon could hear the wolves growling and snapping, and when he could finally see again, he was staring at a room full of seraphs. Feathered wings and weapons drawn, the warriors were in formation, ready for a battle, and standing next to Rordan was Dexter.

"I am so utterly disappointed, Tessie," Dex sighed. He took a step towards her, but Nylah was there, snapping her massive jaw. He curled his lip in disgust. "I gave you every opportunity, and you still chose . . . *this*. You will have to beg Achaz for mercy for this betrayal."

"You can beg Arius for mercy all you want when you greet him in the Pits of Torment," she replied, slowly raising her bow, where she already had an arrow nocked. She must have summoned it when Rordan had blinded them all. "But I will ensure he makes your eternity agony."

She released the arrow, but Dex Traveled a moment before it struck.

Instead, it hit another seraph. The being froze before disintegrating into nothing but embers and ashes.

"So be it," Rordan sneered. He turned to the Ladies. "She has started a war, and your kingdoms will be the cost of it." With a look at the seraph to his right, he added, "Kill them all."

Then he was gone, stepping through a portal of light as the seraphs attacked.

"You have got to be kidding me," Luka growled, already throwing dragonfire at an incoming warrior. "This is *not* how I expected this day to go."

"Me either," Theon muttered, drawing his short swords from his magic.

The Ladies and their Sources were fighting too, but it was the Serafina Lady who left first. Creating a portal and disappearing through it. She was powerful, but her Source was also missing.

Theon lifted his blade to block an attack as Tessa's light arced from her palm. The seraph screamed, and he felt her shudder through the bond. Her power was taking, refilling her depleted reserves.

Keep going, tempest, he said down the bond. *Luka, stay with her.*

Before they could argue, he fought his way to the other Ladies. One by one, he told them to leave. That they would reconvene later and strategize. Kyra was last, her flames burning wings while Theon shoved a blade into the chest of a seraph.

Blazing amber eyes held his as she said, "Welcome to the revolution."

Then she tugged her Source through a fire portal.

There were only a few seraphs left when he turned. The wolves took down one, and Luka was standing back, his arms crossed as Tessa—

As she let her power *devour*. The seraphs screamed as their veins lit up, gold threads crackling along their skin. Blood dripped from their noses, mouths, and ears.

Tessa's feet were off the ground, her wolves circling around her when the two seraphs finally crumpled to the ground. They were clearly dead, but Nylah and Roan pounced anyway, ripping out throats.

With a glance and a nod to Luka, they each sent their power to her, letting it tangle with her magic and brush along her skin. She turned, her head tilting to the side as she took them in, eyes and Marks glowing brightly.

Time to come back, little storm, Theon coaxed.

Time to go home, Luka added.

She blinked at the words, her toes touching the floor a few seconds later.

They stood back, letting her wrestle with her magic and take back control, ready to intervene if she needed them. Until finally, she relaxed, her shoulders rolling inward, and she sucked in a shuddering breath.

Luka reached her first, taking her chin between his thumb and forefinger. "Are you back, baby girl?"

She nodded, stepping into him. His arms came around her, clutching her close. Resting her head on his chest, she met Theon's gaze.

"Do you feel okay? Your reserves are full?" Theon asked.

She sighed and nodded. "I'm fine, Theon."

He moved to their side, saying, "Let's go home and get cleaned up. I'll have the kitchens prepare some food."

"Nothing gross," she sighed again as he dropped a kiss to the top of her head.

He hesitated. Not about the food. He'd deal with that later, but—

"We're going to the townhouse in the Acropolis, Tessa," he said. "Luka went this morning and made sure it was vacant."

She looked up at him. "You did?"

He nodded. "While you were sleeping."

"But it's only temporary," Theon added. "Until we can be sure we can return to Arius House."

She stared at him for a long minute, worrying her bottom lip. "Do I still get my own wing of the house and only have to see you when I want to?" she finally asked, batting her lashes.

"Oh, little storm," he said in a low growl as he grabbed Luka's arm, the male snickering. "As if you could ever hide from me now."

"But I can run," she crooned, mischief dancing in her eyes.

"Please do," he answered. Leaning in close, he added, "But I'm not responsible for what happens when I catch you."

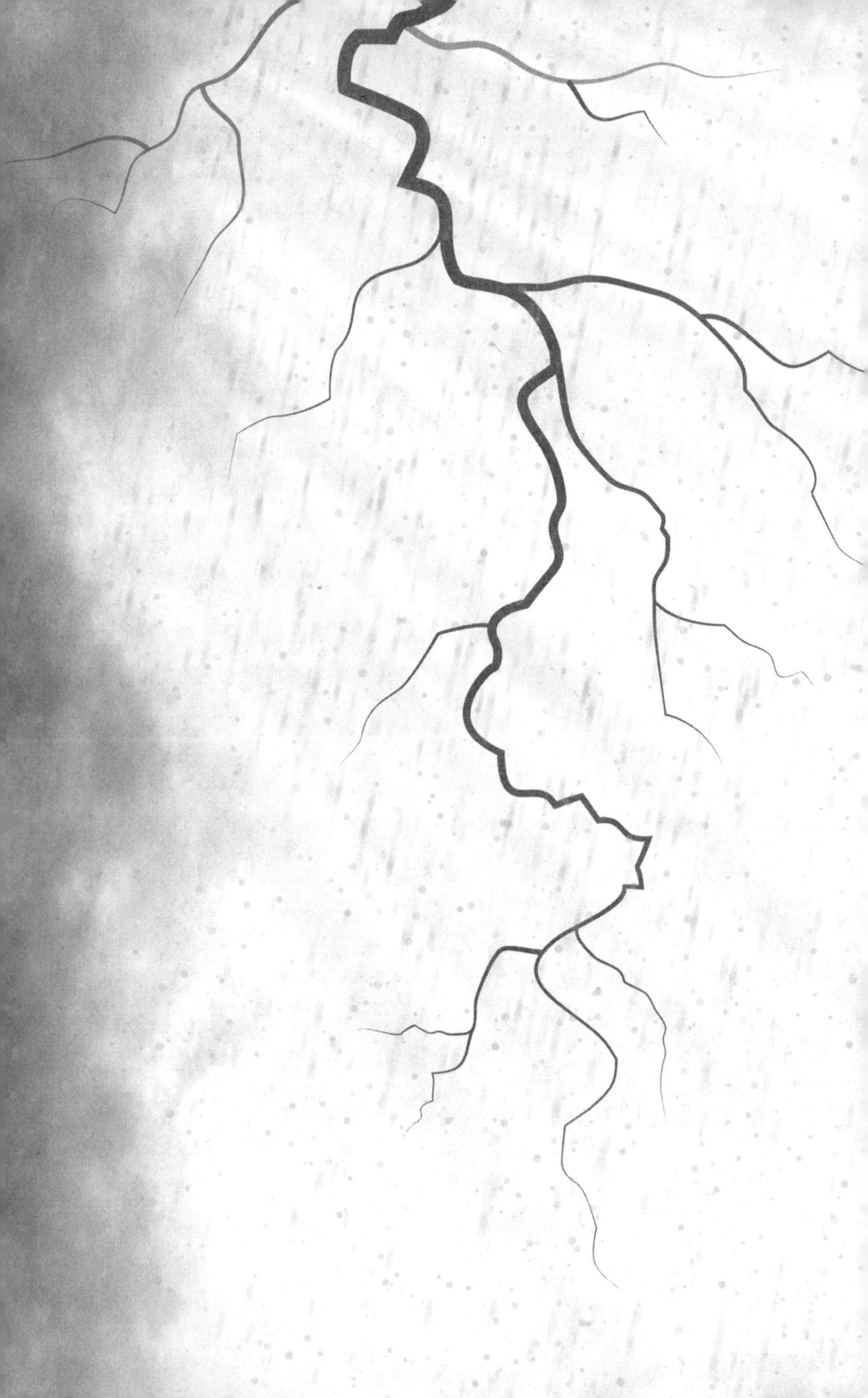

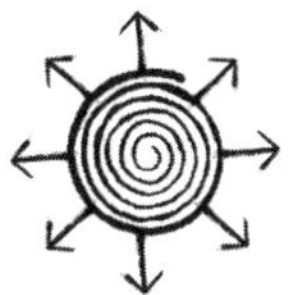

38
TESSA

She blinked from her place on her knees in the mud. Her hands were at her back, and at her throat was a thick band of metal. She couldn't see it, but she could feel it. Knew the thing was the same material as the cuff that Dex had put on her wrist that day in the mountains that absorbed her power. It would require the blood of three different First gods to remove it, and right now, it was containing and weakening her.

"Tessa," Theon rasped. He was several feet away, and he was on his knees too. Blood was seeping from beneath his hand where it was pressed to his side. "Don't listen to them. Don't—"

He hissed out a curse as a seraph appeared behind him, a fist slamming into his other side.

"Theon!" she cried, lurching to stand, but a hand gripped the collar at her throat, yanking her back.

"You've done enough," Dex hissed. "For the love of Achaz, stay put and stop creating messes for me to clean up." She glared up at him, and he smirked. "The attitude is pointless. Look around you. You've already lost."

Her eyes swept the scene, taking in the . . . carnage. It was utter carnage. Broken bodies and bloodstained earth. Seraphs were moving among the fallen, making sure the dead stayed that way. There were some Legacy still alive, but she was certain none of them were Arius Legacy.

She sucked in a gasp when she recognized the bright red hair of the Anala Lady, the light gone from her amber eyes. Her Source was nearby, along with another female who had an arm outstretched toward . . .

Luka.

Luka and Xan were off to the side, matching white-stone collars at their throats where they knelt. Luka's eyes were on her, and it was the first she had ever seen him look so . . . helpless as he looked between her and Theon. His wife and his Ward. Xan's gaze was fixed on the female reaching for them.

A seraph stopped in front of Dex, standing at attention.

"Speak," Dex barked.

"We've been searching everywhere and can't find them," the seraph reported.

"They have to be there. He rules the Underground."

Oh, gods. They were searching for Axel. Axel and Kat—

Her gaze whipped to Theon, where he'd been shoved face down. The seraph's boot was on his back, but still he struggled. Still he fought, despite his power being completely depleted. He was the only one of them not yet bound.

"Burning it will be pointless," Dex muttered. "His wife controls flames. Then again, the only ones we need dead are the vampyre and the child."

"No!" Tessa cried, once more trying to get to her feet.

"You are trying my patience, Tessa," Dex snarled, his hand moving from the collar to her hair, fisting it sharply and yanking.

"Let's just leave," Tessa cried. "Dex, please! We'll use a mirror gate, and I'll go to Achaz willingly. I'll—"

"No!" Luka snarled. "No, you will not."

"Enough! All of you!" Dex bellowed. "This is not a fucking negotiation. An entire First bloodline must be eliminated from this realm in order for Achaz to come here. There are three left of the Arius line." He looked down at Tessa. "You are other and do not count, but you will let Achaz enter once this is done."

She shook her head. "No. No, I won't. I—"

He crouched down before her, taking her face in his hand. "You act as if you have a choice. How many times did I try to give you one? How many times did I try to help you?" Forcing her head to turn, he leaned in and whispered, "And now you can watch them die knowing it's all your fault because Chaos can never reign."

And she screamed as the seraph shoved a blade into Theon's back and he went still.

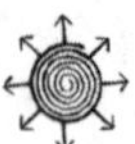

"Tessa, hey. Little storm, you're all right."

His voice cut through everything, and her eyes snapped open. Theon and Luka were both leaning over her, but she launched herself at Theon, wrapping her arms around his neck and legs around his torso. Tears were streaming down her face as she buried it in his neck, and she had no doubt she'd been screaming based on how raw her throat felt.

"Easy, beautiful," he murmured, holding her just as tightly.

Luka was there too, his hand smoothing down her hair, and once she was able to catch her breath, she turned to look at him. Resting her head on Theon's shoulder, Luka reached over and swiped her tears with his thumb. At some point, he'd draped a blanket over her and put on pants. They'd all been naked when they'd gone to bed.

They were back on the third floor of the townhouse, the familiarity of the room somehow comforting despite having not been in here since she'd discovered Felicity in it. Too tired from the day, they'd come back here. Food had been prepared and delivered as promised, and thank the gods, because she'd been famished. Roasted pork, salad, rice, and bread. Everything full of flavor, and nothing like what she'd been served the first time she'd been here. She'd fallen asleep on the sofa while Theon and Luka had discussed plans. She'd tried to stay awake and be part of them, but the next thing she knew, she was nestled against Luka's chest in a warm bed.

"Tell us, Tessa," Luka said softly, gathering her hair and pulling it back over her shoulder.

"We're going to fail," she whispered. "It's the only vision I have repeatedly. It changes, but not enough to matter. Either I die or Theon does, and everyone else . . . Never once do I see us all survive."

"The future is ever-changing," Theon said, still letting her cling to him.

"I know that," she said, listening to his heart beat beneath her ear. "I've seen evidence of that, but this one is different. It's always in the same place. It always starts the same. And this time, they were searching for Axel's child. Luka and Xan were captured. I had a collar at my throat, and you . . ."

"I'm fine," he soothed when she tightened her hold on him once more. "I'm going to be fine. We have a plan, remember? Let's get up and make some coffee. You can tell us everything."

A half hour later, she sat at the counter with her hands wrapped around a steaming mug. The guys were on either side of her listening while she told them how that vision had changed over the months. Starting with Theon killing her, then shifting to her killing Theon, and now this.

"Why does Achaz want to come here so badly?" Theon asked. "It's been centuries and centuries since Devram was created."

She shook her head. "He wants something here, but I don't think that's all of it. He believes it's his purpose to rule the realms. All of them."

"You've seen him in your visions?"

She hesitated, keeping her eyes fixed on her coffee cup.

"Tessa," Luka said in that voice that said he knew he wasn't going like what she had to say.

"Yes, I've seen him in visions, but I've also . . . talked to him in a mirror," she answered.

"You've what?" Luka demanded at the same time Theon asked, "When?"

"When I was with Rordan. It was the same day Luka came to the Tribunal."

"You were in the loft, and you left," Luka recalled.

She nodded. "And I went to the Pantheon, found my way to the mirror, and called him."

"By the gods, Tessa," Theon muttered, swiping a hand down his face. "You are . . ."

She winced, waiting for it.

Impulsive.

Wild.

Chaotic.

"So fucking fearless," Theon finally finished, and her head snapped up.

"But also, please stop summoning gods to the fucking mirrors," Luka added, getting up to get more coffee.

She looked over at him in confusion. "Why?"

"Because it puts me on edge," he muttered under his breath, and she huffed a laugh.

"I've sent a message to the others," Theon said. His hand was on her thigh, fingertips absently dragging up and down her bare skin. All she'd put on when they came down here was a short robe.

"Oh?" Tessa asked, watching Luka gather some oranges and pastries before pulling a small bowl of hard-boiled eggs from the fridge and bringing them to the counter.

"We need to figure out how to transfer power," Theon said.

She nodded, watching Luka peel an orange and hand slices to her. "From Dagian?" she asked.

"To start with, yes," Theon answered. "Razik, Xan, and Tristyn are the most knowledgeable. I asked Kat to come, but Axel is too worried about her going into labor."

Tessa nodded again. "That makes sense," she said around her orange.

"But before we talk about that anymore, we need to talk about yesterday."

She frowned. "What about it?"

"You were a godsdamn vision, Tessa," he breathed. "But there was a moment when you were—Can you . . ."

"I felt you yank on my power," Luka provided, placing a plate of bacon in the microwave and starting it. "The other Ladies felt it too. So did Rordan."

"Can you draw from them? Like you do from me? To refill your reserves?" Theon asked.

Tessa shook her head, thinking about it. "No. I'm . . ." She sighed. "I'm Chaos. We all know that's what my power is. It's drawn to power. It doesn't choose. It calls to it, and I think—" She paused, trying to figure out how to put this into words. "While my Chaos can't take theirs, it can make them lose control of their own hold on their magic a little bit."

Theon stared at her, and she bit her bottom lip, waiting to see what he was going to say. But he only sat back on his stool, his hand still on her thigh.

"Gods, that makes so much sense," he murmured. "My power was constantly drawn to you. I mean, yes, it was *you*, but also . . . Before your power was even allowed to emerge, there were times it felt like it was fighting me for control."

She gave him a small smile, reaching for a muffin as Luka slid a plate of bacon, an egg, and more orange pieces to her.

Because Theon wasn't staring at her like she was wild and untamed, too reckless or too other. He was staring at her like she was a goddess, and when she slid her gaze to Luka, he was watching her too.

"That vision isn't going to come true, baby girl," Luka finally said, reaching for her mug to refill her coffee.

"You can't know that," she argued, biting into the egg.

But Luka only shook his head. "*We* will be left standing when you come to reign."

She was pacing back and forth before the fireplace, her hand dragging along the mantel mainly so she wouldn't pull at her hair. It was afternoon now. Theon and Luka were in casual clothes. Or what was considered causal to them. Black pants and button-down shirts rather than suits and ties. She was in leggings and a long-sleeve shirt, her bare feet leaving prints with each pass she made.

Razik, Eliza, and Tris were here.

And Xan.

Xan who was telling them once again their best option was to bring her mother here.

Did she want to see her?

No. Yes. No.

Gods.

She turned again, trying to focus on the smooth marble of the mantel. She knew they were watching her. All of them were watching her, waiting for her to go too far.

"You say she's the best option, but how do we get her here? Use a mirror gate?" Theon asked.

"No," Tessa muttered. "No, no, no. Something will follow her through."

"She's right," Tristyn said, toying with a roll of lull-leaf in his hand. "Akira is powerful. Something will follow. Or a god will use the opportunity to send something else here."

"Which is why we need to destroy them," Tessa said. She met Tristyn's russet gaze. "We could go back tonight—"

"No," Luka and Theon both snarled at the same time.

"You're the Arius Lady now," Theon added. "You can't simply go to another kingdom, Tessa."

She rolled eyes. She didn't give a fuck about the title she suddenly carried.

The Arius Lady.

How ridiculous.

"We'll deal with the mirror gates in a bit," Luka said. "But if we can't use them, how else do we get Akira here?"

"Tessa can bring her here," Xan said. She stilled her pacing, her fingers curling into fists at her sides. "But it has to be Tessa," he added.

"Why?" she asked, wishing she sounded more confident than she felt. "Because of my Chaos?"

"Because of your father," Xan corrected. The male held up his hand, a ring on his finger with a large onyx stone in the center.

It looked exactly like the one Theon used to wear. The one Axel still wore.

"The ring?" Theon asked. "What will that do?"

"By itself, nothing," Xan answered. "But when the stones from the three are fused, they create a portal key."

"What the fuck is a portal key?" Theon asked at the same time Razik said, "Why haven't you said anything before now?"

"Portal keys have various uses," Xan said. "But there aren't any whole ones left. Only pieces of them."

"They are like the mirror gates in a way," Razik interjected with a glare at his father. "They can be used to create portals between the realms. They came into existence after the World Walkers were defeated and the power to walk the realms was close to being lost."

"Three pieces then?" Theon asked. "You have one. Axel has one, and I . . ." He turned to Luka. "Gave you mine for the bargain with Rordan."

Tessa watched him, and it was perhaps the first time Luka's emotions slipped. Fury and regret streamed down the bond. "That fucking bastard. We thought it was a power play."

"Why would you think that?" Razik asked. "This entire realm is all about strategic moves to gain more power."

"I thought it was an insurance policy of sorts," Luka retorted. "Proof I wasn't going to fuck him over. The goal was to get to Tessa at that point."

She winced internally. Another thing she was responsible—

No, Theon said firmly down the bond. *We're not doing that, Tessa. We all played a part in this.*

"Wait a minute," Tessa said. "None of this makes sense. How did Theon and Axel get two of the rings?"

"I found them," Luka said. "Gave them each one."

"You just *found* these two rings?"

Luka hesitated, as if debating his answer.

"He stole them," Xan answered, fighting a small smile, clearly proud of his son for this.

Tessa looked at Luka expectantly.

"I found them someplace I wasn't supposed to be. Valter found me, but I'd heard him coming and hid them. He demanded to know where they were, and I told him I didn't know what he was talking about. I took a beating for it too, but in revenge, I gave them to Theon and Axel. We later discovered they can't be forcefully taken. Only found or willingly given," Luka said.

"Which is how you still have yours. Why Rordan couldn't take it," Tessa said, turning back to Xan.

He nodded. "But these three have a companion. Temural altered them with the help of Anala and Taika. They will open a portal, yes, but they will only portal to each other."

"Not necessarily a place, but a person," Eliza said in realization, but Tessa was still holding Xan's stare.

A person.

"She has it, doesn't she," Tessa said, the words void of any emotion.

"She does," Xan confirmed. "Temural and Akira's story is . . . dark. They knew Achaz would discover them at some point, so Temural hunted down a set of portal keys with his Trackers and Huntresses. When they finally found one and altered it, he gave half to Akira and he kept half. So he could always find her and get to her. But then there was you . . ."

She could feel everyone's eyes on her now, and she didn't know what to do with herself.

"Temural sent me to Akira because he couldn't get to her. Another story for another time. You were born, and she sent me here with you to keep you hidden until you came into your power. The rings were supposed to take us back to her when the time came. But when things went so wrong upon our arrival . . ." He shifted where he stood. "The portal key was split in the enchantment. I found the three pieces and had them forged into rings. Cienna put an enchantment on them that only my blood could stumble upon them by accident, which is how Luka found them."

"And I have to be the one to use it because?" Tessa asked, her arms wrapped around herself tightly.

"Because the key was altered to bring them to each other, but it does so by blood. It's all Blood Magic, Tessalyn, and you are both of them. Wild and Fury."

There was too much. She was feeling too much. And she had questions, but she didn't want an audience for them.

"I'd like to speak with Xan alone," she finally said, keeping her eyes fixed on the male.

"Tessa, I don't think that's a good idea," Theon hedged.

"I wasn't asking, Theon," she said quietly.

There were a few seconds of tense silence before Theon said, "Yeah, all right." Everyone started making their way to the kitchen, but Theon stopped beside her, tilting her face up to his. "You call us if you need us."

When it was just her and Xan, she dropped her hands to her sides. Her power was floating around her, breathing and stretching, and she curled her fingers into her palms when she said, "No riddles and no half-truths. Just answers."

Xan gave her a soft smile. "I couldn't tell you things when you were wavering on your loyalties, Tessa. Your father is still my Ward, and I guard what is his as if it were my own."

"And yet you left her in another realm," Tessa countered.

"It is not only Akira I guard."

Tessa scoffed, crossing her arms once more as her eyes bounced around the room. "So she was the one who ultimately sent me here?"

"To keep you safe and hidden," he replied, leaning back on the arm of the sofa. He braced himself on his hands, crossing his ankles.

"Why not send me to Temural?"

"Because that was the obvious place, Tessa," he said quietly. "It was the first place Achaz would go when he learned of your existence."

"So she abandoned me instead?" she demanded, trying to swallow down the tears that were threatening to pool in her eyes.

"That wasn't the intention, Tessa. I was supposed to be with you. Raise you with Luka. Make him your Guardian. Don't punish them for my failures."

She couldn't believe what she was hearing.

"Don't give me excuses for them," she cried. "They could have fought for me. They could have tried. They could have done anything. Instead, she chose to send me to a realm where Temural couldn't even come for me. She cut me off from everyone who was supposed to care."

"Just because they're gods and Furies doesn't mean they're perfect. Just because mistakes were made doesn't mean they weren't doing what they thought was best," he said gently.

"Everyone is always thinking they know what's best for me," she sneered. "Maybe it's just more pretty words. Maybe I was never wanted from the beginning."

Xan moved then, suddenly in front of her. He gripped her shoulders, bending down to peer into her face. "We make mistakes, Tessa. Even when trying to do what we think is best at the time. Look at your last months. And I don't say that to shame you, only to prove a point. You have hundreds of years ahead of you. If you think you won't make more mistakes, you are in for a rude awakening."

A lone tear broke free, sliding down her cheek.

"I am not saying your feelings are not valid, but I am saying this may be one of those things you will not understand until you have a child of your own. Until you are so desperate to keep that innocent soul safe from the monsters of the stars that you sacrifice a piece of your own heart in an attempt to do just that," Xan said. "Only to one day learn that sacrifice was a mistake you will pay for dearly the rest of your years."

"Do not project your relationship with Razik onto me and my lack of relationship with Temural and Akira, Xan Mors. We are not the same," Tessa whispered harshly, swiping at the tear.

Xan straightened, taking a step back. A tense silence hung between them before Xan finally said, "It is your call. I will help you bring Akira here, but only if that is what you wish."

"It doesn't appear I have any other option."

"Indeed," Xan said, carefully sliding a finger beneath the collar at his throat to adjust it.

She turned away from him, walking to the kitchen where the others were gathered around the island. Everyone turned to her when she entered, Xan a few paces behind her, and she made her way to Theon and Luka. Theon immediately pulled her into his side, while Luka eyed his father from where he was leaning on his forearms.

"We need the rings," Xan announced. "Tessa's decision. Not mine."

Luka turned his head to her in question, and she nodded mutely, tracing a nonexistent pattern on the countertop.

"We'll have to ask Dagian to get it," Theon said. "He's really our only option at this point. Tessa won't get close. Brecken is . . . gone. Tristyn's cover is blown. He's our only option."

"There will be a cost involved," Eliza warned. "There always is with something like this."

"He's already risking everything to offer me his power," Theon replied. "He agreed to help however he could. This is the easiest and quickest path to that ring."

"It is the most logical," Razik agreed.

"I'm not saying it's not logical," Eliza said. "I'm saying they need to be prepared."

"We are all—" Theon cut off as Luka straightened suddenly. "Someone crossed the wards. Someone is here."

"Two someones," Luka murmured. "Stay here."

Tessa rolled her eyes, but she didn't bother following, staying back with Theon while Razik and Eliza followed Luka to the front door. Theon was tense beside her, and she rested her elbows on the countertop, her chin in her hands.

"How are you doing, wild fury?" Tristyn asked with a small tilt of his lips.

"Did you have a child with Lilura?" she asked, and Tristyn lurched back so suddenly, he knocked a stool over.

"Why would you ask that?"

She shrugged. "You loved her—"

"*Love* her," he corrected.

"Right."

"We do not have a child," Tristyn said tightly. "It's complicated, but the long story short is that it's forbidden."

Tessa hummed, seeing Theon glance at her with a small frown.

"Where is Tessa?"

She jerked upright at the familiar voice.

"Tessa—" Theon started, but she was already running, racing from the kitchen and to the foyer.

She didn't slow when she saw them, leaping into Lange's arms and wrapping herself around him in a tight hug.

"By the gods, I've been so worried about you," she murmured. She squeezed him another few seconds before pulling back and dropping to her feet to go to Corbin. The male embraced her, kissing her cheek as she stepped back.

They looked . . . exhausted and a little haunted. She peered around them, searching for another.

"Where is Eviana?" she asked slowly.

"That's why we're here," Corbin said. "But first . . ."

He hesitated as if unsure if he should ask, but Lange said, "We haven't had a proper meal in months."

"Of course," Tessa said, turning and leading them back to the kitchen, everyone following.

She started pulling food from the fridge, needing something to do with her hands, and as Luka helped her make sandwiches, she asked, "How did you get here?"

"It hasn't been easy. We've been traveling for weeks," Corbin said.

"Two Fae traveling by themselves without proper paperwork," Lange added, refilling his glass of water after drinking the first in a few gulps. "I still don't know how we made it."

"Traveling from Arius Kingdom?" Theon asked with a frown, arms crossed over his chest.

"No," Lange answered around a bite of bread he'd swiped. Gods, when *had* they eaten last? "We came from Serafina Kingdom."

Luka stilled, the knife still in the mayo jar as he looked up. "What were you doing there?"

"She made us go with her," Lange answered. "Spent weeks in the Dreamlock Woods."

"And survived?" Theon asked, the shock evident.

Lange arched a brow. "Obviously."

"Lange," Corbin hissed, nudging him with his elbow. "He's still the Arius Heir."

"Actually, *she's* the Arius *Lady*," Theon said with a small smile and a nod at Tessa.

"Oh my gods," she grumbled, returning to making the sandwiches.

"Wait, really?" Lange asked, sitting taller on his stool.

"I guess," she mumbled, passing a plate over to him.

"That's great news, Tess," he said, picking up the sandwich. "You can help us get Eviana back."

"Where is she?" Tessa asked again, sliding another plate to Corbin.

"We don't know," Corbin said grimly. "But we know who she's with," he added, his gaze sliding to Theon.

"My father," he said, dread in those two words. "I knew he'd surface sooner or later."

"If Eviana is back with him, this is not good, Theon," Luka said.

"She's not back with him," Lange interrupted sharply. "Not willingly anyway. Valter found her. He has—He found her and took her. He didn't take the time to search the woods for us."

"And you two made it here how?" Luka asked, narrowing his eyes. "Like you said, very unlikely for two Fae."

"They're not entirely Fae," Tessa said softly, holding Lange's sky-blue eyes when they slid to her. "At least not Lange. He has Sefarina blood. He's part Legacy."

She looked at Corbin then, finding her friend already staring at her. "You're not fully Fae either, are you?" When he didn't speak, she added, "I'm the Arius Lady, Corbin. You're safe here."

He took a deep breath, glancing at Lange, who shrugged. "There's no one left to trust, Cor."

Eyes on his plate, Corbin said, "I can Shift."

She couldn't have heard him right. "But you . . . You have water magic," she stuttered.

"*And* I can Shift," Corbin said, lifting his gaze to hers. "We don't know how, but—"

"Your mother is a Shifter," Theon said, and Tessa turned to find him staring wide-eyed at Corbin.

"How do you know that?" Tessa asked.

"Because the Shifters in the Underground refuse to be any sort of help to me until I find their missing Shifter Prince, whose mother had a relationship with a water Fae," Theon answered. Then, more to himself than them, he said, "He's been right under my nose this entire time."

"None of that matters," Corbin said tightly. "We need to help Eviana. We need to find her."

"I know where she is," Theon said. "And because of you, we'll be able to find her."

"Me?" Corbin asked, brows arching in surprise. "I just said I don't know where she is."

"She's where my father takes all things he doesn't want found," Theon said, and Tessa could feel excitement flowing down their bond. "He's at his secret holdings in the Underground. The same place he's hiding my mother."

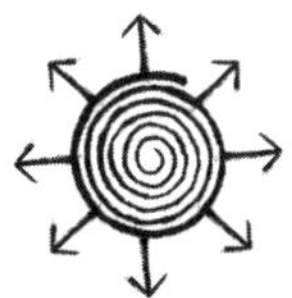

39
EVIANA

She stood next to his chair, her hands clasped in front of her and staring straight ahead. He hadn't spoken to her in hours, but she didn't dare move. Gone was her usual chair near the window. Not that it mattered. They were in the Underground. There was no nature down here. No plants to indulge in, and she wouldn't have been able to anyway. Not with the two bands on her wrists, steadily draining her magic. She couldn't touch it, but she could feel it slipping from her day by day.

Valter could speed the process up. He could add more bands. Could take them off altogether and force her to expel her magic until there was nothing left. Eliza had told her that was the only way the Mark that blocked their bond could be erased. She had to be so depleted of her power that there wasn't any magic left to hold the Mark in place. She wasn't sure if Valter knew that or if he was simply keeping her from accessing her gifts as additional punishment. Either way, the choice to have it slowly trickle from her soul like this was an intentional one. Not being able to expel her magic or have access to it was slowly driving her mad.

Or more mad than she already was.

Valter was flipping through ledgers and reviewing files on his computer, when her stomach growled. Of course her food allowance was limited right now. It would keep her reserves from replenishing.

Valter paused what he was doing before flipping another page.

"For so many years, you were taken care of, Eve," he said casually. "Had everything you needed. The highest of honors for a Fae. I gave you everything."

She said nothing. Didn't dare to breathe too loudly. This wasn't the first time he'd berated her about this since they'd come here. She actually preferred the days he completely ignored her and just made her stand around all day. Those days she slept on his floor. The days he was chatty, she ended up in his bed.

"Ungrateful," he spat, and she tensed, sensing the shift in his mood. "Everyone is so godsdamn ungrateful for what I have given them over the years. My advisors. You. My own fucking sons." He was flicking the pages of the ledger harder now, one of them ripping with the force. "I give and sacrifice for you, them, this fucking realm, and still I find betrayal everywhere I turn. I should kill them all and start over. Do it right. What do you think of that, Eve?"

She still didn't move, unsure if he wanted an answer or wanted her silence. She used to know. Used to be able to read him and could use the bond to her advantage. But now she didn't know, because he was on the brink of losing control and there was nothing he valued more.

Valter sat back in his chair, legs spreading wide as he tapped his forefinger on the desk over and over.

"I could, you know," he mused. "Dispose of my so-called advisors. Get rid of my offspring and create new ones. Sons that actually respect me." He paused, tapping his finger on the desktop. "I've already started in that regard."

She didn't know what that meant, but she didn't have time to think about it as he continued.

"But what of you, Eviana? What do I do with you?" He spun in his chair, and she remained still. She could feel his eyes on her as she stared straight ahead. Heard him shift and reach for her hair, winding it around a finger. "Your betrayal was the biggest of them all," he said, his voice too low and calm. "Death is too merciful, but I also need a Source I don't have to question. Don't have to wonder if her loyalty has been swayed. Even so, I had a feeling this day would come. Realized my mistake all those decades ago leaving you to grow up at that Estate alone. Never spoke to you or visited you until you were old enough to claim."

Eviana wanted to vomit knowing exactly why he was telling her this.

"I realized I need that loyalty to be there from the very beginning. Not something forced later," he continued. "I'd say it's working quite well, wouldn't you?"

As if on cue, the door opened, and Priya came skipping into the study. Her hair was falling out of its ponytail, and her face had a smudge of dirt on her cheek. In her hands was a small potted plant, and she was alight with excitement.

"Hello, Valter," she sang, not even glancing at Eviana.

"My sweet Priya," he said with a smile, dropping Eviana's hair and pushing back from the desk. "What do you have there?"

Priya came around the desk, passing so close to Eviana, her little arm brushed against her. She couldn't hide the sharp breath she sucked in, and Valter didn't miss it either.

"You were right, Valter," Priya said, that excitement growing. "I was able to bring this plant back. Do you think it will grow a flower?"

Valter pretended to study the plant as though unsure. "I don't know," he said with fake confusion. "But you know who does know a lot about plants?"

Priya's brows pinched. "Who?"

"Eviana," he said, gesturing to where she stood. "Eviana has a special gift for plants and flowers, just like you."

The girl's eyes widened. "She does?"

"Tell her, Eviana," Valter said, and with Priya's attention on her, Valter gave her a sharp, knowing smirk.

But she couldn't find the words. Her daughter was staring up at her, not knowing who she was, and this was crueler than anything Valter had ever made her do.

"Eviana," Valter said in warning, that finger tapping on the desk again.

She swallowed thickly, squeezing her fingers where they were still clasped in front of her. She had no idea how to speak to a child. "Yes," she managed to rasp. "I find plants and flowers fascinating."

"Will this plant make a flower?" the girl asked sharply, holding the pot up for her to see.

She glanced at Valter, and he nodded once, his eyes narrowed. Unclasping her hands, she ran her fingertips along the leaves, her power weeping at being separated from what it could use to save them.

"Yes," Eviana whispered, knowing exactly what type of plant this was. "It will produce the most beautiful and bright flower."

Priya's face lit up, and she turned back to Valter, Eviana already forgotten.

"Did you hear that, Valter?" she asked excitedly. "A flower. Maybe it will be like the ones in the woods!" Then she paused, and Eviana could just make out the small frown from her side profile. "When will we go back there? I miss my friends in the woods."

"Ah, I'm afraid it might be some time, my Priya," he said. "Remember we are staying safe right now."

"But there aren't even trees here," Priya said in confusion.

And Eviana's eyes fluttered closed in heartache. She was so powerful, her magic was already starting to make itself known. Priya would feel drawn to nature, find comfort in the trees and soil. She was already feeling the effects of being away from her gifts, too small to understand any of it.

But Valter would make sure he was the one to help her discover all of that. He would ensure that everything that little girl came to love was associated with him in one way or another. It was already starting with this simple potted plant. He would never stop. He would find every possible way to make sure Priya was his. Take her. Break her. Be her savior. Repeat the cycle.

For the next hour she stood in silence, listening to Priya chatter on and tell Valter one thing after the next. How her favorite food was vanilla pudding. Her favorite color was green. How a Spryte had taught her how to call a bird to sit on her shoulder and how the trees had once caught her when she slipped while climbing one. She sat on his lap, drawing on a piece of paper while he continued to flip through ledgers, and she sang and kicked her feet because this is what she knew as happiness. What every child on the Estates dreamed of having.

Someone who cared.

Or appeared to.

Too young to understand the world was full of villains who survived on innocence.

A knock sounded, the Fae nursemaid Valter had brought with them at the door to collect Priya to prepare for dinner. She skipped from the room with her plant, her face alight with a joy Eviana was sure she'd never felt in her decades of existence.

The door clicking shut behind her was loud in the ensuing silence, and her eyes fell closed as she waited for Valter to speak.

"She will hate you some day," her Master mused. "She will grow up knowing that to be a Source is the greatest honor she could ever hope to achieve, and she will love me. She will hate you because you are my Source, which means she cannot be."

She heard him stand, felt him stop in front of her. He cupped her face gently, waiting. And when she opened her eyes, she found his hazel ones on her with a cruel smile on his lips.

"She will blame you for everything she cannot have. Everything that goes wrong in her life, every hurt and treachery, I will make sure she can trace it back to you." A tear slipped free, and he leaned in, pressing his lips to the wetness. "She will hate you, and she will love me," he murmured against her skin. "She will want me and blame you for not being able to have me. It will not be me who ends your life one day, my flower. I will be many of her firsts, but you will be her first kill."

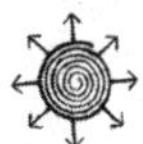

Eviana stared up at the ceiling, listening to Valter's steady breathing beside her. She'd had to sit through another dinner of him doting on Priya. Coaxing her to trust him more and more while she watched on, unable to do anything. A part of her wondered what he'd do if she suddenly shared his secret. Not that she could. She was still bound by the vows and bargains she'd been forced to take over the years, including keeping his secrets. But the more she observed them, the more she watched Priya stare at him and hang on to his every word, doing everything in her power to keep his attention and earn his praise, the more Eviana realized she couldn't do this.

She couldn't sit back and watch this. She had to do something. Maybe Corbin and Lange would come. Maybe they'd bring help, but she couldn't depend on them. She'd never been able to depend on anyone. Plans needed backup plans, and she'd been putting one together these last weeks.

She waited another fifteen minutes before she carefully slipped from the bed. If she waited any longer, she risked waking him. He always slept deepest the first hours of the night. Pulling a dress over her head, because that was all she had here to wear, she silently opened the door of Valter's bedroom and stepped into the hall.

This place was as familiar as Arius House. They came here often, and Valter preferred it to the penthouse in the Charter District. A decent-sized manor house built into the depths of the mountains, just like the Shifter home. This house was just on the other side of the Charter District border, and there were so many wards and enchantments around it, it was only possible to discover if you already knew it was there. Even the Shifter Alpha and Beta didn't know its exact location. Valter kept his secrets here, and she was on her way to perhaps his greatest secret of all.

The hall ended with nothing but the rocky wall, but on the left side was a small closet door. She winced when it creaked, holding her breath to see if Valter heard it. When everything remained silent, she entered, finding not a closet, but a narrow stairwell leading up. Her steps were fast and light, knowing she had little time to waste, and when she reached the top, she used her own teeth to bite hard enough to draw blood. Then she drew a symbol on the wall, the stone pulsing with a faint glow before it dissolved, and she stepped through.

The female sat on the bed, shifting to face her fully and her emerald eyes settling onto hers.

If only Devram knew how deep the corruption ran between the Achaz and Arius Lords.

"Caris," Eviana greeted in a flat tone.

"It has been some time since you accompanied him," the female replied, her voice hauntingly beautiful. "And never alone."

Her black hair was dark as midnight and was longer than the last time Eviana had seen her, reaching halfway down her back. She sat on the bed in a simple black gown with off the shoulder sleeves that hit right above her elbows. The dress allowed room for the two onyx cuffs that were around her biceps and showed off the Marks across her collarbone.

An empty tray was on a small table with two chairs, the dinner dishes empty. A small stack of old leather-bound books was on the bedside table, the room lit only by candles. No windows to even give the illusion of an outside. The rug on the floor was the only source of warmth outside the heavy fur blankets at the foot of the bed. A small chamber off to the left held a washroom, and while the room itself wasn't tiny, it certainly wasn't spacious.

It certainly wasn't large enough to spend the last two decades in.

She should have brought her something.

That was all Eviana could think as she stared at the female. How stupid of her. That was what Tessa had done. Brought her small things to build trust. She didn't have anything to give Caris, and it probably wouldn't have helped in the end. Not when she'd had a hand in why she was here to begin with. Not when she was the reason those cuffs were on her arms.

"My mind has not changed. I will not do what he wishes," Caris finally said, her hands in her lap. "I will spend the next millenniums in this room and not change my mind."

Eviana believed every word.

Caris Emersyn. Once, she was to be a Lady of Arius Kingdom. Then she became the caretaker of the Heirs, and now she was locked away until Valter needed her bloodline.

"That's not why I'm here," Eviana said, clasping her hands in front of her out of habit. "I came to make a deal."

Caris's brow arched, her head tilting. "With me? On his behalf?"

She shook her head. "He doesn't know I'm here, and my time is short."

"No," she said simply.

"You haven't heard what I have to offer."

"Is it returning me to Penelope? Because if it is not, I do not care," Caris said dismissively, reaching for a book on the nightstand. She had to have read that book thousands of times by now.

"What if it is your son?" Eviana countered.

Caris didn't look up from the pages, but her breath stalled.

"I cannot offer you Penelope. I cannot call her back from death." She paused, knowing Valter had told her when he'd had Pen killed. Eviana had been here then and watched the female break all over again. Had watched her beg for death to follow Pen to the After. "But I can offer you your son and the ones who may as well have been your own."

The female's gaze flicked to her, then back to her book, as if bored with this conversation. Eviana didn't know why. At least it was company. A conversation with someone other than oneself. Theon was so much like her, able to keep his emotions hidden so no one could read him.

"Does he know? That I live?" Caris asked.

Eviana shook his head. "If he does, I am unaware. Seeing your presumed death . . . did what Valter wanted. It broke him in a way he hadn't been able to do before."

"And where is he?"

"I don't know," Eviana admitted.

"Then it appears you can offer me nothing, Eviana," she said, standing abruptly and placing the book on the table. "You can leave."

"What will be required of me?" Eviana blurted, desperation winning out.

Caris turned at the words, her gown swishing on the cold floor. Eviana forced herself to stay still under her scrutinizing stare. Several minutes ticked by, and she grew worried. She needed to get back to Valter's bed.

"There is nothing you can offer me," Caris finally repeated.

"His death?" Eviana asked, backing towards the door. She'd already spent too much time away.

"Tempting," Caris mused, filling a glass from a pitcher of water. "But even his death will not free me. And even if I found freedom, where am I to go? The kingdom was taken from my family nearly two centuries ago."

"You . . . *want* to stay here?" Eviana asked, unable to believe that was possible.

"Where else would I go? Who do I have left?" she repeated.

"Perhaps *outside*," Eviana all but drawled. "Anything has to be better than these four walls."

Caris's lips turned up in a bitter smile. "I think you, of all people, understand there are things far worse than these four walls."

"You have a child," Eviana tried one last time, scraping open the scab on her arm to access her blood once more. "You do not wish to know him?"

"If he broke him and is now like him, then no. I do not wish to know him," she answered.

"He's not," Eviana said. "Despite Valter's greatest attempts, all three of them somehow turned out honorable. Pen looked after them and loved them as her own, like she did when you were at her side. And the Fates . . . they had plans for Theon."

Caris stared at her, long and hard. "What kind of plans?"

"A . . . love," she answered, unable to think of a better way to describe it. "Despite it all, Theon learned to love. That didn't come from Valter. That came from you." When Caris only continued to stare back at her, staying silent, Eviana turned and pressed her palm to the wall as she said, "I'll come back."

"No need. It is pointless," Caris called after her.

But she knew it wasn't.

Because she had said the same thing to Tessa, and all those visits hadn't been pointless.

She'd go back as many times as it took because deep down she knew. Caris was a mother, just like her. In the end that would win out. It had to.

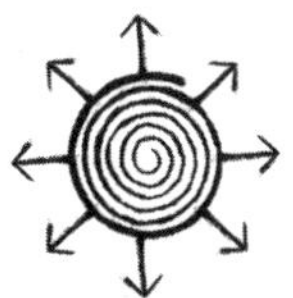

40
AXEL

"We could have gone with them," Kat grumbled from the sofa.

Axel just smiled as he followed Miara to the lift. She'd started coming here for Kat's exams rather than having them cross half the Underground, especially after that dinner.

"Thank you, as always," Axel said, pressing the button for the lift.

Miara nodded curtly. Reaching into her bag, she pulled out a small flask. "Cienna sent this for you."

That saint of a Witch.

That was all Axel could think as he took the flask. He'd refused to drink from Kat again after the dinner despite her protests. Not until the babe came.

"Tell her thank you," Axel said. Then, dropping his voice so Kat couldn't hear anything, he asked, "Have either of you seen anything else? Cienna said she can't see anything regarding the birth or Kat or any of it?"

Miara shook her head. "You know that's not how visions work."

He sighed, tapping the flask against his palm. "A guy can hope though."

The lift doors opened, and Miara stepped in, saying only, "She needs to rest as much as possible."

As soon as she was gone, Kat said in irritation, "Don't ignore me, Axel."

"I'm not ignoring you, kitten," he answered, turning back to her. "You know why we couldn't go."

"A few hours wouldn't have hurt."

"They've been gone for two days."

"We wouldn't have had to stay two days," she huffed.

Razik and Eliza were still in the Acropolis. They were all trying to work out how to transfer power from Dagian to Theon. Axel hadn't been thrilled with everyone leaving, but there were extensive wards around the penthouse. At least his father had done one thing right.

"Miara said this is the month the babe is coming, Kat. It isn't *logical* to leave right now," he said carefully, because by the gods was she in a mood today.

"It's not *logical* to keep me locked up in a tower, but here we are," she retorted.

He swallowed his bark of laughter, knowing she would not find this funny. It took him a few seconds to compose himself before he said, "You're not locked in a tower. We can go for a walk if you'd like?"

"I would not like," she fumed. "I would *like* to leave the Underground. I can have a baby anywhere, Axel."

"Cienna is here, Kat."

"And she can Travel."

"If we can get in contact with her," he argued.

"That same logic can be applied here," she countered.

Axel took a deep breath, rubbing at his brow. He knew this wasn't her. This was the pregnancy and everything else going on, but fuck, he was running out of logical arguments. Because she wasn't being logical, and he didn't know how to handle her when she wasn't logical.

Finally, he said, "If we were to leave, where would you want to go? What would you want to do?"

She stared at him, and he stared back, and it was one of the most ridiculous things he'd ever encountered.

"I don't know," she finally admitted, and he smiled, moving closer.

He set the flask on the coffee table, leaning down and placing a hand on either side of her on the back of the sofa, caging her between his arms. "You know what you *should* do, right?"

She sighed heavily. "Sit on this sofa and rest," she grumbled.

"Because . . . ?"

"Miara said it would help, but she also said she doesn't know when anymore. I heard you ask without wanting me to hear," she groused. "She said she's seen nothing else regarding the birth. Neither has Cienna. Maybe things changed completely, and we'll make it to full term. Visions are useless. No wonder Tessa is half-mad these days."

He huffed a small laugh. "We're almost there, Kat," he said gently. "I know you're tired. I know you're restless and going a little stir crazy."

Her eyes welled with tears.

Well, shit. He hadn't meant to make her cry.

Godsdammit.

"I'm sorry," she whispered.

"Don't be sorry," he said, cupping her cheek. "You're strong, kitten, but these last months have been stressful. These coming months will be more of the same, and—"

She winced then, and his eyes went wide as she brought a hand to her stomach. She'd been doing that more and more lately, and this was exactly why they hadn't gone with the others to the Acropolis.

"What's wrong?" he demanded.

"It's nothing, Axel," she sighed. "It's always nothing." When he still didn't move, she emphasized, "I'm fine."

He straightened, still eyeing her. "Do you want some tea? Something I can get from the kitchen?"

"I can get it," she muttered. "Just help me up."

He didn't like it. He'd rather just get it for her, but he'd concede on this if she'd stop pushing him to leave the Underground.

Helping her up, she made her way to the kitchen, and he listened to her rummage around. For a moment he debated going to help, but ultimately decided against it. She was already on edge today.

Sighing, he sank into an armchair and grabbed the flask, uncapping it. Things had been fine with Miara and the Fae after that disastrous dinner last week, but the Shifters were still unreliable. He'd sent a request for a meeting, but they hadn't replied yet. They wouldn't until they were ready, and who knew when that would be.

And then there was that nagging feeling that wouldn't go away.

It'd seemed too easy.

He took a long drink, letting the blood soothe the hunger and need that had been nipping at him all day. Back to monitoring his rations, he felt like he'd been holding his breath ever since that dinner, waiting for the other shoe to drop. It *had* been too easy. Bree wasn't just going to roll over and move on. She wasn't done with him. He needed to be proactive, but that was hard to do with Kat and the babe.

Kat reappeared with a plate of food and a glass of juice. Axel immediately stood to take it from her, helping her back onto the sofa, and when she winced again, he knew it was only a matter of time.

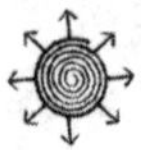

Where was he?

That was all he could think. Or try to think.

He couldn't seem to form any coherent thoughts as he tried to open his eyes.

Blood.

He could smell blood.

He *needed* blood.

But where the fuck was he?

A groan slipped from him, and he tried to sit up. Everything felt too heavy. Even his godsdamn eyelids felt weighted down as he struggled to open his eyes.

Swallowing, he nearly gagged. His throat was sandpaper, and when he finally managed to pry his eyes open, the room spun.

By Arius, he'd never felt so sick in his life, save for the times he was experiencing bloodlust, but that was different. This was . . .

He squeezed his eyes shut again, the room spinning too much. Start small. That was what he needed to do. Wiggle his toes. Flex his fingers. Feel the cool floor beneath him.

Wait. Why was he on the floor? Why wasn't he in bed with—

Kat.

Fuck.

Fuck, fuck, fuck.

With strength he didn't have, he rolled to his stomach and pushed onto his hands and knees.

"Kat?" he rasped out, his voice hoarse and gravelly. "Kat?" he tried again.

Opening his eyes, he stared at a spot on the floor, willing the room to stop spinning.

It didn't.

And he vomited. Or tried to. There was nothing in his system to vomit, so instead he gagged and dry heaved, his stomach muscles clenching and spasming.

Kat.

Get up and find Kat.

He repeated it over and over. She had to be here. There were wards. She had to be safe. She had to be—

Grabbing on to the side of the sofa, he pulled himself up, fighting another wave of nausea. Blinking several times, he tried to clear the fog from his vision, everything blurry and swimming.

There was a nearly empty plate of food. A glass tipped over with a puddle of juice. Pillows were on the floor, sofa cushions askew.

"Kat?" he called again, still not loud enough. Dread filled his stomach, making him want to vomit for an entirely different reason now. "Katya? Kitten? Answer me."

Upstairs.

She had to be upstairs and sleeping.

He turned, readying himself to tackle the stairs, when his foot nudged against something metallic. It slid across the floor, and he looked down to see the flask of blood Cienna had sent. Mostly empty, a few drops of red still left a trail behind the open container.

But that wasn't the blood he was smelling.

His heart rate picked up as his head cleared a little more and his Night Child instincts took over.

There was more than blood. Citrus. Jasmine. Fire.

"Kat!" he called, his voice a little stronger.

Still nothing, and he limped his way into the kitchen. Reaching into a cupboard, the first glass slipped through his fingers, shattering on the floor. He left it, grabbing another and stumbling to the sink. He downed glass after glass of water, trying to wake himself and flush out whatever the fuck was in his system. It was the only explanation, and one he couldn't dwell on right now.

Glass crunching under his shoes, he went back to the living room. Drops of perspiration ran down his neck and back, and he wiped at his brow with a chilled hand. The room was still out of focus, the edges of everything hazy, but he could function. He could smell her, and everything narrowed in on that.

He let himself descend into a place he'd been too ashamed to go. Where his hearing was impeccable and his instincts unmatched. Because when a Night Child gave over to their basest nature, they were a predator that could match any Fae or Legacy. Vicious and cunning, with speed and strength.

He climbed to the second floor, each step pulsing through him as his head pounded. Making his way to the study, he yanked open drawers and pushed aside hidden panels to pull out daggers and knives. He couldn't pull them from shadows anymore, but he sure as fuck still knew how to use them.

"Kat!" he bellowed, slinging a bandolier of knives across his chest. "If you're here, you need to answer me right fucking now!"

He knew it was pointless. She wasn't here. The smell of her blood was though, and he followed it back downstairs. There was nothing on the floor or anywhere nearby. Someone had cleaned it up, but that didn't erase the scent.

Heading to the lift doors, he found it. A faint handprint. As if they'd tried to wipe it away as they were leaving.

Her handprint.

Her blood.

Someone had her.

And he knew exactly who.

Adrenaline and instinct were the only things driving him now. He'd deal with the ones who drugged him later. Right now, all he could focus on was finding Kat. The edges of his vision were tinged with red as he followed her scent. He had a feeling he already knew where she was. The only place Bree would take her.

He really should have checked a clock before he left. How long had he been out? Hours? Days? This godsdamn Underground. He had no idea if it was day or night. How long had they had her? Was she still bleeding?

He prowled across the Underground, moving quickly and quietly. He didn't see the people moving to the other side of the street as he went. Missed those who averted their eyes or slipped down side streets to avoid him. The bloodlust he was feeling now had nothing to do with hunger or need; this was pure vengeance and wrath.

Time was lost to him, all of his focus on moving forward and staying on his feet. The scent of her blood was getting stronger, more prevalent. She'd bled the whole way there, and each step had him giving more and more over to the monster his father had turned him into. This is what Bree had wanted after all, right? May as well deliver.

It could have been minutes or hours before he stalked across the bridge that led to the House of Four.

"Hey, stop!" a vampyre called out.

He didn't even slow, one shirastone knife flying from his hand a second later.

The male cursed as he sank to his knees. Axel grabbed the knife as he passed, yanking it from his chest and fisting it as another vampyre came running from the security post.

"You can't—"

Axel paused, slowly turning to look at him. "My wife is here. Where is she?"

The vampyre held up his hands, taking a step back. "I don't—"

He didn't get to finish. Axel lunged, his fangs sinking into the vampire's throat and tearing as he shoved the same knife into his stomach, slicing wide.

Dragging his forearm across his mouth, he felt the warm blood smear, but he kept moving. It was the first time he'd truly descended into his new vampyre being, and a dark part of him wondered why he'd waited so long. The speed was everything, even against beings of the same. He met them blow for blow, the strength behind his hits fiercer than they'd ever been. It was a song he'd been listening to his entire life, only now he'd learned how to dance to it.

Flipping a dagger in his hand, he let it fly, grabbing another and dropping to a crouch as more vampyres descended. His hand snapped out, snagging a female by the arm. She hissed, baring her fangs, and then she was screaming as he snapped her forearm in half with a quick move. Another knife was in her chest a moment later.

An arm wrapped around his throat from behind, and Axel smiled. Leaning back, he used his newfound strength to flip the male over his head. He grabbed his skull with two hands, twisting hard to one side. The male stilled, but Axel still sank a blade into his chest. None of the fuckers would move again. They wanted to serve Bree? Then they could face the same fate she would.

A mess of bodies and blood was left in his wake. He *wanted* the bitch to know he was coming. He'd warned her this would happen if she came near Kat and his child again. He was, after all, a male of his word.

Veering to the left, he avoided the lift and opted for the stairwell, still following the scent of Kat's blood. It was growing stronger, and there was a lot of it. Something was wrong. Very wrong.

The stairwell was narrow, but it was perfect for fighting his way up. Before he'd turned, he thought that vampyres were savage beings, but he understood now. Understood the *power* that came from sinking fangs into flesh and inflicting agony and death. He didn't need his shadows. Didn't need magic when *he* was the weapon.

Kicking off the wall, he propelled himself over the next vampyre to meet him. A knife was in his back before he shoved him down the stairs, hearing the pained howls as he went. Blood was everywhere now, smeared on his hands, his face. His shirt was torn, and his shoes left red prints.

He didn't know how many floors he climbed when the scent had him pausing. He inhaled deeply, smelling and tasting. A female came through the doorway, and he grabbed her by the throat, slamming her against the wall. His forearm pressed on her airway, and her eyes went wide, fangs snapping.

"Where is my wife?" Axel demanded in a low, cold tone that was nothing but death.

She shook her head, and he slammed her into the wall again. She coughed as the air was forced from her lungs, and then she was gasping as he pressed on her throat more. He didn't ask again. Only held her stare, knowing he could be the face of Arius himself when needed.

"You are too late," the female hissed around gasping breaths. "The babe is almost here, and then—"

Her words morphed into a scream as he dug a knife into her chest, dragging it down. No, this wasn't going directly into her heart. She wanted to be the one to deliver the news he was too late? Then she would pay the price for saying the words.

The knife sank in again, dragging once more. Carving through flesh and bone, his vampyre strength cut through everything with ease until he could reach a hand in and wrap his fingers around her heart.

"Tell me again I'm too late," he said with deadly calm. "Or tell me where the fuck my wife is."

"Down the hall," the Night Child cried, tears of red streaming down her face. "On the left."

He yanked his hand back, taking her heart with it, and letting her collapse in a heap on the ground. His knife still in his other hand, he sank the blade into the muscle, feeling it die in his palm.

Letting the organ drop onto the still body, he stalked down the hall. The smell of her blood getting stronger as a scream reached his ears. Then he was running, another cry piercing the air as he threw open a door.

Only to find himself thrown against the wall and being held in place by a large Night Child. Dirty blond hair hung to his shoulders, and he bared his fangs as another appeared to help detain him.

Cade and Rayell.

The whole lot of the vampyres were in on this.

"Stay back, St. Orcas," Cade snarled.

"I'm going to kill you," Axel promised, jerking hard against their hold. One he might have been able to handle, but two of the most powerful vampyres? There was a reason they held their places in the House of Four.

"Let him go," a feminine voice lilted. "He's so lost to his true nature, he'll kill her anyway."

"Axel!"

His name dissolved into another scream, and it was the only thing that could penetrate this bloody haze that wouldn't let him go.

He shook his head, trying to focus, but everything was still tinted red. Cade. Rayell. The walls. The bed. Kat.

Kat.

He blinked, unable to believe what he was seeing. Trying to comprehend Kat on the bed, curled in on herself with tears streaming down her face. Then she was seizing and crying out again, her back arching as what was clearly a contraction tore through her.

Bree stepped in front of him, blocking her from view. Her long fingers gripped his face, and her nails dug in.

"Axel, darling," she purred. "Color me impressed. I underestimated how long it would take you to get here. I hear you left quite the trail of destruction. The Underground is terrified of you." Her head cocked to the side. "Thank you for that."

Kat screamed again, this time clutching at her stomach, and his chest twisted in agony. He needed to get to her. She'd already done too much of this alone. There was no way he was going to let her give birth by herself.

Bree moved to the side, turning to watch Kat suffer on the bed.

"Poor thing," she tutted. "She's been in this state for hours."

Hours.

That was all he'd heard.

"Nearly an entire day," Bree added with faux sympathy. "Thinking she can stop this." She crossed the room, leaning in to gather Kat's hair in her hands. "But you can't, can you, poppet? That babe is coming whether you like it or not."

"Don't fucking touch her!" Axel roared, surging forward and freeing one of his arms.

"Fuck," Cade barked, trying to grab him again, but Axel was too fast.

He already had a knife in hand and was bringing it down. Cade shifted just in time, the blade sinking into his shoulder rather than his chest.

"Motherfucker!" Cade snarled, grabbing Axel and shoving him back into the wall so hard his head snapped against the stone, cracking loudly. Spots flashed in his already hazy vision, but Kat's cry of agony reached him once more.

"Stop!" Axel yelled. "Let me help her! Let me go to her! Why don't you have a Witch here?"

"She's on her way," Bree said calmly, her hands on Kat's shoulders now. "Lie back, poppet."

Kat shook her head frantically, panting, "Your father—The babe."

Axel went still. He couldn't have heard her right.

"Oh, poppet," Bree tutted. "Spilling secrets I shared with you. Shame on you." Kat cried out again, and Bree used the moment to help her onto her back. "See? Isn't that better?"

"What about my father?" Axel demanded, pushing against Cade and Rayell, but they held firm. Cade looked like he wanted to punch him, the knife still in his shoulder, and Rayell looked . . . not exactly bored, but not like she cared either.

Bree reached for a nearby cloth, dipping it into a basin of water and wringing it out. "This is really your fault, you know," she said, moving back to Kat and bringing the cloth to her brow. She smirked at the low growl that rumbled from Axel. "I tried to let you be a part of this. Tried to bring you to my side. Even said you could have the Fae and the child. But you didn't want any part of that, did you?"

Her voice had turned cold and vicious, and when another contraction ripped through Kat, Bree smiled. "So I had to go elsewhere. This could have all gone so differently."

"That babe is going to be here any minute, Bree," Rayell said suddenly, her honey eyes fixed on Kat. "Where is Miara?"

Miara?

That traitorous bitch.

Had she been feeding Bree information this entire time? Every time they had an appointment, she reported it?

But it all fit. She was the one who'd given him the flask, saying it was from Cienna. She would have known how close Kat was to giving birth. Maybe she'd been having visions all along and not said anything.

Bree frowned, looking down at Kat as she stood. "I don't know," she said curtly. "Go find her."

"You go find her," Rayell retorted. "I'm not beneath you, Bree. This is your godsdamn mess."

Bree straightened, glaring at Rayell. "Fine," she said tightly. "Keep him restrained."

Rayell rolled her eyes. "Someone's going to have to deliver a babe if you don't go find the Witch."

Axel could tell Bree wanted to say something in response, but she turned, striding from the room, her heels clicking. Kat cried out again, throwing her head back, and Axel could only look on, utterly helpless.

Until he wasn't being restrained anymore.

Cade was cursing as he pulled the knife from his shoulder and tossed it aside, the string of words so vulgar, Axel nearly laughed. Then he realized Rayell was moving towards Kat, and he lunged for her. She was faster though, moving to re-wet the cloth and pressing it to Kat's brow.

"There isn't a lot of time," the Night Child said. "I waited until she was on the precipice before telling Bree to go."

Axel was frozen, trying to figure out what was happening. "We're on your side here," Cade growled, shoving Axel forward. "And I'm sure as fuck not delivering your child."

"I can't deliver him," Axel said, slowly dragging his eyes back to Kat.

"Well someone needs to," Rayell snapped. "Because this babe isn't waiting anymore, and I promise you she's coming back with more than just Miara. Valter will be with her."

"Someone tell me what my father has to do with this," Axel demanded, lurching to the bed as Kat cried out again.

"The short version is when you refused her, she made other plans. Your father is currently in hiding in the Underground. Recouping after these last months. They've made a deal," Cade answered, standing near the door with his arms crossed. "She delivers your child to him, and he will give her the Underground."

"And you are okay with this?" Axel demanded.

"Of course not," he retorted. "Why do you think we're helping you right now?"

"Axel," Kat cried. "I can't wait. He's—I can't—"

"Okay, okay," he said, rushing to the other side of the bed. He smoothed her hair back, pressing his lips to her brow. "We'll figure this out. We'll—"

She thrashed, her head shaking back and forth. "Now," she panted. "I've been in labor for nearly a day. He's coming now."

"I don't know what to do," he said, looking from her face to her contracting belly and back. He'd been wrong. *This* was the most helpless he'd ever felt.

"Fae births are long," Rayell said, climbing onto the bed behind Kat. "She's nearly at the end. They take hours to progress, and by the time they get to this point, the mothers are exhausted."

"But her power," Axel tried.

"The . . . tonic," Kat panted. "She had one."

Miara had told them about that. How females drink it to stifle their magic so they don't lose control of it during birth. This had all been planned from the beginning. Bree had been prepared with one.

"Axel!" Kat cried.

"I'll help her push," Rayell said.

By Arius, this was not how he imagined this going.

"Maybe I should help her push, and you deliver the babe," he ventured.

"Axel! Get down there and deliver your son!" Rayell ordered. "We don't have a lot of time. Cienna is handling Miara, but as soon as she realizes this was a setup, Bree will be back. We need to be gone."

Rayell hadn't been wrong. When he moved down the bed and adjusted Kat's gown, he could see just how close they were. He glanced at Cade. "Do not let anyone in that door."

The male nodded, turning away from them, and Axel turned back to Kat. Lifting his eyes, he met her gaze. Her eyes were muted and exhausted. Tears were streaming down her face, and her hair was matted to her brow.

He took a deep breath. "Okay, kitten. I'm going to wash this blood off my hands, and then we're going to do this. Together. Because it's always been you and me against the realm."

She nodded, a broken sob escaping her.

Axel climbed off the bed, stripping off his torn and stained shirt and quickly washing his hands in the small, connected bathroom. There wasn't much he could do about the pants, but he cleaned up as best he could in the minute he had.

When he came back, he stopped at her side and took her face in his hands. "Let's meet our son."

In the end, it was as awful as he'd expected it to be listening to Kat scream as Rayell helped her push. Contraction after contraction came and went, and Axel could tell she was lagging, her strength and energy gone.

"We're close, kitten," he urged. "We're so close. You've been so strong this entire time, trying to keep him from Bree, but I'm here now. She's not touching him. It's you and me and him. One more time, Kat. Ready?"

"No," she cried, shaking her head. "No, I'm not."

But nature didn't care as another contraction came.

"Push, Katya," Rayell demanded, holding her hands and helping her lean forward.

"Last time, Kat. I swear it," he urged, and gods, he hoped he wasn't lying to her.

She screamed, and there was a head. He didn't know what to do. Did he pull? Help? Just . . .

But Kat knew, pushing one last time, and the babe was there, his cry filling up the space. And holy fuck. They'd done it.

"Cade, towels," Rayell commanded, easing out from behind Kat.

Everything was muffled and muted for a different reason now as he held a tiny life close to his chest.

"Take him to her," Rayell said, her voice low and hushed.

He nodded, moving ever so carefully to Kat's side and gently placing the babe on her chest. She was crying, fresh tears on her face as she clutched their son close.

"You did it," he murmured, sitting beside her and pulling her in. "You were so brave and strong, and look at what you did, kitten."

There was a knock on the door that had Axel on his feet.

"Relax," Cade said, reaching for the doorknob. "It's our help."

"Help?" he repeated.

The door opened and the Shifter Alpha and Beta strode in, Cienna behind them.

"We can't stay here," Rayell said, moving out of the way as Cienna strode forward. "We're going to Kylian and Giselle's."

Cienna was at Kat's side, checking the babe over while Kat still held him close. Then violet eyes lifted to his. "You did well, Axel," Cienna said. "I tried to get here sooner, but I had to—"

"Handle Miara. I know," he said. "Can we get the fuck out of here?"

"Let me look over Kat and make sure we can move her. I need a few minutes."

He nodded, moving back to Kat's side. Everything quieted down around him as he stared down at his wife and son. Cienna did the barest amount before they all Traveled from the House of Four, and an hour later, they were settled into a small suite at the Shifter home.

"Sleep, kitten," he said softly.

He was sitting against the headboard, Kat nestled into his side with the babe in her arms. The babe had just eaten, and Kat hadn't slept yet.

"I can't," she whispered. "The last time I fell asleep, I woke up to . . ."

Guilt clawed at him, and he pushed it away. He was drugged. They were played. This wasn't his fault.

"No one is touching him," he said, gently reaching for the babe. "Cienna is here. The Shifters. Rayell and Cade have more than proven their loyalty. We've sent word to Theon. I swear to you, no one will touch him."

She nodded, already scooting lower on the bed. She was asleep before her head hit the pillow, and then it was just him and the tiny sleeping thing in his arms. Black hair, but he'd expected nothing less. A mix of his white complexion and her dark skin. Emerald eyes that matched his, and a set of lungs that let everyone know when he wasn't happy.

Perfect and innocent.

He glanced down at Kat, her chest steadily rising and falling as she slept. Cienna had said the tonic she drank should wear off anytime, letting her magic wake back up.

Axel ran his knuckle along his son's cheek, drinking in the sight of him. "No one will touch you," he murmured low.

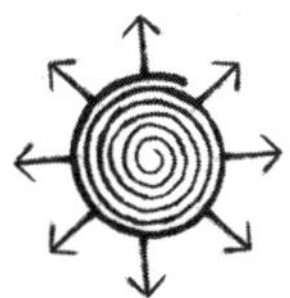

41
THEON

"Where are they?" Theon demanded as they were led into the main foyer of the Shifter house.

"Hello to you too," Giselle said pointedly from where she stood next to Kylian. She eyed everyone trailing in after him. "Your entourage grows every time I see you, Theon."

He paused, helping Tessa with her jacket before passing it to Luka to hang on a hook.

"Introductions can wait, Giselle," Theon answered. "Show me to Axel and Kat, please."

"It's rude," Kylian said, arms crossed over his broad chest.

"It is," Theon agreed. "But I do have some developments to discuss with you *after* I have seen Axel."

They weren't happy about it, but they finally acquiesced, leading them down a hall to a guest wing. Theon knocked once on the door, and the moment he heard Axel call "Come in," he was pushing it open. A rush of relief washed over him at seeing them whole and safe, and in Kat's arms was a tiny bundle wrapped in a forest green blanket.

"Axel," Theon said, his name a little hoarse as he took the scene. His younger brother, a father.

Tessa cleared her throat, standing back near the door with Luka. "Congratulations."

Axel smiled wide, walking over as he said, "Thank you, baby doll."

Theon reached for him, pulling him into a hug. "You're a father," he said, his voice low.

Axel huffed a laugh. "Yeah. How fucking weird is that to say?"

Releasing him, Theon glanced at the bed where Kat was watching them with a small smile. "Can I see them?" Theon asked.

"Of course," Axel replied, leading him over to the bed.

Theon bent down, pressing a soft kiss to Kat's cheek. "Congratulations, Katya."

"Thank you, Theon," she murmured. She looked tired, but her eyes were bright as she snuggled that babe closer.

"He's healthy?" Theon asked, seeing dark hair and a mix of his parents' complexions.

"He's perfect, according to Cienna," Kat said with another tired smile. "Do you want to hold him?"

And the next thing he knew, *he* was the one holding that little bundle close. He adjusted the blanket to see his face more, and they were right. He was absolutely perfect. Sleeping and healthy and whole. He'd made it.

He turned to find Tessa still by the door, but Luka was striding closer, coming to a stop to peer at the babe.

"Did you settle on a name yet?" Luka asked, glancing up at Axel.

"Maddox," Axel answered. "Maddox St. Orcas."

A small bark of laughter came from Tessa, and they all turned to her. She was watching Axel in amusement. "You really named him after the lead singer of your favorite music group?"

"Who said that?" Axel asked, trying and failing to look innocent.

"Axel, is she serious?" Kat demanded.

"Of course not, kitten," he said, throwing a wink at Tessa. "Besides, it's too late now. We already named him."

Kat tipped her head back, her eyes falling closed. "I swear to Anala, Axel. First, I get kidnapped, then you name our child after a singer."

"Kidnapped?" Theon demanded, his head snapping up. "What is she talking about?"

Axel sighed before launching into the story of Maddox's birth. Waking up from being drugged. A bloody rampage through the House of Four. Delivering the babe himself.

The more Axel spoke, the closer Theon pulled Maddox to his chest. It shouldn't have surprised him that his father was involved in this, but to learn how close he and Bree had come to succeeding?

"Easy, Theon," Luka said, reaching to take the babe. It was only then Theon realized some of his darkness had appeared, creeping along the floor.

Luka turned, and Theon followed his gaze, finding Tessa leaning against the wall. Corbin and Lange had drifted in and were chatting with Kat now, but Tessa stayed back, listening to everything from afar.

"You can come closer, beautiful," Theon said with an encouraging smile.

But she just shook her head, glancing at Axel. "I'm fine."

Focusing on the bond, he tried to feel out her emotions, but whatever she was feeling, she had it blocked from them. Which was worrisome. They all blocked their thoughts from the bond most of the time, but she hadn't blocked her emotions since the bond had been repaired.

Tessa? Are you all right? he asked, Luka watching her now too.

I said I'm fine, she answered.

"You're really not going to come and see your nephew?" Axel asked, sauntering over to her.

She gave him a weak smile. "I figured I'd keep my distance. After everything."

Axel frowned. "We're past that, Tessa. I'm sorry if you thought otherwise." Tessa gave him another weak smile but didn't reply. "Wait, did you think I was still holding that against you?"

"No," she answered quickly. "I was just . . . giving you space."

"Well, stop," he said, taking her hand and pulling her across the room in excitement.

"Axel, really I—" She snapped her mouth shut as Luka shifted a little so she could see Maddox. Her violet eyes slid over the babe, and she curled her fingers into her palms. "He's beautiful, Axel," she said softly, staring at Maddox a few moments longer. "I'm going to say hi to Kat."

She slipped away, crawling onto the bed to join her friends. Theon immediately felt some of the tension lift down the bond, her shoulders relaxing as she fell into conversation with them. He could hear bits and pieces while they filled Kat in on what they'd learned of Lange and Corbin's lineages.

"That was weird, right?" Axel asked in a low voice.

"Yeah, a little," Theon agreed. "There's been a lot going on though. Speaking of, we have some good news."

"That's a nice change from the fuckery we've been experiencing lately," Axel grumbled. "What is it?"

"With Tessa now the Arius Lady, we can go back to Arius House," Theon said. "You and Kat can come home."

Axel stared at him, his brow furrowed. "I can't go to Arius House, Theon. Not right now anyway."

"Father is in hiding here in the Underground, trying to take your son. Cressida is taken care of for now. It's safe there for the three of you."

"Yeah, but that's not my place anymore."

"What do you mean, it's not your place? It's our home, Axel," Theon argued.

"Don't be stupid. Arius House never felt like a home, Theon," he said. "But that's not why. I've built alliances here. Relationships with the leaders. I can't just leave. Not when Bree is still a threat to the Underground."

"She's a threat to *you*. Kat. Your son," Theon emphasized, motioning to Maddox. "Staying here puts you all at risk."

"And others just risked their lives for us," Axel shot back. "Cade and Rayell turned on her. The Shifters solidified their alliance by sheltering us here. Cienna has taken over the Apothecary District and leads the Witches. I cannot just abandon them after all that. I'm one of them."

"He makes good points, Theon," Luka said. "From a strategy side, he needs to stay. He's built something here."

"It's not safe," Theon argued.

Axel scoffed. "It's never been safe anywhere."

"Axel—"

"We're staying here, Theon," he said, cutting him off. "I cannot leave the very people I've spent months convincing we care. Besides, I have a score to settle with Bree. I'm not saying it's forever, but I am saying I need to stay here for now. Starting a war with Bree and then leaving before it's finished is not an option."

Maddox started fussing then, and Axel scooped him up from Luka's arms and took him back to Kat. The three of them were somehow already this synchronized unit. His entire life he'd been protecting Axel, and now he was a husband and a father. A leader of the Underground.

"If we're sticking to the plan, you have to let him do this," Luka said in a low voice as Tessa came closer. "We need him and the Underground."

"Yeah," Theon said quietly, watching his younger brother. Because he could still see the child, eyes wide with fear when Theon told him to go find his best earbuds. The brother he'd taken the blame for so many times to keep their father's wrath from him for as long as he could. The one who'd somehow kept his sense of humor throughout their sordid childhood. The one who'd somehow, *despite* that sordid childhood, become one of the most noble people he knew while he had nearly become his father.

"We should go speak with the Shifters," Tessa said, shifting from one foot to the other.

"Tessa, are you all right?" Luka asked, eyeing her.

"Of course," she said, tucking her hair behind her ear.

"You're acting uncomfortable."

"We're in the Underground," she said dryly.

"Right. That's it," Luka said, conveying just how much he didn't believe that.

"We should go speak with Kylian and Giselle," she said again, clasping her hands in front of her. "Corbin is anxious."

"He's not the only one anxious right now," Luka muttered.

"Luka, drop it," she snapped, her power flaring slightly.

Theon's brows rose in surprise, and he glanced at Luka, a mutual understanding passing between them. They'd drop it for now, but they'd be bringing this up again later.

She turned away from them, clearly done with the conversation when she said, "Corbin, are you ready?"

The male was standing near the bed, and he pulled at the back of his neck. "I mean, can you ever really be ready for something like this?"

Lange was climbing off the bed. "It's going to be fine. If you're not comfortable, we say fuck 'em and leave."

"Saying 'fuck 'em' to the Alpha and Beta is not advisable," Theon said.

"Kylian and Giselle are formidable," Kat cut in. "But only because they are fiercely protective of their family. Which you are a part of."

"We'll be back after this," Theon called to them, Axel holding Maddox while Kat prepared to feed him.

Closing the door behind them, they followed their escort back down the hall. Tessa had fallen back with Corbin and Lange, speaking softly with them, but everyone fell silent when they were led into the meeting room. The Alpha and Beta were in their usual seats. Kylian was eyeing them with disapproval, while Giselle had a sharp smile on her full lips.

"Thank you for giving them a place to stay," Theon said, stopping before them.

"Of course," Giselle said, her light grey eyes skimming over their company and pausing. Theon didn't need to know why. Corbin had taken a tonic to mask his scent for a time. They would have known right away who he was otherwise, but a Shifter's instincts were still there. They knew there was something.

"We hope it has provided an understanding of where our loyalties lie," Kylian said, his brow pinched as he also homed in on Corbin. "Introduce us to your company."

"You know Luka," Theon said. "But you have yet to meet our wife, Tessa Ausra, the newly crowned Arius Lady."

"*Our* wife?" Giselle asked, sitting up straighter. "Both of you?"

Theon nodded. "Correct."

Her smile widened. "Congratulations on your unions, my Lady."

"Thank you," Tessa said tightly. The bands of light at her wrists were pulsing, and she was tense beside him.

"How refreshing to have a female on that seat rather than . . ." Her eyes slid to Theon. "Well, you understand."

Tessa huffed a small laugh, some of the tension lifting. "I do, your grace."

Giselle arched a brow. "Your grace? How thoughtful, but you can simply call me Giselle, and my mate, Kylian."

Tessa gave a small nod. "I understand you have a sister, Kylian."

The male straightened, his eyes narrowing. "I have a few."

She glanced at Corbin, the male's hand holding tightly onto Lange's. "Khari," Tessa said. "She should be here for this."

Kylian and Giselle both lurched to their feet, Corbin stumbling backwards.

"You found him?" Giselle asked, her steps quick as she approached, but Tessa stepped in front of her, blocking the path.

"Please summon Khari," she said.

"I will not," Kylian said. "Not until we are sure. I will not get her hopes up and fail her once more. Why can't I scent him?"

"Because we didn't want you to know until he was ready," Tessa answered, lifting her chin in challenge. "It is *his* choice to be here."

"He belongs here," Kylian snarled.

Tessa's lip curled up. "You will find I am not one to pander to what others believe is someone's duty and purpose. Corbin will decide where he belongs."

"Corbin," Giselle said softly. She stepped forward again, and Corbin eyed her warily. "That is your name?"

He nodded, gesturing to his right. "This is Lange."

"Your mate?"

Corbin didn't miss a beat when he said, "Yes."

"What is your Shifted form?" Kylian demanded.

"Summon Khari," Tessa interjected. "I will not ask you again."

Her power was snaking out, tendrils creeping and winding, and the Shifters stepped back.

"You protect him as if he is your own," Giselle observed.

"Because he is. Bring me his mother," she snapped. "Or I will find her myself."

She held Kylian's stare for a long moment before the Alpha dipped his head, motioning to someone nearby to do just that.

As they waited, Giselle said, "Thank you, my Lady."

"For what?" Tessa gritted out, clearly annoyed.

"For protecting him as your own."

Tessa blinked, some of the irritation banking. "Thank you for doing the same for Axel and Katya."

"While we wait," Theon cut in. "I fulfilled my end of this bargain."

"We can't know that—" Kylian started, but he cut off when Theon twisted. Unbuttoning his shirt just enough, he showed them the back of his shoulder where their Bargain Mark had once been. Now there was nothing.

"My father's holdings," Theon asked, re-buttoning his shirt. "Tell me again where they are suspected to be?"

"On the border," Kylian said tightly. "Between our territory and the Charter District."

"You will take us there when we are ready," Theon replied.

Kylian nodded. "Of course."

They all turned at the sound of the doors opening, watching a female enter. She was beautiful with her brown skin and brown hair, olive eyes that matched her brother's scanning over them all in confusion.

"Kylian?" she asked, coming to a stop beside him. "I was told my presence was required?"

His smile was warm and genuine, something Theon had never seen from the male. He took his sister's hand, squeezing her fingers. "Today I fulfill an oath to you," he said, and her eyes went wide. "A lost prince has been found."

She turned towards them slowly, her eyes immediately finding Corbin, and he gave a weak smile, pulling on the back of his neck.

"Meet Corbin, Khari," Kylian said gently. "Your son."

Tears were already streaming down her face as she clutched her hands to her chest, clearly wanting to reach for him and unsure if she should.

"You look like your father," Khari whispered.

Corbin swallowed thickly, glancing at Lange, who gave him a reassuring smile. Then he turned back to Khari as he said, "I'd like to hear about him."

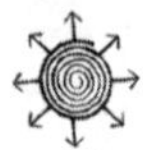

"When's the last time Tessa had her contraceptive shot?" Luka asked, entering the living room.

Theon looked up from his laptop. "What?"

"You heard me," Luka said, crossing his arms. "When was it?"

Theon sat back on the sofa, sorting through things in his mind. It couldn't have been her assessment last fall, right? Because that was . . .

He reached up and slowly closed his laptop, setting it aside. They'd come back to Arius House after making sure none of his father's staff remained. With his father hiding in the Underground, they were safe to come back here, although they'd come back to Theon's suite. None of them were ready to brave the private wing his father had resided in for decades.

"She can't be . . . right?" Theon said.

"I sure as fuck haven't been doing anything to prevent it," Luka said, dragging a hand down his face. "Things have been so fucked lately."

They used to. Both of them used to take their own precautions simply because of who they were. Neither of them wanted a random fuck to end with a child, not to mention females like Felicity who would have gladly used that against him. But ever since it had only been Tessa, he hadn't even thought of it.

"Do you think it's why she was so weird with Maddox?" Theon asked.

Luka shrugged. "It would make sense, but we would scent that, right?"

"Kat hid her pregnancy for months."

They stared at each other, and then they stared at her when she came into the room with her empty mug. She'd been sitting outside on the balcony, soaking in the fresh air. The last he'd looked, Roan had been curled at her feet.

She paused at their attention, her eyes narrowing. "What?"

"You didn't hold Maddox today," Theon blurted.

Her eyes went wide before she turned away from them and continued to the kitchen. "And?"

"And . . . why?"

The sink turned on, and she rinsed her cup.

"Are you pregnant, Tessa?" Luka asked bluntly.

The mug hit the sink, the sound of it breaking carrying to them. Turning the sink off, she turned to face them. "Why would you think that?"

"Because you were obviously uncomfortable today," Luka said flatly.

"So you assume I am pregnant?"

"When was your last contraceptive shot?" Theon asked.

Irritation crossed her face as she folded her arms and pressed her lips together. "Rordan made sure I had one when Luka started staying in Faven," she said tightly. "And I was *grateful* for that, but I also asked Tristyn to get me one a few weeks ago. When was *yours*?"

"We . . . haven't been . . ." Theon started, trying to explain just how colossally they'd fucked this up. It should never have been all on her to make sure they were preventing this possibility.

"I know," she drawled, her gaze bouncing between them. "Were you hoping my answer was going to be yes?"

"Neither of us are ready for a child," Luka said carefully, clearly sensing just how much they'd pissed her off with this. "But with the way you acted today, we thought it might have been possible. There's been a lot of fucking lately, baby girl."

"You're both idiots," she deadpanned, before turning to rummage in the pantry for something to eat.

"But . . . then why were you so uncomfortable today?" Theon pushed.

She sighed, placing a bag of popcorn in the microwave. "You were both very excited about the babe," she said. "I was just giving you the room to enjoy it."

"You weren't excited?"

"Of course I'm glad he made it here safe and sound. I'm happy for them," she replied tightly.

"But?" Luka asked.

"You both seemed . . . enamored with him," she said carefully.

"I don't understand. He's our nephew. Of course we are," Theon said.

"If I *had* been pregnant, would you have been excited?"

His brows shot up. "It would have been unexpected, but we wouldn't have been upset."

"Luka just said neither of you are ready for a child," she countered.

"We aren't, but that doesn't mean . . ." Theon stood, shoving a hand through his hair. "This conversation is confusing."

"When neither of you were doing anything to prevent a pregnancy, a part of me thought maybe you *wanted* that," she said. "And seeing you with the babe?"

"Tessa, children are a discussion the three of us will have when we're ready. We would never try to trick you into that," Luka said, sounding at a loss. "Surely you know that?"

"And what if I'm never ready?"

They all fell silent, staring at one another.

"This isn't something that needs to be discussed or decided right now," Theon finally said. "We're all immortal and have scarcely lived."

The microwave beeped, and Tessa turned away to retrieve her snack. Grabbing the bowl and a bottle of water from the fridge, she headed for the bedroom once more, not saying another word.

Theon and Luka stared after her, and Luka was rubbing at his jaw when he asked, "Did you ever discuss children with her, Theon?"

"No," he answered, because it hadn't even crossed his mind. Sure, his father had pushed for it with Felicity, but even then, it had been more of an abstract idea. The idea of a family was so far down the line, he'd never given it much thought. Something he knew would eventually be required of him. There was too much other shit going on right now.

"You?" he asked Luka.

Luka shook his head. "But I think our wife has thought about it quite a bit."

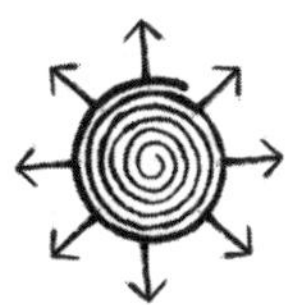

42
LUKA

"Again," Eliza ordered, stepping back so Tessa could get to her feet.

"When are you going home again?" Tessa grumbled, pushing off the ground from where Eliza had knocked her on her ass. Again.

"Stop whining and focus on your footwork. You're putting too much weight on your front foot. Your magic can't do everything," the female retorted, getting into a defensive stance. "Go again."

Luka had been sparring with Razik on the other side of the training room, but they'd stopped long ago to observe the females. He still couldn't get over not only how well trained Eliza was, but also her training style.

"How long has she been the Fire General?" Luka asked.

"Longer than you've been breathing," Razik replied.

Luka sent him a frank look. "Obviously. She's centuries old. I'm a few decades."

"She was the general long before I met her."

"And the two of you have been together for . . . ?"

Razik's eyes flicked to him before going back to the females. "Why does that matter?"

He shrugged. "Just wondering. Tessa has been acting strange since we went to see Axel's son."

"And that has what to do with me and Eliza?"

This broody asshole.

"Nothing," Luka muttered, turning to grab his shirt and water bottle. "It was just conversation, Razik."

He left the training room through the back door that led into the gardens. More than a little restless, he needed to get out. Stretch his wings. They'd been back to see Axel, Kat, and Maddox every day since that first time last week. Or he and Theon had. Tessa had only been back once, and once again, she'd hung back. Chatting with Axel and Kat but avoiding the babe.

Tossing his things to a bench, he summoned his wings. But just before he launched into the sky, the doors opened again and Razik came out.

"Need something?" Luka asked in annoyance.

"No," Razik said gruffly.

"Then . . . ?"

Luka waited, trying to figure out what was happening here.

"I take it Tessa never told you about her conversation with Eliza regarding children," Razik finally said.

Tessa had spoken to Eliza about this?

"When?" Luka demanded.

"A few months ago. When you two were not what you are now."

"What did she say?"

Razik side-eyed him. "I'm not going to gossip with you."

"Then why bring it up?"

"Because I don't want you to ask Eliza about it," Razik retorted, summoning his wings now, still shirtless from their sparring. "But Tessa asked about the Mark over her heart, and it's a Curse Mark from the male she once believed to be her father. It prevents her from having children."

Luka stared at him for a long moment. "How long ago?"

"When she was younger than you," Razik answered. "And it's part of the reason I was keen to go to another realm."

Luka's brow furrowed. "I don't know a lot about Curse Marks, but isn't the one who bestowed it the only one who can remove it?"

"Yes, but Eliza burned him from the inside out, so we need a different option."

"But . . . there isn't one," Luka said slowly.

"There are worlds older than this one and new realms being born every day," Razik said. "Somewhere out there is a workaround, and I will find it."

"You want children that badly?"

"No," Razik scoffed. "I mean, possibly. We've discussed it, but that's not the point. The point is, the choice shouldn't be made *for* her. If she doesn't want children, fine. That's her choice. Not because some bastard made it for her."

Luka nodded. "And have you found anything?"

"I've found some possible leads. Tristyn is looking into some things for me," he answered.

"Tristyn? Blackheart?"

"Do you know another Tristyn?"

"No, but—Just surprised, I guess," Luka muttered.

"You know he's how we got here, right? Yes, Scarlett helped us pass through the mirror gates, but Tristyn saw Scarlett in the mirrors a few years ago. Around the same time Theon did."

That had Luka straightening. "He did what now?"

Razik scoffed. "Anyway, that wasn't the only reason I came out here. While searching for a way to remove the Curse Mark, I may have come upon something else to pass along to your father."

"Our father," Luka corrected.

Razik glared at him. "Do you want this information or not?" When Luka only stared at him, waiting for him to go on, he said, "I've found a way to remove the collar around his neck."

Luka lurched back in surprise. "You've been researching how to remove it?"

"That's not what I said," Razik grumbled.

"You figured it out? You know how?" Luka demanded.

"I can't do it, but yeah, I know how," he replied. There was a burst of black flames before a piece of paper appeared in his hand. Extending it to Luka, he said, "You'll need Tessa. For her Chaos."

Luka grabbed the paper and skimmed the words. If this was true, Tessa could break the collar. It was designed to restrain descendants of Arius and Sargon. The same material Dex had used to stab him by Lake Moonmist.

He glanced up at Razik. "You figured this out when Tessa healed me, didn't you?"

"It gave me the idea. I just looked into it more," he said flatly. "Anyway, you can let him know."

"Or you can," Luka said, extending the paper back to him.

But Razik didn't take it. Instead, he leapt into the sky, done with the conversation.

Abandoning his own plans to go flying, Luka turned and went back through the training room. Eliza and Tessa were nowhere to be seen, apparently done with their training. He climbed stairs to the main floor, checking rooms as he went. Arius House was still massive, even if they were only using one wing and the main part of the house right now.

He finally found Xan in the library, and he shouldn't have been surprised. Theon was still researching everything he could about transferring power, needing to do something while they sat around and waited for Dagian to come through on getting that ring back.

Theon and Xan both looked up, Theon reaching for his mug of coffee while he asked, "How'd training go?"

"Fine," Luka said quickly, attention fixed on Xan. "There's something I need to show you."

"What is it?" Xan asked, getting to his feet and crossing the room, taking the paper Luka extended to him.

Xan's eyes went wide as he read the words scrawled on the page. "You figured out how to remove it?"

"Not me," Luka answered, shaking his head. "Razik."

Xan's head snapped up, followed by a grimace as it jostled the stone at his throat. "Razik?"

Luka nodded.

"Where is he?"

"Went flying," Luka answered. "But he said we'll need Tessa for this."

Xan nodded again, reading the notes on the paper once more.

"I can find her. Ask her to help now. If you're ready?" Luka ventured, glancing at Theon, who had stood and come closer. Theon nodded, already striding for the door.

"I've been ready for twenty-five years," Xan said, still staring at the paper.

A half hour later, they were gathered in the gardens. Razik was still off somewhere, despite Eliza speaking to him down their bond.

"He won't come," she said simply, curling her hands around the ends of her sleeves.

"Then I will go to him," Xan replied. He turned to where Tessa was standing next to Theon, worrying her bottom lip as she read over the paper.

"Are you sure about this?" she asked. "What if something goes wrong?"

"You can do this, Tessa," Theon said. "Luka and I are here if you go too deep."

"That's not really the part I'm worried about," she murmured. "It's more so the channeling that power at his *throat*."

"If you're not comfortable, you do not have to," Xan said gently, but Luka could see the dread in his father's eyes at the idea of having to wear that collar even a day longer.

She glanced at Luka, concern on her features.

I can't do this, she whispered down the bond. *What if I hurt him? I already stole time with him from you. What if I take him from you completely?*

We'll be right here beside you, Luka replied. *Like Theon said, we know how to help you now.*

Just . . . If I can't do it, please don't look at me differently.

Nothing will change the way I look at you, baby girl.

But he felt the hesitation down the bond, and he couldn't really blame her since he *had* looked at her differently when he discovered the truth of his father. She didn't argue further, though, squaring her shoulders and pulling one of her daggers from a swirl of chaos.

She closed the distance between her and Xan, his father dropping to a knee so she could reach easier.

"Thank you for this, Tessa," he said quietly as she pierced her finger.

"Don't thank me yet," she muttered. "Wait until we're sure I haven't killed you."

He smiled in encouragement, but she was focused on her task now. Placing her finger on the collar, she circled him, dragging her blood all the way around it. When she closed the circle, it flared faintly.

"Good, Tessa," Theon said from where he'd come up behind her.

She stepped back. "That was the easy part."

Theon placed his hand on the small of her back. "We're right here. You can do this."

Luka readied his own power, letting it linger just beneath his skin. He didn't want to call it forth completely and distract her magic, but he wanted it ready, just in case.

Bringing a hand up, she let her magic pool, and Luka gritted his teeth. Even without trying, her power called to his. She knew the others were feeling it too. Eliza's lips were pressed into a thin line, and Xan had leaned closer, as if her mere presence could set his power free.

He felt her letting herself slip a little deeper into her magic, her eyes glowing violet and her aura shimmering with that golden mist. But it was dark embers of onyx that floated among her hair. With a shuddering breath, she used her other hand and swiped her fingers through the storm in her palm. As if pulling a thread, a thin strand of chaos unraveled, and she sent it to the collar. That thread settled along her circle of blood, flaring brighter still.

But that wasn't enough. Achaz had been thorough when he'd created this cursed stone, and it required more than blood and chaos to break it.

It required light from beginnings.

Her brow furrowed in concentration, lightning flickered in her eyes as she slowly pulled the light from the chaos on the collar. It splintered, tiny fissures of lightning appearing slowly. This was the part she'd been worried about. All the chaos and power so close to Xan's throat. One wrong move or thought, and they had no idea what would happen.

His father was scarcely breathing, and Luka found himself holding his breath as they waited. A frustrated growl came from Tessa, and she shifted her feet, pitching closer.

Theon followed, maintaining contact with her to keep her grounded. The light on the stone flared brighter, a crackling sound filling the air. Then she pressed her fingertips to the collar, more chaos seeping out. She sucked in a sharp breath, her eyes snapping to Xan's.

"I feel your power," she lilted. "It is angry."

"That it is, Tessa," Xan answered. "Twenty-five years is a long time."

Her head tipped to the side. "How did you not go mad?"

"Maybe I did."

A terrifying grin filled her face. "Is that why we got along so well? Two souls lost to madness?"

"We have to be a little mad to dream, Tessalyn," he said, his throat bobbing with a swallow.

She hummed in thought, clearly slipping deeper into her magic. "And have you dreamed of flying?"

"Every fucking day," Xan gritted out, and it was then Luka realized his father was trembling. With restraint or need, he didn't know, but he was also realizing that the calm demeanor he'd come to know of the male wasn't fully him. It was only a part of him he'd been forced to embrace because the rest had been trapped by that collar.

Tessa pulled her hand back, a thread of pure gold between her fingers. With a final flash of a smile, she tugged on that magic, and the collar shattered, pieces of it dropping to the ground.

In the next blink, his father had shifted, a roar of fury ringing around them. Theon had thrown himself over Tessa, dragging her back as the massive dragon whipped his head around, glowing sapphire eyes taking them all in. He was the same dark midnight blue as Luka, but his wings, along with the ridges on his back, were the inky black of Theon's darkness.

Then he leaped into the sky, the draft from his wings stirring the air around them. Several mighty flaps of those wings, and he was high enough in the air to release a stream of dragon fire into the clear sky. Twenty-five years' worth of trapped power finally free.

A hand brushed his arm, and he looked away from his father to find Tessa looking up at him in curiosity. Her eyes were still glowing, and she was still a little lost to her power when she asked, "Are you going to fly with him?"

"What?" Luka asked.

"Go fly with him," she said again.

"Go, Luka," Theon added with a grin.

With a grin of his own, he shifted and was in the sky with his next breath. The air was cool against his heated skin, and he let out a roar when his father flew higher, twisting and turning as he chased the thrill of flying. Luka couldn't imagine not being able to do this for twenty-five years. He got in a mood if he went two days without flying, let alone twenty-five fucking years.

Luka banked in midair, and then stalled, hovering in place as he spotted the male perched on the roof of Arius House. He still only had his wings, but he was watching them both, his features expressionless. His wings flared, and Luka waited, willing him to join them. He was the reason this was even happening after all.

Razik's head tilted, and Luka knew Eliza was speaking to him down the bond. But Razik shook his head, and Luka wondered if he'd ever get to a place where he could admit he wanted a relationship with Xan. Maybe someday, but he wouldn't let his brother keep him from enjoying this moment. For twenty-five years, he'd thought he was the last of his kind, and now he was in the sky with his father while his brother watched on.

He looked down, finding those on the ground watching them. He could make out Tessa's smile where she was tucked into Theon's side. Without her, he wouldn't have any of this. It all went back to her.

The female he'd told Theon not to Select.

The one he'd swore wasn't the one for this.

Too wild.

Too impulsive.

The perfect one for chaos.

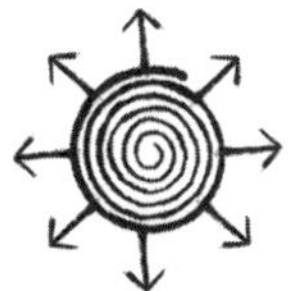

43
EVIANA

There was a burning sensation beneath her skin that she couldn't shake. A constant ache that pulsed with each beat of her heart and with every drop of magic that drained away with the bands. More than that, she was exhausted. Between Valter's demands of her and sneaking off to Caris's prison room every chance she could, she knew she was making it worse. Knew she was only helping Valter's cause of weakening her to the point of restoring their bond. If it got to that point, she was fucked.

"Sit, Eve," he said, pointing to the chair at his right.

She sank into it with as much grace as she could muster. "Thank you," she murmured, knowing if she didn't, she would be reprimanded and possibly made to stand once more.

Valter reached for a small plate in front of him laden with mixed fruit, scrambled eggs, and a chocolate chip muffin. Sliding it across the table, he placed it in front of her before returning to the reports he was looking over.

Eviana froze, unsure of what was happening here. He'd given her things like this in the past, but that was before the betrayal and the running and the blocking of the bond. Since they'd been reunited, it had only been bland foods. Oatmeal. Plain rice. Unseasoned vegetables.

"Eat, Eviana," he ordered, his shadows snaking out and nudging her silverware closer to her.

Tentatively, she picked up the fork, scooping up a bite of scrambled eggs. This was a trap. Food restored her reserves, kept them from depleting. It was a trap, but by the gods, she was *hungry.* Forcing herself to go slow, she took measured bites, despite wanting to shovel everything into her mouth. She hadn't had a proper meal since before they'd left Raven Harbor for the Serafina Estate.

She saved the muffin for last though. A treat she rarely got, even when Valter had thought she was under his thumb. She nearly moaned at the first bite, the sweetness of the chocolate dancing across her tongue. Try as she might, there was nothing slow and measured about the way she ate that muffin. Valter didn't say a word. Didn't even look up at her. One would think it a blessing to have his attention diverted elsewhere, but one would have to be favored by the gods to receive blessings. She was most certainly not favored by the gods or the Fates, or anything else for that matter.

The doors to the dining room opened, and Priya came skipping in. She was in a lavender dress with flowers along the hem, and her hair was braided in two plaits that hung over her shoulders.

"Good morning, Valter," she sang, climbing onto the chair to his left.

Valter immediately put the reports aside, giving the child his full attention. "Good morning, my sweet Priya," he greeted with a smile. "How has your morning been so far?"

"Great," she answered, shifting to the side so the nursemaid could place a breakfast plate before her. The girl frowned as she studied her plate of toast, eggs, fruit, and sausage.

"Is something wrong, my sweet?" Valter asked, a plate being placed before him as well.

Eviana hid her confusion. Had she been served before him? He had waited to eat with Priya?

"I just thought . . ." She looked up at him, her turquoise eyes somewhere between disappointed and upset.

"You thought what?" Valter pushed with faux concern.

"You said I could have those muffins in the kitchen for breakfast."

Eviana glanced at her plate where nothing but crumbs remained.

"Ah," Valter said, sounding as disappointed as she did. "I know I promised you that, but unfortunately, the muffins are gone."

"Gone?"

He nodded gravely. "I told her not to eat it, that I had promised it to you, but she ate it anyway."

Eviana's stomach sank as she realized exactly what the trap was.

"Who?" Priya asked, and she wasn't on the verge of tears like one would expect. She sounded . . . angry.

Valter didn't answer, but he did glance at Eviana pointedly. Then he reached over, patting Priya's hand. "I'm sorry she made me break my promise. I will think of a way to make it up to you."

Priya glared across the table at Eviana, her eyes hard chips of ice. That hatred Valter had promised was already building, and he was adding layer upon layer to it.

"Why is she at the table?" Priya asked, her tiny hands in fists on either side of her plate.

Valter clicked his tongue. "You know she is my Source, Priya."

"But she hasn't been eating with us this whole time."

"I know, my sweet," he said with more fake sympathy. "But she is still mine to care for."

Her gaze snapped to his, and *now* there were thin pools of tears there. "But I'm yours too, right?"

"Of course you are," he answered, reaching over and cupping her chin. "But in a different way."

Eviana watched as she shoved down her tears, her mouth pressing into a thin line of determination.

Everything that goes wrong in her life, every hurt and treachery, I will make sure she can trace it back to you.

"Let's eat our breakfast, hmm?" Valter said, sitting back and picking up his fork once more. "Then later you can show me how your plants are doing. I'm sure Eviana could help some too."

"I don't want her help," Priya bit out, stabbing at a strawberry a little too harshly.

Valter sighed. "I know, but you must learn to get along with her. She will always be with me."

For the rest of the meal, Eviana sat as her daughter cast glares at her across the table in between her conversation with Valter. When she spoke to him, those glares morphed into smiles, and she held on to every word he said. Soaking them in. And when breakfast was done, he sent her on her way with the nursemaid for her studies, promising to meet her when she was done to look at her plants.

The dining room doors shut with an ominous thud, and Eviana sat frozen, her hands in her lap and eyes on the plate of muffin crumbs. She heard his chair scrape. Heard him get to his feet and stop beside her chair. Then he cupped her face, tilting it up to his. Hazel eyes studied her, full of triumph and cruelty.

"We have visitors coming and new alliances to build. Your services will be required," he said sharply, still holding her face.

"Yes, my Lord," she whispered, his hold tightening at the soft answer.

"Who did this, my flower?" he asked, leaning in so his words fanned across her lips. "Whose fault is this?"

"Mine," she answered.

"And who must pay for their betrayal?"

"Me."

He stepped back, reaching for his belt, and she already knew what was next as she slid to her knees.

She had to pay for her betrayal, but not Priya. Not that little girl. This would never be her life, on her knees for a male who had groomed her to adore him. Being passed around to secure deals and punished for not being grateful for the life she'd been forced into.

His grip tightened in her hair as he thrust down her throat, and she winced, knowing he liked it when she hurt.

This would not be the life for Priya. She could hate her for it, but she would make sure she was never Valter's.

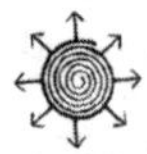

This is stupid.

That was all she could think as she stood outside the wall in a sheer nightgown with a photograph she'd managed to find. It was Theon's commencement photo with Luka and Axel. His formal commencement portrait was too harsh. His features and expression were a mirror of Valter, but this one was different. A spark of defiance lingered, and his smile was genuine. A few years before he went through his Staying, he looked a little younger.

She'd brought Caris extra food and clothing. A new book to read. Little things she could steal and hide until she could bring them here. Nothing like the weapons Tessa had smuggled in to her, but the effort had to count for something, right?

With a surge of determination, she drew blood, smearing it across the secret panel. Desperate and all that, she supposed.

Caris was seated at the small table, eating her dinner and reading the book Eviana had brought her last time.

Progress.

"Caris," Eviana greeted flatly, the same way she greeted her every time she came here.

The female slowly closed her book, leaning back in her chair. "This was an interesting choice," she said, setting the book aside.

"Did you find anything of interest in it?" Eviana asked, staying by the entrance.

Caris's smile was sharp and sarcastic. "I know my own history," she replied. "I didn't need a book to remind me what my life was supposed to look like."

"It was the only one I could find."

"Somehow I doubt that," Caris said. "I always knew you were clever, Eviana. Many times while we watched the children play, I told Pen that there was more to you than met the eye."

"There is nothing more to me than what I am."

"And what are you?"

Nothing.

It was the answer that came to her immediately, but she didn't speak it, instead curling her fingers around the photograph.

Caris studied her, and Eviana did the same in return. It was hard not to see the resemblance. The emerald eyes and high cheekbones. The stubbornness and intelligence. And if those cuffs on her biceps were removed, she'd have the same darkness at her beck and call.

"You were there when Pen died?" Caris asked.

"What?" Eviana asked at the sudden question.

"You heard me."

This was the most Caris had deigned to speak to her over her few visits. But it had taken her a while to warm up to Tessa too, so this had to mean she was getting somewhere.

Eviana lifted her chin. "He made me do it."

"He never does his own dirty work," she scoffed.

She wasn't wrong about that.

"And they saw it? Like they did with me?" Caris pushed.

Eviana nodded. "Valter left the body for them."

"Of course he did. She was truly dead. If he'd left mine, they would have known," she said simply.

"It . . . changed them more," Eviana tried. "Made them more determined to overthrow him."

"It will never work. The whole of Devram would need to fall for anything to change," Caris said, reaching for her book and turning back to her paltry dinner. A dismissal if Eviana had ever seen one.

"They aren't alone," Eviana blurted. "They . . . Theon has fallen for someone. Chosen her against Valter's wishes, and she is changing things. It has caused division among the kingdoms."

"Nothing will change in Devram unless the gods come and destroy it all to start anew," Caris said again. "Good night, Eviana."

"Not the gods, but what of Chaos?"

Caris stilled, slowly setting down the soup spoon she'd picked up. Moving the book aside once more, she turned back to Eviana. "You speak of the Revelation Decree."

"I do," Eviana answered, not sure how this was going to convince Caris to help her. She just needed to find a bargaining chip. *Something* to entice her.

"That is not really a decree," Caris went on.

"Theon figured that out early on. He was only in his adolescent years when he started digging into it. Initially, Valter was happy, but Theon became preoccupied with it," Eviana said, and as she spoke, Caris leaned forward imperceptibly. Almost as if she was hanging on to every word.

"Pen was from the Falein Estate," Caris said softly.

"I know."

"She would have encouraged his love of academics."

"She did," Eviana confirmed. "Something Valter was often irritated with her for when it interfered with what he wanted Theon focused on. Theon can be . . . obsessive."

"And all of this relates to Chaos how?"

"That obsession carries over to his personal relationships," Eviana said. "The female he has fallen for was to be his Source, but she is not Fae. Hidden in the realm, she is the granddaughter of Arius and Achaz. Both."

Caris's brow furrowed. "Beginnings and endings cannot be in one."

"But they are, and more. I do not understand it all as it is not my place, but her magic is Chaos itself," Eviana continued. "She is the most powerful being in Devram, and she will bring the realm to its knees. She has already destroyed the Pantheon, and I am told Theon is now at her side once more."

"And you? Where are you in all this?" Caris asked, crossing one leg over the other and resting her chin in her hand.

"What do you mean?"

Her smile was sharp. "I watched you with him for years, Eviana. Endured torture at your hand while cut off from my power. For decades, I have not been able to touch it." Her emerald gaze darted to her wrists. "But you understand that some, I suppose."

"It's been days for me. Not decades," Eviana deadpanned.

Her smile didn't falter. "But it is still driving you mad."

"How are you not?"

"Pen helped me learn to endure it long ago," she answered, her smile turning dark and cold. "I had to endure many things, thanks to you and Valter. Forced to conceive a child against my will. Watch another claim my child as her own. Care for my son and be unable to tell him who I was."

"I was . . ." Eviana trailed off, understanding the pain of what she was describing.

"Just trying to survive," Caris supplied.

Eviana nodded, holding her stare. "But more and more I find myself wondering why I bothered."

"Why did you?"

Silence hung in the air as she debated what to say. For seven years she'd kept this secret. No one knew about Priya, and it was part of keeping her safe. And yes, Priya was why she was here, trying to gain Caris's trust to begin with, but she suddenly felt like she was telling her secrets to everyone. Tessa knew. She could assume she'd told Theon and Luka. Corbin. Lange. The more people who knew, the more she would be used against her. Caris wasn't the only one who had a rightful grudge against her.

Finally, Eviana said, "If I was gone, he would just do the same to someone else."

Caris's head tilted, her raven locks slipping over her shoulder. "Why do you care?"

Why did she care? If she'd been gone, she wouldn't have had to worry about anything. She'd be in the After with no cares. Priya wouldn't exist to worry about, spared from this poisonous cycle.

"I don't know why I cared back then," she answered honestly. "But now, it's because of an innocent girl he lords over me the same way he did to you with Theon."

Caris sat up straight at the words, her eyes wide. Eviana crossed the room, placing the photo on the table.

"I didn't get to care for her. She didn't even know I existed until a few weeks ago, and she still doesn't know who I am to her," Eviana said. "I don't know her favorite foods or what scares her at night. I didn't get to see her first steps or watch her wonder the first time she felt a flower call to her. I know it's not the same, but she is why I care now. Because even though I didn't get those things, I will still sacrifice whatever I must for her, just as you did for them."

She stepped back as Caris reached for the photo, her hand trembling. Eviana didn't know if Valter told her anything about Theon. He wouldn't have cared to tell her of Luka or Axel, despite her being their caretaker as well. Judging by her reaction though, she hadn't seen them since the day Valter tortured her in front of them.

"The bargain isn't for me," Eviana said. "It's for her. Even if I never see her again in the end."

"I don't know what you think I can do," Caris said quietly, still fixated on the photo.

"I just need to get her out of here," she answered. "If I can get you out, will you take her with you? Get her to Theon? There are two males who will be with him. They will take her from there."

Her eyes filled with pity. "Even if you could do that, what about you, Eviana?"

"Does it matter?" She gestured around the room. "Did it matter to you that this became your reality as long as they were safe?"

"Come to me with a plan, and we'll talk," Caris said, holding the photo with two hands now.

It wasn't a yes, but it was something.

Eviana turned to leave, but just before she stepped through the hidden panel, Caris called out, "Thank you, Eviana."

She didn't stop or look back. There was nothing to thank her for. It was the least she could do after being part of the reason she was there in the first place.

Now to finalize her plan and hope that Corbin and Lange would be on board.

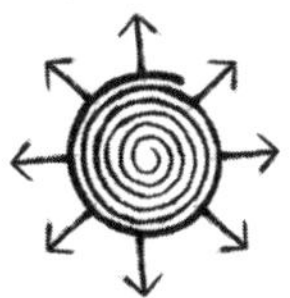

44
AXEL

Perfect.

That was all he could think as he leaned against the doorjamb, watching Kat softly talk to Maddox while she rocked him. Her hair was down, framing her face, and her finger gently stroked his cheek. Everything about that tiny babe was perfection, and now, nearly two weeks later, they'd discovered his perfect cry when he lets them know he needs something and his perfect soft sighs as he drifts to sleep. It was unfair for something to be so gods-damn perfect in this fucked up realm, and more than once he'd tried to figure out how his father had looked at him or Theon when they were that small and new and still only saw them as a means to an end.

Kat looked up when he softly cleared his throat, and the pure joy from seconds ago faded into disapproval. Her eyes narrowed and her lips pursed as she looked him up and down once, taking in the black pants and fitted black long-sleeve shirt. The boots and weapons. Everything he wore when he was out scouting with Cade and Rayell as they made their plans for Bree. Maddox squirmed as if he could sense the sudden tension, a soft cry coming from him as Kat stood from the chair.

Crossing the room with purpose, she held him out, forcing Axel to take their son. "You may as well hold him. It might be one of the last times," she said sharply.

He sighed as he cuddled the babe close, Maddox instantly settling down. "Kat, we've talked about this."

"No," she hissed in a low tone so as not to wake Maddox. "*You've* talked about this. Planned this entire thing without me."

"That's not true," he argued, keeping his voice just as low. "You know what we know. You've been part of the plans, and you know this needs to happen. She won't stop."

"I know that," she snapped in a whisper, angrily beginning to fold blankets. "But I deserve this vengeance too, Axel. I'm the one she kidnapped, forced into labor from the stress. I'm the one who labored for hours and hours without you because of her. It wasn't just *your* son she tried to steal."

Hot and angry tears were filling her eyes, and Axel's chest twisted at the sight. He reached out a hand, halting her aggressive folding and tidying. "Kitten, I'm not keeping you from the vengeance because you don't deserve it. If something goes wrong . . . Maddox can't be left alone."

"Something is less likely to go wrong if I am with you," she argued. "I'm the one with the magic now. Even without his shadows, my fire is still something."

He winced at the words. Even knowing they weren't meant to be cruel, it still hit that way.

He swallowed thickly before he said, "I know that. Which is why if something happens, and he can only have one of us, it needs to be you."

Katya went still, her eyes going wide at the words. They'd argued about this several times since Maddox's birth, but he'd never said those words. Never put it out there so plainly, but it was the truth. Bree needed to be dealt with to keep Maddox safe. Then his father. And Axel didn't have his power. Sure, he was a lethal predator, but so were Fae and Legacy. He was the disadvantage here, and Maddox deserved every advantage. If only one could stay with him, it needed to be Kat.

"Axel," she started, clearly choosing her words carefully. "Maddox needs both of us."

A small, sad smile curled on his lips as he looked down at the sleeping babe in his arms. His tiny fingers curled around the edge of the green blanket. His lips twitching in sleep. "I know, kitten," he said thickly. "But that's not always how life works, and he deserves to not be hunted. I plan on being with you for decades, but I'm not naïve. If it keeps you both safe . . ."

"Because love to you is defined as safety, and you know loving someone as protecting them," Kat said, moving closer until she stood in front of him. When he didn't answer, she reached up with one hand, cupping his cheek.

"That's noble love, Axel, and while I understand it, I'm also telling you that is not how I need to be loved right now."

"And I'm telling you if something happens to me, I don't give a fuck. But if something happens to you—"

"If something happens to *you,* I give a fuck, Axel," she interrupted. "Are you dismissing everything I went through to find you?"

"Of course not. I—"

"Because if something happens to you, Maddox may still have me, but he won't have all of me. You'll take a part of me with you to the After."

Axel curled his palm around the back of her head, hauling her mouth to his while being mindful of the sleeping bundle between them. His tongue skated along hers, her lips soft against his.

"You'll pluck the stars from the sky for me," she murmured against his lips. "But I'll burn them to ashes for you just so we can build something new for him."

They both looked down at their sleeping son as emotion clogged his throat.

"Who do we trust to stay with him while we do this?" he asked thickly.

"Corbin and Lange," she answered instantly. "Even if we don't completely trust the Shifters, we can trust they won't do anything to Corbin after finally having him back."

That was fair. Those two had opted to stay here for the time being, and Axel couldn't blame them. Tessa, Theon, and Luka were still figuring out their new relationship. Not to mention Luka's family was broody as fuck. At least here they had Kat—another Fae—and Corbin was slowly getting to know this side of his bloodline. More than that, they were searching for Eviana, which was a whole other matter—learning his father's Source had a child.

One thing at a time, or he was going to go mad.

"Okay, but . . ." he started, and her eyes narrowed. "Kat, you gave birth two weeks ago. It was long and exhausting. Not to mention traumatizing," he continued in a rush. "Are you sure—"

"We do this, Axel. We do this, and then we rest," she interrupted.

"I don't like this."

A coy smile tilted on her lips. "But?"

He sighed. "You've finally figured out I can never deny you anything."

"I love you," she whispered, pushing onto her toes.

"Yeah, yeah," he muttered. "We don't have set plans yet. Remember that."

She pressed her lips to his jaw before she left the room to shower.

He looked down at the sleeping babe, his gut churning with unease. "I promise she'll come back, Mads," he said softly. "You'll never be alone."

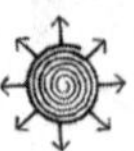

"We know where she is," Rayell announced, striding into the study they were using for their plans.

Axel set down the book he was looking through with Maddox asleep on his shoulder. "Really? That's great."

"I know," she said, dramatically dropping into a chair. "But we need to make our move tonight."

"Which means you better have come up with a way to contain her," Cade added, crossing his arms over his broad chest where he stood beside Rayell.

"And if we haven't?" Axel asked, because that was, in fact, the case.

"Then I don't know when we'll get another chance," Cade said simply. "Could be days. Could be years."

"Years is not acceptable," Axel said darkly. "And you're certain we cannot kill her?"

"She is older than anyone I know. Than anyone here," Cade said.

"That doesn't mean she can't be killed," Axel argued.

"But what if she's *not* from here?" Kat said, sitting up a little straighter.

Axel frowned, rubbing his palm along Maddox's back as he stirred. "You think she came through a mirror gate at some point?"

That was plausible, he supposed, but it still didn't explain why she couldn't be killed.

"Maybe, but I don't think that's the case," Kat said, pacing the same way Theon did when he was putting pieces of something together. "I don't know exactly how, but . . ." She paused, turning to face him. "I think we're going to need Tessa to imprison her. Maybe there is a way to kill her, but if we can imprison her until we figure it out, then we do that tonight."

"Tonight," Axel repeated.

She gestured to Cade. "They just said it might be our only chance for a while."

"We're nowhere near ready," Axel argued.

"Something has her on edge," Rayell cut in. "It's the only reason she's come out of hiding. She's at the House of Four, but she won't stay there long, Axel."

"If Tessa comes, Luka has to come because of that Life Mark. And if Luka comes, then Theon is going to come. That is too many people to do this quietly," Axel said.

"So Theon and Luka stay here with Maddox while the rest of us go," Kat said, as if it would be that simple.

"Right," Axel deadpanned. "You convince them of that, and we'll go tonight, kitten."

"Great," she answered, lifting a palm before flames carried a fire message to Arius House.

There was no way in all the Pits of Torment she was going to convince Theon and Luka to let Tessa do this alone with them.

The three of them were escorted into the room several minutes later, and Theon was immediately taking Maddox from Axel. Tessa watched him, her lips thinning, before she focused her attention on Kat.

"You said you needed me?" she asked, drifting closer and perusing the books scattered about.

"I think we're going to need your magic to imprison Bree," Kat replied.

"Of course," she answered, flipping through pages. "Just let me know when."

"Tonight."

She looked up, her brow arching. "Tonight?"

Kat nodded. "Rayell and Cade have found her, but it might be our only chance for a while." She paused, glancing at Axel. He smirked in response, gesturing for her to continue. "And it needs to be just you. Theon and Luka need to stay behind."

"Not happening," Theon said immediately while Luka said, "Fuck no."

"It's too many people for us to be covert," Kat argued. "We understand Luka and Tessa can't be too far apart. We're just going across the Underground. We've done this before. You two can stay with Maddox."

"No," Theon said simply while Luka just crossed his arms.

"Theon, you can't be serious. We need Rayell and Cade to guide us through the House of Four. With Tessa, that's five people trying not to be seen. Adding two more is simply unjustifiable."

"And if she gets lost to her power and you cannot call her back? What then?" Theon countered in a harsh whisper, and Axel swallowed his huff of laughter at how ridiculous this was. An argument with quiet voices to avoid waking the sleeping babe.

"I think I'll be fine," Tessa said simply, her magic now drifting across the books and papers.

"Forgive me for not being okay with you *thinking* you'll be fine," Theon said flatly.

She shrugged, her head tilting. "I am keen to meet this Bree."

"You shouldn't be," Axel muttered.

"I could just . . . take care of her," Tessa added.

"Everyone seems pretty convinced that can't be done for some reason."

"We don't think she's from here," Kat added. "Rayell and Cade said she's the oldest being they know of in all of Devram."

"That's silly. Cienna and Tristyn have to be older," Tessa murmured, her power still swirling.

Axel blinked at her statement, then turned to Kat. "Is there a reason we haven't asked them?"

She looked just as alarmed. "I suppose we've been a little preoccupied," she answered slowly.

Saying nothing else, Tessa lifted a hand, a swirl of chaos appearing while her magic continued . . . whatever it was doing.

"What do you think she is?" Theon asked, attention back on Kat.

"I don't know," she admitted, pacing again. "She said some things at that dinner, but it doesn't seem to fit."

"What kinds of things?"

"About the Fates watching all the power players. She's also the one who told us we can't kill her. That we have no idea what we're dealing with," Kat answered.

"The fucking Fates," Tessa muttered, making her way around the table. "I'd kill them all if I could."

"Tessa, what in the name of Sargon are you doing?" Luka finally asked.

She glanced up at her name, blinking as though she'd been lost to something. "Nothing." When he gave her a frank look, she sighed. "Sometimes my power finds things for me."

"That makes no sense."

"Are you saying your magic is . . . reading all of that?" Theon asked, coming closer.

She looked up at him, her eyes moving from Maddox and back to the papers. "Sort of. I'm not absorbing anything, but if it's something of importance, I kind of just . . . know."

"How long have you been able to do this?" he demanded, but before Tessa could answer, the door opened once more and Tristyn strode in, his usual cocky smirk in place.

"You called, wild fury?" he asked, hands slipping into the pockets of his jacket. He had a messenger bag draped across his chest.

"How old are you?" Tessa asked.

He barked a laugh. "You summoned me here to ask me that?"

"Not *only* that. Are you and Cienna the oldest beings in Devram?"

His brow bunched. "We're some of them, yes."

"But not *the* oldest?"

"Tessa, where is this going?"

"We're discussing Bree DelaCrux," Axel cut in. "We have been told by a few people we cannot kill her."

"You can't," Tristyn said simply.

"Do you know her?"

"Not personally," he answered slowly. "I cannot interfere with the Fates."

"Back to the godsdamn Fates," Tessa muttered.

"Okay, so we save the killing for later," Axel said. "We need a place to hold her. Or ideas on how to do that."

"Well, the ideal place would be the cells beneath the Pantheon, but . . ." Tristyn trailed off.

"Yes, yes, they were destroyed," Tessa sighed, but then she froze. "But were they?"

"You did it, Tessa," Luka said flatly.

"Yes, I destroyed the mirror and the Pantheon, but can't we still keep her *beneath* the Pantheon? It's still the center of the continent. It's still a nexus," she insisted.

"What do you know of nexuses?" Theon cut in.

She waved him off. "Not now, Theon. That would work, right, Tris?"

His russet eyes were studying her as he said, "I suppose, but you'd have to get her there."

"So we Travel."

"Yeah, but we don't know what it's like under there," Tristyn argued. "If it's just rock and rubble and nowhere to stand or move or breathe, what are you going to do?"

"Do you have a better idea?" Tessa shot back.

Tristyn rolled his lips. "No. Your idea is actually brilliant if we can pull it off."

"You go make sure a cell is ready, and I'll go with them to get her," Tessa said.

"Not without us," Theon interjected again.

She flicked her eyes to him once before glancing at Luka. "You two have babysitting duty with someone other than me tonight."

"No, Tessa," Luka said tightly.

"I'm not sure when you two decided I needed your permission to do anything," she said casually, shuffling papers around and pulling out a book from the bottom of the stacks.

"Since you and Blackheart got yourselves in trouble. Do you need a reminder of the cost of that night?" Luka retorted.

Her head whipped to him, eyes flashing. "This is different, and you know it. You know where I'll be, and they have been planning this. This isn't a spur-of-the-moment choice, and I can call you through the bond if we need help."

Axel smirked, leaning against the side of the sofa and watching this little power struggle play out.

"Tessa, you're the Arius Lady," Theon started, clearly trying another angle.

"Correct," she said, flipping the pages of the book.

"You can't just—"

"I believe because I am the Arius Lady, I *can* just," she interrupted. "I could *just* use your own magic to keep you here while I go help stop the person trying to kidnap your nephew, but I'm not. I'm *telling* you so you can be prepared if anything goes wrong."

"I call that growth," Axel piped in.

"Shut up, Axel," Theon grumbled, shifting Maddox onto his shoulder.

"How about if Theon stays with Maddox, and I go with," Luka tried.

Tessa shrugged. "This isn't my mission. Take it up with them."

"Truly it's too many people," Kat said. "We need Cade and Rayell, and this is personal for me and Axel. Tessa's right. She can contact you down the bond, and you can Travel, Luka."

Luka glanced at Theon before he sighed. "Fine, but this is the last time the three of you gang up on us."

"It's cute you think that," Tessa said with a smirk, snapping the book closed. "When do we leave?"

And that was how Axel found himself outside the House of Four two hours later.

All of them were dressed in black, the females with their hair pulled back. They went as soon as possible because the vampyres weren't sure how long Bree would hang around.

Hiding in the shadows across the cavern, Rayell and Cade instructed Tessa on where to Travel them so they wouldn't have to cross the cavern bridge.

They couldn't risk Traveling directly into the House of Four though, so they were entering through a hidden entrance at Rayell's house and making their way over to Bree's.

Rayell's section of the House of Four was far different from Bree's. He'd expected them all to be the same—extravagant and formal. But Rayell's house was more homey. Warm colors of beige, coral, and blues. Everything airy and welcoming, somehow reminding Axel of being by the sea rather than stuck under the mountains.

"It gets tight in here," Rayell warned as she led them towards the back of the house. "There is a passage behind the Houses that connects them all, but it is narrow. Only wide enough for one at a time."

Axel glanced over his shoulder at Tessa, who was trailing her fingers along the wall. Her head tilted, and he knew then Theon and Luka were talking to her.

"Tell them where we're going, Tessa," Axel said. "So they can talk you through it."

His focus was entirely on Kat. While he loved Tessa like a sister, he wasn't going to be the one to talk her through her phobias when his wife was here. Bree could be anywhere.

Rayell hadn't been kidding about the tight passage. More than once, Axel wondered how the fuck Cade fit through here. The male was as big and broad as Luka, but even Axel had to turn and shuffle through a few areas, his shirt getting caught on the stone wall more than once.

When they finally emerged in Bree's House, Tessa shoved past him, leaning against the wall with her eyes closed and breathing deep.

"Tessa?" Kat asked, going to her and tentatively placing her hand on her arm. "Are you all right?"

She nodded, her chest heaving. "Just give me a moment. "

"We don't have a moment," Cade said gruffly. "We're in her home now. We need to keep moving to find her before she finds us."

Kat took Tessa's hand, tugging her forward. "We're all leaving here together, Tessa."

Tessa nodded, visibly trying to calm her breathing as Kat stayed close and followed Axel and Rayell. Cade took up the rear again, and while they moved, Axel tried to figure out where exactly they were.

"Isn't it odd she came back to her house?" Axel asked Rayell in a hushed tone.

"Yes and no," the Night Child answered. "She's been around a long time.

A lot of her secrets are here. We knew she'd come back eventually. She always does."

"What made you turn on her?" Tessa asked from behind them.

Axel glanced back, Kat giving him a reassuring smile.

"She kept refusing to fill Henry's position," Rayell answered. "We were already growing suspicious of her motives. For nearly two hundred years, we have led the Dispensary District together and always been on acceptable terms with the Arius Lord. We gave respect, and in return, we were left alone. Bree was suddenly threatening our way of life and the lives of the people in our care."

"Do you think she instigated that attack on me? The one Theon killed Henry for?"

"It wouldn't surprise me," she answered.

Axel looked at Rayell because he'd never thought of that, but now that Tessa had brought it up, he wouldn't be surprised either if Bree had planted the seeds for that little rebellion. She was cunning and clever. She'd likely been sowing seeds of discontent for decades. Little things here and there, letting them fester and grow until she was ready to make her move.

They rounded a corner, and Axel slowed when he saw the large iron doors that lay ahead of them.

"The dragon dick room?" Axel questioned.

"The what now?" Tessa asked.

"There's a ton of treasure in there," Axel replied. "Gems. Gold. Weapons. I remember thinking Luka's dragon dick would get hard in there."

Kat's eyes were wide. "What is wrong with you?" she asked incredulously.

"You haven't seen his cave, kitten."

"Yeah, he's right," Tessa said, eyeing the doors with new interest. "Luka has random trinkets and things everywhere, and he gets really annoyed when people touch his things."

"That's an understatement," Axel scoffed.

"Can we please focus?" Cade interrupted.

"Right. We just need to incapacitate her," Axel said. "Then we can Travel her to the Pantheon." He turned to the only two people with power. "Ready?"

Kat and Tessa both nodded. Flames flickered in Kat's eyes while the bands of light around Tessa's wrists sparked and crackled with energy.

"We won't be able to simply walk in," Cade was saying. "She has the doors warded."

"That won't be an issue," Tessa said, placing her palm on the door. Her magic seeped from beneath her palm, racing along the doors. Then she reached back and grabbed his hand. "Make sure we're all touching."

Pulling open the heavy door, she stepped in. Axel felt the wards ripple, but nothing else happened.

"Do you even feel them?" he whispered to Tessa as they took tentative steps farther into the room.

She shook her head, gaze darting around the room. He did the same, watching for any movement among the stacks of things. Nothing had changed. Weapons of all kinds were along the walls, and chests full of coin, gold, silver, and all manner of jewels and jewelry were stacked on the floor.

"Are you sure she's here?" he whispered after several tense minutes ticked by.

"She's here," Cade muttered. "She's already seen us."

"Then why are we hiding?" Tessa asked.

That . . . was a good question.

But before they could contemplate anything further, Bree appeared, stepping out from behind a pillar. "You brought them just as I asked," Bree said with a cunning smile. "Thank you."

Axel whirled on Cade and Rayell. "You tricked us?"

"No," Cade barked. "This is all part of her games."

"She's lying. You know she's lying, Axel," Rayell said, for once appearing alarmed at what was happening. "If we were betraying you, we've had plenty of opportunities to grab Maddox and disappear."

Axel bared his fangs at the mere mention of that, but Tessa was asking, "This is Bree?"

"Tessalyn Ausra," Bree purred, sauntering closer. Her black hair was straight and swayed with every step. In her signature red dress, her honey eyes were fixed on Tessa. She held that stunning sword in her hand. The gold and ruby hilt. The deep crimson blade. "I've been waiting quite some time to meet you."

Tessa turned to Axel. "This is her?"

"Yeah," he answered, trying to watch Bree but perplexed by Tessa at the same time.

"Tristyn was right," she said with a frown, more to herself than anyone else. "She even survives the destruction of the realm."

"Have you met her?" Axel muttered.

"No, but I've seen her."

"Are you going to properly introduce us, Axel?" Bree asked, stopping several feet from them. "It's the least you could do after all I've done for you."

"All you've done for me?" Axel repeated. "Am I supposed to thank you for nearly killing my wife, forcing her into labor, and then trying to abduct my son?"

Bree tsked in disappointment. "I'm hurt, darling. Did you not find your beloved because of me? Learn what she was to you? If I hadn't set you free, would you even have known she carried your child? If I hadn't saved you to begin with, would you even be standing here? Or would you be so lost to your bloodlust, you wouldn't even be able to make sense of love and hate?"

He could only stare at her because words were failing him. She couldn't be serious. *Thank* her?

"She's right, Axel," Kat said suddenly. "We should be thanking her."

Bree's gaze slid to Kat, her eyes lighting up with intrigue. "That's right, poppet. It's because of me you learned to use that little bond."

"I know," she said softly. "Because of you, I at least got to feel that bond for a little bit before it was lost to us."

"So tragic," Bree said with mock sympathy.

"Kat—" Axel started.

"Don't be rude, Axel," Tessa interrupted with a pointed look. "Please introduce me properly."

"Tessa, this is Bree DelaCrux, a leader of the Night Children," Axel said slowly, trying to catch on to what these two were up to.

"I've heard a lot about you," Tessa replied, and her voice made the hair on the back of his neck stand on end. He knew that eerie ring that was slipping in.

"All dreadful things, I'm sure," Bree said with a sharp smile.

Tessa tipped her head back and forth, as if debating. "Not necessarily dreadful, but interesting nonetheless. I'd thank you for saving him, but at the time, I didn't really care."

Axel's gaze snapped to her because what in the actual fuck?

Bree's smile grew. "And why is that, my dear?"

"An ex-Legacy? Now powerless? I didn't need him. Eventually, I'd have to find him to kill him," she said plainly. "But for the time being, what was there to be concerned about?"

Bree's head tipped to the side as she studied her. "Chaos come to reign indeed. And now?"

Tessa shrugged, letting some of her magic pool around her, spreading across the floor in a slow crawl. "I still seek power."

"I hear you've taken two for your own," Bree said.

Tessa sighed. "And they are fairly attached to him despite what he now lacks, but I can't say he's entirely useless."

"That he is not," Bree agreed, stepping closer to Tessa.

"I'm assuming that's why you took him from Valter to begin with."

"Finally, someone who understands," Bree purred.

"Saw the potential," Tessa continued. "The way fate could play out."

"Not like I once could, but perceived powerlessness can be so deceiving."

Tessa hummed in agreement. "And what of these two? Were they once like you?"

Bree let loose a bitter laugh. "That's insulting."

"So they don't matter?"

"Not in the slightest."

Tessa nodded. "And Kat and Axel? Is there someplace we can . . . keep them for the time being?"

"Tessa?" Kat asked, her eyes going wide as Tessa's power started winding up Kat's legs.

"Tessa!" Axel barked, lurching forward, only to be ensnared by her magic too.

Bree's eyes were bright with surprise and delight. "And their son?"

Tessa shrugged again. "I grew up with no one. I'm sure he'll be fine."

Bree's eyes narrowed. "My agreement requires their son."

"Fine, fine," Tessa sighed in irritation. "We take them first, and then I get the babe. It makes no difference to me. I don't understand why everyone is so enamored with it."

"Tessa," Axel snarled again, because he knew this was an act. It had to be, right?

But she'd never once held Maddox. Always slipped to the other side of the room or left the room entirely if she could. But Kat. She at least cared about Kat. She wouldn't . . .

"And I can take care of these two," Tessa added, gesturing to Cade and Rayell, who were as frozen as Axel and Kat. All four of them were being held with her chaos.

"Then do it now," Bree demanded, lifting her chin.

Tessa clicked her tongue. "I'd think long and hard about trying to give me orders," she replied in a deadly calm. "But why would I give you something without a guarantee in return?"

"What do you want?" Bree snapped.

"I already told you," Tessa retorted sharply. "I need a place to keep these two for the time being. Until Theon and Luka understand why this has to be done."

"And why, exactly, is that?"

Tessa's answering smile was all power. "I do not want the Fates stepping foot here, Miss DelaCrux. I can only assume you desire the same? There are too many distractions right now, and they are keeping me from destroying the mirror gates. Once the mirror gates are dealt with, we can deal with . . . an Arius Heir that is not mine."

"Tessa!" Kat gasped in horror.

"You don't mean that!" Axel said, feeling the blood drain from his face.

"You think I have spent all this time taking the Arius seat only to have a potential rival heir?" Tessa spat. "I will have the Arius Kingdom and the Achaz Kingdom. I will have this realm. Not Achaz. Not the Fates. It is mine." She turned back to Bree. "And if you wish for a place in it, this is the time to show your allegiance. I have no need of the Underground. Only of someone to keep it under control."

Cade and Rayell were on their knees now, gasping as her power wound around their throats. Kat had two tears sliding down her face, and he was staring at Tessa in complete and utter loss. How could she have deceived them all?

But then she turned to him, her lip curling in a sneer as she said, "Injustice wrapped in pretty words is still injustice thousands of years later. Even the Fates can understand that."

"I will help you," Bree said, striding forward, that blade still at her side. "But I want your word I will not be harmed."

"Done," Tessa said, her attention back on the vampyre.

"Valter has holdings just inside the Leisure District. They are warded and can only be accessed by him, so I'm not sure how we'll get them in," Bree said, drifting closer.

"Leave the wards to me," Tessa said. "Just take care of them."

Bree stopped in front of Kat. She reached up, twirling one of Kat's curls between her fingers. "Looks like I win the game, poppet." Her gaze slid to Axel. "And you'll regret betraying me."

Then her hand was in Kat's hair, yanking her head to the side as Bree's fangs snapped out.

"No!" Axel bellowed, struggling against Tessa's magic, but to his surprise, he could move.

And Bree was thrown back a second before her fangs pierced flesh. Axel was beside Kat in the next blink, but then he was lurching back as flames coiled around her, leaping for Bree. His wife stalked forward, letting that fire wrap around Bree where she lay on the floor. Tessa's power had created a ring around the female, keeping her trapped.

He glanced at Tessa, and she jerked her chin to Kat. Axel didn't need to be told twice. He stepped through the chaos to stand at Kat's side, looking down at Bree.

"You will pay for this," Bree snarled on a rasp, the flames around her throat burning. "Fire cannot kill me."

"Oh, we're aware," Axel said coldly. "We have a special place waiting just for you. Cold. Dark. I'm told the craving can be such a bitch."

"I have lived hundreds of years. I will live hundreds more, and I will come for you. Both of you. And your son," she spat.

"Unless the Fates find you first," Kat said darkly. "I've read some very interesting things about the Fates as of late. They're as difficult to kill as a god." She paused before adding, "But not impossible. I'm sure we can figure something out one day."

Bree's eyes went wide.

Axel bent down, picking up the beautiful sword that Bree had dropped when Tessa had slammed her power into her. "And if you do escape your prison in the meantime, we'll be ready and waiting."

"Luka is waiting to Travel with us to the Pantheon," Tessa said, coming to his side. "Are you ready?"

"It's destroyed," Bree cried with a hysterical bark of laughter. "You can't keep me there."

"Between me and a couple deities, we've rectified that situation," Tessa said sweetly. "That way, if Achaz ever does find his way here, you'll be the first person he sees. Like a happy little reunion, wouldn't you say?"

"This isn't over," Bree sneered. "The Everlasting War is just that. Everlasting. Achaz will never stop until he has what he wants."

"Perhaps," Tessa agreed. "But the battle for Devram is coming to an end."

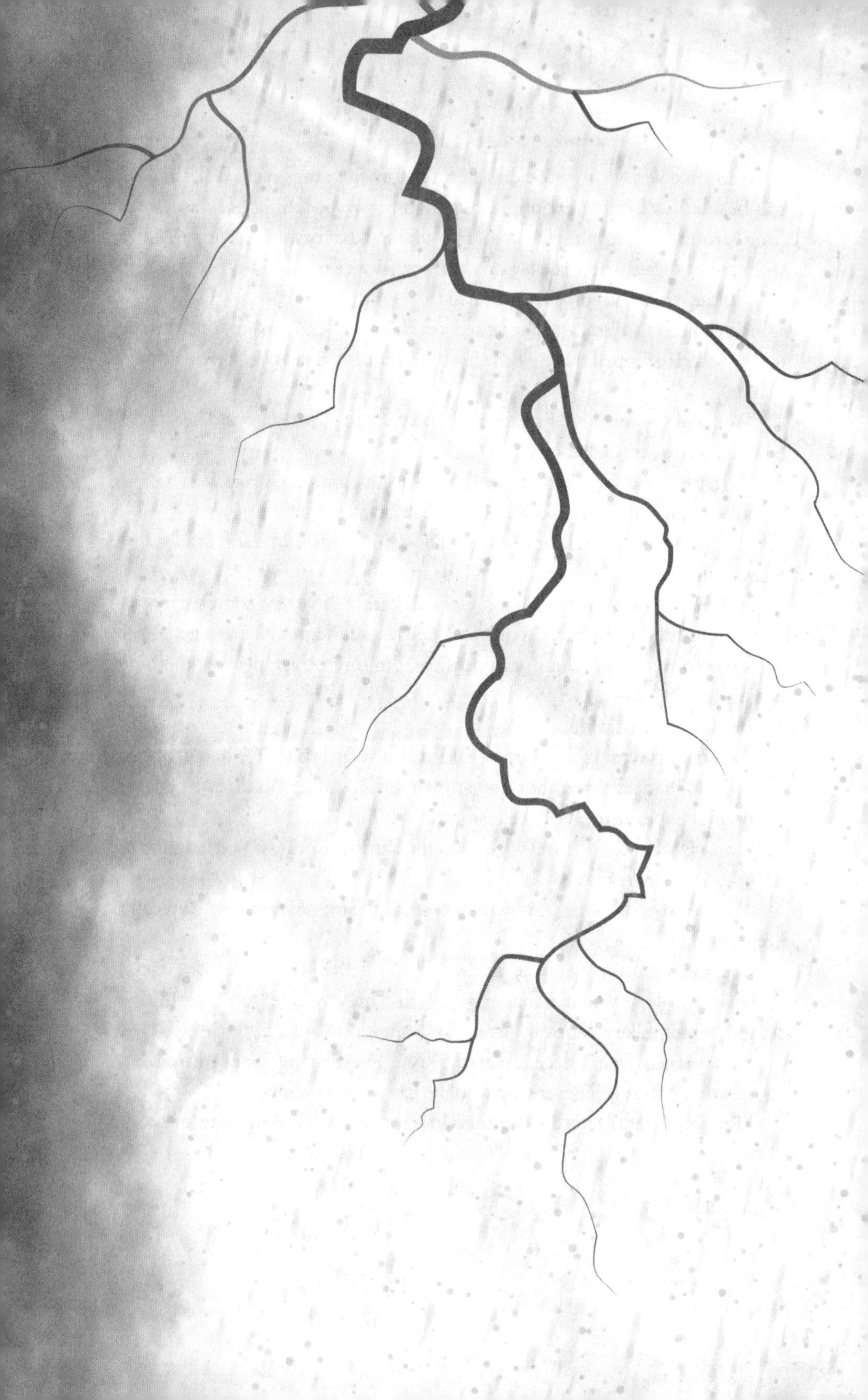

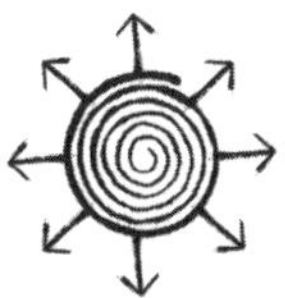

45
TESSA

“Are we certain that is going to hold her?” Axel asked.

“More than certain,” Tristyn replied. “Those cells are designed to hold a god. She is not that. You know what it took to get Tessa out of one, and even then, there was a cost.”

“She’s not a god, but she’s . . . something,” Axel said, standing next to the chair where Kat was feeding Maddox.

The moment they’d come back here, Kat and Axel had gone straight for their son. The weight of his safety now lifted from their shoulders, at least in regards to Bree. There was still Valter to worry about though.

One villain at a time, she supposed.

“She’s a Fate. Or she was one,” Tessa said simply. “But Kat already knew that.”

They all turned to the female, and she looked down at Maddox, her cheeks flushing. “I had an inkling based on how she spoke at the dinner, but I didn’t know how it was possible.”

“What do you mean she *was* a Fate?” Axel asked. “How is that possible?”

“The same way you *were* a Legacy one would guess,” she said with a shrug.

“Arius cursed the Legacy who took advantage of the Fae with bloodlust,” Tristyn offered.

“But others found it to be a blessing,” Axel said slowly. “Cienna said that once.”

Tristyn flashed a smile. “She is always telling you things. No one listens.”

“Maybe she could just spell it out once instead of speaking in fucking riddles,” Axel bit back.

"We can't interfere with the Fates."

"But didn't you do just that?" Tessa asked, fidgeting with her power. She'd been hoping she'd get to *take* on that little expedition to the Dispensary District. Her power was wanting, and it made her feel reckless.

"Yes and no," Tristyn said. "She's not technically a Fate any longer. That sword should stay hidden though," he added, nodding to the weapon Axel had discarded along the wall.

"I'll take it back to Arius House," Luka said, striding for it.

"Arius House or your cave?" Axel asked with a smirk.

Luka flipped him off before picking it up and inspecting it.

Tessa startled at the feel of Theon's hand on her back, and she glanced up to find him watching her. She gave him a weak smile. She was more than ready to leave the Underground.

"In addition to the enchantments that were already around those cells, we added more wards and protection charms," Theon said. "Cienna and Tristyn did everything they could. Bree is not leaving that cell. Either we figure out a way to end her, or she lives out her immortal life there. If she somehow does move beyond those bars, we'll be notified immediately. We also have a schedule to check on her regularly."

Axel nodded. "There's nothing else we can do, I guess."

"We have taken every precaution," Theon insisted. "Next we deal with Father."

Axel nodded, not saying anything else as Kat handed Maddox to him. Everyone was exhausted. Between the venture into the House of Four and then time below the Pantheon ruins, it was nearly dawn. Or so the clock said. It wasn't like she could see outside to know.

Looking over her head at Luka, Theon said, "Let's give them their space and go home."

The next moment, she was in Arius House. Or rather, on their balcony, and she sucked in the fresh air. He always knew.

"Better?" he murmured.

"Not quite," she sighed. "But it will do."

He dropped a kiss to her head before leaving her with Luka and that sword.

"Do I need to be jealous of a blade?" Tessa asked flatly.

Luka looked up. "Why would you be jealous of a sword?"

"Because you're looking at it in the same way you look at me."

A dark grin pulled at the corner of his mouth. "And what way is that, temptress?"

"Like you want to fuck it or hide it away," she quipped. "I'm hoping it's the latter."

Luka huffed a laugh as he muttered, "Brat."

She flashed him a fake smile before her face dropped, and she turned to follow Theon into the bedroom. She stripped down, opting to take a shower later. Food was calling her name. Food. Shower. Then sleep.

Slipping into loose pants and a Chaosphere sweatshirt, she piled her hair atop her head in a messy bun before wandering out to the kitchen. But she'd no sooner opened the fridge when Theon said, "I'm having food sent up for breakfast, but tonight we have dinner plans."

Tessa looked over her shoulder. "We do?"

He nodded. "Just the three of us."

"Isn't it always just the three of us?"

"Not always," he replied. "But I wanted to make sure tonight was."

"What's so special about tonight?"

He reached over her and closed the fridge before cupping her jaw and kissing her soundly. When he pulled back, his words feathered across her lips. "Happy birthday, clever tempest."

Her birthday?

She blinked in surprise. She'd never celebrated her birthday. Hadn't even known when it was until last fall. Only that it fell in the fifth month.

"How do we even know it's my actual birthday?" she blurted.

Theon stepped back, a small smile playing on his lips. "Why would you think it's not?"

"How can we be sure it is?" she countered. "Xan brought me here, and then I was taken. Someone probably just made that date up for my files."

"Does it matter?"

"Does it . . . Of course it matters, Theon."

"Why?"

"I . . . It just does."

Theon hummed, going to answer the knock that had sounded. A moment later, he was helping the staff set a small spread of food on the table. Waffles. Fruit. Sausage.

Luka emerged then, freshly showered and shirtless, setting that gods-damn sword across the desk. "Why aren't you eating?"

"The food just got here," she answered.

"Tessa doesn't want to celebrate her birthday," Theon called out, scooping food onto a plate.

Luka's eyes narrowed on her. "Why not?"

"Because we don't know if it's really my birthday," she replied, exasperated by this entire conversation. Luka hummed in response, and she wanted to throw something. "I don't need the two of you being so dismissive of this. We don't know."

Luka shrugged, grabbing a plate. "I can ask Xan. He'd know."

"Does it really matter?"

Theon looked up from the whipped cream he was scooping onto the waffles. "Does it matter if we celebrate the day you were born to the realms so we could find you? Yes, Tessa. It fucking matters."

Okay, well. That wasn't the answer she'd been expecting.

"Eat," Theon added, holding out the plate to her.

The plate of carbs and sugar and everything unhealthy.

"I suddenly want every day to be my birthday," she said, taking the plate from him while plucking a strawberry from the whipped cream.

"Don't push it," he warned.

She flashed him a smile, plopping into a dining chair. "So, what's the plan with your father now?"

"We'll need to think on it some," Theon answered, scooping extra fruit onto his own plate.

"You'll meet your mother when we go there," she added.

"Yeah," he murmured.

"Do you want to? Meet her, I mean?"

He took a seat on her right. "It's not the same as Akira. At least, I don't think it is. I guess I don't know the story, but I want to hear it."

She nodded, cutting off a bite of waffle.

"What about you? Still undecided?" Theon ventured.

"I can't be undecided. We need her help, so I'll have to face her."

"But do you want to?" he parroted.

Keeping her eyes on her plate, she answered, "It doesn't matter what I want. It's for the betterment of Devram."

Because she'd meant what she'd said to Bree. The final battle for this realm was coming, and she intended to be on the winning side. She didn't want to be a Lady, had no desire to rule a kingdom or the realm, but she'd sure as fuck make sure the people she freed here could live safely. Would be able to live without fear of a god coming to collect something that wasn't his or Fates showing up to destroy the realm. From what she'd gathered, Scarlett was a sort of guardian of her world. Nothing came in or out unless she allowed it.

"Where'd you go, baby girl?" Luka asked, drawing her from her thoughts.

She gave him a weak smile as she shoved another bite of waffle into her mouth. "Just tired."

He gave her a frank look that said he didn't believe her, but he let it go. Perhaps another birthday gift, but she knew he'd be back to push about it later. They both would.

"So Valter is next?" she asked, attempting to change the subject.

"Looks like it," Theon said. "We'll have to figure out exactly where the holdings are and then go from there."

"Bree told us, and I can get us past the wards. After that, it's just facing him. Between all of us, it shouldn't be too difficult, right?"

"Depends on what he's pulled together to control us with," Theon answered.

"What do you mean?"

He shrugged. "He'll have a threat, Tessa. It used to be harming Axel. It's why Pen and Caris died. He has my mother there, and there's still Maddox to think about. If this goes wrong, and he wants vengeance, he'll go after him first."

"It's his grandchild," she said, although she wasn't sure why that would matter. Her grandparents were gods, and one wouldn't hesitate to kill her.

"That is part Fae," Theon said.

Fair point.

They fell silent, each of them eating and getting lost in their own thoughts. She was just rinsing her plate and dreaming about the shower she was about to take when a knock sounded again. Looking at Theon, she arched a brow, but he just shrugged while Luka went to get the door.

"Sorry to interrupt, but there is someone at the door for the Arius Lady," the male said.

"For me?" Tessa asked in surprise.

He nodded. "He said it's a matter of urgency, and that you've been expecting him."

"Who is it?" Theon asked.

"Dagian Jove, sir."

The three of them looked at one another, and then they were all rushing to the foyer. Dagian was there with Sasha, and when her brown eyes fell on Tessa, they flashed in relief.

"Sasha," Tessa greeted, Theon and Luka flanking her on either side. Then she turned to the Achaz Heir. "Dagian."

He nodded once, his features tight and hard. "I got it, but he knows. I can't return home."

Tessa glanced up at Theon. "They can stay here, right?"

When Theon didn't say anything, Dagian scowled. "We made a bargain, St. Orcas. Besides, isn't *she* the Arius Lady now?"

"She is, but she is still ours to protect."

"Sasha?" Tessa asked, watching the Fae.

She glanced at Dagian, clearly looking for permission. When he nodded, she said, "He's not lying. We cannot return to Achaz Kingdom. In fact, I suspect the Achaz Lord will be on your doorstep before long."

"Looking for you," Theon said coldly.

"And you," Dagian shot back. "You are the one who asked me to get this stupid thing."

He tossed something to them, and Luka's hand shot out, catching the ring.

"He did bring it here," Tessa said.

"So we just trust him now?" Theon argued.

She looked back at the Achaz Heir. He appeared thinner. His cheeks a little more hollow. She didn't want to know what he'd had to sacrifice for that ring, but whatever it was, it clearly haunted him. Something she knew all too well.

"He is doing his part. We'll do ours," she finally replied. "Have someone show them to guest rooms. We can meet later today and discuss our next moves."

Turning on her heel, she made her way back to their rooms. She wanted that shower and their bed. The rest of their problems could wait until after.

"You need to be nicer to him, Theon," Tessa groused as they entered their rooms after dinner.

"He ruined our dinner plans," Theon grumbled.

"He brought us the ring to move forward with our *other* plans," she cried, marching across the room and pulling a wineglass from the cupboard. "You cannot seriously be upset by this."

"They didn't have to join us for dinner."

"Theon!"

He sighed, taking the bottle of wine she was attempting to open. "I'm trying, Tessa. There are three decades of animosity we're working through. He wasn't exactly a pillar of manners tonight either."

He had a point.

Tessa had insisted on staying in for dinner now that there were guests here, and while the dinner had been fine enough, Theon and Dagian had spent a good portion of it throwing subtle insults at each other. Since they were staying in, Xan, Razik, and Eliza had joined them too, adding to Theon's sour mood. Xan, however, had confirmed today was indeed her actual date of birth. The rest of the dinner had been discussing how soon they could bring Akira here. Dagian was very insistent on being rid of his power as soon as possible.

In the end, the only decent thing about that dinner had been the chocolate cake.

And the fact the guys were wearing *jeans*.

She could only remember one other time she'd seen them in jeans. Paired with the long-sleeve shirts that hugged muscles and grooves in all the right places, dinner had taken forever.

Theon poured her glass of wine, and when she reached for it, he held it a little longer. "Have I told you how beautiful you look tonight?"

She rolled her eyes. "Don't suck up to me now, Theon. You were an ass all dinner."

"Not to you."

"It doesn't matter," she cried again.

"Will you two stop arguing? By the gods," Luka muttered, sliding a tumbler of liquor across the counter to Theon. "You're ruining the mood."

"What mood?" Tessa grumbled. "The arrogant asshole mood? Or the broody and silent mood?"

"The bratty birthday mood," he retorted, dropping an envelope on the counter.

She took a sip of her wine, eyeing it. "What's that?"

He widened his eyes. "A birthday present, Tessa. It's what people do on birthdays."

She dropped a hand to the counter, her fingertips a few inches from the envelope.

When she only tapped her nail a few times, Luka sighed. "Do you think it's going to bite you? Open it."

"I don't know the proper etiquette here," she snapped.

His features softened, and he reached out, sliding the envelope closer. "You just open it, baby girl. It's a gift."

Tessa swallowed thickly as she gingerly picked it up and slid her finger along the seam. Pulling out the contents, her eyes went wide, flying up to Luka's.

"Chaosphere tickets?" she rasped.

"Whirlwinds versus Firewings," he said with a smirk. "No whining when the Whirlwinds lose."

"We can't go to this," she said, staring at the tickets in her hands. But gods, did she want to. She'd never been to a live game. Only watched it on TV, and this last year had been so fucked, she couldn't remember the last time she'd watched a match.

"Why not?" Luka asked.

"Because the world is on fire, Luka. We can't just go to a Chaosphere game in the middle of chaos. It feels . . . wrong."

Luka came closer, tapping the tickets. "The game is a few months from now. Hopefully this is all taken care of, and if not, we'll need the escape, Tessa. If only for a few hours."

She looked up at him, not knowing what else to say. "Thank you," she whispered.

One of his rare smiles appeared as he slid a hand to her nape and tugged her mouth to his. She melted into him, his tongue licking into her mouth as his other hand found its way beneath the soft sweater she was wearing.

Then a hand was on her shoulder, tugging her back.

"Not yet, fucker," Theon muttered. "We agreed on this."

"On what?" Tessa breathed, because she was more than ready to tumble into bed with both of them.

"Not yet," Theon ground out, clearly having heard her thoughts. "You have two more gifts to open."

"Two more?" she asked with a frown. "Why?"

"Because it's your birthday," he said in exasperation. "You get gifts on your birthday, Tessa."

He shoved a bag towards her. It was nothing special. A plain white paper bag with handles. Pulling it closer, she reached inside and pulled out something wrapped in tissue paper. As she pulled the paper off, her eyes welled with tears as she slowly lifted them to Theon.

He was tapping his forefinger on the countertop, watching her carefully, and he looked *nervous*. As if she wouldn't understand what he was trying to tell her with these.

A pair of gold flip-flops.

And not just any flip-flops. The soles were cushioned and soft, and the straps were a brushed dyed leather. Because Theon St. Orcas would only buy the best, even when it came to godsdamn flip-flops.

"I love them," she whispered.

His eyes narrowed. "Don't lie to me, beautiful."

She shook her head, willing the tears not to fall. "We said no more lies."

Then it was him slipping a hand into her hair and tugging her to him.

Until Luka was pulling them apart.

She let out a frustrated growl, and a dark chuckle skittered along her skin.

"So needy, temptress," Luka said, his voice low.

"Yes," she said, the word bordering on a whine. "I am. So how about my *next* birthday present be you two in a bed with me."

"There's one more, beautiful," Theon said, and she turned to find a small box before her now. "It's from both of us," he added.

Tessa picked it up carefully. This one was wrapped in silver paper with a black bow, and she tugged on the ribbon before tearing off the paper. Taking the lid off the box, she stared down at what lay inside.

A gold ring inlaid with sapphires and emeralds.

Not a ring to suffocate her power.

Not a band to drain her magic.

Not a cuff or a collar.

Just a simple reminder of who she belonged to and who belonged to her.

"I stole that for Luka for his sixteenth birthday," Theon said softly, taking the ring out of the box while Luka gently took her wrist to extend her hand.

"When he became your Guardian?" Tessa asked, watching him slide the ring onto her finger.

Theon nodded. "It seemed fitting it goes to you."

"We were told that night that three is a crowd, but it can also be a perfect storm if properly balanced," Luka added, pulling her hair over her shoulder to press a kiss to the side of her neck. "We didn't understand at the time, but it was always leading us to you."

She swallowed thickly again, admiring the ring on her finger as she said, "Now can we go to bed?"

Both of their auras shifted, darkening with lust. Luka kissed her neck again before he was dragging her sweater over her head. Theon was there, capturing her mouth and kissing her thoroughly. Slowly. As if he planned to drag this out, and he probably did.

She wrapped her arms around his neck, pulling him closer, and then his hands were on her ass, lifting her up. Her legs wound around his waist as he carried her to the bedroom, never breaking the kiss that only grew hungrier with each passing second.

Laying her on the bed, he stepped back, his breaths coming fast as he pulled his own shirt over his head. Tessa propped herself on her elbows to watch, her breath hitching as bare skin came into view, but then Luka was stepping in front of him, already shirtless and pushing her back down to the bed. His hands roamed, ridding her of her bra. His fingers dragged between her breasts, down her stomach, making quick work of her jeans and undergarments.

"Look at you," he murmured, his glowing eyes drinking her in while he removed his own pants before crawling onto the bed beside her. "We have plans tonight, baby girl."

"Do they involve actually fucking me? Because both of you have stopped this twice now," she retorted. Then she hissed as he pinched her nipple hard.

"So ungrateful," he growled.

"I'm not," she insisted, her voice breathy when his hand skimmed down her body again. "I'll just be *more* grateful after I've had both of you inside me tonight."

"Fuck," Theon growled, and she turned her head to see him stroking his cock. Apparently he'd lost the rest of his clothing when they had.

Luka's hands were still moving, squeezing her breasts, while his mouth was working its way along her collarbone, up her throat, nipping at her jaw.

"Enough of that, Luka," Theon ground out. "Get your tongue between her legs."

Luka chuckled against her skin, letting his teeth drag. "What do we think, baby girl? Are we giving him all the control tonight?"

"Gods, yes," she gasped, because she also wanted that tongue between her thighs.

Luka huffed another dark laugh, sliding down her body until he was settled right where she and Theon both wanted him. Now his lips were kissing up her thighs, and she was squirming, more than a little impatient. The bastard knew it too. Licking and nipping and teasing everywhere but where she wanted. And instead of telling him to get on with it, Theon kept his eyes locked on her, all while leisurely moving his hand up and down his length.

Finally, Luka's mouth found its way to her clit, and she sighed as the sensation made her clench in anticipation. Theon's lips curled into a dark grin at the sound, and she was fairly certain the step forward he took was involuntary.

It didn't take long between the sucking and flicking for her to be panting, her fingers in Luka's hair as her hips sought more and more. Then she felt his tongue slide into her center, and she moaned. More. She needed more. Always more with them.

"What's wrong, beautiful?" Theon taunted.

"I need," she whined, her hips rising and grinding against Luka's face.

"Words, Tessa," Theon ordered. "What do you need?"

"More. To be fucked. *Please*," she begged, not caring that he'd conditioned her to know it would get her what she wanted faster.

But it worked because Theon was there, climbing onto the bed. His fingertips slid up her thigh while Luka continued devouring her cunt, and gods, she never wanted to leave this godsdamn bed. Between Luka's tongue and Theon's fingers skating higher, along her ribs, over a breast, the sensations were too much and not enough and all she could think was more.

More, as her power appeared, coiling and taunting them.

More, as darkness and black flames chased her.

More and more and more.

Theon stretched out beside her, and she could feel all of him as he pushed her, rolling her halfway onto her side, away from him. Grabbing her leg, he lifted it while pushing her hips into Luka's mouth.

"Don't stop, Luka," he ordered, and fuck, this was the definition of worshipping her.

Luka didn't stop as she felt Theon's cock nudging her opening. His tongue kept going, and she tried to push back onto Theon, but he held her tight. Forcing her to take it slow. Painfully slow.

"Theon," she whined.

Luka chuckled, the sound reverberating through her core, and her muscles clenched, making Theon hiss.

"I know what you need, beautiful," he rasped. "Trust us to give it to you."

There was a sharp nip at her clit that had her crying out as Theon slid in deeper, and she looked down to find Luka watching. His fingers had replaced his tongue, and he was homed in on watching Theon's cock slowly fill her.

"Fuck, look how well you take him, baby girl," he murmured, his fingers still rubbing her center and brushing along Theon's dick in the process. She loved it when they were this close. Everything in her was hot and needy, and—

"Gods, one of you please fuck me," she snapped, taking back a little control and rocking back against Theon.

"Fuck, Tessa," he hissed as she took him completely, but she was sighing at the stretch. Relishing feeling full.

"So fucking needy," Luka said again, nipping at her inner thigh. "As if we're not both going to fill you up tonight."

"Please," she gasped as Theon started moving, thrusting into her with long, deep strokes.

Then she was crying out as Luka's tongue was back on her clit, licking and sucking. And Theon went faster, harder. Tipping her over the edge with both of them using her and shoving her into pleasure.

She went lax as she came down from her high. Luka had pulled back, giving Theon room, and he flipped her onto her stomach, pushing her into the mattress with each punishing thrust until he was holding himself deep, emptying himself fully.

He rolled off her, settling onto his side as she turned her head to him. He fisted her hair, dragging her closer, his tongue seeking hers. The feel of hands gripping her hips had her sucking in a sharp gasp, and Theon was chuckling darkly against her lips.

"We're not nearly done with you yet, beautiful," he murmured.

She never wanted them to be done with her.

Luka pulled at her hips, lifting her ass into the air, and then he was sliding in fully, a sharp curse leaving his mouth. "Fucking Fates. It's so good when he's had you first."

Gods, his fucking mouth had her clenching around him instantly.

"You like that though, don't you, temptress?" he went on, thrusting into her again and again. "You like when one of us takes you while the other's cum is still dripping down your thighs."

"Luka," she gasped, dropping her head, but Theon took her jaw in hand, lifting it back up.

"Don't give out on us now, beautiful," he murmured darkly, dragging his mouth down the side of her throat. "It's your birthday, after all."

"What's she going to do when we're both inside her at once?" Luka asked, each word labored.

And Tessa momentarily stopped breathing at the words, because what?

Theon chuckled, "Oh, she likes the sound of that, Luka. You should have seen the way her power leapt in her eyes."

"Fuck off," she snapped, feeling her pleasure building once more.

"Theon," she gasped.

But he was already moving, already knowing what she needed. He took her mouth with his again while his darkness slid down her flesh to her core, coiling and pulsing against her clit.

"That's it," Theon murmured against her lips. "Give him what's his, Tessa. Take it from him the same way you take it from me."

Her entire body tensed as she found her release again, Luka gripping her hips tight and holding her to him as he followed her. Her breaths were sharp inhales as she collapsed onto the bed, Theon pulling her onto his chest while Luka settled behind her, his spent cock nestling against her ass.

"Happy birthday to me," she murmured, already feeling sleep pulling her under.

She felt Theon huff a breath of laughter while Luka pressed a kiss to her bare shoulder.

"I told you we're not nearly done," Theon said darkly, rolling her back to Luka.

And they weren't.

They spent the next hours showing her just how grateful they were she'd been born to the stars. It had to be well into the morning hours when they finally gave in to exhaustion, which is why Tessa was groaning in agony at the incessant knocking on the door as the sun came up.

"Make it stop," she moaned, trying to burrow deeper into Luka's chest.

"Someone better be fucking dying," Theon muttered, rolling from the bed. She wasn't even sure he put on pants as he stalked from the bedroom.

But when they heard him shout, "What?," she and Luka both sat up in bed, fully alert as Theon appeared in the doorway.

"Get up. We need to go," Theon said, striding for the walk-in closet. "Rordan is in Castle Pines. We're under attack."

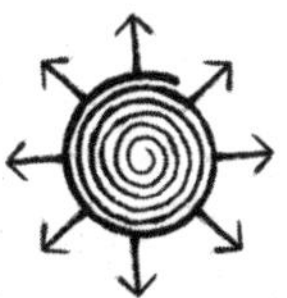

46
LUKA

"How did we never think to get you fitted for fighting attire? Armor? Something?" Luka muttered, eyeing Tessa.

"You're not wearing armor," she retorted.

"I can shift into a dragon, Tessa," he returned, unimpressed.

"Theon's not wearing armor."

"Theon has been training for years, and his darkness covers him like armor. You are wearing a dress. And you're barefoot."

"You are wasting time arguing with me about this," she tossed back. "I can create weapons from my magic, death feeds my power, and Nylah and Roan will be at my sides. You just worry about not falling out of the sky."

"For the love of the gods," he muttered, stalking after her as she threw open the door to the suite and made her way to the foyer where everyone was meeting.

"Reports tell us there are at least a hundred ground warriors and dozens of seraphs," Theon was saying.

"You'll need the dragons in the sky," Eliza cut in. "Dragonfire can kill the seraphs. The ones that make it to the ground need to be burned too." She paused, looking at Tessa. "You need armor or leathers."

She sighed heavily. "I assure you, I do not."

"Anything we need to know about the Legacy on the ground?" Razik asked, reaching over and checking the buckles on Eliza's armor. She batted his hand away, but he brought it right back.

"Their power is light. They'll use it to blind you. Some have the same energy that Tessa and Rordan have," Dagian answered. "The Zinta and Sirana bloodlines are sworn to him as well. Expect priestesses to be with them."

Razik glanced at Luka as he finished checking Eliza's armor, then did a double take. "Where did you get that?"

Luka smirked, knowing he was eyeing the sword that was resting on his shoulder. "Found it."

"You did not," Tessa scoffed. "Axel took it from Bree."

"Give that to Theon to use," Razik ordered.

"No," Luka growled.

"You won't be able to use it as a dragon," Razik retorted. "Tessa is unpredictable, and Theon is skilled. That sword needs to be used."

"He's right," Eliza said, also eyeing the sword.

"Can we go? People are dying," Tessa interrupted.

"Last question," Theon said, turning to Dagian. "Is your father likely there?"

Dagian exhaled a long breath. "I honestly don't know. He might try to exhaust your forces here before attacking somewhere else. He might come straight for the rings and try to entrap Tessa again."

"Improvise as we go. Got it," Tessa said, and Luka could feel her already sinking into her power. "I'm going."

"By Sargon," Luka muttered, grabbing her arm a second before she Traveled out.

Theon had done the same, apparently grabbing Dagian and Sasha. Razik and Xan Traveled in separately, Eliza in tow. Now they all stood in the center of Castle Pines, and Theon muttered a low curse. He'd mobilized warriors nearby, or Tessa had, but most of their forces were stationed in the larger cities like Rockmoor and Dark Haven. The only reason to start in Castle Pines would be if Rordan was coming straight for Arius House.

There were bodies in the streets. Some warriors, some civilians. Seraphs were in the air, power raining down from their stolen gifts. Achaz forces were splitting up and storming down side streets, Arius forces rushing to meet them.

"Kill more than me, *mai dragocen*," Razik said, flashing Eliza a challenging grin before he leapt, shifting into his dragon form in the air and loosing a battle cry as he soared up. Xan was in the air a moment later, the two dragons already engaging and letting their bloodline sing.

The Fire General spun towards them, drawing her sword from her back. "You two come with me. Tell me about the magic we're facing," she said, pointing at Dagian and Sasha.

Dagian glanced at Theon, who nodded in agreement. "She knows what she's doing. Go with her and stay close."

They went right, which left Theon and Tessa to go left. Luka hesitated, wanting to be in the sky, but also needing to be with his Ward and wife. On top of all that, he'd never *fought* in his dragon form. He was far more confident in his abilities with a blade.

Then the howling reached them, Nylah and Roan appearing seconds later from the fray. Which was great for Tessa, but it also announced their presence among the mayhem.

"We're starving," Tessa purred, a dark smile filling her face as Achaz forces came running in their direction.

Luka looked up, seeing Razik and his father taking on the seraphs as ashes started to drift in the air like snow. Is this how they felt when in battles with their Wards? Torn and needing to be in two places at once?

"I'll stay with you two until more forces arrive," Luka said, tightening his grip on the sword he still held.

Theon glanced at him. "Are you sure?"

"There aren't enough here," he said. "We sent extra support to Dark Haven after the massacre."

"Yeah, all right," Theon said, drawing his twin short swords from pools of shadows. "But if you need to go help in the sky, you just go."

"Now?" Tessa asked, her feet already floating off the ground.

"Now, baby girl," Luka conceded as a few warriors managed to break past Nylah and Roan.

They were met with a wave of crackling light, three of them on their backs within seconds. Arching in agony, that light spread beneath their skin, veins bright and translucent until they stopped moving altogether.

Tessa inhaled sharply through her nose, as if savoring whatever she'd just done. Then she turned to face them, violet eyes bright and the Marks on her skin glowing that soft gold color. Her smile was pure wildness before she set off.

"If anything, I need to stay with the two of you to help rein her in when it's time," Luka muttered.

"But for now, we're just going to let her be who she is," Theon replied.

They followed her, like they always did. She didn't race to join the fray, but she seemed to have a certain direction she was going. Luka had no idea what was driving her, but her wolves prowled ahead and she let arrows fly as she moved.

Theon and Luka used their blades, and the first time he swung with that sword, dragonfire encompassed the thing. He didn't have time to marvel at it as he sank the sword into a warrior, his power turning them into nothing. It was just like Eliza's sword, only hers magnified her fire magic.

Theon was the death he always was, his darkness fighting as much as he was with weapons. They'd trained like this hundreds, if not thousands, of times, but these last months were the first times it'd been life or death rather than sparring.

It didn't take long for them to realize the Legacy warriors weren't going to be the issue. It was going to be the seraphs in the skies, but that didn't mean there wasn't just as much work to do down here.

"You need to get up there," Theon barked, his darkness holding two Achaz warriors in place while Luka cut through both of them with his sword.

"And leave you two vulnerable down here?"

"Does that look fucking vulnerable to you?" Theon snapped.

Luka's gaze snagged on Tessa where she was letting her arrows fly while her power took. And she wasn't just fighting the warriors on the ground. No, her chaos was reaching into the sky and grabbing seraphs who made the mistake of coming for her. It dragged them to the ground, and even from here, Luka could see the eerie glee on her face as she stood over them and fed her magic.

She may have let her magic end the seraphs, but with the warriors, she used her arrows or blades, blood spraying and leaving nothing but ashes and destruction in her wake.

A roar of fury rang out, and they all looked up to see a group of seraphs converging on Xan.

"Go!" Theon snarled while Achaz forces tried to take advantage of the momentary distraction. Theon grabbed one by the throat, his darkness seeping into the male's soul. The other—

Tessa appeared, Traveling to Theon's side. One of her daggers sank into the male's side, and as he doubled over, she drove the dagger in her other hand into his neck. Blood splattered on her face, her hair.

A godsdamn goddess of chaos and destruction.

She turned as though she'd heard that thought, her smile wicked and terrifying and fucking beautiful.

"Luka, get in the fucking sky," Theon snarled. "We are clearly fine."

Gritting his teeth, he tossed his sword to Theon. He caught it, and the dragonfire around the blade instantly morphed into darkness. Evidently it magnified whatever power the wielder held.

His gaze connected with Theon's, both of them clearly thinking the same thing.

Do not let Tessa touch that sword, Luka said.

Noted, Theon ground out, shoving the blade into another sentinel.

We could do many things with that sword, Tessa argued, and Luka hated that her voice was *other* even in his mind.

"I've got it handled," Theon bit out again, shoving the male back with his foot.

Another roar finally had Luka shifting fully, and he was in the sky a moment later. His own roar of rage echoed with his father's, and then Razik was there with him, the two of them soaring hard and fast for Xan.

Until a burst of power slammed into them, shoving them back. How in the fuck?

Razik's black diamond-shaped head whipped around, both of them searching for the seraph. The problem was, they had no way to determine what every single seraph's power was. Those who'd stolen elemental powers were easy enough. Water. Wind. Whatever. But those who'd stolen other gifts—altering reality, power detection, and likely gifts they didn't know were out there—there was no way to tell what they were.

Razik snarled, flipping over and sunlight glinting off the faint scarring on one of his wings. His massive tail swiped out, catching a nearby seraph and sending it hurtling straight to Luka. On instinct, his jaw closed around it, teeth sinking in. The crunch of bones and wings snapping echoed with the seraph's cries of pain. And the taste? Vomiting in the sky was not on his list of things to do today.

He released the female, letting her fall, and dragonfire engulfed her, courtesy of his brother. Sapphire eyes connected with his, and Luka could swear Razik huffed in amusement. That fucker knew they tasted awful.

Luka snarled, spinning away from him and once again making his way to his father, who was still battling the same swarm of seraphs. He couldn't just send dragonfire at them without also risking hitting his father. It wouldn't wound him, but he'd still feel it.

With a disgruntled growl, he barreled forward. Teeth snapping and claws swiping, he knocked them, dodging magic attacks as much as he could. It wasn't enough though. He took hits of ice daggers to his flanks, and winds tore at his wings.

Razik was below him, black flames spewing from his mouth as Luka knocked them down, and Xan was finally able to shake off several of them.

His fury echoed again as he broke free of the swarm. He banked sharply, the black and blue of his form shimmering in the daylight, and then Luka was darting out of the way as that fury exploded from him. Dragonfire rained down, but not in the wild way his and Razik's dragonfire was consuming. No, this was *controlled*. It leapt from one seraph to another, the flames never banking or going out, as if Xan could control his magic even from his dragon form.

Luka's head whipped to Razik only to find him watching their father too. Luka had never been able to control his gifts like that when in his dragon form, and while he couldn't read any sort of expression on Razik right now, he was guessing it was the same for him. It was why they preferred to fight with just their wings, not fully shifted. It was no wonder the seraphs had seemed to leave them alone and focus on Xan, and Luka suddenly wondered if the god of war and courage himself had trained his father.

Xan twisted to find them staring, and he snapped at them with a sharp growl, jerking his head to the side. The message was clear: do their fucking job.

Razik snarled, clearly irked about being caught watching, and he banked right, going in the direction of flames below. Luka followed his lead, going left. He'd take care of the skies above Theon and Tessa, while Razik managed those above Eliza. Xan could clearly handle the middle sector.

He didn't know how long they fought, but he sank into it that same way he'd felt Tessa sink into her power. Magic was flying, cries of victory and agony mingling. He could hear the clashing of weapons and the bellows of orders being shouted.

Time both dragged on and flashed by. There was no time to think, just give in to instinct. But that instinct was telling him this wasn't going to be enough. Rordan had bided his time. This wasn't a frivolous attack, but one that had been meticulously planned. He knew their forces were concentrated elsewhere and had attacked Castle Pines for that very reason.

Even with Theon and Tessa, Dagian, a Fire General, and two additional dragons, the odds were not in their favor.

Not as it seemed like three more seraphs appeared for every one they took out.

Not as more and more Achaz forces swarmed the streets of the city.

Not as those forces methodically pushed their own to the city center, effectively surrounding them.

Not as he started to feel his power weaken and drain. If Theon started drawing from him, he'd have to shift back and fight from the streets. Tessa wouldn't need him. She was a godsdamn vision below, her chaos wreaking havoc and her arrows finding their marks. She'd been training with the things, sure, but nobody became that skilled that quickly. Whatever power created her arrows was connected to her on some level, ensuring her wishes were carried out. And with every life that was forced to give, her power took and took.

His father streaked by, making Luka whip around to follow where he was going, only to see a fresh wave of Achaz forces appearing to the south of the city.

Son of a bitch, Luka growled down the bond. *There's more Theon. To the south.*

Godsdammit, he muttered. *We're not going to win this. We need to switch gears. Focus on getting the innocent to safety, and then we can retreat.*

Give up the city? Luka countered. *It's the closest one to Arius House.*

I'm aware.

We're just going to abandon it?

I'll lose the city if we can save the people.

Then her voice was drifting down the bond. *Rordan is here.*

That was all she needed to say, and Luka was diving for them. If he was as powerful as Dagian said he was, there was no way she was facing the male alone. Theon didn't have any additional gifts yet, and Dagian had said it would drain her to the point of breaking to face off with him. That was not happening today.

The ground shuddered as he landed behind them, forces from both sides scattering to accommodate his size. Whipping his head around, he snatched up an Achaz warrior that was coming for Theon, careful not to draw blood because they seriously tasted fucking awful. Taking a few steps closer, he dropped the male on the ground at Tessa's feet. Theon's darkness wound around him, keeping him immobile, and Tessa lifted her gaze to Luka's with a dark smirk.

"A late birthday present?" she crooned.

He shifted then, leaving only his wings on display. He needed to preserve as much of his magic as he could at this point. "Just wanted to see that viciousness in action," he returned, taking in the blood splattered on her porcelain skin.

Then he frowned. There were spots on her arms, her shoulder, her thigh, where Theon's darkness was cinched tightly around her. Luka reached out, gripping her elbow for a closer look.

"Her blood can't touch the ground. It will summon Hunters," Theon said tightly. "I've been making sure it doesn't."

Tessa pulled her arm from Luka's grasp, crouching beside the Achaz male, that same wicked smirk on her lips.

"Please! Don't!" he cried. "I have to follow orders. I have to—"

"You'll have to plead your case with Arius," she interrupted with a dark croon. "Because I do not care."

Then one of her black runic daggers appeared in her hand, and blood was splattering as she dragged it slowly across his throat before plunging it deep into his chest.

She stood casually, dagger still in hand, as she said, "Rordan is here."

"You said that already," Luka replied, watching the mayhem around them. "You're right, Theon. We need to get the fuck out of here."

Then Eliza was there, panting and covered in blood herself. "What's the plan?" she gasped, Dagian and Sasha behind her.

"My father is here," Dagian said.

"We know," Luka growled as Eliza spun and blocked an arrow with her sword before the warrior went up in dragonfire a moment later, Razik dropping in behind her. He'd already shifted, and Eliza was reaching for a dagger.

"No, *mai dragocen,*" he murmured, taking her chin between his thumb and forefinger.

"You need to fill your reserves, Raz," she insisted, still trying to bring the blade to her forearm.

"If you think I am taking what little magic you have left when we are in the midst of battle, you are sorely mistaken," he growled, stepping in closer to her.

"You need it more than I do. I can use my sword," she argued.

"We combine them if needed," Razik said. "Like we did to free Xan."

"Razik, no. This is—"

"End of discussion, Eliza. I am not drawing from you right now."

Her eyes flashed with anger. "Cut me off and tell me 'end of discussion' again, Razik Greybane. I dare you."

"Be violent with me later," he retorted, kissing her hard before she could reply.

"My Lord! Or—My Lady?" a panting Arius captain gasped out, his hands on his knees as he tried to catch his breath.

"What is it?" Theon snapped.

"At the front. There are—We couldn't stop them," he gasped.

"Godsdammit," Luka growled because Tessa was already moving. So much smaller than they were, she slipped through the crowd practically unseen while the rest of them had to shove people out of the way. Her wolves prowling in a radius around her helped some, but not enough. He looked up, trying to spot Xan, but he was nowhere to be seen. Where the fuck was he?

"Tessa, wait!" Theon called, having to stop and use his sword or magic every few steps.

"Tessa!" Luka hollered. He couldn't simply send a wave of dragonfire. Their own forces were too intermingled now. They couldn't afford to lose any more.

She kept moving, and he and Theon kept fighting to get back to her. She was in so much godsdamn trouble when this was over.

Finally, they burst through a throng of fighting, only to go completely still as they took in the scene before them.

Tessa stood there, her aura swirling with light and dark, while Nylah and Roan were at her sides, teeth bared and growling. Across from her stood Rordan Jove, light undulating and crackling around him.

Seconds later, Razik and Eliza pushed through the crowd too, Dagian and Sasha at their heels.

"Well done, Dagian," Rordan said with a small smile.

Luka slowly turned to the male, eyes narrowed. "If you betrayed us—"

"I didn't," Dagian spat, his eyes fixed on his father. "And he knows that."

Rordan's smile turned dark. "He speaks the truth. I raised him to take what he wants. If only he wasn't as big of a disappointment as Tessa turned out to be."

"If only you'd loved me and coveted my loyalty the way you did hers," Dagian returned. "Your entire existence has revolved around finding her to gain Achaz's favor. I was a necessary inconvenience until you found her."

"You would have been given everything," Rordan said calmly. "A kingdom to rule. A Source for your power. A wife to warm your bed and give you powerful heirs. I blame your mother for the way you turned out. She coddled you too much. Intervened too much."

"You tortured her!" Dagian roared. "You used me to manipulate her into giving you more and more power. She—"

"Loves you?" Rordan interjected, his features all cruel amusement now. "This is Devram, son. Love doesn't exist here, and do you know why?"

Dagian held his tongue, his jaw clenched so tightly Luka could hear his teeth grinding.

"The gods didn't want it to. They know how useless it is. How it sways kings and queens. How it causes wars and breaks alliances. And look just how accurate that is," Rordan continued, gesturing to Tessa and Theon. "Five kingdoms that have worked seamlessly for centuries are now broken."

"You did that," Theon retorted.

"No," he countered. "*Love* did that. Why do you think we take the Fae to Estates as babes? So mothers do not have the chance to love and sacrifice for them. Why do you think Matches are contractual obligations? So *this* doesn't happen. Everything we do is to make sure none of that can flourish, and yet, despite our efforts, it does. Look at Maya? So distraught by the death of her Source, she can't think clearly," he said with disgust. "So no, Dagian, I've never loved you. The only thing I've ever wanted from you was your loyalty, and instead, you've brought me betrayal. I can see it well enough on Theon's finger."

Luka glanced over, seeing the ring Dagian had delivered back on Theon's middle finger where it had sat for years.

"The payment for that betrayal is your Source's power," Rordan said.

"No," Dagian snarled. "You will not take that from her. You've taken enough. You have enough!"

"So be it."

It happened so fast, no one could do anything. Not as Rordan's light struck precisely, coiling around Sasha and yanking her violently to the space between them.

"No!" Dagian roared, lunging for her, but Rordan's power wrapped around him too, suspending him in the air as Sasha screamed. His light twisted and coiled, taking the shape of a snake that wound around her before sinking fangs of pure power into her throat.

Her screams stopped, and the world was quiet save for the sound of Dagian being dropped back to the ground. Rordan had subdued his son with scarcely any effort, and Dagian was powerful.

"Sasha!" he cried, crawling to her still body. "No! No, no, no!"

"And then there's *you*," Rordan said, his eyes sliding to Tessa and ignoring his son's broken cries.

Tessa's fury was palpable as she took a single step forward. "How incredibly *weak* of you to pick a fight with someone you know cannot hold their own."

"I am anything but weak, child," he replied too calmly. "But you? We all know your weaknesses now, don't we?"

"No!" she cried, and it took a second for Luka to realize what was happening. Rordan's power moved too fast, and Luka didn't know how he did that. But a wave of swirling golden mist was blinding them, as if the sun itself was laying siege, and Luka was being thrown back, flying through the air.

But not because of Rordan's power.

It was the impact of Tessa's magic colliding with it.

Luka hit the ground hard, banishing his wings a moment before impact. He felt the skin on his back peel open as he skidded across the ground, but he was scrambling back to his feet in the next breath.

"By the gods," someone muttered. Maybe Razik?

Because Tessa's chaos was arcing over everyone like a dome while Rordan's light slid along it, looking for any cracks to gain entrance. Seraphs pelted that dome with magical attacks. Tessa's hands were raised in front of her, power flowing and racing, reinforcing. In truth, Rordan had been stupid for waiting until now to attack. She'd been feeding her magic for hours. If he was going to be part of this, he should have been here from the beginning, when she was at her weakest.

Theon was running, clearly having been thrown as far as Luka had.

Tessa, draw from me! Do it, tempest! he ordered down the bond.

Luka was shoving people out of his way as he took long strides back to her too, and then he stumbled as there was a yank on his power. Because Theon was drained, and she was taking from him, forcing Theon to draw from him as his Guardian.

"Shit," he muttered, finally reaching his side. "This can't last forever."

"I know, but it will give us a little time to . . . try to think of something," Theon answered, looking around as if he'd find the answer somewhere.

They stood back, not wanting to get too close to her and be a distraction. Her features were twisted in concentration, and her power had her off the ground, so at least she wasn't having to hold herself up.

"Where the fuck is Xan?"

Luka turned at the growl from Razik, and he dragged a hand down his face. "I don't know."

"He just fucks off in the middle of a godsdamn battle?" Razik demanded, Eliza looking just as furious at his side. Beside them was Dagian, holding Sasha's body to his chest.

"He is going to come back to a massacre," Razik snarled.

"Tessa is stronger than Rordan," Theon bit back.

"Until her power gives out. Then we're all fucked, even if Rordan's gives out too. They have more forces. He's draining her on purpose, and then we will be overwhelmed because he fucking abandoned us. Not that we should be surprised. It's what he does," the male sneered.

Even Luka had to admit this looked pretty fucking bad.

"Let's just figure out what we're going to do in the meantime," Eliza cut in. "Travel out?"

"We need to do that now. We're all drained," Luka said. "We can't afford to lose any more power and risk not being able to Travel. And we won't be able to take everyone."

"How do you decide who gets left behind?" Theon demanded.

Eliza's lips were pressed into a thin line. "You just . . . do. This is war. Not everyone survives."

"That's not acceptable," Theon bit back. "Look around you. They're still fighting. We can't just abandon them."

And they were. Trapped on this side of the barrier, their forces were easily overtaking the Achaz warriors. But the fact remained that the moment that barrier fell, there were at least a hundred more warriors waiting for them, not to mention the seraphs in the sky.

"We have to go now," Razik said. "War requires making impossible choices."

"He's right, Theon. We can't—"

A roar ripped through the air.

They looked up to find a dark stain against the sky, and he wasn't alone. Those were flames flying beside him. Bright oranges and reds. People with wings of flame. Some were riding flying creatures of the same. They clashed with the seraphs, and a small whimper came from Tessa as some of the strain on her power was eased.

"Stay with her. Tell me when she's almost tapped out," Luka ordered Theon. "We'll do what we can."

Then he and Razik were back in the sky with their wings, not wanting to waste their magic by shifting fully. As he got closer, he realized these were Anala Legacy. He had no idea they had an aerial fleet, but Xan had known. He'd known and gone for backup.

Flames flickered around him as they fought side by side. If they could keep them busy up here, maybe they could figure something out down there. So he fought with everything he had alongside his father and his brother, praying to anyone that would listen that it would be enough.

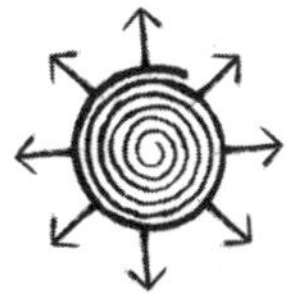

47
THEON

It hadn't been enough.

That was all he could think as they sat in the Penthouse in the Underground once again.

They were all covered in blood and grime, and he was slowly peeling back his darkness from Tessa's scrapes and wounds, letting Cienna do her thing before her blood hit the ground. The last thing they needed was to deal with a fucking Hunter right now.

They'd lost. At least that battle. Even with Anala Kingdom sending aid, it hadn't been enough. They'd needed more people on the ground. Tessa had been godsdamn amazing, her power lashing out and taking as she held that dome in place. But splitting her focus drained her faster. Eventually Luka'd had to abandon the sky because Theon was drawing too much from him, and in the end, they'd done exactly what he hadn't wanted to do. They'd had to abandon Castle Pines and the people who hadn't managed to get out.

He'd failed.

Again.

Everyone was quiet and somber, the defeat weighing on them all. Gia was here, making her rounds while Cienna tended to Tessa. Eliza was curled into Razik where he sat on the floor. Xan was nearby, talking low with one of the Anala warriors who'd returned with them. They'd taken over the entire building, giving quarters to all those they had been able to bring back with them.

They'd only needed one additional floor in the end.

Kat and Axel were here as well, having moved back to the Penthouse after imprisoning Bree. Kat was upstairs with Maddox while Axel sat in a chair opposite him. His elbows were braced on his knees, head hanging. He hadn't been there, but he still felt the defeat in his soul.

Having finished with Tessa, Cienna moved on to Theon, despite his protest to go to Luka when the lift doors dinged. They all looked up, and a moment later, Dagian was stepping into the room. His face was as dirty and bloodied as the rest of them, only there were tear stains streaked through the grime. They'd fought beside each other today. Arius and Achaz. Theon had never thought he'd see the day.

Tessa sat up straighter, as though she was going to go to him, but Luka planted a hand on her thigh from her other side, keeping her in place. They were both too on edge right now to be anything other than overbearing.

"I'm sorry," Tessa said softly. "I knew Sasha. She was . . . I'm sorry."

Dagian gave a stiff nod, rolling his lips.

"Can I get you something?" Axel asked, pushing to his feet. "Something to eat? Drink? Blood now that you can't . . ." He trailed off, shoving a hand through his hair.

"No," Dagian said tightly. He turned to Theon, his eyes somehow hard and hollow at the same time. "I'm only here to find out when you're taking my power, St. Orcas."

Theon stared at him, somewhat at a loss. He flicked his gaze to Xan before coming back to Dagian. "We have all three rings now," he said. "But we still need to find someone to do the transfer. Unless your mother is now an option?"

"She is not," Dagian snapped. "I will not lose another person I love to his madness."

"Won't he kill her anyway?" Luka asked.

Dagian's lip curled. "Not even he's powerful enough to do that. But he will hurt her. Torture her. She's endured enough. We all have." Light sparked at his fingertips, making everyone tense, but he got it under control in the next breath. His gaze raked over them on the sofa, Tessa between the two of them. "It wasn't like that with us," he said, hollowness ringing in his tone. "My father tried, but . . . Sasha was like a younger sister to me. Nothing more. He forced us together from the day she was born, and I . . . She was my sister. I was her protector. I never touched her otherwise."

They all stared at him, and shock rippled through Theon because *how?* That bond was demanding and relentless.

"But . . . she was so nervous on Selection day?" Tessa said tentatively.

"We both were. We'd known about the bond and what it did. Neither of us wanted each other like that," Dagian answered.

"And it didn't . . . try?" Theon asked, trying not to sound like a complete ass with his question.

Dagian shook his head. "There were a few times. Right after the Marks were given. But we had arrangements made. Others willing to satisfy those demands."

"You let someone else touch her?" Theon asked, still trying to comprehend this.

"Someone *she* chose," Dagian said. "It was always her choice, but enough of this. Figure it out, and take this power from me, St. Orcas. I've held up my end of the deal and paid the price. Hold up yours."

Then he turned his back on them, pressing the lift button. The doors opened immediately, and he left, leaving them to stew in their loss once more.

"There are three showers available," Axel said after a beat. "Feel free to use them. I'll get some food fixed up."

Everyone dispersed, and Theon sent Tessa up with Luka, wanting to talk to Axel for a moment. He followed his brother into the kitchen, but as he went to sit down, Axel snapped, "Don't touch anything. You're covered in blood."

"We were just sitting on furniture," Theon replied.

"Which we now have to clean, but I wasn't going to say anything then," he replied.

"Axel?" Kat's voice rang out from the other room.

"And don't touch my kid either," Axel called from the pantry where he was digging for something or other. "Not until you've showered."

Kat appeared a moment later, Maddox in her arms. He was awake and taking in the world, and Theon smiled weakly at them.

"I'm sorry things did not go well today," Kat said, coming farther into the room.

Theon nodded, leaning in closer to see Maddox. "We need to get that power transferred," he said. "Which is why I need to talk to Axel."

His brother reappeared, narrowing his eyes at how close Theon was to the babe. Theon held up his hands. "I'm not touching him. Relax."

"I'm going to tell you that when you have a child," Axel grumbled, dumping bags of rice and cans of beans onto the counter. "I'm going to have to go get some pork."

"Husband, father, and chef," Theon smirked. "What next?"

"Fuck off, or you're not eating," Axel retorted, pointing a finger at him.

Theon huffed a laugh, but it was quickly gone. "I'm going to the secret holdings as soon as my powers are restored enough."

Axel stilled, blinking at him. "Then I'm coming with you."

"You don't have to, Axel. You have a son. A wife," Theon tried.

"Whom he has threatened on multiple occasions," Axel retorted. "Not to mention our whole fucking childhood. If you're going to confront our father, I'm coming with to end him. I'm a godsdamn Night Child because of him."

Theon glanced at Katya, who was swaying with Maddox. She did that a lot, and it had to be some innate mother thing.

"We need to take as few people as possible," Theon tried again. "Tessa, obviously for her power. Luka because he's my Guardian."

"Corbin and Lange," Kat added. "They'll insist on going. They've been restless while waiting."

Theon shook his head. "It's too many people."

"Tell them that," Kat tossed back. "They've become close with Eviana, and we all know if someone has to be left behind, it will be her. Mark my words, Theon, if you don't take them with you, they'll go themselves. Explain that one to Tessa."

That would go over well.

Theon sighed. "We go in. We find my mother and Eviana. We send everyone else away, and we take care of Father."

"Tessa and Luka are not just going to leave us there, you idiot," Axel groused from where he was now rummaging through the fridge.

"I'll talk to them."

"Great. Do that. While you fucking shower. You're too disgusting right now to be standing so close to my wife and child," Axel called over his shoulder.

Theon rolled his eyes, glancing once more at Kat to find a small smile playing on her lips. "You won't win this one," she said softly.

He sighed again, knowing she was right. "I'm not enjoying you two constantly ganging up on me," he said, turning to leave the kitchen.

"Tessa would side with us," Axel called, and Theon flipped him off over his shoulder because he knew that too.

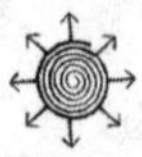

"Are we sure there's something here?" Axel asked, looking around where they stood just inside the Leisure District.

Kylian had shown them the area a few days ago while their powers were still recovering. Theon and Luka had again drunk rations, and they really needed to figure something else out. Tessa had offered to fill their reserves, but then she would be left without full strength because she could only refill her magic by taking life. Checks and balances even when she was an imbalance herself.

"Can't you feel the wards?" Tessa asked.

"They're meant to deter you," Theon answered. "I feel something trying to get me to turn around. Go in the other direction. Like an instinct of some sort."

She shrugged. "We're here. We may as well try it, right?"

"I guess," Axel said, scratching the back of his head.

There wasn't much else they could do. If it wasn't here, then they were at a loss, and Theon refused to entertain that idea at the moment.

"We have to all be connected," Lange said, reaching for Tessa.

Theon knocked him away, taking her hand while Luka took the other.

"Stop being a dick," she muttered.

Theon ignored her. This had nothing to do with her friend touching her and had more to do with him being on edge. He was going in there to meet his mother and kill his father.

With everyone touching, they moved forward, step after step, until he felt the wards ghost over his skin and a two-story stone house loomed over them. Built into the side of the cavern wall, it had a few windows on the front and a stone wall surrounding it.

"There's no gate or way in," Axel said in a hushed tone after they'd all darted to the side.

"Then we go over the top," Tessa said simply.

"And get caught?" Axel tossed back.

She turned her head to him with a smirk. "Don't let anyone see you."

"How are we supposed to scale that?" he asked, gesturing to the wall.

She turned in the other direction. "Lange?"

He winked. "Sure thing, Tess."

A minute later, Lange was using his air magic to lift them over the wall. When the last of them were on the other side, they turned and faced the house.

"Now what?" Axel asked.

"We go in," Theon replied. His magic was tense, as on edge as he was, and he could feel it writhing in anticipation.

"The Mark," Luka said, handing him a dagger.

Right. It was the only way they could come up with to track down his mother. A Blood Mark that would lead him to a blooded relative.

The others studied the house for a way in while he drew the Mark he'd practiced for days on his forearm. When he finished, they made their way to the side of the house. The front door was obviously out, but there had to be other entrances. Except they couldn't find a single one. In fact, there wasn't even a front door.

"He must shadow-walk here," Theon said.

"So we Travel in?" Tessa asked.

"But you can't Travel to somewhere you haven't been."

"I can't Travel somewhere I don't know," she corrected. "If I look in the windows . . ."

He didn't like the idea one bit, but they were wasting time. The longer they fucked around out here, the more likely they were to be caught.

Tessa and Luka crept to the lowest window they could find and peered in. Then they both ducked down in a rush, crawling to another window before making their way back.

"The first window was to your father's study," Luka reported. "He's in there." His eyes flicked to the Fae. "So are Eviana and the child."

"My mother first, then them," Theon said pointedly to the males.

They clearly didn't like that, but the plan was set. They weren't changing anything now.

Tessa took Lange and Corbin while Luka grabbed his elbow and Axel's shoulder, Traveling them inside. They all froze for nearly a minute, releasing a collective breath of relief when no one appeared in the room they'd entered.

"You're up," Luka said, looking at Theon, and he concentrated on the Mark.

In the end, it ended up working similarly to the Tracking Mark they had on Tessa. A pull in his soul had them creeping out of the room and up a set of stairs. They ran into no one, not even a servant. He wasn't entirely surprised by that. His father had too many secrets here to keep a full staff. There were likely only two or three trusted servants here, and they would all be busy with their daily tasks.

Continuing down a long hall, they came to a dead end, only the stone wall to greet them.

"A closet?" Axel asked when he turned to a small door.

But Theon didn't answer, following the pull of the Mark. Sure enough, they opened the door and found a narrow stairwell, making their way up.

"This can't be right," Theon muttered.

They were all crammed onto a small landing. In fact, Corbin and Lange weren't even able to fit on the landing, still standing on the stairs.

"It's just a wall," Axel said.

"I can see that," he snapped.

But the Mark was still pulling him closer, insistent and warming his soul. As if what he was seeking was just out of reach on the other side.

"It isn't just a wall," Tessa breathed, placing both her palms on the stone. "Can't you feel that?"

Theon and Luka glanced at each other. "No?" Theon said.

"There's power here," she whispered, chaos seeping from her palms. "Lots of power."

"Tessa, you're going to trigger something," Luka growled, reaching to grab her.

"Wait," Theon said, holding up a hand to stop him. "Look."

There were tiny fissures crackling along the stone. As thin as strands of hair, they raced out from beneath her palms.

"There's power on the other side," Tessa hummed, slipping into that eeriness as her power took over. "We want it."

"Be ready to stop her," Theon warned.

"What do you think I was doing?" Luka retorted.

He ignored the sarcasm, letting his darkness swarm and billow, creating a shield to protect Axel and the Fae in case the wall exploded. Which would not be great and would probably alert his father, so he was really hoping that wouldn't be the case.

Little by little, pieces of the wall fell to the ground. Tiny pebbles and pieces of shale. It sounded like raindrops as they fell faster and faster until they all crumbled into a pile, leaving them staring into a room. A small sofa for two. A table and chairs for the same. A small bed. And on her feet, wide emerald eyes staring back at them was—

"Caris?" Axel rasped, and Theon was glad he said it, because he sure as fuck couldn't.

He was just . . . staring at her.

A phantom of his past. A female he'd watched be tortured to death in front of his own eyes when he was scarcely ten years. A nursemaid who'd been more of a mother to him than Cressida had ever been.

Her eyes were bouncing between him and Axel and Luka, and she appeared as frozen as they were. No one daring to breathe or move. As if they were looking through a pane of glass.

"She is powerful," Tessa hummed, stepping over the line of crumbled rock and into the room. "But she is trapped."

"Tessa, stop," Luka ground out, going after her and winding an arm around her waist. He pulled her back into his chest, his dragonfire brushing along her arms and stomach.

But now the female's gaze was holding Theon's, and all he could think to say was, "How?"

She smiled sadly as she took him in. "You're tall." Her gaze skipped between the three of them again. "You all are."

"How?" Theon repeated. "You're not . . . You can't be . . ."

"You have to speak it otherwise I cannot say it," she said, still as unmoving as he was.

A vow or oath of some sort then.

"You're my mother?" Theon asked, the words quiet as they passed his lips.

And she nodded, something shifting in her features. A wariness, perhaps? Suspicion?

"We saw you die," Axel said suddenly. "We watched it. What he did . . ."

"You watched the torture," she said, her fingers curling at her sides. "You thought you saw my death."

"We scattered your ashes in Sinvons Lake," Luka said, and Theon could feel his own suspicion down the bond.

"But did you see my body burn?"

"None of this makes any sense," Theon said. He took a step back, pebbles crunching under his shoes. "This is a trap."

"How can it be? The Mark led you here," Tessa said, seemingly back from the depths of her power.

"I hear you have become quite the academic," the female said tentatively, clasping her hands in front of her.

"From who? Him?" Theon sneered.

She arched a brow. "Valter only visits me to gloat or try to force me to aid him. He never speaks of you. Of any of you. It was a torture in and of itself."

"I think you need to explain . . . everything," Luka said, still holding Tessa to him, and she was looking at the female with keen interest.

"She's trapped," Tessa said again.

Ignoring her, Theon said, "Start from the beginning."

She studied him for a long moment, and he felt too godsdamn exposed. Why was he wondering what she thought of him? If he measured up? He'd watched Caris die, and even then, Caris couldn't have been his *mother*. She was a Fae with water magic in love with Pen.

"My family line is the original line to rule Arius Kingdom," she finally said.

"Bullshit," Axel spat, and her head whipped to him, eyes narrowing.

"Language, Axel St. Orcas," she snapped.

His eyes went wide, and he stumbled back a step. "Sorry," he mumbled.

"The St. Orcas family challenged my brother for the seat. He was far older than me. Over a century. I was young, around the age you all are now," she went on.

"Wait, I do know some of this," Theon said, taking a tentative step towards her. "Valter's father challenged for the seat nearly four centuries ago."

She nodded, a bitter smile tilting on her lips. "And he won. My brother was killed, and he took the seat. I was allowed to remain a noble . . . until your father claimed his seat."

"But . . . you're a Fae. Not an Arius Legacy," Theon said. "You have water magic."

"Just like Penelope, right?" Caris asked.

"You're saying it was never you?"

She nodded, raising her arms slightly. Two metal cuffs were at her biceps. He'd never seen her without them. In his formative years, they were just accessories. A part of her, but now that he was older and understood . . .

"She's trapped," Tessa repeated.

"He had them custom made," the female said. "I was presented with them the evening of his lordship. He demanded I become his Match."

"That's forbidden. It upsets the balance of power in the realms," Theon replied.

"Because the Lords and Ladies of Devram are so pious," she deadpanned. "I declined, and he accepted that for a time." She shifted on her feet, eyes suddenly darting around the room, looking anywhere but at them. "He and Rordan became close, forming the Augury. Every few months, Valter would approach me with his request, and every time I would deny him. I had found Pen by that time. She'd been assigned to Arius Kingdom, and . . ." She shrugged. "Things happen as things do. I loved her with my whole soul. Valter learned of the relationship and saw it as a betrayal in his twisted mind.

"Valter and Rordan had their falling out, and the Arius Kingdom was shunned more than ever," she went on. "Of course, Valter wanted vengeance against everyone and everything. Kingdom alliances were being threatened, and the rulers held a conclave, agreeing to all attempt to have children the same age. Priestesses were brought in to help . . . better the odds."

"Obviously it worked," Axel muttered.

"It did," she agreed. "But your father wouldn't risk it. By that time, he'd taken a Match."

"Cressida," Theon said.

She nodded again. "But it wasn't what he wanted. He wanted a child that would be more powerful than the others. A full Arius Legacy, through and through."

"Are you saying . . . Theon is two Arius bloodlines?" Tessa asked.

"The next time he approached me, my rejection was not an option. I was brought here, and . . . Well, you were created," she said, gesturing in Theon's direction. "Cressida fell pregnant at the same time. Of course, her child was not fully Arius, and her child was a female."

"Axel's sister," Theon said. Luka had told them all of this, filling them in on what Xan had told them. How his mother had taken the female and fled. How they'd been in hiding all this time in the Anala Kingdom.

"Yes," she said, moving to the table. She rested her palm on the surface, taking a deep breath before she lifted her gaze to them once more. "You were born and passed off as her child. The Arius Heir. Of course, Cressida wanted nothing to do with you, and she was still pregnant at your birth. Her child wasn't born for another six weeks. I was forced into an oath to never reveal the circumstances, but in exchange, I was allowed to be your caretaker and stay with Pen. No longer a noble Legacy, but a Fae in service to the kingdom."

She smiled softly. "It was worth the sacrifice to get to be there. In a way, you were mine and Pen's, even if you were his heir. I got to care for you, see your first steps, hear your first words. I got to . . ." She cleared her throat, eyes darting away once more. "And then Luka came shortly before Axel was born. Soon, there were three mischievous boys running amuck. You became my world, and I became your weakness. Although that day was my fault, not yours."

Theon's brow furrowed. "What do you mean? He was punishing us that day."

She smiled sadly. "I'm sure he wanted you to think that, and I am told he used the moment to his advantage. But that day was about breaking me. He wanted more from me because even then, he was starting to fear you were going to turn on him. He is paranoid, and I can't really blame him in this world. Everyone is always out for everyone. I refused to go through that again. I snuck out one night. I may have been passed off as a Fae, but I still remembered the secrets of the kingdom. Stealing coin, I found passage to the Underground where I paid off a Witch for these." She gestured to the Marks across her collarbone.

"What do they do?" Theon asked.

"Take away my ability to have children."

"Like a Curse Mark?" Tessa asked, and Theon glanced at her in confusion.

"It's not a curse," she replied. "I cannot even conceive a child. The day I returned and he saw them was the day I was tortured in front of you."

Theon blinked, the memory surfacing. She *had* been gone for days. They were more than a handful at that age, and Pen hadn't been able to wrangle all three of them, much less for days on end. That was what they had assumed they were being punished for, but . . .

"You're my mother?" Theon asked, restating what was now an obvious question. The emerald eyes. The midnight hair. Even some of the facial features were the same.

"It's why you look like Arius," Tessa murmured. "Two distant bloodlines with a twist of fate."

"I'm told you are not like him," Caris said. "That none of you are. That you've found love and that somehow, you are not like him."

"Who told you that?" Theon asked, taking another step closer.

"Eviana has been visiting."

Right. Eviana.

He turned to tell the Fae males that they would go find her in a moment, but the landing was empty. So were the stairs.

They'd gone off without them.

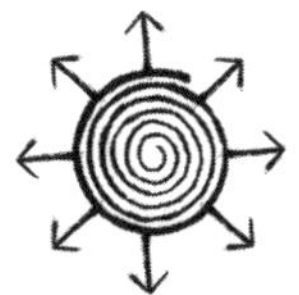

48
EVIANA

A hand covered her mouth, and her eyes went wide as she was dragged into a hall bathroom. Then she went still when the door closed, and she came face-to-face with Lange.

"By the gods, *bellana*," Lange muttered. "Does he only let you piss once a day? We've been waiting forever."

Corbin had removed his hand from her mouth, but he still had an arm wound around her. She wriggled from his hold, facing them both now.

"What the fuck are you doing here? And how?" she hissed, knowing she didn't have much time.

She had been allowed to go to the bathroom, but she also had to return with a new bottle of scotch for Valter. If she took too long, there would be consequences.

"We're here to get you," Lange answered. "Tessa is here, along with Theon, Luka, and Axel. They're with Theon's mother. Did you know she was here?"

"Of course I knew she was here," Eviana snapped. "I helped put her here."

"And you never told him?" She stared back at him. "Right," Lange muttered, rubbing at his nape. "I suppose you couldn't."

"We don't have a lot of time," Corbin stated.

"Obviously. What's the plan?" she retorted.

This time *they* stared back at her.

"You came here without a fucking plan?" she demanded. "Did I teach you fools nothing?"

"We sort of have a plan," Lange countered. "Theon and Axel are here to kill their father. So once that's done, we're good to go, right?"

"They are here to kill him?"

"Well, I'm guessing he's not going to let them simply walk out the nonexistent front door with their mother," Lange drawled. "Speaking of, why the fuck isn't there a door?"

"Oh my gods," Eviana muttered, going over all this new information and trying to pull together a plan. Priya wasn't just going to go with them. She was too enamored by Valter.

"I have to get back or he's going to come looking for me," she said. "Come back *with* Tessa, Theon, and Axel, but first . . ."

She faltered, clasping her hands in front of her. Out of habit, yes, but also out of nerves. She felt the most in control when she was doing something she was used to. Something that came as naturally as breathing.

"What is it, nightmare?" Corbin asked, clearly trying to lighten the mood.

"Have you met the Shifters?" she asked suddenly.

His eyes widened in confusion. "Yes," he answered slowly. "Tessa took me to them shortly after we caught up with her at the Acropolis."

"They were kind? Kylian can be abrasive," she said.

Corbin studied her for a moment. "They were more than kind. My . . . mother especially."

She nodded once, squeezing her fingers. "When this is all over, will you stay with them?"

He exchanged a look with Lange. "We haven't decided where we will settle down," he answered. "I suppose it will depend on what the world looks like when this is all over."

That made sense, she supposed.

"Eviana?" Corbin prodded gently when she remained silent.

She straightened her spine, dropping her hands to her sides. "If you can only leave with one of us, promise me you'll take Priya."

"What?" Lange scoffed. "No. You're both coming with us."

She sighed. "Lange—"

"No," he interrupted, stepping closer and crowding her against the wall. "You're both coming with us. Do you understand me? You didn't drag us across half the fucking kingdoms, through the Dreamlock Woods, and make us godsdamn *care,* for us to leave you behind. You and Priya are both leaving here with us."

"Swear it," she breathed, looking up into sky-blue eyes. "Swear that you will leave here with both of us. That when this is all said and done, you will take us both from here. That you will . . . help me with her. Is it an accord?"

His head tilted as if listening to something, and she swore to the gods, if those winds fucked her over right now . . .

"I swear to you that you will both leave here with us," Lange said, holding her stare. "I swear that when this is all said and done, you will not be alone. You and Priya? You'll be part of our family. That is the accord I make with you."

"Agreed," she breathed, fighting back the emotion trying to claw up her throat. She didn't get emotional. Emotions were pointless.

But she felt the tingling of the bargain Mark on her skin just below her shoulder blade. Then she pushed off the wall, shoving him aside. "I have to go. He will come looking soon. I am already taking too long."

She slipped from the bathroom, rushing to the kitchens and retrieving the liquor and a fresh ice bucket before hurrying back to his study. He looked up when she entered, his hazel eyes hard.

"That took longer than it should have," he said coldly.

"My apologies, my Lord," she answered, dropping her gaze to the floor. "I have been unwell with my power so low."

"And who's to blame for that, Eve?"

"Me, my Lord," she said immediately. Lifting the liquor bottle, she dared to look at him, finding him with a slight smirk. "Would you like a glass now or later?"

"Now."

She nodded, moving to the liquor cart and pulling out a tumbler. She filled it with a few ice cubes and the liquor, trying to calm her racing heart and steady her breathing before she carried it to him.

His fingers brushed hers as he took the glass, and then he stood, forcing her to stumble back a step. He leaned against his desk, studying her while he took a sip.

"How long have you been mine, Eviana?" he mused, swirling the contents of his glass.

"For decades, my Lord," she answered, her mind racing as she tried to figure out where this was going.

He hummed in response, setting the glass down with a faint clunk. Then he reached over, a fingertip trailing along her collarbone. "Decades of training. Decades of investing my time and energy into you."

She stayed silent, his fingers still skating down to her cleavage. It was only then she realized Priya wasn't in the room anymore. She had been here when she'd left to fetch the liquor, but now she was gone.

"And I was studying you all that time too," he went on. "Clearly not well enough. You still managed to hide your thoughts and emotions from me. Not that I'm surprised. You are clever, but your mannerisms . . ." His fingers dragged back up. "You've never once lied directly to my face. Until now."

Her eyes went wide, and she tried to lurch back. But he was faster because she was too weak right now. His fingers clamped around her throat, keeping her close.

"I did not think I could be more disappointed in you," he snarled into her ear. "Yet you continue to prove me wrong at every turn. Tell me how, after fucking decades, this is how you treat me, Eviana?"

But she couldn't speak because he was squeezing her throat. Then she couldn't speak as the door opened and Corbin and Lange were shoved into the room by two of the three servants that were here, one of whom was an Arius Legacy.

No!

"Tell me," Valter said, twisting so he stood behind her now. He tugged her back into his chest, adjusting his grip on her neck. "Tell me why a seven-year-old *child* is more loyal to me than my godsdamn Source."

Corbin and Lange were staring at her wide-eyed, clearly not knowing what to do or say.

Then she was trying to scream around that grip on her throat as shadows sprang forward and wrapped around the males. They both cried out in agony, those shadows biting and twisting and coiling. They fell to their knees, items in the room being thrown about as Lange fought back with his wind. Corbin shifted, but the magic didn't care. It wrapped around the feline as much as it did Lange. Strangling and drawing blood.

No! No, no, no!

She could do nothing. They were here because of her. They'd come for her. To help her. And now they would be dead because of her.

It had been decades since she'd felt anything, but now she felt guilt and regret. She wished she'd never met them. Never coerced them. Never dragged them with her on this pointless quest to do what? Find her daughter just to watch her slowly become what she was?

Those were tears on her face, and she thrashed against Valter's hold. He only tightened his grip on her throat, murmuring in her ear how she had caused this. This was her fault. She was the reason they were being tortured.

As if she didn't already know those truths.

"What are you doing?"

Valter stilled at the small, horrified voice. His grip on Eviana's throat loosened the smallest amount, and she turned her head to find Priya standing just inside the door. If her voice was horrified, it was nothing compared to the look on her small face as she took in a scene no child should ever have to see.

"These Fae are here to hurt you, Priya," Valter ground out. "I am protecting you. Just like I promised I always would."

Her turquoise eyes bounced from Valter to the Fae to Eviana and back, fear pouring off her.

"Leave, Priya," Valter said, his voice getting firmer. Gruffer. "Let me handle this. Go with Benson." Snapping at the Arius guard, he added, "Where the fuck is Annis?"

"I don't want to go back to Annis," Priya said, backing away as Benson approached her.

"Sometimes we don't get to choose what we want to do," Valter gritted out, losing all semblance of patience. "Go with Benson. Now!"

"Don't touch her!" Eviana gasped, Valter's grip loosening more as his attention was split between her, Priya, and keeping Lange and Corbin tied down with his shadows.

Lange had stopped fighting back, instead using his magic to get air to himself and Corbin as Valter's shadows squeezed tighter. Blood marred them everywhere, that magic burning and branding.

"I will restore your obedience if it is the last thing I do," Valter snarled, his hand leaving her throat and grabbing her hair. He yanked her back, throwing her into the bookshelf behind the desk, and she crumpled to the floor. Too weak to fight back. Too drained from these godsdamn bands.

"Stop! Let me go!" Priya was crying, *screaming*, and Eviana grabbed onto the desk to pull herself back to her feet.

Benson was wrestling with Priya, and the girl was fighting back with everything she had. Kicking and biting. She was a fighter, Eviana would give her that, but she didn't stand a chance against an Arius Legacy.

Valter was stalking across the room, a dagger in hand as he approached Lange first.

"Get her out of here, Benson!" he roared.

No child should have to see this, but a part of Eviana was glad. She recognized that made her a horrible person. She also recognized it was why she should never have been a mother, but seeing the truth of the male she was so enamored with? It would mark her. She would always remember this.

Always be wary to trust again, and she should be. Whoever she deemed worthy of her trust needed to earn it.

"Son of a bitch!" Benson barked, and Eviana looked over to see her teeth deep in his hand. He released her, throwing her away from him, and she hit the ground hard.

"Priya!" Eviana cried, and it hurt. Fuck, did it hurt. She had to have broken a rib when Valter threw her into the bookshelf.

Then it was Benson being thrown across the room, light and dark lifting him off his feet and pinning him to the wall. Tessa stormed in, power rolling off her with a hand raised to keep Benson in place. Theon, Axel, and Luka stalked in behind her, the three of them looking like walking death.

"How the fuck did you get here?" Valter demanded, lurching back.

Tessa's smile was pure wrath as she rotated her hand, a crack resounding through the room before Benson dropped to a heap on the floor.

The interruption had caught Valter off guard enough that his power loosened, Corbin and Lange sucking down breaths. Corbin was still in his mountain cat form, hovering over Lange.

"Eviana," Tessa said in a too calm voice. "Get Priya."

She moved as fast as she could, biting down the scream of pain when she reached the girl and scooped her into her arms.

"Don't watch," she murmured, pushing Priya's face into her neck. "Don't watch and cover your ears."

Priya didn't argue, and Eviana clung onto her as she watched Valter's sons cross the room. Valter tried to fight back, his shadows lashing out at them, but it appeared Theon had finally learned a truth. He was stronger than Valter even without a Source. He was stronger than all the Ladies with his double bloodline.

It was something Valter had never let him learn, and it was part of the reason he was brutal with Theon from the very beginning. If he grew up thinking he was the weaker one, he'd never realize how powerful he actually was. It had driven Valter mad that Theon wouldn't discuss his Source options because Valter couldn't scheme properly. He had dreaded the day Theon took a Source. He'd wanted him powerful, but only if he controlled that power. So he controlled his son with threats and abuse. Threatened him with Axel and Luka.

And then Tessa had come along.

Tessa had moved to Corbin, who'd shifted back, and Lange, standing beside them while Luka towered over her. Her violet eyes were homed in on

Valter, watching and waiting. Eviana knew she would intervene if she needed to, but she was letting the St. Orcas brothers have their vengeance.

"My ungrateful, spoiled sons," Valter spat, pressing up against his desk. There was nowhere else for him to go.

His shadows lashed out again, and Theon's darkness *caught* them. Somehow seeped into them. Made them darker and deadlier. Controlled them.

Eviana saw the uncertainty flicker across her Master's face, but then it was gone. He straightened with a sneer, staring back at his sons. "Killing me would be pointless now. I heard what you've done, Theon. Giving our kingdom over to an Achaz descendant? You betray our people."

"We're not here to discuss the kingdom, the people, or my choices," Theon said coldly. "We're here to discuss you."

"You lost any right to discuss anything with me when you gave everything we are to that cunt," Valter spat.

Theon's darkness was at Valter's throat, sinking into his flesh. His veins took on a grey pallor as Theon stalked forward, pulling a dagger from a swirl of black. One of the many daggers Eviana had seen Valter shove into his own children on numerous occasions.

Without any of Valter's flair, Theon plunged that blade deep into Valter's side. "That's my wife, you weak, pathetic piece of shit," he snarled. "Talk like that about her again, and I'll rip out your godsdamn tongue."

"You always were one for empty threats," Valter sneered, reaching for the dagger hilt.

But then Axel was there, moving so godsdamn fast he was a blur. In Eviana's next blink, he had Valter's hands wrenched behind his back, and Theon was shoving rings onto his fingers.

Priya whimpered in her arms, and Eviana clutched her tighter. She should really get her out of here, but she was too weak to do anything other than slide to the floor. She stifled her own scream when she adjusted her hold on the child, her ribs definitely broken on one side.

"My worthless spare," Valter panted, his power no longer working to combat his wound.

With one hand holding his wrists, Axel pulled a knife from the bandolier across his chest. It was a long, thin one, the blade coming to a sharp point, and he dragged that point along Valter's cheekbone.

"I really have nothing to say to you," Axel said, his voice as cold and dark as the death he came from, even if he could no longer wield its wrath.

Axel had wrath of his own to wield.

"But then again," Axel continued, "I know how much you *love* my dramatics."

Without warning, the blade was in Valter's inner thigh, right next to his groin. The ex-Lord howled in pain as Axel twisted the knife.

"The thing is, you threatened my wife," Axel said, each word getting tighter as he clung to his control.

Another knife was in Valter's other thigh. This one Axel dragged down, slicing him open more.

"And came after my child," Axel snarled.

Another knife to the back of Valter's knee, dragging horizontally this time.

Another whimper from Priya, and Eviana knew she was hearing far too much.

"Shh," she murmured, smoothing a hand down her hair. "You're safe. I promise, you're safe. They won't hurt you."

"I've got it."

Eviana looked up to find Lange there, reaching for the girl. His hands covered Priya's where they were clamped over her ears.

"All she can hear now is the sound of the wind," Lange said.

"You stole everything from me," Axel was saying, coming around to stand before his father. "And I want to thank you."

"Thank me?" Valter spat, once again trying to reach for the knives and dagger, but Theon's magic snapped around him, pinning his arms to his sides. "For what? Making you weak enough to give in to bloodlust?"

"For making me strong enough to keep getting back up, even when it feels fucking pointless," Axel returned, his hands sliding into the pockets of his pants.

Valter scoffed. "You are nothing but a slave to the dark now, vampyre."

Axel's lips tilted in his signature malicious smile. "And yet the sun still rises because the dark does not hate the light. It makes it clearer. A balance. Fire and shadows."

Valter huffed a derisive laugh, dismissing his younger son and turning to Theon. "And you? How else will you fail me today?"

"I won't fail you," Theon said, too calmly. Too controlled. "I will return you to your beginnings. Deliver you to your beloved Arius, and you can fall at his feet and proclaim how *you* failed *him*."

And for the first time, Valter stilled, as if only now realizing what his death would mean. Who he would have to face and how that would end.

Eviana blinked as she realized the male had truly thought himself invincible. Then again, all the rulers of the realm did. They were the gods here, forgetting that Devram was the forgotten world of the stars, and in the grand scheme of things, they were minuscule.

Theon strolled forward, pure dominance and power, and he slapped his father's cheek patronizingly. "Because *I* control *your* fate, and I can think of nothing better than letting Arius fall asleep to your screams of agony from the Pits of Torment every. Fucking. Night."

He stepped back, nothing but hatred on his face as he looked down at his father. "And while I could be the one to end you, because I am, after all, far more powerful than you—"

Valter snarled, and Eviana knew Theon's words were hitting harder than any blade embedded in her Master's flesh.

Theon's lips tipped up in a knowing smirk. "I have my own vendettas against you, but they're nothing compared to Axel's when you went after his wife and child." He paused, taking a step to the side. "Or Luka's."

"Luka?" Valter spat. "That ungrateful bastard. He—"

But then Valter was bellowing in pain. Eviana couldn't figure out why until she saw the smoke rising from Valter's shirt as it slowly burned. A perfect hole right over the top of his chest. And it wasn't just his shirt that was burning, but his skin. Bone. Muscle. A cavity slowly burning deep into his chest with dragonfire until they could see his heart beating far too fast.

Axel snickered where he stood nearby, having poured himself a glass of scotch. "I truly thought there would be nothing there."

Theon slapped his father's cheek again, much harder. "Stay awake, Valter. We're not done yet."

"That's for my father," Luka snarled, not moving from his place at Tessa's side. "And for my wife."

"Your wife?" Valter gasped, wild eyes jumping from him to Tessa to Theon. "Somehow you manage to disappoint me even more, Theon."

"As if I give a single fuck," Theon replied casually, taking the glass of liquor Axel passed to him.

"So what now?" Valter spat. "You leave me filleted wide open? Since no one seems to have the balls to carry out their threats? Weak. All of you."

"Your death is not ours to claim," Theon said simply, sipping his scotch.

"I suppose it's the cunt's you share with the dragon?"

Eviana gasped when Theon shot forward, gripping Valter's hair and yanking his head back. Valter opened his mouth with a pained groan, and Theon poured his drink down his throat, Valter coughing and gagging.

"I told you not to speak of her again," Theon snarled, that control gone. "The only one who deserves to claim your death more than me is my mother."

"Your . . ." Valter's eyes flew to the other side of the room, and so did Eviana's where she found Caris standing just inside the door. The stone on her upper arms was gone, and darkness flowed around her like a midnight mist. She glided forward, and as she passed Tessa, the female handed her a gold dagger.

Not a blade of black to end the former Arius Lord, but a blade of light.

Caris stopped in front of Valter, and the male stared back at her.

"Finally taking your vengeance then?" Valter sneered, holding himself up with his desk as his legs trembled from Axel's blades.

Caris said nothing, but she looked over her shoulder, locking eyes with Eviana. Caris glanced at Priya, then back to her, and Eviana gave a nod of her head, smoothing her hand down Priya's hair once more.

"It's almost over," Eviana whispered, even though Priya couldn't hear her over Lange's magic.

But Lange heard her.

"It is, *bellana*," he said. "You're almost free."

"You took my place in this kingdom," Caris said, her tone strong and unwavering. "You took my son. My love. My life." She lifted her other hand, her fingers covered in her darkness, and she reached inside Valter's chest and gripped his heart, squeezing.

Valter gasped, his knees giving out, but Theon and Axel were there, holding him up. Making him face his comeuppance.

"And still this is not for me in the end," Caris said, her voice taking on the edge of death she came from. "It is for everyone who suffered because of you. Me. My sons. The people of the kingdom you stole from my family."

Her hand tightened again, and Valter's eyes rolled back before she loosened her grip.

"But in the end, this is for Eviana and everything you stole from *her,*" Caris said, and then she yanked her hand back a moment before her other hand sank the gold dagger into the muscle.

Axel and Theon released him, letting Valter drop to the floor as if he were nothing, and they stepped back, turning away. Eviana knew they would never think of the male again.

She nodded at Lange, and he pulled his hands back. Priya shifted, and Eviana sucked in a sharp breath as her chest tightened. She reached up, smoothing her daughter's hair back from her brow before taking her face in her hands.

"It's over, Priya. You were so brave," she murmured softly.

The girl's eyes were haunted, her face tearstained as her gaze bounced around Eviana's face.

Eviana was doing the same. Taking in her turquoise eyes. The scattering of freckles across her nose and cheeks. Her wild auburn hair.

She sucked in a shuddering breath, her chest constricting even more. "You are such a bright and beautiful flower," Eviana murmured, her hands slipping from Priya's face.

The world tilted a little, and Lange caught her shoulders. "Easy, *bellana*," he said, brow furrowing in alarm. "Let's get these off you."

He gently pulled the bands from her wrists, her power springing forth at being free. The few potted plants in the room reached for her, leaves stretching, and she smiled.

But removing the bands wouldn't do what Lange thought it would. Her power wasn't going to replenish. It wasn't going to heal her or strengthen her.

Eviana lifted a shaky hand and turned her palm up, a seedling appearing in the center. Priya gasped, staring in amazement as the seedling opened and grew. Sprouting and unfurling until a perfect bright pink *bellana* flower formed.

Priya reached for it, twirling it between her fingers. A wide smile spread across her face, and Eviana marveled at it.

Until her chest tightened further and she was sinking down, her head in Lange's lap.

"Eviana? What's wrong?" Lange demanded, eyes darting from her to Priya and back.

"Take her," she rasped. "Don't let her see."

"See what?"

But someone was there, lifting her daughter into strong arms. She blinked as the room blurred, finding Corbin's features tight with grief as he stared down at her.

"Don't tell her," Eviana whispered. "Don't tell her who I am."

"What? Why?" Lange demanded, trying and failing to keep the panic from his voice.

"I don't want her to remember . . . this," she rasped, each breath becoming harder. Shallower. "But you swore . . ."

"Eviana, stop," Lange ordered, her face in his hands as he leaned over her. "Stop. We'll get a Healer. Cienna. Someone. We'll—

"You swore she would be part of your family," Eviana forced out. "That she wouldn't . . . be alone."

"Eviana!"

Corbin was there then, leaning over her, and Eviana could just make out Caris holding Priya in her arms, softly discussing the flower. Priya was none the wiser, listening intently to whatever Caris was saying. She was a mother. She understood.

"It's okay, nightmare," Corbin said gently, taking her hand in his. "We've got her."

Eviana gave him a weak smile. "Thank you."

"No," Lange snarled, shaking his head in denial. "No, you didn't . . . You hauled us all over the continent for her and now . . . No."

"She always knew it would come to this, Lange," Corbin said softly, ever the observant one. "It's why she took us with her."

He understood. Good. That was good.

"Make sure . . . she knows the trees," she rasped.

Corbin nodded, his throat bobbing with emotion. "Yeah, nightmare. We will."

Because there was always a cost. For every good, there was an evil. For every light, there was a dark. For every sacrifice, there was a reward.

And hers was getting to watch her daughter admire a flower, bright and beautiful, as she took her last breath. Not as a Source on her knees for her Master, but as a mother knowing her daughter would never have to be what she had become.

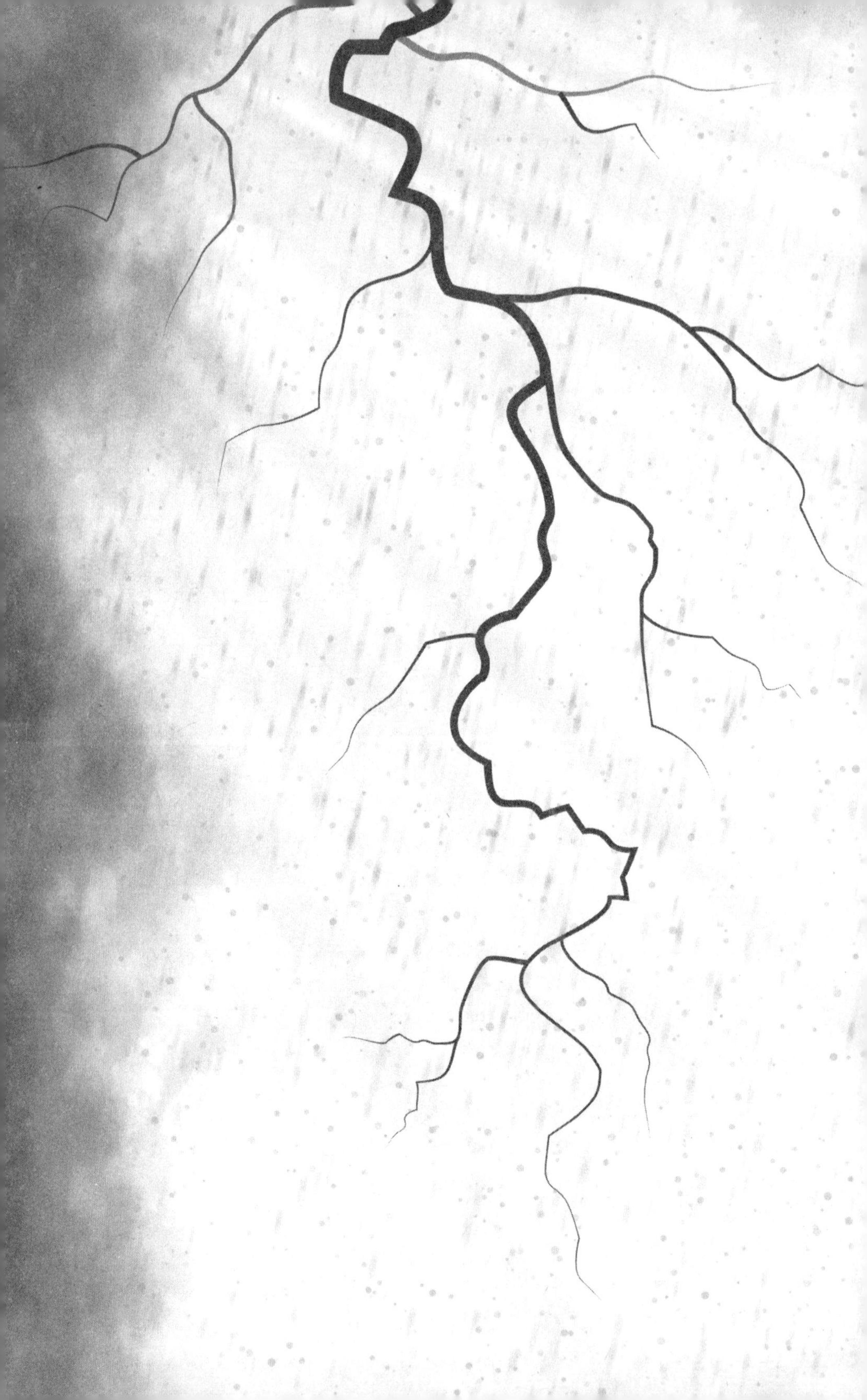

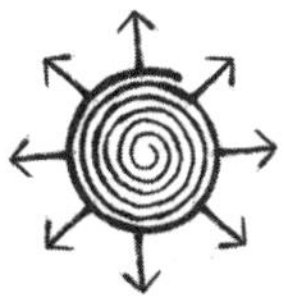

49
TESSA

"I don't understand," Axel said, all of them sitting in the Penthouse living room once again. This time they weren't sitting in jarring defeat, but the shock was still there.

Valter was dead, never to threaten any of them again. Theon. Axel. Maddox. Caris. They were all free of him.

And so was Eviana, though not in the way Tessa had intended.

From the first time she'd visited Eviana at the Faven Palace, she'd intended to free her of the Arius Lord. She'd worked to build a tentative trust, and then she'd trusted Lange and Corbin to be the good souls they were and build it even more. They'd clearly done that, and nothing was more evident of that than the way Corbin was holding a sleeping Priya in his lap next to Lange on the sofa.

"Thank you," Caris said softly as Eliza placed a glass of wine and plate of food on the table before her.

Xan, Eliza, and Razik had all come to the Underground to wait for their return. Even with Bree contained and no longer a threat, Axel wouldn't leave Kat and Maddox alone.

"Do you need anything else?" Theon asked, his voice monotone as he sat with what had happened.

"No," Caris said gently. Her gaze slid to Axel. "But I can clear up the confusion."

"Please do," Axel said, swiping a hand down his face. "Never in a thousand decades did I think I would be upset my father's Source was gone."

"Don't call her that. Her name was Eviana," Tessa cut in sharply.

Axel winced. "Sorry, Tessa. I'm just . . ." He lifted his gaze back to Caris. "Confused doesn't begin to cover it."

"As I said earlier this evening, your father was a very paranoid male. It only grew after Rordan's betrayal. He started taking extreme measures," Caris said.

"Like linking Cressida's life to yours," Theon said.

Caris nodded, toying with the stem of her wineglass. "Nothing was enough for him. He wouldn't risk not having a son, so Cressida and I both carried a child. Then he needed another, just in case." She paused for a moment. "His Sources were no different. Eviana was his second Source."

"We know this," Tessa interrupted. "He had her . . . Well, he chose her before she'd even entered the world."

Caris pressed her lips into a thin line. "You learned of the Sirana Villas."

Tessa gave a sharp nod.

"You're not wrong," Caris continued. "But a bond wasn't enough. He would have required more of her. Forced more vows and bargains with her."

Theon's head snapped up. "He had a Life Bond with her."

"Surely not," Axel gasped, his eyes wide.

Caris nodded.

"What is that?" Tessa asked, looking among them all. "What does that mean?"

"A bond between two lives," Luka told her gruffly. "If one dies, so does the other."

"He would have altered it to only be one-sided. If she died, nothing would happen to him, and she wouldn't have been able to tell anyone," Theon added. "He would have forced her to secrecy like he did with everything else."

"She wouldn't have told us even if she could have," Corbin said, his voice low and soft to not wake Priya. "Eviana was a lot of things, but she knew what she wanted in the end. If we had known, we would have tried to find another way. She wanted Valter gone because he would forever be a threat to her. She didn't care the cost, whether it was her or anyone else, as long as that threat was gone."

"I don't blame her," Tessa said, her fingers curling into the edge of her chair. "She lived a life we were taught to covet, but she knew what it truly was. Forced to bring a child into the realm, she wanted the greatest threat gone. In the end, does it matter? One villain gone out of thousands?"

"We're working on changing things, Tessa," Theon said.

She gave him a fake smile. "Will it be fast enough? For the Priyas of the world?" She looked at Axel. "For the Maddoxes who don't have the privilege of being born into a ruling family?"

"Everything we're doing is to ensure the realm is different for them," Axel argued. "It won't happen overnight, but we'll never stop fighting for it."

Tessa fell quiet, reaching for her glass of wine. She took a long drink, knowing there were eyes on her. Her emotions were . . . undefinable. She didn't understand them or know how to deal with them. It didn't feel like grief, despite the sadness. Failure? Disappointment? Inadequacy? She didn't know.

"Axel?"

Tessa lifted her gaze to find Kat at the top of the stairs, Maddox in her arms.

Axel was already moving, taking the stairs two at a time. He dropped a kiss to her cheek before taking the babe and then grasping Kat's hand.

"Come," he said with a sad smile. "There is someone I want you to meet."

He led her down the stairs, drawing nearer to Caris, and Tessa took another drink of wine.

"Kat, this is Caris. She was . . ." Axel paused, looking down at his son and then at Caris. "She's my mother. This is my wife, Katya."

Tessa didn't know if Kat knew of Caris's history. She was sure Axel would tell her everything later, but she smiled warmly as she greeted the female.

"A wife so young?" Caris asked, her smile kind as she stood and reached for Kat's hands, squeezing them gently. "Aren't you a vision, my dear?" Kat dropped her head, her cheeks heating. Caris's attention went back to Axel. "And this is . . . ?"

"Maddox," he answered, his voice thick with emotion. "Your grandchild."

Tessa drained her wineglass while Axel passed the babe to Caris, and suddenly Theon was there, fingertips brushing down her arm. She was projecting far too many things down the bond, but she couldn't stop it.

"So, what are we going to do about Priya?" Tessa asked, glancing at Lange and Corbin.

"What do you mean?" Lange asked. "We promised to make her family. She'll stay with us."

"Are you sure? Because if that's not something you want to do, we can make other arrangements."

"She's staying with us," Lange replied. "We swore it to Eviana, and even if we hadn't, we'd do the same."

"Corbin?" Tessa asked, looking at the male. "You are fine with this? With essentially adopting her?"

Corbin nodded, pulling the sleeping child a little more into his chest. "Yeah, Tessa. We're fine with this."

Tessa nodded, getting to her feet. "We'll make sure you have everything you need for her. Make lists. We'll get it sorted."

They rose too, heading for the lift to go down a floor to the apartment they'd been staying in. Stopping at her side, Corbin said, "Thank you, Tessa."

"You made the deal with Eviana. Not me."

"But you sent us to her."

And then they were gone, Xan, Razik, and Eliza following.

Without looking at the others, she said, "I'm going to bed."

Minutes later, she was sliding between the sheets. Luka and Theon would be up at some point. They'd stayed to visit more with Caris, and as she lay in the dark, all she could think about were the Priyas and Maddoxes who didn't have anyone to fight for them. The Fae children alone at the Estates. Those with mixed bloodlines born for the single purpose of power. Those forced to bring children into a broken world. The unplanned babes who may be loved but still subject to the wickedness Devram bathed in.

The forgotten children.

The suffering mothers.

The fathers who didn't know.

She sighed, rolling onto her side as she pictured Theon's face when he saw his mother. She could feel him down the bond. Luka too. They adored Caris. Everything a mother was supposed to be, ripped from them before they'd even lived a full decade. Even then, that trauma was used to manipulate them.

And tomorrow she would have to face her own mother. They looked at Caris with adoration and grieved lost time. And she . . .

Tessa heard the door open. Not both of them. Only Luka.

Her back was to him, and she didn't acknowledge him while he shuffled around the room. A few minutes later, the bed dipped, and an arm looped around her waist, pulling her back against his warm body.

"Time to talk about it, baby girl," Luka murmured, pressing a soft kiss to her neck. "You've been tossing and turning for the last hour."

"You were so relieved to see your father again," she whispered, a part of her sighing in relief at having someone to listen. Something she'd never thought she'd feel if she was being honest.

Luka was quiet for a few seconds before he said tentatively, "I was. I thought he was dead. Then I learned he was alive, and when I found him again . . . Yeah, I was relieved."

"And Theon is in awe of seeing his mother once more. Not relieved like you were, but . . . something similar."

"The three of us are all shocked at the way this day has gone. Caris was beloved by us."

She nodded, falling silent. Luka's hand came up, smoothing her hair back. "Keep going, Tessa," he said gently, urging her to keep talking. Knowing this was foreign to her. To have someone listen and not try to manipulate her based on what she said. Someone who was listening because they cared and not because they were trying to figure out how to use her to their advantage.

Still, she hesitated because saying this aloud was . . .

"You are all so grateful to be reunited with a father or mother, and I don't think I want to see mine," she whispered.

"Because of who they are to us," Luka said. "None of us would feel this way if we discovered Valter still lived. There would be little feeling if Cressida was gone."

"But you wish to see your mother? Xan told you she still lives in the Anala Kingdom."

"Yes, Tessa. I still wish to see my mother, but you not wishing to see yours is understandable. There is no right way to feel about this."

"But once again, I do not have a choice."

"You do," Luka said simply. "You are choosing the good of the realm over your own comfort. It's a noble choice. Even so, your feelings are valid."

"Are they?"

"Of course they are, Tessa." He shifted, splaying a hand on her stomach. "You can't change your feelings, and you shouldn't feel guilty about them. You should, however, talk about them instead of trying to shove them aside or face them alone."

"I should want to, though, right? Meet them? Shouldn't I be curious? Anxious? Shouldn't I be excited at the prospect?"

"There is no right way to be feeling about any of this," Luka said gently, his fingers on her stomach dragging loose circles atop her shirt. "Curious. Tentative hope." He paused. "Anger."

"Stop reading my emotions," she muttered.

He huffed a chuckle. "It's a balance, baby girl. You have to let us help you."

She snuggled back into him. "You'll be there tomorrow, right? You're coming?"

"I wouldn't be anywhere else. I'll be where you can see me," he answered. Silent seconds ticked by until Luka said, "When we went to free Xan, Eliza said something to Razik. I didn't understand then, but I do now. She said just because you help here doesn't mean you have to do anything else. No one is expecting anything else from you, and even if they are, you helping here? That's all it is. It is not an offering of anything else. Just because she comes here tomorrow doesn't mean you have to decide right now or even tomorrow how much you wish to know her. Okay?"

She nodded again, staying silent and once more trying to find sleep. Even when Theon joined them some time later, it didn't come, and she knew they didn't sleep either.

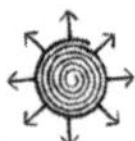

"You're sure we don't need a mirror gate for this?" Theon asked, all of them gathered in the gardens of Arius House.

Theon was focused on the task, and she was focusing on the cool ground beneath her bare toes. The soft breeze on her face. The rays of warmth trying to pierce through the stormy sky.

She was doing that. She knew that. The sky a reflection of her inner turmoil.

Luka and Theon had been unusually careful around her. Fretting and fussing. It was annoying.

"Not with a portal key," Xan said for what Tessa was sure was the hundredth time.

This was not an offering of anything else, she reminded herself. She was bringing Akira here to help the realm. That was it. If her mother had expectations, they didn't matter. No promises of anything more.

She looked up, unexpectedly locking eyes with Razik. The male was watching her, arms folded over his chest and mouth pressed in a firm line. But a strange understanding passed between them. How many times had she told Xan she didn't know if or when Razik would forgive him? She hated that *this* was what she had in common with the broody dragon who was an asshole ninety percent of the time.

Her fingers curled, chaos coiling around her fingers as her breathing became erratic. Theon and Luka both whipped their heads to her, but Razik only held her stare.

"You control when and how the relationship moves forward," Razik said, pointedly ignoring Xan's attention on him. "Some days you will be able to handle a conversation. Other days, you will not want to be in the same room. Both are fine. You hold that control here."

Tessa nodded slowly, something in her chest easing at finding someone who at least understood what she was struggling with.

Xan cleared his throat. "She will follow your lead, Tessa. She will wish for a chance to explain her actions, but . . ."

"But you are not required to hear her excuses," Razik interjected, his features hardening. "And that is a service to her. If you are forced to hear them before you are ready, they will fall on deaf ears."

Tessa nodded again, pursing her lips as she turned to Xan. "What do I need to do?"

"Because Temural altered them, they are not entirely like other portal keys," Xan said, dragging his eyes from Razik and focusing back on her. "You'll need to use your power to pull the stones from the rings and repair them. It will . . . be a lot, but once reunited, the portal key will do the rest. The one she bears should recognize it."

"And if someone follows her through?" Razik cut in.

"Is that a possibility?" Tessa asked, eyes wide in alarm.

"Yes, but highly unlikely. Akira is going to assume she is going to Temural. She will not let anyone follow," Xan answered.

"But if someone is with her when the portal opens?"

Xan held her stare, and it was answer enough. This was a risk.

"With all of us here, if someone follows, we can handle it," Theon interrupted.

"Can we?" Tessa argued. "If a god or goddess follows her through?"

"They can't come here, Tessa," he said calmly.

"Because it will upset the balance?" she drawled. "I'm here, aren't I?"

"If it were that easy, don't you think Achaz would have already come to Devram?"

That was a valid point. All of her visions confirmed the same. He couldn't come here. There was something keeping him from entering.

"Fine," she said, holding out her hand. "Give me the rings."

"Tessa, if you need time—" Theon started.

"I don't. Now," she insisted, her power growing restless as she prepared to let it breathe.

"Tristyn will need to take it from here," Xan said. "This is Witch magic now."

Witch magic. Blood magic. Marks and enchantments. It didn't much matter to her. She was ready to be done with this.

Tristyn had already drawn an upside-down triangle on the ground nearby, and he gestured for her to come closer. "Place a ring at each point," he said, features dark in concentration.

"Have you done this before?" she asked, placing the rings.

"Have I repaired a portal key? No," Tristyn replied. "They are rare, and those that do exist are hidden away." She nodded, letting Tris guide her to the center of the triangle. "Normally there would be incantations involved, but since this one was altered and is keyed to your blood, I think your blood and chaos will do."

"You think?" she asked incredulously as he passed her a small knife.

He shrugged with a wink. "We'll improvise if we need to."

"This doesn't seem like something we should improvise."

"You're altering everything, wild fury," he said. "It's all improvising at this point."

"Right," she muttered, dragging the blade across her palm as Tristyn stepped from the triangle. She couldn't let it drip to the ground in fear of summoning Hunters, so instead she let it pool, her chaos merging with it. Then, just like she had with Xan's collar, she pulled threads of her power and sent them to the rings.

It was innate somehow, letting her power do this. Recreate something. Everything came from Chaos, so it only made sense her chaos would be drawn to making something new.

The rings rose into the air until they hovered at eye level, light springing from each one and meeting in the center. That light turned dark, a churning mass of onyx as streaks of purple and gold flared until a ripple of power radiated out from the thing.

Tessa blinked, the light receding. Everyone around her was getting up from the ground. Tristyn was holding Theon back while Xan held Luka's shoulders.

"You can't go to her right now," Tristyn gritted out. "Not until this is done."

"The fuck I can't," Theon snarled, shoving Tristyn off him, but Razik was there, helping the deity.

"I've seen this done before," Razik snapped. "If you interrupt the process, it could cause something you don't want. The last being I saw repair a portal key didn't survive it."

Theon stilled at that, and his voice was death when he said, "I was never told that was a possibility."

"She's stronger than that Witch was," Razik gritted out. "But I'm assuming you don't want to chance anything."

The stone in front of her was a mix of colors now. Marbled onyx with white and violet running through it. Her magic was reaching for it, coils of chaos wrapping around it tightly and drawing it to them. Tessa reached up, taking it between her fingers. It pulsed in her palm. It was odd to think about. This other-worldly power in the palm of her hand. If she closed her hand, squeezed tightly enough, maybe it could just . . . cease to exist.

Or maybe we could create something new. Use that power. Take it as our own.

Tessa! Luka growled in her mind at the same time Theon snapped, *No, Tessa!*

She slowly turned her head to them once more. Luka and Theon couldn't stop them. No one could stop them. Not the gods. Not the Fates. This was theirs anyway. She was theirs—

"No, you are not," Theon snarled, his darkness slamming into Tristyn and Razik and throwing them back. He prowled forward, not caring about the ritual mark on the ground or the power she held in her fingers. He gripped her chin, forcing her eyes to his. "The only ones you belong to are me and Luka. Not the gods. Not the Fates. And you certainly do not belong to the fucking Chaos. Do you understand?"

You control it. Not the other way around, Luka added down the bond.

Then that key started glowing, and it didn't matter what she thought. Not as it sprang from her fingers, hovering in the air once more.

"Fuck," Theon cursed, grabbing her and dragging her back.

"I told you interrupting this would fuck something up," Razik grumbled as Tessa fought against Theon's hold, trying to get back to that power.

Because he was wrong. She was Chaos, and Chaos was hers. It called to her. It was a piece of her. It was—

The portal key dropped to the ground. The air shimmered as if a clear veil was there, and then a female stepped through it. Hair the same gold as her own, loose and wavy, fell to her navel. Blood-red lips and ethereal grace. An ivory dress that was so sheer it hid nearly nothing with a gold belt slung low on her hips. Gold rings. Gold earrings. Grey eyes swirling with gold and violet.

"I've seen you before," Tessa breathed, Theon still holding her to him.

The female turned, meeting her gaze, and Tessa could see the madness there. Fractured and furious.

"You got back up," she said, energy crackling in her aura as streaks of gold and violet lit up the sky. Her eyes flashed to Theon. "And you have taken what's yours."

She took a step towards her, and Theon pulled Tessa back, his darkness appearing.

"Don't!" Xan barked, but not fast enough.

A maniacal grin spread on the female's face as light arched from her hand, somehow latching onto Theon's darkness and dragging it to her.

"The fuck?" Luka growled, stalking forward and summoning his own magic.

The female tipped her head back and laughed, lifting her other hand and letting her power latch onto his too. Luka stumbled as that light yanked, and it was all Tessa needed to see.

"Come closer, little ones," the female sang, taking another step and reaching with her hand. "Let me taste it."

She grunted when light and dark slammed into her, shoving her back and back and back as Tessa stalked forward. "I become incredibly violent when people touch what is mine," Tessa snarled, fury coursing through her veins.

"No! Stop!" Xan interjected, shoving himself between Tessa and the female. "Akira, stop. We don't harm them. Here."

The male's black flames appeared, sliding up her arms, along her collarbone. Winding into her golden hair.

"Breathe and take," Xan coaxed. "Then look."

Her eyes fell closed, her storm of power winding around Xan's black flames, and she inhaled deeply. When she opened her eyes, gold was swirling in their grey depths, similar to the way Auryon's used to swirl with ashes.

"Xan?" she whispered.

"There you are," he said with a smile. "You have it under control?"

"For now," she agreed, and he pulled her into an embrace. "Where is he? Where is Temural?"

"Not here," Xan murmured, still holding her close. "But there is someone else you should meet."

He stepped back, his hand falling to the small of her back. Tessa could feel Theon and Luka behind her as Akira's eyes widened when they settled on her. Tessa still had her hands raised, chaos at her fingertips. She could feel it swirling in her eyes, knowing they were a mirror of Akira's, only a different color.

"Tessalyn," Akira breathed.

She moved to take a step towards her, but stopped when Tessa said, "Tessa. That is my name."

Akira nodded, her fingers flexing at her sides as she shuffled from side to side. "There is a lot of power here," she murmured, stretching her neck one way than the other as if trying to get something under control. "Too much. There is too much power here." She spun suddenly, Xan catching her wrists when she reached for his shirt. "Did I hurt them? Try to—"

"She stopped you," he consoled, more of his dragonfire skimming across her arms. His brow furrowed. "How long has he starved you?"

"Too long," she murmured. "She is upset with me."

"Who? Anala?"

She shook her head, golden strands swaying. "Tessa. I can feel her fury."

Xan's eyes flicked to her, and Tessa stared back, expressionless. She wasn't entirely sure what was happening here.

"Were you followed?" Tessa asked sharply, and Xan frowned, but she didn't care. "Did someone follow you through the portal?"

"We would have seen them, Tessa," Xan replied.

"You don't know that," she argued. "Phantoms could slip through, and you cannot tell me gods cannot be invisible if they choose."

"She is wise," Akira murmured. Tessa watched her shoulders rise with another deep inhale before she turned once more to face her. "No one followed me, Tessa."

"Where were you?"

"Locked in his world with nowhere to go."

"This whole time?" Tessa demanded.

"For decades."

"Was I born there?"

"No."

Tessa nodded, her fingers curling into her palms as she started pacing.

Until Luka pulled her into him, and Theon slid a palm down her hair.

Akira's eyes narrowed in interest. "Who are they?"

But Tessa didn't answer as her power twisted in her soul, mirroring her conflicting emotions.

"They are her balance, Akira," Xan said softly.

"Two?"

Xan smiled. "She is the daughter of wild and Fury. She requires two to balance her. The Fates delivered."

"The Fates did shit," Tessa snapped, shaking off the males. She felt steadier, drawing from their possession.

Akira hummed. "Which ones did you meet?"

"What?"

"Which Fates? Some are more palatable than others," Akira clarified.

"I didn't . . . You've met the Fates?"

"You haven't?"

"This conversation is going around in circles," Theon grumbled, and Tessa sent him a dry look over her shoulder.

She should feel something, right? Some kind of familial connection? Some kind of . . . *something*.

"The fuck?" Luka barked when Akira suddenly jumped forward a step. Tessa once again found herself being dragged back.

"Do you like stories?" Akira asked, her hands clasped under her chin and face full of hope as she held Tessa's stare.

"By the gods, you can't be serious," Theon muttered under his breath.

"I love stories," Tessa replied.

"Me too. Me too," Akira murmured, starting to pace. Small steps, back and forth, Xan staying close. "In all things, there must be balance. Beginnings and endings."

"Light and dark," Tessa supplied.

"Fire and shadows," Akira said in excitement.

"The skies, the seas, the realms," Tessa echoed.

"Yes," Akira said, nodding as she continued her pacing. Sparks of energy echoed each step. "Beginnings and Endings were once friends, forced to keep the balance in the stars. A common purpose and a trusted bond. Until one desired more. He convinced Endings to join him, and Accords were struck, until Endings uncovered truths and lies woven to create new realities. He turned from Beginnings, taking Dreams with him."

"Arius and Serafina," Tessa said softly.

"Good," Akira said, nodding. She seemed relieved that Tessa understood. "Beginnings was furious. He sought others to help him seek revenge, creating beings and armies, but he wanted more. Always more. He found one to give him a child, but the child wasn't enough either. He stole what was not his, forcing her to keep it. It corrupted her. Twisted into something new. Created fury that could not be contained, but she tried. She tried to contain it, but she was never enough."

The words were shrouded in anguish, Akira's steps quickening with each one.

"She tried to please him. Tried to be what he wanted her to be. Took more and more, forced to keep and keep. Take and keep. Take and keep," she continued.

"This isn't making any sense," Luka muttered.

"Don't interrupt the story," Tessa and Akira snapped at the same time.

But it was making perfect sense to Tessa. She understood every single word.

"Every time she slipped a little more into what she was not supposed to have. It consumed her. She was desperate to please him, so she went in search of something that would make her enough. They were hidden among the stars. Secrets of Dreams and Death."

"Saylah and Temural," Razik said quietly, and Akira spun to him.

"Yes! Yes! Wild and Shadows." She spun in a circle, resuming her pacing. The energy swirling around her flickered in the air, lightning crackling and thunder sounding far off in the distance. "I found him. Or he found me. His Trackers did. He found me, and the world was quieter," she murmured. She paused for a moment, her fingers closing into fists at her sides. Her voice was vicious when she spoke next. "And then Beginnings took me from him." Her gaze snapped back to Tessa. "But not before you. Created from something inevitable and uncontrollable. He could not have you. Never you." Her voice cracked, tears pooling in her eyes. "Never you. So she sent you away, and she fell into madness. It was the only way she could survive losing him and you. She let it consume her. She wasn't strong enough to get back up, so she let it create something new. Something born of vengeance and wrath."

"A Fury," Tessa said on a breath.

Akira nodded, her eyes falling closed as Xan sent another trickle of dragonfire to her.

"Do you understand, Tessa?" Xan asked gently.

And she did. She understood all of it because she'd lived the same. Never enough. Trying to prove herself. Needing more and more. Take and keep, keep and take.

"Tessa?" Theon asked softly, cupping her face to turn him to her. "Are you all right?"

She hadn't realized she'd started crying. Tears trickled down her cheeks.

Tessa turned back to her mother, voice soft when she asked, "Why didn't you send me to Temural? Why here?"

"He was on the run," she answered, her eyes somewhat clearer. "Achaz hunted him, as he does all children of Death and Dreams. He could not have you. Never you," she insisted. "So we chose the one place he couldn't come. Temural didn't know until later, but I sent others. Xan. Nylah. Roan."

"And he sent Auryon once he figured out how to get her in," Xan added. "You were never meant to be alone."

"You were alone?" Akira asked, her eyes welling with tears now.

Tessa nodded, unable to speak past the emotion clogging her throat.

"I never wished for that," she whispered. "Alone is agony. Too many nightmares haunt the in-between. The whispers drive you mad."

"Yes," Tessa said, more tears streaming down her face because someone finally understood.

"I . . ." Akira faltered, her fingers tangling into the fabric of her dress. Her eyes flashed to the males towering behind Tessa. "I wish to embrace you, but I can't. My magic is too much here, and you still have fury. It will try to devour that."

"Okay," Tessa whispered, wrapping her arms around herself.

"But I wish to speak more. When you are ready," Akira added.

Tessa nodded, and Theon cleared his throat lightly. "Actually, there is a reason you are here. Aside from your daughter."

"Who are you?" Akira asked again, her eyes narrowing. "You are too far removed from Death to carry the power that you do."

"That is a tale for another time," Theon said, and Tessa snickered as he avoided the story. "But we are told you can facilitate the transfer of power from one being to another. Or at least, you can teach Tessa how to do it."

"Perhaps," she agreed, still eyeing him. Her gaze shifted to the left. "I know who you are. You were scarcely walking when I saw you last. You are hers?"

"I am," Luka answered.

Before Akira could ask about the rest of their company, there was a burst of flames that had Tessa lurching back. She'd never get used to magic messages. With a grumble of annoyance, Theon reached into the fire, plucking out a piece of paper. His eyes scanned it, brows arching in surprise.

"What is it?" Luka demanded, taking the paper from him.

Theon turned to Tessa, "We've been invited to the Anala Kingdom. We will be escorted in the morning."

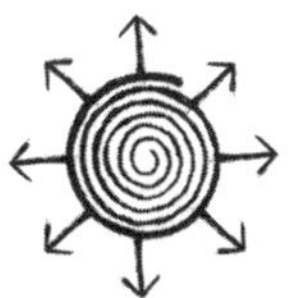

50
AXEL

"Thanks, kitten," Axel murmured, feeling her flames dance around him.

It was cold in Idalia, the capital city of the Anala Kingdom. He'd known that, of course. Geography had been part of his studies, and Idalia sat just on the outskirts of the Sulien Forest. In the northernmost part of the realm, it was always cold, and from his understanding, the forest often had snow even in the summer months. At least in the southern part of the forest, the year-round snowfall didn't seem to affect Idalia quite so much.

Of course, none of that mattered much to the Anala Kingdom. Not when a good number of their population had fire magic. Aside from the Anala Legacy, they never let other kingdoms claim fire Fae. Katya was one of the rare exceptions, and he still wondered how she'd ended up in the Falein Estate.

They'd arrived via portal station, stepping into the daylight, and Axel had immediately pulled up the hood of his jacket to shield himself from the sun. Gloves in place and completely covered, the cool weather helped hide his new nature well enough.

The portal station was on the water's edge, and Axel could see the faint outline of the Ozul Mountains across the body of water between their two kingdoms. It was brilliant really. With the mountains butting right up to the water's edge on the Arius Kingdom side, there were no inhabitants. If they did send anyone to spy, all they'd see was the same thing a person saw if they entered the kingdom through the portal station. Axel had only been to the kingdom one other time, and that was due to the tradition of all heirs touring the capital cities and Fae Estates. Otherwise, Lady Kyra rarely granted entry.

Kat held Maddox to her chest, keeping him plenty warm. They were staying in Idalia for a few days' time, which meant they'd needed to bring him along. There was no way either of them was missing out on entering the Anala Kingdom.

Tessa walked ahead of them, pulling her fur-lined jacket tighter around herself, and Luka stepped to her side, presumably doing the same thing Kat had done for Axel by providing some of his dragon warmth. Theon was at her other side, while the rest of their company trailed behind Axel and Kat.

They were escorted from the portal station and down several blocks into the heart of Idalia until they came to a three story brick building. Topped with a gold dome, the sun reflected off it. Climbing the front steps, they entered an elegant lobby, mosaics of the sun and fire on the floors. A moment later, the sound of heels echoed before Lady Kyra appeared before them, along with her daughter and their Sources.

Kat shuffled nervously next to him, fighting all her instincts to drop to a knee. Tessa had made it clear *none* of the Fae with them were to do so. She'd said if they were pushing for this change and wanted the Fae to be seen as the equals they were, no one should be bowing to anyone. The Fae had been nervous, but none of them defied their own Lady.

Lady Kyra's bright amber eyes skimmed over them, a small smile playing on her lips as she bowed her head slightly. "Lady Tessa," she greeted, lifting her head to meet her gaze. "Welcome to Idalia."

"Thank you," Tessa said tightly, everything about her tense. She was still conditioned to think everything was a trap, and Axel couldn't blame her.

Lady Kyra either didn't notice or didn't care to draw attention to the possible slight as she shifted her focus to his brother. "Theon," she greeted, stepping forward. "You bring quite the company with you."

"Thank you for the invitation, Kyra," he said. "It is such a rarity."

"Out of necessity, I assure you," she replied, features hardening the smallest amount. "We have a light lunch prepared. Come and eat. We can discuss matters, and then you can be shown to your quarters before we meet again."

They all followed her to a large space with a long table in the center. Rather than being served, one wall was set up with various dishes in a buffet style. After everyone had filled their plates, Axel held Maddox while Kat settled in to eat.

Lady Kyra sat at the head of the table, observing everyone as she said, "Now that we all have food, perhaps some introductions?"

"Of course," Theon said, glancing at Tessa, who nodded. She may be the

Arius Lady, but she was letting Theon be the public face of the kingdom. Not that she didn't step in when she needed to, but she was smart enough to know that Theon had been playing the game of politics far longer than she had.

"You know Luka," Theon started.

"Of course," Kyra said. Arching a brow, she added, "Lady Tessa's other husband."

Theon smirked. "Correct." He didn't say anything else to that, gesturing across the table. "And you know Axel. This is his wife, Kat, and their son, Maddox. Together they sit on the Underground Council."

"The lost fire Fae," Kyra said with a nod of her head. "Congratulations on your son."

"Thank you, my Lady," Kat said softly, glancing at Axel, and it took all of him not to ask right then and there how Kat had come to be raised in the Falein Estate.

"A child of fire and shadows will certainly be . . ." Kyra hedged.

"Welcomed," Tessa interjected, her fork halfway to her mouth. "He is welcomed within our kingdom and the realm."

Kyra nodded in understanding, her gaze lingering a moment longer on the babe before moving on.

"Xan Mors," Theon said. "Luka's father, and Razik Greybane, his brother, along with Eliza, Razik's mate."

Kyra settled back in her chair, propping her chin on her fist. "You are not from Devram."

Razik and Eliza exchanged a look, but it was Theon who said, "No, they are not."

Kyra was still eyeing Eliza, and it was enough to make Razik shift closer. Eliza, however, was holding the Lady's stare.

"Any other questions?" Eliza asked, a bite in her tone.

"Several actually," Kyra answered. "But I will save them for another time. Xan Mors, however . . ." She shifted her focus to the dragon. "There is someone here you have been separated from for quite some time."

"There is," Xan agreed. "I would like to be taken to her as soon as possible."

Kyra nodded. "That can be arranged." Before Theon could move to the next person at the table, Kyra said, "Caris Emersyn. I need no introduction. It is nice to see you once more."

"Wait, you know Caris?" Axel interrupted.

"Quite well," Kyra replied. "Her brother was once a Lord. We were working closely on several matters before the St. Orcas line took over the kingdom. Obviously, those relations could not continue until recently."

"It is good to see you, Kyra," Caris said with a gentle smile. "I have missed your company."

Axel sat back in his chair, somewhat shocked. His entire life he'd been told Arius Kingdom had been shunned by the others. To hear otherwise was . . . Well, not entirely surprising considering the ways all the kingdoms had twisted history to match their narratives. Anala Kingdom wasn't innocent in all this either. Even if they claimed to be trying to change things, they were still complacent in the end.

"As for you, Corbin, welcome back," Kyra said. "Thank you for keeping so many secrets."

He smiled, bowing his head. "Of course, my Lady. Although I discovered you were keeping secrets of your own."

She nodded, her face falling a little. "Out of necessity, but it is not something I am proud of." Corbin's mouth pressed into a thin line. "Who is with you?"

"Lange Castellon," he answered, nodding to the male two chairs down. "And Priya Perin," he added. The child shrank back in her chair where she was seated between the two males.

"It is lovely to meet you, Priya," Kyra said. "Do you have enough to eat?"

She nodded, her turquoise eyes harsh for a child so young. Axel couldn't say he was surprised by that either. She was right to be distrusting after what she'd just endured, but true to their word, Corbin and Lange hadn't left her behind once. One of them was always with her. Axel had no doubt they'd earn her trust, just like they'd somehow earned Eviana's.

"And next to Xan is Akira," Theon finished. "Tessa's mother."

"You are also not of Devram," Kyra mused.

"I am from what should not be," Akira said simply, digging into her meal.

An awkward silence filled the air until Lady Kyra picked up her fork as she announced, "Well, now that introductions are out of the way, let's eat. After you have been shown your rooms for your stay, we will take you to areas of our kingdom I trust you will find interesting."

They dug into their meals, small talk taking place among them, and it was about halfway through when Tessa turned to the Anala Lady and said, "May I ask you a question?"

Kyra smiled, setting down her silverware and wiping her fingers. "Of course, my Lady."

All the chatter had died down, and Tessa picked up her wineglass. "Why is it that all the fire Fae stay in the Anala Kingdom?" She glanced at Kat. "Or most of them."

Kyra hummed. "Yes, there are very few exceptions. She was one of them, although not by my choice. I did not learn of it until you were already gone from our borders, Katya."

"I didn't mind the Falein Estate," she said. Then she added, "For the most part."

Didn't mind, my ass, Axel thought to himself, and he must have made some kind of sound because Kat reached over and rested her hand on his thigh, squeezing softly. He was fairly certain if she'd been raised here, she wouldn't have been forced to *service* any scholars.

Kyra cleared her throat, gaze darting away from Axel. "There have been Accords since Devram was created that the fire Fae would serve Anala Kingdom. Anala herself demanded it before agreeing to bring her Legacy here."

"But why?" Tessa pushed. "None of the others made such demands. Silas. Sefarina. Anahita."

"None of them were a First," Kyra said. "They were not in a position to make such demands."

"Not in a position? They are gods."

"Yes, but they are Lessers. Everything in Devram mirrors other worlds in one way or another."

"Like the Source Marks?" Tessa asked with far too much sweetness. Theon and Luka took note too, both of them stiffening at her tone.

Kyra looked more and more uncomfortable as this conversation went on, and Axel was rather impressed. For someone who didn't want to be the most powerful in the room, Tessa was handling it with far more grace than any of them would have.

"Yes," Kyra agreed. "Like the Source Marks."

"That mirror something else."

Kyra shifted in her chair. "I won't deny that there is corruption in the realm, Lady Tessa."

"Do you deny your participation in it? Do you deny going along with it to maintain your seat of power? Of forcing the Fae Anala felt the need to protect to still serve at your feet?" Tessa pressed, lightning flickering in her eyes. Her gaze flicked to Kyra's Source, then to Gatlan. "Forcing Fae to endure such Marks?"

"We do not treat them beneath us here," Kyra tried, lifting her chin.

"It doesn't matter if you do so outside your own borders. You simply prioritize those you deem more valuable," Tessa spat bitterly.

"Tessa," Theon murmured, reaching to take her hand.

"No, Theon," Kyra said, holding up her hand. "If we are to be allies, we need to be able to speak freely."

"You know of twin flames?" Tessa asked, tapping her wineglass with her nail. "You know they're incorporated into the Source Marks?"

Kyra cleared her throat. "Yes, I did know. That was happening long before I acquired my seat."

"And you didn't think to do anything about it?"

"We have all made mistakes. We all have regrets. I think you've learned that well over these last months," Kyra replied. Tessa's eyes narrowed, but she went on. "Changing how things have been done for centuries is not an easy task, my Lady, especially when the majority of those in power do not want change. When they are vehemently against it. Instead, it must be accomplished by making smaller changes. Letting them build into something bigger. Over and over again, even when it doesn't feel like a difference is being made in the end.

"It is making a difference when no one will likely know but the person who receives the gift. It is keeping as many as you can safe and mourning those you lose. It is welcoming those who manage to escape and giving them refuge. It is watching and observing those who show the slightest bit of sympathy because maybe, just maybe, they will end up joining the cause. It is working endlessly for something you may never see come to fruition in your lifetime."

Her voice cracked as she continued. "It is hoping, when all feels lost, that a young heir who Selected someone who could be this world's salvation or destruction will let her be who she was always meant to be. It is hoping she will choose this world too, despite how it broke her and used her and does not deserve her. It is hoping, even when it seems pointless, because hope sees the invisible. What is possible. What hides in the dark, hope drags to the light. Hope is never truly lost as long as one person still dares to dream of something better."

Axel was staring at the Anala Lady. Everyone was. The room had gone silent and still. Something reverent hung in the air.

"I once thought hope was pointless," Tessa said softly.

"What changed your mind?" Kyra asked.

"A friend gave me music," she answered, her eyes finding Axel. "When my world was breaking, he cared enough to give me something to drown in when there was nothing else."

Axel offered her a small smile, and she returned it, even if it was a little muted and sad.

"But I can agree we wish for the same thing, Lady Kyra," Tessa said, picking up her fork once more.

Kyra smiled, doing the same. "Then it will be my pleasure to show you what we've built here."

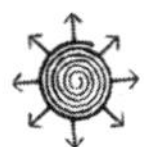

After they were shown their rooms, they were led to a building on the other side of Idalia, and Axel was shocked to find it was another portal station. Portals that anyone could use—Legacy, Fae, mortal. It didn't matter.

The first portaled them to the other side of Sulien Forest, on the east side of the Terrarun River. If he was shocked about the portal station, he was amazed at what they found.

An entire city of Fae.

It spanned for miles and was larger than Idalia.

All of them were Fae that had sought safety from the other kingdoms. Mothers who wanted to save their children. Lovers who were desperate to stay together. Those who had dared to defy the Legacy and were facing the Underground or death. All the Fae from the Sirana Villas, the Celeste Estate, and the Pantheon.

Thousands of them were housed here, and they were clearly running short on space.

"We cannot risk going too far south," Tana, the Anala Heir, was explaining as they walked through the streets. "The cities there are mainly Legacy, but the Fae that are there are employed and paid fairly. Nothing is forced."

"And this city is guarded," Gatlan, her Source, added. "Hundreds of members of our forces are trained outside the city. It is part of their duties to serve on rotation here, as well as the other cities."

Axel had been watching the male and Corbin. They had apparently been friends during their formative years at the Anala Estate. It was yet another reminder of how much the Fae were forced to sacrifice for the kingdoms. Friends. Relationships. Hopes and dreams.

It had him slipping his arm around Kat's waist and tugging her into his side while he held Maddox on his shoulder, the babe sleeping soundly and warmed by his mother's magic.

Tessa had asked to visit a school in the city, and they had opted to stay outside. In a rare moment alone with the Anala Lady, Axel asked, "Lady Kyra?"

She turned to him with a smile, waiting for his question.

"You called Kat a 'lost fire Fae,'" he ventured. "But with all these security measures . . ."

"How did it happen?" she finished when he trailed off. Axel nodded, and Kyra sighed. "We have people on the inside in nearly every kingdom. As you can imagine, it is a dangerous thing to ask of someone, and they risk everything by doing so. But when passion and hope win out, the risks don't seem to matter."

Maddox started fussing, and Kat reached to take him, snuggling him close. Her head was down, focused on their son, but Axel knew her well enough to know she was trying to process whatever Kyra was about to tell them.

"A little over two decades ago, one of our greatest assets found their way to us. He was deep in the Achaz Kingdom and could sense power," Kyra continued, and Kat's head snapped up.

"You speak of Brecken," Kat said, eyes wide.

"I do," Kyra agreed with a sad smile. "He did much for the Fae in Devram. So much more than anyone realizes. But all those noble actions still came with costs, and you were one. I did not know what he'd done until it was over. I was furious, but he swore he'd make it right."

"Brecken is the reason Kat was outside the Anala Kingdom?" Axel asked, not following where this was going.

"He was," Kyra answered. "Brecken had come across a desperate mother. A Shifter who'd had a child with a Fae. She was being held at the Sirana Villas, and she begged Brecken to take the child and hide him. Refused to be told where so she couldn't be forced to betray the secret."

"Corbin," Axel said, the pieces slowly coming together.

Kyra nodded. "Our alliance was still new and tentative. He didn't fully trust me yet, which was fair. We keep strict records of all our Fae, and we knew exactly how many children were at the Estate. He swapped the child out." Another sad smile at Kat. "He took you to the Falein Estate. As I said, I was furious. He wouldn't tell me where you were, but he swore an oath to watch over you and keep you safe. He checked on you often."

"And when my Selection year was getting close, he took me to Tessa," Kat whispered.

"I do not know those details," Kyra said. "I was to claim you that night under the Accords the moment your fire magic showed itself, but . . ."

"I claimed her for Arius first," Axel finished. "You were irate."

She nodded. "So was Brecken, but it appears to have worked out in the end. Fate can be funny like that."

"Don't let Tessa hear you discuss the Fates," Axel snickered.

Kyra hummed. "Yes, the Fates have not been particularly kind to her." A few seconds passed before she said, "Before the others return, there are two people here I think you will find of interest. One you may not wish to speak to. The other, I think you would like to meet."

His stomach dropped.

His mother and his sister.

"I . . ." He pushed out a harsh breath, shoving his hand through his hair. "Cressida," he finally said. "I do wish to speak to her." He glanced at Katya. "Alone."

"I can arrange that," Kyra said.

So while everyone else continued to tour the kingdom, Axel went with Kyra's Source to a small town on the other side of the Terrarun River at the base of the Raghnall Mountains. Just inside Sulien Forest, it was built into the side of a mountain. The kingdom's own mini Underground it seemed. Then again, it wasn't quite a prison. There were not bars, but semi-comfortable rooms that they weren't allowed to leave.

"Just knock when you're done," he said, and Axel nodded as he was let into a room.

It was sparse. A small sitting room with a table for two, a sofa, a small desk, and a bookshelf. A doorway led to what he assumed was a small bedroom and bathroom. Cressida had clearly heard the door, because she emerged from that room a moment later, then froze when she saw who stood in her space.

"Axel?" she gasped, rushing to him and throwing her arms around his neck. "Thank Arius you've come for me."

He was stiff as he reached for her arms and pulled her off him, gently shoving her back a few steps. His lips curled back as he said, "I didn't come for you. I only came to say goodbye."

Because at the end of the day, she *was* still his mother.

"Say goodbye?" she cried. "What do you mean?"

"You kept things from Theon. From me. You betrayed Arius Kingdom and tried to have Tessa killed," Axel said coldly.

"I was forced to keep those secrets," she argued. "And betraying Arius Kingdom? I was betraying your father, not the kingdom. Do you know what he did to me?"

"I do," he answered. "I'm sorry you had to endure that."

"You're sorry?" she repeated, her features turning cold and angry. "As if that changes anything."

"It doesn't. I know that."

"I suppose I should be grateful. After all, I got *you* in the end, right?"

"I could never replace another child," he replied.

"That's not what your father said," she sneered. "A male. A spare heir. I should be honored to provide such a thing after giving him such a *disappointment* the first time."

"But you never really loved me, did you?" he asked.

She lifted her chin. "I did what I could."

"You tolerated me. Used me as a weapon against Valter and Theon. Favored me out of spite," Axel continued, slipping his hands into his pockets. "Tell me I'm wrong."

She was quiet, and when that silence stretched on for nearly two minutes, when she refused to look at him, he knew he was right.

"I have a son," he said, and her head snapped up, emerald eyes wide.

"What?" she gasped. "I have a grandson?"

"One that you will never lay eyes on," he replied. "Because you will remain here. For the rest of your days."

"I am your mother," she cried, lurching forward and clutching at his arm. "You can't leave me here!"

"My mother was kept locked in the Underground for nearly a decade," Axel snarled, once again removing her hands from his body. "She has held my son. She has rocked him to sleep. She is the only reason you are not in the After."

"You cannot leave me here!" Cressida cried again as Axel turned away.

He knocked twice, the door opening a moment later, and as he stepped through the door, he looked over his shoulder one last time. "Goodbye, Cressida."

He could still hear her furious cries echoing while Kyra's Source led him back out of the small incarceration unit, and when they stepped out in the daylight once more, he reached for his hood again.

"Dey? I didn't know you were going to be here," the Fae male said, and Axel turned to see who he was talking to.

Dark red hair was cut to her shoulders, bangs touching brows over emerald green eyes. In fitted pants and a shirt, she had daggers strapped to her thighs. She'd clearly been trained to fight. Her eyes were narrowed, studying him, and he didn't need the shadows drifting around her to know who she was. Knew she was five years older than he was, weeks younger than Theon.

Shoving his hands in his pockets, he stayed put, waiting for her to make the first move.

She stepped up on the first stair, stilling once more. "You're her son?" she asked.

"She birthed me," he replied. "But I don't claim her as my mother."

The female didn't respond. Only studied him more, and he didn't care. He'd long since stopped caring what other people thought of him. He had a family he'd kill for, and an Underground full of people in his care. If his sister decided she wanted nothing to do with him, it'd hurt, but he'd move on. He'd understand.

"Aiyana told me of you," she finally said, moving up another step.

"I've been told of you as well," he replied. "But I'm guessing you've known of me far longer than I've known of you."

"Probably," she answered, venturing another stair closer. "You were speaking to her?"

"For the last time," he said, watching the mist of shadows trail her. "Have you met her?"

She nodded. "Once."

"And?"

Her lips thinned. "She took one look at my shadows and cried. Sobbed about what her life should have been to have produced an Arius heir."

"*Her* life?" Axel questioned.

"You heard me."

He huffed a laugh of disbelief. "Yeah, that tracks for her." He tipped his head, studying her. "And now?"

She was still four steps down from him, spine ridged. "Aiyana will return to her sons, and I . . ." She shrugged.

Axel took a step down this time. "What do you *want* to do? Stay here?"

Her hands clenched at her sides, and he knew what she was going to say before she said the words.

"I've been forced to stay hidden here," she replied.

"Valter is dead. No longer the Arius Lord," Axel said. "Would you like to see the rest of the realm?"

Her shadows thickened, caressing her in a way they used to do to him. "Your brother won't consider me a threat?"

"He's not the ruler, and even if he was, no. He wouldn't, and he wouldn't be a threat to you."

"I've heard . . . things. About him. And you," she ventured, her nerves finally flickering in her eyes.

"Most are true," he conceded. "But much has changed too."

She remained quiet, features hard.

"Think about it?" he said, jogging past her down the stairs. "I have to get back to my wife and son, but when you're ready, we'll be waiting."

"You have a wife and son?" she called after him.

He paused, turning to walk backwards down the street. "I do."

"What are their names?"

"Kat and Maddox. What's yours?" he tossed back.

It was small, but her lips curved up at the corners. "Kasdeya, but everyone calls me Dey."

"Let me know when you're ready," he repeated. "Mads will need someone to teach him to wield his shadows when the time comes."

"Me?" she asked, her brows flying up.

He shrugged. "Who better than family?"

Her power writhed beside her until a panther of shadows took shape. He grinned, and she smirked back. And in that moment, he knew they'd see her again.

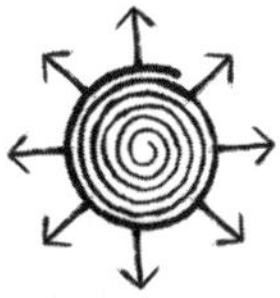

51
LUKA

It was late afternoon when they walked along the streets of Idalia, back from their trip to other areas of the kingdom. Along with the Fae city to the west, they'd been taken to the Anala Estate. Axel had gone to see Cressida while the rest of them had gone to a city farther south. They were headed to their rooms to relax and get ready for the dinner they'd be having later this evening with Kyra and her family.

His father was anxious where he strolled at his side, while Razik hung back several paces behind them with Eliza. All three of them were lost in their feelings as they waited for the same person to appear.

"Are you warm enough, Tessa?" Luka asked.

"Mhmm," Tessa hummed from his right, lifting a hand and letting her power drift along her fingers. The bands of light on her arms glowed brighter too, and she sighed. "It's beautiful here."

And it was. It wasn't the sleek and modern buildings of the Arius Kingdom or the opulent marble architecture of the Achaz Kingdom. The Anala Kingdom was grand brick structures with a simple and practical elegance. Lamp posts lined the streets, burning even in the daylight, and he was certain that even in the winter months, the chill was never truly felt here.

Theon was a few steps ahead with Axel and Kat, listening as Axel filled him in on his visit to Cressida and meeting Kasdeya, but he'd glanced back at Luka's question. Tessa had lost her gloves and coat, Theon carrying them now. She was left in a long-sleeve dress that matched the color of her eyes. She'd lost her shoes at some point too, those now dangling from Theon's fingers.

The sun was out and shining, and Kyra had commented more than once about how unusually warm it was today. Luka was pretty sure it had to do with the mother and daughter in their company.

Akira had stayed close to Xan's side, but since her arrival, Tessa had made an effort. He'd seen it. Theon watched it. They'd both monitored it down the bond. Tessa was still hesitant, keeping her distance, but there was a relief there too as they watched Akira struggle with her magic and fury.

"Will you stay here, Xan?" Tessa asked suddenly.

Luka went rigid, and Xan nearly stumbled at the question.

"What?" Xan asked.

"When this is over, if we all survive, will you stay in Devram?" Tessa clarified, her chaos now twisting in her palm.

"I . . ." He glanced at Luka sidelong before looking away once more. "I can't answer that. To have children in different worlds and a Ward in yet another, not to mention a home world that will someday be reborn, I don't know."

"What do you mean a home world that will someday be reborn?" Luka asked in confusion as they approached the building they were staying in.

But Xan didn't answer him, and it took Luka a second to realize why.

Why the male was shoving past them. Past Theon and the others ahead of them. Why his strides were long and purposeful. Why he was moving like a dragon locked in on his prey.

Because that was a female doing the same. Her brown hair was pulled back and tied up, and she was tall. Creamy skin a few shades lighter than Luka's own slightly tanned complexion. She was toned, carrying herself with the grace of a trained warrior in fitted black pants, shirt, and boots, with only a single dagger strapped to her thigh.

Neither his father nor the female spoke. Xan only grabbed her face in his hands and brought his mouth to hers.

When he finally pulled back, his brow pressed to hers, and Luka could hear him murmuring. He didn't understand what was being said though. The words were in a different language, but whatever he was saying had her turning to look in their direction. Her eyes moved from him, then past him and back again, and Luka watched as tears filled her eyes.

She said something else in that same language, and Xan nodded.

"She asked him if he brought both her sons to her," Akira said simply.

Tessa peered around him. "You know what they are saying?"

Her lips pursed. "I am fluent in many languages of the stars. Achaz made sure of that."

His parents were walking towards them. Both of them. And gods, the moment was surreal. Only months ago, he'd thought them gone. Nearly a year ago he thought he was the only one left of his kind, and now he was watching a resurrection of dreams that had died long ago.

They came to a stop in front of him, Xan's hand on her lower back. "This is—" he started, but she interrupted him.

"I know who this is," she said, her eyes drinking him in. "I've had to watch you grow up from afar, unable to be there when you needed me most. For that, I am so incredibly sorry, Luka, but I am so proud of who you've grown to be."

She was moving forward then, wrapping her arms around him, and Luka clutched her back. An embrace he hadn't felt in twenty-five years. An embrace he'd forgotten despite trying to cling to the memory of it.

"I am sorry for the life you were forced to endure alone," she whispered, her tears seeping into his shirt.

Luka hugged her tighter. "I wasn't alone. I had brothers. We survived together."

She nodded, but Luka knew it wouldn't be enough to assuage her guilt. Nothing ever would.

She stepped back, holding his shoulders. "We have much to talk about, but I need to—"

"I know," he said, leaning in to press a kiss to her cheek before he stepped aside.

Tessa was there, looping her arm around his and leaning her head on his biceps. *Are you okay?* she sent down the bond.

Yeah, baby girl. I'm okay.

His mother had sucked in a sharp breath as she stared across the few feet separating her from her other son. It may as well have been a chasm for the way Razik was staring back at her. The same hard apathy in his eyes that was always there.

Then she moved, not seeming to care that he was rigid and giving every signal to stay the fuck back. She wrapped her arms around him, and Razik didn't return the embrace. The male hadn't seen her in centuries, and he couldn't even return a hug?

Their mother didn't seem to care though. She stepped back, holding his broad shoulders the same way she'd done to Luka. Her gaze raked over him, taking him in.

"And for you, I missed everything. I couldn't even watch from afar. I could tell you I fought for you. I could tell you I thought of you every single day. I could tell you any manner of things, but none of it will matter or make up for the memories stolen from us. For that, I am so incredibly sorry, Razik," she said, her words clear and steady. "Someday, I wish to know who you have grown to be, but I understand today is not that day."

Eliza reached over, intertwining her fingers with Razik's. Luka could only assume she was speaking down their bond. Their mother must have assumed the same thing, and she took a small step back as she said, "I'm Aiyana."

"Eliza," the Fire General answered. She glanced up at Razik before looking back to Aiyana. "His—"

"*Mai dragocen*," Razik interjected. "That's who she is." Aiyana nodded, and then her eyes went wide when Razik spoke in that same language she and Xan had spoken in.

Back and forth they went, and Tessa sighed beside him. *I wish I knew what they were saying,* she grumbled down the bond.

Luka huffed a laugh. *Why?*

Because I'm curious.

Theon barked a laugh, having come up beside her. *Maybe we should give them some time.* He glanced at Luka. *You could stay too. Tessa and I can go get ready for dinner.*

But as much as Luka wanted to spend that time with his mother, this dinner was important. They would be telling Kyra of Dagian's offer and requesting her permission to bring Dagian here for Akira to perform the transfer. They were in for a long night of discussion, and he could find time to spend with his mother later.

"Stay, Luka," Tessa murmured, pushing up onto her toes and pulling him closer so she could press her lips to his jaw. "Theon and I are fine. Take your time."

Take your time.

Everyone kept acting like they had all the time in the world, but he was staring at his mother. His brother. His father. A family who had lost all that time and maybe would never see it again if they couldn't find a way to mend all this.

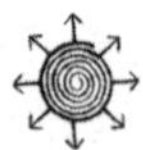

"All the Ladies?" Tessa cried, the door not even fully closed to their room when they returned from a very long dinner.

The sun had set long ago, and Luka had felt Tessa's emotions rising all evening. She'd done well though. Keeping her poise and control. They'd expected the pushback and debate. Kyra had eventually relented to allowing Dagian to come to Idalia. However, they hadn't anticipated Kyra informing them that not only would Dagian be here in the morning, but so would the other Ladies. She would send them word tonight.

"It's not all that surprising," Theon said calmly, removing his suit jacket and loosening his tie.

"And what are we going to do if they oppose this? We don't have days and days to debate this, Theon."

She was already pacing.

"It doesn't really matter if they oppose it," Theon said. "It is Dagian's choice. Not theirs."

"It *is* theirs," she retorted. "We can't simply go against the wishes of the kingdoms. We're trying to *change* one or two people getting their way. Not just . . . do what we want."

"Tessa," Theon cut in. "We are doing this tomorrow. You're right. When things are different, more opinions will be taken into account. But not with this and certainly not with the same four Ladies who have had every opportunity to push for change for decades and have done nothing but preserve their own seats of power. *They* will not alter a godsdamn thing."

"This is . . . What if something goes wrong?" she demanded, having moved to the wall, dragging her fingers along it.

"That is always a possibility," Luka replied, watching her power crackle around her with each step. "We can try to anticipate problems and prepare for them as best we can, but eventually, we just have to jump, Tessa."

She didn't answer them, but she did speak, murmuring to herself. "This is it. Salvation or destruction? We don't know. We don't know. We don't know." She repeated the words over and over, each time sounding more and more agonized. Her fingers were in her hair, and she wasn't pacing anymore. She was turning in place. "A final stand. A final battle. Who will be left standing when Chaos comes to reign? Me? Them? We've seen the visions. Seen the dreams. They never change. No, they do, but never . . . Always destruction. Always—"

She sucked in a gasp, her eyes snapping up as Theon and Luka both sent waves of power to her. Calling to her chaos. Distracting her.

"This weight isn't on your shoulders alone, Tessa," Theon said gently.

"Isn't it?" she asked, desperation ringing in her voice. "Am I not everything that prophecy is? Salvation. Destruction. The realm depends on me, and I did not ask for this!"

"Maybe that is why it was given to you," Theon countered.

"I'm not the one for this!" she cried again. "Luka's been right all along. I'm not—"

"Enough," Luka barked. "Where is this coming from? You've been Traveling around Devram for months now. Destroying mirror gates. Standing up to Rordan. Helping innocent people. And now you question where your place is in this?"

"It's too much for one person!"

"Which is why you have us," Theon retorted. "It is why we are doing this. You are not facing this fate alone, Tessa."

"How is this any different from those who have taken power before us?"

"Because we fucking care," Theon snapped, and Luka could feel his frustration down the bond.

And so could she.

"You're the one who told me to process my feelings. You can't be upset with me for trying to do that," she bit out.

"I'm not upset you're processing your feelings," he ground out from between his teeth. "I'm frustrated because you aren't giving yourself enough credit. You still believe yourself the villain in all this."

Her lip curled back, and Luka was more than perplexed as to where this mood had come from. "This world turned me into one, Theon!"

Her cry of outrage echoed in the suite as Theon threw her over his shoulder. "Luka," he barked over his shoulder.

But Luka only snickered, strolling to the liquor cabinet and pouring three glasses of amber liquid, one slightly less full. He already knew where this was going. They'd been planning this for weeks. Well before her birthday, and Theon had apparently decided it was time.

Thank the gods.

Whether a distraction or to prove a point, Luka didn't really care. Sure, Theon was irritated, but this wasn't being done out of anger or a need for control. Quite the opposite actually.

Tessa needed someone else to take control right now. Take the weight of responsibility and madness from her. Make the decisions so she didn't have to think. She could just . . . be. Be wild and untamed. Be reckless and impulsive. Trusting they would be there to catch her and keep her safe while she was exactly as she was made to be.

The world didn't understand, but they did.

Theon already had her in a chair, his darkness around her wrists and ankles, keeping her in place. The fact she could get up if she wanted to told Luka just how right he was in his assessment. She always picked fights when she didn't know how to ask for what she wanted. Or if she thought they'd deny her.

As if they'd ever fucking deny her.

Make her say it. Make her crawl for it. Make her beg for it. But they'd never deny her.

Luka tipped his head, all predator now while Theon prowled over and took a glass of liquor.

"Look at you, temptress. Tied up and waiting . . . for what?" Luka mused, setting his glass aside but keeping the one that wasn't as full. She glared back at him. "Does she know what we're going to do tonight, Theon?"

"No," he ground out, unbuttoning his shirt. He didn't remove it though, leaving it hanging open. "Give me your tie. I left mine in the other room."

Luka tugged it loose, and then Theon was there, pulling it free. Luka followed him back to Tessa, where he placed the silk fabric over her eyes, tying it behind her head.

She gasped as she lost her vision. "What are you doing?"

"You want to think you're a villain?" Theon asked, his voice harsh. "That's fine for now, but you forget, beautiful."

"Forget what?" she snapped.

He leaned in close, his words a whisper in her ear. "We're your villains when you need us to be."

She went still, and Luka chuckled darkly. "Here, baby girl. You're going to need this tonight."

He brought the glass of liquor to her lips, tipping it up and pouring some into her mouth. She coughed and spluttered, and he chuckled again. "Trust us, Tessa. You're going to want this." He was leaning in now, his words dark as he asked into her ear, "Do you trust us?"

He heard her swallow. Saw her fingers clench around the arms of the chair. Felt her power crackle in nervous anticipation.

"Verbal acknowledgement, Tessa," Theon ordered, the sound of him removing his belt making her head snap in his direction.

"Yes," she bit out. "I trust you."

"Then drink up," Luka retorted, bringing the glass back to her lips. "We have plans for that mouth." She drank it down with ease this time, only a small drop escaping onto her lip. He slowly thumbed the drop, pushing it back into her mouth as he added, "We're taking control right now, but you know you can take it back at any time, right?"

He could swear she stopped breathing for a moment, but she slowly nodded and that nervousness down the bond was coupled with thinly veiled excitement.

"Good," Luka replied, his fingertips dragging along her jaw.

Then he stepped back and his dragonfire burned her dress away, leaving her naked and tied to a chair.

"I liked that dress," she said in outrage.

"You're the Arius Lady. Buy another one," Theon cut in, shucking off his shirt, then his pants. "The Arius Lady. Soon to be the Achaz Lady."

"Don't," she snapped.

"Yes, don't," Luka drawled. "The gods know we don't want someone who cares about *all* the inhabitants of a kingdom to have a say in policies going forward."

"That's not—"

"It is, Tessa," Theon interrupted. "You can say it's not what you want, but your actions show otherwise. Begging me to claim your friends. Destroying the Sirana Villas. Fighting for the Fae. Giving Eviana a chance to fight for her daughter. Destroying mirror gates to save this world. But . . ."

"But what?"

Then she was gasping again. Theon had silently moved to her side, completely naked now, as he poured a trickle of liquor down her chest.

"Luka?" Theon said, arching his brow.

Luka didn't care who was calling the shots right now. He bent over Tessa's bare body, his tongue lapping up the spilled alcohol off her breasts.

"*Oh,*" she breathed, already sliding her thighs farther apart. Not having her sight would be heightening every other sensation at the moment.

"But you're a villain, right?" Theon went on as if none of that had just happened. "So the plan must be to make them trust you, and then you'll leave them to their own fate. Right?"

"That's not—"

Then she was hissing as Theon poured more alcohol down her chest, and Luka was there, cleaning her up. His tongue slid along her flesh, circling her nipples, sucking them sharply.

"Luka," she gasped.

"Yes, please stop, Luka," Theon sneered. "She didn't ask for this."

"Theon, that's not . . . This isn't the same thing," she gritted out, jerking against the darkness keeping her in place.

"It should be," he snapped.

Her brow bunched in confusion. "What?"

"It should be exactly the same fucking thing," Theon snarled again, pouring more alcohol down her front. More than last time. Only this time, he kept talking while Luka dropped to his knees before her, catching the small stream that was making its way to her navel and licking up her torso.

"Here, when it's just the three of us, you trust us to be what you need. To *know* what you need. To be your balance." Theon gripped the back of the chair, leaning down and speaking harshly into her ear. His hand slid under her chin, tipping her head back. "Even out there, you trust us to pull you back if you sink too deeply into Chaos. But you can't trust us to be your balance in *this*? In something we have worked and prepared for nearly our entire lives?"

"To take over Arius Kingdom," she gasped. "Not . . ."

"Say it," Theon ordered. His hand slid from her jaw to her throat when she didn't answer right away. His fingers flexed, massaging her pulse point. "Say it, Tessa."

"They're going to think we're trying to take over everything. That we're no better than Rordan," she cried out. "And how are we any different? You are taking power from others. I am the very thing that has been prophesied to destroy the realm since its inception. The three of us? It's no secret we could bring this world to its knees and make them worship at our feet."

"Baby girl, you have proven time and again that is not your plan. Why would you bother with any of it if that's all you wanted?" Luka asked, his hands settling on her thighs as he watched her torment play out on her features.

His thumbs made small circles, distracting her as she shifted, trying to move them higher. Because when she was in this state, she lost control of her thoughts. Letting them out and saying things she'd never admit to anyone else.

"Because I could," she whispered. "Maybe not now, but the power . . . Maybe not now. Not tomorrow or next year. But some day . . . It wants that."

It.

Not *we*.

"We are yours," Theon said darkly, his hand sliding down to cup a breast. "Are you saying you are not ours?"

"No. That's not—"

"Because if you are ours, you will trust us to make sure that never happens. We are a balance, Tessa. We call each other out. We fight. We fuck. We drive each other mad. We talk. We love. We do this thing *together*."

"I understand," she whispered.

"That wasn't very convincing," Luka growled, his thumbs now massaging the creases of her thighs.

"Are you ours?" Theon demanded again.

"Yes."

"All of you? Every piece of you?"

"Yes," she ground out.

"Then that means we get your insecurities, Tessa," he retorted, his teeth nipping at her throat and making her hiss again.

"We get your fury," Luka said, his thumb swiping once through her center. Fucking Sargon, she was *wet.*

"We get your hate and your love. Your pain and your pleasure," Theon snarled against her skin. "No one else, and when you don't give them to us willingly . . ."

"We take them," Luka finished, pulling his hands away and smirking at her whimper from the loss.

The darkness was gone, and Luka scooped her up, his tie still in place as he laid her on the bed. Theon was immediately there, spreading her legs apart and sinking into her cunt with one thrust that had her moaning and him cursing.

Luka quickly stripped out of his own clothing and climbed onto the bed, stretching out beside her. He trailed his fingers down the same paths he'd licked alcohol from her skin.

"You know, temptress," he taunted. "You could just ask when you want to be fucked instead of throwing a fit."

Her head snapped towards him, and if that tie wasn't there, he knew she'd be glaring at him.

"Fuck you, Luka," she spat.

He laughed a dark thing. "You will be soon enough." He thumbed her mouth. "I'll start here and move lower." He captured her mouth with his lips, licking into it, and forcing her to taste him. Then he nipped at her lower lip, pulling back as he said, "And we're not taking turns tonight, baby girl."

"Wh-what?" she stuttered.

But Theon adjusted his position, lowering over her so their torsos pressed together. His arms slid beneath her, holding her close, and he fucked her with fast thrusts. Luka could tell by the way Tessa was squirming and panting that the position was working for her. Had no doubt Theon was hitting that perfect spot with every push into her until he was forcing her into pleasure.

Because it was all theirs.

Tessa was panting, but Theon pulled out, his cock still hard and pointing straight up. He nodded at Luka, but he was already ahead of him. With a burst of flame, he pulled a vial of oil from his magic.

"Theon?" she rasped, her breaths still shaky.

He was gripping her hips, rolling her to her stomach. "Do you trust us with your pleasure and your pain, Tessa? Your doubts and your needs?"

"Yes," she answered before Theon could demand a verbal answer.

Luka would have demanded it for this too.

Theon leaned over her, turning her head to face Luka as he murmured, "So Luka can use that mouth if he wants to?"

And yeah, he fucking wanted to.

Luka reached over, pulling the tie from her eyes and tipping her chin up. "You can take back control whenever you want," he reminded her. "But we're going to talk you through everything." He ran his thumb along her lip, his other hand reaching down and stroking his cock. He'd been hard since this all started. Since before his first lick of alcohol off her skin. "Trust us to be what you need."

She nodded once, and Luka glanced at Theon, who was already waiting. Luka could feel his impatience down the bond, and he narrowed his eyes because if he fucked this up for them by being too rough right away, she'd never let them do this again.

And he wanted his turn when they did this again.

"Remember to breathe, baby girl," Luka said, bringing his cock to her lips and pushing into her hot mouth. "Fuck," he growled as Tessa whimpered around him, the vibrations of the sound going straight to his balls as Theon slid an oil covered finger into her tight hole. Pressing and readying her. When he added a second finger, she moaned louder, and Luka sank a hand into her hair, fisting as he thrust in and out of her mouth. "You say I have a dirty mouth, but look at you, baby girl. All but begging for him to fuck your ass."

She pulled off him, her eyes wide as she stared up. "By the gods, Luka," she murmured.

He only smirked, leaning down to press a kiss to her swollen lips. "We love you," he said into her mouth. "Let us worship you."

Her throat bobbed in a swallow. In anxiety or anticipation, he wasn't sure. Probably both.

"Remember to breathe, baby girl," he said again, his voice low and dark. "Breathe. It's going to be—It's going to hurt at first. Trust us. Can you do that for us?"

She nodded, lurching forward to take his mouth this time, and he held her there as Theon positioned his cock.

Go slow, Theon, Luka warned down the bond.

I know, he gritted back.

"Have you . . . done this with someone else?" Tessa gasped, and there was no doubt Theon had pressed into her a little because she jerked back. Her fingers were curling into the bedding, and she had her eyes squeezed shut tight.

"Hey, hey," Luka said, turning her face back to him. "None of that. You keep your eyes right here, and remember you can take back control anytime. Your power can throw us across the godsdamn room if you want to stop this."

Her violet eyes were bright with lust and fear as she held his stare, nodding her head.

"And no," Luka answered, stroking her hair, down her back, her arm. "We've shared a female before, but never like this."

Something akin to satisfaction flitted across her features, a determination that hadn't been there before.

Because she was more possessive than they were.

She gasped again, her body tensing, and Luka gripped her nape, massaging the tendons. "You have to relax, baby girl."

"How would you know?" she bit out. "Have you been fucked up the ass, Luka Mors?"

He barked at her snark. "No, temptress, but I've done my fair share of the fucking part. If you can still use that bratty mouth to spout off, we're not doing enough."

Luka readjusted, stretching out beside her once more so he could reach beneath her. Licking his fingers, he pressed them to her center, finding her clit and rubbing in slow, taunting circles. She sucked in a breath, and at the same time, Theon pressed in farther.

"Fuck," she spat, her brow dropping to the bed. "Fuck, Luka. Theon."

"By Arius, it's so good," Theon panted, his self-control on a tight leash.

"You're doing so good, Tessa. Do you hear him right now? Look at the control you have over the Arius Lord," Luka praised, his fingers moving faster, her hips seeking pleasure as the pain chased her.

She cried out when Theon pushed in more, and his fingers dug into her hips. "Keep breathing, beautiful," he gritted out. "I'm almost there. Keep distracting her, Luka."

"I have this handled," he retorted. "You keep yourself under control. How does it feel?"

"So fucking tight," Theon gritted out, and Luka watched as he sank in all the way. Tessa was tense, her knuckles white.

"Breathe, baby girl," Luka pressed, leaning in to nip at her jaw, her shoulder, her arm. Anything to distract her as she adjusted to the new sensations. He knew she was getting there when her hips started moving against his hand, his fingers still massaging her clit.

He glanced at Theon and gave a slight nod, and he pulled back a little before pushing back in.

And she moaned.

Something sinful and dark and needy.

"There you go, baby girl," Luka praised, his fingers moving faster. "How are you feeling?"

"It's . . . *gods*," she rasped when Theon pulled back and thrust in again. "Yes," she moaned.

They gave her a moment, let her adjust and get comfortable with this, and then Luka murmured, "We're not done with you."

"That's . . . a lot," she rasped out as Theon kept moving.

"You can take it. You will," he replied, leaning in to press another hard kiss to her lips.

Then he was helping her onto her hands and knees so Theon could change positions and turn onto his back, never pulling out of her. She gasped, her hands grasping for purchase as Theon pressed his mouth to her neck, sucking and biting.

And Luka sat back, looking at them splayed out obscenely before him. Her back to Theon's chest. Her head settled on his shoulder, and his feet pushed her legs wider so Luka could see everything.

"I remember how your eyes lit up at the idea of both of us taking you at once, beautiful," Theon whispered darkly into her ear. "You already love me buried deep. You're going to love feeling both of us at once."

His hand splayed across her stomach, pushing down and forcing her pelvis to tip down too. Her head dropped back, and Luka had his hand on his dick, stroking as he watched them. He'd never minded watching, but not tonight.

He scooted forward, kneeling between their knees and running his fingers along her swollen center. "Whose are you, Tessa?" he demanded darkly.

"Yours," she gasped, Theon laving at her neck.

"How much of you?"

"All of me. I trust you," she rasped out in a harsh breath. "Just . . . *please.*"

"Deep breath, Tessa," Theon coaxed as Luka pressed forward. "You think it's tight now, just wait."

"Oh, gods," she cried out as Luka pressed into her cunt, forcing himself to go slow. His self-restraint was as taut as Theon's was now. They'd never done this before. Not at the same time, and holy fucking fuck, he was not prepared for how fucking *good* this was going to be.

He could see perspiration on her brow and glistening on her chest as he forced himself in a little more. Could feel Theon's cock separated from his by only a thin barrier. Could feel her muscles spasming against the intrusions. Could feel every fucking thing.

Theon was murmuring dirty praises into her ear, and she was slapping her hands on the sheets, him, clawing at skin as she tried to find something to sink her nails into.

"So good to us, Tessa," Theon was saying. "We don't deserve you, you know that, right? But we need you. We're yours. This is how it's meant to be. The three of us with everything."

She was nodding her head frantically, but her power never appeared. Never once did she ask to stop. Never once did she push them away.

"You're going to take it all, aren't you, temptress?" Luka grunted out, and then he thrust in the rest of the way, and all three of them stilled. There was nothing but their harsh breaths, chests rising and falling without any rhythm. Theon and Luka locked eyes because holy fuck. They'd planned this. Talked about what it might be like to have her like this between the two of them, but it didn't compare to any of their dirty fantasies. Didn't even come close.

"Are you ready, Tessa?" Theon asked, reaching up and smoothing hair off her brow.

And despite everything they were doing to her right now, something in her eyes softened at his touch. At his concern. She reached up, sliding her hand behind his neck and stretched out her other arm for Luka. He dropped his head down, letting her pull him to her mouth for a kiss, and he gave an experimental thrust of his hips.

She moaned into his mouth, spurring him on. His thrusts grew harder, her head turning from his mouth to Theon's and back again. And *this* was how it was always meant to be. Something primal and dark. Something fierce and sacred. Something solely theirs. Something that they somehow found despite everything being stacked against them.

Tessa was thrashing, and Theon was holding her tightly to him, letting Luka have his way.

"Give it to him, Tessa," Theon ordered. "It's ours."

She shook her head, nails digging into his arms. Theon chuckled darkly against her skin. "Oh, little storm. Then we'll take it."

One of his hands slid down to her stomach, pressing down, and Luka felt her clench around him.

"There it is, baby girl," Luka grunted, his hair in his eyes and matted to his brow. "Just like that."

She whimpered, and Theon's fingers flexed, pressing down more. And fuck, every time he did that, she tightened more and more. "If you won't give it to us, we'll take it," he repeated in a harsh pant. "But that's what you want, isn't it? Force us to push you and push you until you can't take it anymore."

"Yes," she gasped. "Yes, *please*."

Theon's hold on her tightened, and Luka snapped his hips forward, his cock dragging deep and fast against her until she was clamping down around him, a cry leaving her lips. He couldn't have stopped himself if he tried. He followed her into pleasure, his muscles contracting just as hard as he spilled into her.

"Fuck, Tessa," he spat, his hips still moving through his release because she was still spasming around him. Her climax rolled on, dragging him deeper, until finally he pulled out and fell onto his back.

Theon was already moving, and Luka had to give him credit for his self-control during all that. But he was clearly done waiting as he rolled Tessa onto Luka. He propped her up and gripped her hips, driving in and out of her other hole while she clung to Luka, a dazed and satisfied look on her face while Theon took his own pleasure.

No.

As Tessa gave herself to him to give him pleasure.

Her choice after everything.

And after Theon found release and they cleaned her up in the shower, after they were all wrapped up in one another back under the blankets, only then did Theon press a kiss to her forehead as he murmured, "You're not a villain, Tessa. We won't let you become one."

Her back was pressed to Luka's front, and he could hear the tears in her voice when she whispered, "I'm scared, Theon. What if we fail?"

Theon's smile was soft as he stroked her cheek. "Failure has never been an option, Tessa. If it comes down to it, we'll be the villains so you don't have to. But never you."

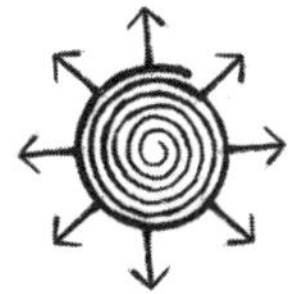

52
THEON

The conference room was silent when Theon finished explaining what they planned to do by transferring Dagian's power to him. The Ladies stared back, seemingly at a loss for words, and the tension in the air was so thick, it was oppressive. Luka was rigid on Tessa's other side, and Tessa appeared almost . . . bored. A far cry from what she'd been last night. He knew she wasn't bored. She was waiting to see which argument they were going to face first. Just like he was. But he'd meant what he'd said. This was happening whether or not the Ladies agreed to it. Mainly because Dagian was not only offering but insistent. The male hadn't been the same since Sasha's death.

He wasn't surprised that the Falein Lady spoke first, nor was he surprised by her question.

"I need to clarify what you are requesting," Lady Farhan said, her palms flat on the table.

"Not requesting," Theon corrected. "Simply informing you of what's to come."

Her eyes narrowed, her words terse as she said, "You want us to approve of you taking power from the Achaz Heir?"

"That he is willingly giving," Theon amended.

"That is not the point," the Celeste Lady interjected. "The point is you will be more powerful than any of us."

"But not more powerful than Tessa," he said with a shrug. "She will still be the Arius Lady."

"Whom you are married to," she retorted. "You have already deceived us once. We will not stand for this."

"If she is the Arius Lady, why are you speaking for her?" Lady Farhan asked.

"He is not speaking for me," Tessa cut in. "He tends to be far less . . . dramatic than I am." Her point was accentuated as she drummed her fingers on the table, a single flicker of lightning appearing and bouncing along the table. "But if you'd rather deal with me, then so be it."

All the Ladies, save for Kyra, sat up straighter. "You have two husbands," the Celeste blurted.

"Yes, yes," Tessa muttered, waving her hand dismissively. "That's already been established and not why we are here today. I do not have time for such trivial matters."

"Trivial matters? What is stopping us from taking second Matches?" Lady Candra scoffed.

Tessa widened her eyes. "Nothing. Take another husband. Take a wife. Take five. As long as they are not forced, I don't care."

Now they were blinking back at her, clearly uncertain what to do or say.

"That is not how things are done," Lady Farhan finally said.

Tessa paused the drumming of her fingers. "Forgive me for not really caring how things are done when, for most of my life, I was forced to bow, and for the last year, everyone has been trying to use me and decide my destiny for me."

"I still don't understand why all these other people are here," the Serafina Lady interjected, although her voice was monotone. As if even *she* didn't wish to be here.

"They are my . . . advisors," Tessa said, settling on a word.

"No one needs that many advisors," the Celeste Lady argued. "Fae? Sargon Legacy? A vampyre? We do not even know them all."

"Perhaps if you had more, and they were more diverse, we wouldn't be facing our current reality," Tessa replied, her hand leaving the table and moving to her hair. But Luka caught it, guiding her fingers to rest on his thigh.

"We need to stay focused on the subject of this meeting," Theon interjected.

"The answer is no," the Celeste Lady said. She turned to the Anala Lady. "I cannot believe you summoned us here for this."

"I thought we should hear them out," Kyra mused, settling back in her chair and taking everything in.

"This is utter nonsense. It will change everything."

"That is the entire point," Tessa drawled, and Theon had to work to hide his smirk. Gone were the insecurities and nerves of last night. He'd like to say they fucked it out of her, but her trepidation was still there. He could feel it lingering beneath other emotions, but he was so godsdamn proud of her in this moment.

"Theon is right," she continued. "This is a courtesy to you all. We are not asking permission. Arrangements have already been made, and this is Dagian's request."

The Serafina Lady turned to the Achaz Heir. Dagian was seated down the table, quiet and haunted. "Is this true, Dagian?"

He nodded, looking them each in the eye. "I came to Theon weeks ago and asked for this."

"Weeks ago?" the Falein Lady questioned. "Why not come to us?"

"Why not come to you?" he repeated derisively. "You, who have served with my father for decades? You, who work to uphold the ludicrous traditions of this realm? You, who twist and scheme and plot with the rest of them? No, Lady Farhan, I would not bring these concerns to any of you only to have one of you whisper them to my father. Your own heirs aren't even in this room to discuss matters that will affect them when they take their seats. I went to the kingdom who loathed him. I went to the one who has the means to end him. I went to the ones who could make a difference, not the ones content to watch the world crumble as long as their thrones remained intact."

"You understand you will no longer be able to hold your seat?" the Serafina Lady asked. "Once your father is dealt with, you will not be the Achaz Lord?"

Dagian's lips tilted in a sardonic smile. "I am not the most powerful Achaz blood at this table, Lady Isleen."

All eyes slid back to Tessa.

After several seconds of tense silence, the Celeste Lady said, "Fine. We transfer power, but we should decide together who will take it."

"No," Dagian said firmly. "It is my power. I will only transfer it to Theon. If anyone else tries, I rescind the offer, and you can face my father as you are."

"He cannot be stronger than all of us together. Not if Tessa is fighting on our side," Lady Farhan argued.

"It will take all of Tessa's power to defeat Rordan, and even then, she could be weakened to the point of being overpowered by the seraphs that serve Achaz," Luka said. "That is not an option on the table."

"It's more than Rordan," Theon added. "Tessa is . . . not a Legacy. She's not a god. She's . . . more. She's something more, and while we've been trying to figure it out, others have been looking for her. Others who will come for her."

"Like who?" Lady Farhan demanded.

"Achaz," Tessa said simply.

"The gods can't come here."

"Not right now," Tessa agreed. "But if they can find a way to create an entire world and then abandon it, I assure you, there is a way to break the Accords of old."

"Achaz is one threat," Theon agreed. "The Fates are another. There is no agreement keeping them from coming here."

"The Fates?" Kyra asked, her brow arching. "This is new information, Theon."

"Since we're all here, and for the sake of transparency, we want to share everything we know. This isn't some grand effort to overtake the kingdoms, but it is a desperate attempt to save this realm and all the people in it."

"By putting *her* in power?" the Celeste Lady sneered.

Theon's lips curled up. "I told her to leave us all and let the Fates destroy the realm. She chose to stay and fight for us. Doesn't get more benevolent than that, does it?"

"But she is not the one who will gain more power," the Falein Lady argued. "*You* will."

"To become her balance," Theon said. "The Fates are looking for her because she is an imbalance. Beginnings and Endings. As we all know, her power is extensive. Something needs to balance it out."

"And that something is you?"

Theon's brow arched. "You're welcome to try."

Tessa's power had already been growing, chaotic embers and sparks of light drifting around her. He could feel her working to keep it under control. There was lots of power in this room. It was the reason Xan and Akira weren't in here with them. Because Tessa's power was seeking; he couldn't imagine Akira in here.

But at his words, Luka's dragonfire wound around one of her arms while Theon's darkness fluttered along her jaw. She visibly relaxed, but the power in her eyes didn't bank.

"The two of us help her control it, but the Fates will require more," Theon said. "Rordan has been stealing power for decades. Even the added expanse of Dagian's gifts likely won't be enough to offset it, but it will give Tessa more to draw from."

"As her Source?" Kyra asked, her head tilting with interest.

"As her Source. As her lover. As her equal. As her balance," he replied. "I'm whatever she needs me to be."

"And you don't believe it will be enough to keep Devram from ruin?"

Theon glanced at Tessa, and her lips pursed at the question.

"Rordan's goal is to bring Achaz here. He believes if he is successful, Achaz will give him this world to rule as a reward for his faithfulness," Tessa said. "I've never seen the true depth of his power, but I've felt it. My Chaos seeks more. It knows who is the most powerful in a room, and when he is in it, it is always him," Tessa said. "As for the Fates, I suppose they will require an equal power. I am the grandchild of three First gods. No, one power being transferred to Theon will not be enough."

Kyra nodded, toying with flames in her palm. "But the power of another ruler would help."

"What?" Tessa asked, but it wasn't in confusion. It was shock. The same shock Theon was feeling. The same thing Luka was processing, because Kyra couldn't mean what it sounded like.

"You've seen what we've built here," Kyra said, and Theon could hear the slight tremble in her voice. "I've been in this position for over a century, and Dagian is correct. I've done much, but I could have done more. I *can* do more to ensure the people in my care are safe. That this realm is safe." She took a deep breath, her eyes pooling with tears. "Because change requires sacrifice. Change requires more than pretty words." She offered Tessa a weak smile. "So I offer my power as well. For the betterment of Devram and all those who deserve more in a world long forgotten by the gods. If I'm not willing to sacrifice to save them, I don't deserve to call myself their Lady."

The room was silent at the proclamation, and Theon didn't know what to do or say. He'd expected arguments and debates, yes, but he'd never expected things to end like this.

"I offer mine as well."

Theon's head whipped to the right where the Serafina Lady was meeting his gaze.

"You?" Theon asked, because it was all he could think of to say.

"You've held a longstanding alliance with Achaz Kingdom," Luka said, voicing Theon's thoughts.

"And he has betrayed that time and time again. I was too foolish to see how thoroughly," she replied. "And now I have lost . . . too much. I have seen too much, and in the end . . ." She cleared her throat, getting herself under control. "Maybe a beginning isn't what is needed, but an ending to make room for something more."

He heard Tessa's slight inhale. Felt her emotions all over the place as the Falein Lady followed suit, and finally the Celeste Lady. As one by one, the Ladies of the realm offered their power and their places alongside Dagian so that Devram might survive. So that they had a chance. So that Rordan wouldn't win.

So that there just might be a balance in the realm once more.

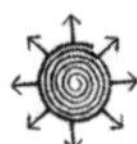

That afternoon, everyone gathered on the banks of the sea south of Idalia. It was the place where the Shade Plains merged with the Anala Kingdom at the base of the Ozul Mountains. They didn't dare do this in Arius Kingdom after Rordan's recent attack. They were told it would need to be some place the power could manifest. The magic would fight being taken from one to go to the other, and as he took more and more, he would struggle to contain it right away.

Introductions had been made, all of them leery of Akira, and Theon couldn't blame them. He was used to Tessa slipping into her chaotic states. Akira seemed to live in that space permanently.

"So, to be clear," the Falein Lady said, "Theon won't suddenly possess gifts from all the First gods?"

Tristyn shook his head. Tessa had requested he come after things had escalated during the meeting this morning.

"That's not how this works," Tristyn explained. "He will have the strength of that power, but it will manifest differently. It will become the darkness he now possesses. Your power will simply strengthen it."

"And what will they become?" Tessa asked, Luka tucking her hand into his before she could start pacing.

Tristyn glanced at the rulers, and Theon could swear he winced. "They won't be mortal, but they won't have power. Only an extended lifespan with a Staying that will remain for some time. For how long, we never know."

Theon looked at each of the Ladies. "This is your choice, your graces," he said. "We are not asking this of you, and we understand if you rescind your offer. No one will hold it against you. To be separated from a gift you have harnessed in your soul your entire life is a tragedy, even if done willingly."

"My offer stands," Lady Kyra said. "My only request is that Tana is still offered a seat at whatever new sense of order is established to oversee the kingdoms."

He smiled softly. "That can be arranged."

"We will value all your input when the time comes," Tessa added.

"But if we do not do this, it won't matter," Dagian interjected tightly. He was on an edge, and Theon would be the same if their roles were reversed. He was moments away from losing not only a power he'd trained much of his life to harness, but also the life he thought he'd have. "Let's get on with it."

"What of their Sources?" Tessa asked suddenly. "If they no longer have power, what will happen to their Source?"

The three Sources that were present went rigid, and Tristyn rubbed the back of his neck. "That I don't know, wild fury. And even if I did, because of the corruption of the Source Marks here, I don't know that it would be the same anyway."

"The only way to sever a Source bond is by death," Tessa mused, pulling her hand from Luka's to pace anyway.

"But if there's no power, is there anything for the Mark to cling to?" Axel asked. "If I'd had a Source when I turned, what would have been the point?"

"Yes, but you lost your power. The magic itself isn't dying. It's just being moved to another," Tessa argued. Then her eyes went wide. "Will those bonds transfer with the magic?"

"Again, because the Source Marks here are not a true Source Mark, we won't know," Tristyn said. "Because of the other Marks interwoven, we can't know."

"It won't be balanced," Akira piped in, drawing closer.

"What does that mean?" Tessa asked, turning to her mother.

"Xan told me of the Source Marks," she answered. "One connects the soul. One intertwines the power. The life force. The heart. It is a balance. If that balance is broken, the whole thing shatters."

"How can you be sure?"

"Nothing is certain in the stars, Tessa," she sang, crouching down and beginning to draw a Mark in the dirt. "But the magic will be strained enough. It will not be able to sustain an unbalanced bond."

"And the Fae tied to them?"

Akira stood, moving a few feet, and crouching to do the same thing again.

"Their lives are not tied to the Marks." Akira frowned. "Although they will likely feel the death of it. That will be as excruciating as losing one's gifts," she said simply, moving another few feet to draw more.

Tessa turned to the Fae, all of them having paled. "This is no longer only the Ladies' choices," she said. "If any of you wish not to do this, we will decline the Lady's offer."

"Tessa—" Theon started, but she held up a hand.

"No. They were already forced into a bond. No one will force them to risk their lives after having so much taken from them," Tessa said. "This is *their* choice because this is what we are fighting for. Everyone having a godsdamn choice."

Silence fell, stretching on until finally the Anala Lady's Source spoke. "My life as a Source has been better than others," he admitted. "But if this means none will be forced to give themselves for this purpose again, I will take the risk. If that is what we are fighting for, Lady Ausra, then I will risk this and stand by your side if I survive."

He placed a fist over his heart and bowed his head, and Tessa lurched back a step. But Theon was already moving in front of her. He'd bowed before her when she took the Arius seat and now he'd stand beside a Fae to show his solidarity in this too. He stood next to the Anala Source, following his actions.

Axel moved next. "You already know this, but the Underground will follow you," he said, stopping next to Theon. "Someone who understands what it is to have their value stripped away to nothing. Someone who fights to ensure the amount of power someone carries—whether vast or nonexistent—does not define them. Someone who does not care what blood runs in their veins or what type of being they are. Someone who sees them as people. You have our loyalty, Lady Ausra."

One by one everyone fell into a line as faint howls sounded. Nylah and Roan appeared, prowling to her side and lowering to their bellies.

The Fae.

The Underground.

The Legacy.

Those of Devram and those from across the stars.

Because destiny beckoned and sacrifice demanded.

And while she had not asked for this, Chaos had come to reign.

And Chaos did not choose.

She would fight for them all.

"A new dawn," Akira said simply, and Theon lifted his head to find her staring at her daughter. "Because in all things there must be balance."

"The sky, the sea, the realms," Tessa echoed faintly. "One was never meant to rule over the other."

Akira smiled wider, her hands clasped under her chin as she nodded several times in excitement. "So Endings discovered because Dreams dared to challenge."

"Yes," Tessa breathed, a laugh of disbelief coming from her lips. Her gaze slid to Theon, where Luka stood beside him. "And so we fight."

"And we will not fall," Theon said darkly before he turned to Dagian. "Are you ready?"

The Achaz Heir nodded once, and Akira clapped her hands twice. "We draw, Tessa," she said, pointing to the Marks. "In a circle."

Mother and daughter drew until the circle was complete, and then Akira was shoving Theon to the center. "Come, come," she added, motioning to Dagian until the two males stood in the middle.

"You must not lose contact at any point," Akira instructed.

"It will be agony, Dagian," Tristyn added grimly. "I cannot perform this, but I have seen it done. You will feel a piece of yourself being torn away."

"It can't be worse than losing Sasha," he said tightly. "Tell us what to do."

"No one else crosses in," Akira said, dancing back outside the circle.

"Or the power may choose another." She glanced at Luka. "Keep her contained. Her Chaos will want it."

"And you?" Theon demanded.

"I have her," Xan said, stepping to Akira's side while Luka slid an arm around Tessa's waist, pulling her back into his chest.

Dagian lifted his hands, turning his palms up when Akira instructed them.

"A blade," she encouraged. "Across your palms to merge your blood."

Dagian drew a dagger from his magic, and Theon knew why. He wanted to feel his power one last time. He drew it across his palms before passing it to Theon to do the same. Theon placed his hands atop Dagian's as he said in a low voice, "One final chance, Dagian. No one will fault you if you change your mind."

But his sharp features only tightened, holding his stare as he said loudly, "Do it."

"Your blood, daughter," Akira said. "On the Marks."

"But the Hunters," Tessa protested.

Akira shook her head. "The Marks are more. If they appear, their power will be taken. They will not venture where sacrifice demands."

Tessa moved along the perimeter, Luka walking with her, and the Marks flared as her blood fell. Akira was speaking in a language Theon didn't know, but nothing was happening. There was nothing but him and Dagian and the awkwardness that came from standing in a circle holding hands.

Until Dagian winced.

That was when he felt it. A tiny beat of power against his palm as Dagian hissed from between his teeth. Theon's hands tightened instinctively, their mixed blood dripping to the ground while more and more power flowed. Small drops that grew and slid along his soul as if seeking a way in.

Dagian grunted in pain, lurching back a step. "Do not let the connection break!" Akira cried. "It is too late to stop."

But Dagian stepped back again, gasping in pain.

"Dagian," Theon ground out, gripping the male with everything he had. "You can do this. For your people. For Sasha."

Dagian nodded frantically, another grunt of torment coming from his lips as he dropped to his knees, dragging Theon down with him. He didn't know what was going on around them anymore. Didn't know what Tessa was doing. Couldn't focus on Akira. Everything in him was homed in on the male who had already sacrificed, and now was giving more. Who was trusting him to make a difference with this sacrifice. To ensure Sasha's life was not lost for nothing.

Dagian gasped, the ground trembling beneath them. Waves were crashing to the shore from the sea, and it wasn't drops of power coming to him now. This was waves of magic slamming into his soul. He grunted for a different reason, forcing himself to stay upright as another burst of power flowed into him. It wasn't light. It wasn't energy. It was darkness and death churning in his soul, and he felt it rip free, his shadow wings forming as he absorbed more and more from Dagian. He was an heir, poised to be the most powerful male in the Achaz Kingdom. If this was his power, what of the Ladies? This was staggering enough. To add more? And to know he still wouldn't be as strong as Tessa?

Someone was calling his name. Someone else was still chanting in an old tongue. All he could do was take the power rushing over him, trying to find another while also latching onto his soul. His darkness swallowed it down, taking and taking.

Because life must give, and death must take.

Until finally it was done, and Theon caught Dagian's shoulders as the male slumped forward.

Akira must have told them it was safe because Tessa was throwing her arms around him, and he clutched her close, letting his darkness envelop her. Luka watched warily while wrapping Dagian's hands in something. Where he'd gotten the cloth, Theon didn't know, but Dagian wouldn't be able to heal anymore.

Tessa pressed her mouth to his, her lips lingering as she asked, "How do you feel?"

"Restless," he muttered, trying to wrangle the new magic in his soul.

"I can help," she whispered, still straddling his lap. He felt her chaos there, wrapping gently around his darkness. Coaxing it. Calling to it. Calming it.

His breathing evened out as he tried to adjust, and she took his face in her hands. "We can do the others another time. This does not all need to be done today."

But he shook his head. "It does. We do it all now. I don't want a slow adjustment. I'd rather do it all at once."

She nodded, pressing her brow to his. "We do this together."

He nodded, taking another minute before Luka pulled him to his feet. Tristyn was with Dagian off to the side, speaking low with him. Theon shook out his arms, feeling anxious and jittery with all the new power. Then he looked at Kyra and said, "If you are still willing, I'm ready."

Her head held high, she stepped forward. "We just witnessed a young male sacrifice everything for a kingdom and realm that wasn't his to protect yet. Decades and decades younger than me, he's made a bigger difference in his short life than I have in my decades on a seat of power. I am not blameless here. None of us are. Change requires sacrifice, not to make amends for our transgressions, but in the hope that those who come after us will learn from our failures."

So they began again.

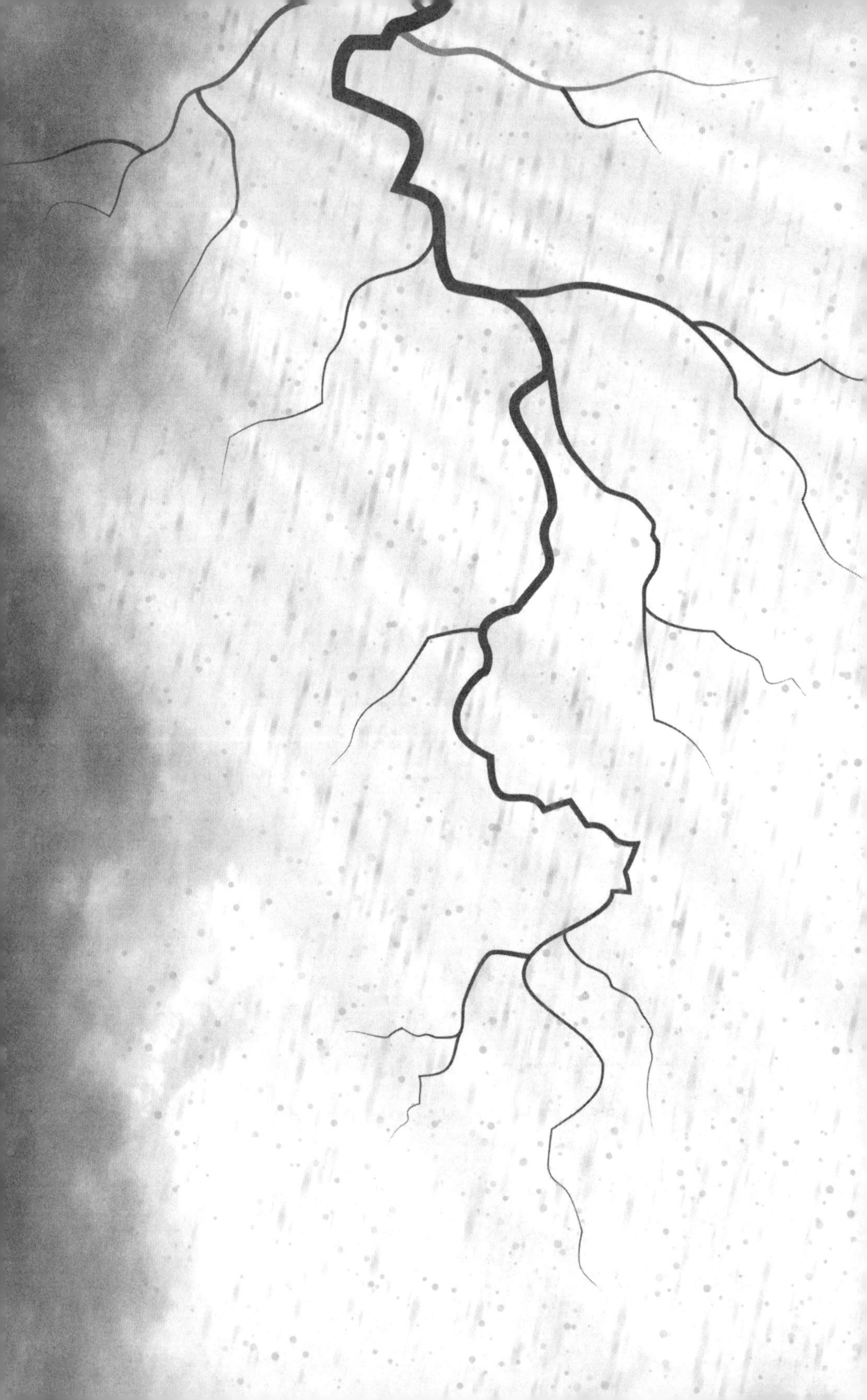

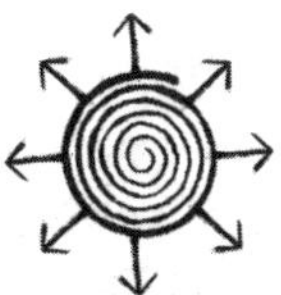

53
TESSA

"I really wish you'd wear some armor," Luka muttered. "What are we going to do if your blood touches the ground?"

She smirked where she stood near the kitchen island, leaning a hip against it. "I'm not wearing armor, Luka. If Hunters appear, I'll take care of them. My arrows kill them. Auryon's did."

"We're going to be facing enough enemies. We don't need to add more," he argued.

She hummed, the bands of light on her wrists flaring brighter as they unfurled and coiled. "I'll be fine," she said, pushing off the counter to return her coffee creamer to the fridge. "Maybe I'll just make armor of light like Theon does with his darkness."

"Great. Then you'll be a beacon calling everyone straight to you," he deadpanned.

"Why so grumpy this morning?" she asked around a huff of laugher. "One would think after the night we had, you'd be the farthest thing from grumpy."

Because it had been a *very* good night that had left her more than a little sated. She'd slept deeply without a single dream, and while normally that was fine, it was also a little worrisome. She hadn't had a vision in weeks. Tristyn had told her it was likely because the future was changing too quickly when she'd mentioned it to him a few days ago, and while that made sense, it still had her on edge.

So her husbands had taken it upon themselves to drive every other thought from her mind.

"What are we discussing?" Theon asked, coming into the room and going straight for her. He pressed a kiss to her temple as he reached over her head for a mug.

"Luka is upset I don't have armor. Again," she sighed, glancing at Theon.

He wasn't in a suit. Instead, he wore black tactical pants with pockets. His long-sleeve black shirt hugged his torso, and his belt already had daggers sheathed to it. Luka was in the same, and she'd been trying to avoid staring all godsdamn morning.

"It slows her down," Theon reminded him, turning to lean on the counter as he took a drink of caffeine.

"See?" Tessa said, gesturing to Theon. "I'll have Nylah and Roan. My power will be feeding the entire time. I can funnel power to the two of you if needed."

"Absolutely not," Theon barked, straightening. "You'll keep your power."

She gave him an exasperated look. "Theon, you've been sleeping off and on for over a week with all that power you have now."

"I've also been training with it and learning how to conserve it and control it," he countered.

"Yes, but a week isn't enough time."

"We're out of time, Tessa," he said quietly, pulling his phone from his pocket when a message sounded.

He wasn't wrong. Each day they delayed this was another day Rordan could make the next move, and they really wanted to be the ones to do that. But they'd had to wait. Theon had taken on the power of the Ladies and Dagian, and by the gods, she'd never seen something so heartbreaking and breathtaking. Never once had she thought she would see the Ladies take accountability for their actions and do something so monumental for the betterment of all those in Devram, not just those in power.

Theon had been beyond exhausted, and while he'd slept and the Ladies had done the same to recover, the rest of them strategized and planned. They'd brought in the heirs and generals of the other kingdoms. They'd studied maps, and Tessa had absorbed as much as she could. But this wasn't her area of expertise. She was the power. She recognized that. Luka, however . . .

Tessa had watched him with a sense of wonder. There were generals from the various forces there, yes, but watching Luka, Xan, and Razik command the room as Sargon's descendants? That was a sight to behold. Eliza had known more about battle strategies and formations than the males who led the kingdoms' forces. Tessa had so many questions, but she knew they didn't have time to indulge her. Later, when they survived this, she'd ask them all. Then again, she'd have lived it by that point. Experience was a better teacher than anything and all that.

There was a sharp knock on the door before Razik entered, Eliza at his side.

"We just received word that the last of the forces have moved into place," the male said.

"Axel had the Underground move in two nights ago," Theon added. "Do you two want coffee?"

Eliza curled her lip. "No. I've never taken a liking to that bitter drink."

"It's why you add cream and sugar," Tessa offered.

"I'll stick to tea," the general replied flatly.

"We're heading to the camps shortly," Theon said. "Is everyone else ready?"

They didn't have time to waste, but they'd needed it. There was no fast and easy way to move hundreds of forces into position. The few people who could Travel used massive amounts of power to do so, and those who could make portals did the same. The thing was, with Theon now having so much more power, he was one of the few who could make portals now. The heirs could, but it drew a lot from their Sources. They'd had to time everything to allow everyone the opportunity to replenish reserves—whether by natural means or rations of blood.

So all the kingdoms had moved forces into place in the Dreamlock Woods of all places. The border between the Serafina and Achaz Kingdoms across from Faven would have been preferable, but then they'd have to cross the Wynfell River when they were ready to move forward. Rordan would have the advantage still, and they'd be fucked. Instead, they were sneaking in little by little into the Dreamlock Woods from the Serafina Kingdom and crossing into Achaz territory. The woods were avoided by everyone, and Rordan would never expect them to attack from the south.

But he didn't know about Priya.

It was Kat who had told them that bit of information one evening when they were debating where to make their stand. Going straight for Faven would be unexpected, but Rordan had come for Arius House. They were going to answer in kind.

Corbin and Lange had confirmed that Priya had somehow befriended the woods, and a small group of them had Traveled there to see it for themselves. They watched a little girl speak with Sprytes and Nymphs. They watched her talk to the trees and witnessed the flowers bloom for her. She was at home and in her element, and when Corbin and Lange crouched before her and asked her to do this for them, she'd done so without question. That child didn't trust another soul but them, and all Tessa could think was if she accomplished nothing else in her life, helping those three find each other was enough.

"Everything is packed and ready?" Luka asked, rinsing his coffee cup and leaving it in the sink, and Tessa fleetingly wondered if they would be back to wash it.

A thought that clearly was heard down the bond because Theon's gaze snapped to her.

Enough. If we start thinking that way, we may as well admit defeat right now, Theon growled.

She thinned her lips, but she nodded in response.

"Let's go," he said tightly, grabbing her hand as they all made their way to the foyer. Axel and Kat were there, and Kat had tears on her face as she pulled Maddox to her chest and kissed the top of his head.

"You can stay," Axel was saying, holding them both close.

She shook her head. "We're doing this for him," Kat whispered. "If we won't fight for this, we are no better than those who came before us."

Kyra was here, waiting off to the side. With the Ladies no longer having power, they were given other tasks and areas to be of help. Kyra would keep Maddox until they returned.

With one last press of lips to their babe, Tessa's heart twisted in her chest as they watched Axel hand his son to another. She had yet to hold him, but not because she didn't adore him just as much as the others. He was perfect in every way.

"We'll be back," Axel said firmly. "Do what you must—"

"With my life, Axel," Kyra said softly. "When you return, the world will look different."

With a lingering look, they walked out the front door of Arius House. Axel and Kat. Xan and Akira. Razik and Eliza. Caris. Everyone else was already in the Dreamlock Woods, waiting for them.

They stood in a circle, and Tessa looked up at the towering house that had once been her prison. She'd believed herself to be nothing then. Too wild and untamed. Too broken to fix.

She'd never wanted any of this, but little by little, they took and took.

Little by little they started a war with her. She didn't belong with their nobility. She didn't want a throne, but she was coming for it anyway.

Rordan thought she would bow to him.

Dexter thought he could control her.

Achaz thought he could use her.

But you can't control the uncontrollable.

Something dark and wicked coursed through her veins as she took hold of Theon's and Luka's hands.

She wasn't taking a throne. She was taking the entire godsdamn realm.

She was taking it all, and she'd decide who would be left standing in the end.

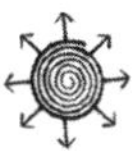

"You should be sleeping," Luka said, coming to her side. "We don't move for another two hours."

She hummed an acknowledgment, but she didn't answer. Standing at the edge of the trees, she stared out at the open area that would soon be filled with warriors of all kinds. Legacy. Fae. Night Children. Shifters. Witches and deities and dragons. They were marching on Faven at first light, and that was indeed hours away. But others were already stirring. They would be preparing, but she hadn't been able to shake this feeling. Something was nagging at the back of her mind, and it was something she should know. Something she should recognize.

"Baby girl," Luka sighed, pulling her into his chest, a large palm running down her hair. "It's the realm against one kingdom."

He was mistaking her mood for nervousness and dread, but she'd oblige him in this.

"A powerful kingdom run by a male who has been stealing power for decades with seraphs in his army. If we win this, it will not be easy," she murmured, pressing her cheek to his chest.

"No one said it was going to be easy. But with you and Theon. All the forces—"

"That we scrambled to put together. Who have never known true war. Who have never truly fought."

"Theon was right yesterday," Luka said sternly. "We can't think like that. If we do, we may as well bow down now."

"I will never bow to anyone again," she said sharply. "Never again, Luka."

His fingers gripped her chin, tilting her face up to his. "Then let's make sure of it. Are you ready?"

She nodded, and he lowered his lips to hers, kissing her deeply on the edge of the woods as they prepared to bring a storm of chaos and fury at dawn.

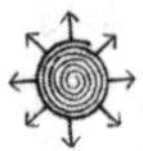

They flooded out of the woods. Hundreds of them at once. Those with wings were soaring above as they all marched on Faven when the first rays of daylight kissed the ground. As they expected, it didn't take long for seraphs to answer in the sky.

Razik, Eliza, and Caris were leading units to the right. Xan, Aiyana, Tristyn, and Cienna had the left, her mother with them. Tessa led the rest in the center, with Theon and Luka at her sides. Axel was with them. Cade and Rayell. Kylian and Giselle.

"Get in the sky, but stay close," Tessa gritted out to Luka. She turned to Theon, her grin pure madness as an arrow appeared in her hand and she nocked it to her bow. "And so chaos rains."

Theon grabbed her neck, hauling her to him, and for a few precious seconds, she savored it.

Then pulled back and let that arrow fly.

And as the sun broke the horizon, the first seraph fell.

Everything after that was instinct as she let herself plummet into her Chaos. It wanted to take, and she was going to let it.

Her arrows didn't miss, seraphs becoming nothing but fluttering embers as she released one right after the other. She didn't worry about the ground forces. Nylah and Roan were at her sides, and they didn't let anyone near.

Her power was thrashing and yanking, tasting the death in the air, but she wasn't ready. Not yet.

Not yet.

Soon.

Theon, however . . .

He was not waiting.

His darkness coated him like armor as it always did. That sword they'd taken from Bree was in his hand, and his darkness wound around that too. He moved like the god he descended from. Power flowed, blanketing the ground around him. Tendrils shot up from the depths of the inky mist like vines. They wrapped around seraphs as they dove, yanking them down where either the Trackers ended them or Theon did.

A roar of fury had her looking up to see not only Xan and Aiyana, but their sons fully shifted too. Black flames filled the sky at the same time thunder cracked, rain starting to fall. Whether it was her or her mother, she didn't know, but a storm rolled in. Lightning flashed, dragon and seraph alike diving to avoid it. They'd have to deal with it though because that cloud cover forced the seraphs lower, allowing those with wind magic to interfere more effectively.

Tessa shot one last arrow before looping her bow over her chest as an Achaz warrior made it past Roan. Her hand shot out, snagging the male's arm as he raised a dagger. She wasn't stronger than him physically, but she finally let her power out. It pounced, sinking deep into his soul, light and dark crackling under his skin as she watched the bands of light on her arms flare brighter. Knew the Marks on her skin were doing the same. The warrior screamed, pitiful and full of agony as her Chaos feasted, refilling the magic she was using.

More.

She needed more.

Each step was purposeful, calm and slow as she made her way into the melee. Weapons clanged around her. Warriors from both sides crossed to the After. But as she sank deeper and deeper into her magic, everything seemed to slow. She ducked as swords swung above her, her power unfurling from her soul. It crackled out, an intricate network of light spreading beneath her feet.

Theon? she gasped down the bond, her power yanking for more of her.

Tessa? Where are you?

Do you see it?

See what? There was a pause. *What are you doing?*

Can you use your power to shield our own?

Tessa?

Please, Theon.

Fuck, he muttered. *Yeah, tempest. I've got it.*

She sucked in another breath as her power pulled enough to distract her, and it cost her. Someone wrapped an arm around her waist, lifting her off her feet as the air was pulled from her lungs.

Until she heard gurgling sounds, and she was dropped back to the ground.

She quickly rolled over, reaching for her dagger while struggling to hold back her magic, only to find Axel with blood dripping down his chin. He dropped a body beside her, the male that had held her now missing half his throat.

"Vicious," she murmured with a smirk.

Axel only winked, yanking her to her feet. Then he was shoving her back down as his hand wrapped around another throat. "They don't fucking stop," he snarled, his fingers flexing.

"I got it," Tessa said, scrambling out from under him and shoving her dagger deep into the chest of a female.

For the next few minutes, it was the two of them. Axel's strength and her blades, her magic moving with her.

"What is Theon doing?" Axel gritted out, snagging another Legacy as he ran by.

Tessa sank a dagger into his back. "Helping me," she panted.

Because everyone on their side standing atop her net of light was being draped in darkness, and gods, she hoped it was going to be enough.

"Go find Kat," Tessa said. "Stay off the light."

He looked down, seeing what she meant, and nodded. "You good, baby doll?"

Roan was slinking to her side, always knowing what she needed, and Tessa nodded. "Tell her to burn them all."

He smiled darkly. "Will do."

Then he was gone, moving faster than she could track. She didn't know how he would find Kat, but she knew he would.

Ready, Theon?

Now, Tessa. This is a lot to hold.

She turned her face to the sky, letting the rain splash against her face, and when the next flash of lightning came, she let the leash on her power snap. It latched onto the energy, pulling it closer. It struck the center of her net of power, all the cracks sparking and exploding out. Anyone not covered in Theon's protection was on their knees, then their backs, screaming while the energy jolted through them over and over.

While her power took and feasted and devoured.

Theon was suddenly at her side, pulling her back to her feet. She didn't even know when she'd dropped to her knees, but now that she'd let it out, her power didn't stop.

"Take some," she panted, clutching Theon's arm. "Take some, Theon."

"No, Tessa. You need—"

"I wasn't asking," she gritted out, planting both her palms on his chest.

Her power halted, recognizing the well it had before it, and it shifted, racing for him.

"Fuck," he grunted as it slammed into him, and she felt his darkness rise to greet it. Latch onto it. Take it for its own.

They hadn't known how this was going to work. The Source Mark worked both ways, but Razik and Eliza had to merge their blood to refill reserves. She'd never had to do that. His power had always been drawn to her, and now that he was more, her power was drawn to him too. Something unexplainable and uncontrollable.

But then his arm wound around her waist, tugging her into him and raising his sword as he spun. The seraph that had come for them was speared on the end, blood raining down as his darkness rose and snapped the male's wings clean off.

"You're smiling, tempest," he muttered, lowering his sword and letting the seraph fall to the muddy ground. "We're in the middle of a brutal battle, and you're fucking smiling."

"We like the madness," she whispered, dropping her hands.

He huffed a laugh, wiping at the blood on her face but only smearing it. "Have you seen him yet?"

She shook her head. "He's here. He'll find me."

And that was how the next minutes went. Or maybe it was the next hour. More? Time became meaningless as they fought. Theon never strayed far, and Luka was always above them. She caught glimpses of fire every so often. Eliza or Kat. Other fire Fae. The Night Children were ruthless, and Shifters sank claws and teeth in alongside Nylah and Roan. A fine dusting of ash from the dragons above mixed with the steady rain. Blood splattered, magic flared, and feet slipped in the mud.

Tessa dropped to a crouch as three enemy forces came for her. Thunder rumbled and lightning struck. Or she did. Her Chaos took it once more, striking true, and a crevice cracked open, much like it had done months ago in a garden. Hunters didn't crawl out of it this time, though. Instead, Achaz warriors fell in. Fae fighting nearby clearly had earth magic as vines and roots snaked out, keeping them in the crevice and dragging more in—those on the ground and those flying low.

She stood still, awed as she watched them work, and after there were several dozen bound to the walls of the crevice, those Fae came together and closed the earth.

Holy gods.

She was powerful, but that was . . .

"Kat! Katya!"

Tessa whirled at the sound of Axel's desperate voice calling for his wife, and she was running without thinking, following that sound. She heard Theon call after her, but it was overpowered by Axel's cries.

"Kat, no! Kat!"

She ran, her power clearing a way as she followed those pleas. Scrambling up a small hill several feet from the mayhem, she reached the top and her heart stopped. She didn't find Kat or Axel, his voice still pleading somewhere nearby, but she did find Tristyn.

On the ground with a blade in his chest.

"Tristyn!" she cried, sliding down the hill and rushing to his side. She dropped to her knees, looking him over. Black pants and shirt. Leather armor like Eliza wore. Sheaths empty where they'd once held blades. Numerous cuts and scratches, and his eyes were a faint sage green when she took his face in her hands.

"Tristyn? Tris, can you hear me?"

"Wild fury," he gasped, coughing with the exhale. "Didn't expect . . . you to find me."

"What do I need to do?" she demanded, panic in her voice as she released his face to focus on his chest. "Pull it out or leave it? I can—I'll get Cienna. We can—"

Tristyn coughed again, wincing with the movement. "There's nothing . . . I failed," he rasped.

"No." The word a denial, she shook her head frantically. "No. No more. I will not—"

Tristyn's icy fingers grasped hers, squeezing. Or trying to.

"How?" she demanded. Screamed it at him. "You're a deity! You can't just—No. No!"

"Can you tell her—" He coughed again, blood coming up with it. "Tell her I'll save her that dance, yeah?"

"No!" Tessa cried. "You tell her. You tell—Tristyn?"

Because his eyes were no longer glowing. They were still and vacant, and his chest wasn't moving. And he couldn't just *die*. He was a fucking deity. He couldn't. He—

A roar pierced the air, breaking through her panic, and she looked up to find a midnight blue dragon with black wings and a dragon a few shades lighter. Xan and Aiyana. It was the two of them against twenty or more seraphs. Black flames met magic attacks, both sides taking hits. Aiyana dove suddenly, as if going after something, but then she banked hard, narrowly avoiding a . . .

Tessa pushed to her feet, running several feet and peering around a small clump of bushes. Seraphs were there, loading a contraption with bolts of white stone. That was what Aiyana had barely avoided. They had weapons against the dragons.

In her next breath, her power erupted. It crackled in the air, latching onto any seraph it could find. Veins and wings lit up as Tessa took their last breaths, watching them all scream and writhe before her. Too consumed by her fury to notice that her power was killing, but it wasn't taking. Those deaths weren't refilling anything.

"Kat? Kat, where are you?"

She spun around. Where in the fuck was he? It sounded like he was right here. Like he was—

Another sound had her spinning to find a body rolling down the small hill, coming to a stop face down in the mud. Dark hair. Tall. If that was Axel . . .

Her feet were moving of their own accord, and she felt like she wasn't in her body. Felt like she was hovering above, watching herself walk far too calmly across the space to the unmoving body. Watching her muster all her strength to roll him over.

And then watched her magic explode when she found not the younger St. Orcas brother but Theon.

She was screaming, and she was burning with fury. This wasn't . . . He was as powerful as she was. He couldn't be.

No.

No, no, no.

She'd save him the same way she'd saved Luka. That was what she'd do.

Her hands on his chest, she ripped at the gear he was wearing. His shirt. Her power shredded through it all as she lost all control. Lost herself completely to her magic. Anyone who came near met an end, and she wasn't even sure if they were all Achaz forces at this point. If Theon was taken from her, they were all enemies. If Theon was taken from her, she was going to destroy the realm herself. If this didn't work, she was—

Tessa paused, her gaze landing on his left arm. His left wrist where a union mark was . . . missing. That couldn't . . .

She glanced at her wrist where the Union Mark was still fully intact.

She blinked, trying to understand. Because that Mark wouldn't fade in death. And even if it did, hers was still there. And she could . . . feel his power. Strong and unyielding. Not as strong as it could be because he'd been using it all day, but still . . .

This wasn't right.

Tessa pushed slowly to her feet, her heart hammering and breaths coming too fast. The world around her was blurred on the edges as she took in the surroundings. Her Chaos was churning in her soul, stretching and taking. Feeling that other power pulsing around her. Then, as if reaching out a hand, it peeled back a layer of magic.

That was Dex on the edge of the clearing, watching her with a smirk on his face. In his hand was a stone collar, just like the one she'd seen in her last vision. He was just standing there as if waiting for something.

She looked down where Theon's body lay, only it wasn't there. Dragging her gaze across the space, she found Tristyn's body gone too. No screams from Axel. No roars of dragons overhead.

This entire thing had been Dex luring her away from the others. Altering her reality. Making her expend her magic on nothing. That was why her reserves weren't refilling when she'd set it free earlier.

Tessa watched him a moment longer. He hadn't seemed to realize that his magic wasn't affecting her anymore. Her own Chaos had countered it so carefully, had turned it back on him, that he thought he was still watching her lose herself over Theon. His own reality altered.

Trembling with a fury she couldn't have described if she'd tried, she pulled a dagger from a swirl of her magic. A long, thin onyx blade with a hilt just as dark. A blade that had taken the life of Brecken.

A blade created to end seraphs.

A blade Tristyn had brought to her after he'd taken care of Brecken's body.

A blade she'd been saving just for this.

It wasn't until she was standing directly behind him that she let her magic shatter his completely. Let it sink in with claws and teeth. Let it shred that power to nothing.

Dex straightened in alarm, likely at not finding her sobbing over a body. His head swiveling around frantically, she waited until he turned.

Then she plunged that blade into his chest.

"Tessie?" He gasped, eyes dropping to the blade she still had her hand wrapped around, then slowly dragging back up to her face. "What are you doing?"

Her smile was sharp as she gripped the hilt and twisted. "Cleaning up my own fucking mess," she snarled.

Dex staggered, dropping to his knees, and she stepped back. Reaching up, he yanked the dagger from his chest, examining it before asking, "Where did you get this?"

She was circling him now. Hunter and prey. Light and dark swirling at her fingertips.

"Apparently you didn't clean up your own messes very well," she sneered. "Oralia was rather slighted that you kept denying her a power."

"Oralia gave you this?" he demanded sharply, and her smile grew when he tried to hide the pained gasp he sucked in.

"She killed Brecken with it," Tessa said darkly. "And after I killed her, I kept it."

The tips of his pristine wings were already turning grey as death came for him, but this wasn't enough for her.

"After all these years, this is what it's come down to," Dex spat, chucking the dagger aside. "When I've been there for you. Tried to help you. Laid the fucking world at your feet."

The bark of laughter that left her was shrill. "I didn't need you to lay the world at my feet. I'm taking it all on my own, Dexter."

"A puppet of Arius," he said with disgust, sagging onto his hands and knees as death seeped into him more and more. Those eyes too dark against the sickly grey skin. Feathers decaying. Cheeks sinking in.

"I'm no puppet," she said darkly, circling back to stand in front of him. Summoning a black sword, she used the tip of the blade to tilt his chin up. "You, however, know all about being a puppet, don't you? What was Achaz going to give you? Had he promised this world to you the same way he promised it to Rordan?"

He pressed his lips together in a clear refusal.

"I'd answer that question, Dex," she sang. "I can become incredibly . . . wild."

His lip curled back, but he couldn't hide the wince when he dragged in another breath.

"Last chance," she offered, her blade still poised at his throat.

"You are a disappointment," he growled. "And for what? Achaz will deal with you himself. The outcome will not change. Look around you, Tessa. When has the outcome ever changed?"

But then he was bellowing in pain as the blade sliced not through his neck—no, that would have been far too fast for him—but down his back, cleaving a wing and letting it fall to the ground. She left the other wing, bringing the blade down on his arm, slicing it clean off at the elbow. Then a foot. An ear.

"All you had to do was do as you were told," she mocked with each swing of her sword. "Answer a fucking question." She struck out with her foot, forcing him onto his back, and then she shoved her blade straight through his gut, pinning him to the earth.

"I'm done being who you wanted me to be. Now? I'm who I was meant to be," she snarled, letting her power wind around what was left of his limbs, his torso, up his throat. She wasn't waiting for the blade to take his last breath. She wanted it. Wanted him to know that his life would only fuel her more.

Standing over him, she shoved her power into every crack of his soul. Listened to his bellows of agony. A song that gave her life.

And when he fell still and silent. When vacant dark eyes were staring blankly at nothing. When her chest was heaving from the adrenaline of everything, she whispered coldly, "To fury you lost."

"Tessa?" a low voice said carefully. Black flames and silky darkness licked at her soul, calling her back. Calling her home.

She turned, finding Luka and Theon standing there, both wide-eyed and staring at her in a way she couldn't read.

"So fucking vindictive," Luka growled, prowling forward while Theon stayed back, alert and clearly keeping others away.

"We felt . . . too much coming from you," Theon ground out, his magic undulating around him. "Grief and agony. Heart-wrenching sadness. And then . . ."

"Fury," Luka supplied. "Ungodly fury, and then we found a goddess exacting her revenge."

She smiled weakly, working to take back control. That same unsettling feeling from this morning was back.

"Look at you," Luka went on, circling her now. "Once more covered in blood."

Look around you, Tessa. When has the outcome ever changed?

Luka paused, feeling her sudden panic. "Tessa?"

She spun, taking in the surroundings.

The stormy skies casting everything in grey.

Dead grass and scorched earth.

Bodies everywhere.

Blood and mud.

The rain.

It hit her then.

That thing that had been nagging at her since they'd come here as she looked around at the fighting and the fallen.

This was her vision.

Every godsdamn time.

This was it.

And they never won.

Not a single time.

A hand cupped her chin, forcing her to look into emerald depths. "What is it, Tessa?" Theon demanded.

"Only one can be left standing," she whispered, just as blinding light erupted.

She scrambled, casting her power out to grab Theon and Luka. She felt them both, their power reaching for her too.

Then that light swallowed them whole.

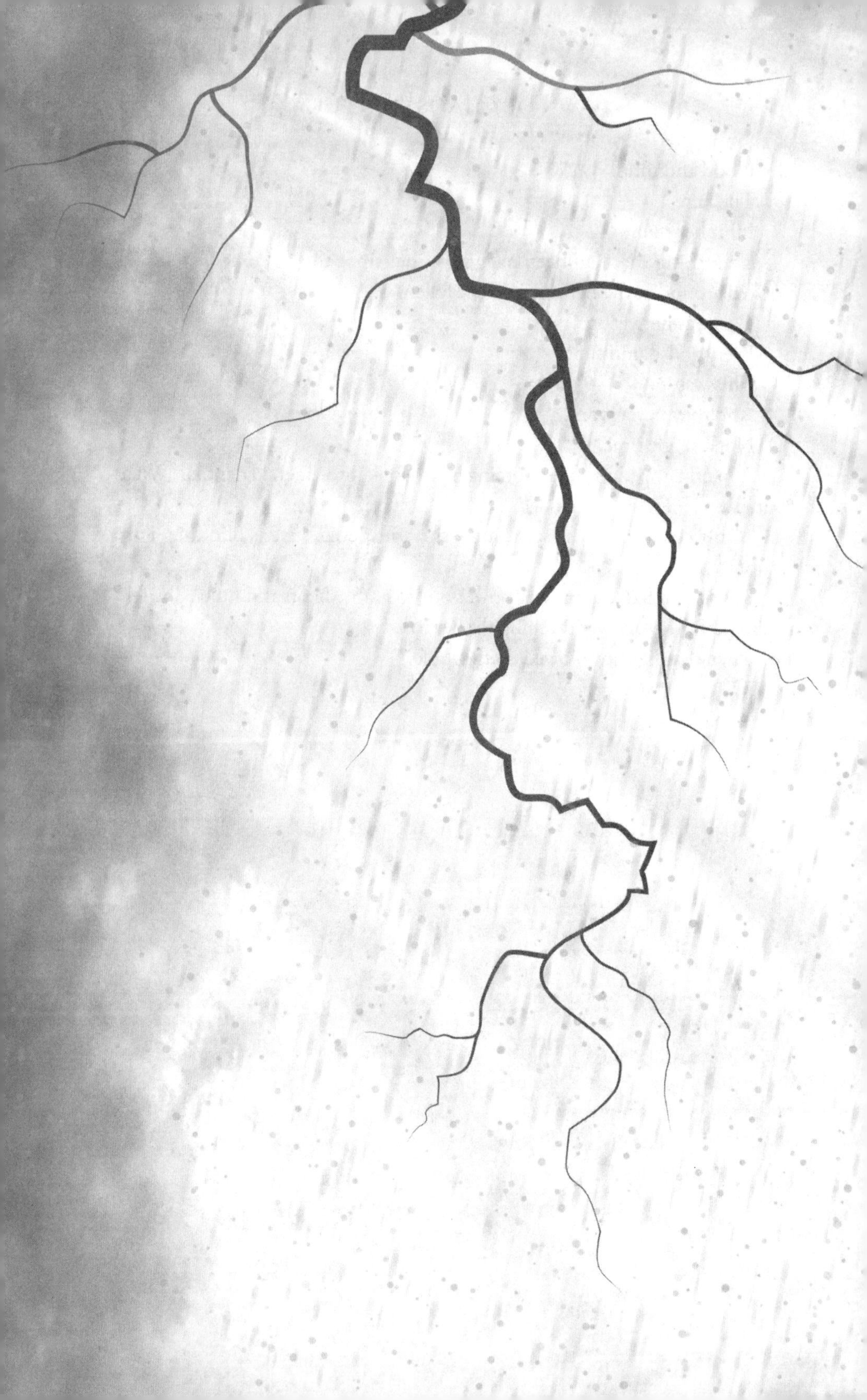

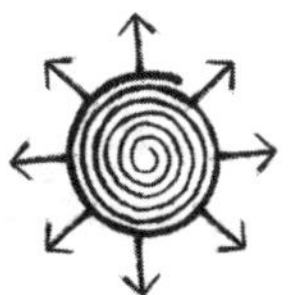

54
TESSA

Tessa hit the ground hard, rolling several times across a marble floor. Scrambling onto her hands and knees, she saw Theon several feet away doing the same. But Luka? He couldn't be too far from her or—

A furious roar echoed, the floor beneath her shuddering, and she looked up to find a domed ceiling of glass. The sky was spitting rain, drops streaming along the panes, and perched atop it was Luka, fully shifted and sapphire eyes glowing with wrath as black flames hit the glass. The water evaporated into nothing, but the glass didn't even crack.

Light was suddenly hitting the dome from the inside, the glass seeming to absorb it and letting it pass through, jolting through the dragon. Luka back-flapped, another furious roar sounding from him as he hovered outside . . . wherever they were.

She took in the space. Pure white and gold, the walls were the same glass as the ceiling. The entire room was circular, the marble floor beneath her boasting streaks of red and brown from her rolling across it. Theon was on his knees, that same godsdamn seraph who never spoke standing behind him while five . . . Hunters closed in.

Fuck.

She looked down, seeing the gashes along her arms that were steadily dripping to the floor.

"They won't hurt him yet."

Theon was watching her, lips pressed into a thin line and eyes blazing with the same wrath as Luka's.

Stick to the plan, Theon said down the bond.

Tessa turned away from him to the source of the voice.

Rordan was across the room, bent over what appeared to be raised garden beds. His crisp navy suit was in place, his back to her. As if she wasn't a threat. "I find gardening rather soothing," Rordan went on. "I think it's in the blood. Light and beginnings. Creating something new and bringing it to life."

She didn't reply, instead trying to take in everything else. The glass walls overlooking a city where a battle raged beyond. The Faven Palace. They were in a room in the palace. A room he'd never brought her to, and now she knew why.

In the center stood a mirror. The stone frame was etched with symbols, and in the back of her mind, she wondered how in the fuck he'd gotten a mirror gate into this room. She wasn't surprised that the mirror was in his palace. She should have known. He'd never risk it being found by anyone else, especially not with who stood next to it.

One of the most beautiful females she'd ever seen was watching her. Golden hair a few shades lighter than her own. Golden skin. Pristine wings. High cheekbones. Eyes the color of a clear sky. Ethereal and radiating with power, her floor-length white gown was sleeveless with metal clasps at her shoulders. A gold belt was slung around her waist with gold sandals on her feet.

Dagian's mother.

She watched Tessa with apathetic features, wings rustling at her back. The bargain with Dagian was that they left her out of this, but Tessa wasn't sure how they were going to do that when she was standing in this room.

Then again, that bargain was with Theon, not her.

Tearing her gaze from the seraph, her magic yanked at her restraint. There was so much power in this room. Rordan. Theon. The seraphs. The mirror.

She shook her arms out, still taking in everything until her focus landed on another heap across the room. A broken body, she realized. A body that looked like . . . Elowyn?

"She failed in her duties," Rordan said, and her gaze snapped back to him, finding him watching her now. His hands behind his back, his head tilted towards the heap. "She was useful for a time. Creating the tonic to keep your power hidden, and then altering your tea so we could . . . enhance your visions."

She arched a brow at that.

He smiled, chuckling to himself. "The one of Ms. Davers carrying

Theon's child was a particularly brutal one. Pushed you right into our arms." The mirth fell. "Then you had to ruin everything."

She had . . . That hadn't been a real vision? Which ones had been real? Any of them? Had she been running around these last months trying to change visions that weren't even real?

No.

Yes.

They couldn't affect her from so far away, right?

She suddenly understood on a whole new level why Cienna insisted on not focusing on the visions. How trying to change a potential future could bring about that very future.

"Once we lost control of you, her usefulness had run its course," Rordan continued, coming closer. "But we couldn't just let that power go to waste, could we?"

"You took her magic," Tessa murmured to herself, staring at Elowyn's broken form. Is that what happened when your magic was forcibly taken from you?

Another roar sounded, followed by claws dragging on the glass. Rordan snarled in annoyance, lifting a hand and sending another wave of light to the ceiling. Luka roared in defiance as he was forced back yet again.

"Dragons and their godsdamn tantrums," Rordan muttered. "They'll be taken care of soon enough." He was before her now, reaching out to finger her hair.

"Don't fucking touch her," Theon growled, his darkness snapping out, but a Hunter stepped in front of the attack, absorbing the magic with a sickening grin of too pale lips. Another Hunter drifted closer, inhaling deeply.

"Blood of death," he hissed, that ethereal voice grating on her bones, and her magic writhed, dragging her down a little further.

"Don't worry, Arius blood," Rordan gritted out. "We're preparing for you too."

He nodded at the beautiful seraph, and her gaze flicked to Tessa. "You know my son?"

"We do," Tessa answered cautiously.

"He spoke of you. Uncontrollable."

Her words were jilted and selective, as if she wasn't sure she was using the right ones. This clearly wasn't her native tongue.

Tessa flashed her a sharp smile. "Some call it uncontrollable. I simply call it madness."

"We are not here to speak of my traitorous son," Rordan barked. "Begin."

"Here?" the female questioned, gesturing around them. "With a child of Achaz?"

"It isn't for her. It's for him," Rordan snapped. "Draw the Marks."

Her clear blue eyes flicked across the room to Theon, the other seraph, and the Hunters before coming back to Tessa. "He is a reflection of Arius."

Tessa's brow furrowed as the female dropped to a crouch and began drawing a Mark.

"But first, what am I to do with you?" Rordan asked now that the female was doing as she was told.

Tessa's fingers curled at her sides, her magic claiming her a little more, while she watched the female move and draw another again a few feet away.

"There is nothing you can do with us," Tessa answered, lifting her chin. "I am still more powerful than you."

"Is that what you believe?" he sneered.

"It does not matter what I believe. Truth is truth," she said, following the path of the seraph. "But more than that, you are not valued as much as I am."

Rordan scoffed, light flickering in his eyes at the snub.

"You think I'm wrong?" she asked, tracking the female as she continued to move, disappearing behind the mirror now. Rordan couldn't see her, but Tessa could, and she paused, studying the floor. Those piercing blue eyes flicked up to her again. Then she turned as if assessing the Marks she'd started drawing in a circle off to the right.

"A reflection of madness," the seraph murmured. She gestured to the Marks. "It flows the wrong way."

"I know I'm not," Tessa said with a shrug, returning her attention to Rordan. "I'm his grandchild, and you? You're so far removed from him, it's laughable to even call you an Achaz Legacy."

"And yet I am the one serving Achaz with steadfast loyalty while you betray him at every turn," Rordan ground out.

"Do I?"

"You're married to an Arius Legacy and a dragon. He will find those betrayals unforgivable."

"Perhaps I am like him," Tessa said simply, wandering over to the mirror and staring at her reflection. Understanding settling in as she watched the female move in her periphery. "Perhaps I find betrayals just as unforgivable. I think it runs in the family." She paused, glancing at Rordan. "Not that you would know."

Rordan's face was flushed, and his words were forced as he ground out, "Achaz will deal with the dragon in time. As for the *Arius Lord*, I will deal with him myself. Achaz can deal with you."

She hummed, dragging her fingers along the stone around the mirror. "He will still choose me. I am his blood, and I have something he craves." She lifted a hand, chaos spinning in her palm. "You are just someone who has taken too long to please him." She closed her fist, the power snuffing out. "But I can help you with that."

"You're going to help me?" he scoffed. "You cannot possibly expect me to believe that?"

She shrugged again. "Fine. Then I will present the Arius blood to him." Looking over her shoulder, she caught the gaze of a Hunter. "Bring me a dagger."

The Hunter went unnaturally still, his white eyes moving from her to Rordan.

"You're playing games, Tessa," Rordan barked.

"I told you I was bringing them to Achaz. I was simply offering you a way to gain favor with him. I'm sure Achaz would love to watch you take power from an Arius Legacy before he meets his death. Maybe then he would find you a little more . . . worthy of him."

Tessa . . . This is not the plan, Theon said down the bond.

He was right. This wasn't the plan they'd discussed, but she wasn't very good at following others' plans for her anyway.

So she shoved him out. Shoved them both out. Because she needed to focus, and her magic was already loud enough. She couldn't handle them in her head too.

She saw Theon's eyes widen at the action. Luka roared again, tail smashing into a wall of windows now as he tried to find a weakness. But there was none. The Faven Palace didn't have a weakness.

"But you're not going to keep me from proving my loyalty," she said. Then to the Hunter she snapped, "A dagger. Now."

Thunder echoed her words, and gold mist was swirling at her feet.

The Hunter appeared, bowing his head and handing her a gold dagger. "Your grace."

"Wait," Rordan interjected. He snapped his fingers at the seraph. "Start over. Here," he said, motioning a circle around the mirror.

"Here?" the female repeated. "Make it flow here?"

"Yes," he clipped out. He turned back to Tessa. "Prove that loyalty then."

His eyes narrowed as she snatched up the dagger the Hunter was offering her, and she wasted no time dragging it across her palm.

"Tessa, wait. Stop!" Theon said, trying to get to his feet, but the seraph behind him planted his hands on his shoulders, keeping him in place. The seraph's hand moved as if gesturing to something. Or halting something. Tessa couldn't split her focus to figure it out right now.

A Hunter moved closer, but he stilled when Tessa hissed, "Do not touch him. He is for Achaz. Will you steal from him?"

The Hunter froze. "We never steal from the Light King."

"Good answer," she replied before she slid her hand atop a symbol of three interlocking triangles.

"Tessa!" Theon said again, his eyes wide. "Tessa, what are you doing?"

"Come now, Theon," she said patronizingly while the mirror swirled. "You keep telling me you want to meet a god. Now you can."

Rordan was standing ramrod straight, his eyes fixed on the mirror. "If you are lying to me, child . . ."

She stepped to his side as the seraph finished the circle, taking a wide step back.

"You can see the symbol as well as I can," Tessa drawled. "Is that not Achaz's symbol?"

Rordan didn't speak as the mirror continued to eddy, gold and silver embers and sparks flitting throughout until a form took shape. A small gasp came from the male beside her, as though he hadn't truly believed she was summoning the god they descended from, and she was glad because the sound hid her own whimper as her power reached for the mirror.

No. We can't have that.

But we want it.

No.

Yes.

A little longer.

It took another few minutes. It always did, and she was fairly certain it had more to do with the gods favoring dramatics than anything else. But finally, there he stood. Blue eyes with brilliant flecks of gold. A glowing aura surrounding him. Tan complexion. Golden hair that reached nearly to his chin.

Rordan had fallen to a knee, and Tessa did the same, bowing her head as the god formed fully in the mirror.

"Tessa!" Theon barked.

The Hunters hissed, and Theon fell silent. She didn't dare look at him.

"Has my granddaughter learned respect?" Achaz asked, his voice ringing in the circular room. She lifted her head, meeting Achaz's gaze as he added, "Then again, that can't be true because your mother is missing."

"She is here. I can be rather impulsive," Tessa answered, a sliver of her power breaking free. Achaz homed in on it, a hunger filling his eyes. "But I had to know. I had to meet her."

"I offered to bring you to her," Achaz chided. "This could have all been avoided. Misunderstandings could have been rectified. I would have taken care of both of you."

"I know," Tessa said softly, eyes dropping to the floor where the Marks sat in front of her. "I am not very trusting. Too many people have tried to use me."

"You can still fix this. You know what you need to do to regain my favor. I can still take you from that world like I promised," he went on.

When she didn't immediately answer, his attention shifted to Rordan. "What do you have for me?"

"The Arius Lord, your grace," Rordan said, lifting his head. "I will rip his traitorous power from his soul before your eyes."

Achaz's smile was anything but light and life. It was cold and wicked, eyes glowing brighter at the idea of taking anything from Arius. "Bring him."

The seraph shoved Theon into the circle before the mirror, and Achaz's lip curled in disgust. "You look just like him. A prophecy then. I will watch you die as a preview of the day I get to watch him do the same."

"That's not how the prophecy goes," Tessa cut in. "Do you want to hear a story?"

Achaz's eyes flashed to her, narrowing. "No," he gritted out.

"That's disappointing," Tessa said, pushing to her feet. "I tell great stories. Right, Theon?"

Theon was watching her, his features tight. "The best stories, clever tempest. In fact, it'd be great if you could tell me one of a female who went rogue and nearly killed them all."

"She sounds delightful," Tessa replied wistfully, letting more and more of her power out. Watching it spread across the floor. Up the glass walls to the domed ceiling. "But I have another to tell."

"Not now," Achaz snapped.

"In all things, there must be balance," Tessa recited. "Beginnings and endings. Light and dark. Fire and shadows. The skies, the seas, the realms. But when the scales tip, and Chaos rains, who will fight and who will fall?"

Her magic swirled faster, her bow appearing in her hand.

"For Dark must bow." Her gaze slid to Theon, his lips curling into an amused smile as he bowed his head to her. "And Light must rule."

She nocked an arrow to her bow, Rordan lurching forward, but Theon snapped out a whip of darkness, throwing him against the mirror. The Hunters glided forward, and she let that arrow fly. Then another. And another.

"But Chaos does not choose. Control the uncontrollable, or to Fury they both lose," she recited as the last Hunter faded into nothing.

Light and dark exploded, colliding as Theon and Rordan both summoned the full extent of their gifts, but her magic encased the room. While they fought for dominance, she sliced her palm, finding those Marks on the floor. She danced around them, her blood spilling and the Marks flaring as she fell deeper and deeper into her Chaos.

"Life must give, and death must take," she sang, her voice rising with each word. "But Fate requires more."

"No!" Achaz bellowed, hands slamming against the mirror. "Impossible. He is not Arius. He cannot hold that much power."

Tessa had completed her circle, the glass walls around them cracking now. She could hear Luka slamming into them over and over. Staying near. Good. Because she wasn't entirely sure how this was going to end. Not anymore.

Theon and Rordan were an equal match. Power stolen and magic freely given.

But she was more.

She strode into the circle, her Chaos merging with Theon's darkness and strengthening it. Her light merged too, but with Rordan's power, turning it around and pushing it back against him. The same way she'd once turned Theon's power on him. It shoved him against the mirror, and she plucked a blade from Theon's belt.

"Destiny beckons, and sacrifice demands," she hissed, slicing that dagger across Rordan's palms while Theon's darkness held him in place. And when she finished, she tugged on Theon's power, using cords of his magic to turn Rordan. They forced him to his knees and his palms to the glass, his blood smearing on the smooth surface.

Then she shoved Theon out of the circle with a mighty surge of her Chaos.

"Tessa!" he yelled as he went flying, shadows wings bursting free and hopefully keeping him on his feet.

Rordan was thrashing. Light flaring as it tried to fight against her hold, but she was drawing from Theon. Taking and taking as she lifted her eyes to meet Achaz's in the mirror once more.

"Who will be left standing," she continued, feeling her feet lift from the floor. As her light and dark wound around her. As energy erupted, bouncing off the glass keeping them enclosed.

Then she started reciting the words. Words she'd listened to her mother recite over and over again as the Ladies sacrificed their power for their kingdoms, atoning for the wrongs they'd brought upon the realm. The lying. The deceit. The hunger and the greed.

She'd memorized those words. Internalized them. Tucked them away, and now as she spoke them, her Chaos snarled and snapped, trying to take the power that was flowing from Rordan into the mirror gate.

Achaz was cursing her. Theon was yelling her name. Luka was still trying to find any way in.

And still she recited the words, letting her power build and build.

She'd planned to come find this mirror gate after the battle was done. Still planned to find the others. She'd call it luck that Rordan had brought her here, but luck had never played a part in her life. Neither had coincidence. Call it fate. Call it destiny. She didn't really care anymore. This forgotten realm was her purpose, and she didn't like it when people touched what was hers to protect.

Rordan was crying out in agony now, trying desperately to pull his hands from the glass, but Theon's magic held them there. She watched as his limbs snapped and twisted at unnatural angles. Watched as blood dripped from his nose, his ears, his eyes. Watched as all that power he'd stolen was violently cut from his being and funneled into the mirror. Watched as the mirror gate absorbed it all, beginning to crack, small shards clinking to the marble floor.

And as the last of that power moved from Rordan to the mirror, as the Achaz Lord went silent and still, Tessa met Achaz's furious stare in that fractured mirror one more time as she said, "Chaos has come to reign."

She let the leash on her magic snap, and it leapt for the mirror gate, crashing into it like a wave. She could swear the world went silent, that the realm held its breath while all that Chaos pulsed and inhaled and stilled.

Then it exploded, the force radiating out. She'd cloaked the room in her power, trying to contain it, but it broke through even that. She was thrown into the air, clutching at any thread of her chaos, trying to keep the destruction in the air. Praying to any being that might intervene that innocent lives would not pay the price yet again.

Glass fell, mixing with the pouring rain. The seraphs had taken to the skies, and she wondered if the two that had been with her had survived.

She hoped she had at least.

Hoped she'd done enough.

And Theon . . .

Tessa? Tessa, where are you? his voice echoed down the bond, and she smiled as she tumbled through the air. She'd done it. She'd saved him.

That was good. Arius Kingdom would still have him.

And Axel and Kat. Maddox was safe.

This was good.

Her magic stuttered, and it was the strangest feeling. She'd never actually experienced her power running out. It had been locked up and caged, forced to slumber, but she'd never truly expended it all. It left an ache in her soul.

Or maybe that was the thought of never seeing Theon again.

You're not getting rid of him by fucking dying.

Luka's snarled voice came down the bond a moment before a dark shadow was there, diving fast. His wings snapped out as he neared, pulling that massive body up while a clawed foot wrapped around her, hauling her back into the sky.

Tessa let her eyes fall closed, feeling the rain splash against her face. Heard Nylah and Roan howling in the distance. Felt the rumble of the thunder in her bones.

Tired.

She was so, so tired.

The next thing she knew she was being placed on the ground, and hands were on her face.

"Open your eyes, little storm," Theon said, the words an order. "Open them, godsdammit."

Everything hurt, and a low groan came from her as she lifted her heavy lids. Theon and Luka were both leaning over her. The rain had slowed to a gentle drizzle, and when she moved her fingers, she felt the mud beneath them.

"You didn't die," she rasped. "That's good."

Theon huffed a laugh as Luka said, "You didn't die either. You're lucky."

"Yet you're still an ass," she muttered, and he smiled—a real one—as he reached for her and eased her into a sitting position while Theon pushed hair off her face.

She blinked as she realized where they were.

The stormy skies casting everything in grey.

Dead grass and scorched earth.

Bodies everywhere.

Blood and mud.

The rain.

But that was Xan and Aiyana, still in their dragon forms and guarding the perimeter with Nylah and Roan.

That was Razik and Eliza, weapons still out and ready for violence.

That was Cienna and Tristyn, brother and sister, alive and breathing.

Her mother and Caris.

Kat and Axel.

"We did it?" she asked, leaning into Luka's chest as he scooped her up and stood in one strong movement.

"You did it, baby girl," he murmured.

She nodded. Or tried to. She just wanted to go home.

Home.

She had one of those now.

How odd after all this time.

Salvation among the destruction.

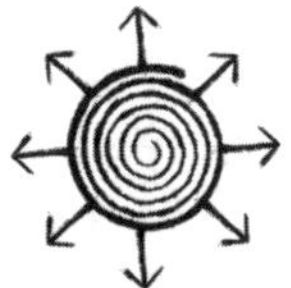

55
LUKA

Luka smiled while he watched his wife take, her head tipping back with eerie laughter as her magic made the seraph in her grasp open its mouth on a silent scream.

It had been nearly three weeks since the day she'd destroyed the Achaz Kingdom mirror gate. Then again, she'd destroyed more than that. The Faven Palace had been as thoroughly desecrated as the Pantheon had been. Cienna had figured out what was going to happen—because of course she had—and she and Tristyn had rushed to get the innocent servants from the palace. Tessa had shielded most of those outside, and those she hadn't been able to shelter, Theon had. Silver embers and gold mist had filled the sky while darkness had coated the ground, keeping the destruction as contained as possible.

Lives had still been lost. Whether from the explosion of the mirror gate or in the battle on the ground, sacrifices had been made. The destruction of the mirror gate had effectively ended the battle and the war. Rordan was gone. Valter was gone. Bree was imprisoned. The Achaz forces had conceded at the instruction of Dagian with Rordan gone. No one had known that he no longer held his power at that time.

They did now though.

The strongest Achaz blood now oversaw the kingdom for the time being.

The Arius Lady *and* the Achaz Lady.

The other kingdoms were being overseen by the heirs with their mothers' help. In a month, a Tribunal was being held that would be nothing like the Tribunals of the past.

But while the Achaz forces were under control, the seraphs had fled, and every few days, he took Tessa hunting with Nylah and Roan so she could refill her power. Power that had been nonexistent when he'd plucked her from the sky as she'd fallen among the rubble and rain.

She let the seraph drop to the ground, inhaling deeply. They were at the river just outside the Acropolis. With the Faven Palace gone, they were staying at the Arius Manor on the outskirts. The sun beat down on them, summer well and truly here, and the rays of warmth glinted off the gold sparks drifting around her, as though she was absorbing the light too.

"Are you quite done for today?" Luka asked flatly when she sauntered over to him. Barefoot. Her bow looped across her chest. Her black pants looking like they were painted onto her skin while her shirt stopped just above her navel.

She rolled her eyes, coming to a stop before him. "As if you're not thinking about throwing me on the ground and fucking me right here after watching me be so wild."

He smirked, looping an arm around her waist and tugging her closer. She was right. He *had* been thinking about doing that. If only they didn't have something else to prepare for later this afternoon.

Something he was dreading.

Tessa clearly felt his shift in thoughts, and she reached up, brushing back strands of hair that had escaped where he'd had it tied up.

"Today will be hard," she said.

He shrugged because he shouldn't really care.

She nestled into his chest, her cheek resting over his heart. "My loyalty is to you," she murmured.

He frowned. "I know that. Why are you saying that?"

"I just want you to know. During the hard days, you're still not alone."

He rested his chin on her head, looking out over the black waters of the Wynfell River.

Knowing standing here wouldn't make time stop, a few minutes later he Traveled them back to the front yard of the manor. They walked up the front steps together, and Luka pushed open the door, ushering her through first.

"Theon?" Tessa called.

"In the sitting room, beautiful," he answered.

Luka followed her in, and then he nearly ran into her when she stopped abruptly.

"What's going on?" Tessa asked slowly.

Luka understood her suspicion. Blackheart was here, and with him was a seraph.

Eyes that were a few shades darker than his grey wings. Neatly trimmed black hair.

"This is the one that never speaks," Tessa said, her head tilting to the side in a predatory manner Luka recognized. "What is he doing here? A present?"

Tristyn barked a laugh. "No, wild fury. He came to me with a request."

"A request," she repeated, sounding a little disappointed, and Luka sent a few wisps of dragonfire to ease the tension of her magic that had clearly been ready to take more.

"He helped me," Theon said, slipping his hands into his pockets. "The day Rordan took us to his palace. While you were . . . keeping Rordan and Achaz busy, he was keeping the Hunters back. Helped me understand what the fuck you were doing."

"You're saying he's on our side?" Luka deadpanned. "I find that hard to believe."

"There are seraphs who are working on the inside," Tristyn ventured. "Look at Brecken."

He had a point. Dex's mother had survived too, the two of them living quiet lives in Coveyll as requested. Luka had his reservations about that. She was one of the original seraphs. Surely someone would come looking for her, but it was one of the many things they'd have to look into in the coming days.

"And what is this request?" Tessa asked, fingers curling at her side.

Tristyn glanced up at Luka before back at Tessa. "When we leave today, he wishes to go with. Scarlett can get him where he needs to go from there."

Tessa was dragging her fingers along the back of a sofa while she asked, "Illithor, right? That's your name?"

The seraph's eyes narrowed, and he nodded.

"And where will you go? Back to Achaz?"

Grey eyes flashed to Tristyn. "He doesn't have a choice, wild fury. But he uses his position to help when he can. Just like Brecken did."

She studied the seraph a moment longer, her power creeping forward as if testing him. He stood perfectly still, holding her stare.

"You trust him, Tris?" she asked.

"I do."

"Then he will be your responsibility."

He arched a brow. "I can accept that."

She nodded, glancing back at Luka, and her features softened. "Then let's go."

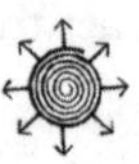

"You have a very anxious king and queen waiting for you," the silver-haired female drawled as she stepped from the mirror gate, her husband at her side. Then she was laughing when Eliza wrapped her in a hug. "I've missed you too, my friend," Scarlett murmured, holding her just as tightly. Her silver gaze flicked to Razik. "Dragon prick."

"Pain in my ass," he said tightly.

Scarlett stepped back, Eliza moving to hug Sorin next.

And then they were all just . . . staring at each other.

Tessa and Theon were here, of course. Axel and Kat as well, since they were in the Underground.

But the ones Luka was focused on were his parents.

This was likely the last time the four of them would stand in a room together. A blooded family he'd just found, but was now being separated once more.

Introductions were done, and when the room fell quiet once more, Razik was the one who reached for a pack on the floor. "Keep that sword somewhere safe."

Luka swallowed his amusement. "We have it covered. Thanks for the concern."

"What sword?" Scarlett demanded.

"They found a spirit sword," Eliza sighed. "Razik is upset he didn't find it first."

"I'm not upset," Razik growled.

"Why?" Scarlett asked, her nose scrunching in confusion. "It's not a bowl."

"By the gods," Razik muttered. "Can we go?"

"Razik."

The male stilled at the sound of Xan's voice. Slowly, he dragged his eyes to where they stood.

Aiyana had tears tracking down her face as she watched her older son, that she hadn't seen in centuries, prepare to walk away from her.

"I need more time," Razik finally said.

Xan nodded, pulling Aiyana into his side. "I understand."

"I'm not saying it'll be never, but—"

"We'll be waiting. When you are ready," Xan said somberly.

Razik nodded stiffly, and Luka watched their mother pull from Xan's hold and approach him. She reached up, clasping his shoulders as she said softly, "I never stopped fighting for you. I won't stop now."

A muscle feathered in Razik's jaw, and she pulled him into a hug before pressing a chaste kiss to his cheek. "We'll wait for you." She stepped back and turned to Eliza. "Thank you for loving him so deeply where we failed."

Eliza gave her a sad smile, glancing up at her mate. "I think we'll meet again."

"Thank you both," Theon said, stepping forward and holding out a hand to Eliza. "Your aid was invaluable."

"More helpful than when they were here, I'm sure," Razik said, jerking his chin to Scarlett and Sorin.

"Not now, Raz," Eliza grumbled, elbowing him in the ribs as she bent to grab her pack, but Razik was snatching it from her fingers a second later.

A jolt of heartache down the bond had Luka turning to find Tessa and Tristyn off by themselves, talking in low murmurs. She was crying, and he was thumbing at the tears before he pulled her into his chest.

"You'll find her," she murmured into his shirt. "I know you will."

Tristyn was leaving with Razik and Eliza, going to their world. Apparently there was something he was working on with Razik, and in return, his brother had agreed to help him track down the Witch he loved.

Tristyn led Tessa back to Theon, handing her off, and Theon held out a hand to Tristyn as well. He'd already said goodbye to Cienna, who was staying here to be with Gia and to help them all rebuild Devram.

"Blackheart," Theon said tightly. "Thank you. For everything."

"Especially the pizza and lull-leaf, right, wild fury?" he said with a wink.

Theon stiffened. Tessa laughed, but the sound quickly faded. "I'll miss you, Tris."

He reached out, thumbing her cheek once more. "If you are weak enough to fall . . ."

"You are strong enough to rise back up," she whispered through her tears.

"It's been an honor to witness."

Her tears came faster now, and it took her a minute to get them under control. But when she did, she turned to where Scarlett and Sorin were waiting quietly near the mirror, as if they understood the pain of these goodbyes all too well.

"Achaz came for your world?" Tessa asked.

Scarlett's brow pinched. "He tried."

"And now? How do you keep him at bay?"

The female's smile was pure wickedness. "He would have to get past me. He is a god, but I am more. I suspect he will try again at some point, and when he does, we'll be ready as the guardians of our realm."

"You control the mirror gates?" Theon asked in that tone that told Luka he was putting something together.

"I do, lordling," she drawled. "It's why I'm here, after all."

"Is there more than one in your world?"

"There is."

"And you don't find that to be a risk to your world's safety?"

She sighed. "Only World Walkers can activate the mirror gates for traveling between the worlds. As I am the only one left, no, I don't find it a risk."

"So we could leave the three remaining mirrors here. In case," Theon said, gaze flicking to Tessa.

"In case what?"

"We can ever be of assistance to you. Or another realm. To return the favor," Theon answered, straightening his cuffs. "I am told the battle for Devram was only one of many in an Everlasting War."

"You would be correct," Scarlett said. "And yes, the mirrors can remain. The gods still cannot come here, or Achaz would have done so already. But I would monitor them."

"Noted," Theon said with a small dip of his chin.

"We should go," Sorin cut in.

Suddenly there was emotion clogging Luka's throat, and he didn't know why. But Eliza approached, uncharacteristically apprehensive. "He cares," she whispered. "I promise he does."

Luka nodded, and the female pushed up onto her toes to wrap him in an unexpected hug. She stepped back, and Razik was there, two packs in hand and that impassive look on his face.

"If you ever find yourself alone again, you know where to find me," Razik said stiffly. There was a swirl of black flames before the male was holding out an empty frame, small and silver.

Luka's eyes narrowed, and he snatched it from his hand. "This is mine."

Razik shrugged a shoulder.

"You stole this?" Luka demanded.

"I gave it back," he grumbled.

Scarlett snorted a laugh, but the humor fell away as her starfire and chaos swirled in her palm. "We really do need to go."

There were final farewells and gratitude exchanged. More tears from Tessa and his mother. They watched as Tristyn went first with Illithor, stopping to throw one last wink over his shoulder at Tessa. "Salvation or destruction, wild fury."

And Theon was pulling her into his chest as she silently sobbed.

Razik and Eliza went next, Axel and Kat thanking the Fire General once more for her help with Kat's pregnancy. Razik didn't look back at their parents, but he caught Luka's eye, giving the barest dip of his chin.

Then it was Scarlett and Sorin, and the queen's silver eyes took them all in before settling on Tessa.

"I am told the winds speak of new beginnings," Scarlett said, shadows drifting around her. "They speak of beings and worlds awakening. They speak of a new dawn."

"What does that mean?" Tessa asked.

Scarlett shrugged. "I don't know, but I do know we weren't the only ones chosen, Cousin."

Then she and Sorin stepped through the mirror gate.

The rest of them stood in silence long after the mirror stopped swirling and became nothing but reflective glass once more.

Eventually, they all left together, Traveling back to Arius House, and later that evening, he sat around a full dining table, listening to conversation and laughter. Two things that had never filled Arius House before, but that were commonplace since Axel and Kat had moved in here permanently.

Family chosen and family found.

Theon said something, and Tessa snapped a sharp retort that had Luka turning to them, finally feeling like he'd found his place in all the fuckery.

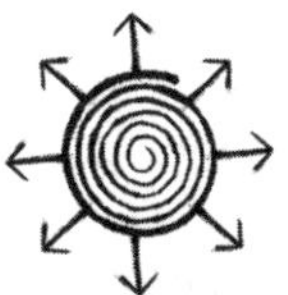

56
AXEL

"Where's Mads?" Axel asked, looking up from the book he was reading when Kat entered their bedroom.

"With Dey," she answered, closing the door behind her and leaning against it. "She's keeping him with her for the next few hours."

Axel's brow furrowed.

With Tessa the only real option for an Achaz Lady right now, they'd moved into the Arius Manor outside the Acropolis and given Arius House to him and Kat. It had been weird for a while, and he'd had the private wing his father had occupied for decades deep cleaned. Then he'd asked Cienna to cleanse it with all her Witchy ways. They'd had the main bedroom completely gutted and hired some earth Fae to remodel it. He was doing the same thing to every fucking room in this house, but at least the rooms he shared with his family were being done first.

Rooms that were once dark and foreboding were being brought back to life. Curtains thrown wide. New flooring and brighter walls. With soft grey walls, the space felt lighter, while the red and orange accents made it feel warm and familiar.

His sister had come to stay at Arius House as well after all was said and done. She was helping with the restructured academies, particularly with those Legacy who were coming into their power. She'd had to learn to control her shadows all on her own, and she'd seemed to have found a niche in helping others hone their own power. Axel was enjoying having her close, and she spent a lot of time with Maddox; however, her rooms were also in another wing of the house.

"And why is Maddox with Dey?" he asked, setting the book aside and watching her. She dropped his gaze, her eyes looking anywhere but at him, and it had him sitting up straighter. "Kat, what is it? What's wrong?"

"Nothing's wrong," she said quickly. "I just . . ."

"Katya . . ."

"I cancelled your next delivery of blood," she blurted.

Axel's brows shot up, and it took him a few minutes to find words. "Okay," he said slowly. "Is there a particular reason you cancelled the delivery of my sustenance?"

"Because Maddox was born. It's been a few months now," she answered, still not looking at him, but her cheeks were flushing.

A smirk pulled at the corner of his lips, realizing what she was trying to convey, but she was going to have to ask for it.

"Maddox's birth doesn't negate my need for blood, kitten," Axel said, his voice dropping low as he pushed to his feet.

"I know, but you'd said—" She gasped when he was suddenly in front of her, and she shoved at his bare chest. "Stop doing that," she snapped.

He caught her wrists, bringing them above her head and pinning them to the door with one hand. With the other, he used one finger to tip her chin up.

Leaning in, he brushed his cheek along her jaw. "I love it when you get jealous of little glass bottles."

"I'm not—" she cried in outrage, his mouth on hers before she could finish whatever she was going to say.

His hands dropped to her hips, and that outrage turned to a whimper as she pressed herself against him. He could feel her nipples through the thin silk fabric of her top, and he pulled back to drag it over her head before plastering his lips back to hers. His breath fanned across her face, and her arms were looped around his neck, keeping him close. Frantic. Desperate.

Sliding his hands around, he cupped her ass, and she immediately hopped up, her legs coming around his waist as he thrust his hips into her, pushing her back against the door once more.

"There are conditions, kitten," he murmured into her mouth, one of his hands coming back to grip her delicate neck and hold her still.

Her amber eyes were bright with exhilaration and lust. She'd been wanting this for a long time. She'd never liked him getting something he needed from someone or something else.

"This is always your choice," he murmured, sliding his lips along her jaw. "Always. If you ever don't want—"

"I will," she panted, pulling him somehow closer with her legs.

"But if you do," he insisted. "You are not a blood source. You are my wife. Understood?"

She nodded, her chest rising and falling with each stuttered breath she took.

"And you will use your magic against me if I can't . . . If I lose control," he said, holding her stare. "Swear it, Katya."

The need dissipated for a moment, and she cupped his cheek. "I trust you," she said softly. "You need to trust me too. This is logical. I'm right here, and—"

He broke into a dark laugh because she was going back to logic with this. "You're nervous," he teased, his thumb sweeping over her pulse point. She always reverted to logic when she was nervous.

"A little," she admitted. "I think this will be different from when you drank from my wrist at the House of Four."

"Undoubtedly," he nearly growled. "There will be fucking involved this time, kitten."

She sucked in a sharp breath, and he smiled darkly.

They stared at each other for a long moment, and then he swallowed thickly, his control about gone. Because she was right here, and he'd been shoving down this desire since the day he'd become a Night Child. Knowing he was seconds away from having the blood he never stopped craving?

Desperation was about to win out.

"Are you sure?" he asked, the words gravel.

"Yes, Axel," she whispered, her fingers winding into his hair. "I still choose you."

He inhaled a shuddering breath, running his lips along her jaw once more. His hand dropped back to her hips, holding her to him as his mouth skated down her throat. Then he scraped his fangs gently along her flesh before pausing.

Her breathing was erratic, and her other hand was squeezing his biceps.

"Relax, kitten," he murmured. "It should only sting for a second."

"I—"

But she gasped as he sank his fangs into her throat, the first rush of coppery fire dancing across his taste buds.

"Fuck," she gasped, the fingers in his hair tightening and keeping him at her neck.

He took a deep pull, and she moaned, her head falling back and thudding softly against the door.

She was *everything.* Jasmine and citrus. Smoke and heat. He was groaning into her neck when he took another long pull. Her life force feeding him, as if she wasn't the reason he was alive the way it was.

He took another pull before forcing himself to pull back, studying the two puncture marks and the blood dripping from them now. Down her neck, her chest, to her breasts.

"You good, kitten?" he asked, slowly letting her slide down the length of his body until her feet were back on the floor.

"Yes, but did you take enough?" she asked breathily. "That didn't seem like enough."

"It's not even close," he murmured, pitching forward to drag his tongue between the valley of her breasts, tracing the blood trail. She gasped again, shifting beneath him, and he smiled. "Just checking in."

He lowered down, pulling her silk sleep shorts down with him. She stepped out of them, and he tossed them aside as he settled on his knees before her. Fingers skating up a calf, he lifted behind her knee, draping her leg over his shoulder. With his other hand, he brushed his thumb along her center, learning just how good she was as he started massaging her clit.

"Axel," she breathed, her head falling back once more. Then she whimpered when he pressed a kiss to her inner thigh, moving higher and doing it again, his tongue flicking out with each kiss until he paused, looking up at her. Embers flickered in her eyes as she watched him sink his fangs into her thigh and drink again.

Longer.

Deeper.

He pushed a finger into her wet core, still rubbing her clit. For several minutes, this was them. Him taking and her giving. Her fingers were tight in his hair, tugging at his scalp, but she never moved to stop him. There for him in every possible way. His, not because of a lost bond, but because they chose to be everything for each other.

After one last suck, he pulled back and slid his mouth up, feeling the blood smear along her flesh. He brushed his nose along her cunt, inhaling all of her with the taste of her blood lingering on his tongue.

Now he wanted to taste something else.

Slowly pressing forward, he parted her with his tongue, flicking her clit.

Her hands slammed onto his shoulders, nails digging in as she inhaled sharply. Lifting her other leg, he hoisted that one over his other shoulder, leaving her at his mercy as she pressed against the door. His mouth closed around her, sucking and licking and swirling his tongue, this taste far sweeter than her blood had been.

"More, Axel," she choked out, her hips rocking against his mouth now.

Not one to deny her a godsdamn thing, he sucked harder at her throbbing clit beneath his tongue while sinking two fingers into her dripping core. Her cry only spurred him on as he felt all of her trembling, right on the precipice.

She wanted to be the only one to give him blood? He would forever be the only one to give her this.

He didn't stop, didn't let up, until she was clamping her thighs around his ears and pulling at his hair. His mouth was fused to her center as she rode out her high, and he drank it all down just as he'd drank from her throat and thigh.

Not until she slumped against the door did he pull back, dragging his tongue along the smear of blood on her thigh. She was working to get her breathing under control as he scooped her up and carried her to their bed, gently laying her among the blankets and pillows.

And later that night, after Dey had brought them Maddox and Kat had fed him, he was walking around their dark room with his son in the crook of his arm. Kat had already fallen back to sleep, exhausted from him taking blood from her.

Who would have thought he'd end up here?

Night Child and a leader of the Underground, working to bring them all out of the dark.

Things he'd resisted and feared, fought against at every turn.

No longer a spare heir, but a husband and father, rebuilding a world from ash so their son would know how to dream.

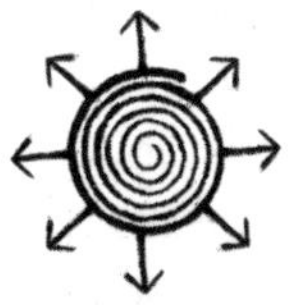

57
THEON

"You two are up early," Theon said, strolling across the courtyard to where Tessa and his mother were throwing sticks for his hounds.

He was used to finding Tessa with Akira, trying to build some sort of tentative relationship, but finding her with *his* mother was new.

"I was just leaving to get ready," Caris said, turning to him with a smile. "I'll leave you two alone."

Theon pressed a kiss to her cheek as she passed before he closed the distance to Tessa's side. She brought her hand back, ready to throw the stick once more, and Theon caught her wrist. She looked at him, startled.

"Use this," he said, a ball of darkness forming in his palm.

The hounds had been excited before, but now they were yipping and prancing about.

"Show off," she huffed, reaching for the mass of magic.

She chucked it, and the hounds took off, racing to be the first to retrieve it.

"Are you worried about how today will go?" Theon asked, Tessa shoving her hands into the pockets of her jacket.

"No," she replied, smiling as the hounds came tearing back, Rigel with the prize.

"Then . . . ?"

"I just wanted to ask Caris some questions," she said. "That's all. Are you ready to go?"

She turned to look up at him, her smile a little too bright. He cupped her cheek and leaned in, running the tip of his nose along the length of hers. "You are keeping something from us, little storm," he murmured.

"Not really," she replied. "Just . . . We'll talk about it after the Tribunals. We have long days ahead."

He was in his suit, and she was in a dress beneath her coat. Everyone else was meeting them at the Acropolis. So for now, he let it go.

Tessa Traveled them, and they strode up the steps of the brick building hand in hand. They'd needed something large enough to hold all the people who would be attending, and an academy in the western part of the Acropolis ended up being the best option.

They were led to an auditorium, where Tessa, Luka, and Theon joined Axel, the Ladies, their heirs, and several others at the front. The seats were full, and not just with Legacy. Fae. Night Children. Witches. Shifters. Even some mortals were here. Which was good. If this was going to be successful, everyone needed to feel they were part of the process.

Everyone took a seat behind the tables that were facing the crowd. Not in grand thrones, but simple chairs, and the room fell silent.

"I guess we should start with how we want the kingdoms to be run going forward," Theon said, unbuttoning his suit jacket and settling back into his chair. "All ideas are welcome. There are microphones throughout the room for anyone to use. We're in for a long several days, so let's get going."

"The most powerful of a bloodline will no longer be the sole leader of a kingdom," Tessa said simply, speaking into the microphone before her on the table.

"Then who will?" the Celeste Lady asked. "The reason the most powerful has maintained that seat of power was for protection, yes. But it was also for simplicity."

"And even then, it often took hours or days for the six rulers to come to agreements," the Serafina Lady chimed in.

"So we maintain a primary Lord or Lady for each kingdom," Theon suggested. "Only they are accountable to a Council within their kingdom."

"A Council of more than just Legacy," Tessa added. "Fae need to be included. Mortals." She glanced to her left where Axel was sitting. "And those from the Underground who wish to rejoin the kingdoms."

Arguments and debates went back and forth on the subject for the next few hours until most of the details were agreed to.

"One primary Lord or Lady for each kingdom," Theon was saying. "Councils will include three Fae, three Legacy, a Witch, a Shifter, a Night Child, and a mortal. Elections can be held, and we can figure out the details down the road. We need interim leaders for now."

"I suppose Tessa is simply going to maintain her place in both the Achaz and Arius Kingdoms?" the Serafina Heir asked, and Theon hid his smirk. The Ladies may have come to terms with things, but the heirs were still adjusting to undoing years of learned animosity.

"Actually, no," Tessa said simply. "There isn't really another option for the Achaz Kingdom at this time, but there is a better option for the Arius Kingdom."

"Theon?" asked the Anala Heir.

"Axel," Tessa replied.

"Wait, what?" Axel asked, lurching forward in his seat. "Tessa, what are you talking about? I don't even have magic anymore."

"No, but your wife does," she said with a smile. "A Night Child and a Fae leading the Arius Kingdom seems fine to me. You are prominent in the Underground and have more than proven your loyalty."

"But he's not the most powerful Arius Legacy," the Falein Lady cut in. "Which is what we just determined would dictate who would hold that seat."

That was true. The heirs would assume their seats as Ladies of the Celeste, Falein, Anala, and Serafina Kingdoms. Tessa couldn't lead both Arius and Achaz though. It would stretch her too thin, and while Theon could go back to Arius Kingdom, he didn't want to split his time and focus. He would stay with Tessa, and so would Luka.

"His son will be," Tessa said. "I propose Axel and Kat hold the position until Maddox is old enough and ready to assume it."

Axel was staring at her, clearly in shock, and murmuring broke out among the people.

"More than that," Tessa continued, the crowd falling silent once more. "I will only be the interim Achaz Lady until we learn who should take over the position. I will work closely with Dagian regarding this matter."

Tessa? Luka growled down the bond. *We never discussed any of this.*

Agreed, Theon said, working to keep his features impassive. *What are we doing, Tessa?*

"We are to believe that you are going to step down from everything after all this?" Lady Isleen asked, her suspicion evident in her tone. "What of you and your . . . husbands?"

"We have other responsibilities," Tessa said.

"Such as?"

"While Rordan and Valter are gone, Achaz is not. There are still realms beyond that will face the same, and Achaz will likely try again. More than that, we have the Fates to contend with," Tessa said calmly despite her chaos that had been thickening a little more as time passed. "I put forth that the three of us become the new Keepers. Guardians of the realm to ensure that no one from the outside comes here without our knowing. So that history just might not repeat itself yet again, and the people we are protecting will not be the cost."

"The three of you would be the Keepers? We're going to vote on everything else and not that?" the Celeste Lady asked.

"You are welcome to nominate another who would be as effective in the position," Theon said, recovering quickly from Tessa's little surprise.

"There isn't another who would be effective," Kyra said. "I believe Tessa, Theon, and Luka have all proven beyond a doubt they care for the realm, not just their own kingdoms. Tessa is the grandchild of three First gods. She is not demanding we bow to her. She is not demanding a throne. She is offering to take on the responsibility of protecting the realm so we can focus on protecting the people. That is a noble offering, and I agree to the proposal."

"We will still have a say in the realm's policies," Theon interjected. "That is important to all three of us."

"So you are, what? Simply Keepers of the Realm?" the Falein Heir asked.

"Yes," Tessa said at the same time Theon said, "No."

She turned to him, eyes wide with incredulity. "What?"

"You are not simply a Keeper of the Realm, Tessa," he said. "You bled and sacrificed for a world that only tried to break you. You fought for a realm that only wanted to use you. You're still here, fighting for all of us in a forgotten world. You could leave. You have that power. You could leave, Tessa, and you are choosing to stay." He shook his head, her wide eyes fixed on him as he stood and took her hand, dropping to a knee before her. "You are the reason this realm still exists. So no, Tessalyn Ausra. You are not simply a Keeper of the Realm. You are a High Goddess of Chaos, because in Devram? Chaos reigns."

"Theon, stop," she hissed. "This isn't—"

But she stopped speaking as chairs scrapped. As people in the crowd stood. As everyone in the room dropped to a knee before the one who could have left them to answer for their depravity, and instead chose to become a villain with the rest of them.

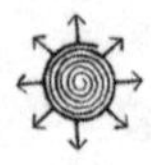

"You need to see something."

"Fucking Arius," Theon barked as he came face-to-face with Axel when he opened the bathroom door, fresh from a shower. "Boundaries, fucker," he muttered, shoving past him.

"Get dressed," Axel said. "I need to show you something. Luka is already there."

"Fine," he grumbled, grabbing some lightweight pants.

Twenty-two days.

It had been twenty-two days of sitting for hours in that auditorium debating new policies and restructuring. Integrating the Underground population into the kingdoms. Dismantling the Fae Estates. Debating where new communities could be set up. Wages for the Fae and giving them the freedom to decide where they resided.

And Sources.

Gods, that had been three entire days in and of itself. Tessa refused to back down on Sources and demanded no more Selections be held. Instead, every five years, Tribunals just like they'd sat through would be held to make changes, elect new Council members, and more. But Sources? Any Legacy could now have one, but only if a Fae was willing. A new registry was being put together at Lilura Inquest where Fae could voluntarily offer to become a Source. Pairings would go through several counseling sessions to ensure it was mutually beneficial, and then it would be one Source Mark.

The true Source Mark.

But after twenty-two days of mentally exhausting debates, he'd been looking forward to falling into bed with Tessa and Luka and not having to be up before the sun tomorrow.

They'd gone back to Arius House and were planning to stay for a few days as a sort of holiday until they would return to the Acropolis. The Pantheon wasn't being rebuilt, but there was a home that was going to be built there.

Their home.

For the Keepers and the High Goddess.

In the meantime, they would stay at the Arius Manor.

Theon followed Axel across the house to the private wing, which still felt strange to be in so freely. They climbed a few flights of stairs, coming to what he knew were Axel and Kat's private quarters.

"Axel?" he sighed. "This couldn't wait?"

He shook his head, leading him through their sitting room and then their bedroom. Luka and Kat were standing in a doorway, and Theon's brow pinched. They were standing in the doorway of the nursery, and when Theon came up behind them, he stilled.

Tessa was in the nursery, asleep in the rocking chair, and nestled on her chest was a sleeping Maddox.

"She found me and asked if she could hold him," Kat whispered. "I left her with him while I went to shower real quick, and when I came back . . ." She gestured to them.

"Do you want us to . . . take her?" Theon asked because Maddox was a few months old now, and this was the first time Tessa had held him.

"She's fine," Kat said. "You can stay as long as you want. I'm sure he'll be waking in the next hour to eat."

Theon nodded, Axel and Kat wandered out to the sitting room, and he and Luka ventured into the dim nursery, taking seats on the small sofa.

"Any ideas on what instigated this?" Luka asked, stretching his legs out and crossing them at the ankles.

"No idea," Theon said, watching her with the sleeping babe. "Maybe she just needed time?"

"Doubt it," Luka said. "This has been a thing since Maddox was born."

"Yeah," Theon sighed because he was right.

And so was Kat.

It was maybe twenty minutes later when Maddox started to stir, and Tessa's eyes snapped open. Her features twisted as she tried to figure out what to do, but Theon was there, scooping up their nephew.

"I've got him, beautiful," he said with a soft smile.

She looked a little embarrassed when her gaze darted to Luka. "I didn't mean to fall asleep."

"We're all exhausted, Tessa," Luka replied, reaching for her hand and pulling her to her feet. "Let's go to our rooms."

They delivered Maddox to his parents and made their way back across the house, and as soon as the door closed behind them, she spun to face them.

"I need to tell you something," she said, her teeth sinking into her bottom lip.

Theon and Luka both froze, waiting for her to go on.

"I . . ." She cleared her throat and crossed her arms, clearly working up the courage to tell them this. "In a few days, I'm going to see Cienna, and she is going to give me some Marks. I wanted to tell you before I went."

"Okay," Theon said tentatively as Luka made his way to the liquor cart. Guess they weren't going to bed quite yet. "What are these Marks for?"

"I—" Her hands were in her hair, tugging at the ends. "I don't want children," she blurted.

He and Luka both froze again because where was this coming from?

"It's not an impulsive decision," she went on. "I don't know the first thing about being a mother."

"That is something that would come in time, Tessa," Theon said carefully while Luka passed out liquor and wine.

"That's not . . ." A sound of frustration came from her. "My existence nearly destroyed a realm. Can you imagine my child? With either one of you? With Luka, it would be a great-grandchild of four gods. With you and your surplus of power? A child would be hunted. They would upset the balance."

"It would be different, Tessa," Theon argued. "Our child wouldn't be left alone."

"You think Temural and Akira didn't think the same thing?" she countered. "Because they did. I've been spending time with her. This isn't what she wanted, but that's not always how life goes. I cannot bring a child into the stars knowing what fate would await them. This isn't like Maddox. Even if I had a child with a random mortal—" She paused when he and Luka both made unimpressed sounds at that idea. "I just mean *any* child of mine will be hunted. That is not fair to them. And I . . ." She was looking between them, her eyes pooling with tears as she begged them to understand. "I can scarcely handle my own Chaos most days. It is a constant battle, even with your help." Those tears broke free. "I am sorry if this is a dream of yours, but I can't."

"And Maddox tonight?" Luka asked after an extended silence.

"I've avoided him," she said, sounding utterly defeated. "Because I think that is something you want, and it is not something I am willing to give you. And tonight? I wanted to hold him. Just to see if something changed. If I had any inclination to want that, and I don't. I wish I did."

Luka had set his drink aside and was taking her wineglass back before he pulled her into him. "Baby girl, how long have you felt this way?"

"Since before he was born, and I didn't—Look at everything we had to do to ensure his safety. My child would require so much more," she answered. "And even if that wasn't the case, it is something I do not want. I am content to be with you two for the rest of my days. To spoil Maddox and

Priya and any other children others may have. Because some day, we may have to defend this world again, and I cannot have a child in it when I do so."

"Okay, Tessa," Luka murmured as she cried silently into his chest. "We would never force you. This is your choice. No one else's."

"But an heir—"

"Does not matter," Theon interjected. "As someone who was being forced to produce an heir, that will never happen again. To any of us."

"But it is something you want," she whispered, so much pain shining in her eyes.

Theon was crossing to them now, taking her chin in his hand. "There is nothing I want as much as you, Tessa. Do you understand?"

"But—"

"No buts. Like Luka said, this is your choice. Tell me of these Marks."

She swallowed thickly several times, getting herself under control. "When Eliza was here, I asked of the Mark on her chest—"

"You are not getting a Curse Mark," Luka growled.

"No. I know. I mean, I did think about it," Tessa admitted. "Until we freed Caris."

"That's what you were asking her about the morning I found you with her and the hounds," Theon said in understanding.

She nodded. "Her Marks are permanent, and they differ from Eliza's. I understand it's permanent. Even if I ever did change my mind, I cannot bring a child into the stars," she repeated. "If that is something we ever want, we could find a child in our own realm to give a home, right?"

"And you've been thinking about this for some time?"

She nodded. "I've never dwelled on it. Not until Maddox was born, and I know I should have said something before we all bound ourselves to one another, but—"

"Tessa," Luka interrupted, easing her back so he could look into her face. "Children were an option far into the future. You were never an option because you've always been inevitable."

"You're not upset?"

"Surprised? Yes. Will we need some time to process? Sure," Luka answered, tucking her hair behind her ear. "But the only thing I'm upset about is you taking so long to talk to us."

"I just wanted to be sure before I did," she murmured.

Theon took her hand, tugging her to him. "We're going with you for the Marks," he answered.

She nodded, settling into him, a weight clearly lifted from her thoughts.

And later that night, as he watched her sleep with his head propped on a fist, he thought back on everything they'd survived to get to this point. He'd never really thought of children as a dream. It had always been an expected responsibility. The only thing he'd truly dreamed of was a family different from what he'd grown up with, and he had that right here in his bed. Unconventional and different in every possible way.

Because this had always been more than a bond.

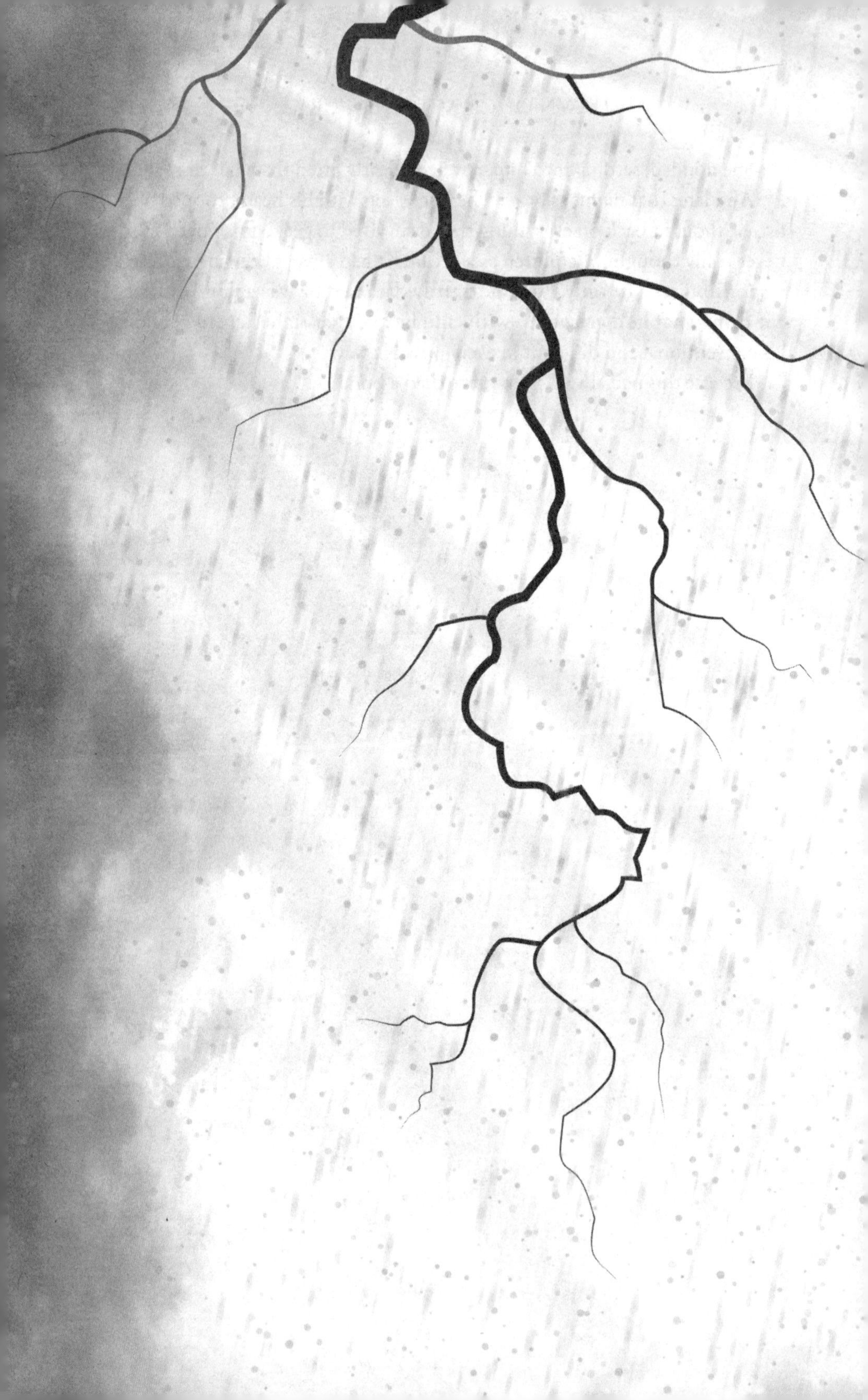

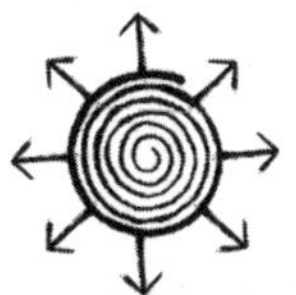

58
TESSA

She blinked in the bright sunlight, her bare feet in the surf as waves gently rolled to the shore.

"Where are we, little storm?"

Tessa turned, seeing Luka and Theon walking down the beach, and she smiled. Even in her dreams, they found her.

"I don't know," she answered, turning back to the endless glittering sea. "It's beautiful though."

"Better than the last vision I was pulled into," Luka muttered, and she sent him a flat look.

"I can't control them, Luka."

He shrugged. "Doesn't change the fact I'll take this over your other visions of death and destruction."

She rolled her eyes, feeling the sun's warmth seep into her soul. For several minutes, the three of them stood there, taking in the tranquility. It didn't last long, though. It never did.

This time was no different, as several figures appeared. Not on the beach, but on the sea, walking atop the waves and making their way towards them. They all wore robes of varying colors with the hoods up, hiding their features.

Theon and Luka dragged her back, sand sticking to her wet toes, and they made sure there was several feet between them and the newcomers when they stepped onto the shore.

There were five of them, but one stepped forward. Tessa could only assume she was the leader of the group as she pulled back her hood. Honey-colored eyes skimmed over them, her loose ashy-blonde hair flowing in the sea breeze, and the sun highlighted how pale her skin was.

"Tessalyn Ausra," she said, her voice as smooth as silk.

Tessa tilted her head. "If you know my name, surely I should know yours?"

The woman's lips curled into a smirk. "Avana," she answered. "My name is Avana, and I am one of the Fates."

Tessa lurched back, but Theon had already looped his arm around her waist, dragging her back farther. She could feel Luka fighting a shift into his dragon form as they stood face-to-face with a threat they thought they'd contained.

"What do you want?" Theon demanded.

"We simply wanted to meet her," Avana said, lifting a hand and gesturing to the four behind her.

"All the Fates came just to meet me?" Tessa deadpanned. "Somehow I doubt that."

She smiled again, sharp and knowing. "This is not all of us. Only a few," she replied, clasping her hands before her. "In truth, we wanted to meet all three of you. We were . . . unable to interfere with you."

"The genesis bond," Theon said.

Avana nodded. "That was part of it, yes."

"And the other part?"

"We are forbidden to interfere with the gods again," she said. "But we still watch, hoping things unfold in particular ways." She paused before adding, "Although the addition of Luka Mors was unexpected. You seem to share an inclination for creating your own fate with your Arius bloodline."

"I still don't understand," Tessa said, her fury starting to creep in. "Are you here to thank me? Because that should be the reason you're here."

Luka snickered at her side while Theon tightened his grip on her.

"A born being of Chaos," Avana said, looking her up and down. "It is interesting, really. Not something we could have foreseen, and it created an issue."

"Which we have solved," Theon retorted. "I am her balance."

"Not just you," Avana answered. "But the two of you together, yes. We have discussed it at great length and have decided we do not need to interfere here anymore."

"As if we would have let you," Theon snarled.

She gave him another knowing smile. "Keep that tenacity, blood of Arius," she said, pulling her hood back up. "You may have altered your fates once, but that does not mean destiny will not find you again."

"Is that all?" Tessa demanded.

"For now," she agreed. "But we all know the future is ever-changing. Enjoy the calm moments, Tessalyn. They are as important as the storms."

"You're sure you won't come with us?" her mother asked as they made their way through the Dreamlock Woods.

The woods housed the Serafina Kingdom mirror gate, and she should have known, really. Of course the mirror was in the center of woods where nightmares came true.

Tessa had left this one intact, along with the one on Ekayan Island and the one in the Underground. The Falein Heir had helped them find two upstanding scholars to be the sentinels of the Ekayan mirror mate, monitoring and reporting any activity immediately to Tessa. Cienna and Rayell monitored the Underground mirror, and here? Corbin and Lange were the Dreamlock mirror gate sentinels. They had a home with the woods in their backyard just outside of Sanal, the Serafina Kingdom capital city, and Corbin also served on the Serafina Council.

Tessa gave her mother a weak smile. "My place is here. With Theon and Luka."

"But . . . Temural can't come here," her mother said with a frown.

No, he could not. Because gods and goddesses still couldn't set foot in Devram. Whatever Accords were in place were a magic that could not be broken. If she'd learned anything this last year though, it was that the gods weren't the ones they had to worry about. Or rather, it was who the gods sent to interfere.

"I'll be all right, Akira," she said.

Her mother nodded. "Because you're not alone anymore."

"That's right," she whispered, watching Akira struggle to keep her magic in check. Tessa sent a wisp of her own magic to calm her soul, and she sucked in a shuddering breath.

Ultimately, this was why it was time for Akira to go. She had stayed these extra months, and Tessa had been grateful. They weren't close by any means, but there was . . . something for them to build on. Not that it would be easily done when they were in separate worlds, but maybe it was another reason she'd wanted an excuse to not destroy the last of the mirrors. She would have—to keep the realm secure—but she was also a little relieved to still have them.

"Welcome back," Xan said with a sad smile when they emerged from some trees.

She'd gone on one last walk with her mother. One last moment to soak in having her here, and now they were facing another goodbye.

Or, more accurately, three of them.

Because Xan and Aiyana were leaving too.

Scarlett and Sorin stood next to the mirror once more, and her cousin was far more subdued than last time. Perhaps it wore on her to be the one to ferry others across the stars and constantly have to be present for these farewells.

Aiyana was hugging Luka, tears on her cheeks as she murmured low to him. Her husband's features were emotionless as always, but she could feel the pain down their bond. So much more than her own. Luka's relationship with his parents was far different from what she shared with Akira.

"How is Tristyn?" Tessa asked her cousin.

"He is well," Sorin answered. "Spends most of his time in Avonlcya with Razik."

Tessa nodded, tipping her head back as Xan stepped before her.

"A path to salvation by way of death," the dragon said, sapphire eyes searching hers.

She gave him a half-hearted smile. "Thank you. For keeping me company when I was too . . ." She swallowed thickly. "Just thank you. It may not seem like much, but it made a difference."

He was pulling her into him then, and she embraced him back. "Those visits were just as valuable to me, Tessa. After years of silence, you were a welcome reprieve. And thank you. For loving him."

"You will come back?" she whispered. "He will miss you both deeply after just discovering you once more."

Xan released her, stepping back as he said, "I think you know more of what the future holds than I do, do you not?"

"The future is ever-changing," she retorted.

"That it is, my dear," he said with a huff of laughter. "That it is."

Tessa caught Scarlett's eye and nodded, and her cousin called forth her magic, funneling the power into the Temural symbol. Minutes later, a male stood among the swirling darkness and white embers.

He was tall, like all the gods and goddesses seemed to be. His long black hair was tied back at his nape, and there were twin swords at his waist. A crown of gilded leaves and feathers sat atop his head with a black eagle at his shoulder, and his pine green eyes were pinned on Akira.

"Vixen," Temural greeted, and Akira was before the mirror, her hands under her chin as she looked up at him. The god's gaze flicked up, landing on his Guardian. "Xan. Well done."

Xan bowed his head. "Like they were my own."

Tessa wasn't sure what that meant, but she suddenly found those pine green eyes on her. Theon and Luka were at her back, but she lifted her chin as she beheld her father for the first time.

"I'm Tessa," she said lamely, because what else was she supposed to say at this point?

"I know who you are," he replied. "The fury of your mother and the wildness of the untamed."

"She was alone, Temural," Akira said, fingers in her hair. "All alone this whole time. We could do nothing."

His eyes flicked to Xan, who sent a swirl of dragonfire to Akira a moment later.

"I know, Akira," Temural said, far more softly than he'd spoken to any of them. "As soon as I found a way in, I sent Auryon and the Trackers." His eyes came back to Tessa. "I sent you every advantage I could and bargained with the High Queen of the World Workers to send additional aid." Tessa nodded, still not knowing what else to say. "Will you be coming home with your mother?"

"*This* is my home," Tessa said. "So, no. I will be staying where my home is."

Temural nodded as Nylah and Roan appeared, slinking to her sides and lowering to their bellies. "Keep them close then, daughter," he said. "And know should you ever need it, there is always a place for you here."

"Thank you," Tessa said softly.

"I'm sorry," Scarlett said around a grimace. "But it is getting difficult to keep the mirror gate stable. They need to go."

Aiyana hugged Luka one more time, and Xan did the same. Tessa hugged her mother, and then Akira was breezing through the mirror gate, headed for the calm to her storm. The one who could silence her Chaos and let her breathe.

Aiyana went next, and before Xan stepped through, he met Luka's gaze one last time. "We are proud of who you've become, Luka, but more than that, know that we love you, even across the stars."

Then he was gone, and Tessa was stepping back into Luka as he pulled her back to him.

"No offense, but I hope I don't see your faces for quite some time," Scarlett said, drawing from Sorin before she opened the mirror gate one last time.

Tessa huffed a laugh as Theon said, "The feeling is mutual."

The female tossed him a smirk over her shoulder. "Until next time, lordling."

Then they were gone too, the mirror gate once again a stagnant piece of glass. She turned in his arms, looking up at him when she said, "Luka?"

But he just pulled her back into his chest.

We can be lonely together, she whispered down the bond, and Luka held her tighter.

For a long time, they stood there like that in the middle of the Dreamlock Woods until they heard footsteps and the chattering of a little girl.

Corbin winced, finding the three of them still reeling from the goodbyes.

"Sorry," Corbin said, a glass box in one hand. "She was getting restless."

"If anyone understands that, it's me," Tessa said, wiping the last of the wetness from her face. "Hello, Priya. Did you find the perfect place like I asked you to?"

The girl nodded her head, eyeing the wolves still on their bellies. They'd perked up at the sound of their approach, but they'd since relaxed once more.

"There are trees and flowers deeper in the woods. The Sprytes showed me," Priya said. "Lots of flowers."

Tessa gave her a sad smile. "That sounds perfect. Can you lead the way?"

Priya smiled again, grabbing Lange's hand and pulling him down another path.

"She has adjusted well," Tessa said, falling into step with Corbin.

"She likes living near the woods," Corbin said with a grin. "We just had to set up rules about not going into them without one of us."

"I don't think the woods will hurt her," Tessa said in confusion.

"Not her, no, but when we have to go looking for her?" He dragged a hand down his face. "It only happened once, and once was more than enough."

"Does she know? Whose ashes are in that box?"

"No," Corbin sighed. "Eviana asked us not to tell her. Didn't want her to remember that she was present for her mother's death."

That made sense. No one understood making hard choices about children better than her. Eviana didn't get the choice she was given though. A daughter she was forced to carry. A daughter she chose to love when she could have simply not cared.

Sometime later, they emerged in a small clearing deep in the woods. Truthfully, the only way Priya could have found it was if a Spryte had shown her. That's how far off the path it was, but by Silas, was it beautiful.

Trees with low-hanging branches made her feel like they were stepping into another world. There was a small pond in the center, water lilies floating on top, while wildflowers of all colors surrounded it. Bright oranges and purples, pinks and yellows. Moss covered fallen logs, and ferns and other small plants were everywhere.

"Will this work?" Priya asked, turning to Tessa. There was a hardness in her turquoise eyes that Tessa wasn't sure would ever go away, but there was also a glimmer of hope. Something told Tessa she was worried about disappointing them.

Tessa crouched before her, holding out a hand for the glass box. "This is perfect, Priya," Tessa said softly. "Thank you for helping us find it. Can I ask for your help one more time?"

She nodded slowly, eyes darting from Tessa to the box.

"Someone very special died to save someone she loved very much," Tessa said, her voice wavering on the words. "She loved the flowers and the trees."

The child's eyes went wide. "Like me?"

"Yes," Tessa said, trying to swallow her cry. "Yes, Priya. Just like you. Which is why I was hoping you could help us return her to the trees and flowers she loved so much. You'll know which ones are the best."

"I can do that," she said seriously. Then she looked up, searching for the males who loved her. "Lange? Corbin? Can you help?"

"Of course, *bellana*," Lange said, flashing her a sad smile. "Let's find the prettiest ones, okay?"

Tessa stepped back, and Theon pulled her into his side as they watched the three of them give Eviana's ashes back to the element she loved so dearly. Priya may not know who she was giving a resting place to, but they did. They knew, and her sacrifice would be remembered always.

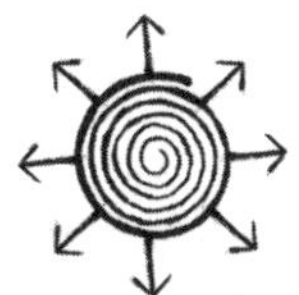

When Chaos Comes to Reign

TWO YEARS LATER . . .

"Yes!" Tessa cried, lurching up from the sofa and jumping up and down, popcorn spilling everywhere. Axel was there with her, picking her up and spinning her in a circle. She tipped her head back, laughter spilling from her lips. "The Whirlwinds aren't even your favorite team," she managed to get out between giggles.

"Yeah, but I bet Mors a good amount of money that they would beat the Firewings," Axel said, setting her back on her feet with a grin.

"There's still three more games in the series," Luka grumbled, arms crossed where he sat on the sofa.

"You know," Tessa said, sauntering closer and straddling his lap. "Every time the Whirlwinds and Firewings play, you tell me not to whine if the Whirlwinds lose."

His hands were on her hips, and he leaned in closer. "And every time, you throw a fit."

"I do not," she scoffed.

"Last time, all my Firewings items mysteriously disappeared."

She arched her brows. "Still a mystery."

"Mhmm," he hummed, sitting back once more and shoving her off his lap. "I get to be grumpy after that game. The Firewings played like shit. The Whirlwinds were missing half their starters, for fuck's sake."

Tessa laughed again, looking up at Theon from where she lay on the sofa now, her head at his thigh. His nose was, of course, in a book. It always was during Chaosphere games. She reached up, batting at the pages. He ignored her, but she saw his mouth twitch.

"I better go help Kat," Axel said, setting down the bowl he'd just filled with the spilled popcorn. "You guys heading back in the morning?"

"After breakfast," Tessa said. "We promised Mads we'd stay for pancakes."

It was the only way they'd convinced the child to go with Kat when it was well past his usual bedtime.

"Good," Axel replied, grabbing his sweatshirt off the back of a dining chair. "I guarantee he's still awake and will ask again as soon as he sees me."

"Good night, Axel," she called after him.

"Night, baby doll."

The door clicked shut behind him, and Tessa stretched out. They stayed at Arius House more often than she thought they would.

The three of them had a large house in the center of the Acropolis, but they always ended up here at least once a week. It felt more like home than anywhere else did, and she knew Theon and Luka felt the same.

She reached up, shoving at Theon's book again. "The game is over."

Turning a page, he said, "I'm aware, beautiful."

The fire was crackling in the fireplace, and Luka clicked off the television, letting silence fall over them. This was her favorite way to spend their nights. Either here on the sofa watching Chaosphere games or on a balcony under the stars.

"Luka is grumpy," she sighed, shoving at the dragon with her foot, which he promptly batted away.

"That he is," Theon agreed. Emerald eyes flicked to hers, a glimmer of hunger swirling in their depths. "What are you going to do about it?"

She hummed. "There's so many options," she mused. Then she pushed herself up onto her knees and leaned in so she could whisper into the dragon's ear. "Am I crawling tonight, Luka?"

And later, after the three of them had tumbled into bed, after they were sated and breathless, curled up with her between them, she couldn't help but think that Luka had been wrong all those nights ago when he'd told her she wasn't one of the monsters. That she couldn't be one because monsters take their happy endings.

She'd done just that, leaving a blood trail in her wake. Leaving broken dreams and tears behind. Casting off shackles and settling for nothing less than what she wanted. Battling back against everything that tried to drag her under. Unearthing secrets and shattering expectations.

She fought for it, fought *them*, and still they got back up. Over and over. This push and pull between the three of them never really died, it just changed.

Because while they were her villains, she was theirs.

A perfect balance that defied the stars.

Bonus Content

Need more from Devram? Who doesn't? You can find all kinds of bonus content on my website, including a brand new bonus chapter!

You can find it all at www.melissakroehrich.com under Book Extras.

Playlist

I adore when books come with playlists that follow along with the story. You feel everything more. It immerses you more. It brings everything to life. If you find this to be true for you too, here you go! I spend a good chunk of time meticulously picking a song for each chapter (usually when I'm avoiding writing, haha!)

The full playlist can also be found under Book Extras on my website:

www.melissakroehrich.com

Enjoy!

A Note From Melissa

It's a Sunday morning as I write this. My house is quiet while my family still sleeps. My coffee is hot. The sun is shining, and the Border Collies are wrestling outside my window. It's almost as if the universe knew I'd be writing this note to you this morning.

This note is one of the last things I write as we prepare to launch a book into the world. I save it for the end because it's when I'm so close to being done. There's a light at the end of the tunnel. A tunnel that consists of drafting and editing, spending endless hours at a computer and having to miss out on family things due to deadlines. Some truth? When I'm in the middle of all that hard, especially during edits, I hate the characters a little bit. We've spent so much time together, and we're all a little (okay, *a lot*) sick of each other. But this point? When we're almost done? When I can take a breath, look back, and reflect—especially at the end of a series? Yeah, this point is surreal and bittersweet.

I've said before, The Legacy Series was something that was never supposed to see the light of day. It was something I started writing just for me in between two of the Darkness series books when I needed a break from that world. Obviously, it became something more than a fun, little side project. It became the series that changed our lives. Yes, things were going great with the Darkness series. We were doing just fine, but this series? This series—with messy characters, challenging world views, and fractured hearts—took us to heights I'd only ever dreamed of. But therein lies the secret.

I dared to dream.

The Legacy Series is a lot of things, but I hope at the end of the day, you realize that your balance is just that. Yours. It might look different from others. The world might sneer and try to force you back into the box that makes them comfortable. But their comfort isn't your responsibility. As long as your balance isn't harming others, yourself, or the world around you, it is yours to claim.

To be clear, there's nothing easy about it. It's hard. Sometimes lonely. You'll question your sanity more than once. You'll push boundaries, and you'll learn to set boundaries. You'll fail. Good gods, will you fail, but if you're weak enough to fall, you're strong enough to get back up.

Make sure you get back up.

Because at the end of the day, we have to be a little mad to dream.

At this very moment, I'm not sure what's next. By the time this book releases, I'm sure I will have announced my next series, but at this exact moment in time, I don't know. I'm debating a few different things and waiting to see which characters become the loudest. It's both freeing and absolutely terrifying. I like to have a plan, and in usual fashion, the people in my head are laughing at me and my plans. With that being said, while The Legacy Series had closure, if there were some minor things that felt a door was left open a crack, rest assured it was purpose. There's so much to come in the Chaosverse.

But whatever comes next, I hope to see you there. I can promise it will have mental health rep. I can promise it will have emotional whiplash. I can promise we'll be back in the Chaosverse soon, but until then, make sure you get back up. Know your worth. Be wild and untamed.

May Chaos reign.

XO,

Melissa

Content Information

Below please find the potential triggers for The Legacy Series as well as tropes and tags. Note this information is current as of July 2025. For the most up-to-date content information, please visit Melissa's website: www.melissakroehrich.com

Trigger Warnings

Depression, Sexual Scenes, Threats of Sexual Assault/Rape (not between the FMC/MMCs), Death, Anxiety, Physical Abuse (on page and memories), Forced Medical Procedures, Murder, Torture, Claustrophobia, Suicidal Thoughts, Blood, Hostages, Alcohol Abuse, Kidnapping, Sexually Explicit Scenes, Gaslighting, Slut Shaming, Profanity, Needles, Graphic Violence, Branding, Drugging, Psychological Manipulation, Addiction, References to Past SA, Pregnancy (not the FMC), Grooming

Tropes

Forced Proximity, Touch Her/Him and Die, Unknown Powers, Who Did This to You?, Meddling Gods, Kingdom Politics, One Bed, One Horse, He Falls First, Enemies with Benefits, Vengeful FMC, Wanted Bonds and Unwanted bonds and Are They Bonds?

Tags

Anxiety Rep, Trauma Rep, Fae, Shifters, Witches, Vampires, Gods, Dragons, & More, Queen Normative, M/F/M/Polyamorous Relationship (inc. main), M/F Relationships, M/M Relationships, LGBTQ+ Rep, Morally Gray characters (Yes, we know they're all walking red flags.), Everything is Not as It Seems, Fae Courts, Multi-POV (as the series progresses), Third Person, Extensive World Building, Interconnected Universe, Contemporary High Fantasy

Acknowledgments

Every single time, I have to start with you, the reader. Without you, this would not be my life. You make an impact in so many lives by simply reading. Thank you.

To the team at Kensington: Alexandra Sunshine, Jackie Dinas, Alexandra Nicolajsen, Cassandra Farrin, and everyone else on the team, for believing in not only these books, but me, thank you from the bottom of my soul. Your passion, knowledge, and partnership mean the absolute world to me, and I am honored to be part of the Kensington family.

To my agent, Katie Shea Boutillier and the Donald Maass Literary Agency, thank you for all the endless emails and phone calls. I simply could not navigate all the new without you, and I am beyond grateful for your continued guidance and letting me talk things out on the phone with you.

To my Book Slut Besties: Brit Irvin, Sara Abel, and Tracey Goodson, can you believe we did an entire series together? The whole dang thing! Thank you, Brit, for managing my never-ending chaos. And Sara—thank you for jumping into your role with both feet and never looking back. I'm honored to call you all my team.

To my soulmate, Miranda Lyn: What is there to say? Even going a single day without talking to you is too much. I am so honored to call you my best friend.

To Sarah Mori and The Realm Studios, for constantly rolling with it when I pop in with a last minute need for a graphic, thank you. You make my world a whole lot brighter.

To my colleagues and friends, LJ Andrews, Frankie Diane Mallis, Penn

Cole, Charissa Weaks, Amber V. Nicole, Helen Scheueuer, Emma Hamm, J.M. Kearl, Emily Blackwood, and L.R. Friedman, thank you for the encouragement when we're fighting for our lives in the trenches. Some of us talk every day, and some of us every few months, but knowing you're there, in the hard times and the celebrations, means the world to me. It was something I didn't know I needed until I had it, and I don't take any of you for granted.

To my beta readers, Ashley Nolan and Rachel Betancourt, thank you for pushing through this one. I know our timeline got tight.

To my editor, Megan Visger, you make me and my writing better, even if we argue about em-dashes. Thank you for all your effort and time with this one. I know it nearly killed us both. I'd have gone to the After with you, Friend.

To my audiobook narrators, Laura Horowitz and Christian Leatherman, thank you for bringing these characters to life. Your talent is unmatched.

To my ARC/Street Team, your love and enthusiasm are unmatched. I am so honored you continue to choose to be part of my little world. Thank you.

To the Chaos Archives Patreon Members, look at you, little dragons hoarding as much chaos as you possibly can. I know the world is a mess right now, and I'm honored you choose to spend some of your resources by hanging out with me in Patreon. And a very special thank you to the Chaos Tier—Alyssa Hollis, Amelia Gage, Ashley VanDurmen, Rita Olander, Lauren Bollen, Tyla Smart, Jen Brisbois, Reem Santrisi, Missy VanDiepen, Alexia Nice, Heather Kerby, Michaela Cason, Cait Juntti, Christina Smyth, Kate Broderick, Bridget Meyer, Charlee Umstead, Rachel Hatley, Malika Meidinger, Lauren Rando, Stuti Shah, Allison Arkle, Moira Reid, Bre Rivers, Olivia Klinkhammer, Rachel Rubio, Corina Clem, Katie Clark, Alli MacManus, Leyna Bertelli, and Cara Barbardo.

To my boys—Your balance is unique to you. Don't let the world define it.

To my husband—Thank you for enduring my endless dramatics and unhinged ideas. I love you.

About the Author

Melissa K. Roehrich is a dark fantasy romance author living her best life in the Middle-of-Nowhere, North Dakota. She resides on a hobby farm where she homeschools her three boys with her husband. They have four dogs, several barn cats, and chickens. When she's not writing or reading, she's probably watching reruns of *How I Met Your Mother* or *Gilmore Girls* while trying to convince her husband they need to add goats to the farm. She loves coffee and traveling and dreams of owning a dragon someday.

LUKA MORS

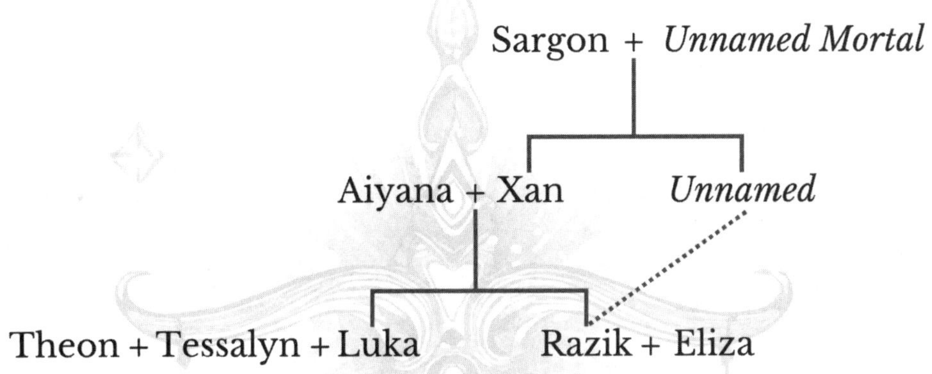

THEON & AXEL ST. ORCAS

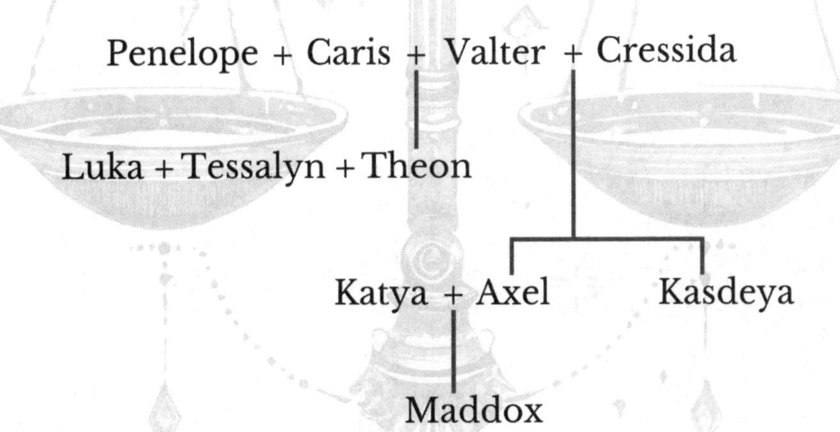

TESSALYN AUSRA

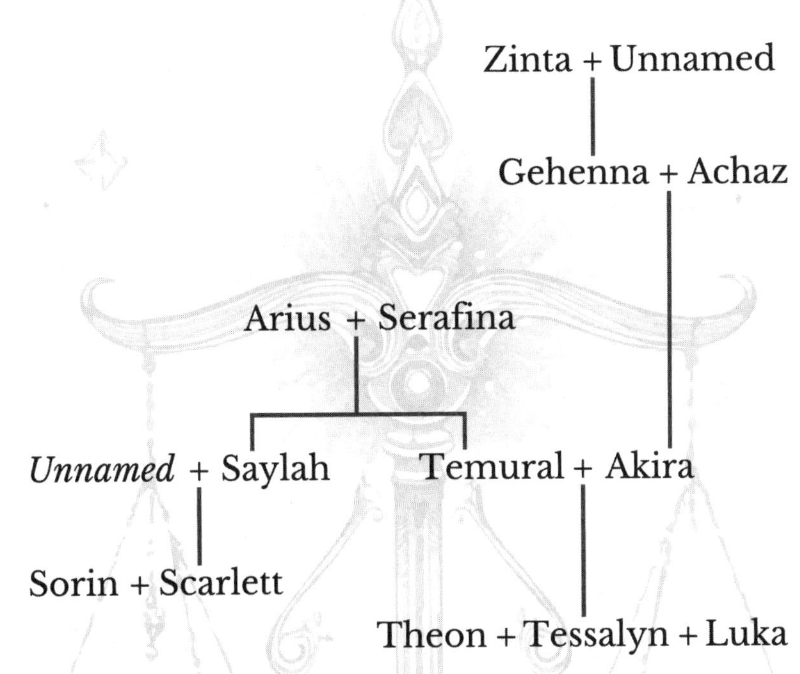

CIENNA & TRISTYN BLACKHEART

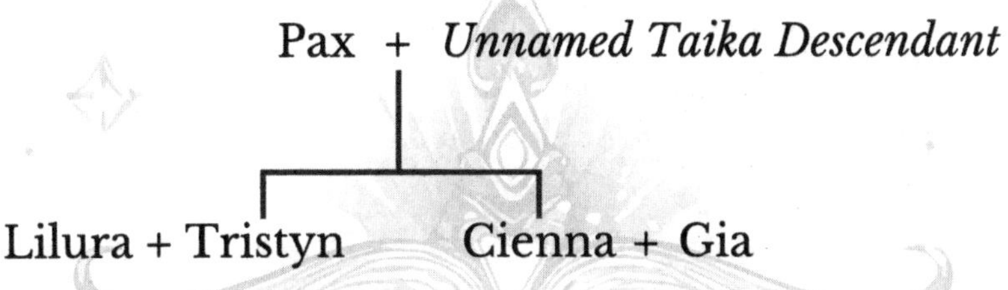

CORBIN

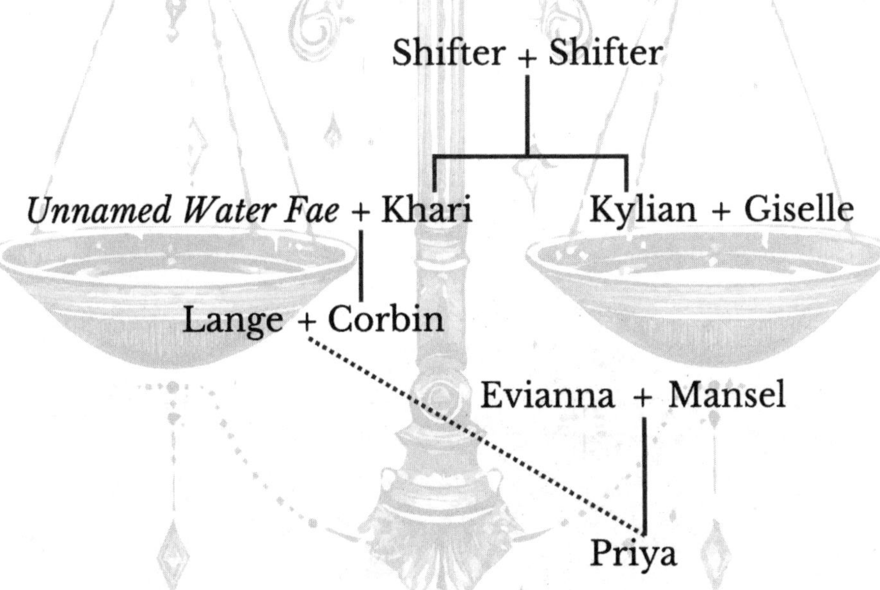